Scorpion

Scorpion

THE MYRIAD SERIES

Christiana,
Is it luck or
is it destiny.
Enjoy the journey and
experience the magic
C Stone

CINDY STONE

REBEL
PRESS

SCORPION
The Myriad Series

Published by Rebel Press
Las Vegas, Nevada
www.RebelPress.com

ISBN: 978-1-68102-153-9
Library of Congress Control Number: 2016947820

Cover Design and artwork: Megan Fisher
Photography: William Edwards
Eyes: Destiny Fava

Printed in the United States of America

To all those dedicated to being a force for good in the world.

The Soul of humanity is like a bird with two wings;
One wing is wisdom, the other compassion;
The bird will only fly if both wings are in perfect
balance...
An ancient Buddhist saying

Definition: Myriad: 1. Ten Thousand (Greek); Classical Greek word for the number 10,000; Origin: mid-16th century (in myriad (sense 2 of the noun)): via late Latin from Greek *murias, muriad-*, from *murioi* '10,000'; constituting a very large or indefinite number (modern English) Miriam-Webster/Oxford Dictionary of Words

Scorpion

Acknowledgements

First and foremost, ten thousand thanks to my sister, Wendy Gregg, for without her this book would not exist. One day on a Saturday morning dog walk, The Myriad series was born. Our walks became brainstorming sessions and her contribution to the story invaluable. She is truly a co-author to this tale.

Many thanks to Alex Kozma, my Bagua teacher, who magically appeared in Toronto late one summer, a decade or so ago, and has been instrumental in helping me make this book much richer in authentic detail. Not only is Alex a master internal martial artist, with a depth and breadth of knowledge rarely surpassed, he is a fantastic writer, with his own series of books. Without Alex, the fight scenes in this book would be sorely lacking. With him, the scenes take on an authenticity that only a real martial artist who has fought in street-style situations could write. I am grateful for his unwavering support and friendship over many years. Our times of sunrise Bagua training sessions on the beach remain some of the most magical in my life.

Thanks to Shun Yuan, Adept from the Order of the Heavenly Dragons, a small esoteric sect of Buddhists from mainland China, who taught me the Five Element WuXing Gong, elevated my meditation practice while introducing me to fascinating inner practices. He helped me with many minuscule details and fine distinctions.

So many magical synchronicities occurred throughout the story creation. During a visit from Shun Yuan, sitting in conversation, late on a summer evening, I told him about three ancient stones I had been given from the first, second and third century AD; one etched with a Scorpion, one, Minerva and one with a Dog and an Eagle, and how the story of The Myriad was being woven around them. Shun Yuan is a Chinese and linguistics scholar and he told me that the ancient Chinese character for the number ten thousand is the same symbol for scorpion. This is only one example of the myriad synchronistic events that took place.

Ten Thousand thanks to Master Bing Zhong, of the Wudang Mountain, who generously lent me video clips and to Lindsey Wei, (Wei Cheng Ling, 24th generation Chun Yang Sect of Wudang Daoism, trained under her master Li Song Feng of the Five Immortals Temple, White Horse Mountain, Wudang.

Thanks to Shifu, Andy James, my current Bagua and meditation teacher, and Shifu Donna Oliver, my teacher of Qi Gong.

Early on in the series development, Marilina Renna, helped me hammer out a structure for the larger story and Kerry Knoll, contributed to the research into the history of the three stones. He discovered that the word Myriad referred to the specific number 10,000, that led to the series title.

Ten Thousand thanks to Arlinda Stonefish (White Feather), and Chief Stephen Augustine for helping me with all of the scenes connected to First Nations history and culture. Stephen J. Augustine is Hereditary Chief and Keptin of the Mi'kmaq Grand Council, Curator of Ethnology, for the Eastern Maritimes. I am deeply honored to know him and to be the beneficiary of his wisdom and advice. White Feather is Lenape, Delaware, born in Moravia town and has been a good friend of mine for many years. Another unexpected synchronicity.

Thanks to Eric Mercury who gave me insights into The Dakota Building that only those who have lived there would know.

Many thanks to my dear friend, Deborra Ellis who took on the role of first reader with a diligence I had not expected. To Deb Dorsey who is not a fan of this genre yet became a champion of the story once she read it.

Thanks to all of my readers who took the time to read, review and critique the work. Thanks to all of my friends, who tolerate my many obsessions with ironic smiles, and the knowledge that I will be lost for a time, immersed in a world that I am compelled to learn as much as possible about. Thank you to Lezlie Mayers for whittling away at my copious words to get closer to the heart of the story.

A special thanks goes to Ffion Lloyd-Jones in Wales, for coming with me and photographing the secret room of the Masons in London in spite of how it made her feel, and accompanying me on one of my many research days in the rare manuscripts room at The British Library.

Ten thousand thanks to everyone at Rebel Press and Next Century Publishing, particularly Simon Presland and Sara Davison. Their editing magic made my book come alive.

Thanks to Larry Robins, my manager, whose belief in The Myriad made it possible to take this dream and make it a real entity in the realm of form and substance.

For more information about the Internal Martial Arts, links to teachers and schools, please see my website www.cindystoneauthor.com. There you will also find a suggested reading list.

Chapter 1

AVERY

The visible world is the invisible organization of energy.

—Heinz Pagels, Physicist

I despise subways and the crowds that swarm them every hour of every day, like so many rats clambering to squeeze into an abnormally small space. I avoid them now, like I try to avoid the totally annoying Norman the Boreman, the wastoid freak my dad always pushes on me. But today I'd rather face the rats than take an extra second to get home. All day my body has been buzzing with the strangest sensations, every cell vibrating and my head whirling.

I headed towards the busiest part of the platform, wondering why I felt compelled to go smack into the center of hordes of strangers. I touched the pendant I wore for the first time, the stone warm, as if alive with its own pulse. My mother gave it to me the night before she died, exactly one year ago today, and I just had to put it on. I needed to feel her close to me.

Every painful detail of the day she died is burned into my memory, like a bad tattoo. I had reached the subway stairs when my dad called me to say I had better get home fast. By the time I pushed through the turnstiles and stumbled towards the platform, I no longer heard anything but the excruciating pounding of my heart. I could see the subway buskers; a cellist, violinist, and bassoonist moving rhythmically while they played. I could see the loud-mouthed school kids shouting. I could see the couple ahead of me laughing and talking, completely absorbed in each other. The world moved inside the station in its usual cacophonous way and my isolation was palpable. I broke into a sweat. Dread seeped into my body from the subway walls. The floor and ceiling closed in around me. I wanted to run, but I had to get home. I had to get to my mom. She couldn't die. She couldn't.

I waited. The train didn't come. I waited some more. Panic rooted my limbs to the spot. A muffled announcement came over the loudspeaker. People reacted, but I was stuck, frozen inside my horror. A woman yelled at me when I didn't get out of her way. Her lips moved as she pushed her face right into mine, her eyes flashing rage. I couldn't stand it anymore. I bolted from the platform, back through the people, the buskers, the turnstiles and up onto the street.

I ran all the way home, but I knew it was too late. I knew she was already gone. I knew it the moment I left the subway. As if the moment her spirit left her body, mine left along with it.

After that day, I could never go in a subway again without dreading the walls, floors and ceiling steadily creeping towards me, suffocating me. My dad sent me to a therapist who told me what I already knew. He thought he was so clever, telling me I was experiencing an existential crisis. Well, Sherlock, nothing like suddenly losing a mother to a mysterious flu to question the meaning of life. I wished for something to end the soul-numbing boredom of my meaningless existence, but my dead feelings just stretched out before me like an endless grey sky. That's why being on the subway platform today was so bizarre, with all my senses so strangely heightened.

I felt things I didn't want to feel, floundering in a sea of bodies, the heat of them pressed into me. I smelled their sweat, even tasted their foul breath. I heard their hearts beat and the blood swish through their veins. The buzzing in my head grew, but I couldn't stop moving forward.

Waves of bodies churned, shoving me to the very edge of the platform. Staring down at the train tracks made me dizzy, so I turned and caught sight of an Asian girl, whip-thin and crouched low, ready to pounce. Strands of purple hair stuck to her blood-red lipstick. She leapt with hands outstretched, her kohl-rimmed eyes seared into her target, somewhere to the left of me.

The train screamed its arrival at the station. As the wiry girl soared towards her mark, she noticed me and twisted in mid-air, her eyes scorching into mine. Her lips curled into a cruel smile as she reached for my chest, for my necklace. My hands shot up to protect myself. She banged into me and knocked me backwards. I shrieked, but no sound came. I reached out for something, anything to stop me from falling. I raked at empty air and turned to see the conductor's eyes, wide in the front window, as the train hurtled towards me. The whistle screeched an urgent warning. The brakes squealed, metal on metal; sparks flew from the tracks as he tried to stop.

In the time it takes from one heart beat to the next, strong, sure hands latched onto my wrists, sending tiny electrical shocks through them. Air whooshed by my face as I was yanked out of the path of the train. Our lips almost brushed as my savior pulled me toward him, his sweet breath dizzying.

He held me until I regained my balance, his eyes searching my face. A crowd gathered around us. It was eerily quiet, except for the buzzing inside my head, a million bees returning to their hive. I stared up at him. His eyes swirled with color, sea-green and brown, fringed with dark lashes. His head was shaved. Instead of appearing tough, he seemed open and vulnerable. He was tall and slender with iron strength in his hands. His smile was shy as our eyes locked, his hands filling my insides with energy. Something inside of me let go, like the wall around my heart broke open and I could breathe more deeply than I had for a very long time. Then he released my wrists, turned and blurred into the crowd, a glide more than a stride. Where he had stood, the space still shimmered with the strange whitish imprint of his body.

"Thanks," I yelled. His long arm reached above the mass of bobbing heads to wave, and I watched his backpack, embroidered with a British flag, disappear into the crowd. For one fleeting moment, I saw what must have been the auras of everyone around me. Angry reds, sick yellows and greens, dark greys and blacks. They all seemed to move around me in some strange slow-motion, muted shadow world. Then the buzzing inside my head stopped. The sounds of the station flooded back, hurting my ears. I stared into the throng but he was gone. The pure white imprint where he had stood started to fade. I searched for the girl with the burning eyes who had pushed me off the platform. She was gone too.

"Is she all right?" came a voice from the crowd.

"I'm a doctor," came another.

I recognized the voice and murmured, "You're not a doctor." My legs shook and my knees buckled.

The world went dark.

AVERY

*One who is too insistent on his own views,
finds few to agree with him*

—Lao Tzu

The ancient elevator inched its way up to my apartment on the seventh floor. One water cylinder drained while the other filled, wheezing like a huge, congested lung. The Boreman had his arm around me and I shrugged him off.

"What were you doing there?" I asked him, noticing things I hadn't before, like how dark and creepy the elevator felt. The velvet bench where we sat was musty and emitted the unmistakable scent of moldy wood. I would think that a building like The Dakota, with its ultra-wealthy tenants, could afford to retrofit the elevators, but so many of the owners here hated change. Everything was done by committee and no one liked to be on one, so the building stayed the same.

"Lucky I was there to catch you when you fainted."

"You didn't catch me," I mumbled. "I didn't faint." But now I was not at all sure about what had happened, though I could still see those dark, dead eyes of the Goth girl burning into mine, and the beautiful face of the man who saved me.

"Of course I caught you. Of course you fainted ... You look different today, Avery. What have you done?"

"Didn't you see him?" I inspected my wrists, still tingling from the touch of the angel man. No marks. Instinctively, I reached for the necklace, hidden beneath my clothes. I could feel it, slightly warm.

"I didn't see anyone, Avery. You were having one of your panic attacks so I ran up to help you."

"I wasn't…" I didn't want to be talking to Norman. I wanted to relive the moment when my lips almost brushed the lips of that man, and my insides vibrated as he took hold of me to lift me to safety. I wanted to remember exactly what he looked like as I watched him glide away.

"I was coming for dinner with your father and Simon. That's why I was there."

The water cylinders stopped their draining and filling, and the doors slid open. I stood up to walk and my legs wobbled. I pressed my hand to the elevator door, refusing to allow Norman to help me.

"Uncle Simon? Dad didn't say he was coming," I said, more to myself than Norman.

He opened the door to my dad's apartment. My father stood in the entryway, waiting for us.

"She's not hurt, Peter," Norman reassured my dad, as we walked into the apartment. I blinked in the sudden brightness. Rasta came bounding up to greet us, looking more like a black bear than a dog.

"I'm fine." I reached down to ruffle Rasta's ears. I wanted to escape. Dad tells me I've changed, keeps asking what happened to his wonderful, loving little girl. Next time he asks, I'm going to tell him. His little girl is almost nineteen and she can no longer hold her tongue.

I don't feel truly connected to anyone, other than Uncle Simon. Not even my best friends. I love them, but they don't understand me. They adore fashion, and boys, and parties; all that feels insignificant to me. I don't belong, and while I battle the gray abyss threatening to engulf me, my friends go shopping. I longed for something real and raw.

"Darling Avery." Dad held his arms open to embrace me.

"Why didn't you tell me Uncle Simon would be here tonight?" I said, tearing off my jacket. Rasta panted beside me, hoping I would take him out for a walk.

"Ruby!" Dad yelled to our housekeeper. "Get your damn dog out of here."

"He's fine. Just tell me when Uncle Simon gets here."

"Sorry, Mr. Adams, Rasta just heard Avery an' he had to come to say hi. Sorry Miss Avery, sorry for Rasta bothering you all."

"He wasn't bothering anyone, Ruby." I flashed my dad a look.

Ruby hugged me, then ushered Rasta back to the kitchen with her.

"You look … different today, darling. Are you wearing eye makeup? Well, whatever it is, it's not the way you dress. Really, Avery, can't you get out of those sweats once in a while?" Dad turned to Norman without waiting for me to answer. "Give Avery a Valium or something to help her feel calm."

"No. I don't need anything to make me calm, and Norman isn't even a doctor."

"I do have a medical degree and a PhD in nanobiology. I start at NYP Hospital next week in their research department. Still..." Norman shook his head. "I don't think I should—"

"Oh, nonsense, Norman. You're almost a doctor." Dad waved a hand through the air, as though Norman's credentials, or lack of them, were irrelevant. And you know how much it has helped Avery. Take her upstairs." Dad turned back to me. "I'll get Ruby to serve you dinner in your room. Have you eaten today? Is that why you fainted?"

"Dad. I didn't faint, I don't need any pills, and I want to see Uncle Simon."

"Honey, you have been through so much." Dad pointed at the stairs. "Go ahead, Norman. And have her take one of those sedatives of her mom's that I gave you. "

I hated that syrupy over-concern in my dad's voice. I knew there would be no winning, so I tromped up the stairs to my room. Norman shimmied up behind me and took my arm. I pulled away.

"Really, Norman." I stood outside the closed door. "You think you're going to come into my bedroom?"

"What's with you today, Avery? I've been in there a million times with you, for your pills."

"Well, not this time. I'm not taking any pills, and if I were taking pills, I can open a bottle and take them myself." I held out my hand. When he didn't hand over the bottle, I opened my door a crack and slipped in, slamming it behind me.

"This isn't like you." Norman opened my door and waltzed in. "You're usually begging for more sedatives, which is why your dad has me dispense them to you."

He took a bottle from his jacket pocket, shook out two large pills into his hand, and held them towards me.

I stared at him. "What makes you think it's okay to just walk into my bedroom when I told you not to, and I closed the door?"

"Come on Avery, take the pills. Your dad wants you to take the pills. So take the pills." He stepped closer and lifted his hand.

I never wanted to be drugged again. Something had awakened in me today and I wanted it to continue. It was true, I was usually eager to take the pills and slip into a deep sleep, find some relief from the depression I had felt since mom died. Not today. I sat on my bed, crossed my arms, and stared at him. "You can't force me."

Norman sighed. He shook his head and then grabbed both sides of my jaw, forced open my mouth, and deposited the pills on my tongue. He clamped my mouth shut. I refused to swallow. I flailed at him, even scratched his cheek with my nails. I fought to get away, but he was bigger and much stronger than I. He forced me down on the bed. He grabbed both my wrists in one hand, yanking my arms over my head and using his leg and body weight to pin me. He held his other hand over my mouth and nose. I couldn't breathe, and writhed to get free as consciousness threatened to slip away. My body went limp, the pills melted, and I swallowed as a reflex, the bitter chemical taste seeping down my throat.

A smug look crossed Norman's face. He looked like some demonic half-wit. His hand brushed across my breast.

"Get the hell off me, you pig." I shoved him away from me. "Don't you ever touch me again."

"Get a grip, Avery. You're acting like a child." He stood, straightened his ugly tie, touched his cheek where I had scratched him, and left.

I ran to my bathroom, shoved my fingers down my throat, and heaved into the toilet. Some foamy bile came up. I hoped I had gotten rid of enough of the medication so that I could still function, but it was the dirty feeling inside me that I wanted to puke up. Something within me was disgusting; Norman's look had confirmed it. He had lain on top of me. His hand had touched my breast. I shook off the feeling and looked at myself in the mirror. I didn't like what I saw. Never did. My eyes were intense even when I wasn't feeling that way. They were deep gold and startling like an animal's eyes, a hunted animal. My body was proportioned all wrong. I was too long and too lean, except in my hips which were too wide for the rest of me. *Really Avery, you do need to get a grip.* As if anyone would want to cop a feel of me. It was a mistake. A slip of the hand. Nothing intentional.

The random events of the day creeped me out. Is life really random after all? Something about the encounter with the angelman forced itself to the forefront of my mind. I wasn't in control of anything, was I? Control was some kind of grand illusion. I touched a finger to my lips. Those sea-green eyes had looked at me, into me, in a way I had never experienced before.

I strode to the French doors leading to the narrow, iron balcony that looked out on Central Park and the row of trees planted in tiny squares of dirt carved out from the sidewalk. Those trees confined within their circular framework of scrolled iron used to make me feel secure, as if things could be easily contained, kept safe within a border. Now they just made me feel as trapped as they were.

I pulled my cell phone from my pocket; the glass face had cracked under Norman's weight. I used my watch phone instead. I had to talk to Whitney before I fell into the stupor I felt coming on. Whitney was my best friend and the daughter of my mother's best friend. "Oh, please, answer. Please." I opened the door and stepped out, taking hold of the railing to steady myself. The crisp, early spring air temporarily cleared the cottony sensation taking over my mind.

"You've reached the cell phone of Whitney Rose. I'm not available right now, and I'm way too fabulous to listen to voicemail. Shoot me a text! Byeeee!" I turned back inside my room and flopped onto my bed.

Katie. I can call her! I desperately wanted to connect. The day felt surreal and I needed everything to feel normal again.

"Hi, Av..." Katie said brightly.

Hearing her voice undid me and I started to weep. "Katie, something awful just happened. But something incredible too. I..."

"Whoa, slow down a bit. What? What happened?"

"So much, I don't know where to begin." I had already pushed the experience with Norman far away. That I wasn't ready to deal with, but I had to tell her about the angelman. "I was on a subway platform, and when the train was about to come into the station, someone pushed me onto the tracks, literally pushed me, and then this guy grabbed me just before I landed and he pulled me back up onto the platform. He stood there for a moment and our eyes, his eyes..."

"You were on a subway platform? You don't take subways."

"Well, I did today. And someone pushed me, tried to kill me, and then this beautiful guy saved me at the last second."

"Are you on drugs or something? Someone tried to kill you? You've gone all emo, Avs. Why would someone want to do that?"

Saying it out loud did make it sound kinda crazy. "Yeah," I whispered. "You're right, who would want to kill me?"

"Come on. Sorry to burst your bubble. But there would have to be a good reason. Now, if I were you, I would want to kill your father for constantly setting me up with Norman the Boreman."

"The Boreman's here for dinner."

"Do you want me to come over and say inappropriate things to liven up the evening?" She giggled.

"Uncle Simon will be here soon. Hey, thanks for listening."

"Have fun with the Boreman!"

The telephone clicked. I felt very alone. I picked up a book, but the words were a blurred dance. My limbs grew warm, then weak as I fought the effects of the drug. I wondered what Norman had given me. Then wondered what was going on with me that I suddenly cared what was going into my body.

Uncle Simon arrived at the door and I heard my father tell him I wasn't home. Their voices wafted up the sweeping staircase, echoing to the second floor. I tried to get up to tell him I was here, but I couldn't get my legs to cooperate. Everything became muffled as they moved away from the entrance. Wine glasses clinked in the distance. I had to see Uncle Simon. Why would my dad say I wasn't here?

Simon was my father's half-brother and lived in Europe, working for one of the family businesses. When Mom got sick, he made sure to visit as often as possible. Her eyes always flared back into life when he walked into the room. His smile was captivating, as though he had a delicious secret. I wondered if Dad was jealous. He always seemed to pick a fight with Simon, forcing him to leave.

I managed to get off the bed and to the door. I entered the hallway, heading for the stairs, but the stairs weren't there. *Today was so strange.* I stumbled down another hallway that looked familiar, and it led to another, narrower hallway. I retraced my steps, but the hallways kept getting smaller and smaller and I couldn't find the stairs anywhere. I had to see Uncle Simon. I ran faster, but the ceiling sloped down lower and lower until I had to crouch. Footsteps crossed the marble-tiled entry and a door slammed. The air became thick. Mud sucked at my feet. I had to reach the door. I had to see Uncle Simon. My heart raced. My legs moved slower and slower. A black cloud grabbed at my ankles, yanking me away. A blood-curdling scream of terror filled the air. It was my voice. My scream. Footsteps ran towards me.

"Avery! Avery! What's wrong?" My father burst through my bedroom door, Rasta bounding in at his heels. Norman scrambled in right behind them.

"It's okay, Rasta. Down, boy." I pulled the covers up over me, although I was still fully dressed. I didn't want Norman to see me in bed, so vulnerable, after what had happened.

"You screamed..."

"I just had a nightmare, Dad. I'm sorry. It must have been the sedative. I couldn't move. I was paralyzed and it terrified me." I sat up, still clutching the covers to my chest. I looked around the room. "Where's Uncle Simon? I heard him come in."

"He got mad and left, but don't worry, he's like a damn boomerang. I can't get rid of him for long."

When I was alone again, I pulled the burner phone out from under my mattress. Uncle Simon had given me the device in secret. He had said, "Just in case you ever need me and you don't want anyone to know."

I dialed. His call answer clicked on. I lowered my voice, even though no one was with me in the room. "Simon. It's me. I was here tonight when Dad said I wasn't. So much has happened since we met last. We have to talk."

Chapter 3

AVERY

The dream is dreaming itself.

—Kalahari Bushmen

"Katie." I waved a hand in the air. "Katie. Over here." Standing outside the Bobst Library, close to the front entrance and across from Washington Square, Katie stood with the commanding presence of a lead dancer. Beside her, Whitney and Prya, an actual East Indian princess, inspected Whitney's latest watch phone. Whitney looked like a small stick of dynamite with her flame of gorgeous red hair, just like her mom's. The three of them glanced up as I sprinted across the street, dodging traffic.

"Hey, Avery, are you still bent out of shape about the subway?" Katie grabbed the tag at the back of my shirt. "You've got your sweatshirt on inside out."

"Oh." My cheeks warmed as I ran my palms down the front of the shirt, trying to smooth out the wrinkles.

Whitney tilted her head. "Avery, you look … different. Really different."

"Yeah," Prya nodded, "you really do look different, more lively or energized or something."

Katie laughed. "Don't tell me. You and Norman the Boreman passionately kissed last night."

"You're sick, Kates." I stuck my finger in my mouth and pretended to gag. "But I did have a dream about kissing the beautiful man who saved me in the subway station."

Whitney's eyes widened. "What? You don't go on subways. And why haven't I heard about this beautiful man?"

27

"Guess I'm the new best friend." Katie flashed her a smile. Whitney scrunched up her face but Katie just laughed. "Really, aren't you the same Avery Adams who claimed that she would never obsess over a guy, like I did in Europe last summer?"

I crossed my arms. "This is different. I'm not obsessing. I'm just..."

"Obsessing," Katie said, "Definitely obsessing."

The hair on the back of my neck bristled and heat bored into the back of my head. I whirled around. A girl stared at me. I recognized her from one of our classes. She had tried to talk to us before.

Katie followed my gaze and frowned. "What does Raven want? She gives me the creeps."

Raven approached us. Her black eyes pierced into mine. The intensity of her presence pressed against me, almost pushing me back.

"What do you want, Raven?" Prya jammed her hands onto her hips. Whitney and Katie giggled.

I cringed. I wanted to say something to the girls, but Raven didn't look away. I was mesmerized. Locked in a visual embrace.

"My mom told me I had to tell you about my dream last night," she said.

My chest tightened and I gasped for air. *I have to get out of here.* I stepped back but her hand shot out and clamped onto my arm. "I dreamt you were in a field weaving straw into gold. The field ignited with fire all around you and there was no escape."

"Why ... why are you telling me this?" Her dream flashed vividly in my mind, the fire's scorching heat surrounding me and the dream became more intense as everything faded from view.

I heard Whitney's voice, surreal in the distance. "Let go of Avery!"

Raven continued, undeterred. "A huge bird swooped down and carried you away."

The bird's claws dug into my shoulders; my feet lifted off the ground. The hairs on my arms stood on end. I looked at Raven, as if maintaining eye contact with her would help me make sense of what was happening. A thin white band of energy surrounded her and she glowed. Like my angelman with the wide, white band of light that left an imprint when he moved. Everything felt utterly still and locked in place.

Then I snapped back to reality.

"Come on, Avery." Katie moved to my side. "Don't get spooked. It's just a dream from some weird, poser wannabe." Katie grabbed my hand then flinched as she dropped it. "You just gave me a wicked shock."

"I don't know what it means," Raven continued as if the others didn't exist. "My mom says I have to tell you, to warn you that something of great consequence is happening. You need to pay attention." Her eyes cut deep into mine as she tightened her hold on my arm.

Prya stepped towards Raven. "Hey, freak, get lost."

Raven released my arm. The spell was broken. Hurt clouded her face. She didn't move. Barely took a breath.

"I can't believe you guys are being so mean." I turned to face my friends. "You sound so high school." I didn't want to see the hurt in Raven's face. I knew that hurt. Knew it all too well.

"Prya, remember you told me how you were bullied in high school when you first moved here? How awful you felt? What are you doing?" I stared at each of my friends. They responded with silence and a horrible tension that I couldn't stand. I turned back to Raven. "I don't understand your dream-thing, but I'll see you around. Ok?"

She nodded and turned to go.

I reached out and touched her on the shoulder. "Hey, wait a minute. I'm coming with you." I flashed the girls a look of disgust and turned to leave.

"You're right, Avs," Whitney stepped up beside me and placed her hand on Raven's. "We're really sorry, Raven." Whitney stared at Prya. "Aren't we?"

"Yeah, Raven. I'm sorry. I don't know why I said that. I do know how it feels, really I do." Prya poked Katie in the arm.

"Oh, me too." Katie pushed some dirt around on the sidewalk with her shoe. "My sister was bullied and I didn't even think. I am so sorry."

A small smile escaped from Raven's lips before she turned and disappeared into a crowd of students crossing over to the Park.

Chapter 4

AVERY

By letting go, it all gets done.

—Lao Tsu

E ach minute at home seemed like an empty hour, an eternity really, since I had seen the angelman in the subway. I felt strangely compelled to find him. Every day before class, I rushed Rasta's walks, leading him around the edge of the park, while he pulled to no avail to go in. Then I would race to the subway like a crazy person, hoping to see the beautiful man again. Saturday morning ballet class would be a welcome distraction from what was becoming a childish compulsion.

I was out of breath when I dashed into the changing room. Katie wore a dance wrap with her hair meticulously braided. I envied her perfection. Every detail attended to. I glanced in the mirror and was sorry I had. Everything about me looked messy and mismatched. I was drawn to my necklace; the orange-red stone seemed on fire. It made the gold in my eyes and the color of my hair too luminous.

"Hurry up, Avs," Whitney whispered. "You're going to be late." She bashed around a new pair of pink pointes, taking the toe box and hammering it with her fists. "I hate it when they're too rigid." She whacked them against the wall.

I slipped on an old pair of pointes, tying the satin ribbons around my ankles. I bunched up my hair in a thick pony tail and wrapped an elastic band around it. Tendrils of hair shot out, tickling my face, as I darted into class; my toe shoes lightly tapped the floor in time with old Mrs. Marsby beating out an unrecognizable melody on the barely-in-tune piano.

I assumed my position at the bar.

As we arched toward it with our arms curved gently over our heads, Katie whispered, "What are you wearing tonight?"

We arched back out towards the center of the floor.

"My blue dress."

We bent back in towards the mirror.

"Hardly a dress worthy of your nineteenth birthday party."

Our bodies arced away from the bar. I didn't answer.

"Is Boreman your date?"

On the movement back, my fingers almost jammed into the mirror.

"Absolutely not."

Away again in a graceful curve out.

"Bet he is."

To the mirror.

"Told my dad no way."

And back.

"As if your dad ever listens."

"Silence!" the Grande Dame shouted. She paced along the row of girls and stopped when she got to Katie. Everyone in the class remained perfectly still, holding their position.

"You American girls are so spoiled; you wouldn't last a day at the Bolshoi."

Smack! Madame slapped the backs of Katie's legs with her yardstick. "Your line is sloppy." She tucked her yardstick under her arm to take Katie's head in her hands and tilt it infinitesimally towards the mirror. "There, that is better. Yes, much better. Like a swan."

Madame pasted a smile on her face, turned her slight frame, and marched back down the row, her posture upright and rigid. We all knew that look. The one that said she owned us.

The last part of class, corner work, was my favorite. Madame—who was Russian, not French—choreographed dance steps on a diagonal across the studio. Today was the once-a-month special when she brought in an African drummer, a gorgeous man with dark, smooth, air-brushed skin and translucent green eyes. He had huge hands with large silver rings on all his fingers. All the dancers speculated at length about whether she was having an affair with him. We waited in threes for our chance to dance across the room.

The walls sweated with the accumulated humidity of our steamy bodies. I reveled in the sensation of being on some exotic tropical island.

The drummer beat out a trance-like rhythm, sending heat, like flames of fire, flickering across my skin.

"Behind the beat, Miss Ratcliffe. You are behind the beat." Madame's voice cut into my reverie.

I waited for my count. Two beats. I surged forward and stepped back rhythmically, a wave of unbridled energy, the choreography already firmly imprinted into my body. Forward again, flat-foot wide stance, my spine undulated first left, then right. A few hip-hop style arm and body movements with a grand jeté into a deep knee bend. Chasse forward, another back and in the air again.

"Higher on the grand jeté, Miss Adams. Deeper when you land. That's right."

The drumbeat reverberated throughout my body. The rhythm infused me, effortlessly moving me. I was across the floor without realizing how I got there, and our group scurried back along the edges of the room to line up again. Every two beats, a new line of dancers advanced across the diagonal. The beats got stronger, faster, and the rhythm grew more and more insistent. On and on we went, three at a time, two beats apart. Each time I danced with greater abandon.

"Not like elephants, girls. You are gazelles. Now go." Madame pounded her stick on the floor in time to her African prince.

We pushed off across the floor. Faster and faster. The music crept deeper into my mind, transporting me. The heat of Africa made my body slick with fevered sweat. The drumming fired up the desperate need inside me to break free of everything and everybody, driving me to move in ways I hadn't ever imagined before. The gazelle gyrated through my body, instinctive, sexual, and wild.

Clap! Clap! "Okay, class. Thank you very much. You all looked quite wonderful. Really." She added that last word as if she didn't quite believe it. "Miss Adams?"

"Yes, Madame."

"You were quite extraordinary today."

"I was?"

"Really extraordinary, but since when do we wear jewelry in class?" Madame sighed as she reached out to touch my pendant, recoiling immediately, "Oh! A shock! You must have worked up quite a bit of static today." She examined me with the eye of an eagle. "Yes. Really quite extraordinary."

We collapsed onto the wooden floor, stretching out our tired muscles before traipsing into the change room.

Whitney hobbled in behind us. "Wish I hadn't worn my new pointes for so long." She grabbed my arm for support. "Hey, you really were amazing; what's up?"

"I'm coming to your house to help you get ready for the dinner tonight." Katie flopped on the bench, picking at the tight knot to untie the satin ribbons. "I can't rely on you to dress yourself."

"I'm coming to help too," Whitney said.

I shifted on the bench. "No you aren't." I threw them both my best 'I mean it' look.

"Today is all about you. You're nineteen and it's going to be epic. Jean-Georges for dinner—I can't wait!" Katie shook her mahogany hair loose and it tumbled down around her shoulders.

"I know this is all-about-Avery-day, but I have to tell you guys about Mark." Whitney winced as she eased her sore feet into her runners.

"I never imagined you as an antique jewelry kinda girl. Where did you get this?" Katie reached out to touch my pendant. She yanked back her hand. "Ouch. Another shock."

"Sorry Kates, I've been giving shocks to everyone today."

"Am I invisible or something?" Whitney pushed out her bottom lip, "No one's listening to me."

"Did you buy this in Soho?" Katie asked.

"No, not Soho. Ok, Whitney, where did you go with Mark?"

"Some geeky cult movie. All about robots and monsters."

"And you like him, why?" Katie stuffed her ballet gear into her bag.

I hefted mine over my shoulder and started for the door. "Are you both ready?"

"Hey, what's the rush, girl? Wait up." Footsteps echoed on the studio floor as we left the building and strode towards the West 4th station.

"You know," Katie said, "I heard there's a whole city of people who live under the subway."

"You're creeping me out. I just started taking the subway. I don't want to get all freaked out again." I reached for Katie's hand, but she linked her arm in mine.

"It's just an urban myth," Whitney shook her head. "How could there be a whole city under the subway?"

We headed for the platform and I couldn't help scanning the crowd for the guy who glowed. My brain started to buzz just as it had the other day. Was that some kind of weird symptom or something? Someone slammed into my back. I stumbled forward a step, but Katie still had her arm linked through mine so I didn't fall. I pulled my arm from Katie and twirled around. Two Goth-girls ran toward the stairs that led away from the platform.

"Goth sucks!" Katie yelled at them as they slithered away. "And it's sooo last century."

"They…they pushed you." Whitney turned toward them. "Why did they do that?"

"I have no idea, but it hurt." I leaned against the wall, gulping for air. Fingers had brushed my neck. One of the girls had made a grab for my necklace, but I kept that part to myself.

"What is their problem?" Katie stared after the girls.

Just as they reached the stairs and headed up, a white glow swirled around a man swooping down the stairs in front of them.

I pointed at him. "There! Did you see that?"

The subway doors opened.

"What? See what?" Both Katie and Whitney looked at me blankly.

Maybe it would be better not to mention the white glow. The crowd surging toward the train saved me from having to answer as it swept us along with it. We crammed into the jam-packed car. The doors slid shut behind us.

AVERY

Peace cannot be kept by force. It can only be achieved by understanding.

—Albert Einstein

"There." Katie stepped back and held both hands toward me. "Ta Da." Whitney turned my chair around to face the mirror.

I was transformed. I reached up to touch my face and my hair, staring into the mirror in disbelief. Metallic kohl shadow lined my eyes, and the gold in my irises sparkled. Not in the normally weird, startling way, but in a way that even I liked. A slow smile spread across my face. Whitney and Katie had managed to make me look natural, but better.

"Wow," I whispered. "I like it. I really like it."

"You just like it?" Katie teased.

"She LOVES it!" Whitney danced around me like a little girl, singing. "She loves it, she loves it. She really, really loves it."

"I actually do."

"It's good to have you back." Whitney stopped twirling around and rested her hands on my shoulders. "We've been worried."

"Back? What do you mean?"

"Avs, you haven't paid any attention to how you look since, well since your mom died. You barely get out of your sweats. I can't believe you've abandoned that closet full of the most gorgeous shoes and clothes."

"Avery. It's time." My father's stern voice echoed down the hallway.

I grabbed a scarf and draped it around my neck

"What are you doing?" Whitney threw a hand in the air. "You are ruining the whole effect with that scarf. Now we can't see your necklace."

Katie's eyes narrowed. "Where did you get that necklace, anyway? You didn't answer me before."

"Why would you want to cover it up?" Whitney reached for the scarf. "It's so … unique."

"Norman's here, Avery," Dad announced.

I ducked away from Whitney before she could remove my scarf. "How could he do that?" I hissed. "I told him I didn't want Norman at my party."

My heart quickened and my hands grew clammy. I pushed down the rising panic; I was not going to let Norman do that to me. I took a steadying breath. I hadn't told anyone what he had done in my bedroom that night, and I wasn't going to.

"You okay, Avs?" Whitney's brow furrowed. "You suddenly went pale."

"It's the Boreman, isn't it?" Katie said. "I've never seen you this upset about him."

"I'm fine. It's just that I only wanted my friends with me tonight. I didn't want to look at his stupid ties—or his dumb face."

Katie cracked up first, while mimicking Norman's incessant tie straightening. Whitney followed with her infectious giggling. Soon I couldn't help myself and broke out laughing.

"We'll be there in a sec, Dad." I took one last look at myself in the mirror. "Come on, let's go." I whisked Katie and Whitney out of the bedroom and down the stairs.

"Norman, you remember Katie and Whitney?" Dad held a hand out toward my friends. "We can take them home to get ready while we have cocktails with my date before dinner."

His voice carried through the entranceway as though he were on a stage. My heels clattered across the highly polished marble floor. Norman did a sort of stupid, stiff-looking bow to each of them and mumbled hello.

"Nice tie, tiger," Katie said, barely stifling her giggle.

I kicked the side of her shoe with mine. In my mind, I pretended I was giving Norman a swift kick.

We grabbed our jackets, in case the evening turned chilly, and traveled down in the elevator in stifling silence for what seemed an eternity. Finally the doors opened and we stepped out into the courtyard. I battled my mood; I really wanted to stay upbeat for everyone, but pretending just wasn't in my nature.

Bowen, the sweet boy from our building, hid behind a potted plant that barely concealed his large frame. Physically he was seventeen, though mentally and emotionally he was still a child. A trail of bubbles drifted up and over the leaves.

"Peek-a-boo," Bowen sang as he leapt out to surprise us, waving his bubble wand. His mop of curly hair made him look like a grown-up cherub.

My father snorted at him and moved quickly ahead of us to get to the car.

"Hi Av-or-ee. How are you? I am go-ood. I don't see the pup-pee? Where is the pup-pee?"

"Rasta is staying home tonight, Bowen." I couldn't help but smile at him as warmth flooded through me.

"Look at my bubbles." He blew a long stream of soapy spheres from his bubble wand.

"Hey, B.," Katie said. "How are the bubbles today?"

"One, three, two, four opens the magic door. Your dad-dee taught that to me, Avoo-ree."

"I can't believe my Dad took time to do anything with you."

"Hey Bowen, nice bubbles." Whitney waved at him as she walked past.

"You're too old to play with bubbles," Norman said. "Your parents should help you grow up, not stay a baby."

Bowen's smile faded. He looked baffled. The courtyard went silent. I turned to Norman.

"Shut up, Norman! *You're* the baby." I shook my head. I couldn't believe anybody could be so cruel to such a sweet soul.

"Hey, I'm just saying that if his parents didn't indulge him all the time, he might be able to learn how to do something useful in life, like stock shelves in a convenience store or something." Norman smiled and ruffled Bowen's hair.

Bowen smiled back benignly.

"Hurry up," Dad shouted from the car.

I took a breath, winding up to let Norman have it, but Whitney took my arm and gave me a look that stopped me.

"Bye, Av-or-reee," Bowen said, all trace of his previous discomfort erased.

I smiled at Bowen, but seethed at Norman.

"You truly are an asshole," I said as I pushed past him.

We climbed into the limo. My father, as usual, was oblivious to what had happened. He blathered on to Norman about going hunting on Deer Island. According to their conversation, now that they were both Bonesmen it would be different. Whitney and Katie glanced at me, eyebrows lifted in question. I shrugged, not wanting to talk about anything pertaining to the Boreman.

"Avery," Norman said, "I got tapped this year." He pushed his ring—exactly like my father's— into my face so I would look at it as he continued his explanation. "Surely you know about the Bonesmen, Avery. Your dad sponsored me. It's Yale's elite of the elite. It's the most secret of the societies. I'm in!"

"Am I supposed to be impressed?" I shoved his hand away. "And if your little club is so secret why did you just tell me about it?"

"Avery." My dad frowned. "You are being rude to your guest."

"He's your guest, Dad, not mine."

The car grew uncomfortably quiet. Whitney played with her hair and Katie stared out the window. Our driver stopped to let Katie out at her brownstone.

"See you at Jean-Georges in a few hours." Katie smiled brightly in her inscrutable way as she lunged out of the car and closed the door behind her.

My father fidgeted with the keys in his pocket, then looked up. "Claire is my date tonight. That's why it was no problem to give Whitney a drive home." He folded his arms over his chest to indicate the matter was closed.

Whitney and I stared at each other, mouths agape; shock registered in our eyes.

"No! You can't go out with my mother," Whitney cried out.

"Claire?" I wailed. "How could you? She was mom's best friend. No!"

"I know it's a bit of a shock to both of you, but Claire and I couldn't think of a better time to let you know about us. We thought tonight would be perfect."

"Know about us? Know about us? There's an us?" My entire body went rigid.

"I...you..." Whitney stammered.

"You've been seeing Claire, and neither one of you told either one of us?" I tried to comprehend this simple statement, but it was all too complex for me. "I can't believe you would do this to me. Or to mom. How long has this been going on?"

We pulled up in front of Whitney's. Without waiting for a response from my dad, she scrambled out of the car and up the front stairs of the Upper East Side loft where she and her mother lived.

I fumbled my way out of the car, trying to wrap my head around it all. Whitney blasted through the front door. I was right behind her. Dad and Norman followed me.

"What are you doing, Mom?" she yelled. "You can't go out with him." Whitney leveled a cold stare at her mother. "What about dad? You're cheating on him with my best friend's father."

"Whitney, love. Calm down." Claire, statuesque and elegant, reached out to Whitney. "I'm not cheating on anyone. Your father and I have been divorced for a long time now."

Whitney shrugged Claire away. They looked like dueling firecrackers facing off.

"Two years is not a long time. Dad still loves you. You made him leave and I won't calm down until you stop going out with him." She pointed her finger towards my dad.

I loved Claire. But this was not right. I felt so raw I couldn't hold back. "How could you do this?" I lifted a hand, palm up. "How could you do this to my mom? You were best friends."

"Whitney. Avery...I..." Claire's face crinkled as her eyes filled with tears.

I turned to dad. "Mom's only been a gone a year. Are you already over her?"

"How could you, Mom?" Whitney scowled. "How could you do this and not tell me? It's just like when you made dad leave and you never told me. I had no idea anything was wrong and then he was gone. Like that." She snapped her fingers. "This sucks! I fucking hate you."

"I was waiting for the right moment...I didn't know how..." Claire held out her arms for Whitney, but Whitney turned on her heel and stormed up to her bedroom and slammed the door behind her. The open concept design of their loft made everything sound as hollow as I felt inside.

"Well, that's done." Dad rubbed his hands together, as if to rub all the messiness away.

"We both missed your mother, Avery. We just kind of grew close. We...just..." Claire pressed her fingers to her lips.

I could barely breathe, as if someone had sucked all the air out of the room. "I can't listen to this. I just can't listen to this at all. Dad, you are a supreme asshole." My pendant grew hot and I turned cold. "Did you ever even love her?" I hadn't realized Norman had followed us to the door until Dad spun toward him.

"Norman, do you have those sedatives on you? Avery needs one."

"That's your answer? Really? Give her a pill. I told you, I don't ever want to be drugged again. And I don't want him near me. Not ever."

"Well, Norman's here for your party. You will have to—"

"No, Dad, I don't have to do anything."

Turning my back on Claire, I pushed past Dad and Norman and stomped out of the house. My dad's shoes slapped the walkway behind me but I ran down 3rd Avenue towards Park, in my too-high Jimmy Choo's, faster than I had ever run in high heels in my life. When the footsteps faded behind me, I stopped long enough to slip off my shoes, then I walked the rest of the way home.

Chapter 6

AVERY

From wonder into wonder, existence opens.

—Lao Tsu

The next morning, I woke to Rasta poking his nose over the top of the mattress and panting in my face. I opened one eye.

"It's too early," I groaned, pulling the covers over my head. Rasta leapt up onto the bed and danced around me. "Okay, okay, I'll get up." I rolled out of bed and pulled open the curtains. A pre-dawn light cast a silvery shimmer into the air. "This is way too early. What's wrong with you?"

Rasta just sat at my feet. Then my horrible birthday memory rushed back to me. I had tons of unanswered calls on my watch phone, but none from Uncle Simon. I pulled the phone he had given me out from under my mattress. I knew there would be a message from him. As I listened, his voice calmed me. *Happy birthday Avery. I'm sorry I couldn't be at your party. Your father sent me to León, Nicaragua for a series of meetings. There are things I have to talk to you about, but it has to be in person. I'm staying at the Il Convento, that converted convent I told you about last time I saw you. I'm sitting in the courtyard by the central fountain, about to go for dinner, looking at the photo of you and your mom that I carry with me always. I should be finished here in a few weeks. See you soon.* I played it again and again, looking for clues as to what he wanted to talk to me about.

It was clear that Dad was keeping me away from Uncle Simon, but to what end? It didn't make sense. Just thinking about Dad reminded me how pissed I was at him. I yanked on sweat pants and a sweatshirt from a heap on the floor beside my bed. I tapped the side of my leg for Rasta to follow me. Though Rasta was Ruby's dog, I was the one who walked him and he slept in my room. Ruby had found him years ago in an alley close to her sister's apartment, all bedraggled and worm-infested. Mom forced Dad to allow us to keep him. We called him Rasta when Ruby sang an old Bob Marley song as she bathed him and he started to sing along. "One love" is still one of my favorites.

Rasta trotted to the door and wagged his tail, looking back at me expectantly. I followed him out of my room, grabbed the leash when we reached the front door, and snapped it onto his collar.

This week had been the longest of my life. Since the angelman had saved me, everything seemed different, brighter, more alive.

"You're up awfully early, Miss Adams," said Andy, the weekend night watchman posted in the 24-hour guard box at the entrance of The Dakota. I wasn't even born yet when John Lennon was killed here, but I still got shivers whenever I was near this spot, and Rasta always walked in a wide arc around it.

"Just walkin' the dog, Andy."

"Be careful on your own out there, Miss. But I guess you don't have to worry too much with that bear." Andy laughed.

I waved as we walked on across the street and entered Central Park. Rasta headed towards the Imagine Mosaic. But I was determined not to let him win this odd, week-long power struggle, where he had obstinately tried to pull me into Central Park on every walk. Usually Rasta was happy to do a quick trot around the block. He was more couch potato than active dog. With so many things in my life spiraling out of control, I wasn't going to lose control of him too.

A warm golden glow replaced the pre-dawn silvery light. *Another empty day to get through.* I was pulling one way and Rasta the other when I heard a voice behind me.

"Why aren't you listening?"

I twirled around. A tall, willowy girl with long straight black hair stood watching us. It took me a moment to recognize Raven. In her deer-skin jacket with intricate beading and fringes, there was no mistaking her First Nation heritage this morning. She looked like she had stepped out of a different world.

"I am listening. He wants to go that way, and I want to go this way."

"No. He says you want to go that way. You just don't know it," Raven said. "I had a dream last night that I should come here early. I know your crowd doesn't really like me, but you have to listen. Not to me, to him." Raven tilted her head toward Rasta.

My cheeks flushed. "I didn't know I had a crowd."

"Oh, you definitely do." Raven waved a hand through the air as though that should have been obvious to me. "And I admit I've been really jealous of all of you. Things seem so easy for you. Except I know your mother died, so it probably hasn't been that easy..."

Raven's candor stunned me into silence. No one outside my inner circle ever referred to my dead mother. It was my unwritten code. I wanted to pull away from the girl in front of me, away from the discomfort I always felt around her, but I couldn't.

"My father left my mom and me. He refuses to see me, but pays for my schooling. I think I embarrass him. He pretends he's not native now that he's a rich Wall Street lawyer and wears a suit every day."

I didn't know what to say to her. She was different from anyone I had ever encountered. Again, I felt like running away, but instead I studied her more closely. She was pretty, with her curtain of long, dark hair. For one brief moment, just like that time on campus when she had creeped me out, a faint glow emanated from her body. Just like the stranger who had saved me, but smaller, closer to her body. Warmth radiated through my heart, like her light was shining into me, making me feel lighter, happier, and fuller.

Rasta tugged on the leash and again I hauled him back. Then felt I had to explain to her. "He's being stubborn."

"No. He isn't being stubborn. He knows what you want."

"What is it that he knows I want?"

"I can't tell you that. He's your dog." She spoke slowly, as though I were a little dense. "Dogs can only communicate so much. They have a different language than we do. He says, 'Go that way.'" She pointed down the path. "He's a great dog. Can I come and visit him sometime? And you?"

"Of course you can, and I'll see you in anthro class," I said, suddenly inexplicably drawn to this strange girl.

Raven's eyes brightened. "Anyone who has been given an animal like this is special." She touched Rasta lightly on the head. "I'm impressed. That's all I know." She nodded before turning and walking away.

I smiled as I watched her leave. I hoped the others in my crowd would open their minds to accept her. They had apologized to Raven for hurting her feelings, but hanging out with her might be another story.

"Okay, Rasta, you win." I sighed and started down the path he pulled me towards. He soon left the path and we crossed dew covered grass, the wetness seeping into my runners, and we climbed up over a small hill.

At the crest, a few trees, already in full bloom, clumped together. The rest of the trees in the grove were just beginning to bud.

Then I saw him. Sitting cross-legged by the pond. Completely still. The first light of day shimmering on the surface of the water. I stared at him in disbelief. It was really *him*. His grey knapsack with the little embroidered British flag was beside him. His dark hair was almost shaved, and that whitish glow was all around him, pulsating.

I expected my heart to be pounding, but it was strangely still and quiet. In fact, everything was quiet. Even the city was just a low hum in the background. Rasta stood, one paw poised to take a step, barely a breath taken. I felt as though I had transcended into that shadow world again.

I don't know how long I stood and watched him before taking a small step, then stopping. What was I going to say? Or do? *This is crazy.* I turned away.

"Hey, it's you." His voice was musical.

I slowly turned back, hoping he was calling out to me, knowing he was. He had risen to his feet and was striding towards me. My head filled with the sound of a thousand bees.

"It's you," he said again.

AVERY

The softest things in the world overcome the hardest things in the world.

—Lao Tsu

"My name is Aiden Kane." He reached out a hand.

"You have an accent." I felt foolish for stating the obvious. I held out my hand. Before we touched, an arc of electricity surged between us. As our fingers came together, tingles traveled into my palm and ran up my arm. He held my hand, as if he didn't quite know what to do. Everything seemed strange, my senses alert. I could almost taste the iron tang of the earth, moist from the morning dew, and hear the tiniest sounds, like scratching in the dirt at my feet. I glanced down to see an ant crawling past the end of my running shoe. Angelman looked down, then back at me. Did he hear it too? Was he experiencing everything I was? A soft thudding reverberated in my ears. His heartbeat. In perfect sync with mine.

"Wow, you felt that, didn't you?" His sea-green eyes widened. "I've trained for years to feel subtle energy, but never experienced it like that. Your eyes went a deeper shade of gold." He let go of my hand and the sensations lessened. But not completely.

"I'm from London," he added.

"What?" I blinked. Everything still looked brilliant and sounded intense.

"My accent. You noticed. What's your name?"

"Oh. I'm Avery. Avery Adams." My eyes started to adjust to the brightness. Would my senses ever return to normal? "What were you doing by the pond? You were so still. Were you meditating?"

45

"Yes. I do it every morning before Bagua Zhang practice." He reached down and patted Rasta on his head. "Beautiful dog." Rasta moved closer and leaned against his leg. Aiden held Rasta's lower jaw and lifted the shaggy head to look into his eyes. "Are you pushing me away from her, or sizing me up for a fight?" We both laughed. Rasta shifted to lean his 125 pounds against the man even more heavily.

"His name is Rasta. What's Baw-gwa-Zhang, Aiden?" I wanted to say his name, to see how it felt on my tongue.

"It's an ancient martial art, rare and mystical, that doesn't use muscular force, but develops internal spiral energy. That's some of what we felt earlier when we shook hands, although that was way more intense than usual. Kinda strange."

"Seriously, Aiden? You've only been here a week and you're already picking up girls?" A different accent broke through the private space that Aiden and I had created. I turned to see a tall man with long dark hair, about the same age as Aiden, stride toward us. He reached for my hand, but I felt no arc or tingles when we touched.

He flinched. "Hey, you shocked me! And that's hard to do." He pulled his hand back. "I'm Blaine."

"Avery," Aiden and I said in unison. We laughed again.

"Blaine and I are about to practice," Aiden said. "Why don't you stay and then you can see what Bagua is?"

"That would be great." I rummaged in my purse. "Look, I just got this out of the library. It's on self-defense." I waved the book. "Maybe I could learn some of this stuff." I mimicked a few moves I'd seen in movies. A scene flashed through my head. Me flipping Norman onto his back and rendering him unconscious.

"It's a little more involved than learning a few moves." Aiden opened his hands and shrugged his shoulders. "You'll see what it's like when you watch."

"I'll want to do more than watch." I shoved the book back into my bag.

Blaine and Aiden exchanged looks. "We'll see," Blaine said.

"Ok. Show me," I teased. "Maybe you guys aren't very good at it." I had seen Aiden in action, felt the weird internal energy he had. I was sure these guys were the real deal.

"Let's show her how it's done, Aiden." Blaine waved a hand toward an open patch of grass. "Let's spar."

"We don't want to freak her out. Let's just introduce her to a few basics." Aiden pushed his sleeves up his forearms.

His eyes met mine. A different kind of shock jolted through me. Could he see right inside of me? Every thought, every memory, every feeling seemed open to him, like a book he could read. He looked away.

"First, Bagua refers to the eight trigrams of the I Ching, The Book of Changes." Aiden circle-walked, creating a path in the ground. He held one palm open and towards the center of the circle, while the other guarded his body. Every few circles he would fly into a series of fluid movements, some slow and some so fast they were dazzling that changed his direction. He started to glow, like he had in the subway.

"Wow." My jaw dropped. "You're amazing. It's sort of like Tai Chi. When you do it slowly."

"Yes. There are three internal martial arts, Tai Chi, Hsing Yi, and Bagua. Each with its own qualities."

"Here I'll show you." Blaine slid his arms along mine and moved them into position. He whispered in my ear, "Tai Chi moves in a line, and uses expansion…" he moved his arms out from mine, "…and contraction…" With a quick, downward movement, he closed his arms back around mine and squeezed closer to me. "These movements provide the power. Hsing Yi uses short, explosive steps, all very close up. And Bagua…"

" … always uses redirection." Aiden moved closer to us. "Think of the three internal martial arts as parts of the dragon. Tai Chi is the tail, using whipping motions, Bagua is the center, always coiling, and Hsing Yi is the head, direct and snapping. Maybe we should demonstrate." He tapped Blaine's arm. "We'll show her some internal energy."

"Sure."

Aiden threw a punch at Blaine and they whacked forearms. The sound echoed like two iron pipes clashing. They moved so fast I could barely follow their movements.

"No you don't, show off." Blaine grabbed for Aiden's arm. They twirled around each other, there one moment, gone the next, spinning away like twin whirlwinds. Blaine looked over at me. The loss of focus was a mistake. Aiden held out his palm, barely touched Blaine's chest, and sent him flying into the air to land on the grass a few feet away.

Aiden chuckled. "You looked away, Blaine. It's been a long time since I've been able to move you that far."

"Really, mate. You didn't have to use that much force." Blaine scrambled to his feet, his face red.

"Wow, I want to learn how to do the palm thing." I held my hand out in front of me, as if making a strike.

Aiden caught my palm in his hand in one swift move. "We've never trained any girls. There aren't any in our Order."

"Well, there was Veronika." Blaine dusted himself off and joined us. "She trained for a bit with Old Phoenix."

"Veronika isn't a girl, she's a demon-spirit." Aiden let go of my hand. "Bagua isn't easy. You sure you have what it takes?"

"I'm totally sure. I really want to learn it. Please. I love how it looks. Like dancing." *Except with power.*

"This isn't dancing." Blaine pushed my arm lightly. "The 'palm-thing' is really dangerous and it takes years to learn how to control it."

"You can't do Bagua halfway. It's all or nothing." Aiden ran his hand over his shaven head, as if he couldn't quite believe my request.

"I want to learn how to fight." I crouched into a wide and deep knee bend. "See I can do this. I have great flexibility."

"No one can really teach you how to fight. That's something you discover when you realize the higher purpose of martial art. And that's found inside the individual soul. It takes years to develop that." Aiden peered at me through dark lashes.

"I really want to do this." I held one hand to my heart. "I don't care how long it takes. I'll work at it."

With one eyebrow raised, Aiden eyed Blaine. Blaine shrugged. Aiden turned to me and looked me straight in the eyes. "Ok, Avery, meet us here tomorrow at sunrise. You okay with that Blaine?"

"Sure. I don't know how Luc will be though. He's the best teacher, other than Old Phoenix, but he doesn't mess around."

Aiden reached into his pocket and pulled out a piece of folded paper. He held it out to me.

Was he giving me his phone number? I grabbed the paper and opened it up. A circle drawn with a dot in the center. I frowned as I looked up at him.

"This is a symbol that Luc gave both Blaine and me when we first started training. Just think on it a while."

I bit my lip as I studied the drawing. "Are we the dot, and the circle the universe? Or is the dot the tree and we're the circle? Hmmm. The dot's the inside and the circle's the outside, like everything's connected. This is cool; there are so many ways to look at it."

Dawn gave only a hint of light, as Rasta and I strode through the park. I pulled my hoodie tighter around me in the damp chill of the morning air. I nodded. I would be the first one at practice. *That'll show them how committed I am.* I gasped as I came over the top of the hill. They were already there, Aiden and Blaine, circling the tall, leafy oak trees. I approached slowly. My jaw clenched and my stomach tightened. Whatever made me think I could train with hardcore martial arts fighters? Not that circling around trees looked all that hardcore. I repressed a grin as I approached them. Rasta turned in circles in the shade before dropping down onto the thick grass. I stopped in front of Aiden.

He raised an eyebrow. "Ready?"

I nodded, breathless. He was doing that glowing thing again, and with the brightness of his white t-shirt and loose-fitting jeans I couldn't find the words to speak.

Aiden waved a hand toward a young oak tree. "When people first learn circle-walking around a tree, they can suck the life right out of it."

"Really?" I cocked my head. I had never heard of such a thing.

"Really." He pointed at the oak. "I picked this one out for you this morning. It's not too old and not too young." He patted the tree affectionately. "The idea is to absorb the energy from the ground and return it to the tree through your palm. We learn how to harness the power of nature; it's kinda magical. But that's for later…"

"How do I start?" I raised my hands the way I thought Aiden had done the day before, and took a step forward. I needed the palm-power-thing now.

"Your stance is vital." He maneuvered his feet so one was behind and one forward, toes pointed inward. "Twist from deep inside, a place called the dantien. Pack your energy like a coil ready to spring open, feel the earth through your feet to propel your movement. And, bah!" He leapt forward with such force and speed, I jumped back, my heart pounding. He grinned. "Now you try it."

I didn't get the dantien thing, but I did my best to mimic what he showed me as I walked around the tree.

Aiden smacked my knees with his hand, as if he were Madame in ballet class. "Deeper knees, Avery. Deeper. Twist more … into the center…from inside."

I circled a few times and stopped.

"Keep going." Blaine circled his hand in the air. "You're doing amazing."

"Now use your feet. Connect to the ground. Kobu one foot, Baibu the other." Aiden showed me the footwork as he walked alongside me on the outside of my circle. "You seem to know your body really well."

"I take ballet."

"Ah," Aiden said. "That will help you, although this is different. I'll show you the first palm change. We will focus on that for awhile. You could spend a lifetime perfecting it. The form will remain empty movements until you learn how to direct your intention, the "Yi" while generating internal energy, the "Qi". That's when it becomes powerful."

My forehead wrinkled as I concentrated. In the deepest part of my body, a current of electricity raced through me, as if traveling through a thin copper wire. I sucked in a breath, and stopped moving, but the feeling inside continued. I felt eyes staring at me and my skin prickled.

Another man glided toward us. He came right over to me, air-kissing both of my cheeks, which I thought was pretentious until he said in his thick French accent, "Bonjour Avery. Aiden told me you would be here today, so I dropped by to meet you and see how your training is progressing."

"Aiden told me about you too." This was the second greatest Bagua Zhang teacher? I'd been expecting some kind of warrior. Luc was small and compact, and seemed so gentle, with his delicate, unblemished hands. I could hardly wait to meet Old Phoenix. He was probably ancient and totally decrepit.

"So who have you trained with before?"

Blaine lifted a hand into the air, palm up. "She's never done any training, Luc."

"Mon Dieu! Impossible! Blaine, you rascal. You are pulling my trouser, no?"

I bit my lip to keep from laughing.

Aiden's eyes, twinkling with humor, met mine. "This is her first day."

"Quelle surprise," Luc said and fixed each of us with his stare. "You three have a great responsibility now. Don't forget about the foundations. She'll need to be a lot stronger to handle the influx of internal energie, the alchemie, n'est pas? You boys know what it can do to a body that is not properly prepared." He shook his head, muttering to himself. "One day. Just one day. Impossible."

I exchanged looks with Aiden and Blaine. Luc shrugged. "Well, au revoir. I have to go now to the hospital to teach the surgeons meditation and Qi Gong."

Blaine grinned. "You're going to revolutionize Western medicine."

"That's the idea." Luc turned to Aiden. "Did she help you with the circle dot?" Without waiting for an answer, he spun around and headed for the pathway leading out of the park.

Blaine burst out laughing. "Luc knows you so well, mate!" He slapped Aiden on the back.

I lifted both hands. "What did he mean by all that?"

"Luc is different." Aiden's cheeks turned slightly pink. "You have to get used to him. You did great Avery. I've never seen anyone learn how to move from the dantien so quickly, and generate so much energy."

Blaine touched my arm. "Will you be back tomorrow?"

"Sure. I love this weird stuff." The sound of girls' voices caught my attention and I glanced to my left.

Aiden had turned his head and asked. "Do you hear that?"

Blaine tilted his head. "Hear what?"

"Those girls talking." I pointed off into the distance.

Aiden nodded. "It came from way across the pond."

"What girls? I don't hear any girls." Blaine frowned. "What's with you two?"

"They said your name, Aiden. They claimed that they are going to get you." I shivered, though there was no breeze.

Aiden pushed back his shoulders. "It's nothing."

"It sounds like something to me..."

His jaw tightened. "I said it's nothing, Avery. Let it go."

AVERY

If one aspires to walk the Tao, one should walk in a circle.

—Lao Tsu

My eyes narrowed. "How can you say that was nothing?" I grabbed Aiden's arm. "Those girls are out to get you, Aiden. That's what they said."

Blaine threw his arms in the air. "What are you talking about? What's up with you two? I didn't hear a thing, but suddenly both of you have some crazy, super-power hearing."

Aiden tugged his arm out of my grasp. "Really Avery, don't worry. Someone wants to fight us. It's no big deal." He turned to Blaine. "Probably Veronika and one of her friends on a little jealousy trip."

I wasn't buying it. "Who is this Veronika, anyway?" I crossed my arms. "Wasn't Veronika the demon-spirit you mentioned before who trained with Old Phoenix?"

Aiden frowned. "It's kind of a long story."

"I'm going to crack on, mate." Blaine gathered up his knapsack and patted Aiden's shoulder. "See you tomorrow, Avery."

"You're leaving?" I touched his hand. "I thought we could all go for a tea, and you could both tell me what's going on. I know there's something you guys aren't telling me."

"I want to crash Luc's presentation. I'll leave the explanations up to Aiden, and catch up with you tomorrow."

"Well, Aiden?" I asked. "Tea?"

"Yes. Sure. That'd be grand."

Blaine gave me a warm hug good-bye, then Aiden and I sauntered off with Rasta in the direction of my place and a café. The air was still damp from the spring rains, but they might have a few tables outside. We could drop Rasta off at home on the way.

"You live in The Dakota." Aiden stopped at the red light and looked across the street "That's where John Lennon was killed, isn't it?"

"Ya, right over there. He had just come out of the courtyard through the archway. Do you like music?"

"I love music. I play the guitar. Acoustic."

"I love music too. I wanted to learn electric guitar but my dad wouldn't let me. He wanted me to take ballet. This morning, at Bagua practice, was the first time I was glad about that … What kind of music do you like?"

"Almost everything, but I really love sixties and seventies music. Because of my mom." Aiden took Rasta's leash when the light turned green and we crossed.

"My mom loved that music too."

"Loved?" Aiden paused. "Is your mom…gone?"

"Yes. She died a year ago."

"Oh, Avery," he took my hand. "I'm so sorry. I know what it's like to lose a mother."

"You do?" I swallowed hard. "Your mom died?"

"Five years ago. A car crash on a country lane, in the south of England. I've had a hard time forgiving myself for not being there when it happened. Listening and playing her music makes me feel close to her."

"I wear this." I pulled my necklace out from under my shirt. "She gave it to me the night before she died, and that day in the subway when you saved me, I had put it on for the first anniversary of her death." I forced back my tears. I was afraid if I let one escape, I might never stop crying.

Aiden stepped closer to me. I looked away from his probing eyes and held out my necklace for him to see.

"Wow. The stone and setting look really ancient." He cradled it in his palm. "It's heavy. And it's giving off a vibe or something. Feels sort of like the amulet I wear. I have one of seven that Old Phoenix originally gave to the Bagua Brothers." He pulled it out from under his shirt. An engraved silver oval hung on a leather cord. "It was strange during the ceremony. Old Phoenix said that one of the amulets would call out to each of us. This one didn't just call out; it was like it jumped into my hand. I never take it off."

"I've been giving everyone shocks since I put this necklace on." He released my pendant and I slipped it inside my shirt. "I didn't put that together until you said that you could feel something from it." We walked through the archway.

"Hi, Avo-ree." Bowen entered the courtyard, blowing a trail of bubbles behind him. "Who's your friend?"

"Bowen, meet Aiden." I reached out and touched both of their shoulders. "Maybe you could show Aiden your bubbles while I take Rasta home. I'll be back in a sec."

I raced upstairs to drop the dog off, and rushed back to those old elevators for the painfully slow descent. At the front doors, I peered out eagerly, almost expecting to find Aiden gone. As if he were some kind of apparition that would disappear the moment I looked away. But he was there, smiling.

"Look, Av-oree. Look what Aiden gave me. It's a Kaleidoscope. It's magic. See?" He twirled it as he looked into it. "Your dad-dee has a magic door. One, three, two, four opens the magic door."

"That's really cool, Bowen." I looked at Aiden.

He smiled. "Just something I had in my rucksack."

"You have fun with that, okay Bowen. Aiden and I have to go now."

"Thank you very much, Aiden, for the present." Bowen held the kaleidoscope to his chest.

"You're welcome, buddy." Aiden clapped him on the shoulder before we turned to leave.

Aiden and I walked towards the café in awkward silence. We were finally alone and I had so many questions for him, I didn't know where to begin. So many emotions whirled through me that walking close to him made me ache.

"That was really sweet of you to give that to Bowen. What were you doing with a kaleidoscope in your backpack?"

"I picked it up the other day for my nephew, Tommy. He's a lot like Bowen."

I nodded, then looked down for a moment, sucked in a breath and looked up. "… So, who is this Veronika, anyway?"

"You don't let things go, do you?" Aiden grinned. "I'm going to start calling you Bulldog soon." The tension between us dissolved as we laughed. A few tables and chairs were set up outside the café and I pointed to an empty one.

Aiden pulled out a chair for me. "What'll you have?"

I wagged a finger at him. "I haven't forgotten that you still haven't answered. But I'll give you time to think about it while you get me an Earl Grey Tea and a cinnamon cookie. They have the best ones here."

"Got it." He smiled. "And I appreciate the grace period." He pushed in my chair and went into the café.

I took a few deep breaths as I waited.

Aiden came out with our tray and set it on the table between us then sat down across from me. "Okay." He pressed both palms against the glass table top. "Veronika was sort of my girlfriend. I met her in China."

"Oh." Something cold slithered through me. "So this isn't a competitive, martial arts thing, after all?"

"It's a martial arts thing. Definitely." Aiden looked at me and his eyes softened. "How about I start from the beginning? It'll make more sense. When I was a boy, my dad disappeared one night, and my mom took us to live in East London. It was a tough neighborhood. Skinhead gangs roamed around bullying kids. That's when I started taking martial arts. I wanted to defend myself, rather than get regularly beaten to a pulp. I tried different styles, then one day, Luc appeared, almost magically. He showed me the internal arts, and that changed everything."

Aiden shifted in his seat. "It took some years before I could fight back, but one day, I did just that. Eddy Endicott came after me with his gang of bullies, and I landed a palm strike that threw him a couple of feet in the air. When they all scattered, I knew my days of being bullied were over. I met Blaine through Luc, and we became best friends, Bagua Brothers. Luc sent us to China to train with his master, Old Phoenix, in the Wudang Mountains. They say he is over a hundred years old. Some say two hundred. He is a small, thin man, who is more powerful than the biggest guy. Once when he was telling us a story, he pointed to a boulder with his finger, and it split right in two. I saw it with my own eyes. Even Old Phoenix looked surprised."

"Oh, come on." I giggled nervously. "You don't really expect me to believe that. I think you're just telling me fantastic stories to make me forget about Veronika."

He shook his head. "I was getting to that, Bulldog. I'm not going to get away with anything around you, am I?"

"Not a thing." What was it about him that made me feel so comfortable, so free to completely be myself? I rarely felt that with anyone, even my friends, and I hardly knew Aiden. "Bulldog is not a very flattering name. Can't you come up with something better?"

"Ok, I'll work on that. But back to Veronika. She was a student of Old Phoenix when we arrived, the only girl who had ever been there. She had trained with her father all her life, and was already a gifted martial artist. She is Chinese-American and has lived in both countries."

"So she was beautiful, I'm guessing?" The cold in the pit of my stomach returned.

"Oh yes. Very beautiful. And bright. And talented. We hit it off immediately, and spent all our time talking, training, doing our chores, and spending mealtimes together. Then one day she disappeared without a word. A few days later she came back, in the middle of the night, saying she had discovered a better teacher than Old Phoenix. She said I had to leave with her immediately to join this new clan. Her eyes had changed. There was a darkness in them that I had never seen before. I refused to go. I was loyal to Old Phoenix, and I didn't even want to be near her if she had turned against him. She got angry with me, and told me I would regret the day that I had rejected her. I hadn't seen her again until last week, in the subway station, when she hurtled towards me in her Goth-Girl get-up, with those dead eyes. I almost didn't recognize her. When I saw her grab at your chest in mid-air, I had to do something."

"That was Veronika?" Shivers ran up my spine. "What does she want, Aiden? Is she still in love with you?"

"I don't know what she wants. I really don't know."

My watch flashed a text from Katie, asking about a book for school. I looked up. "Oh no! I'm going to be late. I completely forgot about class."

"I'll fast-walk you to the subway and you should get there in time."

"Hey, I'm a New Yorker. We all walk fast here, and there is no way we can get there in time."

"You've never fast-walked like this before."

He took my satchel and swung it over his shoulder, along with his backpack. Then he slipped one arm through mine and the other around my waist. His touch set my skin on fire. Currents of energy arced between us as he gained speed. I no longer even touched the ground. The people, buildings, everything became a blur. The air parted as we pushed through it, taking my breath away.

"Holy shit, Aiden, this is fast. How do you do it?" Exhilaration coursed through me, sending my heart-rate into overdrive as we reached the subway in record time. No one on the sidewalk seemed to notice us. "I want to do this. Can you teach me?"

"It takes years to learn. And you have to get to class."

"Forget intro to anthro exam review. I want to learn this. It's like The Flash, but real. Please. Just get me started. I'll practice every day."

"Ok. If you learn this like you learned the first palm change this morning, you'll be flying like superman soon." He let go of my arm and waist, then grabbed my hand and pulled me behind a wall, out of sight of the crowds hurrying up and down the subway stairs. "I'll show you the mechanics slowly. Again, it has to do with the dantien, and bursting through into the space you see ahead."

Aiden bent deep, then took a few strides.

I pressed my lips together. "You look like a duck."

"Now imagine how you'll look when you're learning."

The image of me duck-walking made me laugh, but I sobered quickly. I squatted and took a long step forward. I would have lost my balance if Aiden hadn't grabbed me. *Not as easy as it looks.*

"Really concentrate now." He pressed his index fingers to his temples. "Bend deep into your dantien. Connect with the earth, and imagine being pushed through the air effortlessly. At first it feels impossible, then you almost take flight, and it's easy. You can move so fast that you're almost invisible to others. Like this…" He whipped down to the end of the block and back.

Ah. That explained why no one seemed to pay any attention to us as we flew by. "Wow, that's incredible! I would never have believed it possible if I hadn't seen it with my own eyes. Is that how fast we were walking to the subway?"

"Not quite. You were holding me back."

I poked him in the ribs before bending down again.

He held out his hand. "I'll help you."

"No way. I want to learn the way you did. I'm sure Luc didn't hold your hand when you were learning." I managed to do a slow-speed walk for a few feet without banging into anyone. I stopped in front of Aiden and tilted my head. "When do I get to be invisible?"

"Patience, Bulldog."

I shot him a dirty look but he just laughed. "Walk into the spaces. Train your mind to see space instead of solid objects. I'll go ahead and you can catch up to me." Aiden stooped low.

I zoomed along the sidewalk, seeing space in an entirely new way. A wheelchair turned into my path suddenly and I slammed into it. I grabbed the arms to keep from tumbling across the sidewalk. A withered-looking Albino was perched on the chair; his claw-like hand snatched my arm. He

had a shock of long white hair, mirrored sunglasses, and bizarre tattoos all over his face, like Egyptian hieroglyphs.

I tried to pull away, but he clutched me tighter, and jerked me close to his face. "Who's your oracle, girl?"

"What oracle? What are you…?" I craned my neck in the direction of Aiden but couldn't see him. Where was he? At the speed he was traveling, he could be halfway across the city by now. *Please come back.*

"You know me," the man wheezed. "You must. You are the one."

I froze, my hands still gripping the arms of the wheelchair.

"Of course we know you, sir." Aiden appeared at my side.

At last. He relaxed his grip on my arm. He slipped off his sunglasses and blinked in the harsh sunlight. "They sent me to find you."

I released a breath and let go of the wheelchair.

Aiden took my hand and gently led me away from the chair. I couldn't stop staring at the strange face of the man before me. He stopped blinking and eyed me, first with one pink eye, then the other, like a bird.

"She's the one, all right."

Aiden frowned. "Who sent you?"

The man cast a furtive look up and down the sidewalk before leaning forward. "They did," he whispered. "You know who. We can only be guides. We can't intervene."

"Oh, those people. Ok." Aiden took a step backwards. "Um, we have to go now."

"Quickly, they're coming for you. They may not know about her yet. I just realized who she was when I saw her, or rather felt her, coming toward me." He nodded at me. "You have to pull together. Together is better."

"We'll pull together. We have to go now," Aiden said again, tugging my arm as he took another step away from the man.

"Look for the signs along the way." The albino raised one finger as he turned his wheelchair away from us. "Rabelais knew that during the week of the three Thursdays, destinies were set in motion for the coming Myriad Time. Remember…together is better." He wheeled off through the crowd.

Neither Aiden nor I spoke for a moment, then he turned to me, his fingers still clutching my arm. "When you didn't show up at the corner, I came looking for you."

I shuddered. "He was so creepy. Did you know what he was talking about?"

"I think he has a mental illness. I was playing along, hoping he would let you go." Aiden dropped his hand. "Do you remember what he first said to you?"

"Yeah, he asked, 'Who is your Oracle?'"

His eyes searched mine before he sighed. "I better get you home."

Aiden slipped his arm around my waist and again the sense of power flared through my body. I moved closer to him.

He yanked his arm away, stuffed his hands into his pockets, and stepped up the pace.

My forehead wrinkled. What did I do? "I can walk myself home, you know."

"I won't let you walk home alone." Aiden took my arm. "Don't be silly."

I stopped and shrugged his arm away. "Oh, so now I'm silly."

Aiden stopped and drew in a long breath as he turned to face me. "No. Of course you're not silly. I'm sorry. I didn't mean it like that. It's just...I can't. You can't..."

"I can't stop thinking about you, Aiden," I said. "And I think it's the same for you. In fact, I know it is."

He stared at me, his green eyes swirling with something I couldn't quite identify. I swallowed. Had I pushed him too hard? We'd only met a couple of times. Maybe spewing out my feelings like that hadn't been the best...

The flapping of wings overhead caught our attention and we both looked up. Starlings flocked above us. They flew in waves, swelling and heaving, like masses of black clouds undulating across the sky.

I drew in a quick breath and pressed a hand to my chest. "They're beautiful. It's like they're putting on a show just for us."

"In Norway, there's the 'day of the black cloud' that happens during murmuration. The sky fills with so many starlings the sun is almost blocked out." Aiden shaded his eyes with one hand as he looked up. "But it shouldn't be happening in the spring. That's so weird, like the seasons are out of sync or something."

The birds flew out of sight as quickly as they had appeared. At least they had taken attention away from what I had said to Aiden earlier. We trudged toward my home, side by side. When we reached The Dakota, I climbed up the first step and turned around, my eyes looking directly into Aiden's. My breath caught.

Aiden cupped my face in his hands. The electrical force that had arced between us before traveled from his fingertips and crossed my skin. Our bodies lightly touched. He leaned closer and I closed my eyes. For a few seconds, I felt his breath, warm on my face. I waited. Then I opened my eyes and he was gone.

AVERY

There is no greater disaster than greed.

—Lao Tsu

I lay on my bed dreaming about the angelman that I had finally met, when a buzzing from underneath my mattress made me jump. I pulled out the vibrating phone.

"Uncle Simon," I whispered. "Finally. Why has it taken you so long to call?"

"I'm so sorry Avery. I hated missing your birthday. We finally made it to Limon, where there was a labor dispute at the gold mine. I came in to negotiate. My mine manager, Miguel, left the compound to talk down some of the rabble-rousers. They want to set up a union. One of them took out his gun and shot Miguel. Luckily, the guy was a bad shot, and Miguel is okay. The army has shut down the roads that connect Limon, so I'm holed up on the side of the mountain, in the executive quarters, until they open again. Bandwidth is spotty here, so our cell phones don't always work."

"Are you safe?"

"Don't worry, Avs. The army surrounded the compound, and they aren't letting anyone in or out of the main gates. I'm sitting outside in the gazebo where I have a clear view of the village below. My bodyguard, Juan, is with me. He's former Sandinista, one of the very best they had. I've got absolutely nothing to worry about with Juan around…" A sharp crack reverberated in my ear and I tightened my grip on the phone. "What was that?"

"Gun shot. The guy and his merry men are riding through town on their horses, drinking and shooting their pistols into the air. Everything echoes up from the village below. It looks like a scene from a Western movie."

"Please be careful. I couldn't bear to lose you."

"The army's just letting them drink until there is nothing left, then they'll round them up. We've been through this before and it seems to work."

"So what was it that you wanted to ask me?"

"I really wanted to ask you in person, but I'm not sure how long I'll be stuck here."

"Let's not wait. I have questions for you too."

"Did your mother give the necklace to you? The one in the blue box?"

"Yes. The night before she died."

"Good. You can't let anyone know about the necklace, especially not your dad. It must stay in the box. I've been meaning to talk to you about this for so long, but your father has made it impossible to get near you. That's why I gave Ruby the phone to give to you."

"Why is he trying to keep us apart? And what can you tell me about the necklace?"

"You haven't …out of the box … have you?"

"What? You're breaking up. Can you hear me? Is that shooting? Uncle Simon? NO! Uncle Simon? Are you there?"

The line went dead.

It had been days since I'd heard from Uncle Simon. I tried to call him back, but there was no connection. I called the US Embassy, but they were not very forthcoming. Finally, I spoke to someone who said that Limon was still under siege, but as far as they knew no Americans had been killed.

Between worrying about Uncle Simon and my growing fascination with Bagua, I had barely studied for my last exam. Intro to Anthropology was my easiest course, but I still needed to focus. Instead, I kept thinking about how Aiden and Blaine had both commented that I was learning quickly. Already, I felt different internally, stronger and more grounded. I opened the file for my study notes and tried to print them, but my printer was out of ink.

I'll get some from Dad. I went down the hall and knocked on his office door. "Dad?"

He didn't answer. I knocked again and the door opened slightly. No one was there.

A thin streak of sunlight filtered through a narrow, stained-glass window, leaving the room sheathed in semi-darkness. I turned on the brass desk light, revealing a pile of annual reports scattered on the normally impeccably clean desk. Equarian Inc.'s annual report was on the top. I glanced down at it and my eyes narrowed. Something was partially hidden beneath the report. I moved it aside and picked up a small glass vial. It contained a white powder. Cocaine? Could my dad be a coke addict? That would explain his erratic behavior since my mom died. I'd heard about high-powered CEO's getting addicted, that it made them feel invulnerable, endlessly energetic, even visionary. During a recent dinner conversation, Dad had mentioned that Freud used cocaine, as did Sir Arthur Conan Doyle, author of Sherlock Holmes. His comment seemed so random. Still, I never would've guessed my ultra-straight, ultra-conservative corporate dad was a coke freak.

I need to get out of here. I set the vial down and pulled open the top drawer where a dozen neatly organized ink cartridges stood in their boxes. I grabbed one. A noise at the door startled me and I looked up. My father waltzed into the room. I stiffened.

He switched on the light and glared at me. "What are you doing in my office, Avery?"

He strode across the room and seized my hand. His fingers bit into my skin as he twisted my wrist until I thought it might break.

"I'm getting an ink cartridge … Dad, ouch, you're hurting me."

"How did you get in? The door was locked, the security on."

"Why are you hurting me? Let go! Please."

He tore his eyes away from mine and looked down at my hand, still sealed in his vise-grip. He released me.

"The door wasn't locked. I didn't think you'd mind if I got a cartridge for my printer. For my exam notes. I wanted to study." I rubbed my wrist and glared at him. He had never done anything like that before.

"Did you touch anything on my desk?" His face blotched red.

"No, of course not. I knew where you kept the cartridges from the last time you gave me one. "

Dad rubbed his forehead and drew a slow breath. "Of course, honey. Of course. I'm sorry. I was just surprised to find you in here when I was sure the door was locked." He glanced around the room, then rustled through some papers without looking at them. "I must have forgotten to lock it this morning."

"I'm sorry, Dad, I..." My heart pounded. "I didn't think you'd mind me taking an ink cartridge."

He waved a hand through the air. "Go on. It's fine. It's fine." He dropped onto his desk chair. "You go on now, honey."

I took a much-needed breath, and found my legs. Why did I feel so guilty when it was my dad that was hiding something from me? I crossed the room and reached for the door knob.

"Stop."

I froze.

I heard a click of some kind behind me, but I didn't dare turn around.

"Okay, now you can go."

I bolted through the door and back to my room. What was that powder I had found? Was my dad an addict? I fumbled with the ink cartridge, finally coaxing it into place. Not that it really mattered anymore. How on earth was I supposed to study for an exam when the police could come pounding on our door at any moment?

AVERY

To have little is to possess. To have plenty is to be perplexed.

—Lao Tsu

"Hey, Dad." I pointed down the path, past the Imagine Mosaic. "Isn't that Uncle Simon?" We were headed to the bench my father had dedicated to Mom after she died.

"No, it wouldn't be Simon."

"Do you know where he is?"

"No idea." Dad snorted. "Europe? Asia? Wherever he is, I'm sure he's chasing the ladies and breaking hearts. As he always has."

I ran my fingers along the brass plate that announced the dedication of the bench: 'In loving memory of Patience, wife of Peter Adams and mother extraordinaire to Avery Adams.' I missed her so much. I sat down, the heat of the sun warming me in the spring breeze. I stared out across the Imagine Mosaic. Fresh red, pink, and yellow roses had been placed around it to form the shape of a peace sign. Mom said the peace sign was an ancient Sanskrit symbol that represented protection from evil. She told me her grandfather had the sign tattooed on his wrist when he was in India and that's how she learned its meaning. My chest squeezed as I thought about her, and I choked back my tears.

An image flashed through my mind and I blinked. The last time I saw her.

"Avery," she whispered from down the hall. "Avery, come here please." I could barely hear her, but I had leapt out of bed and rushed to her room. I shivered as I danced across the hardwood floor in my bare feet. It was the coldest spring I could ever remember. Her door was slightly ajar. I opened it more. I tiptoed across the room to the side of her bed. The yellow light from the hallway barely lit my mother's sallow skin, her eyes sinking deep into her face. My beautiful mother looked so tiny, so fragile, propped up by the large, downy pillows and billowy, white comforter.

She smiled at me, the corners of her eyes crinkling as she reached for me.

"Avery ... I need to tell you something." She patted the bed. I crept in beside her, like I used to when I was a child. I could almost feel her heart beat in time with mine. It was warm under the covers, but I couldn't stop quivering. In the pale light, something glinted in her hand and I glanced down. A gold necklace. "Quick, we don't have much time. Daddy has gone out for medicine." Her voice cracked but she continued in a whisper, her breath coming in uneven gasps. "This is for you. Remember I told you about the *intaglio* when you were a little girl?"

"Yes, I remember." I took her hand. It felt very cold and bony. "It's Minerva, the Roman Goddess of Wisdom, and it's very, very old." I choked back tears of anger and sadness.

"You do remember. Good. That's good, Avery." Her breathing became more even. "Don't tell anyone, not even your father. My grandfather made me promise I would never tell anyone and I never did, except you, of course. This was always meant for you." Her fingers closed around mine. "Just don't tell him, promise me."

She whimpered and I shifted slightly so I wasn't leaning against her, causing her more pain. "Are you okay, Mom? Do you want me to go?"

"No. Don't go." Her fingernails dug into my skin. "It's a secret. Avery. You can't tell anyone. Promise me."

"Ok, Mom." I bit my lip to keep from crying. My hands went clammy.

Her eyes darted around the room; she looked wild, and frightened, and she wasn't making any sense. *Is she hallucinating?*

"Simon knows." She smoothed the blanket down with her free hand, fingers trembling. "My grandfather taught me ... things aren't always as they seem. Pay attention to ... spaces, the unseen." She drew in a shaky breath. "I ... didn't understand then. Pay attention. There's more... than what you see."

Her head fell back onto the pillow.

"Mom, no. Don't go." Her hand went limp. Her skin, already pale with illness, turned ashen.

"I don't know what you mean." My heart pounded and tears flowed down my cheeks. "What do you mean? You can't leave me like this. Don't leave me like this!" I couldn't go on without her. She was my rock. My strength. My entire body quaked from the inside out. I gulped for air. Her eyelashes flickered and a weak smile spread across her face. "You'll understand, Av." Her breathing was shallow. "You'll understand all in time. There is a diary."

My father's footsteps echoed on the wooden staircase that circled from the first floor to the second floor landing.

"Don't ever let him see the necklace, Avery." Mom spoke through gritted teeth. She waved weakly at a silvery-blue box on the table beside her bed. I picked it up and held it out and she dropped the necklace into it.

I shoved the box into my pajama pocket.

Mom touched my arm. "Make sure he never sees it."

"Avery!" Dad shouted from down the hallway. "Your mother needs her rest. Stop pestering her." The footsteps thudded closer.

Why does he sound so far away?

He gripped my arm. "Avery. Why aren't you answering me?"

I blinked several times; the sunlight suddenly bright. "Sorry, Dad." I looked around. Instead of my mother, the Imagine Mosaic loomed in front of me. "I must have been day-dreaming. About Mom."

"Ah, yes, I miss her too. She was the love of my life. Everything I've done, I've done for her. I loved her more than she ever knew. I am so sorry about your birthday, honey. Claire and I both miss your mom, and we thought...hoped you might be happy for us." Dad patted my hand absently.

"Yeah, I know, Dad. It's kinda like all three of us share her. I was just so shocked."

"By the way, there's something I've been meaning to ask you. Did Mom give you anything before she died?" Dad stretched his arm along the back of bench and squeezed my shoulder.

"Why do you ask?"

"I had hoped that she had given you some of her jewelry." He turned to me, his watery eyes boring into mine. "So I wouldn't have to go through it. Her box is still in my closet, and I can't bear to do it yet."

I returned his gaze, my heart melting. "I'd probably just lose it anyway. Like my cell phones." I resisted the urge to touch the pendant. "We could go through her box together some time."

"Hmmm." My father gazed off into space, as if already distracted by something else. "There was a necklace handed down from your great-great-grandfather Sinnett."

"Really? Was it special?" My stomach knotted. *How much does he know?*

"Not sure, really. Probably just a trinket from India. He worked there as a journalist, and became enchanted with a group of Indian mystics. He trekked into the Himalayas to study with them, and wrote books about his journeys. While he was in New York, lecturing about what he had learned, he visited a wealthy woman who lived in the newly built Dakota Apartments. He revealed certain "secrets" to her, and so she could continue her mystical studies, she purchased an apartment for him, one floor down from hers. That apartment was passed on to your grandfather, then your mother, and now we have it."

I flushed with excitement. I had never heard this story before. Loud shouting interrupted my thoughts.

"Avery! Avery! We're here." Katie waved an arm wildly through the air as she and Whitney walked toward us.

"Dad, I gotta go now. We're going for a walk down to the pond."

"That's okay, dear. I'll just stay here a few more minutes."

On impulse, I leaned over to kiss him on the cheek. "Thanks for telling me about my great, great-grandfather."

When he looked at me, his eyes were sad.

My chest tightened. "You sure you're okay here by yourself?"

"Of course, dear. The memories are hard, but I'll be fine. Just fine." He gripped my hand. "I love you, my little girl."

I blinked back tears. I hadn't seen this side of my dad since my mom died. Were we finally getting past the worst of it? Would we find our way back to each other? I swallowed a lump in my throat as my friends reached the bench and grabbed me by the hands. "I'll see you later, Dad."

He gazed out into space again, already lost in his thoughts.

Katie and Whitney dragged me to my feet and down the path.

"Ouch," Katie whined. She dropped my hand and bent down to pull off her shoe. When she shook it upside-down, a small pebble clattered onto the cement walkway. "I hate the wilderness."

"Oh yeah! It's like trekking the Amazon here." I giggled. "Thanks for getting me away from my dad, though it's the first time in ages I actually enjoyed being with him."

My watch phone vibrated and I glanced down.

"Look, it's a message from Aiden. He's at the Carousel. He wants to meet."

"The carousel." Whitney clasped her hands in front of her chest. "That's so romantic."

"But we're going shopping for you, today, Whit." My shoulders slumped.

Katie pulled on her shoe. "Go and meet Aiden. I can handle the shopping without you."

"I'm not going to abandon my plans, just because a guy calls me."

"Trust me, Avs." Katie tossed her hair back over one shoulder. "You are not much fun on a shopping spree."

"But …"

"Let's leave her to her crushing." Whitney tugged on Katie's arm.

"Oh, come on. I'm not crushing."

"Even so, we're going to leave you. I'd rather be shopping than traipsing around in all this…" Katie waved an arm through the air and wrinkled her nose, "…*nature.*"

"Let's walk her to the carousel first, Katie. I'd like to meet this mystery man." Whitney elbowed me in the side. "And you *are* crushing, Avs. Hard. How the mighty have fallen."

"And what about you crushing on Mark? You've been hopeless."

"Mark's a geek. I curbed him," Whitney said. "Katie, what do you think Aiden and Avery's couple name should be? Aidenery? Or Aidenav?"

Katie shook her head in mock seriousness. "No, no, no good. How about…Averden?"

I shook my head in disgust as they burst out laughing.

"I've been shipping Averden since day one." Whitney let out another snort of laughter.

"Shut up, both of you. We're just friends." I pressed my lips together to keep from smiling. *No way I'm giving them the satisfaction.* Still, the thought of Aiden and me as a couple secretly pleased me.

Whitney and I each grabbed one of Katie's elbows before she could dash off in the direction of Soho and herded her toward the carousel.

I stopped when we got close. Aiden stood with his back to us, one foot propped up on the rail as he watched the carousel go round. His silhouette was striking against the backdrop of shifting swirls of colors, shapes, and forms. My knees grew weak just looking at him. I felt giddy and stupid. I wanted to rush up, throw my arms around him and kiss his perfect mouth, but I held myself back.

"There he is." I pointed in his direction just as he turned around to face us, his almond-shaped eyes searching the crowd. Had he felt me watching him?

Katie turned to me and mouthed, "He's gorgeous!"

Whitney nodded. He strode toward us, a smile spreading across his face. My stomach clenched.

Aiden stopped in front of me. "Hi," he said. "How long have you been here?"

"We just arrived." His eyes probed mine and I struggled to draw in a breath.

An elbow dug into my side and I shook my head. "Sorry. This is Katie and Whitney, my two best friends. Guys, this is Aiden."

"Hi. Nice to meet you both," he said, his voice warm.

"You too. Well, Avs. We're off now," Whitney said.

"So soon?" Aiden lifted a hand in the air. "Why don't you join us?"

Warmth rushed through me.

Whitney nodded. "I guess we could—"

Katie grabbed her arm. "No, we couldn't. Sorry. I don't do wilderness. I need to go shopping before I turn into a feral beast of some kind. Come on, Whitney."

Whitney rolled her eyes. "I guess we're going."

Aiden and I stood side by side, leaning against the rail as the girls retreated down the pathway. He was so close to me my skin was on fire. My heart beat accelerated. *Say something. Preferably something intelligent.* The words wouldn't come. All I wanted to do was kiss him, to be held in his arms, and drown in his scent. I turned around and focused my attention on the carousel. My skin prickled. He was watching me.

Aiden took my chin in his hand and turned me to look at him. My skin tingled from his touch. I held my breath. His face was so close to mine; all I had to do was lean in slightly and we would touch. We were like magnets just before the pull becomes so strong that no resistance remains. His arms brushed mine. My heart pounded so loudly he had to hear it.

"It was my mom's birthday today." My voice was raspy and I cleared my throat. "She used to love the carousel."

Aiden didn't speak. Should I have just gone with the moment? But what if I wasn't what he wanted? I would be mortified. I wanted desperately to reach out for him, but something confused me, made me stop, when all I wanted was to go.

Aiden dropped his hand. "Do you want to go on the carousel?" He looked down, kicking at the dirt with his shoe.

I drew in a breath.

When he looked up, his teasing smile was back. "For your mum."

My heart leapt into my throat. "I'd love to."

He slipped his hand into mine. I quivered, as though as an electrical current still pulsed through me, as we walked to the booth.

"Two dollars a ride, mister," the attendant said.

I opened my purse to pay, but Aiden lifted his hand. He held some crumpled bills out to the attendant. We took our tickets and walked up to the circular platform. The intolerable feeling of being too close, but not close enough, wouldn't dissipate. I chose a white horse, brightly colored with red and gold detail, head held high in a gallop. Aiden climbed onto the horse next to me. The calliope happily wheezed its tune, waiting for the next three-and-a-half-minute ride. Parents helped a few children onto the horses, then stood beside them, hands on the flowing manes. Laughter and shrieks echoed in the chamber. The chariot in front of us was empty.

The merry-go-round moved around slowly at first. Aiden watched me, and laughed when I shook the reins. When I went up, he went down. We giggled like the children all around us. The colors whipped by as the carousel picked up speed. Up and down and around we went until everything was a blur. My vision faded around the edges, narrowing as though I were looking through a long tunnel. Two Goth Girls sat in the chariot in front of us. The girl with the blood-red lips threw an exaggerated kiss at Aiden before her eyes locked on mine. I clutched the reins tightly, my head spinning. From somewhere far away, a child screamed. My horse moved beneath me, powerfully alive. I clutched at its neck, tearing my eyes away from the Goth Girl. I looked over at Aiden.

He reached for me, a desperate look on his face. I stole a glance at the chariot; it was empty again. The carousel slowed. I regained my balance.

"Avery." Aiden grasped my arm. "Are you okay? Can you hear me?"

Slowly everything came back into focus. "Tie a yellow ribbon on the old oak tree…" churned from the calliope.

"I saw them," I gasped.

Aiden pulled me from the horse and held me close. When the pounding in my chest subsided, he led me from the carousel.

We stopped under a tree and he took me by the shoulders and turned me to face him. "I saw them too." Aiden let go of one shoulder and pointed. "They ran off that way, before the carousel stopped."

A lone person next to the carousel caught my eye. Raven. She stood still. Watching us. I waved to her and she nodded. Her voice echoed inside my mind. "It's all right now, Avery. They're gone."

"Raven. Wait," I called, as she turned to leave.

She hesitated, then turned back and walked over to us. "Hi, Avery." Raven fidgeted and glanced at Aiden.

"Aiden, this is Raven, my … friend."

"Hi." Aiden took Raven's hand and shook it.

"I just felt I should come here. I didn't understand why, until I saw you both on the carousel. Then I saw those dark spirits hiding in the chariot. There are more of them here in New York already, and many more are coming. Avery, there is one, a very powerful one, that wants you. Really wants you. Like possessing your soul or something. I've seen him in my dreams. Aiden, you can't leave Avery alone. Together is better. That's what I keep hearing. I don't know where it's coming from. Some things I hear. Some I see. Some, I can just feel happening. Like some major shift in the energy of the world."

"A major energy shift in the world?" I looked at Raven first, then at Aiden.

"Avery, you know how we've been shocking other people, but not each other?" Aiden rested a hand on mine. "How we experienced strange tingling or energy whenever we touched? We haven't talked about it, but we both felt it. We just didn't know what it meant."

"I thought it meant that I was pretty electrifying." My laugh was nervous, and neither of them joined in. I took a deep breath. "Come on, you guys, I can't quite believe what you're saying. There must be another explanation, surely."

"Something is happening. Something we don't understand." Aiden waved his hand to the sky. "Remember the starlings? The murmuration? They are six months off of their instinctual calendar. That just doesn't happen. Animals don't make mistakes like that."

"Avery, I can't explain any of what I see and dream." Raven held up both hands. "All I know is what I feel. What grandfather taught me to listen to, what my mother encouraged me to tell you. I don't want you to think I'm a freak, but I fear for you."

I shook my head. Strange things *had* happened. Even my father was behaving bizarrely. And there was the Albino who used the same words as Raven, "Together is better."

Raven stepped closer, her dark eyes searching mine. "Avery, you heard me from across the carousel, didn't you? When I spoke inside your mind? How do you explain that?"

AVERY

The key to growth is the introduction of higher dimensions of consciousness into our awareness.

—Lao Tzu

I circled the tree, concentrating on my latest lesson. The sounds of the park receded into the background. The warm sun beat down on me.

"Move your center during the palm change, and keep your arms spiraling. It's never a straight strike in Bagua. Always spiral." Aiden shifted his hand from his abdomen to his shoulder, folding himself back and forth like a hinge to illustrate. "That's right, from your dantien into your shoulder. Excellent. Now your wrist. Close. Open. Wow. Awesome, Avery."

"When you can shift your center like that, Bagua becomes really powerful." Blaine made a subtle ripple with his shoulder to thrust out a fierce palm strike into the air, then twirled away in the other direction. "Usually your center stays in one place, but in Bagua you can learn to throw your center anywhere."

I stopped circling the tree.

"Soon, Grasshopper, we'll teach you about uniting the Six Harmonies, and the swimming dragon."

Aiden dipped low to the ground with his weight over his bent leg, his other glided out to the side, one arm reached out and up while his other grazed along his leg. In one graceful swoop he stood up. "Do you like Grasshopper better than Bulldog?"

"A little." Rasta, who had been sleeping under a bush, suddenly leapt to his feet and bounded for the top of the path. "Hey, Rasta. Where are you going?" I whirled around to see what had caught his attention. "It's

Raven." I waved. "Come on over." When she reached us, I pointed at the guys. "Raven, you remember Aiden from the other day. And this is Blaine."

Raven nodded at them both. "We're going to the Ramapo Mountains tomorrow for four days," she said. "Would you all like to come? We go every year when school ends. There's lots of room at Grandfather's cabin."

"How far away are the mountains?" Aiden stepped closer to us. "And Blaine and I are vegetarians. Would that be a problem?"

"My mom is a great cook and the more she has to do, the happier she is. The mountains are about an hour, depending on traffic. Once outside Manhattan, it's a beautiful drive. I have a feeling that something important will happen if you come. I don't know why. I didn't even think about inviting you until it came out of my mouth, but I'm sure it's the right thing. All of you must come. You too, Blaine."

"Sure. I'm in. Things have been getting very weird around here; I could use a vacation."

"I'm in too," Aiden turned to me, one eyebrow raised.

I shrugged. "I have to ask my dad."

Raven tilted her head; her long, dark hair splashed down around her shoulder. "How old are you?"

"Nineteen."

She shook her head. "I know how old you are, I just didn't know if *you* knew."

She had a point. I was an adult. Time to start acting like it. I straightened my shoulders. "Where do we meet?"

AVERY

*Heaven and earth and I are of the same root, the ten-thousand
things and I are of one substance.*

—Zen Master Seng-Chao

The doorman rang to tell me that Marly, Raven's mother, had arrived. The bell sent Rasta into fits of excited barks, as if he knew I was going somewhere special and he wanted to make sure I didn't forget about him.

"Avery," my father yelled from his study. "Get that dog under control. I'm busy."

"Marly's here. I'm about to leave."

"Run up here, then, and give me a kiss good-bye."

I ran to the study where my father stood in the doorway, his foot wedged between the door and the frame. He leaned into the opening so I couldn't see into his office.

"Dad, I..."

"Just go and have a good time, darling. I really have so much to do this morning before my flight."

He bent forward and gave me a quick peck on the cheek.

"I..." Should I tell him about Aiden and Blaine coming to the Ramapos?

"Go on, have a good time." He smiled and waved for me to go.

I turned and left. So I hadn't told him everything. He was obviously hiding a lot more than I was there in his office.

Just as I got to the entrance hallway, the doorbell rang.

"I'm coming, Mar—" I yanked open the door.

"Oh, Avery," Claire pressed a hand to her chest. Like *I* had startled *her*.

"Claire...what are you...?"

"I'm going to Washington with your father. He has only a few meetings and we thought we could..."

"That's okay." I shot my hand up. I definitely did not want to hear any details of what Claire wanted to do with my father.

"Whitney's gone to her dad's for the weekend." She smoothed down her tan, pencil skirt with both hands. Why did she sound so defensive?

"Ok. I gotta go." I lifted my knapsack and grabbed Rasta's leash. I swept past her, fighting the tears that threatened to ruin my excitement for the weekend. I still hadn't come to terms with Claire dating Dad. Does she know about his drug use? I rushed to the elevator, battling my emotions as the ancient water cylinders drained and filled, slowly lowering me to the ground floor.

The heaviness in the pit of my stomach lifted the moment I saw Marly smiling, with her dark, reflective eyes and her long, black hair in a single neat braid hanging to one side. She waved me over to her vehicle, clearly ready to rock at the wheel of her old Dodge Caravan. I let Rasta in the back of the van behind Raven, slid into the passenger seat, and packed all of my feelings about my father and Claire away.

I felt Raven staring into the back of my head, as if she was trying to get inside my mind. Like she had done the other day by the carousel. It was a strange sensation, having someone else's mind walking around inside mine. I needed to know I could block her out. What if she could enter into my mind any time she pleased, even when I didn't want her there? I consciously imagined a wall between us.

Raven touched my shoulder. "Where do we pick up Blaine and Aiden?"

"In front of the Gramercy Park Hotel." Aiden's face flashed through my mind. That momentary loss of focus was all Raven needed. She walked right into my mind. *We can do this, Avery. We can be linked whenever we want to be.* A shiver rippled through me.

Raven leaned forward in her seat. "I can teach you how to initiate the link, if you like."

I hesitated. Did I want that? How could I not? It was the coolest thing I had ever experienced. "Umm, sure," I said. "I think I'd like to try that."

"Try what?" Marly glanced over at me, then twisted to look back at her daughter. "Are you messing around in Avery's head, Raven?"

Raven just laughed.

"There's the guys." Raven pointed out the window. "Mother, you remembered that the boys are vegetarians, right?" Blaine and Aiden stood on the sidewalk in front of the Hotel, their backpacks and Aiden's guitar on the sidewalk beside them. I blinked. Both of them radiated Bagua energy. Did anyone else see it? I glanced at the faces of the people walking by them. None of them seemed to notice.

Marly drove up to the curb and stopped the van. "Yes, I remembered. And I hate it when you call me mother." I jumped out, then scrambled into the back seat beside Raven, and twisted around to watch Blaine and Aiden. Marly climbed out and opened up the back of the van. The guys threw their stuff inside.

"Hi, I'm Marly." She held out her hand to Aiden.

He shook it firmly. "I'm Aiden and this is Blaine."

"Glad to meet you both." Marly shook Blaine's hand then pointed to the front of the van. "Why don't you sit up here with me, Aiden."

Blaine jumped in beside me. A huge grin spread across his face as he nudged me with his elbow. "This is gonna be fair dinkums. I love the mountains!"

Marly climbed behind the steering wheel and looked into the rear-view mirror. "Fairdinkums?"

"Oh, Aussie for ... for, this is going to be the real thing"

"Crack on, Marly," Aiden said. "The mountains are waiting!"

Marly pulled out from the curb and bullied her way into the traffic. "It'll probably take an hour just to get through the city and to the highway." She navigated the city streets, crammed with yellow cabs, like an expert rally driver.

Aiden shifted in his seat to face her. "I read there is a DNA link between the northern Chinese people and the American First Nations."

"Really. I didn't know that."

"Ya, they found the link recently. What tribe are you from, Cherokee? Mohawk?"

"No, neither of those; I'm Lenape, Delaware, Clan of the Bear. Lenape literally means people torn up from the earth. Our circulatory systems are roots, nourished and literally networked into the land. We are people not just of the earth, but interconnected with it."

"You know that famous story about how the Europeans bought Manhattan for twenty-four dollars from the Indians?" Raven said. "What really happened was the Lenape had no concept of owning land, we were the land. So, they didn't know they were selling it. By the mid-seventeen hundreds, the Lenape were resettled to Oklahoma Territory, Southern Ontario, and a bunch of other places."

Marly nodded. "That's when a small group fled to the isolated Ramapo Mountains. They have lived there pretty much undisturbed since. So the Lenape, from the Ramapo, are very much in touch with our ancient roots, connected to the land, to creator, to our old wisdom ways."

"You know the old ways?" Aiden shifted in his seat.

"I've learned a lot." Marly leaned on her horn and blasted a cab driver in front of her, waving a fist.

"How about you?" Blaine turned to Raven. "Are you into the old ways?"

"Raven is very special, Blaine." Marly gripped the steering wheel with both hands again. "Grandfather and Christian, my cousin, whose mother was a deeply religious Jesuit, have developed her. They are all connected in a special way. You'll see. Grandfather is a tough one when you first meet him, but he'll warm up once he gets to know that you're okay. We call him The Old Twisted Tree on account of his wisdom."

In the first moment of silence since the drive had begun, the final strains of a classic rock song filled the car.

"One thing about the old ways that I have learned," Marly adjusted the rear-view mirror to see us better, "is that it is always wise to listen to your elders. My mother gave me a piece of advice when I was young, when I didn't know yet that I didn't know anything, but thought I knew everything." Her eyes met Raven's briefly. "She advised me to not get involved with anyone until I was older and wiser. Well, I thought I was smarter than my mother, because I was going to law school, on a scholarship, with an articling job on Wall Street. Pretty rare for a Native at that time, so when I met Paul, a brilliant law student, I fell hard."

"Mother." Raven covered her eyes with one hand. "Why are you talking about Paul?"

"Paul is Raven's birth father," Marly said. "I should have listened to my mother."

Raven dropped her hand. "You are so subtle, Mom."

We wove our way around the streets, and began our ascent into the mountains, barely a quarter of an hour outside the city.

"Listen to this, Aiden." Marly reached for the volume button on the radio. "It's Donovan. This is one of my favorite 60s songs. It's all about Atlantis." She sang along.

"Oh, Mom." Raven rolled her eyes. "You are so embarrassing."

"My mom loved this song," Aiden said. "She was fascinated by Atlantis and their advanced metaphysics. She told me all about it."

We turned onto Stag Hill Road and drove for a few miles before coming to a rough, unnamed road, mostly hidden from the highway. The Dodge rocked and rolled along it, the suspension squawking its discontent. Finally the van slowed. Rasta barked our arrival.

The sun came out from behind the clouds and bathed the cottage in warm light, the enormous white pines casting long shadows across the lawn. The van had barely stopped when a tall young man came bounding out the front door, the screen door slapping shut behind him. He wore stone-washed jeans and a light t-shirt, though the air was crisp.

"You made it." He smiled.

"We got stuck in a bit of traffic," Marly said, smiling as she unfolded herself from the vehicle with a stretch. "Everyone? This is my favorite nephew, Christian." Christian hugged her, then lifted Raven up in a giant bear hug.

"Sweet," Raven said. "I'm home again." Christian set her down and she reached up and rested her palms on his temples. After a moment, she nodded.

"I'm sorry." Christian turned to Aiden, Blaine, and me with his hand extended. "I haven't seen my people for a while and I miss them. It's been a busy winter for Marly." He shook Aiden's hand and Blaine's, then surprised me when he lifted me up in a huge bear hug. When he let me go, he turned back to Marly. "How's that case going, the one that...?"

"I'm here on my holiday." Marly playfully clamped a hand over Christian's mouth. "No shop talk!" She checked her watch. "I do have one hour-long conference call in five minutes. After that, I'm free."

"Fair enough." Christian waved a hand toward the cabin. "Come on in and meet Grandfather. You can call him that. It's kinda like his name now. Then we'll get settled."

We walked into the cabin. A wood fire blazed in the stone fireplace. Grandfather sat in a rocking chair at the far edge of the rag rug. Rasta had already found his way into the house and had sat down beside him. Grandfather pushed himself up and out of his chair to hug Marly and Raven. He gave me a nod. Aiden and Blaine held out their hands. Grandfather ignored them and turned his face towards the fire. He sat back down on the rocking chair heavily.

"Grandfather, I told you these are our friends, now be nice," Raven scolded.

Aiden flashed a look at me with both eyebrows raised. Blaine, undaunted, grabbed Grandfather's hand and gave it a vigorous shake. Grandfather yanked back his hand and tucked his clenched fists deep in his armpits. He refused to look at any of us.

"Aiden, give me a hand with these backpacks." Christian broke the awkward silence, and grabbed several bags.

"Hey Blaine," Raven grasped his elbow. "Want to come outside and do a little exploring around the area? We can take Rasta with us."

She hadn't included me in the invitation, obviously wanting to be alone with Blaine, but I wished she had. After that cold greeting from her grandfather, I sure didn't want to be hanging around here.

Aiden gave me a sympathetic smile as he lugged a few backpacks up the stairs behind Christian.

Please come back down soon. I shifted against the wall, wishing I could disappear.

It seemed like forever, but it was probably only a couple of minutes before Aiden came back down the stairs. Grandfather hadn't spoken a word to me; hadn't even glanced in my direction. I had held my breath, not sure if I wanted him to notice me or just leave me alone, until Aiden jumped off the bottom step and I let it out in a rush.

He grinned, clearly aware of my discomfort. "Want to go for a walk?"

"Yes." I shot at look at grandfather. The two of us might have been as invisible to him as we had been to the people on the sidewalk when we flew past them. "Please."

He held out his hand toward the door, and I headed toward it. Aiden and I walked along the path into the woods to look for Raven, Blaine, and Rasta. We could hear their shouts, Rasta's barks, and then everything went quiet. Even the birds. Aiden took my hand, and again there was no denying the feelings that shot through my body. He looked at me, and I knew he felt it too.

"Do you believe in destiny?" I pushed away a stray branch from the path. "I never have, but that morning I put on my mother's necklace, I wondered. Something about that day was different. And I've felt it ever since."

"Yes, Grasshopper," Aiden said, "I have always believed in destiny. I felt it when I first met Luc, and discovered Bagua. Then, when I went to the Wudang Mountains and met Old Phoenix, I never doubted it again. Blaine and I have argued about this for years. Blaine believes the choices we make create the lives we live. I believe that the choices we make take us closer to the life we were meant to live, or further from it."

"I don't know what to believe anymore. Everything used to be black and white to me. Now I just feel confused."

"Old Phoenix always said that confusion creates an open mind."

We stepped out into a clearing. A large target hung on a bale of hay, at the far end of the clearing, close to the edge of the woods.

"Old Phoenix sounds very wise."

"He was the one who really made me believe in my own destiny. He …"

I tripped over a tree root, stumbling forward. Aiden reached out with lightning-fast reflexes and gripped my hand to pull me toward him. He leaned into me, and grabbed my other elbow. Our eyes met. A sense of shared destiny filled me.

We leaned into each other, immersed in each other's eyes. His heart beat loudly, its rhythm synchronized with mine. I wondered if this moment would be the one.

"What're you doing here?" a gruff voice cut across the clearing

I whirled away from Aiden as an enormous man, rifle at his side, strode into the clearing from a well-concealed path at the far end.

"This is Blackstone property. You ain't welcome here." He gripped his rifle with both hands and leveled it at us. Dark eyes bulged from under the rim of his hat. Buttons strained against his gut.

Thwack. An object whizzed past my face. An arrow with bright pink feathers arced across the field, landing just in front of the big man's left shoe. He threw his rifle down and raised a clenched fist into the air. Raven stepped out from behind Aiden and me. Someone nudged me in the shoulder and I jumped.

"Sorry, it's just me." Blaine studied my face. "You okay?"

"Yeah. Just a little freaked out at the moment." Rasta pushed his head between me and Aiden and I rested my hand on his back.

"Wayne, go away." Raven notched another arrow in the bow. "These are my friends."

"You have no business bringing these people onto our lands, Raven."

"You said it yourself, Wayne. This is Blackstone property. And you are not a Blackstone." Raven advanced across the clearing, the rest of us at her heels. "Now go on, get outta here."

Wayne took a step back. "I'll be talking to the Old Tree about this."

Raven lowered the bow until the arrow pointed just below his belt. "Get off my land, before I put one of these in a place I'll bet you haven't used in a while."

"Don't you threaten me, girl," Wayne said. He closed his hand into a fist and lunged toward her.

Aiden and Blaine lunged into defense mode, thrusting Raven behind them and blocking his punch in a blur of dazzling moves. Wayne flew through the air and tumbled into the brush.

"Wayne," Grandfather called out from behind us, "Don't you dare touch one of my kin or my friends, ever."

"Old Tree." Wayne staggered to his feet. "You'll see. They's trouble."

"You want to see trouble? Stick around here another ten seconds."

Wayne threw a dark look at all of us before turning and lumbering off into the trees, stopping just long enough to bend down and grab his gun before he disappeared from sight.

"Grandfather?" Raven touched his arm. "How long were you standing there?"

"Long enough to hear your threat." Grandfather laughed. "You remind me of your grandmother. I'm proud of you, Raven. He's nothing but a big bully. And you two, whatever your names are. Thanks, for protecting my favorite granddaughter."

Raven rolled her eyes. "Their names are Blaine and Aiden. You aren't that old that you can't remember them."

Grandfather smiled a little and looked down. "I don't trust too many people. So when I meet new ones … Well, I'm sorry, boys." He straightened up and held out his hand to them. "Forgive an old man. I misjudged you both." He took Blaine's hand in both of his and then Aiden's.

"What are you doing out here anyway?" Raven slung her bow over shoulder.

"I was on my way to make sure you didn't mess up my circle walk. My Wooch-Ah Ga-Po Ay. Our Lenape sacred circle. Then I heard the commotion." Grandfather turned to Aiden and Blaine and slid an arm around both of them. "Come. Let's walk the mountain. You can show me that move you made to throw old Wayne through the air. Getting that body airborne couldn't have been an easy task." Grandfather chuckled as he tossed Raven and me a look over his shoulder. "We will see you back at the cabin. The boys and I have something to do. We'll meet up with Christian."

"Really, Grandfather?" Raven lifted a hand. "Just the boys 'walk the mountain'?"

"Yes, Raven." He nodded solemnly. "You know the traditions. This is men-stuff."

"I know the traditions." She shook her head. "Know more than most men. You'll show them some plants. Teach them some things. Why not take Avery and me with you?"

"We talk about making Pimewakan. Sweatlodge," Grandfather turned to leave. "You girls don't belong there with us."

"We'll see about that," Raven said. "Come on Avery. You and I will do our own 'walk the mountain'."

Aiden twisted his head back and flashed a half smile. Blaine looked over his shoulder at Raven for a moment before the three men headed off together.

Raven and I shadowed Grandfather's walk. She showed me how to recognize different herbs and mushrooms. "The Sweatlodge might be nothing, or it might be something," Raven bent down and picked up a mushroom. "Just be ready for anything." She popped the stem from the cap. "See this one? It's edible." She passed it over to me. Rasta sniffed at it.

"You and Blaine had a nice walk together." I nibbled at the edge of the mushroom. It tasted earthy. "Are you …interested?"

"Yeah, I really like Blaine. He's so funny and interesting. I think we could be good friends."

"Just friends?"

"Well, ya." Raven stopped and looked at me. "Oh, you don't know. I bat for the other team."

"Oh," I said.

She grinned. "Don't worry. You aren't my type, Avery. We're connected. Like Blaine and I are. But just because you're connected doesn't mean you're in love." Raven crouched down and dug through some foliage. Then she added, almost to herself, "It's so funny. Your friend who likes me the least is the one I'm attracted to the most."

My eyes widened. "Who?"

Raven bit her lip. "Katie. She has no idea that I like her. But we talked one day before a philosophy lecture and she surprised me. She's super smart and feminine. So different from me."

"Wow," I said. "I've really gotta learn how to tap into your mind. I was way off-base."

AVERY

The way of Heaven is to benefit others and not to injure.

—Lao Tzu

Everyone gathered at the picnic table in the backyard for dinner time. Marly grasped the handle and pulled the lid off one. "Elk stew. Your favorite, Grandfather." She replaced the lid and lifted the lid on the other pot. "And vegetarian stew. Raven warned me you boys don't eat meat." Grandfather breathed in the aroma. "We're fasting, Marly. For Pimewaken."

Marly slapped the lid down on the stew. "You should have told me."

Grandfather looked at the guys and winked.

Aiden gasped. "Grandfather, you have a split iris. I feel like I've seen that before."

"Isn't that interesting? I've had it since I was a child. Someone threw a stone and it hit my eye and split the iris. My grandfather started calling me Phoenix then. I've been old for so long I almost forgot that I'm not Grandfather, or Old Tree."

Marly grinned at Raven and me. "Well, all the more for us." She spooned some elk stew into a bowl and set it in front of me.

"Avery and I are fasting too." Raven pushed the bowl away. I glanced at Raven and titled my head. I hadn't heard about any fasting.

"Why didn't anyone tell me no one was eating?" Marly sighed as she sat down.

"You are not coming to Pimewaken." Grandfather scowled at Raven.

"We will see." Raven flashed a smile at me. "I have my ways, Grandfather, and you know it."

85

Marly finished her stew and then brought out hot chocolate and marshmallows for around the fire pit, where she had lawn chairs set up. My stomach grumbled. I reached for a mug but Raven placed a hand on my arm, holding me back. Aiden and Christian brought out their guitars and discovered they knew some of the same songs.

They played, and Grandfather sang in his froggy voice, whether he knew the song or not. Marly joined in on the ones she knew. Aiden played a song for me, one he had mentioned before, called Fields of Gold. I was reminded of Uncle Simon, still in Nicaragua, holed up at the Gold mine. A few days ago I had received a text from him. 'OK' was all it said. When I called back, no lines were available. With no mention of it on the international news, it was impossible to know what was going on.

During a song break, Marly stuck a marshmallow on a long skewer. "So I've had a strange feeling all afternoon. Did something happen while you guys were out?"

"You remember Wayne Big Bear?" Grandfather flashed Raven a wink. "Well he just wondered who was hanging around here. Just being protective of the mountain lands."

"Something else happened, I know it." She drew her stick from the fire and popped a gooey marshmallow into her mouth. "Raven?"

Raven held up her palm. "We had a little dispute with Wayne Big Bully. I threatened him, and he threw a punch at me. Aiden and Blaine stepped in and had him punching air."

"Raven." Marly pointed her skewer at her. "What did you think you were doing? You have no fear. And you need to get some. You'll get yourself into trouble one day."

"Oh Mom." Raven waved a hand through the air. "I was fine. I didn't even need their help."

"I'm proud of her, Marly," Grandfather said. "She's like her grandmother, you know. She never backed down from a bully, either. Did I ever tell you about the time Big Bear and I had a fist fight over her? Wayne Big Bear has always liked to push his weight around. He had eyes for your grandmother, Raven. So his nose was pretty out of joint the night she chose me at the dance. When I walked her home, Wayne Big Bear jumped out of the woods and caught me in the nose with a cheap shot. Well, I wrestled him to the ground and punched him in the face. Knocked him right out. That was the day she decided I was the one."

Blaine chuckled. "That's a great story. You must have quite a punch, to knock out that wall of a guy. He's huge."

Grandfather's chest puffed out. "We got married a week later. And Wayne had to come with a broken nose and two black eyes. All from one punch!" He held up his fist and turned it from side to side, admiring it.

Raven chuckled and sat up in her chair. "Grandmother told that story a bit differently. She claimed that Wayne popped out of the woods and wrestled *you* to the ground. You thought he was a bear, and yelled for Grandmother to run. But she pulled Wayne off of you by the collar of his shirt, and she was the one who punched his lights out."

"She told you that, did she?" Grandfather laughed. "All five foot, two inches of her. Blackstones have a long history of bad blood with the Big Bear family. That's why I'm proud of you."

"Well, how about you grant me a wish, if you are so proud."

He smiled. "What would that wish be, my favorite granddaughter?"

"That you would invite Avery and me to the Sweatlodge."

Grandfather frowned.

"It's not tradition to do Sweatlodge with mixed company. I don't ever mess with tradition. It just isn't done."

"Oh, lots of people are doing it with mixed company nowadays," Raven said. "I'm not going to take no for answer."

"No. Not ever." Grandfather shook his head firmly before smacking his hands down on both knees. "And it's time for bed. No more talk of this. There is only one thing that could change my mind, and that isn't going to happen."

"It's the twenty-first century. Ever hear of equality? This isn't fair and it isn't right." Raven glared at him.

"Off you go, everyone." Grandfather slapped his hands together. "No more talking."

"The rest of you go ahead. Avery and I will put out the fire." Aiden stood up and reached for a bucket of water.

When everyone had gone in, we took turns sloshing water on the flames, until we were sure the fire was out.

"Here." Aiden set down the bucket and held out his hand. He led me over to the picnic table and climbed up on the top of it. We laid down, side by side, and stared up into the sky. Stars glittered against the dark sky.

It felt good to be alone with Aiden again. In the city, it was never quiet, even at night. Here the thick silence covered us like a blanket. The sound of crickets beginning their nightly chorus soon filled the air, and I had a sudden urge to talk, to share something of myself with him. "My dad used to take us to a cabin on Deer Island, upstate, when I was a little girl. We would sit on the front porch and watch the stars together. He pointed out the satellites orbiting and named the constellations: the Big Dipper, Ursa Major, Orion. He told me an old story that the two stars at the handle of the Big Dipper are robins. They hadn't saved any food for winter, so they decided to hunt a bear. When they found Ursa Major, they frightened her, and she ran across the sky. The birds chased her for a year. One of the robins grew tired, threw an arrow at the bear, and Ursa Major's blood splattered all over both birds. That was how the robin got its red breast. I loved it when my dad told me that story. "

"I have few memories of my dad. I remember him raging around the house at night waving a bottle around, shouting about how we just didn't understand. And I remember him on sunny days, telling us, promising us, he would always be there to protect us. My mom would smile at those times and I would feel so safe. When he disappeared and we had to move to East London, that's when I decided I would never be like him. Never break a promise, never, ever go back on my word."

I shivered. Aiden slipped his arm under my shoulders and I rested my head on his chest. He pulled me tighter. Was he more upset about his father than he let on?

"My dad changed when my mom died." I fingered my pendant. "I miss her." I tried to choke back a tear but it escaped.

Aiden reached over and wiped it away with his thumb. His fingers brushed across my cheek. Electricity sparked, palpable between us, and before I knew it, our lips just barely grazed. Current charged through my body. The world turned upside down and back again. I struggled to breathe. Aiden closed his eyes, his face close to mine. Bright sparks of energy arced between us. Our bodies moved closer to each other, exerting a will of their own, and again we kissed. This time our mouths knew exactly what to do, how to touch, how to move, how to become one. Aiden wrapped both arms around me and pulled me closer. Our bodies entwined, my lips pressed against his, our tongues probing, searching. My body filled with liquid gold; a sensation like nothing I had ever experienced before.

Then Aiden pulled away.

The electrical connection between us snapped, yanking me back into my body.

He rolled away from me and climbed down off the table.

For a moment, I couldn't speak. I crossed my arms over my chest, feeling naked, vulnerable.

Aiden didn't look at me.

"Why did you stop?"

He rubbed his hands over his shaved head, his face still averted. "I'm sorry. I shouldn't have started."

Chapter 14

AVERY

Because of a great love, one is courageous.

—Lao Tzu

Raven snatched the warm covers from me, and pulled me from the bed by my arm. "Come on, sleepyhead. Time to get to the Sweatlodge. We are not going to be left out of this."

I threw my clothes on and joined her downstairs, my stomach complaining. In the kitchen by the back door, she handed me a fleece-lined plaid jacket. "The air is still cold here in the mornings. Come on." I reached out to grab an apple from a bowl on the counter. Raven playfully smacked my hand. She led me out the screen door and along a series of paths that eventually came to a flat open space. We stopped and listened to the rushing river, swollen from the winter melt. As loud as it was, my stomach grumbled louder.

Christian and the boys were setting up the structure of the dome. Raven glanced back at me before turning and striding into the clearing, her hands thrust into the pockets of her deerskin jacket. I took a few long strides to fall into step with her.

"Hey guys. Need some help?" Raven stepped up beside Christian.

"Grandfather's not going to be happy." He gave us a fleeting look and returned to lashing some saplings together while Aiden held them in place. Aiden didn't look up. My chest squeezed tight. Blaine leapt up from where he had been sitting, holding a branch securely into the ground. He gave Raven and me a big hug.

"Avery and I are going to be at this Sweatlodge if we have to crash it." Raven inspected the structure. "You need more lashings here." She rested a hand on Aiden's shoulder. "Hey, Aiden."

"Hey Raven. Avery." Aiden stole a glimpse at me. My cheeks flushed.

Raven scrunched up her face and tipped her head toward Aiden. I shrugged.

"What are you girls doing here?" Grandfather waltzed up to Raven and wrapped his arms around her, then stepped away and tapped her shoulder with a fist. "You aren't coming to the Sweatlodge, even if you build the entire thing with your own two hands."

"Be reasonable." Raven flicked her long hair back from her face. "You know that I know as much, if not more, than most men." Her black eyes probed Grandfather's. She nodded her head and Grandfather bobbed his in time with her. "You know that I know things that others don't know. Right?" Grandfather motioned yes. Raven touched his arm. "So you are going to let us join this Pimewaken."

Grandfather clasped her shoulder and smiled. "No. That isn't what is going to happen." He turned his back to her and fiddled with a few of the branches.

"But we have to be there." Raven stamped her foot. "You are so frustrating. We have to be there. That's how it was in my dream."

Grandfather wheeled around to her, his eyes alight, one pupil split. "Why didn't you say so in the first place? Why do this …" he waved his hand around in circles, "…All this talking? I don't ever go against the dream speak. That was the one thing that could change this."

"So … we're in?" A small smile spread across Raven's face. "You are inviting us in?" She took Grandfather's face and kissed him.

"The dream invited you in." Grandfather turned to look at me. "Both of you."

"Let's get to work then." Christian hip-bumped Raven. "There is a lot to do."

He handed me some leather strips. "Help Aiden fasten these so they are secure at the top."

Aiden and I exchanged looks. He raised his eyebrows, and held out his hand for one of the straps. I thought about giving him a verbal lashing about his crazy-making, come-close-go-away dance. Instead, as I held out a leather strip, I accidentally brushed back a willow branch next to him. I pulled back and the branch snapped against his arm, leaving a thick red welt. I stifled a giggle.

He gave me a dirty look and picked up the leather straps I had dropped and bound them together without my help. He snatched another of the fasteners from my hand and stomped to the next junction that needed to be secured.

Blaine crawled around the perimeter where mounds of earth held young tree limbs in place. "I need some help here, Raven." She dropped to the ground and soon they were tumbling over each other, laughing and wrestling.

I watched them for a moment, my chest aching at their easy camaraderie. Why couldn't Aiden and I be more like that together? Why did it always have to be so hard?

"Hey." Aiden's low voice behind me tightened up my stomach muscles.

I turned around. The look in his eyes was so intense I could almost feel it moving over me, like his fingers had brushed across my cheek the night before. Leaping to his feet, he bent down and scooped me up into his arms. I squealed and wrapped my arms around his neck as he ran toward the river. Water splashed around his feet. "No!"

Ignoring my protests, he dropped me into the water.

I came up laughing and sputtering, and wiping the water from my eyes.

"That was for this." He pointed at the red welt on his arm before diving into the river beside me. He came up inches from me and wrapped his arms around my waist, pulling me to him.

I bit my lip. Could I trust him? Did he really want me or was he just playing games?

I want you.

My breath caught. I could read the thought as clearly as Raven read mine. This time I didn't protest when he took my face in his hands and pressed his lips to mine.

AVERY

To see things in the seed, that is genius.

—Lao Tsu

The Sweatlodge we had helped build the day before lay like a small dome in the clearing, the morning mist rising from the cold ground surrounding it. Raven leaned into me and touched my hand. "Be ready for anything. The boys think they will get the cool experience, because they're guys, but this is meant for you and me." She giggled.

Christian cocked his head. "What are you girls whispering about?"

"Oh, nothing, dear cousin." Raven winked at me.

Christian had chosen a location where the terrain was flat, the earth on an equal plane, balanced and in harmony. He had dug a pit where the hot stones would go, then taken two large steps outwards from the pit and paced off the circumference. The structure was large enough to fit eight people inside. "You never know who might pop in to join us, neighbors or spirits," he commented as he paced. I wasn't sure whether or not he was joking. Next, he had us swathe the saplings to create a tightly woven dome.

The platform to heat the rocks was built strictly according to Lenape tradition. Some logs faced east, the others west, to support both the fire and the twenty-eight stones, seven for each round.

"Would you all like some cedar tea?" Christian offered. "Drink as much as possible."

"I can pour." I reached to take the ladle from Christian.

Raven intercepted, placing a hand on mine. "Christian takes care of everything today. He is the Fire Keeper. That's the way it's done."

Christian ladled out the tea into tin cups for us. It was thick and sweet. The roar of the fire merged with the sound of the nearby Ramapo River.

We sipped our teas. Christian scrutinized each of us in turn. "We'll do the Sweatlodge in four rounds. One for each direction – north, south, east, west, and for the four elements of earth, air, fire, and water. Each round will last anywhere from ten to twenty-five minutes, depending."

"Depending on what?" Blaine asked. A twig cracked. Sparks flew from the fire.

"Patience, son. You will soon see." Grandfather came up behind us. "Oooohhhweee!" he called out to the sky, his voice echoing into the stillness. A couple of crows, disturbed from the trees, flapped away, cawing their displeasure.

"I think we're ready, Grandfather."

"Let's have another cedar tea, then we'll be ready. Our Grandfathers and Grandmothers are still arriving," he said, and took the cup that Christian handed him. "Kishelemukong, Creator, has given us a special day today. Yes, I feel something special in the air. The time of ten thousand will come, Telentxapxki. It is a time when all things will change. I pray that greater understanding and greater respect will spread across the land."

We drained the last of our cups of cedar tea. Christian used a heavy shovel to pick up each hot stone, addressing it as a Grandmother or Grandfather. He took them into the lodge and placed them in the earthen pit in the center.

Before we entered, Grandfather stopped us. "All jewelry must come off, and strip down, at least to your t-shirts."

Aiden and Blaine took off their amulets, set them aside and stripped down, completely comfortable in their nakedness.

I wanted to stare at them, yet I didn't dare. I saw enough to take in how handsome both of their bodies were before I looked away. Aiden was slightly taller than Blaine, his skin smooth and dark. A hot flush rose up from my chest and warmed my cheeks. I lowered my head to hide my face and removed my necklace.

Raven removed her many silver rings, and moved to enter.

Grandfather held up a hand. "Your necklace, Raven."

"I haven't taken it off since you gave it to me. Besides, they're just trade beads on a leather band. There isn't any metal that can burn me."

"Doesn't matter," Grandfather said. "You must take it off."

Raven shrugged. She lifted her beads from around her neck and set them beside her rings. We took off our jackets and jeans, leaving our t-shirts and underclothes on, and entered the lodge. We made our way carefully around the hot stones, making sure not to fall into the pit in the middle. The only light came from the flap as we entered. When it closed, the lodge was pitch black and cloying hot. We sat cross-legged.

My heart fluttered with anticipation, but at the same time, my jaw clenched as waves of fear pulsed through me. I sat nearest to the exit, in case I had to get out fast. Though I hadn't had a panic attack since that day in the subway when Aiden saved me, the fear still felt real.

My skin prickled with heat. Grandfather intoned prayers in Lenape, and the heat intensified. Christian touched my shoulder and I jumped. He took my hand and wrapped it around a pipe. He raised the pipe to my lips and I took a quick puff before passing it to Raven, sitting next to me. Christian splashed some cedar tea on the rocks and it sizzled, the scent filling the lodge. We all sat quietly. I strained to see in the dark, but it was too dense and impenetrable. All became as quiet as it was black. Perspiration dripped from every pore in my body. Just when I thought I couldn't handle the heat for another second, Christian pulled open the flap; the light from outside blinded me. He nudged my arm to guide me out of the lodge.

Everyone tumbled out of the dome, wet and spent. The guys ran to the river where it pooled into a natural basin before continuing its rush down the mountain. They leapt into the water to cool off and clown around. Aiden popped up from the water and waved a hand in the air. "Come on in. It feels great." He barely got the words out before Blaine jumped on his back, dunking him under. Grandfather frowned at their antics, then dove into the water. Raven grabbed my hand and we both jumped in. The water was deliciously cold against my hot skin. I dipped my head under and came up face to face with Aiden, our bodies touching underwater. I slipped below the surface and swam away from him, my cheeks warming in spite of the cool water. *Are we together or aren't we?* I couldn't analyze my feelings when he was that close to me. Naked.

I surfaced just as Grandfather lumbered back up the river bank towards the dome and gestured to the rest of us. "It's time now. We cannot keep the Tunkasilas, the ancestors, waiting."

We all climbed out of the water, refreshed, and raced back to the dome. The air buzzed with anticipation.

The second round began much like the first. Just a lot of hot dense air, in total darkness. Grandfather whispered prayers again in Lenape. I held my breath, wondering what would happen.

Christian's voice came like a welcome relief in the loneliness of the dark. "First round was for acknowledging creator and for the healing of our world. This round is for acknowledging the elders and the healing of ourselves." He passed the pipe to me.

I puffed and offered it to Raven. The embers briefly illuminated each of our faces as we drew on the pipe. Then it was pure blackness again, until the flap opened up to the dazzling brightness outside. I spilled out of the lodge onto the ground beside the entrance, with Raven crawling close behind me. She rolled onto her back, steam rising from her body. "That was so hot. I don't even know if I can get to the river."

Blaine popped out of the dome with his indomitable smile. "I'll race you all to the river." Aiden slipped out in front of him and dashed ahead. Raven and I helped each other up, limp and spent. We stumbled down to the river and fell into the water. The cold immersion shocked me awake. I submerged myself again and swam underwater.

I bobbed up from the water beside Raven and whispered. "The Sweatlodge is kinda boring. And every time it gets hotter. I'm afraid I'm going to have a full-blown panic attack."

"Don't stop now." Raven brought her hands up from underwater in a prayer position. "This next round could be it."

"Could be what? Nothing is happening. And it's too hot."

"I don't know what will happen. Maybe nothing. But maybe something. Just keep going. Please." Her dark eyes pleaded with mine.

My shoulders dropped. "Ok. One more."

I was last to settle back down, cross-legged in front of the hot stones. The flap closed and again the darkness engulfed us. After Grandfather opened with the prayers, Christian interpreted, saying, "This round will be for the acknowledgement of the spirit world and the healing of our spirits and all others."

We passed the pipe. I struggled to draw in a breath in the smoke-filled vault. My heart raced. *I have to get out of here.* I tried to rise to my knees but couldn't move. Then a golden shaft of light poured in from the top of the structure, illuminating everything. I looked around wildly, but no one else seemed to see it. Aiden had his eyes closed like he was meditating. Long filaments, like silken threads, connected all of us in something that resembled a web. I blinked in the sudden brightness. How did I get outside the dome? I glanced around. Raven sat cross-legged beside me, the air thick with smoke. I was still inside too. I gripped Raven's arm. *What is happening?* What had been solid, was now open space. What had my mom said about that? Ah yes. "Pay attention to the spaces." I studied them and they expanded. Nothing had an edge to it; everything blended together, almost like a pointillism painting. So strange. I forgot to be afraid. How could I be there and not be there?

I surveyed the circle. Was everyone experiencing the same thing? No one was distinct, as if we were no longer separate individuals. Bodies blended together until I couldn't tell where one began and another ended. My lips moved as I called out everyone's name; my voice came out like a high-pitched, electronic scream. *I have to find something solid to hold on to.*

I moved without moving. The sounds of hearts beating, blood flowing, fire crackling, bird wings beating outside, clouds roaring across the sky, and water separating into droplets and reforming into a rushing river resonated in my ears. Fear and peace, hatred and love, flowed through me. *I have lived the lives of every person in the dome.*

The energy shifted and a scorpion formed from the emptiness, a convergence of tiny dots. Its shiny black body became very hard, very distinct. It scuttled toward me as it doubled, then tripled, and quadrupled in size. Its long, segmented tail curled up over its body, poised for entry, the tip glistening with a single drop of a golden substance. I dug my heels into the hard-packed earth, trying to back away, but it plunged its tail into my thigh, its hard shell easily penetrating, the stinger releasing its golden liquid inside me in one long gush. I shrieked.

Suddenly I was outside.

Aiden held me in his arms. Blaine splashed cool water on my face. Raven clutched my hand. Christian smiled at me, and the pounding in my chest eased.

"Ah, Avery, you are the lucky one." Grandfather shook his head, long gray hair swishing from side to side. "Raven was right. The ancestors wanted to talk to you, not to the boys."

"I'm the lucky one?" I trembled in Aiden's arms. "That was the strangest experience I ever had. I don't even know if I could describe it. I was everywhere at once, inside and out. We were all blended together like there were no lines separating anything. Then a scorpion appeared and it stung me." I looked down at my thigh, and I was shocked that there was no mark. "What does it all mean?"

Aiden helped me to sit up and kept one arm around me as Christian handed me a mug of hot cedar tea. Aiden slipped my necklace back around my neck. Instantly I felt relieved.

Grandfather shuffled his feet. "We need to contemplate our messages carefully. They are personal. But a scorpion always means there is a stinging truth that needs to be revealed."

We all turned at the sound of twigs and branches crashing behind us.

"I told you to get out." Wayne Big Bear waved his rifle in the air as he strode toward us. "Pimewaken is sacred. For us only."

"Wayne." Grandfather lifted both hands, his palms toward the intruder. "These people are good. The ancestors gave this one an experience. They have respect. No one wants trouble here."

"Then they shouldn't a come. They're the ones what have brought the trouble." Wayne spat out the words.

"We've come in peace." Aiden held me tighter.

"And they are our guests." Raven stood up, planting both hands on her hips.

Wayne shoved his black fedora back on his head. Anger blazed in his eyes. "You don't belong here."

Grandfather stepped up to him. "Away with you, Wayne. We don't treat our guests this way."

"Your father stole this land from my father, Old Tree, and you know it," Wayne shouted. "This is trouble. We should get rid of them now."

"You're talkin' crazy." Grandfather waved his hand at him. "No one stole anything. This is Lenape land."

Wayne stepped towards me and pointed the rifle in my direction.

A golden eagle, perched on the branch of a tall tree nearby, took flight with a piercing shriek. It dove at Wayne's head, knocking his hat to the ground. Rasta burst out of the woods, covering the clearing in several bounds and leaping at Wayne's chest, a dark shadow flying through the air. A shot rang out. Wayne fell backwards, two large, black paws pinning his shoulders, and two back paws holding his hips down. Blaine dove for the rifle. In one swift movement, he unloaded it and flung it aside. Aiden stood at my side, every muscle poised, tension quivering through him. Rasta lowered his muzzle close to Wayne's face and growled.

Grandfather gasped. "Mwekane and Aiham, Wayne. The Dog and the Eagle."

"Everything's okay, Rasta," I said. "Let him go now." He gave one last menacing growl and stepped away from Wayne, but trotted over to stand in front of me, as poised to attack as Aiden.

Wayne struggled up, dusted himself off, and grabbed his rifle from the ground. He slunk back across the clearing towards the woods. Just before he reached it, he turned back and yelled, "There is more going on here than meets the eye, Old Tree. A lot more than even you know."

"The Dog and the Eagle, Wayne," Grandfather shouted. "You saw it yourself."

"Send them packing, Old Tree. I'm warning you."

"Dog and Eagle."

AVERY

If you want to awaken all of humanity,
then awaken all of yourself.

—Lao Tzu

I bounded up the stairs. I only had an hour to prepare for the Ambassador's Dinner and Ball.

Dad met me on his way down and I stopped and rested back against the railing. He leaned in to give me a perfunctory peck on the cheek. "How were the Ramapos?"

"Fabulous!" I beamed, unable to contain myself.

"Anything you should tell me about? Maybe something you forgot to mention before you left?"

I shifted from one foot to the other. "Not really."

His eyes darkened. "You really must stop lying to me. You will *not* become like your mother. I will not have it," Dad said.

"What are you talking about? Not like my mother?"

"You've had plenty of opportunities to tell me. I know who you were with. I know that Brit was with you. Avery, you're too young..."

"Dad! I'm nineteen years old! And nothing happened; Aiden and I are just friends." I resisted the urge to storm away from him and slam my bedroom door in his face. I needed to learn how to stand up to him. "And what do you mean, not become like my mother?"

He bent down close to my face and gripped my wrist.

"Wayne Big Bear is one of *my* men." He tightened his hold. "He works for me. When are you going to get it, Avery? My reach is very wide and very deep. I know everything that goes on. I don't like being lied to." His eyes bore into mine.

I lifted my chin, refusing to look away.

After a moment, he let out a breath and released my wrist. "I've made all the arrangements for tonight."

"I don't want to go."

"Nonsense, Avery. You will go. I won't be made a fool of, and I won't have my mood dampened by you."

"Dad, I…"

He held a finger to his lips. "It's all good now. We have an understanding, don't we?"

I rubbed my wrist, heat searing through my chest. "How does Wayne Big Bear work for you?"

"He's my mining manager." He rested an elbow on the stair railing. "Iron ore, all along the ridge up there. It's one of my smaller companies – Three Bears Mining Inc. Doesn't turn a large profit, but we keep it running because it supports the Native community. I've taught you the importance of true philanthropy, Avery. Just remember that, while you're idealizing your Buddhist martial artist. Ask yourself, what can a pauper really do to help people?"

"There are a lot more ways to help people than just throwing money at them, Dad. And don't talk about Aiden like that. You have no idea what he is like or what he does."

He smirked, his lips formed a tight line. "Be very careful, Avery. My friends are presidents, prime ministers, princes. You need to remember who you are and where you came from … and that the people who control the puppet strings on the global stage must be careful to cultivate and secure friends in high places." His face softened and he patted my hand. "Your young friends are walking in shoes too big for them, but I thought I would help them out by inviting them to the Ambassador's Ball this evening. I knew it would bring you joy to have them with you, and you know all I want is your happiness, dear."

My eyes widened. "You invited my friends to the Ambassador's Ball?"

"Yes. I got Blaine's cell number from your phone and called him. They're probably on their way here now."

"You took his number from my phone?" I tried to comprehend what he was saying, as though he were speaking another language and I had to translate in my head.

"I pay the bills, Avery. I have every right to pick up your phone and use it any time and in any way I see fit."

I gritted my teeth. "Neither Aiden or Blaine have the proper clothes to wear to an embassy dinner, and you know it."

"Neither Aiden *nor* Blaine *has* the proper clothes. Watch your grammar, Avery. Didn't you learn anything at that damned expensive school I sent you to? I have a few suits they are welcome to borrow. We're all about the same height."

"You're quite a few pounds heavier than Aiden and Blaine." I shook my head. *Are we really having this conversation?*

"I have classic formal wear stored in your mother's closet from when I was about their age. That's why they're coming here first. Claire and Whitney are coming too. We can't stop it now. It's rolling, baby." He rotated his fists, one over the other, and flashed me a disingenuous smirk.

AVERY

*Fill your bowl to the brim and it will spill. Keep sharpening
your knife and it will blunt.*

—Lao Tzu

The doorbell rang and I hurried out of my room and started down
the stairs. I wasn't sure what game my dad was playing by inviting
Aiden and Blaine, but I wasn't leaving them unattended with him for long.

My father beat me to the front door and pulled it open. "Good
evening, gentlemen."

"Hi, Mr. A." Blaine held out a hand. He glanced at me with a glint
in his eye.

I suppressed a grin. No one called my dad, 'Mr. A.' and lived to tell
the tale.

"Crikey, you've a beautiful home here, mate," Blaine said, kicking
up his Aussie accent.

My dad's shoulders relaxed as he gave Blaine's hand a firm shake.
Blaine's charm was hard to resist. Even for my dad.

"Hello, sir," Aiden grasped my father's hand. "Thanks for inviting
us to the dinner."

Dad's haughty glare was clearly an attempt to unnerve Aiden.

Aiden smiled in return.

Dad waved his hand toward the stairs. "I have your clothes laid out in
one of the guest rooms." We followed him as he strode towards his office,
playing with the diamond cufflinks under his new designer three-button
jacket, a jacket suited more to a slim young man than a fifty-something,
beefy-if-still-handsome one. My dad normally oozed confidence, but

he seemed ill-at-ease tonight. Was he still mad at me for lying, or was it something bigger?

He left us at the guest room door. "I will see you all in a few minutes." He nodded before turning to march down the hall toward his office.

I ushered Aiden and Blaine into the room where the suits were laid out. Their unique connection was apparent through the unison of their movements, smooth, almost graceful, with an implicit understanding of what the other would do next.

"If I have to wear a whistle and a flute, I'll go with the brown one." Blaine picked up the jacket and held it in front of him.

My brow crinkled. "A whistle and a flute?"

"Flute, rhymes with suit, so you make it a whistle and flute. It's Cockney rhyming slang, so that no one knows what you're talking about."

"It works. I had no idea." I laughed, the tension draining from my shoulders.

"I like the black one, Grasshopper." Aiden ran a hand over the gleaming fabric.

Warmth flushed through me. "You really like that nickname, don't you?"

My father came to the door holding two pairs of newly polished dress shoes.

"I think these will fit you," he said with a smile.

All of my father's former bitterness and macho maneuvering melted into a sickly sweet attentiveness. I marveled at his ability to switch moods as quickly as a hummingbird switches direction. The boys graciously accepted the shoes. Dad steered me by the shoulders out of the room, and closed the door.

After retreating to my bedroom, I slipped into the champagne satin dress and gold strappy heels that Whitney and Katie had advised me to wear earlier in the day by conference call. I touched the stone on my necklace and felt its pulse in rhythm with my own. Was it possible I had the frightening experience because I had taken it off? I felt protected whenever I wore it. That, and an incredible infusion of energy and wellbeing. But Grandfather said the Old Ones wanted to speak to me. Why me? I grabbed a matching wrap and swept downstairs, feeling both self-conscious and ultra-feminine. Aiden, Blaine, and my father stood in the entryway.

When I stepped onto the marble floor, all three men turned toward me, mouths dropping open in unison. *That may be the only thing these three men will do together for my entire life*. I basked in their looks, my cheeks warming. Katie's latest favorite saying echoed in my head: "Be proud. Hold your head up and be all that you can be. Never hide." I asked her once how she got so wise. She said she had been writing a paper on Nelson Mandela, and in his Nobel Peace Prize acceptance speech he'd said something about letting the world see your light. Katie surprised me sometimes. Like she had surprised Raven.

The four of us left the apartment and walked to the waiting limousine. My father slid onto the seat beside me and directed Aiden and Blaine to sit across from us.

"I'm surprised, Avery, that you look so beautiful tonight," my father said. "I mean, not surprised that you look beautiful, you are beautiful, of course, it's just that—"

"Hey, Mr. A," Blaine held up a hand, "you should probably quit while you're ahead."

I tensed, waiting for my father to take offence and lash out, but instead he started to laugh. Blaine joined in. Aiden nudged me with his knee and I offered him a weak smile.

My father turned to him. "So, Aiden, where do you and Blaine live?"

"We're staying with a friend who's an intern at NY City Hospital. His family has an apartment here." Aiden met my father's intense gaze calmly. "Have you always been a New Yorker?"

"Born and bred."

"Where did you meet Avery's mum?"

I shifted to face him. "Oh, I'd love to hear about that, Dad." The only thing tying me to my father at this point was my mother. I needed to hear him talk about her.

"The boys don't want to hear a love story, Avery. Although I did love your mother very much."

Blaine leaned forward. "Actually, we'd love to hear your love story."

The car pulled up to the curb and came to a stop.

"Ah, saved by two more beautiful women," Dad said with a wink. He opened the car door and got out. Claire and Whitney were ready and waiting for him on the sidewalk. He gave them each a hand into the car.

My eyes met Whitney's. She didn't look very happy, but she shrugged as though resigned to the inevitable. I sighed. *I guess I'm going to have to accept that he is dating Claire.*

Aiden moved over so Whitney could sit beside him, and Claire settled in between me and my father. He cast adoring looks at her as we drove, and laughed and joked with everyone. *Maybe this relationship with Claire is good for him.* I'd experienced too many of his mood swings to relax yet though. I'd wait and see if this good one would last.

We arrived at the Waldorf Astoria and, one by one, the line of black limousines pulled up to the curb. The doorman opened our car door with a white-gloved hand.

"Just follow my lead, when to bow and when to shake hands. Try not to feel too out of place, boys. These people may be the power brokers of the world, but they are very nice, really," Dad said. He stepped out onto the sidewalk and held out his hand for me, all smiles. "Just try to follow my lead, Avery. Don't do anything to embarrass me," he whispered. He took my arm in one of his, and held out his other to Claire. We started for the front door, Whitney, Aiden, and Blaine behind us.

The Japanese ambassador greeted us with a bow as we stepped inside the entry way to the ball room. My father bowed in response and the rest of us followed suit. We moved onto the next Ambassador, wearing a designer suit and lavender polished cotton shirt, his head wrapped in a traditional Arabian scarf.

"Hello, Ahkmed," my father said. "This is my lovely daughter, Avery, and her two friends, Blaine Owens and Aiden Kane. My beautiful friend, Claire Rose, and her daughter Whitney." After exchanging pleasantries with the ambassador, we moved into a large room, following my father's lead as we greeted one person after another.

"Hello, Yang." My father introduced us to a man who responded in English and in Chinese, bowing slightly. Aiden stepped forward and greeted him in Chinese. Mr. Yang clapped his hands. They conversed for a couple of minutes before he invited us to sit with him at a larger table.

"That's very impressive, Aiden. Where did you learn to speak Chinese?" My father held out a chair for Claire before sitting down to my left.

"Mr. Aiden has excellent conversation, Mr. Peter. Very excellent," Mr. Yang said.

"I lived in a mountain region close to Tibet while I studied martial arts," Aiden said, pulling out a chair for me. I smiled at him as I smoothed my gown behind me and sat down. He took the seat to the right of me. "I love languages and learned the dialect there."

Mr. Yang settled onto the chair on the other side of Aiden and the two of them engaged in an animated conversation. I watched them, thrilled to see Aiden so at home at such a major event. Maybe my father would soften towards him.

A very officious-looking man came over to our table and whispered in my father's ear.

Mr. Yang looked over at him. "Hi, Mr. Anthony. What you want here?"

My father cleared his throat. "I apologize, Yang, and everyone." He nodded to the table. "Anthony was just inviting Claire, and the family, to stay on his yacht in St. Bart's next winter. I didn't want to interrupt your conversation."

"No problem, Mr. Peter." Mr. Yang exchanged a look with my father that I couldn't quite grasp.

"I'm so sorry to interrupt you." Anthony backed away from the table.

The waiters began serving white bowls filled with deep green sorrel soup, and the room filled with the sounds of a baroque quartet and spoons clinking on porcelain against a background of muted voices talking and laughing.

Mr. Yang said in English, "You know how China dominate manufacture of thing like appliance and electronic? Now, do same thing with car. Chery and BYD soon replace name like Ford and General Motor. And China has something else – rare earth and vast lithium deposit in highland of Tibet. Soon all of car in world will run on lithium battery. Our lithium supply will permit us to finally end reliance on foreign oil. We are already beyond lithium to power car and onto rare earth magnetics. Experiments already working. Cars float above the road." Mr. Yang nodded emphatically. "Whoever own the road, rule the world."

"Whoever owns the energy, rules the world," Aiden replied as he rested his arm on the back of my chair. Electricity tingled across my shoulders.

"Superconductors, magnetic resonance, and second sound are all possibilities that will someday completely change the way we live," Blaine said. "What once seemed like magic, will soon be explained."

"When we figure out how to harness and use free energy, then we will stop having to fight for resources. Then we will have peace in the world." Aiden squeezed my shoulder.

My father adjusted his cufflinks and cleared his throat. "Aiden, really. Such a naive approach to complex realities. Wars are fought for many reasons, and perhaps most importantly is the meaning and purpose it gives to life and death, nation and sovereignty. And Yang, America will always dominate the car market. Chinese quality just isn't up to snuff.

You're dreaming if you think China's lithium supply will substantially change the market. There is already a surplus of lithium production in the world. Anyone would be a fool to buy stock in lithium."

Another man came up to our table. He rested his hands on the back of my dad's chair. "Hello Peter."

My father twisted in his seat. "Oh, Rick. I didn't know you were in town for this. Everybody, I want you to meet my main man for the reduction of nuclear disarmament, Rick Phillips."

A polite smile flashed across Rick's face as he glanced at us all, then he leaned down to my dad. I couldn't help but overhear. "Peter, what happened after I left the conference? Everything was fine. Why didn't the president sign off?"

My dad shook his head. "This isn't a topic for a party. Why don't we meet tomorrow?"

"I'm flying back to Washington first thing." Rick's knuckles gleamed white around the top of the chair as he bent close to my father's ear and hissed, "I want to know why the agreement changed."

"I'll be in Washington next week. We can talk then."

"We need to get on this fast, Peter. This doesn't bode well for the negotiations coming up in the Stans. Kazakhstan is already reacting to this. It destabilizes the entire region. Plays into the hands of terrorists."

"Oh, we'll be fine." Dad waved a hand through the air dismissively

Rick straightened up. "I'm glad you're so sure. We'll talk soon." He turned and stomped out of the banquet hall.

I watched him leave. "He seems really upset."

"Rick's neurotic. He worries about every little detail."

Claire rested her hand on my father's arm. "You know, Avery, your mom once told me that your great-great-grandfather gave a lecture in this very room. Something about atoms. I didn't even know they knew about atoms back then."

"Aiden." Dad leaned forward to look around me. "You and Yang are having quite a conversation."

"This very auspicious time for Chinese and world," Mr. Yang said. "Time of great transformation, but maybe time of great destruction too. It our choice."

"Oh, Yang." My dad chuckled, but it sounded a little forced. "You always talk about great this and great that for China."

"Mr. Peter. You think you so powerful in world. Just as predicted, there could be polarity shift in world, where what on top, magnetic north, go to bottom and what on bottom, magnetic south, go to top. So too this reflect in culture. Those on top will find themself on bottom, those on bottom find themself on top. Different gift will be needed. It is you who will see."

"The day magnetic north goes south will be the day dinosaurs return to roam the earth." Dad pressed a cream-colored linen napkin to his lips before tossing it onto the table. "There is real power in the world, beyond what most people even know about. You and I are undeniably a part of that. I can guarantee that power will not be toppled."

Yang stood up and bowed again. "With that, I must leave you." He pressed his card into Aiden's hand. *"Hengowshen, renshennei.* It has been a great pleasure to meet you. Take my card and come see me in China. I like you."

I leaned back in my chair, unable to stop a smile from spreading across my face, in spite of the irritated look that crossed my father's. Or maybe because of it. My dad's patronizing advice notwithstanding, the last thing Aiden had seemed that evening, in the midst of all those mighty *power brokers*, was out of place.

Chapter 18

AVERY

Courage is knowing what not to fear.

—Plato

I woke up just before dawn. After rolling out of bed, I eased into a pair of jeans, a T-shirt, my sneakers, and a hoodie in case it was chilly. I left Rasta behind, knowing Rub y would take him out later. I slipped out the front door and was barely down the street when someone whispered in my ear, "Where do you think you are going?"

I froze. Two hands gripped my shoulders and swung me around.

"Aiden! What are you doing? You scared me half to death."

"I'm sorry. I was worried about you. I stayed in the tree outside your bedroom window last night to make sure you were okay."

"What? Why? What's going on?"

"I wish I knew." Aiden whisked me along the sidewalk. "It's just a feeling I have. That something bigger might be going on here. Somehow we are all connected to it, but I don't know how. Yang hinted at things about your father. Unfortunately, Chinese is a language with multiple meanings for words and expressions, so I couldn't understand all of the nuances. I did get that we need to be more alert…he made me wonder who your Dad really is."

"Slow down, please. We're walking too fast." I felt winded, the mental workout wearing me out. Who *was* my dad? Lately, I didn't even know.

"If you know something, Aiden, tell me."

"Just trust me." He snatched my hand and dragged me towards the subway entrance. We flew down the stairs towards the train. At the last moment, Aiden caught my arm and pulled me through the doors of the train going the opposite direction.

He pressed a finger to his lips. His gaze flashed around the crowded car. Whatever he was looking for, he didn't appear to see it. He sat down, scoping out the passengers in the car, then pulled me down beside him. "We're not going to do anything routine for the next few weeks. If we're being followed, we have to change our habits. It's good that school is over so you don't have to be anywhere at a specific time. We won't meet for practice at the same time in the morning and we'll change parks every day."

My mind blurred as I tried to take in everything he was saying. "Is all of this really necessary? What could anyone possibly want with—?"

He gripped my hand tighter. "Don't underestimate what is going on here."

I shifted in my seat to study his face. "Who are you, Aiden? I need to know."

"Who is your dad is a better question. Have you heard of the five families? The Illuminati?" He swept the train with his eyes again.

"Aiden, you're freaking me out."

The subway rolled into the station.

"Your father is a very dangerous man, Avery."

The doors swished open.

I searched his eyes. They had gone hard and cold. Maybe my dad wasn't the only one I didn't know. My stomach tightened. And maybe he wasn't the only one who was dangerous. A whistle blew. The subway doors started to close. I lunged for the opening and squeezed through.

Aiden strong-armed the doors open and bounded out after me. He grabbed at me, but I was far enough away that I easily dodged his grasp.

"Get away from me!" My heart pounded in my chest. I'd had it with all the unanswered questions, the furtive looks, the intrigue, and most of all, the push and pull game that Aiden played. I ran along the platform toward the transit officer.

"What are you doing to that girl?" An officer positioned himself between me and Aiden swiftly coming up behind me.

"You don't understand..." Aiden said.

Three more transit officers arrived. The other commuters scattered. Both trains pulled out of the station and suddenly the five of us were the only ones on the platform. Aiden crouched down, his hands in front of his face. Attack position.

What is he doing?

Suddenly, one of the officers ran up the wall and flipped, dropping down in front of Aiden. The one who had been standing in front of me twirled toward him like a tornado.

"Run, Avery!" Aiden yelled.

But it was too late. Another officer grabbed my arm from behind me. Aiden was surrounded by men who were clearly not official New York subway guards. They kept coming at him, moving so fast I couldn't keep up with the action.

The officer holding my arm let go of me. Knowing there was nothing I could do to help Aiden, I spun around, prepared to run, and stopped abruptly. The two Goth Girls who had attacked me twice before advanced toward me, slowly. I glanced at the officer, but his attention was on the fight in front of him. I stepped backwards, but with platform drop-offs on both sides, and a deadly fight happening behind me, there was nowhere for me to go. Cold smiles crossed both their faces as they approached me and grabbed my arms.

I screamed for Aiden and twisted my head to look back as they dragged me down the platform. He circled around the three guards and ran towards me, but the fourth guard, the one who had held my arm, stepped in front of him. The other three officers caught up. Aiden yelled out, his voice deadened by the squealing of brakes on metal. The Goth Girls pulled me away from the oncoming train, toward the opposite track. I struggled to free myself, but they hauled me down a dark tunnel.

Their hold on me was as strong as my fear. Thick blackness pressed in on me from all sides. Now, instead of struggling to get away, I practically hung onto them in panic. Unable to see anything, my other senses became more acute. The air became dank, the smell of human waste mingling with machinery oil. We seemed to be going deeper and deeper underneath the city, into a world I had only heard about, but never believed existed.

"Who you got there, girlies?" An asthmatic, wheezing voice called out from the darkness.

"Is it dinner time?" cackled another voice.

Slowly my eyes adjusted. Shadowy figures stood against the slick, black walls of ancient tunnels. My feet barely touched the ground as the two Goth Girls pulled me forward. Oily water seeped through my sneakers and crept up my pant legs.

Squeaks, squeals, and cackles echoed through the tunnels. A weak yellow candle lit up a decrepit card table, where a creepy old man sat with something that looked like a dead rat on a dinner plate in front of him. I gagged. He leered at me, his bird eyes unblinking, and held up one finger. Black line tattoos on his face danced in the flickering light. I sucked in a quick breath. It was the albino man in the wheelchair. I craned my neck to watch him as we passed. Would he help me?

"You like rats?" The tall Goth Girl turned her face toward mine; her breath smelled.

The other one squeezed my arm. "There are more where we are going. Rats don't like the vibrations of the subway so they go deeper into the tunnels, where it's really dark."

The tunnels grew narrower and danker the farther we traveled. I struggled to draw a breath. This was far worse than riding a subway. My heart pounded in my ears.

We arrived at a juncture of several tunnels and stopped in front of a wooden door. Water oozed through the cracks in the bricks, trickled down the walls, and pooled at our feet. The stench made me want to throw up.

What is happening to Aiden? How could he fight so many opponents? The thought of him being injured sent pain shooting through my chest. This is my fault. If I hadn't leapt off the train … I swallowed the lump in my throat. Aiden had amazing skills; I'd seen them myself. Even so badly outnumbered, there was a chance he could fight them off. I glanced back in the direction we'd come. *Please come. Please be all right. I need you.* Could he read my thoughts like I had read his when he was holding me in the water? The pain in my chest deepened. I'd give anything to feel his arms around me again, holding me close.

The Goth girls gripped my arms tighter. How could I get away from them? I didn't know enough martial arts yet to fight even one, let alone two, experienced fighters. And even if I could get away, where would I go? Could I find my way back through the dark tunnels? A shudder moved through me at the thought. Maybe the man with the tattoos would show me the way out. My heart quickened, but I had learned enough from Aiden to center myself. I slowed my breathing and looked around, my eyes becoming accustomed to the dark.

The taller girl rummaged through the keys dangling from one of her many bracelets and I saw an opportunity. I lashed out with my arm, kicking out my leg at the same time. The sudden change in me from frightened, clingy girl to rampaging, whirling dervish caught them off guard and they both lost their grip. The thin wire of energy within me had been steadily growing with practice and I surprised myself. I scrambled away from them, not caring what direction I headed.

Footsteps pounded behind me. I ran, pressing the back of my hand to my mouth to keep from retching with the stench of sewage. I tripped over something in the ankle-high water and reached out to steady myself. My fingers brushed cold, slimy walls and I yanked them back. Was I going deeper down or coming up? The tunnel seemed to go on forever, and with the complete absence of light, I had no idea where I was. When I couldn't take another step, I stopped and bent forward, clutching my knees with both hands. My gasping breaths echoed off the tunnel walls. Gradually they evened out and I straightened up, straining to hear in the darkness. The only sound was the beating of my heart and the constant trickle of the groundwater. I took a step, and I heard a one behind me. I held my breath and stopped.

I peered down into the darkness, trying to determine which way the little rivulet was flowing. The same direction I was running. I felt intuitively that was good. The river must be flowing out towards something. *Or it's just flowing deeper underground.* Tears pricked my eyes at the thought, but I blinked them back. Was this all just a nightmare? I pinched my arm, trying to wake myself up. Shock reverberated across my skin, but nothing changed. Darkness, stench, and sliminess threatened to consume me. My head jerked up. *This is just like the nightmare I had when the halls closed in on me as I went deeper and deeper to try to get to Uncle Simon.* Footsteps sounded behind me and I whirled around. Silence.

Desperate, I reached out and trailed my fingers along the wall as I walked forward. The wall ended. Another juncture. *If it's like the others, there are three tunnels.* I could sprint down one, hoping to lose my pursuers. I decided to run straight ahead … no, to the left. Yes, the left. I changed my mind at the last minute and went straight ahead.

I smashed into a body and clutched the arms that reached for me. "Aiden?"

"Ha! Don't you wish?"

The cold, hard voice of one of the Goth Girls turned my blood to ice. I screamed and struggled. I spit at her.

"Bitch!" she shrieked. "Veronika, hold her! She's turned wild on us."

I screamed and clawed, but in a lightning-fast move, she kicked my legs out from under me and I went straight down. I turned my head, coughing and sputtering to clear my mouth of wet ooze.

She yanked both my arms behind my back and wrapped something around my wrists. When she lifted me to my feet, I twisted, turned, and kicked uselessly at thin air.

"She spit at me, she bad." The one holding me yanked my arms further behind me.

I pressed my lips together to suppress a groan as pain shot across my shoulders and chest.

"Shut up, Valerie," Veronika said.

The two Goth Girls each took an arm again and dragged me back down the tunnel. In seconds we were at the wooden door again. I gritted my teeth. I must have been running in circles.

Veronika yanked a key from her bracelet and opened the door. The rush of light and relatively clean air overwhelmed me and I stumbled, suddenly dizzy. Veronika pulled me away from Valerie and shoved me down to the wet slimy stone floor. She crouched at my feet, wrapping a rope around my ankles and pulling it so tight I gasped.

"We wait now," Valerie said.

I looked around, trying to get a sense of what was going on.

"Little girl," purred Veronika. "Are you cold?"

I hadn't noticed how cold and damp it was in the room until she mentioned it. Valerie clutched my hoodie in one hand—*when did she pull that off?*—leaving me in my thin T-shirt, and I shivered.

"Aiden will be here any minute," I said.

Veronika's eyes hardened. "If Aiden comes, he will be coming for me, not for you. I love him and he loves me."

Is that true? Was Aiden working with these two? Had I fallen into some kind of trap that he had set for me? I shook my head. I had no idea what to believe anymore.

Valerie bent down to my face and held my chin, studying me closely. "Veronika, she very pretty. Do we have to hurt her?" She moved closer to me until I could smell strange spices on her breath. Before I realized what she was going to do, she pressed her lips to mine, and stuck her tongue deep into my mouth.

Shock coursed through me and I bit down hard.

Valerie reared back and smacked me across the face.

Stinging pain shot across my cheek, but I watched in grim satisfaction as she withdrew to sit on a chair across the room and glare at me.

Veronika threw a disgusted glance at her before kneeling down in front of me. I pressed my back to the wall behind me as she leaned in, her dark eyes searching mine. "Hey, Bait, do you know who Aiden really is?"

I barely shook my head in response.

"You are so stupid. Of course you don't. You don't even know who your own father is." Veronika cackled and Valerie giggled.

"So Aiden hasn't told you anything?"

"I wouldn't tell you if he had."

Valerie mocked me in a whiny voice, "I wouldn't tell you if he had."

I clenched my fists. "If you know who Aiden is, why don't you tell me?" I sounded petulant. I wished I sounded different, strong, heroic, angry even, anything but petulant.

"If you know who Aiden is, why don't you tell me?" Valerie parroted.

What is this, grade school?

"It's not my job to enlighten you," Veronika snapped. "But if I were you, I would find out who Aiden is … before it's too late."

"You playing with fire and you not equipmented," Valerie added.

"Equipped, she is not *equipped*, Valerie." Veronika sounded exasperated.

Of course I wasn't. Nothing in my life had prepared me to deal with a situation like this. I hadn't realized just how pristine my life was. I had grown up privileged, gone to private school, even had drivers when I couldn't take the subway because of my panic attacks. I hadn't even known this dark world existed. These girls were way beyond the dressed-up Goths I saw on the streets of Manhattan. I thought I had wanted to experience the gritty reality of life, but this was way too much, too weird, too scary, and too evil. An icy coldness penetrated down deep inside of me. I struggled with the bindings on my wrists.

Veronika stood up and pulled a chair over to me, twirling it around so she could straddle it. She smiled as she pulled something from her pocket and flashed it through the air in front of me. My chest tightened. A fish filleting knife.

For a moment I stared, mesmerized by the glittering blade. Then I tore my gaze away.

Valerie was perched on an old credenza, swinging legs encased in black, fish-net stockings with red, high-heeled shoe-boots. The single naked bulb that had seemed so bright when we first entered barely lit the immediate area.

Every now and again, someone passed by the door, water splashing beneath their feet. Voices called to each other in the distance. I straightened as the slapping of running feet grew louder.

"Aiden," I screamed. Running feet passed by the door, the sound receding.

A smirk crossed Veronika's face as she turned the knife over in her hand, the light glinting off it. "See, Bait? No one cares about you down here, so you can yell all you want. There's only one fish we'll catch with you, and that's the one we want."

"Let's put her in chair. We can't leave her on floor."

Veronika shrugged. "Do what you want, just don't let her escape."

Valerie leapt off of the credenza with the ease of a cat and came over to me. She grasped my elbow and pulled me to my feet, then kicked a chair underneath me. Veronika watched carefully as Valerie moved behind me, undid the ropes around my wrists, and re-tied the binds around the chair, practically dislocating my shoulder in the process. When she undid my ankles, I shot out my leg, catching Veronika under the chin. She rocked back on her heels, but before I could follow my attack with another kick, Valerie had leapt around to grasp both my ankles, wrapped the rope around them tightly, and knotted it around the bottom rung of the chair. Even through my jeans, the bindings dug into my skin, but I lifted my chin and glared at her defiantly.

Valerie pushed to her feet and brushed off the knees of her black tights.

Veronika moved to her side and shoved her out of the way. She rubbed her chin. "You will pay for that, Bait." The knife flashed in her hand and I swallowed hard. With a quick flick of her wrist, she cut my jeans, then ripped the opening wider with her hands. Slowly, methodically, she drew the blade across the surface of my skin.

I bit my lip to keep from crying out as fire licked across my leg.

She studied her handiwork with apparent interest as blood bubbled to the surface. "Just a little notice, Bait, in case you're thinking of trying to fight either of us again. I'm not afraid of using this knife." Her hand flew through the air and she slashed the knife across my thigh. Pain screamed through me. My blood flowed, soaking into the light blue denim. I dug my fingers into my palms to keep from letting out a piercing shriek.

Veronika dragged the side of the blade from the corner of my mouth across my cheek to my ear without breaking the skin. "I could give you a permanent smile," she sneered, "but not yet. I'll wait until I'm sufficiently bored with this game. That will give you time to wonder what will get you first. The rats that will be attracted to your blood, or me."

"Hey, look, I want it." Valerie yanked at my necklace, the old clasp giving way easily. As soon as it fell into her hand, she dropped it to the ground. "Ouch, you shock me!"

Veronika swooped down and picked up the necklace, holding it up to the single light bulb and studying the fiery patterns.

"That was my mother's!" I cried out in frustration. I couldn't believe they had it, the stone that connected me to the one person in my life who had truly cared about me.

"You know shit, my little angel." Veronika laughed.

"Give necklace to me," Val begged. "I found it."

"This was what I felt when I first saw you in the subway. I was about to catch Aiden off guard and I had no idea about you." Veronika ran a finger over the smooth stone. "It all makes sense now. This must be what makes you so important to Zheng. How did someone like you get a stone like this?" She dangled it in front of my face, then snatched it back. I yanked on my restraints as she placed the necklace around her neck and closed the clasp.

A tremendous boom rocked the room. The floor shook. Mortar dust fell from the walls and ceilings. Two rats dropped down from the wood beams over our heads. I screamed as one ran over my foot and disappeared into the darkness behind the dim light cast by the bulb.

"What the...?" Veronika stared up at the ceiling, her dark eyes wide.

"Terrorist?" Val pressed her knuckles to her lips.

"Not when we're here." Veronika shook her head. "They don't dare do anything without our permission."

The naked bulb sputtered. For a few seconds the light flickered, then the room was plunged into darkness.

AVERY

Darkness cannot drive out darkness, only light can do that.
Hate cannot drive out hate, only love can do that.

—Martin Luther King, Jr.

I blinked. *Am I dead or alive?* I tried stretching my arms and legs but they were still securely fastened to the chair. A candle flickered, sending macabre shadows dancing across the walls of the room. I strained against the ropes but they only seemed to tighten. I froze at the sound of something sniffing around my leg. One of the Goths stamped her foot and a rat raced away into a dark corner. My head pounded and my mouth was dry. *How long have I been here?*

"Come on now, time to wake up." Veronika prodded me with the end of a long stick.

Valerie sat on the credenza, filing her nails. I felt like an insect caught in a spider's web, partially paralyzed and waiting to be eaten, but conscious. My arms had gone numb. A vague memory drifted back, of Valerie coming in the dark and giving me a sip of water. Had she drugged me? Rage flooded through me and I struggled to sit up straighter in the chair.

"She coming to," Valerie said.

"How much did you give her?" Veronika snarled. "I thought you'd killed her, she's been out for so long."

"So? We not need her."

"Don't be an idiot. Zheng wants her alive. She's part of this. I just don't know what part yet. She must have vital information."

"It my turn to wear necklace now, Veronika."

"No, it's not. And it won't ever be. You let the necklace drop."

"It shock me."

"It shocked me too, but I hung on to it, so I get to keep it." Veronika paced around me, periodically tapping her wooden pole on the stone floor, sending the rats racing for the edges of the room. Every once in a while she prodded me with the rough end. I yanked my arm back and glared at her.

"Something's not adding up. You're Peter's daughter and you hang around Aiden. You had this necklace." Veronika stopped pacing and propping herself up with her pole, tapping a finger against her chin. "No, this isn't adding up."

"She the one Master Zheng want? She the one he say so important?"

"I don't know anything," I said. "I never heard of Zheng."

"Zheng is not telling us everything, Val."

The door flew open and Aiden burst into the room. Shoving Veronika to one side, he reached for the ropes binding me to the chair.

"Hi, Fish. Glad you took the bait," Veronika said. "What took you so long?"

He glared at her, then stepped towards me.

"Aiden! She has my necklace." Fear shivered up my spine as I glanced at the girls. Why did they look so calm?

Just as he reached me, both girls pounced on him. He shook them off like rag dolls, and caught Val around her neck, whirling her around. He reached behind me and quickly loosened the ropes so I could work at untying myself.

"Get out of here, Avery!" Aiden crouched down, his hands in front of him. He didn't take his eyes off of Veronika.

His thoughts whirled through my mind. Energy pulsed from him. In contrast, Veronika and Valerie appeared completely relaxed and in control.

"Where is your focus?" Veronika laughed. "This isn't the Aiden that I know ... and I know you oh sooo well." Lowering her voice, she sidled up to him, murmuring in a mixture of Chinese and English. "We share something, Aiden. Something very special."

I gritted my teeth and gave the ropes around my wrist one final jerk. They fell off and I leaned down, scrambling to untie the ropes binding my ankles to the chair. When I had freed myself, I rose to my feet, my eyes on the girls. All their attention appeared to be focused on Aiden, who looked like he was in some kind of trance. I moved along the periphery of the room, looking for a good angle. When I saw it, I leapt onto Veronika's back, clawing at her neck.

Val grabbed me from behind.

Aiden pounced into action. I could barely follow the Bagua moves, they came so blindingly fast; dragon serving tea, hawk piercing the sky, snake flicking his tongue. Aiden downed Val in a few deft moves. Veronika laughed as she threw her head back and rammed me into the wall. I slumped down to the floor, gasping for breath.

Aiden and Veronika faced off.

"I think Bait should wait until you tell her who you really are," Veronika said, looking pleased with her plan. "Yes, I think that is a very good idea."

They moved on opposite sides of a circular pattern.

"Avery knows you were with me in China," Aiden said.

"Oh, Aiden. Poor sweet, decent, hero-save-the-world Aiden, you just don't get this, do you?" She reached across the circle to stroke his cheek. He jerked away from her touch. Veronika smiled. "You think I'm upset about you dumping me."

I glanced at the door but hesitated. Valerie moaned.

"Get out of here, Avery."

"Come on, Bait. You know you wanna know who he is," Veronika said. "Just give me your amulet, Aiden, then I'll have both of them and you can go."

"What do you want with this trinket?" Aiden patted his T-shirt, where the faint contour of a leather string with an oval hanging from it showed through.

"I would fight you to the death for that *trinket,* my Taoist love."

"It has no worth to you."

"No worth? Old Phoenix hasn't told you what this is really about, then."

Aiden's chiseled face hardened as he stretched out his arms, palms soft and open. He had found his focus. I looked at the open door again. *I can't run through the catacombs alone. I can't.* I lifted my chin. *I have to.* I bolted for the door. Out of the corner of my eye, I saw Aiden spring into a twirling mass of arms and legs.

No idea where I was going, I flew down a tunnel in the pitch-black darkness. Every step I took reverberated, pounding like my frenzied heartbeat. I came to the first juncture where I had to choose from three tunnels. *Which one? Which one?* Nothing moved behind me. Why was Aiden taking so long? Surely he could kick their collective asses in a few fabulous Bagua moves.

The tattooed face of the blind albino appeared suddenly in front of me. "I told you to stay together. Now they know about you." His hands, disembodied in the dark, flailed through the air. "This tunnel. This tunnel is the one." He receded back into shadow.

Should I trust him? I didn't have time to think about it. Something deep inside me said, "He was sent to help you." I turned down the tunnel he told me to take and kept running.

Far behind me, glass shattered amidst loud thuds and crashes. Was that Aiden? I shuddered.

I halted at another juncture. Which tunnel should I take? Aiden had taught me about the three treasures, or powers. Ming Jin is obvious, An Jin is subtle and Hua Jin is almost imperceptible power. I chose Hua Jin, the third power and the third tunnel, and sped along its dark and slimy interior.

I kicked a small stone and it clattered along the floor in front of me. Maybe I could use that to help me get out of here. Feeling along the ground, I found the stone. I snatched it up, using it to scratch a mark on the wall. If I kept taking the third tunnel on the far right, that might get me out of here. But the scratch marks would tell me if I was just going around in circles. I could barely breathe, the air was so thick and torpid. My heart raced with fear and exertion. I came to another juncture; this time there were four tunnels. I swallowed back a scream of frustration. *Stay calm.* This was a good sign. I hadn't been running in circles.

I chose the fourth tunnel; the fourth treasure, Kong Jin, is empty power. The sickening stench of waste dominated the air. A rat dropped from the ceiling in front of me and I screamed, even though it scurried away from me. I followed it, thinking I had probably scared it so badly that it wanted out of the tunnel, too. Then I remembered Valerie saying that rats don't like the subway because of the vibrations. *He's going deeper underground, away from the noise.* I whirled around and ran in the opposite direction.

I came to another juncture; people leaned against the walls of each of the tunnels, some standing, some lying on wet cardboard beds. They blended into the brickwork of the tunnels, their clothes and faces caked with the same grime as the walls. Their eyes peered out at me from the blackness.

"Which way is out?" I asked. My voice cracked. Would they attack me? I pushed back my shoulders, feeling a sudden infusion of strength. I could feel which way to go even if they refused to tell me.

A little boy stepped out and pointed down a tunnel. He had something in his hand and held it out to me. I didn't want to touch him, he was so dirty, but his warm eyes held mine. "For you," he said. "So you won't be afraid anymore."

He pushed the little flashlight into my hand and pointed down the tunnel. "You turn the crank and it lights your way."

I hesitated. This little boy had nothing in the world, yet he was giving me a present.

He squeezed my fingers around it. "You're almost home," he said and he held up one finger.

AVERY

Man's enemies are not demons, but human beings like himself.

—Lao Tzu

I hung over the railing at the entrance to the subway station, fighting to catch my breath, and trying to assimilate what had happened. The city was in total blackout. I grabbed the sleeve of a woman hurrying by. "What's going on? Why is everything so dark?"

Her brows furrowed. "Where have you been? The power has been off for three days." She yanked her arm away and disappeared into the crowds thronging down the sidewalk. Sirens wailed. Someone grabbed me from behind and I jerked around, ready to claw at anyone.

Aiden held up both hands. "It's okay. It's just me."

I threw myself into his arms. "Aiden. You're safe," I breathed into his chest.

He held me close while people streamed around us like we were a rock in the middle of a flowing stream. The sliver of a waning moon peered above the tops of the skyscrapers.

Aiden pulled my hoodie around my shoulders and zipped it up. "Come on, Grasshopper, let's get you home."

"The city's been in a blackout for three days, Aiden. What's happening? How could we have been gone so long?"

"I'm so sorry. I never thought things would get this dangerous. I don't know why I didn't read the signs better. I really underestimated—"

"Who could have imagined any of this would happen?" I waved a hand through the air and looked around. Broken glass was scattered on the sidewalks outside of gaping shop windows; doors hung half-open on smashed hinges. A constant stream of fire engines and police cars whizzed by. Times Square was pitch black; no flashing lights, no moving pictures, just people wandering around with flashlights and lanterns, looking as dazed as I felt. Police officers, soldiers, and mounted officers were everywhere, dressed in full riot gear.

"I've got to get you home, Avery."

"We've been gone for three days." I shook my head, trying to clear the strange, buzzing sound that rang in my ears.

We tucked into each other and headed towards 76th street. The city looked like a bomb had exploded. I pulled closer into Aiden, fearful of what I saw: burned-out store fronts, overturned garbage bins, and bands of looters rushing through the streets with pillowcases full of merchandise. Grey ash floated through the air and several buildings glowed orange, flames leaping from broken windows. A shot echoed in the distance.

Aiden touched the arm of a fireman, standing on the sidewalk watching a building burn as he clutched a useless hose in one hand. "What's happening?"

He shook his head. "Some kind of geo-magnetic storm blew out the grid. Solar sun spots or something."

Someone rushing by stopped to add, "Yeah, we all thought it was a terrorist attack, but the cops have been telling us its sun spots. Come on! Do they really think we'll believe that?"

A lone taxi crept toward us as emergency vehicles whizzed past. Aiden jumped in front of the cab, forcing the driver to slam on the brakes. He shook a fist at us. Aiden rounded the front of the vehicle and leaned into the driver's open window. "I've got a sick girl who has to get home. Can you take us?" He pointed to me, leaning on an overturned garbage container. I must have looked as if I was about to melt down the side of it and pour onto the sidewalk.

I looked up to see the driver shake his head, then watched as Aiden pulled a wad of bills from his pocket. The driver gestured for us to get in.

Aiden waved me over, then helped me into the back seat and slid in after me. He looked down at my blood-soaked jeans. "Should we go to the hospital?"

I shook my head. "No. It will be chaos there. I just want to go home."

Aiden nodded and turned to the driver. "To the Dakota. Quickly, please."

The taxi snaked its way through the traffic.

Aiden leaned forward. "We've been away for a few days. What's going on?"

The driver glanced in the rear-view mirror. "State of emergency declared in Manhattan and most of the Eastern Seaboard. Some kind of electrical storm or something knocked out all the power. Must have messed with everyone's heads too; people have gone crazy."

Suddenly, the streetlights we drove under flickered back to life. People on the sidewalks cheered. Cars honked their horns. When we finally arrived at my apartment, Aiden handed the driver the wad of bills.

A wave of dizziness swept over me and I clutched the front of his shirt.

Aiden pulled me close. "Are you sure I shouldn't take you to the hospital?"

I looked up and met his intense gaze. "No, really. I'm fine. I just need to go in and lie down."

He stroked the side of my cheek with one finger. "I'm so sorry about all this, Avery. I never meant for you to get hurt."

"I know."

He leaned down and I closed my eyes.

Suddenly I felt him pull away. My eyes flew open.

My dad held Aiden's T-shirt in both fists. "Where have you been with my daughter? You're both filthy." Peering around Aiden, he looked at me, his scowl growing fiercer. "Is that blood?" He shook Aiden.

"Dad, he didn't have me anywhere…"

"Enough from you." Dad pushed Aiden aside. He grabbed me by the wrist and dragged me toward the entrance to the building. "Three days! I'm calling the police and having him arrested."

I pressed a hand to the wall beside the door so he had to stop. "Dad, no! Listen, this is going to sound crazy, but two Goth Girls kidnapped me, took me down into the subway tunnels and kept me hostage in a room. Aiden rescued me."

"I'm sorry, sir…I didn't—"

"Goth Girls? The subway?" Dad's face twisted. "What on earth are you talking about?"

"The girls… they…" Aiden reached my dad and grasped his elbow.

Dad shook him off. "Shut up, Aiden." He let go of my wrist. "Avery, did they say why they took you?"

"No," I said. "They just took me."

"Did they ask for money?"

I shook my head. "They didn't ask me for anything. They just tied me up and gave me some kind of drug that knocked me out. I had no idea we were gone so long."

He searched my eyes as if he was trying to decide whether or not to believe me. When he spoke, his voice was softer. "And Aiden saved you?"

"Yes. He tracked us through the tunnels."

He cleared his throat and stepped back. "Oh. I...ah, guess I owe you an apology, Aiden." He didn't look in Aiden's direction. "And a thank you. For saving my daughter and bringing her back to me safely. Ruby and I have been sick with worry. The police have been useless."

"I'm sorry, sir, I found her as soon as I could and brought her home."

My dad finally turned to face him. "What happened to these Goth Girls?"

"I left them in the underground. They'll be sore for a few days, but they'll be fine."

"Hmmm, well, we'll need a description of them for the police." Dad turned toward the entrance to the building. "And you, young lady, will not be going out until I get you a personal bodyguard." He escorted me through the door.

I craned my head to look back and mouth, "See you tomorrow."

The door locked behind us with a loud click.

AVERY

The truth is not always beautiful, or beautiful words the truth.

—Lao Tzu

I lay on my bed, my arms folded behind my head. Outside, sirens screamed and lights flashed across the ceiling, bathing the room with an eerie, strobing red. I shivered and flopped onto my side so I could reach under the mattress for the burner cell from Uncle Simon. A message waited, but I needed to talk to him. I dialed. A Spanish voice informed me that there were no international lines available, the matter-of-fact tone a stark contrast to the craziness swirling around outside my window. I pressed the button for his message.

"Avery. I'm still safe on the mountain. Big revolution might happen. Hard to contact. Don't worry. I'll be…" The line went dead. I checked the corner of the screen. The call had come in three nights ago. Were other parts of the world affected by that electrical storm or sunspots or whatever it was? I hoped he was still okay.

My thoughts raced. Who was Aiden? And who was my dad? What was really going on?

My cell phone rang and I tossed the burner cell onto my bed and reached for it.

"Are you okay?" Raven sounded panicked. "I've been worried sick, and there was no way to contact anyone. This is the first time in days that my cell has worked. Blaine came and got me, and Christian came down and joined us. We hunted for you and Aiden, but couldn't find any trace of either of you."

"Oh Raven, you wouldn't believe what happened." I sank back against the pillows, completely drained. "I feel like I fell down the rabbit hole and I'm Alice in Weird Wonderland."

Someone shuffled past my bedroom door. What was Dad doing up so late?

"Listen, Raven, I'm fine. I'll call you tomorrow and tell you everything, okay? There's something I need to do right now."

I hung up and tiptoed to the door. I eased it open and slipped through the opening. My back pressed to the wall, I crept down the hallway to the top of the stairs. Dad pulled open the front door, then quietly closed it behind him. *Where is he going at this time of night?* I gave him enough time to take the elevator down to the lobby. I jammed my feet into a pair of slip-ons, grabbed my hoodie, and went after him. I wasn't sure what I would say, or do, if he saw me, but I had to know what he was up to. I touched my neck, feeling for my pendant. Grief shot through me. Veronika still had it. I clenched my fists. I couldn't stand the thought of that evil girl wearing my mother's necklace. When the elevator opened on the main floor, I crossed quickly to the main door and outside, where I slid in behind a potted plant. One of Bowen's favorite hiding places.

Energy pulsed in the air. A Chinese man approached from the gate. The security guard ordered him to stop, and told him that he had to check in. The man gave him a brief silent look, and walked towards the inner courtyard. The guard leapt from his security box. The man turned to face him. He reached out calmly and pinched his neck. The guard crumpled to the ground. The Chinese man continued into the courtyard and stopped inches from where I was hidden.

I held my breath.

Footsteps thudded toward us. I swung my gaze toward the sidewalk to see who was coming. My dad emerged from the darkness and approached the Chinese man.

"Zheng, that was unnecessary." He jerked his head towards the downed security guard. "I said I would be here to meet you."

My breath caught. This was the Zheng everyone had been talking about?

He shrugged. "You have diary?"

"You took my daughter for three days." Dad frowned. "Three days! That was never the deal. You will leave her alone, do you understand?"

"I will take your daughter when I want," Zheng said. "And I do want your daughter. But she not ready yet."

"You will leave her out of this."

"The diary." The man held out his hand.

"You will get it when the job is done…"

Zheng lowered his arm and stepped closer. "You are playing dangerous game, Mr. Adams. You and your so-called Twelve Apostles don't know what you dealing with. You think McMurty is your friend and he will help you."

"You obviously don't know my reach, Zheng."

"On the contrary." The man's voice was cold and hard. "You don't know mine."

I didn't sleep all night. My mind raced, going over the events of the last few weeks. The rabbit hole was getting weirder and weirder. Why was my dad conducting a clandestine meeting with Zheng in the dead of night? Zheng said he wanted me. What for? And the Twelve Apostles? *What is that about?* It sounded biblical or something, which made no sense whatsoever.

I left the house just as the sun started to cast a golden glow on the eastern sides of the grey brick buildings. When I reached the park, Blaine and Aiden were huddled together under a tree. I strained to hear their hushed conversation as I approached.

"You've got to tell Avery who you are, mate. She doesn't deserve this…"

Aiden's gaze lifted over his shoulder. "Hey, Avery."

Blaine whirled around to face me, "Are you okay?" His eyes were filled with concern.

"I'm fine, just a flesh wound on my leg." I managed a weak smile. "What were you guys talking about?"

"I was just telling Blaine what happened in the tunnels. How the Goth Girls are going to be hurting for a while." Aiden didn't meet my eyes.

"You should have killed them when you had the chance." I blinked. Where had that come from? I'd never wished anyone dead before.

In the distance sirens continued to wail. The power might be back on, but clearly things were still crazy.

Blaine looked from Aiden to me, then cleared his throat. "I've gotta go meet Luc," he said. "I'll catch up with you both later."

Aiden finally looked at me. "Want to walk?"

I nodded. We made our way through the park in silence, litter scattered everywhere.

Finally I couldn't stand it anymore and I grabbed his arm to stop him. "What did Blaine think you should tell me?"

A pack of early morning joggers pushed past us on the path.

He sighed. "Let's go find somewhere quiet."

Aiden's hand sought mine, but I felt so much confusion between us, I moved away.

"What do you think happened during those three days, Aiden?" I crossed my arms over my chest. "How would a geomagnetic storm knock out all the power on the eastern seaboard? Or solar sun spots? There are so many weird things going on. That Albino guy. The Goth Girls who aren't just playing dress up. What does all of this have to do with you? With us?"

We stepped out of the park and headed toward our favorite coffee shop. Most of the shops were closed, but when we arrived, I was relieved to see that one was already open. Aiden pulled out a chair from a table on the sidewalk. "Here." He patted the back of the chair. "Sit. I'll get us something to eat and we can talk."

I sank onto the chair. I had questions I needed answers to. The problem was, I wasn't sure I wanted to hear them. I forced myself to breathe deeply, to stay centered.

Aiden came back out with two Chai teas and a cinnamon cookie for me. In spite of the angst tightening up my muscles, I had to smile. Was it possible that he really listened to me, really cared about me? Silly, really, that a cinnamon cookie would mean that much. But it wasn't the cookie, it was that he remembered.

Aiden set the teas down on the table and settled onto the chair across from me. He didn't speak for a moment, then he leaned forward and clasped his hands on the table. "Avery, I don't know yet what's going on. But since I arrived here, and met you, everything has turned upside down." He unclasped his hands and wrapped his fingers around his cup, as though he needed the warmth. "The barista said that banks might not even be open for another week or so."

I could care less about the banks. I needed to know about us. I leaned back in my seat. "What are you trying to say?"

He lifted his cup and took a sip, then set it down again. "There's something I have to tell you," he said. "Something you should know about me."

His sudden seriousness deepened my apprehension. *I don't want to know.* I wanted to keep him some mystery man, some arcane martial artist who glided into my life and awakened things in me I didn't even know had been there.

I swallowed. "I know all I need to know about you. I know you are kind, and thoughtful, and decent, and protective, and smart, and funny, and..."

"Avery, stop." He lifted a hand as sadness flooded his face. "You're so beautiful, but..."

"But what?"

"There is a reason I don't kiss you, even though I know you want me to."

I shifted in my seat. "Don't do this, Aiden."

"I have to. I have to tell you why I can't kiss you ever again. I—"

I shoved back my chair and stood up.

"Avery. Please. Don't go." Aiden stood up too.

"I know something horrible is about to come," I whispered.

"Please sit down. This is what Blaine told me I should tell you, and he's right. I should have told you a long time ago, in fact."

When I didn't move, he sat back down on his chair and held a hand out toward mine. "Please."

I studied him for a moment, then drew in a deep breath. I really did need to know. I sat back down. "What is it? What could possibly keep you from—" My head shot up. "Oh my God. You're gay. That's what you're trying to tell me. I totally didn't read that one; you and Blaine..."

His eyes widened. "No! Blaine and I are best friends, as close as brothers, but that's it. If you only knew how much I want you..." His eyes probed mine. "But there is something you need to know about me. I—"

I leaned across the table and pressed my mouth to his. I could feel in his lips, in the trembling hands that framed my face, how much he wanted me.

He pulled back. "You are the most beautiful girl I have ever..." He closed his eyes.

I stared at him, a dawning understanding flashing through my mind. "No way," I said. "It can't be. It can't be." I searched his eyes. "I know what you are."

"You know?"

"Of course I know. The lightning speed, the superhuman strength, your impossibly good looks. Real people don't look that good. I've seen all the movies, read all the books..." I could barely catch my breath. I stood up and paced back and forth beside the table. It was an insane theory, but as crazy as everything had been, this made a weird kind of sense. Or did it? My forehead wrinkled. "No, wait. I've seen you eat pizza. And you go out in the sunlight. There is *no way* this could be real. No way."

Aiden tilted his head and stared at me as if I had lost my mind.

Maybe I have.

"What does pizza have to do with anything?"

"You're a ... a ... vampire."

He let out a shocked laugh. "A vampire? What the hell are you talking about?" Aiden stood up and grasped both my shoulders. All traces of amusement were gone from his face. "I'm not a vampire. I'm a celibate monk. I made a solemn promise to fulfill my destiny. I took a vow."

"A celibate monk?" Relief poured through me, He wasn't, in fact, a member of the undead. "This is great news, this is fine ..." The words registered in my overworked brain. "Wait, celibate means no sex, right?" I staggered back to my chair and dropped onto it. "Celibate. No. No, this isn't great news."

"You see why I had to tell you. I didn't want to mislead you."

"Too late for that." I propped my elbows on the table and dropped my face into my hands.

Aiden sat back down. "I made a promise. To Old Phoenix. To our entire order of monks. One that I cannot break."

"That you would stay celibate."

"That I would remain pure, yes."

I lifted my head. "Pure?"

"Yes. That I would not be with a woman. When you take the direct transmissions from Old Phoenix, you have to be pure to receive the Bagua energy."

"Okay, but once that happens you don't have to be pure anymore. Right?"

He drew in a long breath. "I have dedicated my life to fulfilling my destiny. I chose to take that vow because Bagua expresses all of who I am. I have committed myself to a life of spiritual practice, free of possessions and desires." He took my hand in his. "We can still be friends."

I yanked back my hand. "My *friend*," I said. "You are hardly free of desire. You cannot just friend-zone me. I know you feel the tension between us. You've seen the electricity when we touch. It's special. The connection we have – some people never get to experience that and you're throwing it away. It's not natural. You can't spend your life never having sex, not having a relationship with someone you love. It's such a waste. No one as cool as you is celibate in this day and age."

"Being a monk won't stop me from being in your life. It just stops me from creating a whole life with you. Can't you understand...?"

"Understand?" I wrapped my hands around my cup, barely resisting the urge to chuck the contents of it across the table at him. "No, Aiden. I can't. I don't understand it at all. How can you even consider a life without love, without a family – a life without me? I know you, maybe better than you know yourself. We are meant to be together. And you are throwing it away for some crazy ideal. I know your spirituality is important to you, but you can't do this."

He shook his head. "I'm sorry. I made a promise long before I met you. We can still hang out, still practice together. We just can't...can't..."

"Oh, just say it, Aiden! We can't have sex. We can't kiss. We can't ever get close. That's what you're trying to say."

"Avery."

I clenched my fists. "I love you. With all of my heart. This is about more than just sexual attraction. I've never been so certain of anything or anyone in my entire life." My eyes met his. Something passed between us, so strong I could almost reach out and touch it. This was just so wrong. "I know you love me too. I know what you feel inside."

I reached over and pressed my hand against his chest. His heart pounded beneath my fingers. "Have you ever felt this with anyone else? We have filaments that connect us. I saw them in the Sweatlodge."

He didn't speak. I could see him, feel him, but he was already gone. "It's not supposed to be this way." I pulled my hand away. "Tell me that you don't feel what I feel. If you can look me in the eyes and say those words, I'll walk right out of your life without turning back. My heart will break into a million pieces, but I won't turn back. Tell me, Aiden. Tell me you don't feel what I feel."

He looked away.

"Coward." I stood up and shoved the chair back under the table. "You owed me that much."

Still not looking at me, Aiden pulled my necklace out of his pocket and held it out.

I snatched it from his grasp, then turned and walked away.

AVERY

Watch your thoughts; they become words. Watch your words;
they become actions. Watch your actions; they become habit.
Watch your habits; they become character. Watch your
character; it becomes your destiny.

—Lao Tzu

I snuck back home before Dad noticed I had left. He spent the day in his office, periodically coming to check up on me in my room. Aiden's words consumed my thoughts. When night time finally came, I hoped I could sleep.

But in the quiet and shadows of my room, my thoughts haunted me. Why had I called Aiden a coward? I knew it would hurt him. I had wanted him to hurt in that moment, but not anymore. *I know we belong together. How can he not know it?*

I hated him. I loved him. I hated that I believed, deep inside, that we would always be together. How stupid was that? He'd made himself clear. He preferred to be a monk than be with me. How did someone make a choice like that?

I flopped onto my side and held my pillow over my head. After a couple of minutes, I flipped onto my back and put my hands over my eyes. I glanced at the clock on the table beside the bed. Two am. Ten minutes past the last time I had looked, and twenty minutes past the time before that. I rolled onto my stomach, then back to my side. I curled up into a little ball and felt sobs in the pit of my stomach. I tried to hold them back, but I couldn't for long; slowly they found their way up and I wept in huge gasps of desperate longing. How could he do this to us ... to me? How could he? He made a promise to a bunch of ancient Chinese guys and I'm supposed to still be his *friend?* My mind spun. One minute I was furious with Aiden, the next sad, the next humiliated. I decided I never wanted to see him again, and then I was positive I would die if I didn't.

When the alarm rang for Bagua, I was surprised that I had fallen asleep. I considered missing practice, but I would show Aiden what I was made of. Something had happened to me in those tunnels. As I made my way out, I had found an inner spark of certainty. A confidence that I could deal with anything. I had faced real evil and lived through it, even though I was terrified. I had hit the wall, and instead of just seeing the wall, I saw beyond it, moved beyond it, and now lived beyond it. I stroked my leg where Veronika had sliced me, the thin red scar a grim reminder of what she was capable of, and what she had promised to do to me. That experience had made me stronger.

I stretched, then got up and took extra care in getting ready, still mulling how I would get through this. I wondered about the conversation Aiden and I had in the woods in the Ramapos about destiny. *Do we have control of our choices, or do our choices control us?* Since the morning Rasta led me to Aiden and I finally followed, Rasta had returned to his usual behavior of sleeping in. I left him comfortably curled up on my bed; it would be easier for me to sneak out and get back in without my dad knowing if he wasn't with me. Dad had told me he'd hired a bodyguard who would shadow me wherever I went, starting today, and I didn't want anyone following me where I was going. I grabbed a sweater on my way out to keep the early morning chill at bay and closed the front door quietly behind me.

"Avery!" Aiden stepped out from the darkness behind a tree. "I'm so glad you decided to come to practice. You...you look beautiful."

"Don't mess with me, Aiden. I don't deserve that. Of course I'm coming to practice...why wouldn't I?" I twirled away and stalked down the sidewalk. I had no intention of falling down and weeping a million tears for a life that wouldn't be. "Which park is it today?" I asked, without looking back.

"Ah … um … Battery Park, I think. We better catch the subway, and stay super-aware. We can't get caught off guard like we did the last time. "

"You don't sound sure about the park. Is something the matter?" I was baiting him, but I couldn't help myself. My chest burned with anger, giving me the strength to speak up.

Aiden fell into step beside me. "Avery, are you okay? You're acting... different."

I rolled my eyes. "What kind of stupid question is that?" I quickened my pace and disappeared down the steep stairwell to the subway, with Aiden a step behind me. He wasn't supposed to ask me if I was okay. Of course I wasn't okay, but I couldn't allow him to know that. "I'm fine. Why wouldn't I be? We're *friends*." I fought to keep the bitterness out of my tone. "Can't have too many *friends*.

"Avery, please try to understand."

I stopped and turned so abruptly he almost banged into me. "It is what it is, Aiden. We just have to live with it."

Aiden exhaled; his whole being appeared to be collapsing under the weight of his own decision.

Good. I spun around and strode toward the train. How could he not see how wrong this was for him, for me, for both of us?

We arrived at Battery Park. Raven and Christian had arranged to teach us archery in exchange for learning Bagua.

"Raven, Christian, so glad to see you!" My smile felt brittle. Raven's eyes narrowed, but Christian swept me into one of his bear-hug, twirling embraces.

When he set me down, my eyes met Raven's dark ones. *Don't ask me if I'm okay.*

She nodded slightly. We were really beginning to link.

"Hi, Blaine." I stepped over to him and gave him a big hug and a kiss on the cheek. Surprise flashed across his face before he pulled me tighter. When he released me, he lifted his gaze over my shoulder and I knew he was sending a questioning look at Aiden, trying to figure out what was going on.

I pushed back my shoulders. "Blaine, could you show me that palm strike stuff we did yesterday?"

"I could show you, Avery." Aiden raised his hand to begin the sequence.

"No, it's okay." I turned back to Blaine, who went through the short series of movements.

"Thanks." I acted out the three strikes. "I think I've got it now."

"How are you, Avery?" Christian touched my arm.

Why was everyone suddenly so concerned about me? Had Aiden told them he had brushed me off?

"I'm great." No one looked convinced. I gritted my teeth, hearing the false brightness in my voice. I wouldn't believe me either.

"I mean since the three days you spent underground. It was scary enough up here with no electricity and the city going berserk; I can't imagine what you guys went through."

"Oh … that. Yes, I'm totally fine." Surprisingly, I realized I was telling the truth about that. "It was pretty terrifying, but the funny thing is, I've had this claustrophobia since my mom died. I avoided the subway because of it. But being forced to face my fear, and being able to, may have cured me of my panic attacks."

Blaine frowned. "I didn't know you had panic attacks."

"I didn't exactly advertise it, since I've always been ashamed of having them, but now that I feel different, I'm okay talking about it."

"Christian brought the bows and arrows and we already set up the target." Raven pointed toward a large, open area. "Let's get started."

Christian opened the trunk of his car and carried out a selection of weapons for us to choose from. "I have a few bows here. Spend some time with each of them, and then pick the one that speaks to you."

We touched each one, felt the give in the string, ran our hands down the smooth wooden surface.

"I'll take this one." Blaine gripped one of the bows and held it up.

"Ah. She's a lively one," Christian noted. "Made from Osage Orange."

I paused at one I had been drawn back to several times. "I like this one."

"She's the still one. Taken from where the heartwood and the outer layers meet," Christian said. "You will do well with her, Avery. Aiden, have you chosen yet?"

"He's chosen all right." I studied my bow, refusing to meet anyone's eyes.

Christian tilted his head.

"I'll take this one." Aiden ran his fingers along the curve of the bow.

"Ironwood. Tough as nails she is." Raven nodded solemnly. "You'll need to be careful with her."

"I'm getting that sense." Aiden's voice was low, and quiet, as though the words were for me alone.

The air felt too thick to breathe.

"Take your bows, and place an arrow there." Christian touched the spot on his own string. "That's right. Now, one person at a time, focus in on the target, and in one sweeping motion, pull the bow, take aim, pull and release."

My fingers felt like thumbs. The arrow fell off before I even lifted my bow up to take aim. Aiden's arrow fell off too. Blaine managed to launch one wobbly arrow, but it landed in the ground in front of and to the left of the target. Thankfully, Christian had brought a pile of arrows in a round case for us to practice with.

"Here." Aiden held an arrow out to me at the same time Blaine did.

"Thanks, Blaine." I grabbed the one he offered.

Raven came up behind me. "It's natural," she whispered in my ear, "like a breath. Lean the arrow into the bow as you sweep up in a single motion and let it go. Keep all of your intention on the target. You use intention by committing all of your mental state to achieve the purpose you imagine. Get it? Like your Bagua practice."

I breathed deep as I swept my bow and arrow up in a graceful arch, pulling the arrow back at the same time. I kept my intention on the target and let the arrow go. It soared through the air on a straight trajectory and the arrow stuck into the target, just off the outside circle.

"OMG." I jumped up and down, clutching my bow. "I did it!"

"Some people have the instinct." Christian smiled. "Some have to practice to get it."

I made several more shots, improving each time. Aiden and Blaine both improved rapidly.

"Your intention is strong," Raven said. "All of you."

Christian nodded. "That makes a huge difference."

"Aiden. Aiden!"

Raven looked over my shoulder.

We all turned to see Luc running across the field, waving a hand. He was panting by the time he reached us, and rested his hands on his knees for a moment before straightening up. "Aiden, Old Phoenix is calling you back. You have to get ready. There's a flight leaving just after midnight tonight, I have your ticket for you. You have to come back with me now. Old Phoenix outlined the preparations he'd like you to make before you leave."

"We have to go right now?"

Luc's forehead wrinkled. "You know how this works. It's always sudden."

Aiden took a deep breath. "Avery." He dropped his bow and grasped both my arms. "Will you come with me to the airport?"

I shrugged him off. "No. You have to do this on your own." I stepped back, out of reach. "Besides, I'm in lockdown. It's a miracle I got here without my dad noticing. He would never let me go to the airport after what just happened."

"But…" he ran a hand over his close-cropped head. "I don't know…"

"You do know. You knew yesterday, and you know today. I'll see ya when the monks let you out for a vacation, or whatever monks do. I have to get home before my dad discovers I'm gone. Bye, everyone."

I walked across the field and broke into a run before anyone could try to stop me. Heat roared through me. Go to the airport with him? I didn't even know where he was going. I clenched my fists as I slowed to a jog. *Well, he can go to hell, for all I care.*

He'd made his choice, and he would have to live with it.

Apparently I had escaped the building just minutes before the arrival of my twenty-four-hour-a-day, burly body guard. I spent the day in my room, avoiding Rambo and researching my great-great-grandfather on the internet. Soon it would be time for Aiden to leave for the airport. Not that I cared.

My cell phone rang. Blaine. I snatched it up.

"Really, Blaine? Did he ask you to convince me to come to the airport?"

"No, Avery. *I* want you to come to the airport. We're taking him soon and could swing around and pick you up. I don't know when either of us will see him again. But no matter what has happened, we are linked through Bagua now. All three of us. Please come. It's important. To Aiden. To me."

"Sorry, Blaine. I can't. But I will be at practice tomorrow morning."

I hung up and went back to my research. Most of the books that A.P. Sinnett, my great great grandfather, had written were still in print and I ordered ten of them. I found a couple of original editions on rare book sites, dating back to the eighteen-seventies. One was a collection of hand-written correspondences between Sinnett and his mystical masters, a collection now housed in the British Library's "Rare Manuscripts Room."

I had read an article that mentioned a carnelian stone that Madame Blavatsky had given him so he could gain access to the Ascended Masters in the Himalayas. As compelling as these discoveries were, Blaine's request kept surfacing. I closed my eyes and tried to meditate. It wasn't long before my thoughts paraded before me, and it became crystal clear what I had to do.

I left my room, the bodyguard a step behind me, and found Dad in his library, drinking whisky.

I rapped on the half-open door. "Are you busy?" I jerked my head behind me. "And is this guy really necessary?"

He looked up. "You are not going out unprotected until I know for sure that you are safe."

"Aiden is leaving for China tonight. Can I go to the airport to see him off? I promise I'll let Rambo watch over me."

"His name is Jared, not Rambo. And I'm glad to hear Aiden will be gone. He was taking up entirely too much of your time." Dad waved a hand toward the door. "Go on, but Jared won't let you out of his sight. Take the limo."

"Thanks. We won't be too long."

Rambo and I went out to the limo. He held the door open and I jumped in. He gazed around before getting in as if doing due diligence.

Although I'd convinced myself I didn't want to see Aiden, my heart pounded now at the thought I might be too late. The traffic was awful and it took eons to get to JFK. As we drove up, Luc and Blaine were pulling away in a taxi. They didn't see me in spite of my insane antics, yelling and waving at them. I ran through the front doors, searching wildly for the line-up for checked bags and boarding passes. Rambo shadowed my every step. I stopped and turned a slow circle, but couldn't see Aiden anywhere.

I clenched my fists in frustration. I had to find him. I was angry, but this was no way to let someone I loved, that I genuinely cared about, go on to fulfill their destiny. Blaine was right. We were all linked, and I didn't want him to leave like this, under a cloud of my anger. That wasn't who I wanted to be, or who I was. I wanted to send him away with my blessing. If I could do that, I would not only free him, I would free myself too.

I ran to security, trying to get to the gates, but they wouldn't let me through. Then I saw him, waiting to pick up his backpack from the x-ray belt. He gathered up his gear and left the area; only his shimmering imprint on the air remained.

I pleaded with the guards, but they wouldn't relent. I was too late. I had missed my chance because it had taken me so long to let go of my stupid pride. I trudged back to the cab with Rambo, and huddled against the back of the seat, staring out the window as a China Air jumbo jet took to the skies. Choking back sobs, I reached for the Carnelian-stone necklace at my throat.

It had gone ice-cold.

Chapter 23

AIDEN

A journey of a thousand miles begins with a single step.

—Lao Tzu

The plane lifted from the runway, a languorous climb toward cruising altitude. The air inside the cabin was thin and hot. I was returning to fulfill my destiny, but all I could think about was leaving Avery. Old Phoenix had laid out his yarrow stalks of divination for me the last time I was there. He said my life had been predetermined, from the very moment I was born, under the sign of Scorpio, in the year of the Dragon. Could a person's destiny possibly change?

The man seated next to me tapped the arm rest. "Afraid of flying?"

I nodded, but flying wasn't the problem. Everything in the past few days had happened so quickly. Being close to Avery was obviously torturing her. I didn't want to cause her one more moment of misery. I touched a knuckle to my lips. I had kissed Avery. I shouldn't have, but I couldn't bring myself to regret it. The memory would remain with me forever. Her glorious soft lips pressed to mine. Was Blaine right when he said that she was young and would quickly mend her heart and move on? My stomach twisted at the thought. *I'm glad he'll be staying in New York and watching out for her.* The dark agents of Master Zheng were amassing, and she appeared to be in their sights. I hoped my leaving would draw some attention away from her.

I undid my seat belt when we hit cruising altitude. The jabbing sensation in my gut intensified. I put my palms over my stomach and sent healing energy into the pain. Images of a black viscous substance oozing through my body came into my mind.

I retraced my steps. When I left the security gate, after I picked up my rucksack, I felt distracted, as if Avery's energy was close by. I turned to see if she were there, and a man wearing dark glasses and a wide-brimmed hat jammed into me. I had felt the quick jab in my gut, but I was concentrating on trying to see if Avery had come. One more time.

Had I been intentionally hit with the death palm strike?

My insides felt inflamed. I lifted my T-shirt. A swollen red patch, about the size of a man's hand, had risen on my skin. I knew about the open palm strike, the move that made the internal martial arts so powerful. *But surely the strike is made only in combat.* I knew of rumors that the strike could be delivered in such a way that the victim is barely aware of it until later, when the damage disrupts the internal organs, and by then it's often too late. The hit I took was masterful. Fear gripped me. Why would someone want to injure me in such a slow and deadly way? I poured every ounce of my energy into my body, trying to counter the potentially deadly disruption. The intense pain was subsiding, and the red palm ring on my stomach no longer looked so angry; only a light pink shadow remained.

In spite of the uncomfortable airplane seat, a heavy sleep overcame me. I woke up to the nauseating smell of airline sausages, shocked to discover I had slept almost the entire flight. The flight attendant came by to say we would be landing in two hours. My seat-mate snored on.

I went to the loo, flipped the slide bar, and the lights came up in the tiny cubicle. Pain shot through my entire body and I closed the door behind me quickly. I doubled over and almost collapsed from the sheer intensity of it. I took a deep breath and pulled my T-shirt up to inspect my stomach. The angry red patch in the clear shape of a palm had flared up again. I splashed cold water on my face as heat roared through me. I staggered back to my seat to meditate on healing. My hands hovered over my abdomen as I visualized breaking down the thick black goo I imagined clogging up my system. When I opened my eyes, the fever had abated. Even so, my stomach roiled at the smell of the rubbery omelet that had appeared on my tray table. I pushed it away and closed my eyes. The plane dropped in altitude. We would be landing soon. How would I get to the caves where the seven monks lived? And how will I live the rest of my life without Avery?

The thought brought a fresh wave of nausea, and I rested my head against the back of the seat. I woke when the plane bumped onto the landing strip and the engines roared into reverse to slow it down.

"We've landed safely. You can stop worrying." The man beside me patted my arm and smiled at me.

I could barely nod my head. Beads of perspiration broke out on my forehead and rings of sweat circled my underarms. I stood up but, overcome with dizziness, I fell back into my seat.

The man beside me looked alarmed. "I'll get the flight attendant. You don't look well." The rest of the passengers filed out of the plane.

I closed my eyes.

"Sir? Are you all right?" I looked up. A flight attendant, blue eyes filled with concern, rested on the arm of the seat vacated by the woman across the aisle from me. She held a cold compress to my forehead and told me she would get a wheelchair for me.

I pushed the compress away from my head. "I'm fine." Grasping the back of the seat in front of me, I pulled myself up. My entire body shook, but I managed to grab my rucksack and stumble down the aisle and off the plane. Inside the terminal, I sank onto the first seat I came to.

The same flight attendant came up to me and handed me some water. "Is someone meeting you here?"

"No," I managed to whisper.

"Where are you going?"

"I don't know."

"Let me help you."

"No...no...I'll be fine," I said. "The sick feeling is going away now." Trying to convince her, I stood up to carry on to Customs, refusing to allow the slicing pain in my gut to stop me.

The attendant didn't look convinced. "Here, take my card. I'm in Beijing for two more days if you need me." She slipped a white card in the pocket of my rucksack.

I turned and walked away, feeling her eyes on me as I went. Was she on their side? I couldn't trust anyone. I made my way slowly to customs, pushing doubt from my mind, but anxious thoughts kept intruding. Why was I here? Why wasn't I home with Avery? I blinked. *Home.* A funny word for me. I had always considered the Wudang home. Never England. Never anywhere else, just the Wudang. But now the word 'home' was inextricably entwined with my image of Avery. I automatically handed over my passport to the customs agent and said the customary, "NiHao."

He eyed me, then asked, "Where's visa?"

"My visa is there." I answered in Mandarin before it registered in my muddled brain that he had spoken in English. "I have a three-time visa and I've been here twice. I have one visit left."

"Looks like three times." He held my passport and pointed to a mark that made it appear I had been there a third time already. The man turned his back to me and slipped through a door, its window blackened, behind him. *What's wrong? Could he be one of Zheng's men? There is no escape if he is.* My body felt like it was on fire, but I had to fight the encroaching fever. If the agent noticed anything wrong, I wouldn't be let into the country. Finally the door opened and the customs agent returned to the desk. "Is okay. You only been here twice on this visa. It just looked like three. I had to check."

Relief flooded through me. I wouldn't have survived the flight back if they had forced me to leave. My legs shook. I took the passport he held out to me and shoved it into my pack. The customs agent gave me another look-over. I forced a smile, willing myself to appear strong and healthy. He offered a brief half-smile and waved a hand through the air to dismiss me.

I walked through customs, bypassed the baggage claim since all I had was my rucksack, and exited the area. Hard plastic seats lined the window. I staggered over to them and sat down next to a man whose face and body were obscured by an open newspaper. I leaned forward, the sharp pain in my stomach stealing away my breath.

"Hey, Aiden. What you doing?" a familiar voice sang to me.

I straightened. "No Trace? What are you doing here?" My old friend's name, whose Chinese name denoted special talents, translated to "No Trace" in English. It fit. He was silently ubiquitous, moved without a sound, and appeared in the most unlikely places, always leaving without a trace.

"I came to meet you."

"But I didn't tell you I was coming."

"You know me better. I always know." The monk giggled, shook his closely-shaven head, and folded his newspaper. Both arms rested inside the large openings of his cloak. "You look bad, Aiden."

"Thanks." I showed him the red handprint on my stomach.

147

No Trace commandeered a motorcab, propping me up in the back seat. We raced through Beijing. The cab made a steep bank around a corner. I held my stomach and looked up at a giant portrait of Chairman Mao; he seemed to look straight into my eyes as we crossed Tiananmen Square.

"Someone follow you," No Trace yelled. "Not anymore!"

He pushed the motorcab to its limit, and soon we arrived at the train station.

Once on the train, I tried to stay awake, but the regular rhythm overcame me. Through the misty fog in my mind, I had a vague awareness of No Trace draping a blanket over me. Occasionally I heard the scream of an oncoming train rushing past, or a steward checking tickets, but it all seemed very far away.

I lay on a wooden bench in front of a hand-built cabin. The acrid scent of a wood fire burning inside hung in the air. The air was so bitter cold it burned my lungs, and I ached to go in and warm myself at the flames. Several layers of blankets were wrapped around me. My lips felt dry and chapped. I blinked, trying to clear my vision. A ring of mountains circled us. The Wudang? *Where is No Trace?* I grasped the back of the bench and attempted to haul myself upright, then gasped in pain and slumped back down. A chicken clucked. A dog barked in the distance. The wind whistled through the tops of the trees, and a loose window shutter clapped.

My eyes narrowed. A straw hat bobbed in the distance, then a man's head, his shoulders, and finally the horse he was riding. The pair rose up from behind the ridge and headed towards me. In relief, my eyes fluttered shut and once again I fell into a fitful, disturbed sleep.

When I woke again, I was sprawled on a low bed in the main room of the house. Every wall was lined with shelves holding thousands of colorful glass and ceramic jars, all jammed together. The light from the tiny windows glinted off the glass. The man who had been riding the horse grunted at me, gesturing for me to roll onto my side. I complied with a groan. He ran his palms over my body. His hands barely touched my skin, but I felt a burning sensation as they passed over me. He grunted again and I dropped back onto the mattress. He pulled the blanket back over me and moved to the other side of the room where he lit a Bunsen burner. I watched as he measured powders, ground leaves, and tossed everything into a beaker that belched puffs of smoke.

No Trace burst through the front door. "Aiden, you are awake?" Without waiting for a response, he turned to address the medicine man. "Sheng Li, I found the herb you wanted way over on the far hill." No Trace held out a handful of slim branches with leaves and little red buds. "Is this the right one?"

The man nodded and took the branches from him, carefully breaking off the red buds and adding them to the concoction.

No Trace came over to me and held his hand on my forehead. "Aiden, my friend, hang in there," he said. "Sheng Li tells me you have the rigors. It is a fever that first goes up, then comes crashing down. Your body is trying to fight an internal poison. Someone gave you the 'death hand.' Sheng Li says he is surprised you lived through the flight. The poison is beyond his knowledge. You need the Rinpoche." No Trace took my hand. "You must tell me. What have you gotten involved in?"

I thought of the Goth Girls, Veronika and Valerie, and how they said they were after my amulet, claiming it belonged to their clan. The dark man at the boarding gate must be one of them. How could they possibly have known I would be at the airport? It was a mystery, just like No Trace's uncanny ability to always be there whenever I arrived in China.

"I don't know, exactly," I whispered through chattering teeth. "I really don't know."

No Trace stayed by my side. Hours melted into days. I lost track of how long I had lain there on Sheng Li's narrow daybed. I slept. I ached. I burned with fever. I froze with rigors. I was forced to drink Sheng Li's foul-smelling medicine.

"Too much Yin, must get Yang," Sheng Li said. "Yesterday, too much yang. Difficult balance. Difficult..."

Each day I got a bit stronger. One day I asked, "How long have we been here?"

"Very long time, Aiden." He smiled. "Six weeks ago we arrive. We think you going to die."

"Six weeks." I groaned. Was Avery okay? Sheng Li handed me my medicine. I took the cup in my hand and held my breath as I sipped. "Hey, Sheng Li, it tastes good today!"

"Now you little better. Now you balanced," Sheng Li announced with pride. "Maybe you live now. You need Rinpoche to get cure. You must go see Rinpoche."

After a few days of eating Sheng Li's wonderful food, some of my strength returned. No Trace helped me chop enough wood to last Sheng Li a year. I barely made it for dinner that night, the exertion taking its toll. Sheng Li insisted that I didn't have to do anything to repay him, but I tended his garden, No Trace beside me all the while, making certain I didn't collapse. When we had the root vegetables prepared for Sheng Li for the winter, I felt stronger.

"Aiden, you want come market with me?" Sheng Li asked.

I answered him in Mandarin, attempting to mimic his dialect.

He shook his head. "I want speak English."

We went to the barn and bridled up a tall, grey, dappled stallion. Sheng Li didn't use a saddle. A brand new BMW convertible was parked outside the barn.

"Why don't we take the car?"

"Car is gift from my granddaughter. She is surgeon at Shanghai hospital. She calls it Beemer. I call my horse Wushu. He knows way to market. Beemer doesn't."

"Oh." I nodded, and took up my position beside the stallion.

"No, you been sick. You ride." Sheng Li held the horse for me to mount.

I took the reins and stood back. "No Sheng Li. You ride. I feel better and need to walk."

Sheng Li lifted himself onto the stallion's bare back and swayed easily atop Wushu as we set out to the market.

"How far away is it?" I asked, after an hour of walking.

"Soon. Only one more hours."

I groaned and Sheng Li reined in Wushu and dismounted. He handed me the reins. "You ride now. I walk rest of way." I tried to refuse Sheng Li, but he insisted and so I rode for the next hour.

"Wushu been with me since his birth. I forget how old he is. I forget how old I am. When I get drunk he always get me home."

Outside the village, Sheng Li tethered the grey horse to an old hitching post and we walked into the crowded market place with stalls set up on either side of the narrow road. Sheng Li, one of the gentlest beings I had ever met, suddenly turned into a crowd warrior, all elbows, hands and knees to get to the front of the line. It was every man and woman for himself in this crowd. The young ladies of the surrounding villages traded their vegetables for knock-off Prada purses, Manolo Blahnik shoes, and Armani jeans. The scene felt so anachronistic, I chuckled to myself. For the first time since I left New York, I felt human again. Images of Avery saturated my senses. I could smell her delicious scent, hear her voice, and feel her lips touching mine. My chest ached with her absence.

I sensed the young man before he moved straight toward me. I braced myself, knowing my body couldn't take another bout of internal poisoning, and that I wasn't strong enough to fight him off.

"For you…" He pressed a scroll into my hand and moved on in one fluid movement.

When I shoved it into my jeans pocket, I noticed how loose they were.

"One more stop, Aiden, then we go home. There, there it is." Sheng Li steered me towards an odd-looking stall. Live insects crawled inside jars; containers of coarse and fine powders of varying colors, and tins filled with pastes and salves were displayed on the table. "This Aiden," Sheng Li said to his friend, "he need help."

His friend, who had been studying me from behind the stall, came around to stand in front of me. His hands moved in small circles about two feet away from my body. He stopped and closed his eyes for several seconds before looking at me again. "Sheng Li," he said in Chinese. "This man was poisoned with a rare Tibetan herb. Very hard to come by. Was he in Tibet in past months?"

"No." Sheng Li shook his head emphatically. "He hasn't been to Tibet."

"He need antidote. He need Rinpoche. I am unable to treat." The man shuffled back to his stall.

"Please, you give him something," Sheng Li said.

My brow furrowed. "Where is the Rinpoche?"

"Don't know where Rinpoche is? Maybe he dead. He flee Tibet. No one see him since," the man answered. He contemplated me for another moment, his lips pursed, then he nodded. "Okay. Okay. Sheng Li, I give your friend something that might work to keep him alive a little longer. He been poisoned with very rare herb. Very bad magic."

The man reached over and snatched an empty jar from a shelf at the back of the stall. He rummaged around behind the counter, looking inside various containers. "Here, I have some." He took a fine, iridescent powder from one jar and apportioned some into another. "No charge to you, Sheng Li. No charge to undo bad powder."

"Thank you, my friend, but he wasn't poisoned with an herb. He had death hand strike." Sheng Li held up his palm in front of my abdomen.

"No. Not death hand. He been poisoned with rare Tibetan herb. Very bad magic. This will help until he get to Rinpoche." He pushed the jar into Sheng Li's hand.

Sheng Li nodded as he took the jar and dropped it in the pocket of his cloak. We walked back to where we had left Wushu. "You ride home," Sheng Li insisted. "You not look good again."

I glanced down. My hands and arms had gone ash-grey. We arrived at the hitching post to find Sheng Li's horse gone.

"Wushu, my best horse." Sheng Li clasped both hands to his head. "What is going on here? Aiden? Tell me. What you involved in? Please, tell me."

I held out my hands, palms up. I had no answers for him. Not yet. "Sheng Li, I'm so sorry about your horse."

"What did man in marketplace give you? I know he give you something. What going on?"

I took it out and unrolled the paper. Chinese characters, unintelligible to me, danced along the fine paper.

Sheng Li took it from me. "It say, 'Be very careful, my martial arts son. Master Zheng wants to possess two things very precious to you. Listen and you will hear, follow and you will lead. The balance of the entire universe is at risk.'" Sheng Li continued to study the scroll. He let go with one hand and pointed a finger at a small mark. "There, in bottom corner, is traditional symbol for 10,000; it also mean scorpion. See it look like mother scorpion with 10,000 babies she carry on back after born."

I studied the scroll, more confused now than I had been before. "Who would have sent this to me?"

"I don't know," Sheng Li answered. "But I know of Zheng. He is very powerful. I don't like it."

He handed the scroll back to me and I rolled it up and stuck it back in my pocket. With a heavy sigh, Sheng Li turned and started for home. I trudged along behind him. The sun was warm on my face, and some of the chill gripping me eased.

Sheng Li patted my back. "You can only will yourself to be strong for so long, Aiden. If you have death palm strike, you still need time heal, and if you have rare Tibetan poison, you need antidote. Let us hope your will can get us home for dinner first."

We arrived, exhausted, just after nightfall. No Trace had a campfire burning. He looked relieved when we limped up to the cabin.

"Wushu stolen," Sheng Li said. "My friend think Aiden poisoned by rare Tibetan herb. Got temporary antidote. Need Rinpoche to know for sure, but we don't know where he is." He pulled the jar of medicine from his pocket and handed it to me.

Too exhausted and in pain to worry about measuring it out, I lifted it to my lips and tipped my head back to allow a little of the powder to fall into my mouth.

No Trace whirled toward me. "No!"

Startled, I yanked back the jar, almost dropping it. I slammed the lid back on and tightened it. "What's wrong?"

He shook his head. "We don't know if that medicine good for you."

Warmth seeped into my body. "I feel better already," I said. "I'm just going to lie down here by the fire."

I pulled the rough wool blanket around me, and immediately began to drift off. Avery's hand slid into mine. The camp fire reflected in her eyes. Was she here or was I there? I kissed her, and the fire in my belly became an intense desire to be with her. Ten thousand stars twinkled in the night sky above us.

Avery whispered in my ear, "I love you Aiden."

I held her face in my hands, aching for more of her.

"I have to go now." She pulled away from me and sprang up onto the grey dappled back of Wushu."

"No!" I cried, but she curled her fingers into his mane and they flew into the dark night.

I slept on, dreaming she had returned. Her breath was warm on my lips and it woke me. I opened my eyes to Wushu breathing in my face.

I struggled to sit up, caught in that halfway place between dreams and wakefulness. I wiped the horse's saliva from my face with the back of my hand.

"Look," Sheng Li said. "He got away and found his way back. Beemer wouldn't know how."

No Trace flashed me a wry smile and raised his eyebrows. "Pleasant dreams?"

Warmth flooded my cheeks. He had no idea.

Chapter 24

AVERY

Rhythm and harmony find their way into the inward places of the soul.

—Plato

"Let's go to a movie, Avs," Blaine said. "Come on, it'll be great. We'll see if Raven wants to come, or Whitney and Katie. My favorite's playing in Chinatown – Donnie Yen in *Iron Monkey*."

He slipped his arm inside mine and we walked along the path leading back to the Imagine Mosaic. It had only been the two of us practicing today, with a couple of hip-hop and parkour guys who saw us and wanted to learn Bagua. Blaine didn't give them the hard time that he and Aiden had given me about starting. It was just, "Sure, meet us every morning at dawn."

Aiden had been gone for almost two months with no word, other than the note in Chinese characters he handed Blaine at the airport to give to me. Blaine translated it and wrote on the back of the note: "Lovers' hearts are linked together and always beat as one." Why would he leave me a note like that, and write it in Chinese, when he had made it clear his choice wasn't me? The words pained me, yet I slid the note beneath my pillow and pulled it out to look at whenever I missed him. Aiden's departure seemed like yesterday and a lifetime ago. I had to keep going with my life; I was still mad at him, but I was practical.

Blaine stopped me on the path. "You're quiet today." He grasped my shoulders until I looked directly at him. Then his hands slid from my shoulders to my face. The emptiness that I had been drowning in evaporated in his eyes. A curious connection formed between us and my

154

heart lifted. His eyes drew me into his. I held my breath. The moment lingered.

I jumped when my phone chirped.

"Avery, I have to talk to you." Raven's voice tugged me out of the strange sweet spot I had found myself in with Blaine.

"I'm having lunch with my mom at Rue 57. Come and join us. Please."

"Of course I'll come. Are you okay?"

"I'm fine. It's you I'm worried about, but don't let on to Mom I said anything." She lowered her voice and her words echoed, as though she had cupped her hand around the speaker. "Mom's coming... Hi, Avery. Mom and I are here at Rue 57, why don't you come and join us? ... Okay, great. Bye."

Blaine steered me to a nearby bench.

"What's happening, Avery?"

"I ... I don't know exactly. I thought that since the Goth Girls haven't been around, they must have followed Aiden. You seem to be so calm, I thought that somehow all the danger and craziness had gone away. My dad even had Rambo stop following me. "

"They did follow Aiden, I'm sure. The Goths wanted all of the Bagua Brothers for their amulets, but they focused on Aiden. Veronika knows his weaknesses and now that he is separated from the rest of us, until he gets to the Wudang, he is an easier target."

I touched the pendant around my neck. "That was Raven, and she is worried about me. I think it's about my necklace, Blaine. I think it's all been about my necklace." I pulled it out from under my T-shirt to show him, clutching the chain to ground it. "It's a Carnelian Intaglio, given to my mother by my great-great-grandfather, A.P. Sinnett. He was some famous writer who lived in the Himalayas and studied with mystics. I never told you before, but this is what the Goth Girls took from me down in the tunnels. Aiden got it back for me."

Blaine reached for the stone. He studied it as it lay in his palm. "It's beautiful. Like a fire. What did you say it was? Carnelian Intaglio?"

"Yes, you can see the image when you hold it up to the light. It's Minerva, the Roman Goddess of Wisdom."

"All the great masters and high level monks in the Wudang wear powerful stones." Blaine rubbed a thumb over the pendant. "They believe different stones have energy vibrations that alter the frequency of the wearer."

"I feel weird when I take the Carnelian off, like it's become my second heartbeat, almost as if it talks to me and guides me. Does that sound overly emo?"

"Hey, I've lived in the Wudang, where things get pretty freakin' weird."

"Do you feel anything when you hold it?"

He lifted and lowered his hand. "It's heavier than I expected, that's all. Why?"

"Just wondered. Since I put it on, people have been getting shocked when they touch me."

"Well, you kind of take my breath away when I touch you," Blaine said. "Does that count?" He took my hands in his and gazed into my eyes. His dark eyes were hypnotic. He radiated a calm strength and confidence that made me feel safe. My body leaned into him, then I stopped. I went rigid. *What am I doing?*

Blaine released my hands and patted my shoulder, as if he felt my confusion. "People here don't understand what Aiden and I learned in the Wudang. It wasn't about how to fight, be tough and win competitions. It was about a complete way of life, of meditation, healing arts and evolving beyond what seemed possible."

"Did you want to take vows like Aiden?" I was afraid to ask. "Live as a monk?"

"I have always believed that living Tao was like understanding quantum physics at the most visceral level."

"Quantum physics?"

"Yes. I was doing my Ph.D. in theoretical particle physics when I left it all behind for a life of Bagua with a study of trance, hypnotic and meditative states. The mind is absolute magic. It's so much more powerful than we imagine."

"You amaze me, Blaine."

"I'm a scientist first and always will be. It's built into my DNA. I've experienced amazing things that we don't have an explanation for. That's what I want to bridge, the impossible to the possible. I never wanted to become a monk. That wasn't my path, and besides, Aiden had already claimed that one. He was the one who wanted to learn the most ancient inner secrets the Taoists possessed, that are not ever revealed unless you take the final vows. I want to bring Tao and Quantum physics together and present the combination to the world as a way of life, a way forward for us, so we can live using more of our brains than we ever have before, more of our intuition, our innate, undiscovered gifts. The world so needs us to use more of our brains."

"A Ph.D. in Physics? I always thought of you as more of a dumb jock."

"Haha," Blaine scoffed. "Believe it or not, I wasn't always the studly creature you see before you. I was a skinny geek who had no social life, so had lots of time to study. But I found my way." He held out his hand. "Come on. I'll walk you through the park to meet Marly and Raven."

"Will you wait for me?"

"Sure, I'll wait for you, Avery. I will always wait for you." Blaine took my purse and slung it over his shoulder. He beamed his high-watt smile at me and I couldn't imagine him as a skinny geek.

"You don't have to carry my purse, Blaine."

"I don't mind, I think it brings out my eyes." He laughed. "Besides, it just seems the thing to do when you're with a lady you care about. I promised Aiden I would take care of you. He didn't need to ask though, I would have anyway."

We walked through the park without speaking. Silence for Blaine, usually exuberant and lighthearted, seemed odd. But I had to say there was something charming about a guy who carried a girl's purse in public.

He walked me to the front door of Rue 57 Restaurant and passed my handbag to me. Then he brushed back a lock of my hair hanging over my eye, and tucked it behind my ear. I glanced toward the door, uncomfortable with the intensity of Blaine's gaze. My stomach churned. My mind swirled. *He can't have feelings for me. I can't deal with that.* I shook my head. How could Blaine be attracted to me? I was imagining things. He was just being kind to me because I had been hurt. He would never betray his Bagua brother.

"Why don't you join us?" I said. "Please. Marly and Raven would love to see you."

"I wasn't invited and it seems Raven needs to talk to you alone. I'll be right here if you need me."

"Blaine, you're awesome. Thanks." I leaned in to give him a quick kiss on the cheek, then turned and walked into the restaurant. Marly and Raven sat at a table in the corner.

Marly waved me over. "Avery, so glad you could come." Her phone vibrated. "Ah, I have to get this, girls. It's the office. Again." She stood up and crossed the restaurant to go out into the hallway.

"Avery, listen. I was at my mother's office earlier, and overheard a conversation between her and the DA," Raven whispered. "You know how there are people at the top who manipulate world events?"

"What are you talking about?"

"I heard them talking about a group of men that control world markets and engineer conflicts. You know, wars. I think they said it was *your* father who was being investigated by the DA's office, that he was the one at the top. I shouldn't have heard any of that, but I was meeting mom for lunch and when I got to her door they were talking loudly, like they were upset about something. Shhhhh. She's coming back."

My eyes widened. I couldn't believe Raven had just dumped all that on me and now expected me to act as if nothing was going on.

"Sorry, girls. McMurty is on the rampage. Something's about to blow up, and I've got to go back."

"Are you ready to order?" The server stopped at our table.

"Let the girls have whatever they want, and put it on my card," Marly handed her credit card to the server. "Bye, girls. I'm so sorry."

"That's okay, Mom." Raven lifted her hand. "I'll see you later."

"Bye, Marly," I said. "I miss you."

"Miss you too, Avery." Marly grabbed her purse and left.

Raven and I ordered the French onion soup. While we waited, she dove right back into the conversation, speaking in hushed tones.

"I couldn't hear everything. But I heard enough to know that something isn't right."

I leaned closer to make certain I was hearing properly. "I don't understand. My dad's being investigated?"

"I'm not positive, but I thought they said Peter Adams. That was when Mom asked to be taken off the case. I think it was McMurty who said, 'No way. You asked for this case, you are the best in the office, and you are going to see this through.' I heard that loud and clear."

"McMurty is one of my dad's friends. He's been to our house before." I shook my head as I remembered what Zheng had said in the courtyard that night. "It doesn't make sense."

"I waited before I knocked so I could hear as much as possible. They said that a guy came into the office yesterday saying he had been in hiding for years after his business partner was murdered in an unsolved freak accident. He was an engineer and they had plans for a ..."

The waitress arrived with our soups.

"There you go, ladies, two onion soup au gratin." She set the bowls down in front of us. "Can I get you anything else?"

"No thanks," Raven said. She waited for the waitress to move out of earshot, then began again, leaning over her soup and lowering her voice even further. "The guy had detailed plans for a zero-emissions energy generator, something about using graphene, I think he said, before anyone had ever even heard of it or stable super-conductors."

I scooped up a spoonful of melted cheese and broth. "Why would someone kill for that?"

"Think about it," Raven said. "If we could all generate our own energy, what would happen to the oil, gas and coal industry? What would happen to the utility companies? What about resource mining? It would tip the balance of power in unimaginable ways. You bet someone's going to kill for that. Many have been killed for far less."

I set my spoon back down. "Are you sure this is about my dad?" I asked. "I know he's always telling me he's powerful, but this is inconceivable. It's kinda over-the-top."

"They said they'll get him on stock fraud first, and then go after the big stuff. They want to bring the whole organization down, and this time they are starting at the top. Apparently the Skull and Bones Society has gotten too much power, created too many wars. They have to be stopped."

I pushed my bowl away, my appetite gone. "My dad does belong to the Skull and Bones Society. But they do charitable work. They help their friends. They don't make wars. He has an anti-nuclear proliferation business."

Raven pointed her spoon at me. "I'm just sayin' what I heard. Look them up. If you keep digging deeper and deeper you can find people who are revealing what they are really up to. They are vilified as being crazy conspiracy theorists, but I don't think they are. You need to read up on them. I have. And you'll find out the Skull and Crossbones aren't what they want everyone to believe them to be." Raven reached across the table and squeezed my arm. "You need to be careful, Avery. Super careful."

Chapter 25

AIDEN

A good traveler has no fixed plans,
and is not intent on arriving.

—Lao Tzu

Our journey to the mountain caves was a long and arduous climb. Every now and again I saw shadows following us and sensed it must be Veronika and Valerie. At least one decision I had made would benefit Avery; I had lured those two away from her. Wushu led us up the twisted passage, picking his way along the scree. All of a sudden, he stopped and refused to go on. He stamped one front hoof on the hard-caked path. A well-known Daoist Temple was perched at the edge of the trail ahead, barely visible above the layer of clouds. A deep rumble in the distance broke the silence and shook the ground we walked upon. An ecobus, the only vehicles allowed in the Wudang, and limited to the tourist sections, pulled up at a stop on the road, adjacent to our concealed passageway. Tourists clambered out, their chatter and laughter wafted across the valley, and echoed against the rocky mountain sides. Ahead of us, at the other side of the path, hidden from view, a tiny aperture in the tangled trees appeared.

No Trace and I squeezed through the opening, the branches scratching our arms and legs. As soon as we were through, it closed up behind us. I wasn't worried about Veronika and Valerie. Wushu would lead them away from us. Only No Trace or one of the other cave monks knew the way to the compound of the Order of the Celestial Dragon's Gate, the Order I was about to become formally initiated into as a monk. These monks had been my family for many years. Though I felt I was coming home, the vision of Avery superimposed itself and I felt a longing in my heart that I had never experienced before.

We traveled in silence, single file, No Trace seeming to create the path with every step he took. With every one of mine it disappeared behind us. We came upon my dear old friend and transformation guide, Wao, sitting on a rock meditating, as if waiting for our arrival. He sat tall and relaxed, his face peaceful with his hair twisted on the top of his head and held with a single wood pin. We approached and No Trace crept up to him. Knowing No Trace, he was likely preparing to tweak his nose. Before he could, Wao opened his eyes wide and screeched. No Trace stumbled back. They both laughed. Wao waggled his finger at him, then turned to me. "Aiden, my brother. Welcome home." He unfolded himself from his seated meditation position and embraced me before taking our arms and leading us into the compound, where I was excited to be reunited with all my brothers.

White Feather ran up to greet us, and took my rucksack. "I'll put it in your cave. Same one as last you were here." The others rushed up to say their hellos.

"Aiden, how come you prefer the old ways?" Young Phoenix bounced eagerly beside me. "Don't you miss nightclubs? Cars? Girls?" His eager eyes wanted to know everything about the world beyond these sacred mountains.

"Don't torture poor Aiden about the world he just left behind, Young Phoenix." Old Phoenix put a grandfatherly hand on his shoulder. He turned to me and looked straight into my eyes, a penetrating gaze exactly like Grandfather's. There, in his left eye, was the same split iris.

"Finally, you noticed." Old Phoenix lifted an abnormally smooth hand to his face. "I thought I was preparing a blind man these past years."

My head swam, with the juxtaposition of Grandfather's split iris with Old Phoenix's. I held out the scroll that I had been given in the market when I was there with Sheng Li.

Old Phoenix took it and opened it up to study it. "This parchment is written in ancient symbols. Some, I haven't seen since very long ago …" He looked up, his calm face now etched with concern. "The Myriad Time has begun."

"What's The Myriad Time?"

Before the words were out of my mouth, Old Phoenix was a hundred yards or so away, appearing at the door of the temple as if in a single step.

A shiver moved through me. My protective bubble of peace and safety fell away. These mystic monks were so much more evolved than the rest of humanity; if one could not be safe here, one couldn't be safe anywhere.

Wao came up behind me. "Rest now, Aiden. When you are ready we will practice."`

Dawn's light filtered into the cave, illuminating the walls with a warm golden light. I was surprised I had slept so deeply and for so long, but the mountain air, along with the lavender sprigs mixed into the husk mattress, had lulled me to sleep. I raised myself up from the comfort of the bed to ready myself for practice.

"Hey sleepy head. Let's go," Wao called from outside. I emerged into the light and he steered me away from the other monks in the courtyard, to a clearing not far away. He leaned into me. "If The Myriad Time has begun, we have much to achieve."

"What's The Myriad Time, Wao?"

He shook his head. "Not now. Old Phoenix tell you when time is right. How's circle walk?"

I set up eight bricks on their ends, two large steps from the center of my circle. I stepped around the circumference, landing on the small surface of each brick while performing several difficult palm changes. Other Bagua systems used a mud step, where each step lifts, extends and then slides. Our lineage used a different style, called the Crane step, where, like a Crane, each step lifts up, extends outwards and lightly lands.

"Excellent, Aiden. Now you are ready."

"Ready for what?" I cocked my head. "Wasn't that it?"

"Aiden. Aiden. Aiden." Wao shook his head and chuckled. "At beginning of journey. You have far to go yet." We moved through to another clearing, where long bamboo poles were stuck in the ground at random heights and patterns. The highest one was about five feet. Wao hopped up to one of the poles and bounded around them as if he were flying.

Wao somersaulted down from the poles, giggling.

My eyebrows shot up. "Now?"

"Not now. First you must work on your light body, so you can get up to top of poles." He shoved a bucket and a lightly woven straw basket about four feet in circumference into my hands. "Here, fill this basket with sand." Once I had filled the basket, he had me do my circle walking around the rim of it.

"That good, Aiden. Every day, you must take one bucket of sand out of the basket until empty and you can walk around the rim without crushing it. Then you have light body. Then you reach the poles."

"Really?"

"Really, Aiden. Then we really begin." Wao laughed. "We always really beginning, aren't we?"

I had so much to do to work on my concentration and skills that I barely had to time to dwell on Avery. But she was there in the back of my mind, always. I comforted myself with the thought that I had kept her safe by drawing Veronika and Valerie away from her. They were probably still trying to find their way in the woods.

Every morning I emptied more sand from the basket, making it more difficult to walk around the rim. While my light body work developed, my night-sight training began. During the day I raced through the forest, blindfolded, trusting my instincts and evolving my inner sight. It was like seeing from the inside of my mind, while feeling the energy field, the life force of everything, as I whipped past.

I ran through the forest, perceiving each tree. Everything took a clear shape inside my mind. I pulled up energy from the earth into my feet to push faster; barely a leaf touched my skin. I felt Avery's lips brush my mouth. WHAM! I banged straight into a tree.

"Aiden." Wao waved a hand through the air. "You okay? You were going like the wind. I never saw anyone go so fast before." He ran towards me.

"I'm fine," I said. "I just lost my concentration for a moment." I stood up and brushed the dry leaves from my arms and legs.

"You can't go that fast without the power of concentration." Wao shook his head. "Too dangerous. You must have everything in balance." He waggled his finger at me. "You so fast now. You must be seeing without seeing. Except you didn't see that last tree." He exploded with laughter.

I couldn't help but join him, though my mind was still with Avery.

In the blackness of a starless night, I wandered through the forest on my latest training exercise. The monks could be there, together or separately, or not at all. I wouldn't know. They could have weapons. I could have none. Those were the only rules. I walked silently, "seeing" into the dark. The sky was so black there was no need for a blindfold. The daytime exercises had prepared me well for this. I could now sense the energy of things around me in such a way as to almost see them. I imagined it might be similar to the way a blind man once described to me how his heightened perceptions of sound, sense and vibration allowed him to create a type of visual representation in his mind of the world around him.

I turned statue-still. Something hovered high above me. Eyes followed me. The heat of a body. The miniscule movement of air slowly sucked into lungs without a sound. I gauged its size. *Young Phoenix.* The tendons in my arms and legs came alive. I deepened my stance. I felt the attack before it arrived, a huge mass falling from above. I was ready.

"Ha," I yelled. "Young Phoenix, I got you." I reached up, prepared to roll with Young Phoenix onto the ground. My fingers dug into fur. Not human. *Oh no.* I flipped the heavy beast onto the ground. I could barely make out the vague, shimmering outline. My stomach tightened. A panther. He turned to launch another attack on me. He hurtled in the air, and I lunged with him, turning mid-flight to shove him from behind. One of his claws lanced my forearm as I came around. I was used to fighting men, not animals. I focused on the animal forms I had practiced for years. Each animal had its own distinctive fighting style.

We landed on the ground and circled each other. The eyes of the cat blinked slowly. He was sizing me up. How did I move? Where were my weaknesses? Where would an attack most likely succeed? Our eyes locked in the darkness. His were created for night vision, mine could only just discern his outline, but I felt his magnetism, pulling me into a dance. I matched his steps and the intensity of his gaze. He stopped. I tried to push my mind into his, the way Raven described how she communicated. *With deepest respect, I will do you no harm.*

He lowered his head and ears as he crouched, lining me up in his sights between his powerful front legs and paws. I was ready. He dropped his eyes for barely a moment and stepped backward. I cast my gaze downward, and stepped back. He backed away a few more feet. I did the same. He locked my gaze again and I swear he winked at me with one golden eye, then wheeled around to sprint away through the woods. Adrenalin coursed through me. I had connected with this animal's amazing mind, and he had let me go. I wanted to savor the moment, but there was no time.

I whipped around to grab Purple Cloud's long spear, creating a vibration in it that dislodged him from his perch on a rock. He regained his balance, soared towards me from the rock with a roar and sliced at me with his spear. I snatched his weapon and used it to vault my body into the lower branches of a nearby cedar tree. I scrambled up the rough bark toward the tall tree tops.

"Aiden. Aiden." He stopped his pursuit to call to me. The forest went quiet, as if all the nightlife wanted to hear what he had to say. "I give up. I thought you wouldn't notice me because of the panther. I surrender."

I didn't want to fight anymore that night. The red palm had flared back to life on my stomach. I was tired from the week of drills, and tired of fighting the irresistible urge to think about Avery. I waited on a high, spindly bough, resting my weight against the trunk as Purple Cloud climbed up to join me.

He dropped lightly onto a nearby branch and held out his hand. "Congratulations, Aiden."

I took his hand and he pulled me off the bough and flung me into the air.

"When will you learn?" he yelled.

I crashed through the thick branches, grasping at them without catching anything. Just before hitting the ground, I snagged a branch that held my weight and clung to it, gasping for air.

"Never trust in a fight." Purple Cloud's belly laugh echoed through the night.

AVERY

Goodness in words creates trust, goodness in thinking creates depth, goodness in giving creates love.

—Lao Tzu

Blaine and I crept down the hall of my apartment, even though no one was home. Dad had gone on another business trip, and Ruby had taken Rasta to visit her sister. I felt almost delightfully devious. We stopped in the drawing room and looked around, then continued to my father's study. It was always locked and now I was pretty sure it wasn't just his paintings he was keeping safe. I had to get some answers, even if I didn't know exactly what I was looking for.

"Okay, Avs, how are we getting in?" Blaine whispered.

"Why are you whispering?" I whispered.

"I don't know." He chuckled. "Why are you? Okay, how are we getting in?"

"I don't know. Last time I got in, he accidentally left his door open."

Blaine rattled the door knob. Definitely locked. "So, if we ever get the door unlocked, what kind of security system does he have inside?"

"No idea."

"Great. Did you think I would know how to break in?"

"Well, Einstein, you're the quantum physicist..."

"Was... but that still doesn't help me with breaking and entering." Blaine shook his head, but he was smiling. "Oh, Avs, what am I going to do with you?"

Blaine pulled two long cocktail picks with silver olives on the end out of his pocket and went to work on the door lock. "I grabbed these when we stopped in the drawing room. I had a feeling they might come in handy."

"What are you two kids up to?"

I whirled around, my hand pressed to my chest. "Oh my God, Ruby! You scared me half to death."

Blaine fumbled the two picks and they dropped to the floor. I bent down to pick them up. Blaine reached for them at the same time and our heads banged.

"I have a key, if you need it," Ruby reached into her pocket. "And I have security clearance for the alarm system for when I clean the office. What is it you need, Avery? "

My eyes widened. "You can help us get in?"

"Of course, darlin', you're my girl." She glanced around, as though my dad might have spies hidden behind the furniture, and lowered her voice. "I don't know what your father's into, but I'm sure it's not all good. Someone should find out what he is doing." Ruby pulled out her ring of keys and opened the office door, setting off the measured beeps that signaled the alarm system had been activated. She went straight to the voice recognition module. "Ruby here, cleaning up." There was one long beep and then silence. "There." She waved a hand through the air. "Go ahead. I'll be in the kitchen. When you're ready just call me, and I'll come back to swish my duster around and turn the alarm back on. You have about half an hour, in case your father checks, which he sometimes does. Now, hurry up."

Blaine and I dashed into the office and went directly to his desk. The first thing I saw was a vial of white powder. I couldn't keep the secret any longer. "Look, Blaine," I said, holding up the vial, "My dad's been taking coke."

Blaine picked up the annual report that was under it. He looked closely at the vial. "Avery, I don't think that's coke, that's a vial of lithium. This is the same vial that's on the cover of this company's annual report. Look at all these papers. They're all companies that mine lithium."

I sighed in relief. "Thank God he's not using drugs."

"I think he's doing something, but it's not coke. Let's keep looking. There might be more to this. He's got reports here from Venadium Global Mining, World Lithium, Rare Earth Minerals, NWO Lithium Mining, Lithium Research Labs. Oh, look here, Avery," Blaine whistled at the open drawer. "There are hundreds of stock slips of buys and sells of lithium stocks. What's he been doing?"

I opened another drawer and leaned over Blaine to pick up a printout of a stock tip newsletter. I'd never noticed how good he smelled. It was a little distracting. I gave my head a little shake, refocusing on the page in front of me. I quickly scanned it for information. *Lithium a bad buy ... overabundance of lithium in the world ... the electric car isn't the answer ... vanadium ranked higher than lithium.* The writer of the piece was N.H. "Blaine, I bet this was written by Norman Howel, you know, the Boreman. Look at all these buys. The dates are just after this article was published. They're causing the lithium price to go down. Here's another and the same thing, more buys just after a negative article is published."

Blaine stood near me, paging through the articles.

"Here's an article by someone else." I skimmed the article that trumpeted lithium's potential worth, declaring it a limited resource in a post-fossil fuel world, dominated by the sale of electric vehicles. "Look at this date." I pointed to the slip. "And look at the dates of those sells. He was totally manipulating the market."

Blaine held up another newsletter. "He does the same thing here with graphene."

I glanced at the drawer. A smaller drawer with a keypad on it was half-hidden deep inside. "Blaine." I grabbed his arm. "A keypad. I wonder what he's hiding in that drawer. I have a feeling there is more to this than just stock manipulation. Raven told me she heard her mom and McMurty, the DA, talk about this. So I looked up the Skull and Bones Society from Yale, and there is speculation that this group is part of the Illuminati. Some articles I read said that much of what goes on in the world, goes on because these groups manipulate it. What I don't get is to what end? Why create wars?"

"When you own munitions companies, you benefit from war. I bet if we scratch the surface we'll find more to this. Your father is some piece of work. He has security on top of security."

I sank onto my dad's desk chair. "In three weeks I have to go to St. Barts with Dad, Claire, Whitney and The Boreman. How am I going to go away with them and pretend everything is normal?"

Ruby appeared in the doorway. "Avery, Blaine, you've been here almost forty-five minutes. It's time for me to reset the alarm. I don't want your dad to get suspicious."

"I need more time," I said. "I know there is something I need to find here."

"Avery, luv," Ruby said. "I don't want you to get caught. You need to leave."

I sighed and stood up. She was right. Whatever Dad was into, it seemed extremely dangerous. What would he do to keep his affairs secret?

Blaine and I straightened his desk so it looked just like it had when we arrived, while Ruby ran around with her duster.

"There," she said. "Just like after I clean." She gestured toward the exit. I looked back when we reached it. Ruby sat at the desk and pressed something that made an audible click by the door as we left. Then she got up and went to the voice recognition module. "Ruby here, reset alarm please." One long beep was followed by measured short beeps until she closed the door and locked it.

"Now child," Ruby turned to me and planted a fist on her hip, "You owe me an explanation. What are you looking for?"

AIDEN

*At the center of your being you have the answer; you know who
you are and you know what you want.*

—Lao Tzu

I looked out across the peaks of the Wudang that thrust above the cloud
line, separating the region from the rest of the world. The setting sun
streaked the sky with watercolor shades of red, pink and orange. Here,
the air was thin, and the sky so close, it felt as if I could reach out and
swirl the colors with my hand. Taoist temples were built into various
rock faces, some perched on the edge of sheer drops down into the valley
of the Hanshui River. This area was truly one of the most remarkable I
had seen in the world.

The Eight Immortals Temple peeked out from the canopy of emerald
trees on the other side of the abyss, across from where I stood at the edge
of a rock cliff belonging to The Order of The Celestial Dragon Gate. The
Five Dragon Palace visually leapt out of its background, with vibrant red
buildings. In contrast, no one could see our temple. Centuries of trees,
moss, and vine growth concealed our compound's walls of natural rock,
rendering us invisible.

Wao stayed close to me. He was my shadow, the monk who would
guide me through each ritual for the transformation that I had vowed to
take, and as such, he seemed, to me, omnipresent. Wao and Old Phoenix
spoke in hushed whispers on several occasions, but today they conferred
for longer than usual. Instead of my gut churning, it was my mind that
burned with the memory of Avery. Wao approached me and motioned
for me to walk with him. I followed.

"You need to talk."

I blinked. "I can't."

"You can't hide," he said. "You know that. You know the caves cannot be used for hiding."

I sighed. "I used to be so sure," I said. "I felt I knew my mind so well. Now, I don't know anything."

"Ahh. That is a very good place to start. The not knowing is the place of power."

"The not knowing is the place of confusion."

"Confusion is the gateway to learning."

"Humph," I answered, not enjoying the Taoist banter where everything was true unless it wasn't.

Wao took my arm and led me down a narrow path we had not taken before. We sat on some stones beside a brook, and I listened to the sound of clear water bubbling over rocks. "Aiden. This is not banter." Wao said, as if he were a mind reader. "This is not playing a linguistic game. This is opening a mind. Being a monk is not the only way to live Tao, or to live with Spirit, with God. Being a monk is just one way, not THE way. I can see into your heart, Aiden. You cannot receive the direct transmissions with a broken heart. That is hiding. Being a monk is not hiding. It is being, fully. Too many people use it to hide. I can't let you do that. "

"I don't want to hide, Wao." Relief flowed through me as I finally spoke my truth. "I just don't know how to get back to the state I was before, when I left you here. Happy with my decision. Sure of my decision. Certain of my destiny. I made a promise. To you. To myself. To Old Phoenix. How can I live with myself if I can't keep a promise? What kind of man is one that can't keep a promise?"

"Aiden, don't try to get back to where you were, get to where you are going. If you put your hand into a river, the river moves on. It will never be the same river again." Wao took my hand and plunged it into the ice cold water, then released me. His eyes locked with mine. "Let me tell you a story. I have been a monk for many years now. I was chosen to be your guide for the vows long ago, before you even arrived at the caves. I have often wondered what my purpose is here on earth, but now I think I understand. You know I trained with Master Du, and at a young age my skills were already more than adequate. I met his daughter, Lu Xi, and we fell in love. We were fourteen years old."

"I didn't know Master Du had a daughter."

"He did, and she was dear to my heart. Fourteen wasn't considered too young back then, especially when you lived in a remote village," Wao said. "One day, Mao Zedong's, People's Liberation Army officers, came and raided our village. They raped, tortured and killed Lu in front of me, and forced my eyes open so I could not look away. The officers were angry that we were still practicing our tradition of Esoteric Taoist Martial Arts. According to them, this was something that should have been eradicated during the so-called Cultural Revolution, when all religion and spirituality was deemed illegal. They wanted to destroy Taoism and particularly our tradition. They believed our practice was a threat to the new order. We were to be exterminated, or at least destroyed mentally and spiritually. I survived the torture and years of imprisonment in an earthen pit, until a Bagua Zhang brother arrived to help me escape.

"Old Phoenix?"

"Yes. He was old even back then, all those years ago. He took me to the caves to hide and heal. My heart and my spirit were broken and I wanted to become a monk. There was no other life worth living for me. I was barely seventeen years old, and severely traumatized by what I had witnessed. We talked at great length about hiding in our own minds and losing our souls in a trauma such as mine." Wao stopped for a moment and looked off into the distance.

"Lu was the love of my life. To this day, I believe that love is the ultimate expression of Tao. That love may be expressed through the love for the caves and all nature – as I love now – or the grand expression of love for your partner in life, where two loves join to become a more powerful 'one'." He clasped his hands together to illustrate the powerful connection. "A promise made temporally may transform into something else, something greater, as events in the universe unfold. You are a good soul, Aiden. One of the most pure I have ever known. As a monk, I have not made much of a difference in this world, except perhaps today. As a monk, Aiden, you may not fulfill your whole potential."

I rubbed my temples with my fingers. "But my destiny is to be a monk. We all know that. It was clear the last time I was here. Old Phoenix threw the yarrow sticks."

"The last time you were here, your heart and soul were not somewhere else. Take some time, Aiden. Think about things. Meditate. You do not have to hurry. We will talk again. And again. When you are plagued with doubt about yourself, doubt your doubt. Just think on that awhile." Wao paused while my mind spun out, then he began again. "A certain mind is a closed mind."

"I don't know what you mean." My mind was spinning out even more. "Are you saying to embrace my doubts about being a monk, so I can be free to be a monk, or embrace my doubts about a life outside the caves, so I can pursue that life? I made a promise. You told me not to ever make a promise lightly, because it could never be broken."

"Aiden, Aiden. You know better than that. Embrace all your doubts and your destiny will be revealed. Good night." Wao walked away.

I shook my head and realized I was in front of my cave. I had been so engrossed in our conversation that I hadn't noticed that's where we were heading. Is that what had happened with me and Avery? I had gotten so fixated on her that I hadn't noticed where my path was taking me? I trudged into my cave and dropped down onto my bed of sticks, covered by a straw mattress.

Good night? Ha! Wao had completely uncorked me. I made an unbreakable promise to Old Phoenix to take the transmissions and become a monk, but I loved Avery. *Embrace the doubt. Embrace the uncertainty. This was not a decision to be made; this was a decision that would arise.* The ancient voice of Old Phoenix mingled with Grandfather's. Somehow the lyrics to a Beatles song played in my mind: *Whisper words of wisdom, let it be. And in my hour of darkness, she is standing right in front of me, speaking words of wisdom, let it be.*

I exhaled loudly and flopped onto my side. I would never break a promise. I would never be like my father. But I felt I was going mad. I closed my eyes and fell into another uneasy sleep.

AIDEN

If you gaze for long into the abyss, the abyss also gazes into you.

—Nietzche

I t had been seven days since Wao had spoken so sincerely to me. Every day, he brought me to the still pond for meditation practice. First, he had me sit on a board in the middle of the pond. I didn't know what I was to do, what I was to notice. Then it became clear. My being rippled when Wao, on the far side of the pond, put his hand gently into the water and the surface moved. When I noticed, Wao was pleased. Next he had me sit on a rock in the pond.

When I finally detected Wao ripple the water on my shadow, he was excited.

"Excellent, Aiden, you notice the very subtlest of energy shifts. So much of our being is contained inside shadow. You have learned to feel its connection to you. Very good. Now, if only you could notice the inside of your heart." With those words, Wao left me.

I had to become brutally honest with myself. By staying here, was I hiding from life and taking an easy way out? Or was leaving here taking the easy way out by breaking a promise that was becoming impossible to keep? My mind churned and turned up nothing. What was I meant to discover? Who I am, or who I thought I could be? My gut ached with a slow, dull pain. Not the poison, not the death palm, but my indecision.

I waded out of the water and dragged myself back to the inner courtyard.

For seven days I had fasted, continued my lessons with Wao, prayed, and practiced Bagua. I hoped that by walking the circle some clarity would come to mind.

"Aiden, you can't fast any longer. You didn't have the strength to begin with." Wao slid his arm around my shoulders and directed me to a nearby bench to sit on.

"I have to sort this out." I was determined to gain back the peace I had experienced when I made my promise.

"You can't force peace. Your determination is commendable, Aiden. As always you have iron will to make anything you set your mind to happen. But this isn't mind thing. This is heart thing."

Wao took my breath away. Like a key unlocking a heavy bolt, a burden suddenly lifted from me, then almost as suddenly landed back on my shoulders, heavier than before. I felt I had come close to grasping something my mind found unfathomable.

"I can see you struggling in this decision, Aiden. You don't make a promise lightly, that I respect. I've asked Old Phoenix if we can use Mirror Pond to bring clarity. Mirror Pond need good reason. Mirror Pond used to find Fourteenth Dalai Lama. That was good reason. This, too."

"Mirror Pond?" I couldn't imagine that a Mirror Pond would help me through this. Perhaps I could find the clarity I was looking for, though I feared the truth and what it might mean for the rest of my life. And Avery's.

I shrugged. "I'll try anything."

On the morning of my scheduled trip to Mirror Pond, excitement buzzed through me. To be allowed to go for a vision is a great honor. Wao came to me in the early morning, clothed in a sapphire robe. He carried incense, a burner and nothing else. I think he wanted to see the vision almost as much as I did. He believed the answer to my destiny lay inside it, and that because of who I was, I had a greater role that carried more weighty implications than I had imagined. Wao was rather generous. I found Avery's accusation of cowardice more fitting for me.

I pulled the loose-fitting robe over me as I had been shown, and gathered it together at the waist with a rope cord. When I was ready, I followed Wao along the old stone path towards the western caves, winding gradually up the outside of the mountain face. Our walk was quiet, solemn even.

We stepped through the opening of the mountain pass to the inner circle of the mountain range where the Mirror Pond was cradled like a brilliant sapphire stone. Protected by the surrounding mountains, the stillness created a deep azure glass surface. As we approached, a wind whipped up, as if from nowhere, and changed the reflective pond into a rippling sea. The closer we got, the greater the force with which the wind blew, and the more the pond churned until it was a murky, muddy, roiling mess. The sky darkened with angry clouds, and rain soon pelted down on us with a vengeance. We sat in meditation, although the storm whipping around us stole my hope that I would catch any kind of vision in the brown, opaque water.

Then I saw her. Her golden hair, her golden eyes looking right at me. My heart skipped. Avery was on a boat. Claire and Whitney were with her. Whitney was laughing. I wanted to get back to the vision of Avery, but it was coming in pieces. There she was again. She closed her eyes tightly and held out her cupped hands, an anxious smile lingering on her lips. She peeked, but her father gently passed his hand over her eyes to close them again. Avery still held her hands out. A man I could only see from the back – was it Norman? –slipped in beside Avery where her father had been a moment before. In one swift movement, he took her hand and slipped a diamond ring on her finger.

"Noooooooo!" I screamed out, and dove into the image after her. I had to stop her from marrying someone else. How foolish I had been. I had chosen to come here and leave her behind. I did not deserve her. But I could not forget her, could not stop feeling I had made a terrible mistake. I thought I wanted her to move on. But now that she had, I couldn't take it. The icy cold sent shock waves through me. I had not leapt inside the vision, but into the frigid mountain lake. My robe became saturated with water, wrapping around my body and pulling me deeper down into the water.

My limbs went numb, my arms and legs imprisoned in the heavy folds of material. I ripped at the rope cord, trying to free myself so I wouldn't drown. Peace filled me. I stopped struggling as water filled my mouth, nose and lungs. Instead of gasping for breath, I felt elevated, as if I had no need for air. I belonged to the water now, breathed water now. I sank deeper and deeper into the void.

Abruptly, the cord on my robe was yanked tight, and I was pulled toward the surface. I protested silently. The golden glow of Avery's eyes shimmered below me. I reached toward the light that shone in front of me. That was where I wanted to go. *No, don't bring me back.*

Wao called out to me, but I fought against him. I had already left the world of air, the world of sensory experience, the world of pain. He called out to me again and again. *No, I'm not coming back.*

He pulled me from the water. I sputtered, coughing up brown water and silt. Wao lunged on top of me, pushing on my lungs and giving me mouth to mouth.

My head lolled to the side. I saw the diamond on Avery's left hand, the glow of her eyes. I wanted to go back to where I had been; wherever it was, it felt better than here. My lungs burned, but mostly my heart ached beyond any ache I had ever known.

"Aiden." Wao shook me. "Come back. Come back now. Come back here."

I refused to speak, as if that might help me re-enter the murky place deep inside the void. His voice grew distant. Wao's tone transformed from worry to anger.

"What are you doing, Aiden?" His furious yell broke through. "You lost your mind? You can't dive into the Mirror Pond. No one dives into the Mirror Pond!"

That jerked me back inside my body. I opened my eyes. Somehow seeing Wao as an angry monk sent me into hysterics and I burst out laughing.

"You think this funny?" Wao said. "You wrecked the vision, Aiden. The vision tell you when it's finished. Not you. "

That sobered me quickly. "I'm so sorry, Wao. I don't think it's funny. I'm so, so sorry. I don't know what got into me. I just jumped in … I thought I could touch her."

"You mess this up." Wao shook his head. "Let's put our robes out to dry and then go back. Old Phoenix is not going to be happy. It's going to be my head on the chopping block. I'm responsible for you, Aiden."

We took our robes off in silence and tossed them over rocks to dry. The Mirror Pond returned to its serene, reflective nature. The storm clouds abated and the sun beat down from the cloudless sky, as if there had never been a storm.

"No one ever jumped in after a vision before."

"I'm so sorry, Wao."

"I'm responsible for you. I should have protected you."

Our robes dried, leaving the material brittle from the hard mineral water of the lake. They felt like rough burlap when we put them on.

"You should have seen my face when you jumped in." Wao chuckled. "I was so shocked, you would have thought I had just seen a vision of Buddha himself." He laughed harder. "You screamed like Banshee when you hit water." Tears streamed down Wao's face, he was laughing so hard, and I couldn't resist joining him. Soon we were doubled over laughing, harder than I had ever laughed before.

Finally, completely drained, I straightened up. "I'm so sorry I made you angry. I didn't know you could get angry."

Wao looked surprised, but then his eyes went from laughing to deadly serious. "Well, you weren't coming back here and the only thing that ever breaks through your tough nut," he whacked me across the top of the head like Grandfather used to do, "is to do something you don't expect. You think you know what a monk should be and, well, let's leave the rest of the lesson for another time." Wao rubbed his temples. "What caused you to jump in?"

I rubbed my head. "I saw Avery." Immediately, a deep, aching loss tore at the fabric of my being. The cord that tied me to her had been severed and left dangling, bloody between us. I should feel relieved that my destiny has been spelled out to me so clearly. I was to be a monk, and Avery would marry someone else. "She is getting married."

Wao's eyes narrowed. "What did you *really* see, Aiden?"

AVERY

The measure of a man is what he does with power.

—Plato

I wrenched the ring from my finger. I had to get the offending object away from me and the nausea swelling up in the pit of my stomach. "Never, ever will I marry the likes of you. You are a pig." I flung the ring at him. It bounced off his temple.

For a few seconds, Norman looked stunned, then he dropped to his knees, feeling with both hands around the white pebbled decking. "My ring. I've got to find my ring."

My father leapt at me. I readied myself to use his momentum to twirl away, as I had been taught to do in Bagua practice. He came at me as if in slow motion, mouth open and eyes blazing with hatred. So much hatred. *Why?* I froze. He landed a few inches in front of me. *Why doesn't he love me anymore?* Before I could move, he backhanded me across the face. "You ungrateful bitch."

Claire swooped in, wrapping herself protectively around me. Shouting assaulted my ears, but my mind was spinning and I couldn't tell who was yelling or what they were saying. All I felt was the stinging on my cheek and the flush of shame rising from within.

I pressed my face against Claire's chest. She clutched me so tightly I could barely breathe, but for the first time since Aiden had left, I felt safe. *What had happened to my father?* He had been his old, charming and loving self with Claire by his side the whole time we had been in St. Barts. I had let my guard down with him, believing he was once again the father I grew up with; believing that he would put my happiness above and beyond what Norman wanted.

Claire and Whitney whisked me back to my cabin. I collapsed onto the edge of the bed while Claire cupped my chin and inspected the rising red welt on my cheek. "We are getting you out of here." Her eyes met mine. "I've made a terrible mistake, Avery. I can't stay another minute with that beast after what he did to you."

I couldn't speak. I felt locked inside my mind, churning over everything that had happened. How could I have prevented it? What had I done to provoke such a reaction, to make him hate me so much?

Claire took my face in her hands. "Honey, are you all right? He should never have done that."

I looked right at her, but I wasn't there. I was somewhere else, though I couldn't quite grasp where.

She grasped my arms tighter and shook me gently. "Avery? Talk to me. Come on."

I opened my mouth to speak, but a torrent of tears poured from me instead. A memory flashed through my mind. I was a little girl, and Uncle Simon had come to visit one day. He sat at my table with his knees scrunched up to his chest while we had tea with my dolls and stuffed animals. After a while, he left me to play by myself and went to my mother's room.

My father came home and I told him that Uncle Simon was with mom in their bedroom. My father stormed off and I followed, not understanding why he suddenly looked so angry. I peeked in from the doorway. When Dad exploded into the room, Mom was crying and Uncle Simon was comforting her. She stood up and held her arms in front of her, but my dad smacked her across the face. "You ungrateful bitch."

Uncle Simon jumped in front of her, grabbed my dad's wrist in one hand and punched him in the face with the other.

My father stumbled back, blood dripping from his lip. His eyes flashed hatred. "You are no longer welcome in this house, Simon. You've done enough damage to this family. Now get out."

Simon looked at Mom. "Come with me, Patty. You and Avery." He held out his hand to her.

Tears glistened in her eyes as she looked at Simon.

Dad grabbed her arm and yanked her close to his face." You will never take Avery away from me. Not ever."

Mom looked helplessly at Simon. "I can't Simon. I'm sorry. We have to stay."

When Dad finally allowed Uncle Simon back into the house a few years ago, he never left him alone with my mother or me. Since then, an uncomfortable gnawing, like trying to find a word that had slipped from memory, haunted my mind whenever Uncle Simon was around.

As I came back into the present my insides quaked.

"Avery. Avery." Claire's fingers clutched my arms.

Gradually her face came into focus.

"Okay, good. You're back." Whitney looked relieved as she pressed a cold compress to my forehead and my cheek. "You scared us, girl." Our eyes connected. "Lou put our luggage together and has the shuttle boat, that thing they call the tender, waiting for us. He'll take us to shore where a car is waiting to get us to the airport."

Claire took my arm and helped me to stand up. "Let's get out of here."

"Uh, sure." Moving numbly, as though wading through dense muck, I followed the two of them out of the cabin.

AIDEN

Great teachers can lead you to the doors of understanding, but it is up to you to enter.

—Lao Tzu

Wao and I stood in a queue at the first food kiosk we found in Katmandu. The flight had been short, but my body was weak and the angry palm welt on my stomach burned from the inside out. Since the Mirror Pond, my health had deteriorated, and Wao had insisted we consult with the Rinpoche.

I pressed a hand to my side. "So how far is your friend from here?"

Wao lifted his arms. "I'm not sure. You see, he isn't exactly a friend, just someone I have heard about who performs miraculous cures."

Great. More miracle cures of undrinkable herbs.

A tall, gangly young man ambled up to us; his freshly-shaven head shone white and vulnerable against the rest of his tanned skin. He was obviously a new monk and his eyes were alight. "I just saw Rinpoche, and you can't imagine," the monk said, speaking in English with a foreign accent I couldn't quite identify. "He took a crystal and put it on his palm. The crystal rose up and traveled across the room, touched me on the forehead, then returned to his hand. It was incredible. I feel amazing. You are almost there." He waved an arm through the air. "Just down those streets. Look for the red door in the blue wall."

"How do you know where we are going?" I reached across the counter for our noodles and paste.

"Why else would you be here?" The monk winked at Wao, then shimmied into the queue to order.

"Can you believe our good fortune?" Wao took his bowl from me. "Only here for one minute and we find who we are looking for, and we didn't even have to ask."

We wolfed down our food and hurried off to find the Rinpoche.

We walked through endless stone streets with doors that opened up to reveal other streets, with more doors that opened up to more streets, until we came across the red door in the blue wall. Wao turned the wing-style ringer and a bell sounded on the other side of the thin wall.

A small, stooped man opened the door. "We've been waiting for you." His tone was mildly accusing. "You're late. You said you'd be here an hour ago."

"Oh, no," Wao replied in Mandarin. "We don't have an appointment, but we would like one with Rinpoche. My friend is ill."

The man shook his head. "I know you don't have an appointment, but Rinpoche told me you would be here."

"Please," Wao said. "We need to see him."

"Oh, forgive my manners. Of course, come in." The man waved us through the door. "You are the ones he described. Exactly." The man nodded in my direction and smiled.

Wao shot me a smug glance.

I rolled my eyes, preparing myself for more intolerable cures that didn't cure. It wasn't that I didn't believe in old Chinese 'magic,' I just doubted that, after all this time, anything would solve the red hand print engraved on my stomach.

The little man led us through a dark ante room and into an even darker waiting room. There were no windows and the chairs he directed us to were hard and stick-straight. He turned to us and bowed slightly. "Rinpoche will be with you shortly. He has had a busy day and told me he needed to nap for five minutes; that was four minutes ago."

We sat down on the chairs. In precisely sixty seconds, the Rinpoche opened his chamber door, back-lit by shafts of dazzling golden sunlight.

I blinked at the sudden brightness lighting up the waiting room. Had he planned his opening scene? Did he think I would be impressed with what could have been a magician's trick? My jaw tightened. It would take more than a magician's trick to cure me.

"Come in," he sang, "do come in." His Chenglish was laced with British-accented English and formality. "I've been waiting for you. After Jiang left you at the airport, he called me to say you would be coming."

Wao glanced sideways at me.

So the Rinpoche wasn't a mind-reader. I couldn't help but raise an eyebrow. China was full of so-called legendary healers, mystics and martial arts masters. Many took advantage of trusting Chinese people and naive tourists. There were only a few authentic healers, and they kept themselves well hidden. *If Old Phoenix couldn't do anything for me, how could anyone else?*

"Aiden, you are the one we need to see," Rinpoche said, not looking directly at either of us. "But both of you, come in." He opened the door wider and motioned us into a very large room, filled with ornate carved wooden chairs, old scrolls and magnificent paintings. A monkey was perched on a pole in one corner. The Rinpoche walked slowly across the room, lightly dusting his fingers across the furniture as he went by. He sat down at his desk and turned his head towards me. His eyes were cloudy and unfocused. Surprise tingled through me. He was blind.

The monkey twirled down from the pole in the corner of the room and gamboled over to the desk. He ran up the leg of the chair and settled onto the Rinpoche's lap.

"I know no one should keep a monkey as a pet, but this one came to me as a baby and had lost his mother to poachers. I bottle-fed and raised him, and we remain devoted to each other. He is the sweetest animal ever. I call him Sage, because he is a green monkey. He has a sort of greenish cast to his fur, don't you think?" Sage was small with sweet, dark eyes and very large teeth. "I found him when I was traveling in Africa many years ago."

He rested a hand on the monkey's head. "Now, Sage," Rinpoche said lovingly, "I'm about to work so you must go back to your corner."

Sage touched his face with his little hand, then scampered back down the chair, heading for the pole. Suddenly he changed direction. He romped over to me, clambered up my pant leg to my chest and touched the amulet around my neck. The little monkey looked deep into my eyes, then he leapt to the ground and made his way back over to the pole where he scrambled up to his platform at the top. From there he studied me.

Chills tingled across my skin.

The Rinpoche tented his fingers in front of his chest. "You are being prepared for transformation, are you not?"

I blinked and tore my gaze from the monkey. "Um, yes ..." *How does he know that?*

The Rinpoche waved his hand dismissively. "Wao is your transformation guide? Is he not? And Old Phoenix performs the initiation? Does he not? "

I gave up trying to answer. Clearly the Rinpoche enjoyed asking rhetorical questions.

"And this last transformation, this last initiation you will take, will provide you entry into the mystical secrets of this most esoteric Order of Monks; entry into other dimensions of the mind and of the matter is already underway then? Part of the alchemy. It's just a matter of time, is it not? Please, sit." He gestured toward two chairs facing his desk.

The Rinpoche stood. He walked around the room, then circled my chair. He stopped, changed direction, and walked around my chair again, moving slowly and deliberately. When he had completed the second circle, he stopped in front of me, bent down and touched my amulet, in almost the same manner as Sage had.

"You should already be dead." He tapped the amulet gently. "This is what's been keeping you alive." He went over to the wall of cupboards behind his desk and opened one of the doors. Jars of various colors and sizes lined the shelves. He took down a jar containing a thick viscous liquid and set it down on his desk. After removing the lid, he drew up the liquid into an eye dropper and released seven drops of the amber fluid into an empty bottle. "Scorpion venom is what is needed. And some Cordyceps, along with the larvae of the Ghost moth, yartsagunbu." He pulled other jars and containers down from the shelves and added a measure of their contents into the jar with the venom. "And a pinch of … well, you don't need to know." He chuckled to himself. He put all of the containers back on the shelves and picked up the clear bottle. When he had swirled the ingredients around, he poured half of the medicine in one bottle, and half in a small glass carafe.

"I like it stirred, not shaken," Rinpoche said with a smile. His hands and fingers moved as though they had eyes guiding his every step. He glided over to where I was seated and held out the carafe, only slightly to the left of me.

I reached out and took the carafe from him.

"It's just one mouthful. Drink it all down and you should feel better soon. There is one more mouthful in this bottle that you can take with you, and you must drink that ten thousand minutes from now. For good measure." He tapped a finger on his chin. "Let's see, sixty minutes in each hour, twenty-four hours in each day, so that is seven days from now, minus one hour and one quarter, not before, not later."

"Do you know what happened to me?" I pointed to the mark on my abdomen, even though he couldn't see it. "Was I poisoned? Or hit with a death palm? I think it was the death palm. I remember—"

"It matters not, my young man," he said. "Matters not. Just that you drink in one mouthful."

I tipped back my head and downed the liquid as instructed. A fiery hot lump sank down into my belly, then radiated back outwards to the tips of my fingers, my toes and to the top of my head. My face and neck felt warm and flushed. My insides felt as though they were on fire.

"It is reaching each of your chakras, each of your energy centers, and extending outwards to your fingers and toes. It is eradicating everything poisonous inside, and revitalizing your centers. You will be okay now."

Beads of sweat bubbled up on my forehead, throat and solar plexus. I wanted to tear off my clothes and jump into ice water. Every breath came hot. Surely steam was being emitted from my ears and nose. I gripped the edge of the chair with both hands to keep from bolting out of the room. What was going on? Had I traveled all this way to die a slow, fiery death from the inside out? An agonized scream rose in my throat, but I bit my lip.

Wao watched me closely, fear dancing on his face.

I tried to smile at him, to ease his concern, but quickly gave it up. I was too concerned for myself to try and make him feel better. After what felt like hours, the internal heat diminished. My grip on the chair eased as the sweating stopped and a tremendous burst of energy surged through me. An incredible lightness came over me. I hadn't felt this good since I left New York. Eyes wide, I turned to the old man. "Thank you, Rinpoche, thank you so much."

"You are welcome, my son." He turned away in his deliberate manner, then added, as if an afterthought, "The Scorpion has finally arrived."

AVERY

If you don't change direction,
you may end up where you are heading.

—Lao Tzu

"I can't believe that freak asked me to marry him," I stirred my tea, and glanced around at the other patrons of the coffee shop. I wasn't sure who or what I was looking for, but I didn't want anyone overhearing our conversation.

"Kill me now," Katie said, as she sipped her Chai latte. "Why did you come back so early?"

"I couldn't stay another minute trapped on the same boat as Boreman or … my father." I picked at the cuticles on my fingernails. *How much should I tell her?*

"You okay? Did something else happen?" She set down her drink and straightened in her seat. "Oh, something happened. I can see it on your face. "

I stared down at the table. "It wasn't a big deal. It's just, my dad … he hit me."

"Oh my God, Avery. That rat bastard. I'll kill him myself."

I looked up at her. "It was just a slap, but Claire saw it and insisted we leave. She called my dad a beast and said she couldn't spend a moment longer with him."

"Good for her." Anger still flashed on Katie's face, but she picked up her drink again. "Why did he hit you?"

I put more sugar in my tea and attempted to suck back my tears. "Because I threw the Boreman's ring back at him. I guess that messed up my dad's grand plan for me, whatever that might be. I was so embarrassed that he hit me in front of a boat load of people. *I really don't want to talk about this anymore.* I played with the cinnamon cookie on my plate. "Let's change the topic."

"Fine. Why don't you move in with me and my parents? Now that you're besties with Raven, doing Bagua together every morning, I never get to see you. And I hate the idea of you living with your dad even more than Claire does."

"How do you know what Claire thinks?"

"She dragged you back from the holy land of vacation shopping, didn't she?" Katie grabbed my hand and studied my eyes. "All kidding aside, Avery. I mean it, move in with me."

I glanced over at the next table where a young girl with super-short spiked hair had just honed in on our conversation. She flashed a knowing smile at me.

"Hi, Av-or-ree," Bowen said. He ran up to our table. "I don't see your pup-pee, Where's your pup-pee? I know where your Dad-dee's magic door is. One, three, two, four, opens the magic door."

"Sorry, girls." Bowen's mom rushed over to collect her son. "Come on, Bowen. I said you could get one cookie on the way home."

"But I want to stay with Av-or-reee."

"No cookie, if you don't come now," she said and winked at us.

"Okay. Bye Av-or-ree. Bye Kay-tie."

I was happy for the momentary distraction of Bowen, but Katie's attention clearly hadn't been diverted. Her eyes, filled with worry, still searched my face as she waited for an answer. I covered our clasped fingers with my free hand, not certain which of us I was trying to reassure most. "I'm fine. Stop worrying. My dad's been super sweet to me since he got back."

Katie didn't look convinced, but she let go of my hand and took a sip of her latte.

"Hey, there are two of my favorite girls." Blaine waltzed up to our table and kissed each of us on the cheek. He smiled broadly as he looked at Katie. "Bet you're glad to see your world traveler back." His smile faded. "What's going on? You two look like someone died."

"Just catching up." Katie pointed to the empty chair at our table. "Want to join us? You'll have to have coffee, though. I don't think they have wheat grass shots here."

He playfully socked her arm. "You know I can't desecrate my temple with caffeine. Besides, I really hate to break up the girlfriend thing here, but we have a date … I mean … a movie to get to." Blaine glanced over at me.

"What movie?" Katie's eyes lit up.

"Ip Man," I said. "Martial arts. You wouldn't like it."

"Think about moving in with me, Avs," Katie said. "Please. And Blaine, really? Martial arts movies? Take her to a ballet once in a while."

"Hey, that's a great idea." Blaine touched his temple with one finger. "I'll take you all to the ballet. And Raven too."

"That'd be epic. Raven at a ballet? Gotta see that." Katie rolled her eyes then turned to me, the brief moment of lightness gone. "Avery. Think about what I said."

"I will." I nodded. "Promise." I pushed back my chair and stood. "And by the way, I love martial arts movies." I beamed a smile at Blaine.

He shot a smug look at Katie, then picked up my pink ballet bag and slipped his other arm through mine. We left the coffee shop and started down the street towards the movie theatre. He shifted the handle further up on his shoulder. "My God, this thing is heavier than a yammerin' yobbo!"

I laughed.

He grinned. "You don't know what I'm saying, do you?"

"Not at all, but pink looks good on you." Warmth radiated through my body. The same feeling of safety that had washed over me when I was with Claire filled me again. "You know, when Aiden was trying to tell me why we couldn't be together, I thought at first he was saying that the two of you were in love."

Blaine laughed easily. "I do love him. He's my brother, but he's really not my type at all." His eyes grew serious. He stopped in the middle of the sidewalk and reached for both of my hands. Lifting them to his lips, he kissed the back of them. "You, on the other hand, are very much my type, Avery."

Shock jolted through me. "What? Blaine, no. You can't …" I stammered. My eyes met his warm, brown ones. We had become so close. I couldn't bear to lose him too. "I …don't. Don't do this to me, Blaine."

For a moment, his eyes searched mine. Then he pressed his shut and shook his head. "I'm sorry, Avery." Blaine dropped my hands and opened his eyes. "I'm so sorry. I don't know what I was thinking. Aiden is my brother. You are my best friend. I didn't mean … You're so beautiful, that's all. Well, that's not all. But I'm sorry. I promise I will never cross that line with you again."

"Good." I was shaking. "We can't. I can't. This isn't about Aiden. He made his choice and so I made mine, to move on." A lump stuck in my throat. *Liar. You haven't moved on at all.* I shoved back the voice that shouted at me from deep down inside. "I need you, Blaine. I need you as my friend. I need to not lose you, like all the other people in my life that I have loved. Maybe that's not fair, but I couldn't handle losing you."

"Avery." Blaine shook his head again. His eyes locked onto mine, as if willing me to believe him. "You will never lose me."

I hoped with all my heart that was true. Because if I lost him too, I didn't think I could bear it.

AVERY

Think lightly of yourself, and deeply of the world.

—MiyomotoMusashi

I stepped out of the elevator at the RoofTop Lounge in The Gramercy Hotel. Walking through to the seating area, my eyes latched on to a figure huddled on a couch in a corner. Each area in the lounge was like its own private living room. There were huge potted trees and plants everywhere, with twinkle lights scattered throughout. At dusk, the skyline of Manhattan, visible through the large windows that dominated every wall, winked into life.

The figure on the couch, a man, peered up from his cell phone as though he felt me looking at him. As soon as he saw me, he leapt to his feet.

"Uncle Simon!" I rushed over and threw my arms around him. "I've been so worried."

"I don't have much time. I'm just on a stop-over, but I had to see you." He held me out at arms' length. "I need to know you're okay."

"I'm okay. Really okay. What happened in Nicaragua?"

The server approached us. "What can I get you two?" She gave Uncle Simon the once over.

"I'll have a scotch on the rocks," Simon said. "And you, Avery?"

"Do you have any green-tea soda?"

The server nodded. "Absolutely."

As the waitress walked away, Uncle Simon sat on the couch and tugged me down beside him. "Nicaragua sounded way more dramatic than it was," he said. "We were on the mountain with a mini revolution going on in the village below. We were safe, we just couldn't get out of the country. Cell phone connections aren't great there at the best of times, but with everything that was going on, it was impossible to get a decent line out. And the solar flare that left New York and the Eastern Seaboard completely without electricity affected a lot of other parts of the world too, which didn't help. How about you? Were you safe while all that was happening?"

Where would I even begin to tell him about everything that I'd been through? "We have so much to catch up on, Simon." Dropping 'Uncle' seemed right today. I was finally grown up. The past few months had definitely changed me. "But tell me, how did you finally get out of Nicaragua?"

"When the government sent more soldiers into the village, they quelled the riots. I got out a few days ago."

"I'm so relieved to see you. So much has been going on. I do martial arts and meditation every day now."

He nodded, his eyes flickering with interest. "That's good, Avs. You might need to protect yourself if…" He looked around the room. When he spoke again, his voice was low. "Do you have the necklace? You haven't taken it out of the box, have you?"

"I have the necklace, but why is it so important?" I pulled the pendent out from under my shirt. "Look. I have it here."

Simon glanced around again before leaning in closer to study it. "Didn't she tell you to keep in the box? Not to wear it? Has Peter…er, your dad seen it?"

"No, he hasn't seen it. I keep it hidden. And, yes, she told me to keep it in the box. But on the anniversary of her death, I put it on. I needed to feel her close to me."

"Oh Avery," Simon shook his head. "You have no idea what power has been unleashed. I don't know the whole story of the stone. She would never tell me."

"Doesn't that sound a little crazy to you?" I dropped the pendant back down my shirt. "Come on, unleashing something powerful by wearing a stone? She must have said that when she was dying, because she was saying all kinds of cray cray stuff in the end."

"Your mother was never crazy. Not ever. Not even in the end. She knew exactly what she was saying at all times."

I tilted my head. "Can't I just put the necklace back in the box? Not that I want to. I feel like she is with me when I wear it. I feel way stronger, more powerful. But if it's causing trouble…"

He shook his head. "You can't just put it back in the box and hope that what's been done, will be undone. It doesn't work like that. It just doesn't."

I bit my lip. "I'm so sorry. I didn't know. Well, I did know, but I didn't. I didn't mean to let the genie out of the lamp, or whatever it is I've done." I had a feeling that Simon wasn't just talking about the stone, but something else. Something more personal.

"She told me she didn't believe any of this, you know," Simon said. "Then her father gave her the diary that his father had written when he lived in the Himalayas with the mystics. She said the diary must be kept as safe as the necklace. Have you read it yet? She said it contained some answers and even more questions."

I shook my head. "I didn't get a diary. She never even mentioned one."

"It must still be there, in the house somewhere or maybe in a safety deposit box. You'll have to find it, Avery." Simon gripped my hand. "But there's something else. Something I need to tell you. Something I've wanted to tell you for a very long time."

The server arrived and set our drinks down on the coffee table in front of us. "Sorry that took so long," she said. "They had problems with the taps or something." She straightened up and stood there, waiting.

"Oh." Simon let go of me and dug into his pocket, peeled a few bills out and put them on her tray. "Thanks. I don't need change."

She smiled at him and left.

"What was it you wanted to tell me?" I touched his arm. "I'm so confused by everything. Can you help me make sense of any of it? Please?"

Simon dropped his gaze to the scotch glass in his hand.

Finally he nodded. "Avery, I …I will always be here to help you. That's what I wanted you to know. I gave you the phone so you could reach me any time."

"That's what you wanted to tell me?" My eyes narrowed. "I already knew that. Are you sure there wasn't something else?"

He drew in a deep breath and scrutinized me. "I …I want to know what's really going on in your life. Who are your friends? Who do you have a crush on? How did you get involved in martial arts? And what happened to your ballet? I want to know everything about you, your life, your friends. You are so important to me, Avery. More important than you will ever know."

I leaned against the back of the couch. "When Dad asks me about my life, I feel as if I'm being interrogated. But you never make me feel like that. You really want to know, don't you?"

"I really do."

Warmth flooded my chest. I'd almost forgotten what it was like to have family that cared about me. "I haven't left ballet, but martial arts made an impression on me. And I was crushing on a guy. His name was Aiden, but he went back to China. That's when I decided to move on. He made his choice and it wasn't me, so why keep my heart on a hook?"

"That's my girl." He patted my knee. "You deserve someone who will love you completely. Loving someone who loves someone else …well, I'm glad you've moved on." Emotions flickered through his eyes, but I couldn't decipher what they meant. My watch buzzed with a message. I glanced down and saw the time. "Hey, you're going to be late for your flight if you don't get going."

He set down his glass and stood up. "Avery, there's one more thing." He held out his hand.

"Sure, what's up?" I grasped his hand and he pulled me to my feet.

"I …I love you."

Why does it seem like there is so much more he wants to say? I squeezed his hand. "I love you too, Simon."

Chapter 33

AIDEN

In thinking, keep to the simple.

—Lao Tsu

"Your color better, Aiden." Old Phoenix pointed to a chair beside him for me to sit on. He lit another candle to brighten the dark cave of his library room. The light of the flickering flame sent out shadows dancing across the wall. "Your visit to the Rinpoche was good? I think soon you visit Mirror Pond, once more. Do you think you can stay out of sacred waters this time?"

I nodded. I was deeply grateful that Old Phoenix would allow me to go to the Mirror Pond again. My cheeks flushed when I thought about how I had leapt into the sacred water, thinking I could somehow touch Avery.

"The Mirror Pond isn't a quick method to astral projection, Aiden. The pond is a sacred divination tool that reveals and clarifies deep questions. I trust you and Wao have fasted for the past three days?"

I nodded again.

"I've also fasted for the past three days..."

My eyebrows rose.

"Yes, I am coming this time to make sure that the sacred waters remain that way. Wao has your ceremonial robes. I will meet you at the pond." His eyes, filled with wisdom, probed mine. "The question is always deeper than you imagine," Old Phoenix said softly, again seeming to read my mind. "And then, of course, there are times when we think our question so very deep. Usually that is the one that is not." He grinned at me in a youthful, impish way before laughing his deep belly laugh and sweeping out of the room.

I walked to the door and glanced back, noticing that our shadows still flickered on the wall. *How can that be? I'm over here and he has already left?* I scratched my head and walked out.

Wao waited for me outside. "Hurry, Aiden. The sun is rising. We have to leave soon. Look at me. You have me worried like an old dog. I think I might put a leash on you this time." He laughed as he handed me the sapphire robe. "Take your clothes off. We'll drop them by the side of the road and pick them up later. Come, the sun is almost here."

I changed quickly and we climbed the path that wound its way upwards, passing the time telling jokes and talking about everything except the Mirror Pond. Strong breezes churned up dust on the road and threatening clouds gathered. The sun that had started its journey across the sky was now completely hidden behind angry-looking clouds. Bitter winds chilled us to the bone. At least this time I was a little more prepared for the unusual weather conditions. What I wasn't prepared for was the answer to the simple question that loomed before me. How could I live up to my promise to dedicate my life to being a monk, when my heart belonged to Avery? From the moment I had set foot in the Wudang Mountains, I knew what I wanted—to be a monk and to live a monastic life. I was honored to be the only foreigner ever invited to take the highest initiation into the Order of the Celestial Dragon Gate, where I would learn the most secret esoteric teachings. It had been divined long before I had arrived, long before I had ever even been born: a foreigner would come to live among them.

We rounded the bend and the jewel pond, cradled by massive mountains, came into view. The lake was spectacular. As we approached, the surface started churning into a mud-colored frenzy. Wao sat down and motioned for me to join him. A pair of feet beneath a swirling robe approached us. I looked up and Old Phoenix, tall and steady as an old, deeply rooted tree, smiled down.

Wao shaded his eyes with one hand as he peered up at him. "Old Phoenix? You never come to visioning anymore."

Old Phoenix laughed, looking like Zeus with his beard, long hair and flowing robes, Mount Olympus rising behind him.

"Aiden, time to meditate," Wao yelled out over the howling winds.

Old Phoenix sat down beside us and in an instant his breath was even.

I breathed rhythmically, followed my breath out, and in. My mind settled into a vast space between, and once again I was 'seeing' the reflective surface of the Mirror Pond.

I envisioned the day I arrived at the Wudang. Then the day Old Phoenix gave each Bagua Brother an amulet. The day the yarrow stalks were thrown and my future revealed. As I concentrated, a ripple started at one end of the pond, and like a scene change in a movie I glimpsed Avery sitting on her bed, looking at a photograph. Involuntarily, I started to stand, but Wao grabbed my hand and held me firmly down. I wasn't about to jump in again, but I was shocked to see her there, so close. Her beauty. Her strength. Her vulnerability. Her luminescence.

Avery fingered the pendant at her throat. Beside me, Old Phoenix drew in a rapid breath. Could he see her too? Suddenly, her bedroom door flew open and her father filled the frame. His eyes were flashing, his face red. He held a pile of papers that he shook at Avery as he yelled at her. I strained to make out the words, but the howling wind trapped within the walls of the mountains was deafening.

Avery's father launched himself across the room, struck her on the cheek and ripped the necklace from her neck. Wao grabbed my arm again as I started to rise, fists clenched. How dare he strike her? His own daughter. My Avery.

The winds whipped up, reflecting the fury that roared through me and sending more ripples across the pond. Suddenly the azure blue water returned to its natural calm state. The pictures disappeared. I slid to the ground, completely spent.

Old Phoenix leapt to his feet. "Aiden, you must not allow Avery to stay in the house with that evil man."

Wao looked at Old Phoenix as if he had just grown ten thousand heads. All I could think of was how to get Avery away from her father as soon as possible. My chest ached at the thought of her being hurt. She was in danger. That was what I needed to see. That was what had been eating at me ever since I had met Avery and her father.

Old Phoenix rested a hand on my shoulder. "Before you commit yourself to life as a monk here, you must go back for Avery's necklace and bring it here, along with all the Bagua brothers."

I blinked. Where had that come from? Why would Old Phoenix want me to get Avery's necklace back from her father and bring it here? Shouldn't it go back to Avery? It belonged to her.

"Avery's mom gave her that necklace before she died. When I get it back from her father, I have to return it to her. I can't..."

"I don't care who it belongs to, just bring it here, with Blaine and Luc. This is vitally important, Aiden. You will understand more when you get back."

"I don't—"

He lifted a hand. "You will find out in time. For now, you must rescue this young woman from cruelty and bring the necklace here with the rest of the brothers. And Aiden, be vigilant. Very vigilant. I am asking you to blindly trust me and do what I instruct. All will become clear in time."

"But..."

"Aiden, being part of an order of monks requires one to relinquish control, to surrender oneself without question. Are you willing to do this?"

I grasped at my wildly racing thoughts. I had never been asked to blindly trust before. In theory, I had been absolutely prepared to surrender to a greater will, but in reality, what he was asking me to do didn't make sense. It seemed in that moment that the entire universe and every creature in it fell silent, awaiting my answer.

"We don't get to choose when and why we will be asked to surrender," Old Phoenix whispered gently.

I lifted my chin. I did trust Old Phoenix, completely and unequivocally. He would never do anything to harm another being. A surge of energy poured through me, a wave of certainty. I had to help Avery and, in doing so, place my trust in Old Phoenix. "Of course I will do what you ask of me."

Wao had been quiet throughout the conversation. He had been raised in a country where deference to a master was common. I had been raised to question everything and everyone. Having power over others could be very enticing, but there was power, too, in submission.

Wao and Old Phoenix released a collective breath. Old Phoenix knew my soul better than me. No doubt he was aware that I would trip over being asked to blindly trust.

"I'm coming, Avery," I whispered into the wind. "I'm coming home. I'll be there soon."

Chapter 34

AVERY

Music in the soul can be heard in the universe.

—Lao Tzu

The words seemed to float on a waft of wind that blew through my open window. "I'm coming home. I'll be there soon." My head shot up. Was that Aiden?

My father clutched the necklace he had just ripped from my neck.

I jumped at a loud cracking sound and brilliant flash of light. I turned my head. A transformer exploding outside my window momentarily lit up his hideous smile in a flare of sparks. My TV blinked off, came back on as a screen of static noise, then went blank. It was still twilight so we hadn't been plunged into total darkness.

"What the fuck?" my Dad muttered, pacing my room. "This can't be happening. Not another geomagnetic storm." He stomped over to the window to look out. "Yup, something's happening. Hope those back-up generators the mayor installed after the last storm actually work."

I sat slumped on my bed, still reeling from another stinging blow to my cheek. The chain had dug into my skin before the clasp finally snapped, and something trickled down my neck. I reached up and wiped at it. When I looked down at my fingers, blood dripped from their tips. I looked up at my father, my eyes wide with shock. Like the transformer outside of my window, something exploded inside of me. "Why are you doing this?" I held up my fingers to show him the blood. "Why? What would Mom think of you?"

"Avery, I told you never to lie to me. First you sneak into my office. Then I discover you had the necklace all along. Why are *you* doing this

199

to *me?* I gave you and your mother everything. First she betrayed me, and now you."

"What are you talking about? Mom never betrayed you."

The lights flickered to life briefly, accompanied by the hum of various air systems and electronic devices coming on, then died again, leaving the apartment even more deadly quiet than before. My father looked sad and tired, but his Jedi mind tricks no longer worked on me. He had just stolen my mother's necklace. *I hate him.* If what Raven had told me she overheard, and if even a small part of what I'd been reading about the elite Skull and Bones Society and the Illuminati was true, my father could actually be a Master of War.

"Come on, generators." Dad pressed a palm to the window frame and leaned closer to the glass as he looked out. "Come on, babies, I've got things to do and I need electricity to do them!" He turned to look at me as if just remembering my presence. A scowl crossed his face. "I'll figure out what to do with you later."

He picked up my cell phone and shoved it into his pocket, then grabbed my laptop. "I'll tell your little friends when they call that you aren't well." He stalked to the door. When he reached it, he gave me a little wave. Mom's necklace dangled from his fingers as he offered me a weird smile of victory. Then he walked into the hallway and pulled the door closed behind him.

"No!" I sprang from the bed and scrambled for the door. Just as I reached it and grabbed the handle, a key turned in the lock.

From behind the door, my dad threw out his parting words. "I'll be back in a few days to deal with you."

"But, Dad," I wailed, flinging myself against the door. "I have my dance recital on Saturday. I have to be at rehearsals."

"Guess you should have thought about that sooner." His voice was cold and held a warning. "Remember, I have eyes and ears everywhere. Don't even think that you can outsmart me, Avery. Your beloved Ruby will have to answer for anything you try to do while I'm away."

I gulped and slid down the door, landing in a hopeless heap on the floor.

AVERY

Always be on the lookout for ways to turn a problem into an opportunity for success.

—Lao Tzu

Something rapped at my bedroom window and caught my attention. I spun around. *Was that a hand knocking on the glass? Impossible, I'm seven floors up?* I rushed over and looked out to see Blaine clinging to the iron railing. He used his legs to swing onto the tiny balcony. I tried to open my French doors but they wouldn't budge. I turned to the old casement window and yanked at the crank. It groaned in protest and opened slightly.

"Blaine, what are you doing out there? My dad had the French doors welded shut a few weeks ago, saying they were dangerous. This is as far as I can get the window open."

"Are you okay? There was another geomagnetic storm last night. They couldn't get the new city generators to come on line until about four this morning. I worried when I couldn't reach you on your phone. Then when your Dad answered I knew I had to come."

Footsteps sounded in the hallway outside my bedroom door and I put my finger to my lips to hush Blaine.

"Avery." My dad's voice was muffled through the door. "The generators came online early this morning. The airports are open again, so I'm leaving now for Washington. Don't try anything stupid."

I waited until I heard the front door slam before returning to the window. Thankfully, my balcony was on the park side of the building. Dad would be picked up by Lou inside the courtyard. No chance to see Blaine's daredevil act.

"Hey, Blaine." I recognized Bowen's voice. "Can I be Spiderman too?"

"No, Bowen, stay where you are. You don't have your magic spider web to help you."

"What is going on?" I strained to see where Bowen was.

His voice rose up from below. "I know some magic. One, three, two, four, opens the magic door. It's in Avery's daddy's drawer. I saw him."

"What are you talking about Bowen?" I shook my head and sighed.

"Bye Bye. I'm going to get my magic spider web."

Blaine tried to squeeze himself through the narrow casement window. "I'm like a dolphin. I can dynamically make myself thinner when I need to." He got stuck partway into my room.

"Not dynamic enough." I giggled.

I went to my dresser and came back with a nail file. "I should leave you stuck there. What were you thinking, climbing up seven floors on the outside of a building?"

"I had to make sure you were okay."

I took my nail file and went to work removing the crank mechanism to release the window. When I finished and tugged the window open wider, Blaine slid into the room and landed in a heap on the floor.

"Good morning, sunshine." He gripped the window frame and hauled himself to his feet. "Your father told me you were sick and couldn't see anyone. I didn't believe him, so here I am to rescue you."

"He locked me in. He found out I went into his office and he's furious. He's got my necklace."

"It won't look very good on him, I'm afraid." Blaine smiled. "Unless he's bought a new pair of pumps to go with it."

"Be serious, Blaine." I punched him in the arm. "I've got to get out of here. I need to find the diary."

A light rap on the door jolted us both into silence. Then Blaine nudged me and nodded at the door. Obviously whoever was out there knew I was inside and would wonder why I wasn't answering.

I cleared my throat. "Yes?"

"Do you want anything before I leave for my sister's? I'm taking Rasta with me."

The knots in my stomach eased at the sound of Ruby's sweet voice.

"All I need is some food, Ruby."

"I brought you a tray earlier while you were sleeping. Just over by the desk there, dear."

I glanced over to see the breakfast she'd left me. "Thank you, Ruby. Thanks so much."

"Are you going to be okay, dear? I don't have to go, you know. The subways aren't running because the generators aren't powerful enough. I'm going to start walking, and hope I can get a cab that will take Rasta."

"I'll be fine, you go and have a good visit." I glanced at Blaine and he nodded.

"Your father left for Washington when he found out the airports opened up this morning. I could let you out…"

There was nothing I wanted more, but I couldn't let Ruby suffer because of me. "No, Ruby. He'll fire you, and I know how much your family needs you working. Please go. I'll be okay."

After Ruby's steps had faded down the hallway, I said in a low voice, "I have got to find that diary. I know it's here somewhere."

"Did you hear what Bowen just said to me outside?"

I nodded. "Something about a magic door."

"That's right. He said he saw your father go into his desk and open a magic door with one, three, two, four."

"Blaine." I grabbed his arm. "That has to be the pin code for the security pad that's inside his desk! Bowen knew it all along; we just didn't know what he was talking about."

"Ruby's already gone, so we can't ask her to open the door again," Blaine said.

I let go of him and pursed my lips. "Do you still have those long pins you were going to use on the office door?"

"No, I didn't bring them with me. I didn't know what I was doing with them, anyway. I've just seen it done on TV."

I tapped the nail file on the edge on the window frame as if that might help me come up with another idea. "I've got it. We could start a fire. They put in a new fire alarm and sprinklers about two years ago. The whole building will empty and we can slip into my dad's office. Fire is the only thing that overrides the door lock. We can get in, then open the magic door."

"Hey, I'm impressed," said Blaine. "Let's go for it."

I grabbed the lighter I used for the vanilla scented candles from my bedside table. "Put the waste paper bin under the smoke detector."

Blaine picked up the bin and moved it to the far side of the room by the windows. "I didn't tell you everything your father said when he answered your phone. He said he was taking you away soon. He was just finalizing details."

"What a bastard." I crumpled a few papers and crossed the room to throw them in the bin. "He's locked the door from the outside. It's new and not linked into the fire alarm system. We'll have to figure out a way to get it open."

"No big deal. I'll break it down once the alarm starts."

I swept the room with my eyes, snatched up my knapsack and loaded it with some random stuff. "Okay. Light her up now."

I handed Blaine the lighter. He flicked it once and set the papers on fire. They roared up and died out quickly. The alarm remained silent.

We exchanged looks. I loaded up the bin with more paper and added some cotton t-shirts for good measure. Blaine lit them again. I fanned the flames with a large notebook. Sparks flew into the air.

In seconds, the fire alarm blared. Blaine took a few deep, grounding breaths, then reached his arms up and around and brought his palms together. He turned to the right, and moved his foot back for an open stance. He flew towards the door, his body looking like it possessed the force of a tsunami. With his open palm, he smashed against the wood. His hand hit right above the lock and it gave way with a splintering sound.

"Hey, it worked!" Blaine spun around to face me.

"Wouldn't your foot have worked easier?" I hurried toward the door. The fire alarm pierced my ears.

"Yeah, but there's nothing like feeling internal energy flow from your palm." A huge grin spread across his face and his entire body shimmered with light. "Maybe Aiden isn't the only one with all the power."

I rolled my eyes as Blaine made a dash for my dad's office. I turned back into the room to make sure I hadn't forgotten anything. An ember glowed on the rug by the curtains. I must have fanned the flames too vigorously. Before I could cross the room to step on it, the ember ignited and flames licked up the curtains. "Blaine!" I turned to see him clambering down the staircase two steps at a time.

"There's a fire." I pointed into the room, transfixed.

"I know. But it should burn itself out in the bin. Hurry up. We have to find the diary." He stopped mid-stride and looked back at me.

"No, it's spreading." I rushed back into the room and grabbed a sweatshirt from my bed. I beat at the rug and the curtains, but the fire continued to grow. Flames crawled across the floor and licked at the blankets on my bed. The sprinklers sprang into action as Blaine reached the doorway.

"Get out of here! You have a chance to get the diary now. Let the sprinklers do their job." Blaine latched onto my arm and pulled me away from the fire. He shoved me into the hallway and dragged me down the stairs.

I stumbled trying to keep up to Blaine, who didn't hesitate at the next locked door. Without slowing down, he prepared himself to palm strike another door. I reached around him and opened it. "The sprinklers overrode the lock. Remember?"

Blaine shrugged then dashed to the drawer and opened it. I came up beside him. Fingers trembling, I reached for the security pad and typed in 1,3,2,4.

Something tapped against the office window. I whirled toward it, my heart pounding.

Bowen's nose was pressed against the glass. "Hi Av-or-ee, I love fire. I love to help." "

"It's Bowen. We have to get him out of the building."

"I see him." Blaine hurtled past me towards the window.

Bowen waved to us. "My Fire is better than yours."

"Sure it is honey." I gripped the edge of the desk and stole a glance around the room to see what the security pad may have revealed.

Blaine pushed the window open and grabbed Bowen, pulling him into the room. "How did you manage to climb up?"

Bowen shrugged. "I do it all the time. Look, you found the magic door." He pointed to the far wall.

I followed to where he was pointing. One of the panels was ajar. "I've seen these wooden panels a million times and never once imagined one would open up." I strode toward it and pulled it open. For a few seconds, all I could do was stare, my mouth hanging open. An entire room was hidden behind the walls of my dad's office. But why? What did he keep in here? I shook my head. No time to wonder. We had to be out of the building in less than a minute or we wouldn't be leaving at all. Outside, sirens screamed, getting louder as emergency vehicles approached the Dakota.

"See, Avery?" Bowen beamed. "It's the magic door."

"I see it, Bowen." I stepped into the room. A huge filing cabinet dominated the wall to the right. I yanked open a drawer.

Blaine followed me into the room and grasped my elbow. "What are we going to do with Bowen, Avery? We have to get him downstairs."

I was completely engrossed with what I had found. "There are dossiers on Veronika, Valerie, you and Aiden and … and me. My father obviously had a PI following us and reporting to him. I'm taking all of this to look at later." I pulled open another drawer and scanned the papers tucked into a file folder. "Here's a DNA document, stock certificates, and look at this file full of financial institutions he owns, resource companies, banks and pharmaceuticals. He's into everything." I shoved as much as I could into my knapsack. "We need to find the diary, and my necklace. They must be here."

Blaine tugged on my arm. "We have to leave, Avery. It won't take the firemen long to figure out where the fire started."

"Are you happy Av-or-ee?" Bowen said. "Where's the pupp-ee?"

"Ruby has him. Blaine, get Bowen to safety." I pulled my arm out of Blaine's grasp and shut the filing cabinet drawer. I headed over to a pile of boxes in one corner of the room. "I'll be right behind you."

Blaine didn't move. "I'm not leaving without you. But we have to go—now!"

"Where are we go-ing? Will we see the pupp-pee?"

"Please go. Get Bowen to safety."

I rifled through the first box, the urgent need to find the diary and my necklace over-riding my fear of the fire. I waded through statues and artifacts and papers before I reached the bottom of the box. No necklace. Frantic now, I pulled open another box and looked inside. "Look! There are stacks of unopened letters addressed to Uncle Simon and my mom." I shoved them into my backpack and moved to a third box.

Blaine came over to me. "Let's go." The urgency in his voice finally broke through the spell the room had cast on me. I picked up a book with a magnificently carved wooden jacket just as he grabbed my arm and pulled me out of the room.

"It's the diary, Blaine." I held up the book. "I found it. My necklace must be there too."

He let go of me and turned to slam the wooden panel shut. "If what's in there is so important, these panels are likely fireproof. We'll come back for your necklace later."

He grabbed my hand and Bowen's, and tugged us both toward the office door. Cool water sprayed through the sprinklers, drenching our hair and clothes as we crossed the room. I stopped abruptly at the sight of my phone on my dad's desk. "Wait." I freed my hand from Blaine's and ran toward the desk. Bowen sang his magic number song as Blaine prodded him through the office door and they both went into the hallway. I grabbed the phone and shoved it into the pocket of my jeans. Spinning around, I started for the door behind Blaine and Bowen.

Just before I reached it, a loud click, the same one I had heard when I was in the office before with my dad, startled me and I stopped. A clear Lucite tube flew down from the ceiling, encircling me and trapping me inside. I raised my hands and felt all around the insides of the tube, my heart pounded when I realized there was no escape from the narrow enclosure.

"Avery, what the hell?"

Blaine's voice sounded muffled. The air inside felt hot and thick. "Oh my god, Blaine. Get me out of here."

"Just breathe, Avery." He ran his hands around the outside of the tube. "I'll get you out."

I pushed against the tube, some kind of security feature my father had installed. I felt like a caged animal. Blood pounded in my ears. "I can't get out. I have to get out." I smacked the inside of the hard plastic with both palms. "Blaine, quick. You have to get me out."

"Deep, slow breaths, Avs. Remember the subway tunnels? You got through those. You can get through this."

"I heard a click just before I got to the door."

"I stepped there too, but I didn't hear any click." Blaine studied the apparatus. He was inches away from me but, with thick Lucite separating us, he may as well been on another continent. My throat tightened and I struggled to draw a breath.

Blaine pressed his hand to the cylinder where mine was. "Stay calm. I'll get you out."

I forced myself to take a deep, calming breath. The fog swirling through my head cleared. "Wait a minute. Dad once told me he had been to the White House where they had a top secret room rigged with a security system calibrated so finely to the exact pressure of each person coming into the room that if they tried to leave with even a single sheet of paper, it would pick up the difference in weight and trap them. The last time I needed an ink cartridge to print out an essay, I was about to leave the office with one, when Dad stopped me and flipped a switch. I bet he had the same system put in here. I took some papers and the diary from the room. They're in my knapsack."

"Well, this thing is so tight you aren't going to get anything out of there … Okay, Avery, I want you to take another deep breath. Focus on my eyes." Smoke billowed through the hallway behind him and Bowen coughed.

I shook my head. "Blaine. We don't have time for this. Go on without me. Get Bowen out of the building."

"No, Avery. You don't need to panic. You are standing on a mechanism, that's why you heard the click. Now look at me. Right at me. That's it. We're going to practice a very simple exercise, just like mornings at the park. Take a breath and allow yourself to feel very, very comfortable. Your breathing is already starting to slow down, isn't it? That's right. Very good. Now, does one of your arms feel lighter than the other? Yes, that's it. The left one. I can see it's already starting to rise up. Good. Now think of yourself as much, much lighter than you are right now. Believe that you are becoming lighter, your body is lifting up, reducing the weight load on your feet. That's great, Avery, you are doing great..."

Click. Whirr. The vacuum tube released and shot back up into the ceiling. Blaine snatched me up from the concealed scale under my feet and lifted me to safety. Outside the office door, he set me down on my feet.

The smoke was so thick in the hallway, I couldn't see to the end of it.

"But..." I glanced back at the room, still not sure what had happened.

"The magic of the mind. True alchemy." Blaine flashed me a grin as he grabbed Bowen's and my hands again. "Run now. Ask questions later."

The three of us dashed to the stairwell. Blaine let go of Bowen's hand and reached for the knob, but pulled back as soon as his fingers touched it. "It's hot. There's fire on the other side of this door too."

My eyes narrowed. "How did the fire get behind that wall? That doesn't make sense."

"I love fire," Bowen said. "I made a fire too, just like you, Spiderman."

"Sure you did." I patted Bowen's arm, partly to placate him and partly to calm myself.

Blaine looked around wildly. "We can't take the elevator."

I squeezed his hand. "I bet we can, they run on an ancient hydraulic system, they'll still work."

We rushed back down the hall to the elevator. Blaine pushed the button and I held my breath. Would the elevator still be running, with the power out and the building in lockdown? I felt the heat on my back as sweat trickled down my spine. If the doors wouldn't open, we were out of options. All three of us would die in the fire we had—I couldn't allow myself to think about it.

The elevator doors slid open. Blaine let go of our hands as the three of us jumped inside. He slid one arm around Bowen's shoulders and the other around mine. I was shaking and he pulled me closer.

Completely drained, I let my head fall onto his shoulder.

He kissed the top of my head lightly. "I love you, Avery. I just wish you could open that door with me."

I lifted my head and looked at Blaine. He'd spoken so quietly, almost in a whisper. Had he really said those words?

He didn't meet my questioning gaze.

"What door?" Bowen said. "The magic door? You already opened it."

So he did say it.

"Let's not tell anyone about the magic door, okay Bowen?" Blaine said.

"Is it a secret?" Bowen's eyebrows drew together. "My daddy says I don't know how to keep a secret."

The elevator finally came to a thud at the ground level and the doors slid open. We stumbled through the lobby and out to the courtyard where firemen battled the blaze. Through the thick smoke, paramedics carrying oxygen masks rushed towards us.

Bowen's dad was right behind them and threw his arms around Bowen. "I couldn't find you. Where were you? I've been so worried, Bowen."

"I was in the magic room with Avery and Blaine. They brought me back with them, so the fire wouldn't hurt us."

"Right, the magic room you keep talking about." His dad shook his head as he sat him down. "Okay, Bowen, whatever you say. I'm just glad you're safe, buddy."

Blaine and I exchanged a look. As long as no one took Bowen seriously, like we hadn't, the magic room would stay a secret.

AIDEN

The words of truth are always paradoxical.

—Lao Tsu

"It's a touch-screen TV, Wao." I gestured at the unit set in the back of the airplane seat in front of him.

He tapped the screen, delighted when it responded. "Aiden, this is like touching another world!"

A flight attendant stopped her cart at the end of our seats. "Would you like a drink?"

"Absolutely." Wao smiled. "I'll have the ruby red Cab Sav."

"Cab Sav?" My eyebrows rose. "Since when did you become a wine expert?"

"Oh, Aiden, let loose a little." He giggled as he took one mini bottle of red wine and motioned to the attendant for a second one. "We are going all the way to New York. Maybe we need a third one for my friend, Aiden. These are very tiny bottles."

The flight attendant handed him three mini bottles of the Cabernet Sauvignon and two plastic wine glasses.

I watched him for a few minutes, an inexplicable agitation growing within me. Finally, I touched his arm. "Wao, you shouldn't be drinking."

"I love these little bottles." Wao held one up and examined it. His cheeks had already turned red. "They're so cute. Like you. You're very serious, Aiden. Has anyone told you you're like a disapproving father? You are, you know. Disapproving." Wao cracked open another bottle, poured the wine into a plastic glass and held it out to me. "Come on now, drink up, Denny. That's what I'm going to call you from now on. Denny. Now come on, have some. Wine is very good for you..."

I lifted a hand. "No, thanks."

"Oh Denny," Wao waggled the plastic glass in front of me "This so much fun. Old Phoenix and I enjoy an evening with wine once in a while. No Trace brings it to us. And no one ever finds out." Wao pulled his passport from the back pocket of the seat in front of him. "Why do you think we call him No Trace?" He waved the document at me, winked and continued in a light voice, "No Trace. Get it? He can make passport. He can get wine. He knows where you are even when you don't. No one ever knows where he is, except when he appears."

"I'm surprised," I said. "I didn't think monks drank."

"We have Chateux Neuf-du-Pape, a very fine French wine. And, umm, Malbec, from Argentina. Where's Argentina? Will we be close to Argentina when we get to New York?"

"I know nothing of wine and I want to know nothing."

"What's the matter, Denny? Was your father a drunk? And now you think no one should drink?"

My face burned. Wao hadn't meant to hurt me, but I felt deeply wounded inside.

"You have needed to face the anger you feel toward your father." Wao gripped my hand. "This is good. I have known for a long time you had anger inside, I just didn't know exactly why. Now I do. Now you do. So let's keep drinking..."

I never had any desire to drink. I never wanted to become my father, and I secretly feared that drinking would release the same demon in me that had been released in him when he drank. The pain of my father's broken promises raged inside me. He always promised to quit drinking and he never did. Then he promised the night before he disappeared that he would always be there for us, and after that he never was.

It wasn't long before Wao fell asleep, wedged into the narrow passenger seat beside me. I tried to sleep, but I had so much to think about. Avery. Her father. My father. And why Old Phoenix wanted me to bring Avery's necklace to him, along with my Bagua brothers. I calculated the remaining days for my next dose of the Rinpoche's cure.

Wao woke up disoriented and hung-over. I fed him dense airline croissants and muddy coffee. He rested his head against the back of the seat. "Ohhh, Denny," Wao pressed a hand to his stomach, "I'm not feeling too good."

"Does this always happen when you drink?" I tugged the airsickness bag out of the back of the seat, just in case. "Why would you put yourself through this kind of torture?"

"I have never had more than a small glass with Old Phoenix," Wao whispered, holding his head in both hands. "I just wanted to break through another layer of you, Aiden. Like the first time at the Mirror Pond when I had to swear at you to wake you up."

I kept my eye on him until we landed and then, with a sigh of relief, returned the airsickness bag to the holder in the seat in front of me.

The taxi driver pulled over to the side of the road to let us out. I went to pay the fare, but Wao interjected, "You took us long way. We pay only forty-six dollars."

I shook my head. "It's okay, Wao, I've got this."

"Aiden, you would pay an elephant his weight in gold if I allowed it."

"Wao, it's okay."

"It's fifty-four dollars," the taxi driver said. "I don't care who pays, just pay."

I counted out fifty-four dollars and gave him a dollar tip.

"Gee thanks, cheapskate." The man scowled and shoved the money into his shirt pocket.

I climbed out of the cab after Wao.

"What are you doing, Aiden? You gave him too much," Wao said. "You must learn to negotiate."

"Here, the fare is the fare. You don't negotiate."

"But the meter said fifty-two dollars, and he asked for fifty-four dollars. You should have paid forty dollars, because he certainly took us the long way around; they always do when they think you don't know better. And still you pay him fifty-five dollars."

"The fare was fifty dollars. With toll booths and tax it came to fifty-four dollars, and with a tip its' fifty-five dollars," I explained, dropping my wallet back into the pocket of my jeans. I slung my bag over one shoulder, and picked up Wao's small suitcase.

"Aiden. What kind of world have you brought me to? How can anyone get a fair price for anything if you simply pay what's asked for?

There is beauty in a finely negotiated barter. You have deprived that man of his art!"

Wao stood on the sidewalk, New York traffic whizzing by him, both hands planted firmly on his hips.

I repressed a grin. Haggling over prices had taken me ages to get used to in China. Wao was likewise going to have trouble adjusting here.

I dragged myself from the deep sleep that follows severe sleep deprivation. Wao and I barely arrived at Luc's apartment before we stumbled into our rooms and fell onto the beds. I had been awake for more than forty-eight hours, and had fasted for several days. I was weak and the ache in my gut that had all but disappeared after meeting with the Rinpoche, had returned. Not quite with the vengeance of before, but it was there all the same. The time to take the second vial of medicine was approaching, and I needed to ground myself.

I sat on my bed, folded my legs and rested the backs of my palms on my knees. I followed my breath out while chanting silently, Om Mani Padme Hum...Om Mani Padme Hum. Over and over, I repeated the phrase, looking for the space between the words, the space between the sounds in my mind.

Soon I would learn the deepest mystical secrets of the Order. All of my Bagua, all of my meditation, all of my transformation work was leading to the time when I would learn the oldest mystical secrets left on this earth, held by this very small, very secretive group of monks. Old Phoenix had given me hints of what was to come, the depths of deeper wisdom and the unlocking of great secrets. The ceremony would confer on me greater responsibility than I ever dreamed possible. I rose from my meditation, feeling subtle energies shifting internally. My soul had wandered from its sanctuary and now I felt it returning.

I left my room and went down the hall to see Wao. I found him sitting cross-legged for his meditation, and I backed out of the room out of respect. Lately, I had found the world a little less solid than I had believed, time a little less linear, physicality a little less rooted to reality. A shudder moved through my body.

Wao came out of the bedroom and looked at me, smiled and said, "Denny, I like where you've been in your mind."

I realized then that I hadn't gotten up and left the room earlier, it had just been an illusion created in my meditation.

Wao made the movement of the swimming dragon, dipping low to the ground in one graceful swoop. "Are we going to go save the girl now?"

Chapter 37

AVERY

Great acts are made up of small deeds.

—Lao Tsu

"Bowen tells us that he went to get his magic spider web, then from the balcony of your bedroom, he watched you light the fire. After he saw this, he went back to his room, lit a fire to help you out, then jumped to the balcony of your father's office and witnessed you entering a magic room," snarled the detective with the hangdog face.

"Well, that's what happened, pretty much," I said, resigned to the fact that I was about to go to jail for arson. It seemed I'd been here for hours already, going over the story again and again, and then again. The detective had sat me down in the sparse interview room, after summoning me from Claire's house.

The detective cocked his head, clearly not buying the story. His jowly face was puffy, and his round eyes were soft, like a dog's. He took a deep breath. "Okay, how did Bowen get on the balcony to see into your bedroom, and how did he get to the office window and get in? I gotta say, Ms. Adams, the story doesn't make sense. All testimonies will be cross-checked. Do you want to change any of your statements?"

"No, sir," I said. So many things were fighting for my attention, like the DNA document I had found in my father's secret room. And the fact that Blaine and I had done more damage to the Dakota than we had intended. Luckily no one had gotten hurt.

I knew Blaine would tell the truth, and Bowen wouldn't be able to tell a lie. I just wanted all these questions to end. I had done all of this to get out of the prison my father put me in, and now it was looking like I was headed to a real prison.

"Blaine Wells is saying essentially the same as you, which is essentially the same as Bowen, which isn't really possible. We both know that Bowen couldn't possibly navigate one balcony, let alone two, on the face of the Dakota. And why would you light a fire in your own bedroom? If you're trying to protect Bowen, don't. We won't charge him. He's unable to discern right from wrong; we won't punish him for that. We just want the truth of what happened. The most we will do to Bowen is get him some help."

"Bowen told you what happened. I lit the fire in my bedroom."

"And a magic room? Come on, Ms. Adams. How do you expect me to believe that? I know you and Blaine are protecting that poor child. I know you wouldn't light a fire in your own apartment. I know Bowen likes lighting fires. He has a history of it."

"Bowen is telling the truth. I lit the fire."

"Okay, Ms. Adams, I'm not getting anywhere, with any of you. You and Mr. Wells can go, but don't leave the city. I'll have more questions for you. I don't know what your game is, missy, but you aren't helping Bowen or his family with this bogus story. I can tell you that right now."

"Aren't you going to arrest me?"

"Avery! Don't say anything more!" Marly swept into the room and slapped her bulging briefcase on the table.

"Blackstone? What are you doing here? We haven't called the DA's office. We don't even know what we're dealing with yet."

"I know she couldn't have anything to do with whatever happened."

"This is highly inappropriate. A prosecutor from the DA's office can't behave like a defense attorney. What the hell are you doing?"

"Release her from the interview, and I'll tell you what this is about in private. This witness is part of a much bigger investigation."

"I've already released her." He raised his hands and then dropped them, as if everyone around him was hopelessly stupid.

I stood up from the metal chair, wanting to get out of there before the detective changed his mind. Marly gave me a look that said *scram*. I made my way to the door and left.

Blaine was outside, leaning against the building. His face lit up when he saw me. "They said you can go back to the apartment." He grabbed my hand and whisked me toward the sidewalk.

"Blaine, I looked at some of the papers last night that I took from the secret room."

Blaine stepped up our pace and went quiet. I understood him immediately. I wouldn't say any more until we were far enough away from the building to talk without being overheard.

A block later, he slowed his pace a little. "We're safe now, Avery."

"I don't feel safe at all." I squeezed his hand. "I found something. DNA documents. And they proved that my father is not my father. There is a whole bunch of technical stuff I don't understand, but the date was just before my mother got sick. Am I going nuts here, or do you think my father might have poisoned her or something?"

"I don't think you're nuts, but maybe you're getting paranoid. Your father can be nasty, but killing your mother? That's a whole other level of evil. He's way too smart for that."

"He said the other day that mom betrayed him. What if she did? If he isn't my father, then my mom must have slept with someone else. If he found out, that would explain his strange behavior towards me."

"Well, he's human." Blaine stopped short on the crowded sidewalk. "And he's a man. If the woman he claims to have loved so much betrayed him, I guess there's no telling what he would be capable of."

Someone jostled me from behind and we started walking again, slipping into the flow of the pedestrians. "What if he thinks he's so powerful he's beyond the law?" I stopped and waved my arms around at the grey buildings, the sunless sky, the empty-faced people mindlessly surging along the sidewalks. "I feel like the city is turning ugly, Blaine. It's been dark for days now. No sun. No birds singing. Everything feels dead here. Nothing feels right. Something's going on and I have to get to the truth. Unfortunately, I feel like I can't trust anyone to give it to me."

"Not even me?" Blaine asked, hurt clouding his eyes.

"Oh, Blaine. Of course I trust you. I couldn't have done any of this without you. You have been my rock and I am so ..."

Blaine's eyes probed mine. I struggled to draw in a breath. Before I could move, he wrapped his arms around me and kissed me. His lips were soft and warm against mine. He stopped kissing me, but didn't let go. Our eyes locked and the rest of the world melted away. *It's over with Aiden. Why shouldn't I move on with someone else?* I cupped the back of his head and pulled him to me. I kissed him, our bodies moving together in perfect rhythm. My tongue searched for his, as if I could somehow drink him into me. Some guys drove by, honked at us, and heckled. I stepped back, my cheeks warm. For a moment I had forgotten that we were in public.

"Oh, Avery," Blaine said. "I am so sorry. I…"

"I'm not," I said, and I slipped my hand into his.

AIDEN

When a person's heart and mind are in chaos, concentration on one thing makes the mind pure.

—Lao Tsu

I stood on the other side of the street from Avery's apartment, my eyes sweeping the crowd for her. I had hoped we could blend in, but Wao wore flowing grey robes and behaved as if he had just arrived from another planet. There was a lineup of people in front of her building, which looked as if a bomb had gone off inside it. My stomach tightened. Was Avery okay?

"I can't believe how many people are here. How high the buildings are, like Wudang Mountains. There is so much sound," Wao said, his robes swirling around him as he moved, attempting to take in everything all at once.

"Look, Wao, there she is." I gestured across the street. Relief flowed through me. She was all right. Avery walked hand in hand with Blaine, my Bagua brother, my best friend, the man I had charged with her safety. If possible, she looked even more radiant than before. My heart lodged in my throat and my knees went weak.

"Oh, buddy," Wao mumbled. "You in deep, deep doodoo … no wonder your spirit has been altered. She has big energy."

We watched them navigate through the crowd, Avery in front. Blaine stopped and looked around, searching the crowd. I knew he could feel us watching him. He said something to Avery, who gave a cursory glance around the area before urging him on.

I stepped off of the curb.

Wao pulled me back. "Aiden, what you doing? You not looking where you going."

Taxis squealed, drivers honking their horns impatiently as I hopped back onto the curb. "I'm sorry. I just saw her and started walking."

Wao shook his head. "Like I said, my friend, you in deep doodoo."

We crossed at the lights and headed into the crowd. The police officers stationed at the courtyard entrance looked at everyone's identification before allowing them into the building. *What exactly happened here, anyway?*

I scanned the crowed. Avery and Blaine were almost at the guard box.

"Avery! Blaine!" I shouted.

They both turned around and someone else snuck into the line in front of them. Blaine's face lit up. Avery's did too, briefly, and then she turned dark. My heart sank. *She hasn't forgiven me yet.*

We wove our way through the crowd until we stood beside them, at the front of the line.

"Identification, please," said the officer, sounding bored.

Avery passed him her student card. He glanced down at it and back at her, then studied the rest of us. His gaze landed on Wao. "Who's the Halloween dude? He live here, too?"

"These are my friends. They're helping me clean up after the fire." Avery's voice shook.

I tried to catch her eyes, but they darted away from mine. She couldn't even look at me. My jaw clenched.

"Okay, go ahead." He waved us through.

Soon we were in the building and inside the elevator. Avery sat as far away from me as possible on the red velvet bench. I stayed standing, as did Blaine and Wao.

"Avery, this is Wao," Blaine introduced them and shot me a glance as if to say, *Where are your manners?*

I tore my gaze from Avery's face and cleared my throat. "Wao is my transformation guide."

"Good for you," she said, staring at the changing numbers above the door.

I suppose I should have expected Avery to be cold towards me after what I had done, but I had foolishly imagined a different greeting. One where she was as happy to see me as I was to see her.

I tried to probe her thoughts; find out what she was feeling. But her mind was closed to mine. My insides churned.

Blaine squeezed her shoulder. Avery looked up at him and smiled. I remembered that smile when it was for me.

A sharp pain shot across my chest. They had fallen in love. For a moment, I couldn't breathe. Then I pushed back my shoulders. My destiny was now clearer than ever. I should be relieved. But my heart pulled at me. Avery's golden eyes, even deeper gold than before, her vanilla-almond scent, her voice, filled my senses. The sight of her sent memories crashing through me: teaching her the fast walk and both of us laughing hysterically, her convincing us to teach her Bagua, watching the stars in the Ramapo Mountains.

I pressed a hand over the ache in my chest. I had to let Avery move on. To be with Blaine. My choice had made this happen, had created this reality. Old Phoenix was right. Everything we do—our words, our thoughts, our deeds—creates our reality. *But is this the reality that I truly want?*

Thwack! Wao hit me on the head, and I realized everyone was waiting for me to get out of the empty elevator. *Stop thinking so much.* Grandfather's words blended with Old Phoenix's voice in my mind, as if they shared the same spirit. We walked into Avery's apartment, sloshing through an inch of water on the floor. The air held the distinct smell of burnt wood. My chest clenched. She could have been killed. I grasped her arm and turned her to face me. "What happened here?"

Avery glanced down at my hand and back at me, and I let her go. "It's a long story. Blaine and I—" The phone in the back pocket of her jeans buzzed. She pulled it out and scanned the screen. Her face paled.

Blaine stepped closer. "Avery? What is it?"

"It's a text. From my dad."

A shadow crossed Blaine's face. "What does he say?"

"*You got out of this one, but not for long. I have to stay an extra day in Washington but will be back tomorrow and you have some explaining to do.*" Avery looked up, her eyes wide. "How could he even know?"

Blaine shook his head. "He has a lot of connections. He may even have someone watching you, who knows?"

My eyes narrowed. "What's been going on here?"

Avery whirled around to face me. "What difference does it make to you? What are you doing back here, anyway?"

She'd changed since I'd been gone. Suddenly she looked very powerful, very confident.

I swallowed, but before I could answer, Wao spoke up. "Aiden and I came back because we knew you were in trouble."

"I know your father took your necklace," I said.

"H-how could you know that?" Avery turned to Blaine. "Why did you tell him? I thought you couldn't reach him. Why didn't you just leave him in the mountains? He was very busy there, levitating and eating white rice."

Blaine lifted both hands. "I didn't tell him."

I touched her elbow. "He didn't, Avery. I saw it in the Mirror Pond."

Blaine gasped. "You did a Mirror Pond? Lucky dog."

"What is a Mirror Pond?" Avery wedged her hands on her hips.

Blaine and I exchanged a look. He rested his hands on her shoulders. "I'll tell you about it later. Right now, we need to get into your dad's office and find your mother's necklace. Then we're getting you out of here, and away from that bastard who calls himself your father."

My eyes narrowed. "*Calls* himself her father? Isn't he—?"

Avery raised her hand. "It's not your business anymore, Aiden. And Blaine's right. We don't have time for this. We need to get what we came for and get out of here. I promised Madame I wouldn't miss the last dance rehearsal tomorrow."

Her words cut through me like a knife. I couldn't argue with her, though. What was going on in her life really wasn't my business. Not anymore.

"I'll make sure you get to rehearsal, Avery." Blaine grabbed her hand and tugged her toward her dad's office. "We shouldn't be here long. You'll have plenty of time left to prepare for it."

The four of us followed Blaine down the hall. He pushed open the splintered door and stopped. "It looks as though someone's been here." He pointed across the room. "I don't think we left papers on the desk like that."

Avery came up beside him. "No, we didn't, but it could have been the firemen."

"Seems strange you father doesn't have someone here, protecting the place." Blaine moved to the side of the desk and rifled through some papers.

Avery stood beside him. "Apparently he's assigned everyone to keep an eye on me and report back to him instead."

It ripped at my guts to see Avery and Blaine so close. She had been my friend first, and I had been the one to know her heart and soul. Now it was clear that those belonged to Blaine. My insides felt battered by a hurricane and a strange ache throbbed with every beat of my heart.

Avery rushed over to one of the wall panels and pulled it open.

Wao moved to my side. "You can't see the wind blow, but you can see what the wind blows. Unseen forces are at work, Aiden," he whispered.

Blaine rested a hand on the small of Avery's back, guiding her into the room.

If Wao was right, I really wished I knew what those unseen forces were up to. At the moment, it didn't feel like anything good.

The room was dimly lit by a bare bulb in the ceiling. A filing cabinet filled one wall, while the opposite wall was lined with shelves that bent from the burden of supporting stacks of books, papers, statues, and lock boxes. Avery and Blaine combed through papers and looked through boxes. Wao broke open the metal locks by simply holding them with his powerful fingers.

"How do you do that?" Avery asked.

"With Qi," Wao replied.

"Qi can do that?"

"Qi do many amazing things. My energy very powerful now after years of training. The lock spring open for me when I direct attention to it. Very handy." Wao smiled, obviously enjoying impressing Avery. He stole a glance in my direction.

I picked up the box he had just opened and some papers fell out.

Blaine crouched down and picked them up. "These stock certs are for an oil company in Libya, and a uranium company in Northern Saskatchewan." He held a paper up to the light. "And here's one in Kazakhstan."

I bent down to help him. "And these are receipts for enriched uranium from Argentina and a sales receipt to Libya, and one to North Korea." I rummaged through the papers I'd scooped up. "And look here, brochures for anti-nuclear proliferation conferences being held in South Korea, Uzbekistan, and Pakistan. And some certificates from GGMP, Global GenoMod Pharmaceutical Inc., and another for Mondechem—says they specialize in high-nutrient chemicals for low-yield farmlands."

Blaine stood up. "What is your father up to?"

"Who the heck *is* my father?" Avery threw her hands up in the air.

I studied her face. *What does she mean? Her father isn't her father?*

"Look at these." Wao held up a file folder. "Pictures and activity reports on Master Zheng. Why would your father be interested in Master Zheng?"

Avery's eyebrows drew together. "Val and Veronika mentioned him too, and my father met with him in the courtyard of our building one night. Who is this Master Zheng, anyway?"

Blaine and I looked at each other.

"What?" Avery tilted her head, a storm brewing in her eyes. "Do you both know something you haven't told me?"

Aiden cleared his throat. "Master Zheng is Old Phoenix's brother. How would your father even know the brother of Old Phoenix? It's just too weird."

"You aren't keeping something from me that I should know, are you?"

My stomach tightened. It was one thing to not want to upset and worry Avery, but it was another thing to keep information from her—even if we didn't fully understand what was going on—when she asked us for it outright.

Blaine moved to Avery's side. "We know about as much as a fat-tailed dunnart dropped into a city backyard in the midday knows about finding its next meal."

"What's that supposed to mean?" Avery's voice was tight.

"I think Blaine meant..." I stopped. I had no idea what Blaine meant.

Blaine grasped Avery's arm. "We can talk later. Right now, we have a necklace to find, Avery."

We all refocused on the necklace, moving through the piles of papers and searching frantically, but every stack, every box, every drawer netted nothing.

Avery worked silently beside me, close enough that I felt the shiver that rippled through her. She rubbed her arms. "Does anyone else feel a draft?"

Blaine walked past her to the back of the room. "Look. There's another panel open here. That's where the cold air is coming from." He pulled the door open wider.

Avery straightened and followed him through it. I went in after her, Wao's footsteps padding along behind me. The dim light in the room we'd left felt suddenly bright as darkness cloaked the space we'd just entered. I swore I could hear Avery's heart pounding. Unable to see any of the other three, I felt along the walls, waiting for my eyes to adjust. A small green light broke through the darkness and I followed it. When I reached it, I found a utility shaft with a caged cargo platform. I pressed the button and the utility shaft whined to life.

Blaine came up behind me and pulled apart the cage doors, and the four of us clambered onto the shaky platform.

"I've heard about these shafts in the Dakota," Avery whispered. "They were installed when it was first built. There were central kitchens on the first floor where cooks made dinners and sent them up to the apartments on these things. I had no idea one of them was still operational."

The cage stopped. "This should be the ground floor." Blaine reached out to open the doors, but the cage shuddered and began a further descent. Through the bars, it was clear we were going underground. The walls wept water, and the smell of pungent earth filled the air. The cage dropped suddenly, just a few inches, but enough for everyone to look startled. It thudded onto the ground and the doors rattled open.

A long, dimly-lit corridor stretched out in front of us. Blaine took Avery's hand and the two of them stepped out and started down it. Wao and I followed. After about a hundred yards, the corridor turned into a tunnel, just like the ones I had searched when Veronika took Avery into that city under the subway. The dank, rotten smell was the same too. Without the urgency of saving Avery propelling me, I noticed the stench even more. *Avery must be freaking out.* I studied her. Every muscle in her body appeared tense.

She spoke up suddenly, her voice strained. "This is my nightmare all over again."

"It's okay, Avery," I said. "You made it through the last time. Breathe." Everything in me longed to catch up with her and put my arm around her, to comfort her.

She moved closer to Blaine and threw a look at me over her shoulder. "I was sleepwalking through life back then. I'm fine now. And very awake." Avery's fiery look burned through me. Even in her anger, she looked luminescent. My chest ached. I had lost her to my best friend. And it was only right. He had been the one by her side during these past months, helping her and keeping her safe.

I froze at the faint sound of rustling ahead, my night training in the Wudang heightening my senses. Everyone else stopped moving too. The strange albino man in the wheelchair appeared out of the gloom ahead, coming straight at us. His crystal-blue eyes shone like vacant gemstones.

At my side, Wao studied the albino as he approached. They gestured at each other, Wao's hands moving quickly as he performed a mudra, and the albino responding with one of his own.

What are they saying to each other?

The man wheeled by us without changing his rhythm or speed, but his words drifted back to us. "Together! Together is better. Stronger. Put it together. I can't tell you. Just put it together."

Whoosh! I felt, rather than saw, the silver star whizzing toward us, and leaned forward to grab Blaine's arm and yank him out of the way. He stared at me for a second, then another silver star whipped by his ear. We scrambled to hug the sides of the tunnel while a steady stream of silver stars whizzed past us. Ahead, a mass of black, like a surge of boiling oil, hurtled toward us. I stepped in front of Blaine and, as a star zipped by me, I plucked it out of the air. Avery stared at me. I was equally amazed that I could do it, but my training in the past few months had been profound. When I put my mind to it, I could see the stars going by in slow motion. I plucked a few more out of the air. Wao tugged Avery back behind him and did the same.

"Don't touch the tips, Aiden," Wao called to me. "Poisoned."

Wao flung the stars back into the rush of men in black jumpsuits. Two dropped to the ground. I let a few more stars fly and downed another man. We did our best to keep Avery behind us, and out of the fray. These were highly-skilled martial artists, and her beginner abilities didn't stand a chance. Blaine fought beside me, but there were at least six of them against three of us. They were soon on top of us.

An assailant reached me and wrapped his hands around my throat. I held a star in my hand and was about to plunge it into his heart, but I didn't have room to pull my arm back far enough. Instead, gasping for breath, I pinched a place in his neck that should have put him out cold. He didn't let go at first, just kept squeezing his hands tighter around my neck as life seeped from my body. Just as the edges of my vision dimmed, his eyes rolled back in his head and I dropped to the ground, free, grunting when the man toppled down on me. Sputtering for air, I shoved him off and scrambled to my feet.

Wao fought the black-clad men three at a time. Blaine kept two others engaged, and away from Avery. He skillfully stepped into them, spiraling one arm to avoid their thrusts and using his other arm to rain blows on their necks, heads, and chests.

I dove back into the fray, taking on one of Blaine's attackers as another descended upon him.

"Thought you were done, bro," Blaine breathed as he flew past me, tangling one man up in a series of blocks and locks.

"Not quite yet," I said, shooting out both of my palms in the *lion rolls the ball* technique, one arm above the other, fingertips like deadly darts aimed at the eyes and throat. It was one of the most difficult strikes to avoid, but the man in black ducked down and attacked my legs. I caught sight of the cold glint of steel a fraction of a second before the razor-sharp blade cut into my leg. Without conscious thought, my body sprang into the air, in a motion resembling a side cartwheel, preventing the main artery in my thigh from being slashed. The blade left only a scratch and a tear in my jeans.

The knife man followed me relentlessly, this time his blade flashing towards my kidney. The strike would have finished me, but a right foot *Kou Bu* step propelled me over the man in a single bound, leaving him looking totally confused as I vanished like a ghost and landed behind him. *How should I finish him off?* Before I could decide, Avery hurtled towards him. My right and left palms struck him several times on the side and back of the head with a shocking force. He was unconscious before he had even registered that I was behind him. I groaned as her outstretched leg connected with the knife wound on my thigh. Gritting my teeth, I wrapped an arm around her waist, lifted her up, twirled around, and set her down behind me. I gave her a look that I hoped would get her to stay put.

Despite the circumstances, and the pain stabbing through me, the feel of her beneath my hands felt so good, so right. I shot a glance at Blaine. *I can't let her go. Not yet.*

Blaine stepped aside from a vicious, hooking punch to the head, moving in to close range and grasping his assailant's face. He pulled the man off balance, then with a spiraling arm, slammed his right palm into the man's temple. Blaine caught me watching him. "Much has happened since you've been gone."

"I can see that," I said, as I engaged one of Wao's opponents who had vaulted onto me and grabbed my arms in a technique I recognized as coming from classical Chinese "fast wrestling."

Instead of resisting, as a fast wrestler would hope for, so that he could instantly change the throw into a brutal sweep of the legs, I followed his body weight and simply spun around with a back step, slapping a palm to the man's skull. He fell soundlessly to the floor.

"Not the half of it," Blaine continued, and took Wao's second opponent with the *monkey offers peaches to the Emperor,* an ingenious attack technique where both hands fly towards the face, masking the almost simultaneous and very blistering heel kick to the inside of the knee.

Behind us, Avery cried out. We both spun around. One of the assailants had gotten past us and was choking her from behind in a vicious stranglehold.

Blaine and I froze, knowing that any step towards her would turn the choke into a break. A helpless rage roared through me, but I pushed it back. Allowing emotions to takeover would kill us both. *Relax, remember what you learned,* I willed her silently. Avery must have picked up my thought; her eyes locked on mine for an instant while her body slumped down like jelly. Then, with a slight turn of her hips, she sent the man flying over her head towards us. Blaine reached him before me, knocking him out with a kick to the temple before the man even crashed onto the ground.

"Oh, I get the idea," I said. I turned to Avery and clapped my hands. She kept her gaze on Blaine, who gave her the thumbs up.

He shot me a sideways glance. "Are we talking about the same thing?"

"I think so." It was painful enough, knowing Avery had fallen in love with Blaine. *Is he going to make me say the words?*

"I'm referring to my practice with Luc. He's really helped my fighting."

"Oh...yeah. That's what I meant, too. I can see how you've improved." He'd always been able to read the truth on my face. I averted my eyes and looked back at Wao. All six of the men in black lay in the corridor. Wao strode toward us, rubbing both hands together.

I turned back as Avery rushed up to us. "We won! We won! You guys were incredible."

I was about to tell Avery how great she had done, when Blaine stepped forward and said, "You were amazing, Avs. How about that throw, when you were about to get your neck broken? That was impressive."

Her face paled in the dim light. "He was about to break my neck?"

Avs ... He called her Avs. My head started to spin.

Wao reached us. "Why are these guys here?" His question brought us all back to the matter at hand. "They must be guarding something." His moon face shone in the shadowy light. "Come on. We have to find out what's so important down here."

He reversed direction and bolted down the tunnel. We followed him, Blaine and me on either side of Avery, taking her arms and fast walking her along in spite of her protests. Ahead, Wao slowed, turned around, and shushed us. He stopped in front of a doorway and listened.

I let go of Avery and crept closer. Several voices carried on a conversation behind the heavy wooden door. I listened, then motioned to Blaine and Avery to come closer. I stepped back when they got to us so they could hear too.

Wao nudged Avery gently in the shoulder. "Your father is negotiating selling your necklace to Master Zheng. Zheng is demanding the diary as well."

Avery reached for the door knob, but all three of us grabbed her. Before we could formulate a better plan, the door opened and Norman stepped out. His eyes widened and he reached for Avery. I blocked his path and Blaine twisted around to deliver a blow to his solar plexus that brought him down hard. My Bagua brother and I were again working in sync, no need for words.

Wao entered the room, Avery and Blaine close behind him. I went in after them and worked my way to the far side of the room, where Peter was busily shoving papers into a briefcase with one hand, while keeping a tight grasp on a small silvery-blue box with the other.

Avery looked ready to attack her father, but Blaine held her back. She squirmed but he had a good hold on her.

Neither of the men in the room appeared to have noticed our presence. I braced myself. When they did realize we were there, there was no telling what Master Zheng would do, or Peter for that matter.

Master Zheng looked up from the necklace in Peter's hands and locked eyes with Wao. In a flash, they approached each other, circling, sizing up each other's strengths and weaknesses.

I was about to intercede when Zheng took the initiative and flew across the space, so quickly he was nearly a blur, and struck out with a right punch to Wao's head. I immediately recognized it as *BengQuan*, the famous crushing fist attack. Zheng was clearly adept at Xingyi, the *Shape of the Mind* system and brother art of Bagua. Xingyi uses a more direct method of delivering the devastating internal power that channeled the force of the five elements. It consisted of five simple, but deadly, punches. *BengQuan* was the most deadly of all, as effective from an inch as from a foot away. Zheng wasn't interested in fighting; he was going in for the kill shot.

Too far away to help, I watched in horror as the punch seemed to connect with Wao's head, but then Wao was simply not there, his body having spun away to a position behind Zheng. Now Wao was on the attack, his palms descending and slicing with such speed and aggression that Zheng had to leap backwards to avoid being maimed.

Avery's father took the fight as an opportunity to step toward the door, but I caught him by the arm. His face twisted in anger and he struck out at me with vicious moves from a martial art I'd never seen before. I spun away. As long as I could keep circling out of his way, he couldn't land a heavy hit on me.

From the corner of my eye, I saw Zheng take a quick, explosive step into Wao. Peter appeared to see it too, as he edged closer to the door. While his attention was diverted for a second, I grabbed for the small box in his hand, but it slipped from my grasp and clattered to the floor. The lid opened and a bright, blinding light flooded the room. Everyone stopped moving. I bent down to snatch the fallen box, and the necklace spilling out of it, and bolted for the door.

I glanced back over my shoulder. Avery, Blaine, and Wao sprinted after me. The three of us were halfway down the tunnel, with the necklace acting as a beacon, guiding us out, before Zheng and Peter came out the door. Peter grabbed Norman by the arm and yanked him to his feet.

I whirled back around and concentrated on getting back to the utility shaft.

Zheng's angry voice blasted down the tunnel after us. "The necklace is mine. I will get it. And the Scorpion, too."

AIDEN

When I let go of what I am, I become what I might be.

—Lao Tzu

I shoved everyone into the utility elevator, rushing to get us out of the tunnel. Avery gave me a dirty look as I took her hand to help her in. She snatched her fingers back and stepped into the rickety cage on her own. Blaine hopped in behind her, with Wao bringing up the rear. Wao closed the gate behind him as he made a final lurch into the cage. Blaine pushed the button to begin the shaky ascent back to the secret room in Peter's office.

"Why didn't you guys let me get at my father? I could kill him," Avery said.

"You could kill him?" Blaine's eyebrows rose. "He could crush your delicate little windpipe with one squeeze of his hand."

She scowled. "I'm not so delicate."

"I know that," Blaine smiled. "But most Bagua artists at your skill level never meet the kind of opponents we saw today, including your father."

Heat flashed through my body, bearing witness to their easy rapport.

Avery rubbed her forehead with the side of her hand. "What was my father doing trying to sell my necklace to Zheng? I don't get this at all."

Wao suddenly slumped to the ground.

"Wao! Oh my God, Aiden. What's wrong?" Avery dropped to her knees in front of him.

The elevator reached the office floor and I pulled open the cage door gates leading into the back of the hidden room. Blaine and I lifted Wao and carried him out. I took hold of Wao, while Blaine and Avery sprang into action.

"Avery, find the button that disables the weight monitor. It has to be hidden somewhere in the desk."

She ran to the desk and yanked open the drawer. "I've got it, Blaine. Listen for the click."

They worked like teammates, already knowing what the other wanted, only using words to let the rest of us know what was going on. Wao managed a weak glance up at me as I supported him.

Blaine lifted his head. "It clicked." He pulled out his cell phone from the back pocket of his jeans. "Avery, you can't stay here tonight. Grab what you need. I'll call a taxi for us and then I'll let Luc know we're coming."

As soon as Blaine made the arrangements, he and I carried Wao between us and we whisked him out of the apartment and down to the street. Avery was already ahead of us, scouting to make sure the coast was clear. Quiet moans escaped from Wao every few moments. I wondered what move had gotten the better of him. Next to Old Phoenix, he had achieved the highest level of internal marital artist of anyone I knew. His skills were near magical. Zheng was a good match for him, though. I had never seen Zheng fight before, but I knew now that he was one incredibly destructive force. I could feel it in the room, in the tunnel. Pure evil, bone-chillingly cold and damp.

The taxi was waiting for us in the inner courtyard when we exited the building. Against the driver's protests that he wasn't an ambulance and wouldn't take a sick man, nor could he allow four people in his cab, we squeezed in and sped off to Luc's house in Gramercy Park.

We carried Wao up the walk to Luc's house. He stood in the doorway, gesturing for us to come in quickly. He led us to a guest bedroom, where we laid Wao down carefully on the bed. My cell phone alarm beeped, signaling the final countdown to take my medicine.

Luc was by his side immediately, running his hands a few inches above Wao's body, feeling for what was wrong. After a moment, he looked up. "Leave us. I will come out and talk to you when I know more."

In the living room, the three of us took turns pacing. No one spoke. I clenched my fists in frustration. I'd never been one to stand around waiting for someone else to do something. Avery and Blaine both looked as helpless as I felt. My timer chimed a final warning. I had three seconds to complete the cure. I took the vial from my chest pocket, undid the cork and tipped the bottle to my lips. The heat scorched down my throat to my stomach and radiated throughout my limbs. I felt as though I was breathing fire, then the feeling stopped abruptly and was replaced by a surge of energy.

Avery scrunched up her face. "What was that?"

"My last dose of medicine." I basked in her gaze and remembered what I had in my pocket. I took the blue metal box out of my pocket and handed it to her.

"Here. I got your necklace back for you."

She stared at me as she took the blue box from my hand. I tried to decipher the emotions roiling in her eyes, but she looked away from me and opened the box. Her eyes widened as she lifted the pendant out of the box and held it up to the light. The clasp was still intact, the safety shattered. The fiery stone reflected in the deep gold of Avery's eyes.

When she wrapped the braided gold chain around her neck, I stepped forward to help her with the clasp, but she turned to Blaine. "Would you…?"

"Sure." He took the two ends from her fingers and fastened it. My stomach tightened as his fingers brushed over her throat. The ache in my heart deepened. The stone shone in the light; the faint outline of Minerva, the Roman Goddess of Wisdom, appeared to be on fire.

Avery glowed in its light. "I feel better already." She met my gaze, finally. "Thank you, Aiden, for getting it back."

Warmth flooded my chest. It wasn't much, but every little step forward felt like a victory. Then she tore her gaze from mine and the spell was broken. "Blaine. Thanks. Thanks for …everything." She threw her arms around his neck and kissed him on the lips.

I struggled to take a breath. If her looking at me was a small victory, her kissing Blaine right in front of me felt like a full-on defeat.

Blaine lifted his head and gently removed her arms from his neck. For a brief moment, his eyes met mine, his cheeks flushing slightly.

Avery didn't seem to notice. She stepped back and shot a glance at the living room doorway. "What are we going to do about Wao? I only just met him, but already I feel close to him."

I cleared my throat. "Luc is a gifted healer. If anyone can help Wao, he can. He is both an Eastern healer and a Western-trained surgeon."

Blaine took the blue box from Avery's hand and studied it, then put it down on the table. His forehead wrinkled and snatched it back up and studied it closer. "This box is made of Niobium." He held it up toward Avery. "Is this the box your necklace came in?"

"Yes."

I stared at the box. "What's Niobium?"

"It's atomic element number 41."

"Layman's terms?"

"Oh. Niobium is number 41 on the Periodic Table. The number of protons in an atomic nucleus determines the number given on the table. So Niobium has 41 protons in its nucleus so it's atomic element 41. But where it gets really interesting is that Niobium is a metal with a very high density and has incredible superconducting properties at various temperatures. Niobium is used for particle accelerators such as the Large Hadron Collider in Cern. But it's also used to shield against powerful electromagnetic waves."

"So my necklace is electromagnetic?" Avery sank down onto a chair.

"Has to be." Blaine turned to Avery. "Do you ever feel anything weird when you wear the necklace? Like dizzy, or your heart races, or … I don't know … anything different from normal?"

"Yes!" Avery leapt to her feet. "Absolutely. I always felt weird but I couldn't put my finger on what it was, exactly. The first time I wore the necklace, I had to take the subway home because I was dizzy, breaking out in cold sweats, and my head was buzzing. That was the day I met Aiden and he saved me from being crushed on the tracks. I thought … well, never mind."

"That's Aiden, our hero." Luc came into the living room and quietly closed the glass French doors behind him before striding over to give me a quick hug. "We missed you, brother. Wao is resting now. I don't know yet if he will be okay. The next twenty-four hours should tell us. What the heck have you gotten yourselves into? The hit that he sustained is not from any ordinary martial artist. Who was it? And why is Wao even here? He's never been out of China in his life."

Blaine and I exchanged glances.

"I have to know what I'm dealing with here, guys. Wao could die."

"Wao is my transformation guide," I said. "We are here … well … Old Phoenix asked … there's this old Chinese guy …" I took a deep breath. "I'll start from the beginning. As I understand it, Avery was given a necklace by her mother, who was given the necklace by her grandfather, who got it from his grandfather who lived with the mystics in the Himalayas. The day Avery put the necklace on for the first time was the day I arrived in New York and saw her in the subway. Two of Zheng's ..."

Luc gasped. "Mon Dieu. Zheng? What does he have to do with this?"

I swallowed hard. "Zheng wants Avery's necklace. So when Zheng's two girls found out about Avery, they kidnapped her in the subway tunnels, took her necklace, and held her there for three days. That was when the electromagnetic storm took out the Manhattan electrical grid."

"Hey, I bet Avery's necklace caused that blackout," Blaine said. "If it needs to be kept in a Niobium box, it has more power than we imagined."

Luc lifted a hand. "Two-Brains, there's a reason they threw you out of your physics program. Your mind is working overtime."

Blaine frowned. "For the record, I didn't get *thrown out* of my physics program. I left because they were all a bunch of close-minded pin-heads who couldn't see past an electron to a quark if their lives depended on it. And this is important. Bear with me." His eyes bored into a void that only he could see and his words came in fast-moving waves, culminating in a tsunami of ideas. "If Avery's energy had become symbiotic with the necklace after wearing it for a while, then when someone with a very different energy tore it off her neck and put it on, it could cause a sudden massive electromagnetic wave that could instigate a CME, or coronal mass ejection, on the sun so powerful that it could blow an electrical grid quite easily."

Avery nodded. "It kinda makes sense. For awhile, everything and everyone I touched got an electrical shock. And I was getting weird sensations. Remember Aiden, when you first told me about Bagua and internal energy? Even you said the energy we felt between us was extremely intense."

I snapped my fingers. "That's right. It was different. Like nothing I had ever felt before."

Avery's eyes glittered. "I wonder if that's what happened when my dad took the necklace and we had that second power failure in the city."

Blaine rubbed his hands together. "The stone might be resonating with your bioelectricity, and then enhancing or even amplifying it. It could be extremely powerful. The stone, that is." Blaine blushed. "Well, your bioelectricity is pretty powerful too. And together—well, something beyond what I imagined could be happening.

A noise echoed in the hallway. Luc strode toward the French doors and flung them open. Wao lay in a heap on the floor. Luc helped him to his feet. Wao appeared to be in a semi-conscious state, awake but not aware of what was going on. We all followed as Luc guided him back to the guest room and pulled the covers over him. Wao's ashen face gradually relaxed into deep sleep as we stood at the foot of the bed and watched.

I gripped the metal footboard with both hands. "Wao nursed me back to health in the Wudang. He thought I had been hit with a Dim Mak, a quivering palm. We went to see..."

Luc raised a finger to his lips and nodded at the exit. After we all filed out of the room, he closed the door behind us. We started down the hall toward the living room. Luc slid an arm around my shoulders. "Okay, Aiden…Tell me all of it."

Two hours later, after I finished telling Luc the whole story, the three of us joined Luc in the guest bedroom. Wao looked smaller, like years of his life had been sucked away from him. His bright face had lost all of its vitality and his cheeks had sunk into his bone structure. Avery stood close beside me. I could feel her intense vibration as she took hold of Wao's hand.

"I barely know you, Wao, but you can't leave us yet."

I reached for Wao's other hand, and Blaine took mine and Avery's in his. The four of us completed an energy circuit and Wao opened his eyes and smiled. But it was only a temporary surge and his smile faded quickly.

I looked over at my first teacher. "Luc, can't you do anything?"

"I'm afraid I've done everything I can. His injury is nothing western medical science can fix. I've exhausted all of my herbal remedies, and the best of my energy medicine. Look, Aiden." Luc pulled aside Wao's robes to reveal a fiery-looking, dark-red palm print over Wao's heart.

I gasped, recognizing the print as the same one I had endured on my stomach for so many months.

"I'm afraid Wao might have decided that this is his time. If that's the case, no one can do anything about it."

I shook my head. "No way, Luc. No way has Wao decided this is his time. He is my guide. I can't do it without him. His time isn't up yet."

Wao's small rucksack was propped up in the corner of the room. I picked it up and turned out its contents on the small night table. There was a toothbrush, a beat-up copy of the Tao Te Jing, some yarrow sticks for throwing divinations, a Swiss army knife, and a tin cup with a burlap bag inside. It was the cup with the same twigs and herbs that No Trace had made me drink when we were hiking up to the Wudang, while I was still very sick.

Hope ignited inside me. "Can someone fill this up with boiling water?" I held up the cup.

Blaine leapt up and grabbed it. "I've got it," he said and left the room.

Mix blood from the palm of your hand to the twigs and herbs after they are mixed with the water.

I blinked. *What? Why would I do that?*

Old Phoenix's voice drifted through my mind. *The antidote from the Rinpoche is still running through your veins. It's in you.*

Blaine came back in the room clutching the cup I'd given him. I added the twigs and the herbs to the steaming water. I hesitated, then grabbed Wao's Swiss Army knife, folded my hand around it and sliced the surface of my palm.

Avery gasped and pressed a hand to her mouth.

Drops of blood dripped from my hand into the cup, mixing into the herbal mixture. I held it to Wao's slack mouth and let a little of the liquid drip onto his lips, then a little into his mouth, then a little more. He looked dead, but still had a faint heart beat in his wrist when I checked. I slid a hand to the back of his head and lifted it gently so I could hold the cup against his lips. He took a sip, then stopped, as though that small action had worn him out. I gave him a few seconds, and then tipped more of the mixture into his mouth. Another sip, another rest. *He needs more.* I lifted my cut palm directly to Wao's lips and let a few drops fall into his mouth. A little color came back into his cheeks.

It was so still in the room I swear I could hear Wao's faint heartbeat. He had trained me to tune in my listening to an almost impossible level. Or was it just that he had grown so thin, and his chest so sunken, I saw the slight rise and fall of his breaths and imagined I could hear the beating of his heart. I held his limp hand in mine, barely noticing that the blood had ceased to flow and the fine slice had already healed. Someone's fingers slid into my other hand and squeezed. I looked up. Avery. My chest tightened. Blaine took her free hand and once again we completed the circle. For a long time we stood that way, surrounding Wao's bed and willing him to wake up, to live.

AVERY

*Love is of all passions the strongest, for it attacks simultaneously
the head, the heart and the senses.*

—Lao Tzu

We left Wao sleeping in the room. During the night, Aiden had added more of his blood to the healing herbs. By morning, Wao looked as though he had slipped into a peaceful coma.

When a pink, hazy sunrise filtered into the room, giving it a rosy glow, Luc stood up from his chair in the corner. "You've done well, Aiden. Wao needs to rest now. And you three must get some sleep."

We protested, none of us wanting to leave Wao's side, but Luc herded us to the door. "I promise I will let you know if there is any change in Wao's condition, however small."

Blaine slipped an arm around my shoulders as we went out into the hall. "I don't think you should go to that dance rehearsal today, Avs. You must be exhausted. You need rest."

I shook my head. "No, I need to go. I promised Madame I'd be there. Besides, dancing will make me feel better."

Aiden had been walking down the hallway in front of us, but he stopped and turned around, a grim look on his face. "I don't think you should go either, Avs. Not after what happened yesterday. Zheng's agents of mass destruction, those men in black we grappled with in the tunnel, will be looking for you. You're safe here, but as soon as you leave this house, they could find you and there's no telling what will happen if they do."

I cocked my head. "Come on. What are they going to do, pick me up from the sidewalk in front of everyone and carry me away?"

"It's happened in this city before," Blaine said. "Even if people see what's happening, no one wants to get involved. That's often how people go missing."

I crossed my arms over my chest. "Well, that won't happen to me."

"You're right, it won't," Aiden said. "Because we won't let it happen."

I rolled my eyes. "I'll be with Katie and Whitney. Nothing will happen."

Aiden looked at Blaine. "What do you think?"

Blaine shrugged. "It's really important to her. And we won't leave her side. Except when she's dancing, of course. I'm not doing that."

The image of Blaine and Aiden doing ballet broke the tension that had shimmered in the air between us since Wao and Aiden had shown up at my building. We all laughed and the weight that had been pressing down on me for days lifted slightly.

They walked me to the dance studio. No one spoke on the way. No doubt Aiden and Blaine were as absorbed in their own thoughts as I was, trying to figure out everything that had happened to us and between us. Aiden brushed against me and electricity shivered across my skin. How could I still react to him that way, after he had hurt me so badly? I moved closer to Blaine. I needed some time away from the two of them. Some time to figure out why I felt so confused, why so many of the feelings I'd had for Aiden, that I thought I'd moved past, were bubbling up again, threatening the happiness I had found so recently with Blaine.

Blaine reached for my hand. I shot a sideways glance at Aiden. His jaw tightened, but otherwise no emotion showed on his face. I bit back a groan of frustration. How could I not know what was going on in my own heart? Blaine did not deserve my uncertainty, and after our kiss in the street the other day, uncertainty was the last thing I wanted to give him.

When we reached the studio, Blaine opened the door and held it for me. "We'll be waiting here for you, Avery."

"You don't need to. I can walk home with—"

"We'll be right here." Aiden's voice was firm.

Obviously there was no use arguing with either of them. "Fine. I'll see you in a couple of hours."

Katie and Whitney appeared in the doorway. They greeted Aiden coolly, but as soon as the door closed behind the three of us, they descended on me. "Aiden's back?" Whitney grabbed my arm. "When did that happen? And why didn't you tell us?"

Katie pulled her off me. "Give her room to breathe, Whitney. Are you okay?"

"Yeah, of course I'm okay."

Whitney shook her head. "You don't look okay. Seriously. You have to get over this crush. You look like your heart is breaking."

"It's not just Aiden. His friend, Wao, might be dying. And it wasn't just a crush, Whitney. It was real. I felt it here." I placed my hand over the middle of my chest. "And here." I moved my hand to my belly.

"That doesn't look like concern over a friend you barely know to me," Whitney said. She hesitated.

I tilted my head. "What?"

"He abandoned you. He gave up the right to your loyalty and love. Blaine has been solid as a rock for you; he doesn't deserve to be treated like this."

"Blaine is my friend, and Aiden's Bagua brother."

"Blaine loves you. You can see it written all over him. He would do anything for you. Anything. Including not leaving you to pursue some strange idea about being a monk."

My shoulders slumped. "I did kiss him. I kissed Blaine. So you guys have it all wrong. I thought I loved Aiden. I had these overwhelming feelings when I was around him, when we touched, like nothing I had ever experienced. I thought those feelings explained the intensity between us, but it turns out that was because of the stone in the pendant that my mother gave me. It wasn't real. What I have with Blaine is real, that's why I kissed him."

My heart was pounding and I took a deep breath, trying to slow it down. Whitney had a point. Aiden had chased his destiny, which nearly destroyed me. But Blaine made everything bearable. I knew in my heart that he loved me. I never doubted that. In contrast, Aiden had been ambivalent from the beginning. He was hot and cold, pulling me towards him and then pushing me away. I should have taken that as a sign. The leopard can't change his spots. He was what he was. A monk. Even if he did wear jeans and a sexy t-shirt. Even if our hearts felt as though they beat as one. That didn't have to mean romantic love. That could be friendship. And I couldn't deny that my feelings for Blaine had grown over the time that Aiden had been away. I had come to depend on him being there, always. And he always was.

"I do love Blaine," I said. "But I don't hold anything against Aiden. He had to go, Whitney. It was his destiny. His calling. It wasn't his fault."

Whitney grabbed her hair with both hands. "You are so frustrating. Are you saying you love them both?"

I shrugged. "I'm just being truthful."

Katie looked down at her watch. "We better get in there. Madame will kill us if we're late. We can talk more later."

My thoughts whirled as I followed the two of them to the dressing room. Did I love them both? Was such a thing even possible? My thoughts returned to Blaine, who had been so wonderful to me. He made me laugh even when I was in a bad mood. I loved his nonchalant swagger when he carried my pink ballet bag, or my purse. He looked so funny, and he didn't care a bit about it. He just wanted to make me happy, to lighten my load a bit. Our friendship was so deep, I felt him in my very bones. With Aiden, the experience in the subway was like none other I had ever had. He saved me. He glowed. Even after spending such a short time together, we shared our hearts. I felt him in my blood, like liquid gold. But maybe Whitney was right. Maybe he was just a crush I needed to get over. I had felt safe with him, yet I was anything but safe. He seemed to invite trouble.

I sighed. I couldn't think straight when I was around either of them. Maybe I could find a way to ditch them after rehearsal. I needed to find a quiet spot to sort out my thoughts and feelings before I saw either of them again.

Katie changed and waited as I tied my hair back in front of the mirror. "I hope Madame lets you dance. You've missed so many rehearsals."

I didn't need anything else to worry about. Madame had to let me dance. It was the only way my mind would stop rehashing the events of the past few days. I wanted to dance Blaine and Aiden out of my mind. I patted the necklace around my neck. It looked a little out of place against my ballet outfit, but there was no way I was taking it off. I finished with my hair and walked out of the dressing room with Whitney and Katie.

I needn't have worried. When we entered the hall, Madame ran up to me, trilling, "Oh darling, Avery. We have missed you. I planned to replace you in the lineup today. Thank Gawd you've arrived." She twirled me around. "You look … different." She stepped back and held out both arms. "Luminous is the word. Oh, dahling, I am so glad you're back."

It wasn't the greeting I had expected, but I was thrilled I didn't have to beg to get back into the recital.

She gestured toward the line and the three of us ran over to the mirrors to join the others. Madame picked up her yard stick and beat out the rhythm on the rehearsal hall floor. Even without warming up, I found myself dancing like I hadn't danced in a long time, maybe ever.

I contemplated what Blaine had said about my necklace having some sort of energy vibration in it. *Is that what's different with me?* I soared when I leapt. My pirouettes were perfectly still in the center, while I whirled around faster than ever. Exhilaration coursed through me. The ballet did what I had hoped it would do. My thoughts slipped away into nothing and I became totally present in the moment of the movement.

AIDEN

Truthful words are not beautiful; beautiful words are not truthful. Good words are not persuasive; persuasive words are not good.

—Lao Tsu

Blaine rose up from the sidewalk and brushed off the back of his pants. "Avs should be coming out of rehearsal soon. I just saw one of her friends walk past."

"You know all of her friends?" I stood up too, and shoved my hands in my pockets. He knew so much of Avery now, and I really knew so little. I was gripped by the same intense feelings that had plagued me since the first moment I saw her and lifted her from the subway tracks.

Blaine shot me a look. "Get a grip, mate. You've got to get your head together." He glanced over at the dance studio door. "We have to stay completely focused on her safety now. If we don't, we'll miss something and Avery could get hurt."

"It doesn't help that she's refusing to believe how dangerous this all is, and she's not being careful enough." I leaned a shoulder against the wall and watched another group of girls come out of the building.

"She's pretty stubborn. I think it has to do with how her father treats her. She doesn't want anyone else restricting her freedom." Blaine lifted a hand as the group of dancers reached him. "Hey, have any of you seen Avery? Is she coming out?"

A girl with short, red hair shook her head. "I think I saw her and Katie and Whitney leave through the side door a few minutes ago."

I shoved away from the wall and the two of us sprinted for the corner of the building. Half a block away, I spotted her. She was walking close to the curb, her pink ballet bag slung over her shoulder. Katie and Whitney walked beside her. The knots in my stomach loosened slightly. She was okay. So far.

Blaine and I pushed our way through the hordes of pedestrians on the sidewalk, ignoring the dirty looks and cries of indignation as we knocked people out of our way. I strained to keep track of Avery through the crowd of people in front of us. Just as we drew close, a black limousine pulled up to the curb beside her and the back door opened. A man in a long black coat who had been walking right behind Avery suddenly grabbed her by the shoulders and shoved her toward the vehicle. Arms reached out for her from the backseat. A head appeared briefly through the opening. Norman.

My heart dropped to my stomach as I pushed my way frantically through a group of people, trying to get to her. "Avery!"

Avery splayed her legs, struggling like a feral cat about to be bagged. Whipping her head around, she bit one of the fingers digging into her shoulder. The man in the coat yanked back his hands. A siren wailed in the distance, and he dove around her and jumped into the backseat of the limo. The door slammed shut and the vehicle peeled away from the curb. A police car approached and Avery waved it in the direction of the limousine. The whole scene took just seconds.

Breathing heavily, Blaine and I rushed to her side. Whitney and Katie, who had been staring in shock at what was going on, got to her at the same time. Blaine grabbed Avery's arm.

She snatched it from his grasp. "Were you following me?" Her eyes burned into him. "You don't need to baby-sit me; I can take care of myself."

Blaine's eyes met mine over her head.

I touched her shoulder. "Avery, I don't think you have any idea how dangerous these guys are. They could—"

She spun around to face me, eyes blazing. "Aiden. Go away. Leave me alone. I don't need your help. Since you've been gone there have been no Goths abducting me, no epic blackouts that shut down the city, no weird albinos freaking me out, or people trying to kill me. You were fine to leave me when you thought my life was in danger before. What happened to the great hero then? Just go. Go away. Go back to the bald-headed guys and do your transformation thingy and live happily ever after."

"But …" I lifted both hands, feeling as helpless as Blaine looked. "You're in danger."

"I'm in danger of being smothered by you two."

"What do you think just happened? Norman almost got you," Blaine stammered.

"But he didn't get me, did he? I fought him off without either of you helping me. So just go away and leave me alone. I want space. Space away from both of you." Avery raised her hand and a taxi squealed to a stop. She slid into the backseat before Blaine or I could protest. Katie and Whitney both started toward the vehicle, but Avery slammed the door and pushed down the lock before they could reach it.

Just as the cab pulled away from the curb, I caught a glimpse of the driver. My blood froze. Zheng's man. The one who'd almost squeezed the life out of me the day before. I leapt for the door handle but the driver stepped on the gas and it ripped out of my fingers. The cab squealed off.

Blaine hailed another taxi and he and I dove into the back seat. "Follow that cab!" he hollered at the driver.

"Youz two kiddin'?" the cabbie said in a thick Bronx accent.

I followed his gaze. A sea of yellow taxis spread out before us. I spied the back of Avery's head through the rear windshield. "There! That one just up ahead." I pointed. "Go. I'll keep my eye on him till we catch up."

The car lurched forward. The cab driver slung his arm along the top of the seat and glanced back at us. "I charge double for a car chase." He laughed and turned back to the front in time to squeeze between two rows of almost stopped cars, miraculously slipping through without a scrape. The other drivers honked and shook their fists at us as he maneuvered himself ahead of the pack, closer to the speeding car whisking Avery away from us and toward who knew what.

Another car lurched in between us and Avery, but I kept my eyes on the other taxi. "Don't lose them! We're right behind them."

The cab we were following suddenly shot ahead. "Hurry up! We're losing her!" I was coming completely unhinged. Blaine gripped my arm, but I shook him off. The thought of Avery trapped with the brutal man who had tried to kill me the day before was driving me insane.

The cabbie zigged and zagged, leaving a trail of angry motorists in our wake. Another car slipped in front of us and I couldn't see Avery anymore. Our driver gassed it and swerved out and around the car to get back in front. I scanned the horizon desperately but Avery was gone from sight. All I could see was an endless line of cars ahead. Our cabbie pressed on, accelerating to come up beside each taxi. Each one was empty.

The cab driver banged his fist on the dashboard and yelled, "Damn it. I had them. I had them right there. Right there."

He slowed down and turned around to look at me. "I'm so sorry, man. I don't know how they got away. I was on their tail and then a car got in between us and they were gone. I'm so sorry."

I slumped against the back of the seat.

"This is the most direct route outside the city to upstate New York, so I'll bet they're taking her there," the cabbie offered. "Do you need a ride to the police station?"

Blaine shook his head. "Let's go back to Luc's." He sounded as defeated as I felt. "We need help and maybe he'll have an idea where Zheng's men might be taking her."

AIDEN

In the spiritual world there are no time divisions such as the past, present and future, for they have contracted themselves into a single moment of the present where life quivers in its true sense.

—D. T. Suzuki

We arrived at Luc's to find Wao resting comfortably. He looked up at us and a thin smile spread across his face. Grasping my hand, he pulled me close and whispered, "Avery needs you now more than ever. You must go to her."

"You need rest, Wao," Luc said.

"It's my time," Wao replied. "I've never been kept out of the field before."

"What field?" I asked.

"The field, Aiden. The web of life, the meshing of the universe, the place where all things are possible, all things created. Something is wrong. I lost my connection to the field and to Old Phoenix. He wasn't there. He's the one who taught me how to move among the dimensions. It was like there was a super-scrambler interfering with my entry."

Blaine rested a hand on Wao's arm. "The field is a concept in quantum physics. A place where the entire universe intersects, a place where creation sparks to life, just like the Tao taught us so long ago. The language is different, but the ideas are the same. I talked to Old Phoenix about the field last time I was at the caves."

Luc ushered us out of the room and shook his head. "Wao told me he's leaving us today."

An agonizing sense of loss gripped me and I nearly doubled over from the pain. Luc gripped my shoulder. With Avery in danger, and Wao about to die, the threads of my life were unraveling and feared his touch would undo me completely. Instead, it grounded me and filled me with strength and resolve. Wao's voice grew in pitch inside me as Luc took hold of my shoulder. It was as though his hand was a channel opening a door into my unconscious, allowing Wao's words to come to me. *You already know where she is. She needs you now.*

As if Luc had heard Wao's words, he turned to me. "Aiden. Where would Zheng go with Avery? You already know. Think."

A bird trilled. Blaine pressed a button on his watch phone. "It's the ringtone I gave Raven," he said. "I'll put her on speaker. Hello?"

"Blaine, Avery's in trouble. Mom and I are outside in the van."

"We're coming now." Blaine hit the button and headed for the door.

I hesitated, conflicted about leaving Wao.

Luc squeezed my shoulder. "He wants you to go."

I nodded and followed Blaine down the front steps. The side door of the van slid open and we both jumped in. I was relieved to see Christian there.

"I saw them," Raven said, "In a vision."

I had a blinding flash of clarity. "I know where they are," I snapped my fingers. "Deer Island. Norman invited us to go hunting with him there."

Her mother started the van and pulled out onto the street.

"That's it," Raven tossed her long dark braid over her shoulder. "They were in a dense woods in my dream, surrounded by water."

"I'll GPS it," Christian said, and entered the coordinates.

Raven placed a finger to her temple and squeezed her eyebrows together. "We have to get Rasta from Ruby. He knows Avery's in trouble."

Marly shot a look at her daughter. "You are not coming with us."

"I am. I have my bow and I'm a better shot than Christian."

"This is not a video game or target practice. This is life-threatening. I won't allow it."

Raven lifted her chin. "Avery is my friend, and I won't let her down. I can talk to Rasta. No one else can."

Christian leaned forward from his seat in the back and touched Marly's shoulder. "She's right, Marly. Raven is the best shot. We need her."

"We need to pick up Rasta now, Mom."

Blaine looked out the side window. "Ruby's at her sister's house in Harlem. We're not far from there now."

"Deer Island is a five-hour drive, and they've had about an hour head start." My head throbbed. "If we're going to stop, we'll have to be quick."

Raven snatched the phone out of her jacket pocket. "I'll text her now to be ready."

Marly sighed. "Fine."

"There." Blaine pointed toward the front windshield. "That's the street."

Marly wheeled around the corner.

I drummed my fingers on the armrest, anxious to be on our way. "What is this Deer Island, anyway?"

Marly dodged a young man dancing across the road, wearing oversized earphones not paying attention to where he was walking. "Deer Island is owned by The Skull and Bones Society. They're a secret and highly exclusive group that originated from Yale University. Many of our presidents have been Bonesmen, as they are called. Their members are in the CIA, they are bankers, financial power brokers, judges …well, you get the picture. They comprise a powerful cabal who run the world."

Blaine's forehead wrinkled. "If they're so secretive, how do you know that much about them?"

Raven twisted herself around to face Blaine. "What they do is secret, but who they are isn't. In fact, they often brag about making it into the Society. They even wear a ring that designates them as members. It's well-known that Bonesmen hold the highest-level positions in the most influential global organizations. I overheard some men talking about Avery's father in my mom's office one day, and since then, I've been doing some research. Peter Adams isn't just one of those men; he is the top man, sitting up there with five other families from around the world – sometimes referred to as The Illuminati. They run the world, and the rest of us just live under the illusion that we have countries, leaders, and global economies, with allies and enemies. The Illuminati turn all of that on its ear."

"He's definitely a Bonesman." Blaine nodded. "I saw his ring. My dad had a friend who was a Grand Mason and told me a lot about how it worked at the highest levels. He wanted me to join, but I had already learned some of the secrets of esoteric Taoism."

"Avery's father has his hands in every type of energy resource that exists," Marly yanked on the wheel and pulled over to the curb. Ruby waited for us on the sidewalk. "Lately he's been holding hands with Master Zheng, leader of a known Chinese Triad. He and some of his men entered the US a little while ago, and they are trained in deadly internal martial arts. Zheng has been lobbying the Chinese government for management of the largest deposit of lithium in the world, which happens to be in Tibet."

Rasta strained at his leash. We barely opened the door, and Rasta leapt into the back of the van. We waved at Ruby while Marly squealed away from the curb and headed for the edge of the city. Rasta maneuvered his way past Blaine and me, and stuck his head into the front seat between Marly and Raven. He panted, and every once in a while a low throaty growl escaped from him.

Marly patted his head absently. "Zheng is on the DA's watch list right now, and he showed up on their radar because of his connection with Avery's dad. When the CIA showed up to tell him Zheng and Adams were in their territory, old McMurtry really began to dig into it. There was a string of highly unusual killings and everything pointed towards Zheng's men, but there was no hard evidence." She looked over at her daughter. "And all of that is why I didn't want you involved, Raven."

Raven straightened in her seat. "They have my best friend. I am already involved."

AIDEN

A certain amount of opposition is good for man. Kites rise against the wind, not with it.

—Lao Tzu

Marly slowed down the van on the stretch of an empty two-lane highway and pulled onto a barely visible road. She looked at Christian for confirmation.

"Yes," Christian said, nodding his head. "This is the road that Grandfather said to turn down. The GPS showed a different one, but I'd take Grandfather's advice any day."

I heard Grandfather and Old Phoenix blended again as one voice, deep inside my mind. *Trust your instincts. Trust that we are with you.* The road was overgrown with deep hidden ruts that threatened to swallow the tires on the old van and stop it in its tracks. Marly drove in silence through the dark as tree branches scratched the outside of the van.

"Marly," Christian had lowered his voice, but it echoed through the quiet van. "According to Grandfather, we're almost at the dock. In case they left someone behind, we don't want anyone to know we're coming."

She slowed down and turned out the lights.

I blinked, waiting for my eyes to adjust to the dark. Slowly the trees took shape around us and the narrow road ahead began to form.

We drove for a few more minutes, then stopped. Christian put his finger to his lips and motioned for us to get out of the van. We slid the side door open and climbed out carefully, leaving it open behind us. Rasta leapt out of the vehicle and went straight to Raven. He looked into her eyes, then bolted through the woods without looking back. His black coat vanished into the darkness. *How will we ever be able to find him?* The crickets and other night noises were so loud, even if there were people here, surely they wouldn't be able to hear us over the racket.

Christian reached into the van between the seats and pulled out a high-powered crossbow. I raised my eyebrows. As far as I knew, he only used hand-made bows and arrows for target practice. He must have noticed my questioning look, because he held the crossbow to his chest. I understood. This was not going to be target practice. This was not going to be a polite gathering of martial artists testing each other's skills. This was not even going to be like the last few times we had encountered Zheng's men. This was going to be a fight to the finish.

I looked over at Blaine. Our years as Bagua brothers gave us an almost telepathic ability to understand each other. We had done martial arts to the point where it was no longer about fighting, no longer about anything other than the spiritual significance of walking a circle, generating energy, and bringing light into a world that sorely needed it. We wanted to be a force for good in the world. We wanted to be healers. Blaine joked about wanting to fight, but he didn't want to have a real fight to the death any more than I did. But here we were, and it was clear that Avery's life hung in the balance.

We had no choice.

I barely had time to reflect on that sobering reality, barely had time to even consider that tonight I would likely have to kill someone. I thought of Wao dying at Luc's house, and anger rose up inside me. Then I heard my teacher's voice over the night sounds. *Not with anger, my young warrior. Not with anger. Always with honor.*

Christian glanced at me and so did Blaine. We all nodded. Raven had already disappeared into the brush with a full quiver of arrows and her favorite bow.

We entered the woods and crept through them stealthily, avoiding twigs or branches that might crack beneath our feet. Something outside my conscious mind directed my steps with absolute certainty toward our destination. Christian, Marly, Blaine and I moved together, as if we were one.

We crept out to the edge of the woods where the rocks met the lake. Marly came up beside me. I heard a slight splash and caught a glimpse of a slick black object swimming away from the mainland. A dock pointed towards an island a few hundred feet away, as if showing us the way.

A man with a machine gun slung across his chest walked out onto the dock, his form barely silhouetted against the sliver of a moon, high in the night sky. A shooting star streaked across the inky backdrop, like a single tracer bullet. *How many more would fall tonight?*

Christian touched my shoulder and pointed to the man on the dock. He gestured that there were three of them. I looked around but couldn't see anyone else. Then I felt, more than saw, a figure take shape near the edge of the woods. Another man followed. *Where is Raven?*

Blaine and I looked at each other. Christian already had his bow set up to take out the man on the dock. Blaine and I could reach the other two in a few seconds. I circled my finger through the air, indicating that we should come up behind them. Blaine nodded. We snuck along the edge of the woods and got into position. The moment we heard the thwack of the arrow leaving the bow, we downed our men simultaneously with quick strikes to the neck, leaving them temporarily unconscious.

The men were equipped with belts full of everything one would need on a guerrilla terrorist mission. *Should we have killed them?* I sent the thought to Blaine, but he shook his head. I agreed. We had been taught to kill only when absolutely necessary. Taking these two out of commission was all that was needed. For now.

As I tied my man's hands and feet together with the nylon rope that I took from his belt, I looked over to see Christian bent over the man he had killed. He looked as though he was reciting a prayer. Behind him, a man stepped out of the shadows. My heart leapt into my throat. He raised his rifle. Just as I opened my mouth to warn Christian, I heard another thwack, then watched the rifleman crumple to the ground.

Raven emerged from the shadows and, like Christian, went down on bended knee over her kill.

I took the silver gaffer's tape hanging on the belt of the man I had downed, tore off a strip with my teeth, and slapped it over his mouth. A twig snapped softly behind me. I froze, readying myself for a twirling surprise leap in the air, but Marly came out of the trees. She bent down to pick up the remote communications device lying near the man. It squealed and settled into static before a disembodied voice broke through. "All quiet on the western front. What about the east? ...East...East...Come in East. Quan? Are you there, Quan? Over."

Raven and Christian joined us.

Marly dropped the radio and ground it into the dirt with her foot. Then she yanked the automatic weapon off of the man on the ground and barked, "Let's go kick some butt."

Nervous chuckles escaped from both Blaine and me. Automatic machines guns had never been part of our repertoire. Maybe the odd ceremonial sword, and Christian's handmade bows and arrows, but guns were a whole other matter.

Christian stared at his cousin. "Do you know how to use that thing?"

"How hard can it be? Point and shoot." Marly laughed and trudged off to the dock. When she reached the edge, she slung the gun over her shoulder, as if she'd been doing it her whole life, and planted both fists on her hips. "Great. No boat. How are we going to get there?"

"Rasta swam over." Raven nodded toward the island.

Marly shuddered. "There's no way I'm getting into that dark water."

"She doesn't get into any water unless it's a shower," Christian said.

Marly snorted. "I never learned how to swim and I don't think now is the time."

Blaine had left the dock and gone down to poke at the water's edge with a stick he picked up. "Hey, guys," he whispered loudly. "There's an old row boat here on the shore. It's got a hole in it, but it's not far to the island..."

Blaine lifted up one end of the boat and shoved it into the water. He helped Marly and Raven in. I pulled my sweatshirt over my head and balled it up so I could stuff it in the hole and buy us a little time.

Blaine stepped into the boat, holding onto both sides until it stopped rocking. When he'd settled on one of the wooden slats, he handed Marly and Raven each a cup for bailing. Christian grabbed the paddle and I walked the boat away from the shore, giving her a good shove out into the water before I jumped in. We had traveled only a few feet when the boat caught a swift current and glided effortlessly towards the island shore.

Another shooting star tore through the sky. An illuminated messenger breaking through from another world. A lone loon called out into the darkness, its haunting cry hanging in the air like mist across the surface of the water. It would have been a beautiful night ride if we didn't know what awaited us at the shore of Deer Island.

AVERY

The power of intuitive understanding will protect you from harm until the end of your days.

—Lao Tzu

My father twisted my arm behind my back and brought his mouth close to my ear.

"Where is it, Avery? Where is the necklace?"

I winced. "You're hurting me."

"Peter, that's enough," Norman said. "That's your daughter! Come on now." He moved around behind me and lowered his voice. "Come on now, Peter. Lighten up. That's it. Lighten up."

Some of the strength drained out of my father's grip and my shoulders relaxed a bit.

"She's got the necklace. I can practically feel it." His hold on my wrist tightened again.

"Peter, Avery will give you the necklace if you just ask her. Isn't that right, Avery?" Norman spoke in a voice usually reserved for very young children, or someone you were trying to talk down off a ledge.

I nodded, hoping my father would release my arm. I wanted to say, "You aren't my father. I hate you. You're a liar and a bully!" But that would have to wait. I had seen my father in this emo-amplified state recently and it was terrifying.

"You don't want to hurt your daughter, now do you? She has the necklace that you want." Norman kept his gaze trained on Peter.

I nodded each time my father loosened his grip on my arm. I glanced around the room to orient myself to the surroundings. I knew there were armed guards outside, somewhere, but they were looking for people trying to get into the lodge, not out. If I surprised my dad and Norman, I might be able to dart to the wooden door, fling it open, and bolt into the woods.

Someone knocked on the door. My dad's fingers tightened around my wrist again in response.

"No one answering at the eastern dock, boss. The radio battery might be dead. What do you want us to do?"

Norman finally managed to pry my father off me and lead him around to stand in front of me. I shook my arm out and watched them both warily.

Norman slid an arm around my father's shoulders. "What do you want them to do, Peter?"

Dad shoved his fingers through his already-wild hair. "Where's Zheng? He should be taking care of this."

"Zheng will be here soon. His boat was right behind ours. So what do you want them to do?"

"Get down there. See if anyone other than Zheng docks," Peter snarled.

Boots tromped along the veranda towards the docks. Someone called out, "Let that pair of Karelian bear dogs out. They'll make sure no one gets on or off the island."

Peter and Norman both turned toward the voice. I took my cue and sprinted to the back door. I was already outside by the time their footsteps creaked on the wooden floor behind me.

I flew across the lawn and into the woods. I barely felt the branches slashing at my face and arms. My ballet tights and my jeans kept my legs protected. I ran as fast as possible, trying to put as much distance between me and them as I could. They might be stronger than me, but I had better speed and took up less space so it was easier for me to make my way through the thick brush. Hours of ballet and Bagua had built up my endurance, and I also had the necklace. I had taken it off in the back of the taxi and wrapped it around my ankle where it would be harder to find, and I could feel it pulsing now, just above my ankle bone where it was held tight to my skin by my ballet tights.

I pressed on, completely lost in my surroundings. I only knew I had to stay away from my father, who wasn't really my father. The look in his eyes terrified me and suddenly all the warnings from Raven made sense. I could feel death on him, and a vision of that same chilling look on his face when my mother took ill flashed through my mind. I hadn't understood it then, and I never spoke to anyone about what I had seen in his eyes. I just never quite forgot it.

Wham! My foot came down between two exposed tree roots and I tumbled forward. My head banged against another tree root, and I lay stunned on the cold, damp forest floor.

When the world stopped spinning, I sat up and tried to yank my foot out from between the roots, but it was wedged in tight; the shooting pains up my leg didn't help, and neither did the pendant digging into my skin. I ripped at the roots to pull them apart but they were thick and wouldn't budge. I twisted my foot in a last ditch effort to set it free it. I bit my tongue to keep from screaming in agony. I gave it once last tug and I was out. I used the tree trunk as a support to help me stand. My eyes filled with tears when I put weight on it. I wasn't sure how far away my pursuers were, but I couldn't stay here for long.

I leaned down and rubbed my anklebone as I had seen Aiden do when someone hurt themselves at practice, but that only made it throb more. Blood trickled down my leg. Grabbing a stick as make-shift cane, I began to hobble forward. The woods grew denser, and a canopy of leaves blocked the guiding light from the moon and the stars.

I had never felt more alone.

AIDEN

When armies are mobilized and issues are joined, the man who is sorry over the fact will win.

—Lao Tsu

I followed Blaine as we crossed the lawn and approached the lodge. I knew Marly and Christian were behind me, but they moved so silently they were little more than shadows. The sound of dogs barking had receded into the thick woods; Rasta must be leading the guards away from us. I crept along the veranda behind Blaine, stepping carefully in an attempt to keep the old, rotting boards from creaking. At the oversized wooden door, we crouched down and listened. An enormous stag's head was mounted above the opening, its massive antlers reaching out to either side, its large dull eyes looking out into the void. Inside, I could hear men talking, my hearing acute.

"You've let the girl go? With the necklace?"

"She's on an island. And she's a city girl. How far do you think she can get? Norman and I know every inch of this land. We can track her, no problem."

"We may have company. Someone found an old rowboat down by the south beach."

I motioned for everyone to be at the ready.

Peter spoke up again. "Zheng, I'll worry about the necklace, you worry about..."

Blaine shot me a heated glance. He was as ready as me to bust down the door. It looked heavy. We would only have one chance to break through if we hoped to use surprise to our advantage. Blaine nodded and we both stood up and moved to the edge of the porch, facing the door. He held up a finger. I drew in a deep breath. When he pointed, we both charged toward the door. We hit it at the same time and the bolts and hinges gave way.

The door slammed to the floor and we tumbled into the room, with Marly behind us. A guard reached for his gun. A spray of bullets from an automatic weapon drilled into the ceiling and the chandelier rained broken crystal. Blaine and I scrambled behind a large leather wingback chair. The sharp staccato rain of bullets stopped almost as quickly as it started. I peeked out and saw Marly looking dazed, staring at the automatic weapon in her hand as if it had a life of its own. I jumped to my feet, almost as stunned as Marly, and surveyed the room. A few men were hunkered down, but no one appeared injured. Peter and Norman were gone. The back door slapped shut, and I looked over to see Zheng between us and where we needed to go. Men carrying weapons streamed into the room from other parts of the cabin to line up in front of him.

I'd say it wasn't going as planned, except we really didn't have a plan. Although we hadn't discussed it, I'm sure we all thought we'd bust in, have a fight with a couple of guards, Peter, and Norman, save Avery and leave. I glanced at Zheng and his men again, then looked back at Blaine. No way would either one of us would be getting to the back door, right now. From the corner of my eye, I could see Blaine sizing up the situation, and heard his thoughts when he came to the same rapid conclusion. The only way out was through Zheng and his men.

Through meant hand-to-hand combat against a team of highly skilled martial artists all committed to protecting their master. Blaine and I were highly skilled too, but not at killing. Marly still seemed to be in shock, although Christian stood at attack stance, clearly ready for anything. Where was Luc when we needed him? He could easily take on five or six men. We did have Raven who, like a ghost, appeared and disappeared at will. I hoped she was close by. The stream of automatons lining up to protect Zheng stopped. I let out a breath. Then Valerie and Veronika strode in and stood in front of them all.

Veronika turned to stare at me. "Did you think we'd still be wandering in the foothills of the Wudang?" she sneered. "Do you understand what you did, Aiden? Really understand?"

I scrutinized her, confused, but trying not to show it. I still hadn't mastered the art of the poker face.

"Sheng Li is gone," Valerie whispered with relish. "Gone like that!" She snapped her fingers.

Rage surged through me. Blaine grabbed my arm to hold me back. I struggled to contain a mounting anger. If I allowed my emotions to take over, we were done for.

The wall of automatons surged forward in a tidal force of destruction.

Blaine and I leapt into the fray. Arrows hissed past my head. I managed to disarm and render one guard unconscious, then Veronika was upon me, striking at my head and chest.

"This is what happens when love turns to hate," she said through gritted teeth, "and I really hate you." Her black fingernails clawed down my face, leaving a trail of searing pain as I arced out of the line of attack. "You really should have killed me when you had the chance, Aiden the Great," she taunted. Veronika moved into Xingyi crushing fist and attacked me with rapid-fire movements that seemed synchronized with the rapid fire of the automatic weapon Marly had apparently figured out how to use.

I called on every bit of training I had ever received to center myself. The noise dulled and my vision sharpened until I saw everyone with such clarity they appeared to move in slow motion. I found myself in the eye of the storm. Bullets flew, legs kicked, and Veronika raged around me, but nothing seemed to touch me.

Blaine attacked the automatons, knocking them down one by one. Christian worked his magic with the crossbow, while Marly, who must have run out of rounds, used her weapon as a club. I scanned the room, looking for Raven and Zheng.

Veronika slashed at me with a knife. I reached out calmly and squeezed her delicate neck with two fingers until she went limp. After all that had happened, all she had done to Avery, to Sheng Li, and to me, I still couldn't kill her. I could not bring myself to take the life of another living being. And I had loved her—once.

I honed in on Zheng and my breath caught. He had come up behind Christian and was about to deliver a fatal blow to Christian's head. I lunged toward them.

Zheng felt me coming and whirled around to take a powerful step into me to deliver his signature crushing fist to my face. I barely managed to circle out of his attack, and he was on me again. "It will be my pleasure to take down the Scorpion." He squared off, both hands held up in front of him. "Wao must be gone by now," he mocked. "Soon, you will be too." He lunged forward in percussive steps and thrust out his fist, catching me on the side of the head as I tried to spin away.

Pain exploded in my head. I stumbled backwards as a mist drifted in front of my eyes. Zheng was doubling, and tripling. His laugh amplified, sounding like a ringing bell inside my mind. My vision so distorted I thought I saw Luc join the fray. Zheng rushed towards me. I tried to spin out of the way, but my feet felt rooted in cement. Just before the killing blow descended, Old Phoenix stepped in front of me.

I blinked again. The radiance of Old Phoenix glimmered in the room, creating a swathe of bright light among the shadowy Zheng and his henchmen. Was I hallucinating? Was this for real? I shook my head; Old Phoenix could not be here.

I looked up to see Luc with Young Phoenix at his side, leaping into the fray like a whirling dervish. Old Phoenix honed in on his target, Zheng. Like magnets with opposing polarities, the two masters came towards each other and locked in position, one north, one south on an axis.

Everyone in the room froze as Phoenix and Zheng stood within striking distance of each other. Zheng dropped into a deep stance, his hands taking on the shape of the head of a snake. His body writhed, conjuring the spirit of the snake. Old Phoenix stood with his hands limp by his sides. Zheng burst forward in one quick snap, like the attack of a cobra. Old Phoenix wrapped his hands around Zheng's, his gentle, flowing hand movements looking more like prayer mudra than martial art. A blinding flash lit up the room, followed by a crack of thunder.

Blaine caught my eye and jerked his head toward the back of the building. My head still pounded and I fought the fog threatening to engulf my brain. When it retreated, our minds connected. Blaine meant for us to slip out the back door to find Avery, now that we had help.

We worked our way towards the back door. Everyone else in the room stood silently, mesmerized by the confrontation between two former blood brothers whose intents were as different as the paths they had chosen.

Chapter 46

AVERY

Respond intelligently even to unintelligent treatment.

—Lao Tsu

A sky-splitting fork of lightning streaked, momentarily illuminating the ghostly trees. Sheets of rain pelted down. *How long have I been wandering in the woods?* With my sprained ankle, it felt like hours, but it could have been far less. I couldn't tell any more whether I was going straight or in circles. I tried to pay attention to my surroundings, but in the dark everything looked the same.

I didn't want to leave any obvious signs of my passing through. My father had talked often about tracking deer. A trained hunter like Norman knew exactly what signs to look for.

Whenever I came across a clear deer path, I limped on it for a while before drifting off into the dense woods. I kept my eyes on my running shoes, trying my best not to ruffle a single leaf, or crush a twig under my feet. My head whipped around at a sharp, staccato sound. *Was that machine gun fire?* A shudder flashed through me. If it was behind me, maybe I was still headed in the right direction, away from the cabin. I pressed ahead with renewed determination.

For a long time, the barking of dogs had shattered the stillness of the night, but now everything seemed quiet. Too quiet. The only sound was the incessant buzzing of mosquitoes that seemed to be the size of hummingbirds diving in to suck my blood. Not even the rain was stopping them. It hadn't taken long for the downpour to soak through the canopy of trees and I was completely drenched.

I stepped into a small dip in the ground and pain shot up from my ankle. Biting back a cry of agony, I leaned against a tree. My breaths came in short gasps and I forced myself to calm down. I hoped I had not been moving like a scared rabbit. I had to pull myself together. Norman and my father always said that hunting an animal running scared was child's play. It moved on instinct, without thinking, and made too many mistakes.

I tipped back my head to study the tree I stood under. There were enough branches to climb fairly easily. Lightning flashed again and I winced. While it was dangerous to hide under a tree in a thunder storm, I had no choice. If I climbed up a short distance, the next flash of lightning might allow me to see a pathway that could lead me out of the woods. And maybe, if I sat up in the tree and rested a moment, just until my thudding heart slowed, I might be able to hear if anyone was closing in on me.

I grasped the lowest branch. I hauled myself up to the next branch, using my arms and good foot and biting my lip to hold back a sob. I reached for a branch above my head, but a strong hand clamped around my ankle. The necklace dug into my skin and searing pain tore through me, licking up my calf like a flame. I cried out and wrenched my foot out of my father's grasp. The ballet tights ripped as he released me. My shoe flew off and I lifted my leg, then pumped it down as hard as I could, aiming for his head. He didn't move away in time and my heel connected with his cheek. He stumbled backwards.

Adrenaline pumped through me, dulling the pain. Norman grabbed for my other leg and I kicked out with everything I had. He avoided my kick and grabbed my leg. I clung to the trunk of the tree but Norman was too strong for me. He yanked me toward him, the bark tearing the skin of my hands as it slid through my fingers. Just before I hit the ground, I twisted my body as I had seen Blaine and Aiden do many times. It had always looked magical when they did it. I'm not sure how I managed it, but with a full body spin, I flew through the air, landing behind Norman and Dad. I didn't think, just bolted through the woods as fast as I could. Fear overrode pain. For a few seconds, there was no movement behind me. The shock value must have given me a head start.

As the necklace generated heat, I realized my injury was healing more quickly than I thought possible. I could run faster now. My feet dug into the muddy earth. A surge of energy pulsed through me, fueled by my necklace. I was learning how to use its power, my ankle fully healed now.

I charged on, thrashing through the brush. When I still didn't hear the sound of pursuit, I risked a glance back over my shoulder. That break in concentration was all it took. I slammed full speed into a low hanging branch that knocked me backwards onto the ground. For a moment, I lay still, the world spinning around me. Hot, moist breath dampened my neck. I sat up. My blood froze at the sight of the snarling, wolfish grins of what must be the two Karelian Bear dogs inches from my face. Their breath stank of raw meat. Their eyes penetrated mine. As one, they stepped closer to me. I tried to scream, but no sound came out of my mouth.

Norman and my father came up behind the dogs. "You thought you could outrun Norman and me, when we know every inch of these woods on the island?" My father sneered. "And why are you running away from your own father, anyway?"

I shifted on the hard ground. One of the dogs growled, snapping his teeth close to my face.

"Norman," my father waved a hand through the air. "Call them down and leash the beasts. We might need them again soon."

Norman pulled out the thick leather leashes and gave a short, sharp whistle. The pair of dogs tilted their heads towards the path, as if listening, then bounded away from him.

Raven, you are talking to them, aren't you? I would have smiled, if the situation wasn't so dire.

"Come, you damn dogs. Come back." Norman spun around, clearly ready to chase them.

My father bent down and clutched my upper arms in his large hands. "Norman, leave the dogs. We have her now." He hauled me to my feet, his fingers biting into my skin.

I struggled to free myself.

"Avery, darling, what has gotten into you?" My father shook me slightly. "Why are you fighting me?" His eyes softened, his pupils almost as wide as his irises. "I love you, my child. I'm just trying to keep you safe."

My voice cracked as I spat out my words. "Safe? I don't trust you one bit."

He tightened his grip. "It's those two boys you shouldn't trust. They're the ones who have brought this all on. Before they came to New York all was fine. Wasn't it, darling? There was no danger before. We never had any problems between us. You kept your necklace in its box, just like your mother told you to. Right?"

I couldn't argue with him. I had said something similar to Aiden in anger just after rehearsal. Everything *had* been fine before I met Aiden.

My world had been safe. I might have had panic attacks but they were clearly all in my head. Just like that therapist had said.

My father let go of me. "Let's get her to the deer blind, Norman. We have blankets there."

I was shivering. From the cold rain, the night air, or fright, I wasn't certain.

Norman grasped my arm with his free hand. Before I realized what was happening, my father bent down and undid the clasp of my necklace. I yanked my foot away, but it was too late.

"I told you that you would lose this necklace if you weren't careful, Avery." My father's smile was cold as he fastened the chain around his own neck. A streak of lightning cracked overhead, splintering a nearby tree. The earth below our feet shuddered as it absorbed the energy. Electricity tingled through me.

"What the...?" Norman looked up at the sky, his eyes wide.

"Not another damned geo-magnetic storm," my father muttered. "Not to worry. We're on generators here, so we won't be affected."

I felt sickened, weak and tired. My ankle throbbed, now that the healing power of the necklace was gone. Clumps of wet hair stuck to my face.

My father pulled a flashlight from his pocket and turned it on. Waves of nausea overcame me. I had only been a few feet from the deer blind. There it was, just above us, perched on the side of a huge sturdy tree and camouflaged with branches. If not for the narrow slit at waist height for the use of rifles, the blind would have looked more like a small cabin than the makeshift structure I had expected to find. It had a real front door.

My father reached up to release a step ladder and it unfolded itself down to the ground. He climbed up first, and held onto a small safety bar to hoist himself inside. When I reached the blind, he handed me a green wool army blanket. I grabbed it, grateful for something warm and dry, grateful for a chance to rest. I hugged the rough blanket around my shoulders as Norman, pushed me up inside, then pulled himself up into the blind. Two camping-style chairs faced the long, low horizontal window slat.

"Take off your clothes, Avery," my father commanded.

My eyes widened. "What?"

"Your clothes. They're wet. You have a blanket to keep around you. No one will see you." He cocked his head. "Why are you so suspicious?

I just want to hang up your wet clothes so they will dry and you will be comfortable. Comfortable and dry and safe. That's all I want for you."

It all sounded so reasonable. He looked so normal telling me this. Like he was my dad again, and I was a child looking to him for help. He motioned for me to go ahead and do what he'd told me to.

My cold wet clothes stuck uncomfortably to my skin. I held the blanket around me while I pulled off my jeans, what was left of my ballet tights, my leotard and t-shirt, and held them out.

Norman took them and hung them on hooks around the potbellied stove. He'd attempted to light a fire and the wet wood hissed and smoked, but soon a flame grew. When he'd finished with my clothes, Norman took my elbow and led me to a chair in the corner.

I moved mechanically, as if in a trance.

After I'd settled onto the chair, he pulled the blanket tighter around me. I didn't know what my father was up to, but I was too exhausted to fight anymore. *If I can just rest for a moment, I'll find the strength to steal away again.* With the necklace gone, weakness took over me. I had grown so used to its energy that I felt ill without it, almost too ill to care what happened to me.

"Avery, you always did love your luxuries. Just like your mom. You are so lucky to have me as your Dad, because you don't have what it takes to achieve anything of significance. I knew you wouldn't last long out there. Your mom always needed the best of everything, too."

He knows nothing about me, or my mom. My mother never needed all that stuff. She had confided in me that the affluence of our lives made her uncomfortable, and she had often dreamed of having a small bungalow in a small town living a small, simple life.

Another flare of lighting, followed by an explosion of thunder, allowed me to see more of the interior of the hunting blind. Heavy metal animal traps hung from hooks along one wall, and several rifles were propped up in a gun rack. The rain pelted down on the tin roof of the blind in a hypnotic background wash of noise.

"The gods are fighting." Norman pointed toward the roof of the blind. "That's what my dad always used to say when it stormed."

My father nodded solemnly. "Indeed, I think they are, Norman."

Chapter 47

AIDEN

To the mind that is still, the whole universe surrenders.

—Lao Tzu

Blaine and I slipped away from the battle, stealing towards the back door. I glanced behind me just as the two masters clashed again. Another crack of thunder and lightning illuminated the room. I whirled back around. The brief flash of light revealed two empty slots in the gun rack to the left of the back door. I pushed through the door ahead of Blaine, leading him straight into the woods as if I knew the way.

We charged through the dense underbrush. The mud-caked earth had broken apart, creating channels that coursed along the forest floor. All of it seemed familiar – déjà vu – like I had lived this before. Maybe in a dream. I could hear sounds and smell odors with a clarity I had never before experienced. Unfortunately, the rain had washed away any trace of Avery. Tzinggg! I leapt at Blaine and toppled him out of the way as a bullet whipped past his ear, narrowly missing him. Though we were hunting for Avery, we were being hunted.

Blaine hit the ground on his back and I landed on top of him. He raised his eyebrows. I leaned closer and whispered, "This past year in the Wudang was interesting. A lot of night training."

Blaine shoved me off of him, and the two of us helped each other up. He grabbed my arm and pressed a finger to his lips. Branches snapped and a blur of black flew by us, followed by a loud thud, like a body hitting the ground. Then I heard the thwack of an arrow leaving the string and another body fell onto the damp forest floor. Rasta and Raven working as a team. That dog was amazing. I hadn't seen him since he slipped into the water back on the mainland, but I was certain he had been around us, distracting our adversaries. And now he and Raven were taking them down.

Blaine and I dodged down a different path, confident that Raven and Rasta had this section of the woods under control. We trudged on in the thunderstorm.

I nudged Blaine. "She loves you, you know. I can see that." A heaviness draped over me as I said the words, but they had to be said.

"I'm just the stand-in, bro."

"You're more than that. Make sure you take good care of her. She... she's very special."

"We better find her or neither one of us will have her to take care of."

The storm raged on around us. A lightning bolt lit up the sky, followed by a booming thunderclap. The momentary light illuminated a deer blind farther down the path, a large structure cradled in a very strong tree. The ladder leading to the door was exposed. Somehow I knew the blind would be there. I elbowed Blaine and pointed. "She's in there."

"How do you know?"

"This past year with Wao..." I didn't really understand it myself. I had been drawn to this place without thinking, without being conscious of it.

We crept past a salt lick and several cobs of corn scattered on the ground as we approached the blind. Blaine shook his head and whispered, "Nothing sporting in luring a deer to its death."

When we got close, I held up my hand, then gestured, indicating that I would climb up the ladder and he should follow right behind. I'd attempt to break through the door, hopefully surprising Peter, Avery and whoever else was inside, probably Norman. I put up first one finger, then two, then both of us nodded and we were bounding toward the ladder. I reached it first and climbed up, hitting the door shoulder first. It crashed open on impact and I flew into the room. Blaine hauled himself up into the blind right after me.

We both scrambled to our feet. Peter was wide-eyed, as I'd hoped, but his face quickly morphed into controlled rage. I advanced toward him. From the corner of my eye, I saw Blaine make a smooth sweep with his foot, catching Norman's ankles and bringing him down. The rifle Norman had grabbed when we came into the room clattered to the ground. I caught a glimpse of Avery sitting on a chair in the corner. She appeared to be in shock. I couldn't worry about her at the moment, though. In a movement that required no conscious thought, I whirled to the left, my focus honed to a fine and destructive point of intent. I dipped down, just missing Peter's attack from above with a rifle butt. I moved into *snake spitting his tongue* and as I rose up, my fingers dug into Peter's neck. He collapsed to the ground, his mouth open as if emitting a silent scream of agony, his airway temporarily cut off. I straddled him and continued to apply pressure.

I thought I had taken him out, but he was strong. Stronger than I imagined. His right hand shot out and grabbed his rifle. In one swift movement, he flipped me over onto my back and shoved the barrel of the gun against my throat. I gasped for air and clutched the rifle with both hands, trying to pull it away from me. Peter pressed the barrel down. Darkness flickered around the edges of my vision. Then the rifle was gone. I sucked in desperately and a rush of air flowed through my windpipe.

Peter flew off of me. I rolled onto my side and pushed myself up to a sitting position.

Avery, her eyes flaming, clutched a blanket around herself with one hand and attacked Peter with the other, using moves that, as far as I knew, she had only ever seen, but not been taught. She seized his wrist in her free hand and created a wave so powerful I could see the ripple of energy flow up his arm. As his head snapped backwards, I thought his neck had broken.

I waved an arm frantically toward the opening. "Run, Avery, Run!"

For once, she listened to me. She lunged at the doorway and disappeared through the opening. I turned my attention back to Peter.

He scooped up the rifle Norman had dropped and stood in front of the doorway, pointing the rifle in the direction Avery had disappeared.

My heart stopped beating.

His finger closed around the trigger. "Yes, run little deer, run."

"No!" I screamed. My vision narrowed into a single point and I flew at Peter. Norman grabbed my ankles. Instinctively, in midair, I spiraled back into him with my upper body, forcing him to let go of me. I spun back around and kicked out, stretching my foot toward the rifle. A shot rang out, deafening in the small room.

A completely inhuman sound emanated from me. My shoe connected with the rifle, knocking it out of Peter's hands. But it was too late.

Silence. Heavy, heavy silence. Barely a breath taken. All paralyzed.

"You shot your daughter," Norman murmured. "Your own daughter."

"She is not my daughter," Peter said. His voice was flat. His face expressionless. His arms and hands frozen in space.

"You fucking bastard. You fucking bastard. You killed her!" I screamed. I stalked forward and slammed my palm into the side of his head, rendering him unconscious, and took him out at the knee with my foot at the same time. He crumpled to the ground.

Norman took a step towards him.

I spun toward Norman. "Don't you move." My whole being seethed.

Norman stopped mid-step. "I didn't know he would do that. I didn't know," Norman mumbled.

I was stunned as I stared at the door. Fear was something I had learned to deal with in martial arts, but this was a different fear.

"Help! Help!"

I grabbed the rifle and shoved it under one arm. Clutching the sides of the ladder, I slid down the last few feet and hit the ground with a thud. A flash of lightning revealed a sickening sight.

Avery was on her knees, both arms wrapped around Blaine's limp body. "He jumped in front of me right before my dad fired. Help him, Aiden. Please."

The blanket Avery had been wearing lay in the mud. I scooped it up and draped it around them both.

Blood trickled from Blaine's nose and the corner of his mouth. I held my palm in front of his mouth. He was barely breathing. He opened his eyes for a moment, smiled, and lifted his hand. The necklace dangled from his fingers. Then his eyes rolled back and his head lolled to the side.

"Blaine, stay with me. Don't go." A crimson stain spread across the front of his jacket. I ripped away my t-shirt to press it to his chest. "Don't you go."

Avery looked at me. "He saved me," she said, hiccupping. Tears streamed from her golden eyes. "He jumped right in front of me." Her words came out in little explosions of sobs. "My dad tried to kill me. Peter tried to kill me."

Behind me, the ladder creaked. I glanced back. Norman was halfway down. He could escape, for all I cared. No way was I leaving Blaine.

Thwack! An arrow hissed by, pinning Norman's jacket arm to the ladder. He clawed at it with his other hand. Thwack! Now both arms were pinned to the same side of the ladder, leaving Norman helpless to free himself.

Raven and Rasta appeared beside us as I turned back to Blaine.

Marly ran out of the woods. "Aiden, Blaine, Christian told me they need help back at the lodge. Raven, you too." She rushed to her daughter and hugged her. Her eyes met mine over Raven's shoulder. She let go of Raven and pressed a hand to her mouth. "Oh my god, Blaine."

"He's losing blood fast," I said, applying as much pressure as I could to Blaine's chest in an attempt to staunch the flow.

Marly strode toward me and gripped my shoulder. "You need to go. Old Phoenix needs you."

Avery swiped at her tears with her shirt sleeve. "Go, Aiden." She covered my hand with hers. "I've got him."

I hesitated, then slid my hand out from under her fingers. "I'll be back as soon as I can."

She nodded. Her free arm tightened around Blaine and she leaned close to his ear. "Blaine, you stay with me. Don't you dare leave me. You promised."

Marly yanked her cell phone from her pocket. There was nothing more I could do. I looked into the face of my Bagua brother, imploring him silently to fight and not give up, then I tore myself away from the group and started back through the woods at a run, Raven at my heels.

Behind me, Avery's cry echoed through the trees. "Get those bastards!"

AIDEN

Life and death are one thread, the same line viewed from different sides.

—Lao Tsu

When Raven and I entered the lodge, Zheng had fixated on Old Phoenix with a look of such maliciousness that my heart felt sick. Before I could move, Zheng flew at Old Phoenix, his speed accelerating and his energy amplifying with each step. Old Phoenix slipped out of the way of his crushing fist. In one graceful, circular movement, he struck Zheng's head a blow that I knew would resound in his mind for many days. Old Phoenix clearly wanted the fight to end, but not in death.

He noted our arrival with a slight nod. An arrow whizzed by me. Old Phoenix's eyes met mine as a cascade of golden light sliced down from ceiling. Time stopped. The arrow was suspended in the air. Only Old Phoenix and I were moving.

"Aiden," Old Phoenix said, "My connection to the web of life has returned. I know what I must do."

My body shook as I drew in a deep breath. "W … what?" Everything was frozen around us, the shaft of golden light beating down.

"You are part of my inner web, time outside of time, space inside of space," he said. "One will die, so one can live. It's time for me to join the immortal masters and serve the greater purpose. Aiden, things are not always as they seem. You have an important discovery to make. I can't tell you what to do, but I have to tell you that Zheng not only wants Avery's stone, but her soul as well."

"Her soul? But—"

"Every choice you make, Aiden, takes the soul of the world one step closer, or one step further away. I have to go now." Old Phoenix nodded. "Wao will live."

"Wait, I…"

The column of light faded. Time and space returned. The arrow clattered to the floor. Old Phoenix was set up to render his brother immobile. Instead, he stepped back. He held both arms out to his sides. No offense. No defense. Purely open.

Zheng lunged forward. With one, blinding blast of energy, his fist drilled into Old Phoenix's heart. The force of the *Eye Fist* sent Old Phoenix flying backwards and smashing against the wall. Lightning flashed and thunder boomed, over and over until I almost covered my ears to block out the sound.

Then silence fell over the room.

The storm stopped. The fight was over. Old Phoenix collapsed to the ground.

Zheng hovered over his brother's body, made a quick prayer mudra, then turned and charged away, his men falling in behind him like the wake of a boat.

"Raven!" I pointed at the door. "Follow them. Protect Avery and Blaine."

She rushed out of the building behind the men.

I rushed to Old Phoenix's side and dropped to my knees, cradling his head. The life in his eyes drained away. Death was initiated and I knew he would soon be free, passing through the elemental stages of earth, water, fire and air.

My throat tight, I began the prayers for the dead. But I knew that life would never be the same.

Old Phoenix's last, whispered words hung in the air: "The world is in your hands now."

Chapter 49

AVERY

To light a candle is to cast a shadow.

—Ursula K. Le Guin

Machines beeped softly around me. I sat beside the hospital bed and held Blaine's hand. After the surgery to remove the bullet and repair Blaine's lung, Luc had spent time in the recovery room, sending healing energy into him. Though the doctors said he had lost a lot of blood, he looked surprisingly healthy if somewhat pale, against the white hospital sheets.

Blaine opened his eyes and squeezed my fingers. "Hey girl," he said, "Maybe you could stop flying into the face of trouble for a change, so I don't have to catch another bullet."

"I'll do my best." I smiled. "How are you feeling?"

"Not as bad as I would expect, all things considered."

"You've been sleeping for a while." I patted his hand. "I thought you were in a coma. Aiden and I have been pumping you with healing energy."

"I could feel the energy." He winked at me. "I was having some pretty strange dreams because of it. I was levitating three stones with my mind. That was totally cool. I even lit a light bulb. Then I talked to your great, great grandfather. He told me some things … I wish I could remember what he said. Something about the fate of the world and the secret that ends all mysteries. Is there any water?"

I picked up the pitcher of water beside the bed and poured some water in a cup. "Oh Blaine, I'm glad you're okay. I was so scared that I was going to lose you too." I handed him the cup.

"Thank you." He took it from me and lifted it to his lips.

I ran my fingers through his hair. "You crazy nut. You jumped in front of a bullet. I could have lost you."

His eyes closed, a sweet smile on his lips.

"Hey." Aiden walked into the room and stood beside me.

I stepped back from Blaine's bed, my cheeks flushed. "He woke up for a few minutes."

"He woke up? That's a good sign. Is he going to be okay now?" Aiden rested a hand on my arm.

I moved my arm. "Yup. He's going to be okay. He's just tired. The doctor said the transfusion of blood from you was what he needed, and that he had never seen anyone heal so fast from a gunshot wound. We can take him home later today." I looked up and our eyes locked.

"Avery?"

I turned toward the door. "Simon. You came." I rushed over to him and threw my arms around him.

He brushed the hair back from my face. "I got here as soon as I could." His face grew serious. "How's Blaine?"

"He's going to be fine."

"That's good." Simon held out his hand. "And you must be Aiden?"

"Yes, sir. Good to meet you." Aiden shook his hand. "Avery, I'll let you and your uncle visit. I'm going back to Luc's for awhile. Call me when Blaine wakes up again and I'll help you get him home."

"I'll help too," Simon said. "I'm here for a few days. Avery and I have a lot of catching up to do."

Aiden nodded and left the room.

Simon and I stood in awkward silence for a moment, until I touched his arm. "What was it you wanted to tell me the last time you were here? It sounded important."

"Here." Simon slid an arm around my shoulders and directed me to the chairs beside Blaine's bed. "Let's sit. First of all, about what happened on Deer Island." Simon crossed an ankle over one knee. "I told you not to let your father—or that idiot he hangs around with, Norman—know about the necklace. Your father may be in Rikers now, but he won't stay there for long. As soon as he is out on bail he will go after your friends. Really, sweetie, you are playing with some deadly fire. You don't know who my brother really is."

"I do, Simon. I absolutely do. And he has manipulated me and my mom and everyone else long enough. I'm not afraid of him anymore." I gripped his arm. "I really do know. Skull and Bones. Illuminati. I know."

"How—" Simon shot a look at the open door. His whole body slumped in the chair.

I lowered my voice. "Raven overheard her mom talking in her office, and she came and warned me. But her mom is with the DA's office. They aren't going to let Dad, er, Peter out of prison."

"Don't count on that," Simon murmured. "If you know as much about him as you think you do, you know he has virtually unlimited power and wealth."

"Well, if he gets out, we'll have to deal with that." I let go of his arm. "Simon, I know you have something you want to tell me, but I have something I want, need actually, to tell you too. I don't know how to say it, but I think it's what you want to tell me." I stood up and walked over to my knapsack. Crouching in front of it, I unzipped it and pulled out a few of the undelivered letters between Simon and my mom. I handed them to him.

He looked at the envelopes and ran his finger across my mother's handwritten address to him. "So, I guess you know now?"

"Yes, I do."

"I tried to tell you at The Rooftop Lounge, but how do you reveal to your niece that you were in love with her mother all those years, and that's why I couldn't be around. I couldn't handle seeing her with my brother, knowing what he was capable of, yet knowing it was her choice. Also, Peter kept me so busy around the world, I could barely come to visit when I did summon up the courage, when I needed to see that the two of you were okay."

"Wait a minute," I said. "Did you call me your niece?"

His eyes narrowed. "Y…e..s."

"Then you don't know?"

"Know what?"

I took a deep breath. "I'm not sure how to tell you this Simon, but I'm your …daughter. Peter isn't my father, you are."

He stared at me, mouth agape. *Should I have broken that to him more gently?* He stood up and paced. Scratched his head. "My …my daughter?" He put his hand to his mouth, and tears gathered at the corners of his eyes. "Are you sure?"

"Yes. I've seen the DNA test results." A tear slid down his cheek and I gulped. "I'm sorry. I didn't mean to upset you. I just thought you should know. I thought you did know."

"Upset me? Oh Avery," Simon shook his head. "I'm the one who's sorry. If I had known, I would never have left you there, with him." His face was pale and he sat back down, as if he were afraid he might collapse. When he looked at me again, his eyes were wide. "My daughter. You're my daughter." A smile broke across his face. He wrapped me in a huge hug. I felt warm, knowing he loved me, knowing how much he really cared for me. Then he slowly released me. "Oh my god, Avery. You're my daughter. I can't tell you how often I wished I had a daughter like you. I envied my brother. Wait. Did Peter know?"

"Yes. I found the test results in his office. He must have had my DNA tested without me knowing. The test was done just before Mom died, which makes me wonder if he was so furious when he found out that he had something to do with her death. I've told the DA's office my suspicions and they're investigating now. He will never get out of prison, if I have anything to do with it."

"Avery?" Blaine's eyes blinked open. "I had another dream. Wow, this painkiller stuff is amazing. Do you think they'll send me home with some?"

I laughed. "Blaine," I held my hand out toward Simon, "I want you to meet my father, my real father, Simon."

"Is this the young man that you've been telling me about for the past year?" Simon asked.

Warmth rushed into my cheeks. "Um, this is one of them."

Blaine slowly pushed himself upright on the bed, wincing in pain when he reached out to shake Simon's hand. "A pleasure to meet you, Sir."

AVERY

The One begot the two, the two begot the three, and the three begot the myriad.

—Lao Tsu

Blaine and Aiden sat on either side of me at the antique dining table with Luc at the far end. The other Bagua brothers had collected at Luc's apartment over the past twenty-four hours. White Cloud and Purple Mist had been the first to arrive. They sat opposite us. Whenever I caught Purple Mist eyeing me, he quickly looked away.

Wao had made a full and immediate recovery, exactly the way Old Phoenix had told Aiden it would happen. Blaine recovered more quickly than any of us imagined possible. Luc said it was Aiden's and my combined energy that healed him. The last few days had taken their toll on all of us; our shared grief was palpable. We waited for Blaine to be released from the hospital before we took Old Phoenix's body to Grandfather in the Ramapos for his ceremony.

Marly and Raven had guarded Peter and Norman until the authorities arrived. The two men were now awaiting arraignment. While everyone was distracted with Old Phoenix, Zheng, his men and the two Goths disappeared into the black night. The police were hunting them down, but I suspected they would hide until they thought the heat was off, then they would be back.

The atmosphere was heavy and thick around us. No one said much. Blaine didn't even try to make us laugh. So much had happened, I was having trouble wrapping my mind around everything. Wao drifted into the dining room with the soft, lucid look of one who had just experienced a long and deep meditation.

A knock disturbed the solemn mood.

I stared at the door. "Who on earth could that be?"

"No Trace," said Luc, "Our dear friend of endless wanderings." He went to open the door.

Aiden jumped up from the table to greet No Trace. "How did you find us?"

"I always know where you are, Aiden." No Trace ushered Aiden back to the table, his long black robes rustling around him. He put a hand on Blaine's shoulder, avoiding the injured side of his body. "You are going to have to practice getting out of way of speeding bullet."

"We heard you were in Peru!" Wao glanced at No Trace.

"Machu Picchu. Wonderful." He laughed. "There I met a man who was ten thousand years old. A shapeshifter. But that story is for another time."

I was suddenly aware that I was the only woman seated at a table of some of the world's most mystical men. A few months ago, I would have been intimidated. But not now. The more I learned who I was, the more I knew who others were.

Wao sat down and folded his hands.

No Trace cleared his throat. "Today, Wao, you become head of the order. Old Phoenix has left his earthly body, and has determined you will take his place. This is a most auspicious day for us."

"Old Phoenix lost the fight," Young Phoenix said through gritted teeth. "Zheng has won. He has proven his power."

No Trace shook his head firmly. "Old Phoenix did not lose; he chose his time."

"He chose his time? He just lost the fight," Young Phoenix replied.

"He gave one thing to achieve another. You are angry and I understand..."

Young Phoenix banged the table and rose to leave.

Wao pointed with one finger at his eyes, then down towards his clenched fist. As if being guided by an invisible beam, Young Phoenix sat down. Wao remained pointing. Young Phoenix tried to lift his hand from the table.

"What's going on?" His eyebrows drew together as he stared at his fingers. "I can't move my hand."

"You will be able to move it again after our meeting is adjourned," Wao said, looking straight ahead.

"I am here at Old Phoenix's request," No Trace continued. "It was his will that I leave my wanderings in order to appoint Wao the next Master of the Order of the Celestial Dragon Gate, to tell the story of the Carnelian Intaglio stones and the coming of The Myriad Time. The ten thousand-year-old man in Machu Picchu helped me understand the story."

"There has never been a female at one of our meetings before. Why is she here?" Purple Mist cast his gaze downward. "No offense, miss, but it just isn't done."

"This is all according to Old Phoenix's wishes. All seven of the brothers must gather to hear the story that Avery Adams is an integral part of." No Trace settled himself on the chair and began to speak in a low, hypnotic voice.

I found myself drifting in and out of a trance, almost seeing and feeling the story come to life as he told it.

"A long, long time ago, before any of us were born, when Old Phoenix became the head of our ancient Order, a man came to visit him in the mountains. This man was very tall with deep, penetrating eyes and flowing white beard. His name was A.P. Sinnett. Avery's great-great-grandfather."

"Wait a minute. My great-great-grandfather met Old Phoenix? But how is that possible? He lived in the 1800's. That would make Old Phoenix..."

"Very, very, old, indeed." No Trace picked up his rhythmic storytelling. "You will remember the details of the story only when the time is right for you to remember. A.P. Sinnett went to the place between two mountains, where the five energies return, and the mystic pass is revealed. There he found the wise and holy man, Old Phoenix, to tell this story." No Trace slowly lowered his eyelids, until his eyes were shut. His voice changed, taking on the clipped tones of a faintly British accent.

"I was the editor of the first English newspaper in India, when one day, I happened upon a certain Rajah of reputed mystic gifts. He asked me if I had been given two stones by a woman who lived somewhere beyond Mongolia. I indeed had two stones, given to me by a Russian woman who had lived, as a child, close to the Mongolian border, and had been deemed to possess certain extraordinary gifts. The gardener of her parent's estate was rumored to have been a direct descendant of the great Kublai Khan, and he gave the child two Carnelian stones. These stones were said to have been two of three given to Kublai Khan by Marco Polo, and passed down through subsequent generations. Each stone became an intaglio when it was etched with a symbol. She was told that one day she would need these two stones to gain entry to The Mysterious Gate in the Himalayas, where she would learn mystical secrets. Then she would pass the stones to a man, deemed pure of heart and spirit. That woman was Madame Blavatsky. We met in India when she came to stay with me and my wife, Patience."

My eyes grew wide. "That was my mother's name." I glanced around the table. All of the monks had their eyes closed, as if in a trance.

Wao opened one eye, winked at me, and smiled.

"Madame Blavatsky had just returned from her lessons in the Himalayas, and I was most impressed with her abilities, though my wife and I found her to be a somewhat irksome guest. In spite of that, we maintained a deep friendship for many years. During one particularly long stay with us in our summer home in Northern India, Madame Blavatsky cornered me in a room. I found her behavior most bizarre at the best of times, but this was different. She grabbed my hand roughly, deposited two stones on my palm, curled my fingers around them and told me to find a safe place to hide them. She could no longer hold onto the stones because some dark forces had discovered them in her possession and were tracking her with harmful intent.

"She said the stones would one day allow me entrance through The Mysterious Gate, the home of the Ascended Masters and a place few human beings are ever allowed. Her extraordinary feats of mysticism made me quite certain that she had gained their arcane knowledge. She warned that I might feel unusual symptoms while holding the stones and she was correct. Almost immediately, I became dizzy, nauseated, and a strange tingling ran up and down my spine. She said the energy of the stones would eventually synchronize with my internal vibration, and great internal strength would ensue. Her words proved to be true. All of them.

"The poor woman was hounded by dark spirits attempting to steal the stones from her. Her life and reputation were eventually ruined. When the dark spirits began to pursue me, the Rajah suggested an element called Niobium, to shield the energy of the stones. I sought to procure it, only to discover that no one had ever heard of such an element. It was not until many years later that I found the suggested material. By that time, my beard was long, and the dark spirits had done much damage to Blavatsky's and my friendship, and our lives. I kept one stone, Neith, The Weaver of Creation, from Egypt also known as Minerva, in Rome, secure in the Niobium box for my great-great-granddaughter, who appeared to me in dreams. She would have deep gold eyes. Gold eyes of inner alchemy. The other stone I took to the holy man in the mountains, in the hopes the spirits would leave us alone. When I found Old Phoenix, I shared my story with him. He said he had been waiting for me, though he displayed reluctance in taking the stone.

"According to an ancient legend that may go back to the Atlanteans, the two stones will seek each other and reunite during the time of the Myriad, and together they will seek the third, the whereabouts of which I know not.

"Close to this time, I had written about the coming of the next dark time in European history, 1911 to 1918, but an even darker time would come. It would begin in 1939 and end in 1945. This wasn't psychic on my part; the Ascended Masters told me about the dark lord they called Hitler. They said he would first attempt to change the face of Europe, and if successful he would march across the oceans to spread his evil. If someone with that depth of depravity were to get his hands on one of the stones, it would almost certainly be the end of the world as we know it, but if he found two together, the result could be catastrophic, on many dimensions. This was how I knew I must separate the stones and hide one in the most secret and sacred part of the world, safe in the hands of a man of pure light, and the other safe with me in the Niobium box.

"The stones were Carnelian, the stone of enlightenment. "Speculation is that the Atlanteans were taught by highly intelligent beings to mine the carnelian forged in the earth from the red-orange dust of a passing star. These beings took three carnelian stones, and infused them with a powerful, non-terrestrial material, giving them the highest vibration for metaphysical evolution. They were of a particular energy that held massive power for the wearers, assuming they possessed the vibrational capacity to wield it. If not, over time the stone would break apart their insides—like some internal scourge leading to a horrendous death—and even darker forces would be unleashed into the world. On the ten thousandth year of the stones' first appearance on the earth, in Atlantis, The Myriad Time would commence.

"When all three stones reunite, a time of great enlightenment is promised. Many mysteries of the universe will be revealed, but only if the light of those who have the stones outweighs the darkness of those who want to possess them. The bearer of the stone must fully understand its significance and be prepared to fight the dark forces to protect it. To keep the historical record of the stones safe, I used a coded language in my diary. To my knowledge, their history is only recorded in one other place – the letters of the Ascended Masters, called the Mahatma Papers. However, stories of powerful stones were embedded in our planetary culture from the time of their appearing until now, in order to help humanity to accept them when The Myriad Time arrives. Discover the original story and you discover unfathomable power."

No Trace's face subtly changed, and his voice returned to its usual tones, as he opened his eyes. "Last year, Old Phoenix felt the coming of The Myriad, the awakening of our world, the awakening of Master Zheng, and the dark forces beginning to collect on all the planes of existence." He nodded at each of us. "The Myriad Time brings a choice, a choice of light or of dark; it is a time when the fate of humanity hangs in the balance. It will be a time of global linking, a global neural network that marks the transformation on Earth, when we all begin to understand the web of life. When all three stones unite, The Myriad Time will begin and the world will change, either for good, or for evil. Nothing is certain. Good has not always triumphed in the past," he said.

A chill shivered down my spine.

"Old Phoenix took the stone he had held safely in his possession for all of those years and hid it in one of the amulets he gave to each of the seven Bagua brothers. Other stones were chosen to go into the other amulets, each with very special properties of their own. No one, including Old Phoenix, knew which amulet held the Carnelian. The stone chose the wearer as much as the wearer chose the stone. When Aiden saw his vision in the Mirror Pond, Old Phoenix recognized the sister stone that A.P. Sinnett had shown him all those years ago. Do you all remember the day we chose our amulets?"

Everyone nodded.

"There is a hidden clasp at the top that opens each amulet."

Everyone around the table took the amulet from his neck and inspected the clasp at the top. Young Phoenix triggered his with one working hand, his other still stuck to the table; the amulet popped open, revealing a beautiful rose crystal.

"Not me," Young Phoenix said.

White Cloud was next. He fumbled with the clasp. When his amulet opened, a clear crystal with a cloudy center glowed from within. "Me neither."

No Trace opened his, and a deep azure sapphire shone in the center.

Luc offered to go next. I held my breath as he opened his amulet. Was it him? His amulet opened and an emerald was revealed.

I released my breath.

Wao went next. He opened the clasp and a single wooden bead popped out and rolled onto the table. "Ha! It's not the stone, it's the bead. I have the bead! It chose me. This is from the Buddha's own prayer beads. Old Phoenix showed it to me once, long ago."

Only Blaine and Aiden were left. I wasn't sure which one I wanted to have the stone more, or what it would even mean when we found out. Blaine and Aiden looked at each other, and then down at their amulets. If Blaine had the stone, would it mean that he was destined to be with me, or would it mean he would have to become a monk, like Aiden? If it was Aiden, did it mean he never really had a choice, that free-will is an illusion and his life had always been driven by the desires of the stone?

Wao said softly, "There will be much for you three to say to each other. Be true to your destiny."

Blaine and Aiden opened their amulets at the same time, exposing the contents to all seated at the table. Blaine had a multi-colored gem that shone differently as he turned it into the light. Aiden took the stone out of its amulet and there, delicately etched in the fiery orange translucent stone, was the Scorpion.

AIDEN

The wise man looks into space and he knows there are no limited dimensions .

—Lao Tsu

"You know, things make a little more sense to me now." Avery sat at the table and studied the stone in her pendent. "I just don't get what Peter has to do with all of this, and how he got connected to Master Zheng."

I fingered the amulet around my neck. "Master Zheng must have known the history of the stones all along, so he has been looking for the sister stone."

Blaine strode to Avery and placed a hand on her shoulder. "Peter has connections everywhere in the world, with anyone who has anything to do with energy resources. And once Zheng learned Peter was married to the great granddaughter of A.P. Sinnett, he probably stuck to him like spandex on a fat man."

Avery laughed.

The easiness between them jarred me into realizing that I had to confront a truth. Avery and Blaine had developed a deep relationship over the time I had been gone. I cleared my throat. "Blaine, I have to say something. I …I won't stand in your way with Avery. You are free to love her. All of this Scorpion stuff has confirmed for me that my destiny is with the monks, ushering in The Myriad in a pure way, with a pure heart and pure intent. I must fulfill my promise to become the man I wish to be and to honor the stone that chose me."

Blaine shook his head. "You are making a huge mistake. Avery is your destiny, you idiot. Not mine. I admit that I hoped Avery would fall in love with me while you were away and I was by her side constantly. I hoped that she would see I was there for her. But I don't want to be anyone's consolation prize, and we all know that's what I would be."

Avery stood up and slammed her hands down on the table. Her eyes flashed deep, fiery gold. "Enough. You guys are talking about me like I'm not even here. Like it's your choice who I should love and what my destiny is. What if I don't believe in destiny? I don't even know if I believe in this Carnelian stone stuff. I know the stone is powerful, but this is all too weird for me. I'm sick of it. I'm sick of hearing about dark lords, and Atlantis, and Himalayan gates. I don't believe in any of this weird, mystical stuff, and I'm sick of hanging out with people who do. Can we just maybe, I don't know, watch TV once in awhile? Or get drunk at a concert or something normal? I'm tired of being kidnapped. I'm tired of getting caught up in ancient fights with old Chinese dudes who look like wizards from *The Lord of the Rings*, and I'm definitely sick of watching my two best friends trying to pass me back and forth to each other, like I'm some kind of … some kind of prize. What makes you think you have the right to do that?"

Blaine and I exchanged a look.

Avery stomped around the room. "I have faced my fears. I have learned to believe in myself, when I never did before. I have grown up. I want someone who has the courage to face their fears too. And you know what? I don't think either of you are doing that. Blaine, find the courage to know, truly know, how awesome you are. You jumped in front of a bullet! You are a hero. Why can't you see that?"

"I didn't even think about it, I just jumped. I don't think that's gold-star material."

"If you really believe that, then there's nothing more I can say to you." Avery swung toward me, her lioness eyes boring into mine.

I gulped.

"And you Aiden? Really? Get over yourself. You think just because you are about to get initiated into the secrets of the universe, that you know the mystery of a woman's heart? It takes more than twirling a few circles to understand that. You would keep yourself in a Niobium box if you could. What are you afraid of, Aiden? Really afraid of? I know what you aren't afraid of: A battle to the death. An evil being so destructive it threatens the existence of the world. Living alone in a cave, away from civilization. So what is your real fear? Your own darkness? Your own feelings? If you think being a monk is going to help you avoid your inner demons, it's not. You have to figure out what they are and confront them on your own. Here are two hints: Your dad abandoned you and, maybe because of that, you don't let yourself feel."

"Aiden," Blaine grasped my arm. "You didn't promise to become a monk at the ritual, you promised—"

I held up a hand. "I know what I promised."

"Hear me out, mate. I don't think you do know."

Avery threw her arms in the air. "You guys have spent way too much time with a bunch a celibate monks. What didn't you understand about what I just said? Whatever Aiden promised, he doesn't get to decide who I am going to be with. I do. And at the moment, I don't choose either of you."

She turned, as if to storm away from both of us, but stopped when a stream of light burst out of her Carnelian stone and joined with a stream of light bursting out of mine.

Blaine let out a low whistle. "You may not believe in the Carnelian stones, but tell me you don't see that light."

The three of us stared, mesmerized, at the light suspended between the two stones.

All color drained from Avery's face. "What does that mean? Is this the fulfillment of The Myriad Time? Is it over?"

I reached for her hand and held it tightly. "Actually, Avs, I think it's just beginning."

—

(Continued)

Reading ^ACROSS^ Cultures

TEACHING LITERATURE IN A
DIVERSE SOCIETY

EDITED BY

Theresa Rogers and Anna O. Soter

Foreword by Rudine Sims Bishop

Teachers College
Columbia University
New York and London

Published by Teachers College Press, 1234 Amsterdam Avenue, New York, NY 10027

Copyright © 1997 by Teachers College, Columbia University

Library of Congress Cataloging-in-Publication Data

Reading across cultures : teaching literature in a diverse society /
   edited by Theresa Rogers and Anna O. Soter.
      p.   cm.—(Language and literacy series)
   Includes bibliographical references and indexes.
   ISBN 0-8077-3552-3 (cloth : alk. paper).—ISBN 0-8077-3551-5
(pbk. : alk. paper)
    1. Literature—Study and teaching—United States. 2. Pluralism
(Social sciences) in literature—United States. I. Rogers,
Theresa. II. Soter, Anna O., 1946-   III. Series: Language and
literacy series (New York, N.Y.)
LB1576.R396   1997
808'.0071—dc20   96-32594

ISBN 0–8077–3551–5 (paper)
ISBN 0–8077–3552–3 (cloth)

Printed on acid-free paper
Manufactured in the United States of America

04 03 02 01 00 99 98 97   8 7 6 5 4 3 2 1

Contents

PART II
Authors, Teachers, and Texts

Foreword

To sit and dream, to sit and read,
To sit and learn about the world
Outside our world of here and now—
    Our problem world—
To dream of vast horizons of the soul
Through dreams made whole,
All you who are dreamers too,
    Help me to make
    Our world anew.
I reach out my dreams to you.
      —Langston Hughes, "To You"

MUCH OF THE PROFESSIONAL writing on the teaching of literature in elementary and secondary schools has, in recent years, focused on reader-response theory and on multiculturalism in literature for children and young adults. Reader-response theory has provided the foundation for instructional approaches that emphasize the role of readers in constructing meanings and interpretations of texts, while multiculturalism has called for an expanded repertoire of authentic literary works to reflect the cultural diversity that characterizes American and global society. READING ACROSS CULTURES stands at the confluence of reader-response theory and multicultural literature or cultural studies, moving both in a new direction.

The professional writing on the role of multicultural literature in classrooms has primarily focused on the need to make visible underrepresented groups and to counter negative images and stereotypes. The main educational benefit of these strategies for readers who are members of such groups has been presumed to be that such literature would, by legitimating their images, their heritage, and their cultural experiences, provide opportunities for building self-esteem. This would in turn lead to improved scholastic achievement, particularly in regard to written literacy. For readers who are members of dominant groups, the assumption has been that becoming acquainted with and finding their own connections to literature about people from nondominant groups would help them to value all peoples, accept differences as a natural aspect of human societies, and even celebrate cultural pluralism as a desirable feature of the world in which they live. Less attention has been paid to the specific kinds of instructional strategies that might accomplish these ends, to the effects on response of the sociocultural identities that readers assume, and to the influence on those responses of the social and cultural environments in which readings take place.

READING ACROSS CULTURES helps to fill a gap by presenting stories of actual classrooms and the ways that teachers and students in those classrooms, from third grade to college, make and take meanings from a variety of texts. In so doing it takes us well beyond being satisfied with merely exposing readers to a variety of texts. It reminds us that the goal of multicultural education, and the role of literature within that context, is ultimately to help "to make our world anew," to transform society into one in which social justice and equity prevail, and that reaching that goal will require schooling in which teachers and students are able to confront and critique some of the thorny issues and -isms (such as racism and sexism) that are at the root of past and continuing inequities. READING ACROSS CULTURES shows how literature, through the power of its artistry, can be a catalyst for engaging students in critical discussions and for eliciting multiple perspectives and multiple voices in pursuit of understanding. It also reminds us that among those multiple voices are voices of resistance. Real change will not, therefore, be easy, nor will it come solely as a result of reading and responding to literature, which is, after all, an art form, not an instrument of indoctrination. Nor can literature, even with all its potential artistic power, be expected to carry the major responsibility for transforming the world.

In the classrooms portrayed in the first part of this volume, emphasis is mainly on the readers, the teachers, and the texts. They are not, however, the only players in the game of reading and interpreting literature, particularly cross-cultural texts. One of the main issues in the criticism of so-called multicultural literature, especially literature for children and young adults, has been the extent to which an author's sociocultural background influences or interferes with the ability to create literature about characters who are members of a different social group, particularly when the author is a member of a dominant group writing about those who are not. In READING ACROSS CULTURES the author is included in the conversation, as is the critic concerned with patterns in the representations of social groups or with critical interpretations of literature across cultures and the teacher educator aware that his or her instructional strategies will have an effect across generations of readers. In short, Theresa Rogers and Anna Soter and the other authors in this collection take on the complexities of reading, writing, interpreting, and critiquing literature in the context of both culturally diverse and more nearly monocultural classrooms as well as the pluralistic larger society. In so doing they clarify issues and indicate some possible steps toward resolution of some of those issues.

Teachers, teacher educators, and researchers with an interest in cultural studies, multicultural literature, and reader-response theory will find that READING ACROSS CULTURES can be a guide through some of the swiftly flowing waters of contemporary literary theory and criticism. It does not simplify the issues, because they cannot be simplified, but with its own set of multiple perspectives and diverse voices, it helps to clarify our vision and point the way forward toward a better understanding of the role that reading literature can (and cannot) play in helping to transform schools and society, the ways that reading, writing, discussing, teaching, and critiquing literature can help "to make our world anew."

Rudine Sims Bishop
Ohio State University

Acknowledgments

WE ARE INDEBTED to many people for helping us to develop this book from the seed of an idea to published form. We would like to thank the chapter authors for keeping faith and for contributing such fine work within some very tight deadlines, especially toward the end. We are also grateful to Rudine Sims Bishop for agreeing to open this book with her graceful prose and thoughtful insights into the issues raised. We also would like to thank Carol Collins, Sarah Biondello, Karen Osborne, and Lyn Grossman at Teachers College Press for all their helpful advice and careful editing along the way, as well as the anonymous reviewers who have helped to make this a more coherent volume. Finally, a special thanks to our much-loved husbands and sons (Dan, Rob, Ben, Shaun, and Christopher) for their patience and support during this long process.

Introduction

THERESA ROGERS AND ANNA O. SOTER

IF WE THINK of literary criticism and the teaching of literature as having its own narrative, we might say that there has been a turn in that story toward the social, cultural, and political contexts of literary creation and reception. This narrative, which is more recursive than linear in nature, has taken us from the author/audience relationship (e.g., Aristotle), to the authors themselves (e.g., the romantics), to the text and to language itself (e.g., structuralists and New Critics), and back to readers and contexts, as well as to the impossibility of intention and determinacy of meaning (poststructuralism, including reader-response theory). It is a narrative that requires an "ever necessary retelling" (Jauss, 1982) as new readers with new expectations and in new contexts approach a text (Rabinowitz, 1989).

This recent narrative turn, most notably for elementary and secondary classrooms, emphasizes both the need for multicultural literature and (paradoxically) the limitations of reader-response theories (as they are currently constituted) to speak to the actual responses of diverse readers. Reader-response theory has been the first major influence on the teaching of literature in schools since New Criticism, although new critical or traditional approaches still hold sway in many, and perhaps most, classrooms. However, as reader-response criticism begins to make itself felt in schools, it has already been through years of scrutiny and criticism, both as a theory and in terms of its pedagogical value.

As a theoretical perspective, reader-response criticism has not adequately addressed either the role of the author and the author's social and cultural influences (cf. Rabinowitz, 1987) or the relationship between literary and other cultural texts (cf. Ryan, 1989; Willinsky, 1991). As instructional practices, response-oriented approaches often fail to encompass the social complexity of classroom communities with students of varying backgrounds, abilities, and experiences (cf. Eagleton, 1983) and the possibilities for critical inquiry into literacy practices themselves, as well as the discourses surrounding those practices (cf. Luke & Baker, 1991).

Cultural studies, on the other hand, offer some new perspectives on literary response for teachers. As Berlin and Vivion (1992) argue, "English studies can no longer treat literary texts as purely aesthetic documents transcending the realms of the political and historical, and rhetorical texts as mere transcripts of empirical and rational truths" (p. vii). This narrative turn toward cultural response helps us to see that the literary canon itself is a social construction (cf. Tompkins, 1985), that literary texts are complex intertextual weavings that refer to other literary and nonliterary texts (Bakhtin, 1986; Barthes, 1977), and that authors themselves, as well as readers, are at least partly constructed by their own social, political, and cultural contexts.

Many of us who have contributed to this volume were initially influenced by reader-response or audience-oriented critical perspectives that have since been informed by one or more areas of cultural studies, such as critical pedagogy, feminist studies, Black studies, postcolonial criticism, and Marxian criticism. At the same time, we are cautious about seeing literature as purely political documents. Rather, it is the power of literature as artistic as well as cultural texts that persuades us and our students to be moved enough to look deeply at both the aesthetic and cultural contributions they make and to look outward from the works to their social meanings. As Parini (1995) recently argued, "knowing how much or how little emphasis to put on ideology in interpretation strikes me as the beginning of wisdom" (p. A52). Since we are educators rather than critics, we are constantly mindful of the very real consequences of our theoretical and practical approaches to teaching, and so we must weigh any extreme positions against the strengths and needs of the students we teach.

The idea of cultural response as a theoretical frame also raises many other important questions and issues when teaching literature to children and young adults: What do we mean by culture? Why and how do we teach literature from a cultural (and multicultural) perspective? What is the nature of response in actual interpretive communities? Why, and in what ways, do readers resist cultural texts and readings? What is the role of the author in creating literature and how is the author configured in cultural readings? These issues are themes that run through this volume and are answered in various ways across various contexts: the first half of the book focuses on actual classroom stories of reading from grade 3 through college, and the second half on the role of the literature itself, on authors, and on teachers, when we read literature within and across cultures.

In the early chapters of this book, "culture" often refers to race and to ethnicity, as well as to related issues of class and gender, as they are raised in classroom conversations. Since these are stories of American—mostly urban—classrooms, race is often seen in terms of African American or Latino/a as opposed to white, or European American—cultures that Sims Bishop (cf. Cai & Sims Bishop, 1994) has referred to as "parallel." In the second half of the book the notion of the cultural "other" is also extended to religion (e.g., Jewish), to homosexuality in a heterosexist society, and to cultures beyond our borders.

While these are the very real concerns of the teachers and students represented in these pages, we also recognize that some may see this as a theoretically limited definition of "other," particularly in contrast to recent postmodern critiques that plead for an even more inclusive and complex notion of multiculturalism (cf. Keating, 1995; Schwartz, 1995). These critiques point out that the idea of race, gender, and class, of culture, and of the "other" are themselves, to some degree, socially constructed and must be contested in an effort to create curricula that "move against and beyond" traditional boundaries (hooks, 1994) and reach toward social critique and social change.

Many of the chapters in this book do, either implicitly or explicitly, address the role of social questioning and critique in the context of literature teaching, as well as the goals of providing more inclusive communities for our students. Until now, there has been more rhetoric about these goals than stories of how inclusion is, or might be, effected. The stories told here provide ways to understand what issues arise when real students resist, "talk back to," or engage with literature and each other; the stories also create some road maps for teachers who struggle with these issues on a daily basis.

For instance, literature classrooms in which teachers face resistance (several examples of which can be found in these pages) are not the bounded, consensus-building communities imagined by some reader-response critics (e.g., Fish, 1980). Readers resist texts and readings, as well as real and implied authors, because of their cultural memberships and various identity positions: as female, as African American, as homosexual, as white students who resist challenges to their own privilege, or as Americans who cannot grasp the cultural meanings and values in stories of other countries. These communities, then, become sites of struggle

(Eagleton, 1983) that we must navigate with a deeper understanding of culture and of difference, and of the way we create, and the consequences of, our cultural interpretive practices.

PART I: CLASSROOM STORIES

Chapter 1, "Negotiating the Meaning of Difference: Talking Back to Multicultural Literature," by Patricia E. Enciso, describes a fourth- and fifth-grade classroom in which the students "talked back" to the novel *Maniac McGee*, by Jerry Spinelli, as they constructed their own social positions for themselves and others. Enciso argues that cultural metaphors, mappings, and dehistoricizing strategies in the novel challenged the students to renegotiate the meaning of difference in the text and among themselves. Enciso also points out that allowing these cultural conversations into our literature classrooms provides a space for all children to negotiate difference, not just those children whose cultural references and perspectives are already understood and valued.

In Chapter 2, "Re-Visioning Reading and Teaching Literature Through the Lens of Narrative Theory," William McGinley and colleagues, providing examples from two very different upper elementary classrooms, remind us that stories are a means to personal and social explorations and reflections—that they provide life-informing and life-transforming possibilities. Drawing on narrative theory, they argue that stories endow experience with meaning, provide culturally shaped ways of organizing that experience, and reflect prevailing theories about the "possible lives" and "possible selves" in our culture. They also point out that we still know very little about how children actually draw on these life-informing possibilities of narrative—or of the nature of the personal and social understandings that children acquire as they transact with stories in classrooms.

In Chapter 3, "Students' Resistance to Engagement with Multicultural Literature," Richard Beach explores the many forms of resistance that students adopt when their values are challenged—stances that reflect their own privileged perspectives as well as resentment toward alternative versions of reality presented in multicultural literature. In a study of high school students' responses in a variety of settings, Beach found that some students in largely white suburban high schools adopted stances of white privilege that reflected an individual ideological perspective on portrayals of racism in American literature. In contrast, students who were more engaged with multicultural literature were more likely to perceive racism as an institutional phenomenon—a stance that was based on personal experiences.

In Chapter 4, "No Imagined Peaceful Place: A Story of Community, Texts, and Cultural Conversations in One Urban High School English Classroom," Theresa Rogers describes a classroom in which the teacher struggled to create a community in which many, sometimes competing, voices could be heard. By looking at the role of community, intertextuality, and cultural conversations in this classroom, she illustrates the ways in which one teacher moved away from a focus on authoritative interpretations of canonical texts toward inquiry into a wide range of texts as personal, social, cultural, and historically placed constructions. Rogers argues that this approach to teaching literature is not sanctioned by the larger cultural norms of high schools in the United States, since few teachers see issues of race, class, and gender, or literacy practices themselves, as open to critical inquiry in the classroom.

In Chapter 5, "Multiplicity and Difference in Literary Inquiry: Toward a Conceptual Framework for Reader-Centered Cultural Criticism," Mary Beth Hines draws on various approaches to teaching literature at the middle, high school, and college levels to explore a framework for a reader-centered cultural criticism. Noting that we have failed to create communities, or "homespaces," for nonmainstream and oppositional students in schools in general, as well as English classrooms in particular, she suggests that we develop conceptual frameworks for literary inquiry that invite students to read "selves, texts, and worlds" in communities that foster multiplicity of meaning, and an interrogation of difference and diversity.

PART II: AUTHORS, TEACHERS, AND TEXTS

The second half of the book focuses on issues related to the teachers, authors, and literature that are at the center of the struggle to create new ways of reading within and across cultures in elementary, secondary, and college classrooms. One issue that is raised is the role of the author in a time when the focus has shifted toward a critical view of literature in our schools. There is a tension in how we understand the role of the author in this new context that was not present when canonical literature was at the center of the curriculum; that is, when we introduce literature that is meant to "authentically" represent the "other" (or ourselves as the other), the role of the author is rescrutinized. We face a tension between the author as creative individual responsible to craft or muse, and the author as having a social responsibility, as described by the African writer Chinua Achebe:

> The writer cannot be excused from the task of re-education and regeneration that must be done. In fact he should march right in front. . . . I for one would not want to be excused. I would be quite satisfied if my novels . . . did no more than teach my readers that their past—with all its imperfections—was no one long night of savagery from which the first Europeans acting on God's behalf delivered them.

Achebe refers to his writings as perhaps "applied" as opposed to "pure," indicating a role for literature as educative as well as aesthetic. When dealing with literature from other cultures, then, teachers are faced with aesthetic as well as cultural differences: Can we use the same literary critical practices with literature that is not only from a different cultural but also from a different aesthetic tradition?

Finally, as several of the chapters in this volume illustrate, the role of teachers is also an issue when dealing with cultural as well as aesthetic readings of literature. Teachers may need to reconceptualize their own understandings of literature as historically and culturally placed and literature classrooms as "cultural sites"—places of interrogation, struggle, and social questioning and critique.

Behind all of our discussions of what we would like to see happen with respect to the teaching of literature from a multicultural perspective is the issue of how teachers are educated to read and teach from such a perspective. In Chapter 6, "Exploring Multicultural Literature as Cultural Production," Arlette Ingram Willis addresses this issue directly as she adopts the frame of critical literacy for "improving the current generic approaches to literacy training of preservice teachers." Through "sagacious use of multicultural literature," Willis argues, we can enable preservice teachers to become critical thinkers about the "choices they make when teaching literacy." Using herself and her own teaching as a model, Willis shows how we can position ourselves, identify who we are relative to our goals in our teaching of literature, and, through articulating our own values, become correspondingly aware of the values that permeate all literacy instruction.

In Chapter 7, "Reflections on Cultural Diversity in Literature and in the Classroom," Laura E. Desai points out that when looking at the role of culture in a reader's response, we must first consider the multiple communities that frame our social, cultural, and political context, and then we can begin to consider the role that a teacher and the classroom play in this process. She attempts to answer two questions: How can responses be ethically negotiated among the multiplicity of voices in a classroom community? How is the teacher to bridge these voices? Based on her experiences in an urban fourth-grade classroom, Desai shares her conversations with the teacher about dealing with uncomfortable issues raised by the multicultural literature and describes their collaborative search for an "ethics of response in a society framed by multiple communities."

In Chapter 8, "Out of the Closet and onto the Bookshelves: Images of Gays and Lesbians in Young Adult Literature," Mari M. McLean extends the notion of "other" to those who, as she observes, are "conspicuously absent" in multicultural educational materials. Arguing that gays and lesbians are ignored in the selection of groups represented by the descriptive use of the term "multicultural," McLean presents a case for widening that term by drawing on Boas's definition of culture. She also argues that, like members of other cultural groups, members of the gay and lesbian community can identify a history, cultural artifacts, and notable individuals who have made significant contributions. McLean suggests that as young adults begin to define themselves in terms of personal and social identity, positive images in gay and lesbian literature can provide "mirrors" for the "minority youth's culture and experience." She focuses on the need of many adolescents for acceptance by their peers, and specifically on the challenges that gay and lesbian young adults face as they seek validation of their experiences and perspectives.

The question of who should write multicultural books for children is at the center of Chapter 9, "Reader-Response Theory and the Politics of Multicultural Literature." Mingshui Cai argues that embedded in this question are many complicated issues that range from whether or not outsiders can write authentically about the attitudes and experiences of those in another culture; to the role of the author's own cultural identity in his or her aesthetic creation; to relationships between imagination and experience; to authors' social responsibilities; to tensions between author/reader relationships; and to tensions between principles of aesthetic freedom and reader responsibilities. Using real author/implied author relationships as a frame for discussing the foregoing issues, Cai illustrates how complex and politically and aesthetically sensitive these issues are.

In Chapter 10, "Reading Literature of Other Cultures: Some Issues in Critical Interpretation," Anna O. Soter acknowledges that literature has always had the power to move us, to reach us through its natural connection with the worlds of our imagination. At the same time, she presents us with challenges teachers face when students resist literature that represents other cultures that, in turn, represent other value systems. As students respond to content that, at times, presents aesthetic, ethical, and moral values that may be repugnant to them, Soter examines how teachers can use initial connections as the ground for subsequent interpretive criticism and aesthetic appreciation. To do this teachers can create "spaces" that allow student readers to become accustomed to the nuances and rhythms of these different aesthetic models so that they can move from "aesthetic restriction" to "aesthetic distance." The greatest challenge, she suggests, is that when using literature representative of other cultures, "the teacher, as often as his or her students, must be prepared to not know, to learn how to experience the unknown afresh."

With this book, we hope to move beyond simple assumptions about the value of multicultural literature and the ways readers respond to that literature. READING ACROSS CULTURES involves exploring who we are, participating in the lives of others, negotiating social relationships, and critiquing our cultural assumptions about difference. This process does not occur without struggle and resistance, and there are no operating instructions for teachers who choose to create classroom communities with spaces for sustained dialogue about literature and culture. Instead, we offer you these stories and insights from a range of students, teachers, and classrooms in order to continue the conversation about literature, culture, and teaching.

REFERENCES

Bakhtin, M. M. (1986). *Speech genres and other late essays* (V. W. McGee, Trans.). Austin: University of Texas Press.

Barthes, R. (1977). *Image-Music-Text* (S. Heath, Trans.). New York: Hill & Wang.

Berlin, J. A., & Vivion, M. J. (1992). *Cultural studies in the English classroom*. Portsmouth, NH: Boynton/Cook, Heinemann.

Cai, M., & Sims Bishop, R. (1994). Multicultural literature for children: Towards a clarification of the concept. In A. H. Dyson & C. Genishi (Eds.), *The need for story: Cultural diversity in classroom and community* (pp. 57–71). Urbana, IL: National Council of Teachers of English.

Eagleton, T. (1983). *Literary theory: An introduction*. Minneapolis: University of Minnesota Press.

Fish, S. (1980). *Is there a text in this class: The authority of interpretive communities*. Cambridge, MA: Harvard University Press.

Jauss, H. -R. (1982). *Toward an aesthetic of reception*. Minneapolis: University of Minnesota Press.

hooks, b. (1994). *Teaching to transgress: Education and the practice of freedom*. New York: Routledge.

Keating, A. (1995). Interrogating "whiteness": (De)constructing "race." *College English, 57*, 901–918.

Luke, A., & Baker, C. (1991). Toward a critical sociology of reading pedagogy: An introduction. In C. Baker & A. Luke (Eds.), *Toward a critical sociology of reading pedagogy* (pp. xi–xxi). Philadelphia: Johns Benjamin.

Parini, J. (1995, November 17). Point of view. *Chronicle of Higher Education*, p. A52.

Rabinowitz, P. (1987). *Before reading: Narrative conventions and the politics of interpretation*. Ithaca, NY: Cornell University Press.

Rabinowitz, P. (1989). Whirl without end: Audience-oriented criticism. In G. D. Atkins & L. Morrow (Eds.), *Contemporary literary theory* (pp. 81–100). Amherst: University of Massachusetts Press.

Ryan, M. (1989). Political criticism. In G. D. Atkins & L. Morrow (Eds.), *Contemporary literary theory* (pp. 200–213). Amherst: University of Massachusetts Press.

Schwartz, E. (1995). Crossing borders/Shifting paradigms: Multiculturalism and children's literature. *Harvard Educational Review, 65*(4), 634–650.

Tompkins, J. (1985). *Sensational designs: The cultural work of American fiction, 1790–1860*. New York: Oxford University Press.

Willinsky, J. (1991). *The triumph of literature/The fate of literacy: English in the secondary school curriculum*. New York: Teachers College Press.

PART I

Classroom Stories

CHAPTER 1

Negotiating the Meaning of Difference

Talking Back to Multicultural Literature

PATRICIA E. ENCISO

Talking back meant speaking as an equal to an authority figure. It meant daring to disagree and sometimes it just meant having an opinion.

—*bell hooks,* Talking Back

IN HER REFLECTIONS on her experiences as a child among adults in her southern black community, bell hooks states that "to speak . . . when one was not spoken to was a courageous act—an act of risking and daring" (p. 5). She is concerned with the silencing that marked her childhood and the struggles she has engaged in to be heard as an African American feminist and activist. Her purposes for understanding what it means to speak one's mind in the face of domination may seem far removed from the conversations children and teachers have about literature. However, like hooks, children encounter versions of the world in literature that are new or in conflict with constructions of themselves and others. They must, as Dyson suggests (1993a, 1993b), act as social negotiators with this new material, creating meaning about themselves and others while drawing on other cultural materials (equally infused with meaning) from home, peers, school, and other public spheres.

As children read about racial, ethnic, and class differences in literature, they encounter metaphors of and meanings about difference; these new metaphors and meanings must be negotiated by children as they struggle to understand how they will see themselves, their peers, and their teacher in light of the literature's new possibilities. As Dyson (1993a) outlines:

> Although the teacher governs the official school world, in which children
> must be students, the children are also members of an unofficial peer world,
> formed in response to the constraints and regulations of the official world,
> and they are members as well of their sociocultural communities, which may
> reform in the classroom amidst networks of peers [citations omitted]. (p. 5)

In multiple social arenas within the classroom, children "talk back" to the materials presented to them as they simultaneously create social positions and definitions for themselves and others. This dynamic operates as much around any classroom assignment as it does around reading and responding to multicultural literature. However, multicultural literature raises questions about how we construct differences and how we have enacted and continue to enact social practices related to difference. In this chapter, I describe and analyze constructions of difference in a current, popular piece of multicultural literature,[1] *Maniac Magee* (Spinelli, 1990). I also describe the ways a group of fourth- and fifth-grade children negotiated authoritative constructions and meanings of difference—about themselves, their peers, and myself—while they read and responded to this story. As we read and discussed *Maniac Magee*, it was apparent that popular culture was often their primary vehicle for claiming and explaining differences about themselves and others. Thus I will consider ways in which popular culture was used to both control and "talk back" to multiple constructions of difference within the intersecting spheres of the children's definitions of themselves and one another in and out of the classroom.

RUNNING INTO DIFFERENCES IN *MANIAC MAGEE*

The opening chapter of *Maniac Magee* offers a cryptic, puzzling introduction to the legend that has grown up around a young boy after his year of running in and out of the segregated town of Two Mills End. The narrative soon turns to a recounting of the events that have formed his legendary status. Jeffrey Lionel Magee, a 12-year-old Anglo boy, has run away from his foster home into the East and West sides of Two Mills End, performing one fantastic feat after another. He appears to be an indomitable, open-hearted sort of kid, whose fame has spread along with his new name, "Maniac."

Maniac Magee's new world is racially divided, although Maniac himself is indifferent to these divisions during the first part of the story when he runs at will from one end of town to the other. The East and West sides of Two Mills End are peopled with characters who are kind and generous, playful and spirited, hardworking and hopeful. Some are also angry and bigoted, in particular Mars Bar, the African American male whose cool pose and tough demeanor set him up as Maniac's antagonist. Also in conflict with Maniac is John McNab, the leader of a white supremacist group called the Cobras, who lives with his raunchy father in a home dedicated to winning the race war. More commonly, Maniac finds people, black and white, who recognize racial differences but who just get on with life and who seem to be silent or ignorant about how and why racial prejudices are developed, enacted, and upheld. Regardless of all indicators of racial segregation, indifference, or intolerance, Jeffrey Lionel "Maniac" Magee steadfastly ignores the communities' accepted norms of attitude and interaction. Spinelli (1990) writes, "Maniac Magee was blind. Sort of. . . . He could see things, but he couldn't see what they meant" (p. 57).

Through Maniac's actions and the narrator's perspective, readers learn that prejudice takes many forms and has seeds that may be planted and fertilized or uprooted and replaced. Maniac's innocence and openness to all people instruct us that racial divisions may be reconciled through mutual understanding. Indeed, in the narrator's view, Maniac's transparent vision and purity of intention not only fosters but also achieves racial harmony:

"And sometimes the girl holding one end of the rope is from the West side of Hector [Street], and the girl on the other end is from the East side; and if you're looking for Maniac Magee's legacy, or monument, that's as good as any" (p. 2).

This story, which addresses and reconciles racial differences, was read and discussed by 16 fourth and fifth graders and myself—all of us bringing our own racial, ethnic, gender, class, political, intellectual, and linguistic differences to our reading. We met, in two groups, several days a week for four weeks at the end of the 1992 schoolyear. The groups were heterogeneously mixed, based on the teacher's determination of diversity of ability, gender, ethnicity, and race. My intention with the children was to find out how they made sense of the themes, characters, and plot of the story. Although we had our personal histories and perceptions of difference from which to build interpretations and voice opinions, we had to place these in relation to one another, the authority of the book, the author, and the meanings of difference inscribed in the story (Belsey, 1980). In other words, the official world of the classroom and its materials had to be socially negotiated through the children's unofficial peer world as we not only read the story but also positioned ourselves and one another in relation to it. We had to find ways to "talk back," to make a place for ourselves alongside or apart from Maniac Magee and company.

From the beginning of our meetings, the official world of schooling was cause for "talking back." The book itself held authority for the children insofar as it was selected by me, an outsider/adult, and was the focus of our discussions and activities. We did not engage in an open discussion about my choice of this book, nor did we talk at any length about my role in their classroom. Thus the representations of race relations in the literature could be seen by the children to represent my perspectives. My authority as an adult, then, was interwoven with my choice of our reading material. To talk back to the book would be, in many respects, to talk back to me.

The authority of the book and my association with it was further elevated by the Newbery gold emblem on the front cover. Implied in the award and in its selection as a classroom set is the teacher's recognition of a "good book" that is deemed useful and of interest to children. Cathy, who enjoyed reading but who was often excluded by other girls during group writing and reading activities, questioned teachers' ways of elevating books and reading: "How come most teachers, most adults like it when kids read? It's like if someone says they like to read they say, 'Oh. You're such a good little girl or boy'?" Through her question she has talked back to a hidden curriculum of values and valuing that carries a suspect reward for compliance with the adult world's view of literacy for children (Stuckey, 1991).

A third layer of authority is related to the book as an art form that uses metaphor, characterization, setting, narrative perspective, and genre to construct representations and meanings of difference. Belsey (1980) and others have argued, from Althusserian theory, that literature is, in fact, an "ideological apparatus" (Belsey, 1980, p. 56), meaning that it is "a *system* of representations (discourses, images, myths) concerning the real relations in which people live" (p. 57). This does not mean that literature is simply propaganda or that it is opaque to any critical analysis of those representations. However, the majority of children's literature constructs characters as "consistent subjects who are the origin of meaning, knowledge and action" (p. 67); that is, the characters appear to be "free agents," speaking and acting for themselves, outside of the complex sociopolitical contexts in which they were imagined. Thus it is difficult to recognize the ways language operates as an ideological and identifying force in the making of "their" meaning. Belsey suggests that this literature, "classic realist fiction," of which *Maniac Magee* is representative, places the reader as a participant in the story, "unfettered" by an awareness of the power of language to form ideologies and representations about "others" that are part of the story and part of the reader's life.

While these metaphors and meanings are not necessarily consciously constructed by authors, they are drawn from the author's experience of living as a racialized person in a racialized society. Spinelli (1991) wrote, in his Newbery acceptance speech, of Niki Hollie, a black childhood friend who had been raised in an orphanage and who, like Maniac, became a tireless runner. Unlike Maniac, however, the impetus for Hollie's running was an incident at the local swimming pool, from which he had been shut out because of his race. Spinelli writes that Hollie's story was "the first patch in the quiltwork that became *Maniac Magee*" (p. 430).[2] He recalls that in contrast, for him, "There were the summer afternoons on the Elmwood Park basketball court, myself the only white skin among fifteen or twenty blacks. I remember a small, quiet feeling of gratitude, of pride of admittance. There was no turnstile for me" (p. 430). Thus Spinelli is situated as a European American writer in a racialized society.

Toni Morrison, writing about nineteenth-century authors and their work, makes a point which is pertinent to today's writers for children. She explains in *Playing in the Dark: Whiteness and the Literary Imagination* (1992):

> Responding to culture—clarifying, explicating, valorizing, translating, transforming, criticizing—is what artists everywhere do. Whatever their personal and formally political responses to the inherent contradiction of a free republic deeply committed to slavery, nineteenth century writers were mindful of the presence of black people. (pp. 49–50)

Spinelli is not bound to the kind of selective discourse about African Americans that belied white writers' views and opinions more than 100 years ago. He is, however, part of a culture that continues to create and sustain codes and meanings that become linguistic shortcuts for representing and, in turn, interpreting racial differences. Morrison outlines a number of these linguistic moves in her analysis of white writers' use of what she refers to as "the Africanist presence" in American literature. Among these codes are two, in particular, that are significant to this study because of their power to foreclose dialogue among characters: the *dehumanizing metaphor* and the *dehistoricizing allegory*. These foreclosures, I will argue, became the subject of the students' efforts to position themselves in relation to the hegemonic representations of difference found in the voices of the author/narrator and characters, and in the ideologies about difference expressed by their classmates. Talking back meant challenging these foreclosures and creating and negotiating transformative definitions of difference that could sustain further dialogue.

In the rest of this chapter, I first consider the linguistic strategies that construct the Africanist character through *metaphor;* in relation to this literary construct of difference, I describe and analyze the ways children negotiated the meaning of difference in the text and among themselves. Then I turn to the linguistic strategy, which Morrison calls the *dehistorizing allegory*, whereby "history, as a process of becoming, is excluded from the literary encounter" (p. 68). In this study, Morrison's term refers to Spinelli's use of a timeless, larger-than-life, legend genre to situate and amend race relations. Again, I relate this authorial choice to children's interpretations and social negotiations of difference.

MEETING MARS BAR AND MANIAC: CONSTRUCTING DIFFERENCE THROUGH METAPHOR AND MAPPING

Morrison refers to the ways social and historical differences—such as those created through racial categories—can be transformed, through metaphor, into universal differences such as the differences between humans and nonhumans (p. 69). Africanist characters may become pseudo-human, for example, and their speech may be equated with animal sounds so that the possibility of dialogue is obliterated. As I read Morrison's analysis, it is not only the strategy of universalizing that is critical; it is the linguistic possibility that is used by writers to preempt black speech so that the protagonist, an Anglo character, can encounter the racialized world without directly questioning or discussing its implications for and with black characters.

This construction of difference through a "universalized difference" is evident in *Maniac Magee*. Although Spinelli's black characters are not entirely speechless, nor unintelligent, their speech is often interrupted or stylized in ways that reproduce both literary traditions and popular cultural stereotypes.

Mars Bar, Spinelli's black male counterpart to Maniac, is characterized by his intimidating presence. He is larger than life, as is Maniac, but his only unquestioned "move" (as opposed to Maniac's innumerable athletic and social accomplishments) is his ability to stop traffic with his glare and swaggering, threatening walk. Spinelli describes him as mean and essentially lacking in insight or self-control. Already, these codes for Mars Bar's character are, metaphorically, akin to the protective territorial moves made by animals. When these images are set in motion in relation to the character of Maniac, Mars Bar becomes even more a metaphor and a reinvention of popular, media-constructed images of black dangerous, inarticulate males.

In an early episode in which Maniac first meets Mars Bar in the East End, Maniac asks directions. Instead of giving an answer, Mars Bar cynically offers Maniac a bite of his trademark candy bar. To everyone's astonishment, Maniac accepts the offer. Spinelli writes:

> Maniac shrugged, took the Mars Bar, bit off a chunk, and handed it back. "Thanks."
>
> Dead silence along the street. The kid had done the unthinkable, he had chomped on one of Mars's own bars. Not only that, but white kids just didn't put their mouths where black kids had had theirs, be it soda bottles, spoons or candy bars. And the kid hadn't even gone for the unused end; he had chomped right over Mars Bar's own bite marks.
>
> Mars Bar was confused. Who was this kid? What was this kid?
>
> As usual, when Mars Bar got confused, he got mad. He thumped Maniac in the chest. "You think you bad or somethin'?"
>
> Maniac, who was now twice as confused as Mars Bar, blinked. "Huh?"
> . . .
> Mars Bar jammed his arms downward, stuck out his chin, sneered. "Am I bad?" . . .
>
> "I don't know. One minute you're yelling at me, the next minute you're giving me a bite of your candy bar."
>
> The chin jutted out more. "Tell me I'm bad."
>
> Maniac didn't answer. Flies stopped buzzing.
>
> "I said, tell me I'm bad."
>
> Maniac blinked, shrugged, sighed. "It's none of my business. If you're bad, let your mother or father tell you." (p. 35)

Maniac's polite befuddlement is counterpointed by Mars Bar's angry confusion. Neither character is able to understand the other's perspective, but Maniac's blindness is definitely less threatening than Mars Bar's confusion and anger. In this public street scene, they speak past one another while the narrator provides the subtext for their actions and reactions. It is the narrator/author, then, who speaks for Mars Bar and his community. Mars Bar is not humanized—able to tell his own story—until the end of the book, when we hear his reflective voice in dialogue with Maniac about fear and family.

The characterizations of Maniac and Mars Bar can be found in earlier books about black and white relations, particularly in the books Sims (1982) has described as emphasizing "social conscience," such as *Iggie's House* (Blume, 1970), that were written primarily during the late 1960s and early 1970s. These are stories, written by white authors, about the problem of segregation and the white protagonists' roles in understanding and rectifying the situation. Black characters certainly have a part in these books but are typically not self-determining. Rather, they are the beneficiaries of the efforts of white characters, like Maniac, who want to change society.

Mars Bar's character can also be found, as has been mentioned, in the popular mainstream press and throughout American literature. He is found in news stories about violence in America, in stories of school failure, and in fabricated stories of murder. In the context of our reading of *Maniac Magee*, the children and I had repeatedly seen (at home) the video footage of Rodney King's arrest and subsequent beating as it was broadcast on the evening news. More recently, a white woman in South Carolina—Susan Smith—had blamed a black man for kidnapping the children she had murdered. The local police and the national and international news media accepted and pursued her story as if it were true. In both of these media events, the black male's behavior was portrayed and interpreted as predatory, out of control, and inhuman.

Maniac also has counterparts in popular media. He is made to be "out-of-this-world," as if he were an E.T., unfamiliar with and utterly innocent of the social constructions of racial difference that permeate everyone else's lives. He does not, then, have to understand his own whiteness or his own implication in the history or future of a racist society. Morrison's (1992) analysis of whiteness in American literature explores the paradox of creating a "new" self, an "innocent" self in relation to "the presence of the racial other" (p. 46). Innocent whiteness deployed in relation to the Africanist character, she argues, is one "strategic use of black characters to define the goals and enhance the qualities of white characters" (p. 52). In my view, the placement and meaning of racial difference in *Maniac Magee* makes possible a divided, ahistorical setting through which Maniac can explore the meaning of race and home, while it simultaneously creates a setting of personal and historical silence for Mars Bar.

As a European American child, Maniac can maintain his innocence as he makes forays into opposing neighborhoods and homes. However, he senses "in some vague way" that the white children, brothers to John McNab, were "spoiling, rotting from the outside in, like a pair of peaches in the sun" (p. 155). His belief is that he must take action to save the children: "Soon, unless he, unless somebody did something, the rot would reach the pit" (p. 155). But by the time Maniac reaches this realization he has already humiliated Mars Bar during a footrace and will humiliate him again when he tricks him, in the hopes of attaining racial harmony, into meeting the McNabs at their white supremacist fortress. Maniac's innocence is understandable, given that he is a child, but it is also a pretext throughout the story for his view of difference, for his misinterpretations of volatile situations, for his "recovery" by the black community. As will be shown, the children with whom I worked regarded Maniac's utter innocence as implausible but within the realm of explanation. In other words, innocence in a racist society does not really make sense, but the pairing of innocence and racism *can be made reasonable* when the alternative discourse—questioning the construction of social and racial categories and their accompanying privileges—is both difficult and disorienting.

Maniac Magee's stature and innocence are further heightened by his legendary status. This construction allows him to be seen (and rationalized) as better than anyone at any sport or game. He unties the knot at Cobbles Corner that had rested, undefeated, for years in the East End's [read African Americans'] favorite drugstore. He even outplays "Hands Down," the glory of the East End's football team. Maniac's legendary persona is new and exciting to readers. However, his ability to be a better insider than the insiders is not unusual in popular, Hollywood portrayals of cross-cultural encounters. In *Dances with Wolves,* for example, Kevin Costner portrays a white soldier who learns the ways of the Lakota people and eventually leads them into battle. The portrayals of white outsiders' moves toward the inside appear to be sympathetic to the lifestyles and sensibilities of the "other." However, such sympathies can also be read as an appropriation of the "other" that inevitably limits and diminishes the self-determining potential of a people. Indeed, in the story of Maniac Magee, this sense of distrust and outrage at being "bettered" is expressed through graffiti and the destruction of precious books by some anonymous members of the East End's black community. It is implied that Mars Bar had a hand in this sign of rejection of Maniac.

Clearly, Mars Bar and Maniac are more than the unique constructions of one author's imagination. They represent the linguistic choices of an author who is situated in a racialized society. The characters' differences in *Maniac Magee* are created through metaphors that construct a humanitarian, heroic white child who is innocent of color and social meanings of race, in contrast to a threatening, status-driven young black man who is situated in a black community, where he is a leader, yet neither self-determining nor accomplished in relation to the white outsider. Such differences create a dualistic, essentialized view of whiteness and blackness, suggesting that black males are "naturally" angry and white males are "naturally" in search of a resolution of racial disharmony. (Mars Bar never expresses a desire for harmony.) As essentialized characters, Maniac and, particularly, Mars Bar are unable to realize the complex selves they might be in a multitude of social settings.

Readers are, likewise, situated in a society that persistently invents and naturalizes dichotomous racial relations. Thus, while reading *Maniac Magee,* young readers may also construct (or reconstruct) meanings of difference, already informed by popular and personal experiences, that will define themselves and others.

As Britzman, Santiago-Valles, Jiménez-Munoz, and Lamash (1993) argue, it is an ongoing project among individuals (teachers, children, parents, school board members, etc.) to "set themselves off from the 'others' that they must then simultaneously and imaginatively construct [citing Anderson, 1983]" (p. 193). In the process of imagining and then claiming these differences as "real," we are also in danger of constructing an ideology or a view of our relationships with one another that reproduces long-standing hierarchies and inequities. In the following section, I describe the ways the children and I borrowed from cultural referents to define others and "make real" the metaphors of difference represented by Maniac and Mars Bar.

CULTURAL MAPPING: PLACING THE MEANING OF DIFFERENCE

The differences between Maniac and Mars Bar, as portrayed in literature and the media, are not new. They are constructed out of the language and society that construct differences in the first place. The question for response to literature studies, however, has to do not only with the social, political, and cultural context in which literature is produced but also the complex, intertextual, identity, and power relations that are part of the reader's interpretation of the literature. I have found the concept of cultural mapping (Britzman, Santiago-Valles, Jiménez-Munoz, & Lamash, 1991; Hall, Critcher, Jefferson, Clarke, & Roberts, 1978) to be useful in analyzing the ways children made Maniac Magee and Mars Bar familiar and, in turn, illustrative of their meanings of difference.

Hall and colleagues (1978) have argued that our interpretations of social experiences are based on cultural maps that provide the framework for constructing the meaning of new events. They state:

> An event only "makes sense" if it can be located within a range of known social and cultural identifications. . . . This bringing of events within the realm of meanings means, in essence, referring unusual and unexpected events to the "maps of meaning" which already form the basis of our cultural knowledge, into which the social world is *already* mapped. (pp. 54–55, quoted in Britzman et al., 1991, p. 90).

Related to Hall and colleagues' concept, Belsey (1980) refers to advertisements and our reading of the signifiers of identity such as names, clothing, hairstyle, and speech patterns that construct a meaning, or "signified." She describes the relationship between the familiar ground we use to make interpretations, the construction of that ground by readers and authors, and the ways such signifiers become apparent in the kinds of characterizations I have just described. She states:

> These advertisements are a source of information about ideology, about semiotics, about the cultural and photographic codes of our society, and to that extent—and only to that extent—they tell us about the world. And yet they possess all the technical properties of realism. Literary realism works in very much the same kind of way. Like the advertisements, it constructs its signifieds out of juxtapositions of signifiers which are intelligible not as direct reflections of an unmediated reality but because we are familiar with the signifying systems from which they are drawn—linguistic, literary, semiotic. This process is apparent in, for instance, the construction of character in the novel. (p. 49–50)

Authors, students, and teachers "[refer] unusual and unexpected events to the 'maps of meaning' which already form the basis of [their] cultural knowledge" (Hall et al., 1978, pp. 54–55). Although we may not intentionally invoke maps of meaning that create racially based exclusions and inequities, we have learned ways to interpret signifiers that refer us to larger maps of meaning about ourselves and others. As will be shown, some of our maps unintentionally, but nevertheless successfully, foreclose more complex, alternative ways of describing and analyzing who we are in relation to others. In the following excerpt, the children and I try to "place" Mars Bar, using the textual signifiers constructed by the author and the maps of meaning we know that make the signifiers familiar and meaningful.

After reading the street scene episode described above, I attempted to engage one small group of children in a consideration of prejudice by comparing Mars Bar to John McNab, the white supremacist bully. However, their focus was on Mars Bar, the tough guy.

KEVIN: I think Mars Bar thinks he's so tough but he's really not 'cause he wasn't really tough 'cause the kids . . . he gave him that glare from his eye 'cause he was just like born or something with it. So he gives them that and they all . . .'cause they never ever took a chance at him. So they don't. He thinks he's tough, but he really isn't. He's just trying to cover it up.

PAT: OK. The people think he's tough, and he thinks he's tough, but actually there's more to him than that. What about McNab? Is he really tough?

THOMAS: (*From the background. He's standing to the side of the round table rather than sitting with us.*) Uh huh.

KEVIN: Yeah. He's the one that doesn't try covering up.

PAT: He doesn't try covering up. OK. Why would Mars Bar cover up, and McNab wouldn't?

MARK: 'Cause it's like some people act really strong when they aren't. And they take up as professionals.

. . .

PAT: You were saying something too Shaun . . . about how TV shows work. . . . You were saying that you weren't surprised about Amanda stepping in.

SHAUN: 'Cause like. The star like gets beat up by the bully but really at the end someone, like a girl, has to come out an help him 'cause he can't fight for himself or something. So that's why that's what I see on a lot of TV shows.

PAT: Were you glad that Amanda stepped in?

SHAUN: No.

As we interpreted Mars Bar's and Maniac's responses to each other, we had to make sense of what they were doing by placing their actions within an already familiar framework. In this case, the children speculated that Mars Bar was born a tough guy and would become even tougher and "take up as a professional." Their interpretation could make sense to them, given negative mainstream news media images of black males and the pervasiveness of representations of black "professional" tough guys on television sitcoms and sports programs. The signifiers they read—such as "glare" and "jutting out his jaw"—related to the familiar maps of meaning that could explain Mars Bar's persona. We did not consider the fact that Mars Bar is a *constructed* character—constructed as a "universalized" dehumanized metaphor in contrast to the innocent, heroic whiteness of Maniac. By not foregrounding the constructed nature of the character and its multiple signifiers, we, as readers, became participants in the ideology of the text that sees difference in terms of dualisms, that is, either/or, good or bad, innocent or "streetwise," threatening or inexplicable.

The culturally familiar meanings of black and white, good and bad were played out by the children and by me, in part, because we did not understand, at the time, the possibility of examining these dualities in the first place. Britzman and colleagues (1993) suggest a pedagogy that works against such dualities:

[G]esturing toward [naming and examining] the constructed real—of the narratives, of the classroom dynamics, of the identities of every participant, and of the . . . [s]tory—may [allow] students to perceive experience otherwise, in more ambivalent and contested ways. (p. 197)

Although I recognize their argument as powerful and potentially transformative, it was not a guide at the time I was teaching and learning with the children about *Maniac Magee*.

From another view of pedagogy, it has been argued that the metaphors in *Maniac Magee* should be viewed as "imagined" and as literary vehicles for a more compelling story about the nature of truth and the perception of reality (Rosenthal, 1995). I found, however, that the children were continually trying out their understanding of other cultural material and the definitions of their own identities in relation to the story's signifiers of difference. Regardless of the "official," intended focus of our discussions, the story and its signifiers turned us toward ourselves, one another, and our definitions of differences. The social, unofficial negotiations that surrounded our reading were marked, over and over again, by efforts to situate ourselves in relation to the characters' and one anothers' perceived identities.

"WHAT IF": CREATING AND EXPLAINING OURSELVES

The above excerpt illustrates the ways in which children referred to cultural maps of meaning to explain Mars Bar's actions and "nature." In the following excerpt, the children interpret the signifiers within the story while they simultaneously interpret themselves for one another. Even though they cast themselves in the imagined realm of hypothetical situations in an attempt to remove themselves as participants in a racialized society, it was impossible for them to talk about "the other" without also talking about themselves.

We continued our discussion of the street scene episode but began to speak—and not speak—about race as a basis for the characters' thoughts and actions. In the moments when they speak of race, the children simultaneously attempt to say, in effect, "this is not me speaking." However, their pointing to themselves as "not speaking" is, I believe, a code for speaking about their racial differences in relation to the book and to one another.

PAT: What about the part where Maniac eats Mars Bar's Mars Bar?
SHAUN: I'd never do that. That's sick, I think.
PAT: Thinking about somebody else's . . .

MONICA: Well, it's not that I wouldn't, it's . . . but . . . like . . . If I was in that situation, I would *not [eat the candy bar] because he was black or anything*. But just because . . .

MARK: Germs.

MONICA: Yeah.

PAT: So it doesn't matter about who is black or white or green or orange. You just wouldn't take a bite out of *somebody's* . . .

SHAUN: If he was orange or green, I would never take a bite. (*Laughter from others.*)

MARK: (*Sings*) "He's my brother. No matter if he's green or orange." [Tune from the song, "He Ain't Heavy, He's My Brother"] That would be strange. One time I had someone who had a green cat for a day. It was really green. It fell into green paint.

PAT: Oh, that's funny. So, uh, you probably would not have eaten the candy bar. Why do you think Maniac did?

MARK: Because /he's hungry!/ [slashes indicate overlapping speech]

MONICA: /Because he's hungry!/

MONICA: He's hungry and he doesn't know.

MARK: He probably thought, ah. It's just a . . .

MONICA: He thought he was being nice.

PAT: Yeah. He thought Mars Bar was being nice.

SHAUN: Man, I wouldn't have ever. Still, *even if a white person offered me a candy bar.* I'd say, first I take a bite, then you can. (*Laughter.*)

MONICA: I wouldn't have tooken a bite. Also, because you could tell he didn't want him to take the bite really. But he just said that.

PAT: But Maniac didn't understand that.

MONICA: Right. He didn't understand anything.

THOMAS: Mars Bar probably gets Mars Bar candy bars.

SHARON: He probably steals them.

All of us talked *around* race, even dismissed it as relevant—and thereby implied our recognition of its presence. As members of a racialized society, we began to implicitly situate ourselves within it—in the classroom, among peers, with this literature. Kirin Narayan (1993), writing about the multiple identities practiced and interpreted by anthropologists, states that "a person may have many strands of identification available, strands that may be tugged into the open or stuffed out of sight" (p. 673). The story of Maniac Magee tugged identities into the open, identities that had to do with race and belonging.

Monica referred race to the hypothetical world of "what if." As she picked up references to racial conflict from the episode, she situated herself as white, while imagining someone opposite her as black. But she claimed that race was not the real problem for her—germs were the problem. It is possible that the narration of white and black relations (e.g., "white kids just didn't put their mouths where black kids had had theirs") made it impossible for Monica and her peers to openly admit to the race relations in this scene. It was more tenable for them to overlook or laugh at this essentialized construction of difference than to see parallels in their own experiences.

My comment about "any color" unintentionally created an affirmation of their emerging perspective that color could be a laughable characteristic rather than a construction—worthy of dialogue—about human relations. Indeed, Mark followed my "multiple colors" reference with a transformation of a popular song and a brief story about his green cat. And then Shaun, who intended to pose the conflict between Mars Bar and Maniac as a matter of one tough guy meeting another, invoked Mark's and Monica's versions of race and germs to argue that not only would he not eat the candy bar because of germs, but he would not eat it even if the other guy was white (like himself).

The combination of these references points to the ways children not only made sense of a literary text but also constructed their own racial differences in relation to the text and one another. Although none of the children declared themselves as "white" or "black," they implied an allegiance with a naive white perspective, similar to Maniac's.

The conversation described above took place among a predominantly European American group of children. Only Thomas, who is African American and usually soft-spoken, offered one comment that upheld Mars Bar's humanity and the possibility that he and the others could imagine a positive relationship with him: "Mars Bar probably gets Mars Bar candy bars." However, his hypothesis was dismissed. Sharon ended any discussion by implying that Mars Bar had not earned his name (as Maniac had), he had stolen it. Thus she situated herself alongside Maniac while excluding the possibility of dialogue with Mars Bar or Thomas.

MEETING ONE ANOTHER: TRANSFORMING CULTURAL RESOURCES INTO SOCIAL ALLEGIANCES

The children's interpretations of *Maniac Magee* can be seen as the transformation of a cultural product into a cultural resource that enables them to explore and express their ideas about difference and their alignments with one another's definitions of difference in the specific setting of their classroom's social network. In *Understanding Popular Culture*, John Fiske (1990) examines the power relations and meaning relations between cultural products (such as the book, *Maniac Magee*, or the song Mark quoted), cultural resources, and social allegiances. According to Fiske, cultural resources, such as Mark's song reference, are the transformed products of a culture, used as the material through which we can express our own meanings of difference about ourselves and others.

Viewing the book as a cultural product, transformed into a cultural resource for the purpose of defining social relations, enables us to examine the following excerpt as more than a naive understanding of race relations. In Chapter 16 Maniac puzzles over the nature of skin color and the meaning of black and white. Maniac believes that we are all many colors—black and white are meaningless. In an impromptu discussion following our reading of that section, Monica, Shaun, and Cathy, who are European American, expressed their agreement with Maniac's view:

> MONICA: 'Cause black and white are the total opposites, and we're not that much different.
> CATHY: We're not white. *We're skin color.* We're not white.
> MONICA: And there is no light brown here.
> SHAUN: And there is no color white. There's a whole bunch of different colors of white.
> PAT: Just like there are a whole bunch of different colors of brown.
> CATHY: Actually, we're kind of red, too. Look at yourself.
> PAT: Yeah. We are. Some people have a lot of red tone to their skin. OK. Uh. So you're saying there are different kinds of skin color, but people tend to call it one thing, and that separates us. And something Maniac has done is say . . . He begins to recognize that skin color matters. He slowly begins to recognize that.
> MONICA: *No.* He doesn't know it matters. He knows that people *think* it matters.
> PAT: Good point.
> MONICA: But *he* might not think that it matters.
> SHARON: He doesn't think that the color of your skin matters. But you should be friends.

The cultural product, a character, Maniac Magee, who is trying to understand why people are defined and divided on the basis of race, became a cultural resource for the children as they not only expressed their understanding of race but also implied their social alignments with one another. In the context of this discussion, denials of race also designated alignments with race. When the children proposed that white either does not exist or is part of a spectrum of colors, they also implied that definitions of difference are not dependent on a consideration of skin color. Ferdman (1990) argues that such a view is often held by children who are white or "mainstream" because the world they exist in "normalizes" white, thus making skin color irrelevant. Cathy stated as much when she said, "We're skin color."

This view of racelessness permeates American literature and classroom discourse. But as Morrison (1992) argues so eloquently:

> The world does not become raceless or will not become unracialized by assertion. The act of enforcing racelessness in literary discourse is itself a racial act. Pouring rhetorical acid on the fingers of a black hand may indeed destroy the prints, but not the hand. (p. 46)

The hands of Marisa and Richard are brown and black. In the context of rhetoric meant to erase differences, Marisa and Richard also had to examine and begin to specify their social alignments with the characters and their peers, but from the perspective of the "racialized other." When Richard joined the book discussions after a week's absence, he immediately identified with Mars Bar, but jokingly so.

MARISA: Uh. Is Mars Bar black?
PAT: Uh hmmm.
RICHARD: Me and Mars Bar are black.
ALAN: (*Laughs.*)
PAT: What are you thinking, Marisa?
MARISA: Who is chasing Maniac?
RICHARD: That's me!

His alignment with Mars Bar has to be seen in the context of the group. He was outspoken and playful about his African American heritage and was the only child who asserted race as a significant dimension of the story's meaning. Later, in our discussions, Richard aligned most strongly with a minor character, Mr. Beale, the African American father who was part of Maniac's East End foster family. Richard painted several pictures of the entire Beale family but spoke of the father as a strong male with self-respect and a sense of responsibility. Thomas also identified with a minor African American character named Hands Down, an inventive, winning football player who invites Maniac to play in the East End street games.

Marisa was much more circumspect about her alignments and the meaning of racial differences. As our discussions of the book began, it was clear to the group that racial segregation was part of the story. Without identifying herself explicitly, Marisa commented, "This is weird.

'Cause you know how like [they] talk about it and there's a black part and a white part. Where would like Mexicans or Chinese or *someone like that* [emphasis added] be? Could they be friends with either of them?" She also stated that she was tan and could, therefore, go to both sides of Two Mills End, like Maniac. Recognizing her ambivalence about speaking of herself as "different," I attempted to elevate the status of "brown skin" by speaking to her and the group of my Mexican American heritage. Marisa listened, but the conversation went no further. Implicit in Marisa's inquiries and racial identification is the sense that she is not white or black and is therefore uncertain how to claim an alternative definition or alignment in the context of this book or her peers' understanding of race and difference. Her negotiations of the meaning of difference had to be more delicate, it seemed, than Richard's.

GROUNDING THE LEGEND AND OURSELVES: TALKING BACK TO A DEHISTORICIZED NARRATIVE

Marisa and Richard seemed to be far more aware of the implications of racial identification than their classmates. What became difficult for them was positioning themselves when the terms for defining difference were essentializing and dichotomous. Both children held significant positions in the classroom network of friends. Richard was outspoken among his African American peers and playful and friendly with many other class members, but he often felt that his popular cultural referents and playful ways were dismissed or punished while other "white" children's referents and mannerisms were allowed (Enciso, 1994). Marisa saw herself as a member of the "smart" girls who were also mischievous but "good students." It was difficult for Marisa, in particular, to define herself as "other." The story of Maniac Magee created a dilemma for her: She was neither white nor male, though she was attracted to Maniac's heroics, and she was not black, like Mars Bar or Amanda Beale. She could not claim either identity, but the narrative assumed she could or must find a place for herself within that literary world. Richard found a place for himself within the story's world, but he recognized that alignments with Mars Bar would be problematic while alignments with Mr. Beale might seem insignificant to others. Their dilemma was related to the narrative's metaphors, to cultural referents related to those metaphors, and to the nature of language in social contexts that "fix" us in relation to one another.

Even when our statements about ourselves and others are made subtly, it is difficult to escape the culturally formed referents and ways of using language that construct differences. Our statements and cultural referents specify not only with what and whom we identify, but also with what and whom we *do not* identify. How do children talk back to such linguistic mazes?

The source for Marisa and Richard's challenge to the fixed descriptions of difference in *Maniac Magee* is found in their responses to the genre itself. They became aware of the timelessness and lack of historical context that accompanies a legend genre. They puzzled over the lack of signifiers that would have helped them understand both the existence of and resistance to segregation and prejudice.

Morrison (1992) has recognized the "dehistoricizing allegory" as a powerful linguistic strategy that allows American writers to "construct a history and context for whites by positing historylessness and contextlessness for blacks" (p. 53). As in *Maniac Magee*, we know where he has come from (his foster aunt and uncle and the death of his parents), we have a sense of why he is determined to reconcile differences (people should talk to each other), but we have no sense of this same viewpoint from the black characters in the story. They seem to regret the situation of segregation but do not speak of resistance, let alone of its economic and political impact on their lives. White characters, on the other hand, are either blind to racial differences or possess an animosity and separatist view that is derived only from deplorable parenting. No historical framework is provided for the division and attitudes existing in Two Mills End. We only know that Maniac has landed in the middle of it and wants things to change.

Such "dehistoricizing" allows for the remarks shared by Mark, an outspoken European American boy who often exaggerated and extended ideas for the sake of creating interest and humor. The history he creates is parodic and effectively diminishes the past dimensions and present influences of the civil rights movement in this country.

PAT: What do you think about the division between the East side and the West side? Is that something that you know?
MARK: Oh, sure.
PAT: In what way?
MARK: Well, not in these days . . . I mean.
MONICA: Well, like, if . . .
MARK: Before, you would have like, uh, separated bathrooms, fountains, chairs, tables . . .
MONICA: Schools.
MARK: Pencils.
THOMAS: Pencils?
MARK: Yeah!

MARK: Like seriously, they had separate brands or something so they wouldn't even know it.

MONICA, KEVIN, SHAUN: (*Laugh.*)

MARK: I remember one case where they, uh, ride on the bus or something.

PAT: It was really. Yeah, it was very, very segregated before. So that could be what you know historically, but that's not something that you know now?

MARK: Like the blacks' territory and the whites crossing over. Get ready to ruuuummmble. (*Sings/talks words from* West Side Story.)

Mark fills the void of history with cultural references and social positionings that appear to align him with his classmates and me. Although Mark does not intend to be dismissive or mean-spirited, he does succeed in claiming a space for himself at the expense of his African American classmate. Perhaps it is not the place of this book to explore social history. However, in its absence, it is imperative that educators be alert to the slippery ground created by the popular cultural and social alignments that take its place.

One piece of history alluded to in the story did make a difference to Marisa and Richard. A minor East End character declares his disdain for Maniac's presence and in so doing implicates white people in the history of segregation: "You got your own kind. It's how you wanted it. Let's keep it that way" (p. 61). This brief reference to the past prompted an extended dialogue among Marisa, Richard, and myself about our understanding of ourselves in a racialized society. Joining our discussion was Alan, a European American boy who often teased other children but listened closely to Richard.

I began our discussion by asking Marisa what might have happened to the older East End black man that made him tell Maniac to leave the East End. Marisa moves my questions about history to her present life, to the context through which she views and must negotiate racial differences. Both Richard and I are surprised by her family relationships; they are completely counter to the erasures and dualities that defined difference throughout our discussions of *Maniac Magee*. But her exploration of difference encourages us to join her in naming ourselves as "racial [and ethnic] other."

PAT: What might have happened to that old man? 'Cause he's older remember.

MARISA: He grew up when things were really prejudiced. Maybe he was a kid when his parents were slaves or something.

PAT: I'm not sure when this story happened but if it happened a long time ago, like even in the thirties, that's possible. But even his grandparents would have been enslaved and you'd be angry about that.

MARISA: I have some black relatives in my family.

RICHARD: Who? How?

MARISA: They're on my (inaudible) (*She continues talking about her little cousin who is often in her care and often up to some mischief*).

. . .

MARISA: I have some aunts and uncles who are black.

PAT: Uh hmm. A lot of people . . .

RICHARD: By marriage?

MARISA: Well my cousins . . .

RICHARD: By birth?

MARISA: And my (inaudible) I have a black cousin. And her dad's black.

RICHARD: Her [referring to Marisa] mom's Mexican. Right?

MARISA: White.

RICHARD: Uh. OK. I know. 'Cause your mom married a black Mexican right?

MARISA: (*Nods.*) So my dad's colored and not white.

PAT: Uh hmm. And my dad's Mexican American.

MARISA: It's like my mom has blonde hair and I have black hair like my dad.

PAT: Like my dad, too. His complexion is like a deep brown and he has very dark brown eyes and dark black hair.

MARISA: I have dark brown eyes.

PAT: Yeah. Most of my family has dark brown eyes. Just like his. But some of us are fair and some are darker skinned.

RICHARD: Not like me (*smiles*).

PAT: So we all think about our skin color. And we know that people notice our skin color. Right?

ALAN: Not mine.

RICHARD: /*Yeah, they do, boy!*/

MARISA: /*Yeah!*/

Where the story lacked historically and personally meaningful sig-nifiers of difference, Marisa and Richard supplied their own. They ex-pressed an implicit understanding that they did not land in the middle of a racialized society; they saw themselves, instead, as an integral part of our society's perceptions of difference. More importantly, they recognized that speaking of racial difference and its construction is crucial to self-understanding and social transformation.

When Marisa moved the story of segregation to the present, she "talked back" to a construction of difference that renders her invisible. Her story is a pointed reminder that "multicultural literature" may not be as representative of children's lives, desires, and relationships as it may strive to be. Indeed, Britzman and colleagues (1993) argue that much of what we present as "multicultural" to students presents old stories in the guise of new configurations and settings. Furthermore, the literature labeled "multicultural" creates the impression that it is somehow more informed, more capable of embracing a complete understanding of differences. Rather than assume that any literature can possess such redemptive qualities, it is more tenable to assume that difference is constructed always, everywhere. Many constructions, however subtly imagined, will adhere to long-held versions of racial hierarchies and essentialisms. The power of the literature is not in its capacity to present a "truer" version of differences (and resolutions of difference) but to open up dialogues about the construction and negotiation of differences we observe and live. *Maniac Magee* presents a possibility for such dialogue, but its foreclosure of dialogue among the characters and across historical experiences makes open negotiations a difficult, if not risky, maneuver for children.

Richard and Marisa, however, are prepared to "talk back." In a reflective dialogue following Marisa's story, Richard and Marisa explored a hypothetical history of negotiations about difference and how it might be possible to rework the language and practices of segregation. Richard moves, then, to cultural referents that have guided his understanding of race relations. His referents are part of a "cultural map" that places racial hatred in the context of an ongoing struggle to transform it through a liberatory theology and social action.

MARISA (*to Richard*): Are you prejudice?
RICHARD: Yep. I'm prejudice. No. I'm just kidding.
ALAN: [*Laughs.*]
RICHARD: Not on my life.
   . . .
RICHARD: Why do you ask me this?
PAT: How do you think it happens?
RICHARD: Learn it from the older generation and pass it on—the negatives is all.

PAT: Do you think you have to be brave not to be prejudiced in this country?

RICHARD: It is prejudiced in this country.

. . .

PAT: How can *you* not be prejudiced?

MARISA: Well, you don't care what color your friends are. Like, say, your mom. Say like (inaudible). OK. Like . . . The great grandmother could have taught her daughter to be prejudiced and probably the last mother whatever had a kid and didn't teach her about prejudice and so they weren't prejudiced and . . .

RICHARD: Women can be prejudiced but the Ku Klux Klan wouldn't let women join them.

PAT: Hmm.

MARISA: And like, then that her child wouldn't grow up to be prejudiced and it would be easy for her child to make friends with all different colors of people. And then her mom would wonder why she [the mom] don't have much friends like her kids.

PAT: Hmm. So it's going to be hard for one generation and the next generation. . . . It will be a bit easier after that.

RICHARD: Did you ever see *The Little Boy King?* [About] Martin Luther King?

PAT: No.

RICHARD: You never saw it?

PAT: No. I bet it's a good movie.

RICHARD: I watch it just about every day.

PAT: Really?

RICHARD: I got the movie and the movie *Roots* and *Gandhi.*

PAT: Yeah. I saw *Gandhi.*

RICHARD: Four hours long. And, uh, what's it called? *The Ten Commandments.*

PAT: Uhm hmm.

RICHARD: I got that. I love that movie *The Ten Commandments.*

PAT: Do you think Amanda Beale's family knows about Martin Luther King?

RICHARD: Probably not.

PAT: Why?

MARISA: Probably so.

RICHARD: What year was this?

PAT: That's a good question. I don't know. What year do you think?

RICHARD: About 1930 something.

MARISA: Let's check the date.

Marisa lets us know, through her story and her ideal familial discourse, that difference is defined and shaped by the people you know and love. She implies that a younger generation of girls must defy older women's constructions of difference if we are ever to form friendships across racial lines. Her version of social change is similar to Maniac Magee's insofar as both assume that by reimagining ourselves in relation to others, we may be able to help others do the same. However, Marisa's ideal is grounded in a personal racialized history, not a race-free past. Similarly, Richard's ideal is grounded in a personal history that is informed by the visions and social actions of revered spokespersons of civil rights movements across time and around the world: Martin Luther King, Jr., Gandhi, and Jesus Christ. Richard "talks back" to the representations and reconciliations of difference in *Maniac Magee* by invoking the images and stories of those who led social movements. Although the leaders to whom he refers are individuals, like Maniac, they are not innocent or solitary heroes. The films Richard knows show people acting against racism in the midst of enormous social turmoil and at the risk of innumerable lives. With these references, Richard is able to more fully define the meaning of "being Black." He is clearly and positively aligned with an African American tradition of theology that strives for social justice and resists oppression. Together, Marisa and Richard rework the absence of context and history in *Maniac Magee* and construct a more viable setting for resistance to prejudices and racism.

TALKING BACK

Multicultural literature is often considered to be the primary symbolic material through which children might define and redefine meanings of difference. As we mediate this literature with children, it is critical that we recognize that they are not simply responding to these stories as if they are creations of a singular imagination. In the midst of discussions, children borrow and often "talk back" to constructions of difference found in literature, popular culture, and in the words of their classmates and teachers. In this chapter, I have examined the ways difference is constructed in one piece of children's literature and, in turn, the ways children spoke with and against the authority of those constructions.

When the literature itself is granted authority through its awards and position as the focus of discussion, it is often difficult for teachers and children to recognize and question the images and ideology inscribed within it. As a Newbery award–winner, *Maniac Magee* has considerable authority; it is among the elite few books for children that will remain in publication and in use in classrooms for years to come. Because it engages with racial differences and speaks from a child's perspective, it is akin to the much-loved (and critiqued) classic *Huckleberry Finn*. Yet, as in the case of *Huckleberry Finn*, as Morrison (1992) argues, it may be easy to overlook

> the implications of the Africanist presence at its center [because it] appears to assimilate the ideological assumptions of its society and culture; because it is narrated in the voice and controlled by the gaze of a child-without-status—someone outside, marginal, and already "othered" . . . and because the novel masks itself in the comic, parodic, and exaggerated tall-tale format. (pp. 54–55)

When I critique *Maniac Magee*, I "talk back" to a canon in order to awaken my own and others' awareness of the linguistic strategies that can bind and blind the complicated junctures of difference in our literature, in our lives, and in our classrooms. Furthermore, a critical awareness of an Africanist presence in literature enriches the literature and its infinite readings. As Morrison (1992) argues, "when one begins to look carefully, without a restraining, protective agenda beforehand . . . the nation's literature [is rendered] a much more complex and rewarding body of knowledge" (p. 53). Thus, it is not my intention to censor this or any literature for children, but rather to initiate a more complex dialogue about its representations of difference.

Popular cultural references were a significant medium through which children talked with and against the meanings of difference found in the story and among themselves. The reference points they used could be understood as cultural maps that allowed them to place the "new" story of Maniac Magee within an already familiar framework of relations and meanings of difference. For many of the European American children, cultural maps were based on popular images that treat whiteness as a norm. Through these maps children were able to both interpret the story and define differences within and among themselves. Richard and Marisa, on the other hand, referred to personal and historical cultural maps that allowed them to "talk back" to the ideal of a raceless society and thus create strong positions for themselves within a racialized society.

Children also transformed cultural products such as films and songs into cultural resources. As cultural resources, their citations were no longer benign interpretations of the story; they were powerful indicators of social alignments. In several respects, the children "talked back" to *Maniac Magee* when they used the story as a cultural resource to define themselves and others. The official world of our meetings was not, intentionally, about negotiating the meaning of racial differences. But that was, in fact, the subtext of the students' dialogue with one another, the author, and me.

What might be the teacher's and researcher's role amidst this matrix of ideologies, cultural references, and social positions? Some would argue that, regardless of a story's representations, it is always most important to develop enjoyment and appreciation of the literature so that children will continue to seek reading as an enriching activity. I have argued, however, that such enjoyment is made difficult when children are placed in positions that require them to align with problematic representations of themselves and others. Rather than mask these difficulties, we can begin to talk about the ways characters and characters' relationships are constructed. I believe such "talking back" to multicultural literature makes the literature more interesting and the possibilities and definitions of being a reader more empowering. Pleasure in a story can be related to both reading and talking back. It can be enjoyable and rewarding for children to recognize their own authority in relation to the significations and interpretations that accompany a story.

POSSIBILITIES AND IMPOSSIBILITIES FOR NEGOTIATING THE MEANING OF DIFFERENCE

If we hope children will tell their stories and "talk back" to literature, we have to learn what constrains and what opens possibilities for such performances. The construction of difference in a story raises two key questions for readers that might constrain or open the possibility of dialogue: Who is the audience for this book (Sims, 1982)? How does the portrayal of difference relate to a wider circle of sociohistorical attitudes and practices (Bourdieu, 1984; Morrison, 1992; Taxel, 1992)? In the case of *Maniac Magee*, readers might ask, "Is Maniac like me? Is Mars Bar like me? Is his story my story? Are his experiences ones I have had or would like to have?" These are questions implied by any reading, but they may be left unstated or unexplored. If we choose *not* to explore these questions with children, it seems to me that all of the negotiations of the meaning of difference will be left to those children whose cultural references and perspectives are most understood and valued within the classroom. Recent studies of process writing (Dyson, 1993b; Lensmire, 1994) suggest that this is, indeed, the case. Further research on children's response to literature could benefit from a similar analysis.

Part of classroom-based research would also examine the ways children and teachers use popular cultural and multicultural literature as resources to position one another and define differences. Because, in a sense, it is not what we think defines someone else that matters (because that is always shifting) but how we continually place ourselves and others in relation to those shifting definitions. Given this view, we may begin to study the ways children's ideas about differences within and among themselves are intentionally and unintentionally invoked by multicultural literature and how we can work together to call out the contradictory stories and relationships that lend more possibility to our places in the world.

NOTES

1. Multicultural literature is variously defined as that literature representative of the perspectives of people of color (Harris, 1992; Kruse & Horning, 1991; Bishop, 1994) and as literature that reflects the lifestyles and viewpoints of marginalized cultural or social groups that are traditionally underrepresented in publications, mass media, and school curricula (Banks, 1993). Scholars have also grouped the literature by genre and by its intention to represent primarily an insider's perspective, cross-cultural relationships, or root-culture stories and traditions (Cai & Bishop, 1994; Barrera, Liguori, & Salas, 1992).

2. It is curious to note that the key source for the character of Maniac Magee is actually a black child in Spinelli's childhood experience. It is not surprising that Spinelli would choose not to write from the black child's perspective given numerous and pressing questions about representation and authenticity of voice and experience (cf. Cai, Chapter 9, this volume). However, this reversal meant that Spinelli had to equate the white child's first encounters with racism with the black child's first encounters with racism. So then the question has to be answered: How does a black child's view of skin color equate with a white child's view? Are they comparable? Spinelli has created a character who refuses to see the differences as meaningful. He writes, however, that his friend Niki Hollie knew that skin color was meaningful: "There was a turnstile—only one child admitted at a time. When my friend's turn came, a brawny hand clamped the metal pipe and held it still. It would not move. And my friend, who until then had known merely that he was black, discovered now that it made a difference" (p. 430). The replacement of Niki Hollie's perspective with Maniac Magee's creates a significant shift in the story of racial segregation.

REFERENCES

Anderson, B. (1983). *Imagined communities: Reflections on the origin and spread of nationalism.* New York: Verso.

Banks, J. (1993). The canon debate, knowledge construction, and multicultural literature. *Educational researcher,* 22(5), 4–14.

Barrera, R., Liguori, O., & Salas, L. (1992). Ideas a literature can grow on: Key insights for enriching and expanding children's literature about the Mexican-American experience. In V. Harris (Ed.), *Teaching multicultural literature in grades K–8* (pp. 203–241). Norwood, MA: Christopher-Gordon.

Belsey, C. (1980). *Critical practice.* New York: Methuen.

Bishop, R. S. (Ed.). (1994). *Kaleidoscope: A multicultural booklist for grades K–8.* Urbana–Champaign, IL: National Council of Teachers of English.

Blume, J. (1970). *Iggie's House.* Englewood Cliffs, NJ: Bradbury.

Bourdieu, P. (1984). *Distinction: A social critique of the judgement of taste* (R. Nice, Trans.). Cambridge, MA: Harvard University Press.

Britzman, D., Santiago-Valles, K., Jiménez-Munoz, G. & Lamash, L. (1991). Dusting off the erasures: Race, gender and pedagogy. *Education and Society, 9*(2), 88–92.

Britzman, D., Santiago-Valles, K., Jiménez-Munoz, G. & Lamash, L. (1993). Slips that show and tell: Fashioning multiculture as a problem of representation. In C. McCarthy & W. Crichlow (Eds.), *Race identity and representation in education* (pp. 188–200). New York: Routledge.

Cai, M., & Bishop, R. S. (1994). Multicultural literature for children: Towards a clarification of the concept. In A. H. Dyson & C. Genishi (Eds.), *The need for story: Cultural diversity in classroom and community* (pp. 57–71). Urbana, IL: National Council of Teachers of English.

Dyson, A. H. (1993a). *Negotiating a permeable curriculum: On literacy, diversity, and the interplay of children's and teachers' worlds* (Concept Paper No. 9). Urbana–Champaign, IL: National Council of Teachers of English.

Dyson, A. H. (1993b). *Social worlds of children learning to write in an urban primary school.* New York: Teachers College Press.

Enciso, P. (1994). Cultural identity and response to literature: Running lessons from Maniac Magee. *Language Arts, 71,* 524–533.

Ferdman, B. (1990). Literacy and cultural identity. *Harvard Educational Review, 60*(2), 181–203.

Fiske, J. (1990). *Understanding popular culture.* New York: Routledge.

Hall, S., Critcher, C., Jefferson, T., Clarke, J., & Roberts, B. (1978). *Policing the crisis: Mugging, the state, and law and order.* New York: Holmes & Meier.

Harris, V. (Ed.). (1992). *Teaching multicultural literature in grades K–8.* Norwood, MA: Christopher-Gordon.

Kruse, G. M., & Horning, K. T. (1991). *Multicultural literature for children and young adults: A selected listing of books 1980–1990 by and about people of color* (3rd ed.). Madison, WI: Cooperative Children's Book Center.

Lensmire, T. J. (1994). *When children write: Critical re-visions of the writing workshop.* New York: Teachers College Press.

Morrison, T. (1992). *Playing in the dark: Whiteness and the literary imagination.* Cambridge, MA: Harvard University Press.

Narayan, K. (1993). How native is a "native" anthropologist? *American Anthropologist, 95,* 671–686.

Rosenthal, I. (1995). Educating through literature: Flying lessons from Maniac Magee. *Language Arts, 72,* 113–119.

Sims, R. (1982). *Shadow and substance: Afro-American experience in contemporary children's fiction.* Urbana–Champaign, IL: National Council of Teachers of English.

Spinelli, J. (1990). *Maniac Magee.* Boston: Little, Brown.

Spinelli, J. (1991, July/August). Newbery Medal acceptance. *The Horn Book Magazine,* pp. 426–432.

Stuckey, E. (1991). *The violence of literacy.* Portsmouth, NH: Heineman.

Taxel, J. (1992). The politics of children's literature: Reflections on multiculturalism, political correctness, and Christopher Columbus. In V. Harris (Ed.), *Teaching multicultural literature in grades K–8* (pp. 1–52). Norwood, MA: Christopher-Gordon.

CHAPTER 2

Re-Visioning Reading and Teaching Literature Through the Lens of Narrative Theory

WILLIAM McGINLEY, GEORGE KAMBERELIS, TIMOTHY
MAHONEY, DANIEL MADIGAN, VICTORIA RYBICKI,
AND JEFF OLIVER

AFTER READING *Song of the Trees* (M. Taylor, 1975), 10-year-old Joseph reconsidered the hardships associated with being separated from one's family and the experience of growing up apart from one's father or other family members. Specifically, in reading about the struggles that the characters Cassie, Stacey, Little Man, and Christopher-John experienced while their father was away from home searching for work, Joseph was reminded of the time when his own father left home. His comments further reveal the joy he shared with these children upon learning of their father's surprising return:

> These people, Casey, Stacey, Christopher-John, Little Man, momma, and pappa, their pappa has been away for many years. . . .'Cause he was looking to find a job and it took him that long. He had to work for some white men. . . . When I heard that, I wondered how could they miss their father that long. Christopher-John and the others didn't even know their father. . . . My first dad had been away, but see, he never came back. And I just liked it because it was about the whole family and the family meeting, like um, how the children met their father [in the end] and how the ma met, saw their father, saw their father again.

Similarly, after 8-year-old Jamar had finished reading *I Have a Dream: The Story of Martin* (Davidson, 1991) and *Encyclopedia Brown Gets His Man* (Sobol, 1982), he reflected on the meanings he associated with these books that allowed him to envision the possible selves and future responsibilities he might assume as a member of the African American community in which he lived:

> They [these books] make me think that I want to, that I could help the community or go up in space or be an actor or have all three. I have three choices to choose from [when I grow up], helping the community, going up in space, or being an actor. . . . See, if I think about my life, I only think about being an actor, but if I read Encyclopedia Brown or a book about Martin Luther King or Abraham Lincoln, it helps me to think about different things instead of being an actor.

When Joseph and Jamar read these and other stories, they were students participating in two different language arts classrooms in different regions of the country. As part of their participation in these unique programs, they were provided with opportunities to read, write, and talk about themselves, their family and peers, and their communities and cultures. Through a variety of instructional activities that encouraged them and other children to reflect on their own lives and experiences in response to their reading, they were introduced to the idea that stories can be a means of personal and social exploration and reflection—an imaginative vehicle for questioning, shaping, responding, and participating in the world. As Joseph, Jamar, and the many other children who were members of these two classrooms shared their thoughts and feelings about the stories they read, they brought to light a wealth of ways in which reading and responding to literature led not only to an understanding of the conceptual content of the stories but also to a process of reflection that helped them to understand themselves, others, and the world in which they lived.

Taken together, the written and spoken words of the children with whom we have worked over the past few years echo recent themes in the theoretical realms of narrative theory (e.g., Bruner, 1986) and transactional theory (e.g., Rosenblatt (1978, 1983). Collectively, these themes have spawned a renewed interest in the life-informing and life-transforming possibilities afforded by story reading that have only recently begun to be examined by researchers in literacy and literature.

In focusing on this dimension of children's reading, we draw upon data collected during several related ethnographic studies in the classrooms of Joseph and Jamar. Across these studies, we explored some of the ways that reading and writing functioned in children's lives as sources of personal, social, or political understanding and exploration. In addition, we sought to understand children's literacy as a function of the particular communities of practice in which they were socialized and enculturated to value reading and writing (McGinley & Kamberelis, 1992a; McGinley & Kamberelis, 1992b; McGinley & Kamberelis, 1996; McGinley, Mahoney, & Kamberelis, 1995). In this chapter, we draw upon this work in arguing that without a better understanding of the specific ways that stories may function as a means of organizing and interpreting experience, we stand to miss significant dimensions of students' development as readers, as well as an understanding of the possibilities that such reading might offer both children and adolescents who are also coming to know themselves, their family and peers, and the society in which they live. In addition, although conceiving of stories as a unique source of knowledge about self and world is certainly not a new proposition, a more complete understanding of the life-informing dimension of reading literature is essential if we are genuinely to evaluate, revitalize, and refine our understanding of the purpose for reading and teaching literature in school.

In the first part of the chapter, we review many of the constructs from the theoretical domains of narrative theory and transactional theory as they serve to outline the interdisciplinary framework and rationale with which we began our studies of the nature and meaning of children's story reading. Second, we present brief portraits of the classrooms of two teachers who sought to provide children with opportunities to reflect upon both literature and life. Third, we offer the written and spoken words of several children from these classrooms, communities, and cultures, as they provide insight into some of the ways that stories functioned as an imaginative resource for exploring, understanding, and re-creating themselves and their world. Finally, we conclude by discussing the implications of such findings for literacy pedagogy and for reconsidering the role and function of story reading in school and in students' lives.

PERSPECTIVES ON THE FUNCTIONS OF STORIES

The potential of narrative to function as a way of understanding one's own and others' experience has received renewed attention from scholars in both the humanities and the social sciences in recent years (e.g., Booth, 1988; Bruner, 1986, 1987; Carr, 1986; Martin, 1983; McAdams, 1993; Narayan, 1991; Ricoeur, 1984; Rosen, 1986; White, 1987; Witherell & Noddings,

1991). In general, these theorists have argued that because narratives are organized around the dimension of time in lived experience, they allow us to interpret our pasts, envision our futures, and understand the lives of others with whom we interact.

Participating in Storied Worlds

The importance of story or narrative in understanding both self and world has been given careful treatment by Bruner (1986, 1990). According to Bruner, the narrative models and procedures for interpreting and organizing experience are embodied in the written and told stories that a culture provides. Drawing on the work of Greimas and Courtes (1976), Bruner (1986) argues that the imaginative use of the narrative form in literature engages readers in the exploration of human possibilities by situating them simultaneously in a "dual landscape" of both action and consciousness. Stories, he explains, locate readers in a particular pattern or "grammar" of events, situations, and goals while also revealing the subjective worlds of characters who are involved in such events. In this way, stories provide "map[s] of possible roles and possible worlds in which action, thought, and self determination are permissible or desirable" (p. 66). In order to achieve such an effect, stories rely upon particular discourse properties that invite readers to enter into the fictional landscape and participate in the lives of protagonists. As Iser (1978) notes in *The Act of Reading*, the meanings of fictional texts are largely open-ended or "indeterminate." This "relative indeterminacy of text" provides readers with the incentive to develop or construct "a spectrum of actualizations" or formulations about themselves and the social world (p. 61). In sum, the discourse of a story invites a certain ambiguity of meaning and events that induces readers to participate in the production of meaning.

In building upon this idea of indeterminate meaning, Bruner (1986) emphasizes the notion of "subjunctivity" to explain the process through which readers enter a fictional landscape and experience or participate in the life and mind of story characters. Stories derive their power to render reality subjunctive or hypothetical through the depiction of the subjective consciousness of protagonists and the consequential alternativeness of the worlds they inhabit. Through the triggering of subjectification and the presentation of multiple perspectives, narrative discourse succeeds in "subjunctivizing reality" by "rendering the world of the story into the consciousness of its protagonists" (p. 28). As readers, we do not see the world through "an omniscient eye" but through "the filter of the consciousness of protagonists in the story" (p. 25) In this subjunctive state, we know only the realities and experiences of the story characters themselves and we are induced to identify with the plights in which they find themselves. Ultimately the "fictional landscape" achieves a reality of its own as readers construct and "act" in self-made story worlds. This power, Bruner (1986) insists, is at least partially dependent upon the subjunctive force or quality of a given narrative. The plights of characters must be rendered with "sufficient subjunctivity" so that their storied lives and experiences can be "rewritten" through the readers' own "play of imagination" (p. 35).

Moral and Ethical Functions of Stories

In relation to these points, several theorists have focused attention on life-informing and life-transforming possibilities that such a "play of imagination" might afford. For example, some scholars have foregrounded the ethical value of reading literature and the influence that stories may have on the development of an individuals' character or self. Coles (1989), for example, developed the idea that stories achieve their particular force through characters and events that engage readers in a psychological or moral journey. Such a journey or "personal expedition" allows readers to explore life's contingencies and dilemmas through the "moral imagination" of an author and, in so doing, enables them to "take matters of choice and commitment more seriously than they might otherwise have done" (p. 90).

According to Coles, the act of listening, reading, or responding to the stories of others can have important consequences for the ways in which we think about our own lives. The indirections and vicissitudes that inhabit a story and the lives of its characters become our own. A story's energy and emotion solicits our own involvement in the thoughts, feelings, desires, and fears of its characters. As Coles (1989) further explains:

> The whole point of stories is not "solutions" or "resolutions" but a broadening and even a heightening of our struggles—with new protagonists and antagonists introduced, with new sources of concern or apprehension, or hope, as one's mental life accommodates itself into a series of arrivals: guests who have a way of staying, but not necessarily staying put. (p. 129)

According to Booth (1988), the ethical and moral influence that stories exert on our lives and the development of our individual character is simply inescapable. In his exploration of the "efferent effect" or "carry-over" from our narrative reading to daily life and behavior, Booth explains that "anyone who conducts honest introspection knows that 'real life' is lived in images derived in part from stories" of themselves and others both real and fictional (p. 228). So spontaneous and unrehearsed is this narrative process that individuals often "cannot draw a clear line between what [they] *are*, in some conception of a 'natural,' unstoried self, and what [they] have become" as a result of the stories they have enjoyed, experienced, and appropriated over the course of their lives (p. 229).

Similar to Booth, other theorists have argued that individuals' understanding of both self and society is a function of the repertoire of stories that they have read, heard, and inherited throughout their lives (Bruner, 1990; MacIntyre, 1981; McAdams, 1993; Stone, 1988). As MacIntyre (1981) explains, these stories constitute the "dramatic resources" that individuals use in constructing their own moralities and evaluating the moral and ethical sensibilities of others in their world. Depriving children of stories of social traditions and moral life, he writes, "leave[s] them unscripted, anxious stutterers in their actions as in their words" (p. 201).

The personal, social, and moral functions of stories (or literature more broadly conceived) have also been a central focus among reader-response theorists (e.g., Beach, 1990; Hynds, 1990; Iser, 1978; Rosenblatt, 1978, 1983). According to these scholars, the literary experience can function both as a source of personal, social, and political exploration that provides readers with a means to interpret human experience and as a vehicle through which readers broaden their cultural understanding and sensibility. In her now classic work, *Literature as Exploration* (1983), Louise Rosenblatt argued that literature represents "an embodiment of human personalities, human situations, human conflicts and achievements" (p. vii). Through stories, Rosenblatt explains, we "do not so much acquire additional information as we acquire additional experience" (p. 38).

Similarly, Iser (1978) emphasized literature's power to reveal a "new reality" to readers—one that is different from the world they have come to know, such that the "deficiencies inherent in prevalent norms and in his own restricted behavior" are disclosed (p. xiii). More recently, Straw and Bogdan (1990) argued that the act of literary reading should be understood as "part of the lifelong experience of coming to know . . . part of a person's repertoire of experience to be remembered, reflected upon, and recomprehended" over the course of his or her life (p. 5).

In spite of these theoretical accounts of the processes through which narrative discourse succeeds in rendering reality subjunctive, as well as accounts of the moral, ethical, or political force that stories are believed to exert on our lives, several important questions remain concerning the kinds of insight into one's self and one's world that narrative experiences actually call forth. Though it may indeed seem from recent theoretical perspectives on narrative that children's story reading would be associated with particular life-informing possibilities, these theories are still largely without empirical foundation. In relation to this point, we might ask what the nature is of the understanding about themselves and the social world that young readers acquire as a result of their transactions with the stories they read and discuss in school. How do young readers emerge from the feelings and possibilities portrayed through the storied lives and experiences of the characters they encounter in books? In addition, according to a recent comprehensive study across a number of different schools (Applebee, 1993), knowledge of such theories is seldom reflected in current classroom approaches to the teaching and learning of literature. As a result, we know little about kinds of classroom practices and experiences that might engage students in reading both literature and life. These discontinuities among theory, research, and practice formed the basis for our initial interest and subsequent exploration into the nature and function of students' story-reading experiences in school.

STORIES OF READING IN TWO ELEMENTARY SCHOOL CLASSROOMS

Over the past several years, we have spent numerous hours on school playgrounds, on the floors of classrooms, in hallways, and in libraries, listening to children talk about a wide variety of books and stories. In sharing excerpts from students' written and spoken responses to literature, we hope to illustrate some of the ways in which stories provide them with a uniquely powerful means through which they might explore and reflect upon experience. In documenting the meaning that children in these classrooms evoked in relation to the literature they read, we relied upon our analyses of small- and whole-class literature discussions, children's literature journals and response notebooks, the in-depth interviews we conducted with children about their reading, and our field notes of classroom literature-related activities.

The Teachers and Their Classrooms

Vicki. Vicki was an experienced third- and fourth-grade teacher in a neighborhood elementary school in northwest Detroit. She had been living and teaching in the city for approximately 20 years. Throughout those years, she had devoted a considerable amount of her time and energy to trying to improve the community in which she and her students lived and attended school. In addition, she often provided children with rides to and from school; she took them to cultural and recreational events; she developed personal relationships with some of the children's parents; and she became involved with interest groups and activities in the local community. In the classroom, Vicki searched for ways to validate children's personal interests and experiences while also negotiating the numerous school district imperatives to improve children's standardized reading and writing scores. Although she made a special effort to prepare children for such tests, she also wanted students to view their own lives and experiences as important subjects about which they might read, write, and talk.

Motivated by her desire to provide her students with literate experiences that would involve reading and writing both text and life, Vicki searched for literacy activities that "would celebrate the children's voices"—voices that she believed teachers needed to listen to and encourage. Grounded in her "ethic of care" and based on her child- and community-centered educational philosophy, classroom activities were structured to provide children with reading and writing experiences that would be sensitive to their personal, emotional, and communal needs.

Three key events helped to initiate and anchor literacy instruction in Vicki's classroom. At the beginning of the year, Vicki arranged for the children to get to know one another by inviting each child to tell a story about him- or herself. In order to encourage the children and initiate the storytelling, she first asked them to think about what they do when they want to "become friends with someone." In response to this question, children offered a variety of ideas from "talking to them" to "sharing some things" to "asking their name." Vicki then suggested that we could also "tell a story about ourselves." The children then arranged their desks in a circle, and everyone shared some experience or details about themselves or their family.

Second, children were invited to plan and videotape a tour of the neighborhood where they lived and attended school. During the tour, children offered extensive commentary about a variety of local landmarks and related experiences that had particular meaning for them (e.g., churches, homes of relatives and friends, favorite restaurants, neighborhood stores, parks, abandoned homes, and local hangouts). This commentary included historical information about featured landmarks, as well as information about the personal, communal, and political significance of these sites.

Finally, Vicki involved the children in drawing and constructing a number of colorful signs or posters about the particular street where their own home was located. These signs were to be different from those commonly found in most neighborhoods. In constructing these "signs of community life," as she referred to them, children were encouraged to reflect upon and share those aspects of their community that they wished to celebrate, as well as those they wished to change. After sharing their ideas, the children were presented with the following question: "If we could place a sign in our neighborhood, what would it say?" Vicki then explained that the yellow-papered bulletin board in the back of the room would be like "house lights" illuminating their street signs and pictures. In a few days, these "signs of community life" were displayed across the bulletin board, revealing many of the children's hopes, interests, and concerns as they pertained to their lives and their community. The following examples were representative of the many messages and accompanying drawings that children constructed: "Please Don't Take Down The Basketball Rims," "Be Kind to One Another," "Stay in School," "Let's Clean Up Our Neighborhood," "Please Please Be Smart Don't Be a Drug Addict," "Don't Speed Down the Streets Watch For Children," "Keep Community Clean," and "Street of Peace."

Children in Vicki's classroom were also engaged in reading a variety of fictional and nonfictional texts.[1] In general, children's reading took three different forms: shared reading of stories from the classroom basal series, self-selected reading of school library books, and stories that Vicki elected to read aloud over the course of the year. In addition, as children's interest in reading developed, Vicki continued to supply them with books that represented the range of genres and topics in which they had expressed interest. On most days, children began by reading silently from a teacher-selected basal story or from self-selected books. In conjunction with this reading, they were encouraged to "reflect" or "write a sentence" in their reading-response journals about events or characters in the story that reminded them of experiences in their own lives. Each day after reading, several children were invited to share entries from their reading-response journals, and the other children in the class were invited to discuss these entries in small- and whole-group meetings. In both their written responses and in class discussions, Vicki encouraged children to reflect on and share their feelings in relation to particular texts by posing specific kinds of questions (e.g., "Reflect on what you read"; "How did the story make you feel?"; "What did the story make you think?"; "Did the story help you to imagine being a certain kind of person?"; "Did the story help you to imagine doing certain kinds of things?"). She also encouraged them to explore the reasons why an author might have written a particular piece (e.g., "Why do you think this author wrote this story?"; "What did the author want us to think, know, or do?"; "Is the author trying to change our minds about anything?").

Vicki's discussion of *To Hell With Dying* (Walker, 1988) was emblematic of many of the literature discussions in which the children took part. The story is about a loving relationship between a young child (Alice

Walker) and her aging friend (Mr. Sweet). Vicki began by asking the children to share their ideas about why the author might have written such a book. As the discussion developed, Vicki helped the children to identify the qualities and traits of the characters they admired and sought to emulate in this book as well as in other books. In this discussion, as in subsequent conversations about a variety of fictional and nonfictional texts, the children were frequently invited to "read" the experiences of such real and imaginary characters as Alice and Mr. Sweet, Rosa Parks, Harriet Tubman, Malcolm X, Sojourner Truth, Martin Luther King, Maniac Magee, Lulu and Sandy, Encyclopedia Brown, Romona Quimby, and Nate the Great as "dramatic resources" for reflecting upon important experiences and issues central to their own lives and the lives of their friends, families, and members of their immediate community.

Jeff. Jeff was a fourth- and fifth-grade teacher in Boulder who, like Vicki, was concerned with finding ways to help his students bring literature to life. We first met Jeff in 1992. He had been living and teaching elementary school in Colorado for approximately 20 years. In the classroom, Jeff devoted a considerable amount of time to fostering children's interest in reading by providing them with opportunities to understand and experience some of the ways that literature might function in their lives as a vehicle for examining and understanding experience. In particular, children in his classroom were often involved in wide-ranging, literacy-related activities designed to make literature and literacy a meaningful part of their lives both in and out of school. Among the many activities in which children participated, the following are examples of experiences that occurred regularly in Jeff's classroom: storybook read-aloud and personal story sharing in the group center, outdoor nature walks involving poetry reading and writing, storybook writing and reading projects with older adults in the community, student-organized story-reading clubs, student dramatizations of selected storybooks, composing original storybooks, in-class publication of student writing, independent reading, and visits from local writers, poets, musicians, and visual artists.

Although all children participated in these literacy activities over the course of the schoolyear, we became most interested in the story "read-aloud" time that took place in "the group center"—a small carpeted area separated from the rest of the room by a sofa, some chairs, and a bookshelf. On most mornings, children gathered on the floor of the group center to listen to Jeff read aloud from a children's storybook book or a young adult novel. These stories or novels were usually selected by Jeff and often related to particular themes or issues that he believed the children would enjoy discussing.[2] Once children were seated comfortably in a circle near their friends, story-reading time officially began with the ritual lighting of "the dreamer's candle" followed by the whole-class recitation of the poem "Invitation," by the well-known children's author Shel Silverstein (1974). The poem reads as follows:

> If you are a dreamer come in,
> If you are a dreamer, a wisher, a liar,
> If you're a hope-er, a pray-er, a magic bean buyer . . .
> If you're a pretender, come sit by my fire
> For we have some flax-golden tales to spin.
> Come in!
> Come in!

In conjunction with the stories he read and shared, Jeff often encouraged children to respond or react to such stories in particular ways. Similar to Vicki, Jeff's oral story-reading practices were frequently accompanied by invitations to the children to "read" or revisit their own lives and experiences through the lives and experiences of the characters they encountered in books. These invitations usually took the form of questions and often asked children to (1) tell a personal story related to particular story events, (2) share a related personal experience, (3) participate in the consciousness or subjective worlds of story characters, or (4) envision or celebrate a possible self or possible world in relation to a given story. Although Jeff frequently concluded each read-aloud session by asking children if they had "any comments, reactions, or responses," he often used these moments to model a way of reading and responding to literature that involved sharing a personal story or experience from one's own life. Consequently, after Jeff had narrated and shared an experience from his own life, children responded to his story by sharing a personal experience of their own or by responding to one of the specific questions that Jeff sometimes asked. Some of the most frequently asked questions included: "Does the story remind you of anything in your life?"; "Did anything like that ever happen to you?"; "Do you know anyone like that character?"; "What do you think that character is feeling or thinking about right now?"; "What would you do if you were in that character's situation?"; "What do you think the character will do next?"; "How is that character the same or different from you?"

Jeff's discussion of the novel *Everywhere* (Brooks, 1990) was emblematic of many of the literature discussions that took place in the group center each day. The story describes the experiences of a 10-year-old boy and his grandfather, who suffered a life-threatening heart attack. Together with his friend Dooley, the boy dreams of bringing his grandfather "back to life" by performing a "soul switch"—a magical process through which the soul of a dying person is exchanged with the soul of a particular animal with whom the person "got their soul mixed up . . . way back when the world was made" (p. 26). After sneaking a closer look at the grandfather's face, Dooley decides that a turtle would be the most appropriate animal for the switch. The first day's reading concluded with both boys searching for a suitable turtle at the foot of small creek in the woods filled with the wonderfully rich smells of "sap and waterlife" that often inhabit such places. As the grandson openly laments and regrets his decision never to have shown his grandfather this special place, Dooley turns to him and describes the way such places often get "captured" by those who visit them: "When a man gets to a certain spot and it strikes his fancy, he takes it on into his soul, see. It become his. And all the critters in that spot become his right along too" (p. 23).

Jeff initiated a discussion on this first day by asking a question ("Does that remind you of anything?") and then sharing the following memory or personal experience about the woods near his home in Virginia:

> I'll tell you what it reminded me of was, the place. The way he described the place reminded me of being in the woods in Virginia when I was probably about the age of the kids in the book. And seeing turtles and there was a little creek down there. But I liked the way he said, "you can take a place into your soul" because that's kind of how it feels to me even though, like now, when I go back, there are houses built on it, all in there and stuff. But I still feel like I carry around the place. I think that's what he meant by that. I don't know. Anyone else?

In response to Jeff's story and question, nearly every child shared a personal experience or told a story about a special place he or she had visited, often drawing connections to "that place" in the story. In addition, several of these children shared memories of their relationships with older adults (e.g., grandparents). In these accounts, they frequently reflected upon the importance of particular individuals in their lives, expressing personal regrets about missed opportunities for spending more time with older members of their family or immediate community. On this day, story reading was a imaginative vehicle through which students revealed themselves to one another as they shared and reconsidered the nature of their relationships with family members and friends.

On still another occasion, Jeff read *The Mountain That Loved a Bird* (McLerran, 1985), the story of a mountain made of "bare stone" that "stood alone in the middle of a desert plain." Each year a singing bird visits the mountain "carrying in her beak a small seed" that she tucks "into a crack in the hard stone." As years pass, plants begin to grow and eventually the mountain is no longer bare and alone. At the conclusion of the story, Jeff directed children's attention to the mountains they could see from the windows of their classroom. As the children looked out the window he asked, "What might the mountain be thinking?" At this point, children were invited to go outside to think and write in their "writer's notebooks." The invitation to write from the perspective of the mountain—to "experience" the "mountain's thoughts"—was just one of the more common approaches that Jeff used in helping children to understand the possibilities for re-creating and revisioning their world that were offered them by the stories.

Throughout the remainder of the school year, Jeff continued to question children and engage them in similar activities designed to help them draw upon the stories they read as a way to revisit and "experience" a number of important personal, social, and political issues. In reading the book *Teammates* (Golenbock, 1990), a story of the interracial friendship that developed between baseball players Jackie Robinson and Pee Wee Reese, students explored and discussed racism as it was "experienced" through the character of Jackie Robinson. In addition, they reflected on moments in their own lives during which they felt persecuted or oppressed.

The Children's Responses to Their Reading

The majority of students in Vicki's classroom were African American third- and fourth-grade children representing a wide range of academic abilities. The elementary school they attended drew its students from the surrounding neighborhood, a community largely comprised of African American families. The neighborhood in which the children lived and attended school was home to many of the social and economic problems that have become all too commonplace in large urban areas across the United States. Over the course of the year, the children in Vicki's class wrote and talked about many of these problems in response to the literature they read. Although such topics frequently captured students' attention and concern, story-related discussions also focused on the aspects of students' personal and community lives that they sought to remember, embrace, or affirm. Not surprisingly, conversations about family reunions and church gatherings, interesting or unique family members, African American leaders, vacations and family picnics, birthdays and holidays, personal goals and aspirations, and a variety of growing-up memories and experiences were equally popular topics of literature-related discussions.

The fourth- and fifth-grade students in Jeff's classroom were from predominately white, middle-class families. Similar to Vicki's classroom, these children represented a wide range of academic abilities and interests. The neighborhood in which the children attended school was adjacent to a major university campus. In general, although children in the surrounding community had little firsthand experience with many of the kinds of social and economic problems that children in Vicki's classroom experienced on a daily basis, many of their comments and reactions reflected a growing awareness of the problems and complexities associated with growing up in contemporary American society. More specifically, written responses and conversations throughout the year often touched on such problems and issues as poverty and homelessness, racial prejudice, ageism, environmental and conservation issues, health care, religious beliefs, and national and international conflicts as they were experienced at home, at school, in the immediate community, and on the pages of the local newspaper. In addition to these topics, story-related discussions in Jeff's classroom frequently focused on social relationships with family and friends, personal dreams and aspirations, favorite animals and pets, and a wide variety of memorable growing-up experiences associated with birthdays, vacations, holidays, and everyday events in children's lives.

Although the focus of children's writing and discussion about literature in both of these classrooms often differed in specific ways, our interactions and conversations with students over the course of the schoolyear provided insight into some of the humanizing and life-informing possibilities that children in each classroom had come to associate with the experience of reading and discussing stories. In presenting some of these possibilities, we draw upon children's written products, as well as the informal interviews we conducted with them. Our purpose here is not to provide an extensive account of the many ways that reading may function for children (for a more detailed discussion of this topic, see McGinley & Kamberelis, 1996). Rather, we intend to highlight some of the more salient ways that children in both classrooms seemed to use reading to explore and understand various aspects of their life and world.

In general, children's reading seemed to function in personal and social ways. Among the many personal meanings that story reading evoked in children, several emerged as the most salient. Specifically, children's reading often served as a means to envision and explore possible selves, roles, and responsibilities through the lives of story characters, both real and fictional; to describe or remember personal experiences or interests in their lives; and to objectify and reflect upon certain problematic emotions and circumstances as they related to important moral and ethical dilemmas in their lives. Reading also functioned in more social ways, providing children with a means to understand, affirm, or negotiate social relationships among peers, family members, and community members, as well as to raise and develop their awareness of significant social issues and social problems.

Exploring or Envisioning Possible Selves. Children's narrative reading provided them with opportunities to envision possible selves and celebrate particular role models—to adopt and imaginatively explore a variety of new roles, responsibilities, and identities derived from both real and fictional story characters. For example, after reading several books about well-known African American women, Mary wrote the following in her reading-response journal, indicating how the experiences of these women enabled her to reflect upon possible selves and possible roles for herself:

> Leontyne Price is a famous young lady. I read about her and sometimes I think I want to be like her. I read about lots of Black Americans like Duke Ellington, Barbara Jordon, and I forgot Phillis Wheatly. Some of these Blacks are dead already and I wish people would be alive. . . . Harriet Tubman Helped every one when it was slave wartime. I feel like I help people when I think about her.

Another classmate, Tanya, wrote about the biography of Diana Ross in her reading-response journal, emphasizing the qualities of independence and self-respect that she admired in the singer. She began her journal entry by copying a passage from the biography that described the family circumstances and living conditions of Diana Ross's childhood. Then she paraphrased another portion of the biography that juxtaposed Diana Ross's view of her home with that of the mainstream world. Finally, Tanya provided her own commentary on the singer's character:

> "After Diana [was born] came three boys and another girl. They all lived in a small apartment on the third floor of an old apartment house in the northern part of Detroit, Michigan. All the children slept together in one bedroom." I can see that being hard to sleep. The outsiders of Diana's neighborhood called it a ghetto, but Diana called it home. I really think Diana stood up for herself very well.

Remembering and Revisiting Personal Experiences. Children in both classrooms also used reading as a vehicle through which to remember, savor, and reflect upon personal experiences and interests or important people they had met or once known. For example, in an excerpt from her reading-response journal about *Bridge to Terabithia* (Paterson, 1977), Mari, a Japanese American student, wrote about the particular memories of friendship that the text brought to mind:

> When I was in 1st or 2nd grade I had a very close friend her name was Alice. I don't quite know what made he so speical, mabe it was because she was asian and I always felt a little more comfortable around asians. I might have liked asians because they seemed like part of my family.

Similarly, after reading *To Hell with Dying* (Walker, 1989), Gail revisited and reflected upon her relationship with her great-aunt Esther and her grandfather. In particular, she used the occasion to validate and reaffirm the importance of her past experiences with these elderly relatives. As she wrote in her response book:

> MR. Sweet reminds me of my great aunt ester, who dyed a cupple months ago. She was in the hospidle a few weekes and then she dyed and that reminded me of how MR. Sweet dyed. How he was sick and dockders [doctors] would see hem all the time and then he dyed. I thoat that the book was verry sad. and it also remindes me of how the girl would tickle MR. Sweet. I give my grandpa hi fives when ever we pass eachother and we started doing that at north carolina beech on vacation.

Reflecting upon Problematic Emotions. Children also found the experience of reading to be a useful way to objectify and reflect upon certain problematic emotions as they related to difficult or confusing circumstances in their lives. For example, Shanice described how reading *To Hell with Dying* (Walker, 1988) helped her to deal with the emotions she experienced in relation to the recent alcohol-related death of her uncle. In her reading-response journal, she drew a connection between her own experience and the experience of the author, Alice Walker:

> I like this book Because It tells you more what will happen to you if you do those kinds of things. When my uncle died from drinking. I was hurt. and I felt the same way as Alice Walker did. But when I went to the funeral I got Back home and I sat in my room and thought about it. then I learned how to deal with it.

Erika also wrestled with some important problematic emotions surrounding her relationship with her newly adopted infant brother in response to reading *The Cay* (T. Taylor, 1969). The story describes the developing friendship between a young boy named Phillip and his West Indian companion, Timothy. Shipwrecked and lost at sea, the two strangers endure a number of hardships that provide them with new understanding and insight into the differences that have characterized their separate lives. Specifically, the relationship of Phillip and Timothy served as an imaginative vehicle through which Erika revisioned and reconsidered the confusing and sometimes troubling behavior of her new brother.

> I cant sleep when my brother screems ispeshaley [especially] when we just got [adopted] him. he would screem and screem and I would just liy [lie] in my bed and wander what was rong and if I could help him because I felt bad that he had to go through so mach pan [pain] with being with 2 difrnt [different] people [families].

Participating in Imaginary Lives. Children frequently sought to share the exploits and experiences of the characters about whom they read. For example, while talking about the story *St. George and the Dragon* (Hodges, 1984), the story of a "brave and noble knight" who saves a kingdom of people from a "grim and terrible dragon" who was laying waste to their land, Jamar illustrated how the story functioned as a way for him to imaginatively participate in the lives and worlds of fictional characters quite different and removed from his own world:

> The story made me feel that I'd like to be both characters in the story. I would like to beat the dragon, and I would like to be the dragon. I'd like to know how it feels to be something, a giant animal, but then you're defeated by a little person. I'd like to know how it feels to be like, crush cities and stuff, but not hurt people.

Similarly, in response to a series of events in *The Cay* (T. Taylor, 1969), Christa imagined or re-created the "experience" of being lost at sea after Timothy and Phillip tried unsuccessfully to be noticed by a single rescue plane flying overhead. As she wrote in her reading-response journal:

> I would be feeling very sad that the plane had gone and I had been on the island for so long and I for some reason would be thinking

of Timmithy and the storm and the war, my mom and dad and just about my whole life.

Negotiating Social Relationships. Although our work in the classrooms of Vicki and Jeff revealed that children's reading was most often associated with these personal meanings, the children also invoked a number of social meanings that seemed particularly important to their development as readers and within various social groups. Among the most salient of these functions, reading presented children with a vehicle through which to understand, affirm, or negotiate social relationships among peers, family members, and community members.

Billy was one child who engaged in reading (and writing) in order to construct and affirm his relationship with members of his own family. Among the texts that Billy read, several included brief biographical accounts of the lives of famous African Americans such as Rosa Parks, Frederick Douglass, Harriet Tubman, Martin Luther King, Jr., and Malcolm X. When we asked him to reflect upon his reasons for both reading and writing about these texts, he often mentioned experiences and relationships that different members of his family had had with these individuals in the context of the civil rights movement. Thus, through his reading (and writing) he was able to celebrate, reflect upon, and deepen his affiliations with family members who valued and frequently discussed the lives and accomplishments of important African American leaders:

> [I like to read and write about black Americans] 'cause my mom met Rosa Parks and my grandfather he met Martin Luther King, and my dad tell me a story about Malcolm X. And then my dad, and my momma, and my grandfather met Martin Luther King. . . . And then after he was marching with Dr. Martin Luther King they wetted his shirt up. They wetted my grandaddy's shirt up when the firemen came. . . . And then, when my grandfather, he travels a lot, he went to Atlanta, Georgia, and then he put some sunflowers on his grave.

Children's reading also served as a means reflecting upon and rethinking the meaning and importance of friendships and relationships with peers. For example, *Lulu Goes to Witch School* (O'Connor, 1987) is the story of a young girl named Lulu and the difficulties she encountered with Sandy, another young girl who picks on Lulu during her first days at "witch school." In responding to the book, Tanya described how the storied experiences of Lulu and Sandy helped her to understand the difficulties she once encountered in school and the importance she assigned to her developing friendship with a classmate named Mary:

> It brought back memories, when I was little, not when I was little, back when people, when I was picking on people and people picked on me. . . . When I first read the first part of the book, it was talking about Lulu going to witch school and I predict, I said in my mind that this might be how my life was when I first came to school. . . . And as I read on, it kept talking about how I was when I first came to school.
>
> And then it came to the part where Mary [a new student that had just arrived in Tanya's class] came to school, and I started, started thinking on her [Mary]. And then it [the story] went on and on, and started, then we [Mary and I] started being friends.

In later conversations with Tanya, it became clear that reading about the friendship of Lulu and Sandy was a way for her to dramatically revisit the kind of friendship she had developed with Mary. In fact, we believe that in rethinking her relationship with Mary, she refashioned her ideas about the value and importance of friendship in general.

Understanding Social Problems and Social Issues. In addition to engaging in literate activity in order to explore and negotiate social relationships, reading was a means through which children could develop their political sensibilities, especially as it pertained to heightening their awareness of important social issues and social problems. For example, after reading *Farewell to Manzanar* (Houston & Houston, 1973), 9-year-old Mari talked about the experiences and struggles that other Japanese Americans were forced to endure as a result of their imprisonment in internment camps during World War II. In particular, she drew a connection between her own life and the experiences of a young girl named Jeane whose father was "sent away to an internment camp like my great grandfather." Mari used the story of hardship and separation that Jeane and her father experienced as a way of dramatizing and further understanding the difficulties that her own great-grandfather may have encountered in such camps. As she explained:

> The story *Farewell to Manzanar* starts out with an adult and she comes to Manzanar, when, after the war is all over and everything and then she remembers the whole story about when she was a little girl and that and how her father was sent away to an internment camp like my great grandfather was, and didn't come back

'till about five months after the war. . . . I was thinking that one of my great grandparents was this man [in the story] who was very proud, and it was very hard for him to be locked up in this place, so it made him kind of crazy. . . . [And there was a little girl in the story] and I thought that I might be very much like that if I was in the war, 'cause she didn't understand you know, what was happening and why her father was sent away, and what they were going to, like a camp, or something like that. . . . Even though it is something that happened a long time ago, it was a big thing, and it was hard, and I wanted to know just how they got through it.

As demonstrated in children's talk and text, the narrative reading in which they were engaged was associated with a number of life-informing functions and possibilities. As part of their participation in their respective classrooms, children were encouraged to practice and value a way of reading and discussing literature that involved reading both text and life. Over the course of the schoolyear, they used reading to explore new roles and social identities, to affirm their cultural identities, to understand and negotiate human experiences, and to wrestle with vexing social and political issues related to improving the quality of their life and world.

READING LITERATURE AND LIFE

In this chapter, we argued that a more complete understanding of the critical, humanizing, and life-informing dimensions of reading stories is integral to our efforts to further develop and extend our understanding of the meaning and importance of literature (or literacy) in students' lives. In addition, we argued that knowledge of this dimension of story reading is essential if we are to genuinely evaluate, revitalize, and refine our understanding of the role and function of reading and teaching literature in the school curriculum. Toward that end, we examined recent work in the area of narrative theory and reader-response theory as it serves to focus on the important role that stories play in helping us to organize and structure human experience. Although theories of narrative understanding and literary reading are indeed interesting, they have had little influence on the school literature curriculum and the specific manner in which stories are read and taught in classrooms. As Applebee (1993) found, literature instruction is still closely aligned with New Critical or more text-based approaches to literary reading. In the context of such approaches, students have little or no opportunity to experience or understand some of the possibilities for exploring self and world that both narrative theorists and reader-response theorists have come to associate with reading stories.

Unfortunately, recent research in the area of response to literature has done little to mitigate the apparent disjunction between narrative theory and the actual practice of teaching literature in school that Applebee describes. Although a fuller and more comprehensive awareness of the kinds of personal or social insight that literary reading might offer readers would certainly be useful in rethinking the role and importance of literature in the school curriculum, the majority of literature-related research has continued to focus on the *processes* that underlie students' literary transactions (e.g., Earthman, 1992; Garrison & Hynds, 1991; Hancock, 1994; Langer, 1990; Rogers, 1991). So, while some of literature's life-informing or life-transforming possibilities have been suggested by the data from previous studies of students' school-based story reading (e.g., Many, 1991; Many & Wiseman, 1992), few have been made explicit and many have remained largely unnoticed. For example, although many literature researchers have pointed out that children sometimes relate reading and personal experience, the functions of such relations have seldom been investigated.

In sharing a glimpse of the life and language that characterized the classrooms of Vicki and Jeff, we provided a unique look at some of the ways that children were encouraged to use and conceptualize story reading and story-related discussion as unique opportunities for interpreting, negotiating, and reconstructing experiences involving themselves, family members and peers, members of their immediate community, and the larger society. As we explored the talk and texts that emerged from children's reading of literature, we learned that such reading functioned primarily in personal ways. More specifically, children's reading was often related to exploring and envisioning possible selves and identifying with role models, objectifying and reconciling problematic emotions, and remembering and reconstructing important life episodes and events. In addition to these personal uses, children's reading functioned in more social ways, helping them to affirm or transform social relationships in their immediate worlds, to understand and consider possibilities for transforming social problems and injustices, and to fashion social and moral codes.

Through a variety of instructional activities that encouraged children to reflect upon their own lives and experiences in response to their reading, they were introduced to the idea that stories can be a means of personal and social exploration and reflection—an "imaginative vehicle," as Willinsky (1991) suggests, for questioning, shaping, responding, and participating in the world. As Joseph, Jamar, and the many other children who were members of these two classrooms shared their thoughts about reading, they brought to light a wealth of ways in which reading and responding to literature led not only to an understanding of the conceptual content of the stories they read but also to a process of reflection that helped them to understand themselves, others, and the world in which they lived. In sum, reading for these children involved not only constructing textual understanding of the literature they read but also constructing their identities, their moralities, and their visions for social and community life.

The written and spoken words of these children have a number of important implications for the reading and teaching of literature. In particular, children's experiences with stories in the classrooms of Vicki and Jeff suggest the need to reconsider once again the role and function of literature in the school curriculum—to rethink our current conceptions of what it means to read and study literature in classrooms. We believe that this reconsideration would involve shifting attention from comprehending, analyzing, or interpreting literature texts to reading life through texts and texts through life. Indeed, the children whose reading and responses we shared prefigured this shift in the ways in which they readily took up their teacher's invitation to read and talk about themselves, their friends, their families, their community, and their culture. In this regard, these children enacted what many narrative theorists and reader-response theorists have claimed to be one of the most fundamental dimensions of reading stories—their potential to engage readers in the exploration of possible selves and possible worlds through the depiction of the subjective worlds of protagonists. In relation to this point, it may be that literature instruction that focuses primarily on the analysis and interpretation of literary texts denies students access to significant personal, social, and political possibilities and consequences that might be afforded by adopting different and perhaps more life-informing perspectives concerning the functions of literature.

Surprisingly, although our understanding of this dimension of story reading remains only partially developed, assumptions about the life-informing and life-transforming function of literature continue to figure prominently in the conceptual frameworks of recent curricular reforms that fall under the rubric of multicultural education. Such reforms currently place considerable faith in the unique power and quality of literature to transform students' perceptions and understandings of individuals whose life histories, memories, and cultural backgrounds differ significantly from their own (see Desai, Chapter 7, this volume). Literature, from this perspective, is often linked to promoting cultural awareness among students as the basis for social change and the foundation for developing such democratic principles as social justice and equality for all citizens (e.g., Harris, 1993). These assumptions are clearly evident in a recent article by Yokota (1993) in which she revealed some of the more common transformative themes attributed to literature and story reading within recent multicultural pedagogies. As she explained:

> With the increasing cultural diversity of students in American schools, we as language arts educators face the need to provide literary experiences that reflect the multitude of backgrounds from which the children in our schools come. . . . For *all* students, multicultural literature provides vicarious experiences from cultures other than their own; and these experiences help them understand different backgrounds, thereby influencing their decisions about how they will live in this culturally plural world. (p. 156)

However, in a recent study Beach (1994; Chapter 3, this volume) found that mainstream students often develop "stances of resistance" to much of the multicultural literature they encounter in school. According to Beach, such findings raise important questions about the role of multicultural literature in combating racial stereotypes or prejudice. More specifically, several questions related to understanding the functions of stories suggest themselves: Can literary reading and study engender the kinds of transformative possibilities attributed to it by multicultural reformers? What are some of the meanings and functions that students actually evoke in relation to their reading of multicultural literature? In what ways does such reading inform students' lives, as well as their perceptions of others in their school and their world? What is the nature of the instructional context and practices in which students might experience and learn about this dimension of literature?

In light of these questions, possibilities, and consequences, we are led to underscore the importance of developing English or language arts programs that focus on the life-informing dimensions of literary reading and actively engage children in exploring some of the humanizing and transformative functions of stories or literature. The specifics of such programs and the kinds of understanding that literature makes possible are further discussed by Beach, Enciso, and Rogers (Chapters 3, 1, and 4, respectively, this volume). Indeed, we join these authors in suggesting that literature programs should be built upon an integration of the ideas and constructs embodied in the work of narrative theorists and reader-response theorists that we outlined in the beginning of this chapter.

Some of these ideas were embodied quite fully and explicitly in the classrooms of Vicki and Jeff. Others remained only emergent and partial. Yet by providing the children in these classrooms with personally and culturally relevant materials, occasions to read and talk about issues close to their own hearts and lives, we think that these teachers provided a catalyst for children's efforts to explore and understand some of the life-informing possibilities that might be associated with reading stories in school classrooms. As they became familiar with this aspect of reading stories, the children seemed to appreciate more fully the humanizing and transformative possibilities and consequences of such reading. The children's appreciation of these possibilities and consequences suggests the value of articulating, implementing, and studying the ways that stories may function in readers' lives. In addition, they suggest the need to better understand the kinds of pedagogical practices that make such possibilities a reality.

NOTES

The research on which this chapter is based was funded by the National Council of Teachers of English Research Foundation and the International Reading Association Elva Knight Research Award. Special thanks to Daniel Madigan for the intellectual energy he so willingly devoted to helping develop and implement the curriculum in Vicki's classroom. Also thanks to Lucia Kegan for her assistance in collecting and organizing data for much of this research.

1. Some of the more popular texts included *Here Comes the Strikeout* (Kessler, 1965), *Honey I Love and Other Love Poems* (Greenfield, 1978), *Harriet Tubman: The Road to Freedom* (Bains, 1982), *Encyclopedia Brown Gets His Man* (Sobol, 1982), *Diana Ross: Star Supreme* (Haskins, 1986), *To Hell with Dying* (Walker, 1988), *The Chalk Doll* (Pomerantz, 1989), *Ragtime Tumpie* (Schroeder, 1989), *I Have a Dream: The Story of Martin* (Davidson, 1991), and *Maniac Magee* (Spinelli, 1990).

2. Some of the texts that Jeff elected to read included *Bridge to Terabithia* (Paterson, 1977), *A Grain of Wheat: A Writer Begins* (Bulla, 1985), *The Mountain That Loved a Bird* (McLerran, 1985), *Heckedy Peg* (Wood, 1987), *My Name Is Not Angelica* (O'Dell, 1989), *To Hell with Dying* (Walker, 1988); *The Chalk Doll* (Pomerantz, 1989), *Ragtime Tumpie* (Schroeder, 1989), *Everywhere* (Brooks, 1990), *Teammates* (Golenbock, 1990), and *Uncle Jed's Barbershop* (Mitchell, 1993).

REFERENCES

Applebee, A. (1993). *Literature in the secondary school: Studies of curriculum and instruction in the United States.* Urbana, IL: National Council of Teachers of English.

Bains, R. (1982). *Harriet Tubman: The road to freedom.* New York: Troll.

Beach, R. (1990). The creative development of meaning: Using autobiographical experiences to interpret literature. In D. Bogdan & S. B. Straw (Eds.), *Beyond communication: Reading comprehension and criticism* (pp. 211–235). Portsmouth, NH: Boynton/Cook.

Beach, R. (1994, December). *Students' responses to multicultural literature.* Paper presented at the National Reading Conference, San Diego, CA.

Booth, W. C. (1988). *The company we keep: An ethics of fiction.* Los Angeles: University of California Press.

Brooks, B. (1990). *Everywhere.* New York: Scholastic.

Bruner, J. (1986). *Actual minds, possible worlds.* Cambridge, MA: Harvard University Press.

Bruner, J. (1987). Life as narrative. *Social Research, 54*(1), 11–32.

Bruner, J. (1990). *Acts of meaning.* Cambridge, MA: Harvard University Press.

Bulla, C. R. (1985). *A grain of wheat: A writer begins.* Boston, MA: Godine.

Carr, D. (1986). *Time, narrative, and history.* Bloomington: Indiana University Press.

Coles, R. (1989). *The call of stories: Teaching and the moral imagination.* Boston: Houghton Mifflin.

Davidson, M. (1991). *I have a dream: The story of Martin.* New York: Scholastic.

Earthman, E. A. (1992). Creating the virtual work: Readers' processes in understanding literary texts. *Research in the Teaching of English, 26*(4), 351–384.

Garrison, B., & Hynds, S. (1991). Evocation and reflection in the reading transaction: A comparison of proficient and less proficient readers. *Journal of Reading Behavior, 23*(3), 259–280.

Golenbock, P. (1990). *Teammates.* New York: Harcourt Brace Jovanovich.

Greenfield, E. (1978). *Honey I love and other tales.* New York: HarperCollins.

Greimas, A., & Courtes, J. (1976). The cognitive dimensions of narrative discourse. *New Literary History, 7*, 433–447.

Hancock, M. R. (1994). Exploring the meaning-making process through the content of literature response journals: A case study investigation. *Research in the Teaching of English, 27*(4), 335–368.

Harris, V. J. (1993). *Teaching multicultural literature in grades K–8.* Norwood, MA: Christopher-Gordon.

Haskins, J. (1986). *Diana Ross: Star supreme.* New York: Puffin.

Hodges, M. (1984). *St. George and the dragon.* Boston: Little, Brown.

Houston, J., & Houston, J. (1973). *Farewell to Manzanar.* New York: Bantam.

Hynds, S. (1990). Reading as a social event: Comprehension and response in the text, classroom, and world. In D. Bogdan & S. B. Straw (Eds.), *Beyond communication: Reading comprehension and criticism* (pp. 237–256). Portsmouth, NH: Boynton/Cook.

Iser, W. (1978). *The act of reading: A theory of aesthetic response.* Baltimore: Johns Hopkins University Press.

Kessler, L. (1965). *Here comes the strikeout.* New York: HarperTrophy.

Langer, J. A. (1990). The process of understanding: Reading for literary and informative purposes. *Research in the Teaching of English, 24*(3), 229–257.

MacIntyre, A. (1981). *After virtue.* Notre Dame, IN: University of Notre Dame Press.

Many, J. E. (1991). The effects of stance and age level on children's literary responses. *Journal of Reading Behavior, 23*(1), 61–85.

Many, J. E., & Wiseman, D. L. (1992). The effect of teaching approach on third-grade students' response to literature. *Journal of Reading Behavior, 24*(3), 265–287.

Martin, N. (1983). *Mostly about writing.* Montclair, NJ: Boynton/Cook.

McAdams, D. (1993). *Stories we live by: Personal myth in the making of the self.* New York: Morrow.

McGinley, W., & Kamberelis, G. (1992a). Personal, social, and political functions of reading and writing. In C. Kinzer & D. J. Leu (Eds.), *Yearbook of the National Reading Conference: Vol. 44. Literacy research, theory, and practice: Views from many perspectives* (pp. 403–413). Chicago: National Reading Conference.

McGinley, W., & Kamberelis, G. (1992b). Transformative functions of children's writing. *Language Arts, 69,* 330–338.

McGinley, W., & Kamberelis, G. (1996). Maniac Magee and Ragtime Tumpie: Children negotiating self and world through reading and writing. *Research in the Teaching of English, 30,* 75–113.

McGinley, W., Mahoney, T., & Kamberelis, G. (1995). Reconsidering stories. *Statement: Journal of the Colorado Language Arts Society, 31,* 9–16.

McLerran, A. (1985). *The mountain that loved a bird.* New York: Scholastic.

Mitchell, D. (1993). *Uncle Jed's barbershop.* New York: Scholastic.

Narayan, K. (1991). "According to their feelings": Teaching and healing with stories. In C. Witherell & N. Noddings (Eds.), *Stories lives tell: Narrative and dialogue in education* (pp. 113–135). New York: Teachers College Press.

O'Connor, J. (1987). *Lulu goes to witch school.* New York: HarperCollins.

O'Dell, S. (1989). *My name is not Angelica.* New York: Dell Yearling.

Paterson, K. (1977). *Bridge to Terabithia.* New York: HarperTrophy.

Pomerantz, C. (1989). *The chalk doll.* New York: HarperCollins.

Ricoeur, P. (1984). *Time and narrative* (Vol. 1) (K. McLaughlin & D. Pellauer, Trans.). Chicago: University of Chicago Press.

Rogers, T. (1991). Students as literary critics: The interpretive experiences, beliefs, and processes of ninth-grade students. *Journal of Reading Behavior, 23*(4), 391–423.

Rosen, H. (1986). The importance of story. *Language Arts, 63*(3), 226–237.

Rosenblatt, L. M. (1978). *The reader, the text, the poem.* Carbondale: Southern Illinois University Press.

Rosenblatt, L. M. (1983). *Literature as exploration* (4th ed.). New York: Modern Language Association.

Schroeder, A. (1989). *Ragtime Tumpie.* Boston: Little, Brown.

Silverstein, S. (1974). *Where the sidewalk ends.* New York: HarperCollins.

Sobol, D. (1982). *Encyclopedia Brown gets his man.* New York: Bantam.

Spinelli, J. (1990). *Maniac Magee.* New York: HarperCollins.

Stone, E. (1988). *Black sheep and kissing cousins: How our family stories shape us.* NY: Penguin.

Straw, S. B., & Bogdan, D. (Eds.). (1990). *Beyond communication: Reading comprehension and criticism.* Portsmouth, NH: Boynton/Cook.

Taylor, M. (1975). *Song of the trees.* New York: Bantam.

Taylor, T. (1969). *The Cay.* New York: Avon.

Walker, A. (1988). *To hell with dying.* San Diego: Harcourt Brace Jovanovich.

White, H. V. (1987). *The content of the form: Narrative discourse and historical representation.* Baltimore: Johns Hopkins University Press.

Willinsky, J. (1991). *The triumph of literature and the fate of literacy: English in the secondary school curriculum.* New York: Teachers College Press.

Witherell, C., & Noddings, N. (1991). *Stories lives tell: Narrative and dialogue in education.* New York: Teachers College Press.

Wood, A. (1987). *Heckedy Peg.* New York: Scholastic.

Yokota, J. (1993). Issues in selecting multicultural children's literature. *Language Arts, 70,* 156–167.

CHAPTER 3

Students' Resistance to Engagement with Multicultural Literature

RICHARD BEACH

As LITERATURE TEACHERS begin to incorporate more multicultural literature into the curriculum, they are encountering increasing resistance from students (Jordan & Purves, 1993; V. Lee, 1986; Sharpe, Mascia-Lees, & Cohen, 1990). When asked to give reasons for their resistance, students cite their difficulty understanding the linguistic and cultural practices portrayed in the texts (Jordan & Purves, 1993). They are also uneasy with discussing issues of racism, particularly when these discussions challenge middle-class students' privileged perspectives on the world. These students may also respond negatively to literary texts perceived as challenges to their privileged stance, apply negative stereotypes to portrayals of cultural differences, and avoid thoughtful discussion of issues of race and class.

Why this resistance? In this chapter, I discuss some of reasons why students adopt what I am defining as stances of resistance to multicultural literature. I then suggest ways to help students move beyond resistance to develop a more positive engagement with multicultural literature.

STANCE AS IDEOLOGICAL ORIENTATION

For the purpose of this chapter, I am defining stance to mean the ideological orientations or "subject positions" students bring to their response to literature (Beach, 1993; Bennett & Woollacott, 1987). These stances reflect the beliefs and attitudes students apply to texts. Students judge characters' actions and infer thematic meanings according to their beliefs and attitudes. For example, in responding to more "traditional" romance novels, students who bring feminist attitudes to these texts may be critical of the heroine's adherence to patriarchal values.

Students are socialized or positioned to adopt stances associated with their memberships or status in certain communities. These communities subscribe to certain cultural maps (Enciso, Chapter 1, this volume) or discourses constituting ways of knowing or organizing the world (Gee, 1990; Lemke, 1995). By responding in ways consistent with the values of a community, readers demonstrate their allegiance to a community's values. For example, members of fundamentalist religious groups may be socialized to read the Bible as "God's truth." They then affirm their group allegiance by sharing their literal interpretations of the Bible with these groups.

Stances as Constituted by Discourses of Gender, Racial, and Class Differences

Students' stances are constituted by ideological discourses of gender, class, and racial differences. Take, for example, a group of adolescent males watching and responding to a television program. In sharing their responses, these males are primarily concerned with maintaining their own masculine image (Buckingham, 1993). They are reluctant to express their emotional reactions to characters, particularly female characters, for fear of being perceived by their peers as unmasculine. To avoid risking their masculinity, they opt to play it safe by ridiculing or vilifying characters as "stupid" or "ugly." Similarly, female adolescents adopt a gendered discourse based on either/or oppositions between what is considered to be "female"—being outgoing and relating to others—and being "male"—managing events (Cherland, 1994). They also respond to characters in terms of oppositions between "good-girl" or "saintly" behaviors and "bad-girl" or "sinful" behaviors. These male and female adolescent groups are both adopting a stance reflecting a discourse of gender difference that privileges a male perspective (McIntosh, 1989).

As part of acquiring a sense of male privilege, males learn to adopt a "male gaze" stance associated with the masculine practices of assertiveness, physical prowess, and emotional detachment (Bennett & Woollacott, 1987). In a study of adolescents' responses to stereotypical portrayals of females in teenage magazine ads (Beach & Freedman, 1992), secondary school male students frequently described their responses in terms of metaphors of domination and male privilege. Few if any students in the study—male or female—were critical of the gender stereotyping in the ads. Further, some males expressed their resistance to what they characterized as "feminist" perspectives on these gender portrayals.

Readers' stances are also shaped by discourses of class difference. Readers applying middle-class values may object to portrayals that resist these values. In a study of editors' decisions about the selection of books for Book-of-the-Month Club members, Janice Radway (1988) found that the editors preferred those books that did not offend or challenge what they perceived to be their members' middle-class sensibilities. These editors were therefore reluctant to select novels that were experimental or that portrayed topics deviating from middle-class values, anticipating potential resistance from club members to material that challenged the privileged middle-class worldview.

In secondary school settings, students' stances are shaped by a system of ability grouping or tracking that privileges some students over others. It is often the case that students from middle-class backgrounds are placed in "honors" or "advanced" ability groups and students from working-class backgrounds, in "regular" or "vocational" ability groups (Eckert, 1989; Oakes, 1985). From their experiences in these ability groups, students acquire different attitudes toward their own status or privilege in the school. These differences are evident in a study I conducted on students' responses to Richard Peck's (1989) short story "I Go Along" (Beach, 1995). This story contrasts two different groups of high school students: advanced and regular students. I asked students in advanced and regular tenth- and eleventh-grade classes to respond to this story. In the story, Gene, a member of a regular English section, decides to accompany the advanced students on a field trip to a poetry reading at a neighboring college. Gene ends up being the only student from the regular class who goes on the trip. While he is befriended by one of the most popular girls in the school, Sharon, and he enjoys the poetry reading, he recognizes the fact that he lacks the social status associated with being a member of the advanced class.

The regular and advanced students differed in their responses to the story, differences that reflect their stance of privilege. The regular students noted: "I'm glad they have high-potential classes because I wouldn't want to drag anyone back because of my rate of learning." "I used to be in honors classes and then when I switched to regular classes, my teacher was not as nice and treated me and others like us as stupid and as failures." They also perceived the advanced students as being more popular in the school than the regular students. One regular student noted, "Most of the popular kids would not want to sit by a person who is not popular; Gene was amazed that Sharon would sit by him." Another regular student noted that "people who are 'above everybody' usually don't talk to people like Gene." Advanced students attributed Gene's status as a regular student to his lack of motivation; for instance, one said, "I have run across many Genes in my 10 years of schooling and none of them are in advanced classes even though they should be. The average Gene dresses sloppily and doesn't act like they have a care in the world."

These students' responses reflect their beliefs and attitudes regarding power and privilege. Most of the students in the study also conceived of the characters as motivated primarily by their own individual attitudes, as opposed to institutional forces. Few of the students focused on the institutional system of ability grouping or tracking that shaped the characters' actions. Similarly, in responding to multicultural literature portraying racial conflict, students may conceive of racial conflict and prejudice primarily in terms of differences in feelings or opinions as opposed to institutional forces. They may explain instances of racial discrimination as a matter of individual prejudice deriving from a failure to recognize that "we are all humans." Their responses reflect the perspective that Henry Giroux (1983) describes as "private authority"—that subjective responses are constructed primarily by individuals as opposed to institutional or ideological forces. For Giroux, this perspective serves to "suppress questions of power, knowledge, and ideology" (p. 3).

This "individual prejudice" stance is prevalent in mass media analyses of the issue of racism. For example, a "Racism in 1992" series on "The Oprah Winfrey Show" treated the issue of racism as a reflection of individual opinions, rights, and experiences (Peck, 1994). This individualistic perspective reflects a therapeutic model of racism. In that model, racism is defined as an "illness" cured through confessions, release of anger, empathetic understanding of others, and forgiveness. By conceiving of racism as a matter of individual prejudice, whites avoid equating racism with themselves. This allows whites to "assume that every group is racist and to avoid acknowledging the power differential between whites and groups of color" (Sleeter, 1993, p. 14).

For John Fiske (1993), this attitude represents a "new racism" that goes beyond notions of racial superiority. This "new racism" has to do with "the struggle over the power to promote social interests that are always racial but never purely so and that function by putting racial difference into practice" (p. 252). Fiske argues that, rather than a matter of acts of individual discrimination, racism is an institutional phenomenon that privileges those in power, that is, whites. This power has to do with how

> certain social formations, defined primarily by class, race, gender and ethnicity, have privileged access ... which they can readily turn to their own

economic and political interests. [It is] a systematic set of operations upon people which works to ensure the maintenance of the social order (in our case of late capitalism) and ensure its smooth running. It is therefore in the interests of those who benefit most from this social order to co-operate with this power system and to lubricate its mechanisms. (pp. 10–11)

Fiske cites the example of the initial Rodney King trial that led to the acquittal of the police officers who beat King. The trial was moved to a suburban site in which jury members would be more likely to side with the police officers, a reflection of the power associated with the Los Angeles Police Department relative to the power of a black man.

Beverly Tatum (1992) distinguishes between white racism as an institutional force that operates to benefit whites as a group and prejudices, defined as misconceptions or preconceived opinions that all groups may hold. She argues that the prejudices espoused by whites, given their social power in the system, are more likely to be taken seriously than prejudices espoused by other groups. However, whites are often not aware of the power of their prejudices. She also finds that as soon as her white college students begin to sense that they are part of this system of advantage, they deny any personal connection to racism as a system that serves to perpetuate their own economic privilege. While some of her students may perceive the influence of racism on others, particularly people of color, they do not necessarily examine its influence on their own attitudes and behavior. Tatum (1992) notes that students explain their interest in enrolling in her course on racism "with such declaimers as, 'I'm not a racist myself, but I know people who are, and I want to understand them better'" (p. 8). However, their understanding is based on a belief in a just meritocracy in which individual achievement is rewarded, and they are uncomfortable with the idea that society unjustly rewards those who are in power.

One reason for the prevalence of this "individual prejudice" stance is that those students who benefit from institutional power are rarely aware of the advantages of privilege. White students often take for granted their own white privilege because, in their largely homogeneous suburban communities, they are socialized to assume that white privilege is the norm (Scheurich, 1993). In their experience with the mass media, with films such as *Dances with Wolves,* the dominant system of representation positions people of color relative to a white perspective that is presented as the norm (McCarthy, 1993).

These mass media representations are based on essentialist, fixed categories regarding race. As Ann Louise Keating (1995) argues, "despite the many historic and contemporary changes in racial categories, people generally treat 'race' as an unchanging biological fact. Often, they make simplistic judgments and gross overgeneralizations based primarily on outer appearances" (p. 914). Such stereotypical thinking reduces exploration of issues to a sharing of master stereotypes such as "welfare recipient" or polarizing issues such as "affirmative action" (Goebel, 1995). Students may also be reluctant to challenge simplistic equations between academic achievement and race. In a critique of Ogbu and Fordham's notion of the "burden of acting white" hypothesis, Joyce King (1995) argues that this hypothesis assumes that in order to do well in school, students have to "act white." This further assumes the converse: that "acting black" represents a resistance to the school culture and is associated with low academic achievement. However, as King argues, such resistance often stems from students' attempts to protect themselves from exclusionary schooling practices that devalue African American cultural perspectives. Further, the notion of the "burden of acting white" may also include whites who may "experience being and acting white as a 'burden,' particularly in situations where they may begin to feel guilty when learning about 'white privilege,' or having to develop and/or resist 'racial awareness'" (King, 1995, p. 161).

These attitudes were reflected in an unscientific "write-in" survey of 248,000 secondary students conducted in 1995 ("Teens and Race," 1995). About half of the students experienced racial discrimination; 80% of students believe that their peers harbor some form of racial prejudice; 64% hang out with peers of their own race; 47% feel more comfortable with these peers than with peers of another race. These attitudes reflect adults' racial attitudes—64% of students shared their parents' attitudes. The increasing racial polarization in America is evident in changing attitudes toward affirmative action programs. A poll conducted by the Times Mirror Center for the People & the Press (1994) indicates that 51% of whites surveyed agree that equal rights have been pushed too far in this country. This result of 51% contrasts with 42% in 1992 and 16% in 1987, indicating a decline in whites' positive attitudes toward affirmative action programs.

A STUDY OF STUDENTS' RESPONSES TO MULTICULTURAL LITERATURE

All of this raises the question of how these stances of resistance shape students' reactions to portrayals of racial conflict in multicultural literature. In a study of students' responses to multicultural literature (Beach, 1994), I asked eleventh- and twelfth-grade students in three different high schools and in a university course to respond in writing to a range of different multicultural texts. These students also responded to two short stories by African American writers about African American adolescent males. One story, "Judgment" (Thompson, 1990), portrays tensions associated with an interracial relationship between a black male and a white female on a small college campus in the 1980s. (Current attitudes toward interracial dating reflect generational differences; the "Teens and Race" (1995) poll indicated that while 70% of students would date someone of a different race, 51% of their parents would either oppose or disapprove of their doing so.) The other story, "The Kind of Light That Shines on Texas" (McKnight, 1992), is set in a junior high school in the 1960s. It depicts a conflict between a black student and a bigoted white student who bullies the black student. Selected students also participated in taped small-group discussions and were interviewed about their responses to these texts.

It is important to note that the three high schools varied considerably in terms of their racial diversity. Two of the high schools were located in largely white suburban communities and had few students of color. In contrast, the third high school, given its location in an urban area, had a relatively high percentage of students of color. Content analyses of the students' responses indicated that while students in the urban high school were more likely to adopt an "institutional racism" perspective (Beach, 1994), students in the suburban schools were more likely to adopt one of the following "individual prejudice" stances associated with resistance to multicultural literature.

Backlash to Challenges to White Privilege

A number of students were openly resentful of implied challenges to their sense of white privilege. For example, one student, Andy, notes that he is "proud to be white and I'm not going to say oh I want to be something else." Given this stance, he reacts negatively to implied accusations regarding racist or sexist behavior, noting that "when I get accused of something I don't do, I don't like that and I get really violent."

He also defines the relationships between characters in highly competitive, individualistic terms. In responding to the white bully, Oakley, who harasses the black student, Clinton, in "The Kind of Light That Shines on Texas," he notes:

I have no time for people like that, none at all. I was picked on when I was a kid all of the time just because I was different. There is a time when I wanted to be cool and change, like Clinton expressed that he wanted to be white, even though now I am glad that I didn't change, because I am now proud to be an individual, not a number in a large group. I can do what I want, by myself. I don't rely on others for decisions.

Andy's backlash is also evident in a small-group discussion about "The Kind of Light That Shines on Texas" with three other students, Jody, Lori, and Jason. In this discussion, Jody argues that "females are minorities in that they are treated the same ways as blacks were treated back then."

LORI: This is like a big picture of everybody who has been discriminated against in their lives.
ANDY: Yeah, but it's not just women. Everybody is discriminated against.
LORI: Women are discriminated against more than a white male.
ANDY: By some people.
LORI: By most people. Women still make less than males do.
ANDY: I've seen some females get jobs on the basis that they are females.
LORI: That's good. It's about time women rise to power.

Andy's reaction to Lori reflects his defensiveness regarding his own white male status. Later in the discussion, the group discusses Jason's claim that males prefer science:

JASON: Like you can take science and you can find out how you can make your car faster or how you can hit somebody harder but . . .
LORI: Because guys aren't sensitive at this age. All they have in their heads is girls and football.
ANDY: That's prejudice right there.
JASON: That's a stereotype right there.
LORI: I don't think it is, though; it's true.
ANDY: You think it's true about every single male in the school?
LORI: Not every single male but most of them. Don't tell me that you guys don't think about sports and cars and girls more than your school work.

Running through all of Andy's comments is a resentment toward implied generalizations about groups, particularly white males. Thus, in responding to literature, Andy resents implied generalizations from white characters' behavior to the larger white population: "I hate reading stories that tell me that the whole race is to blame; I treat each individual as a person. . . . This story isn't saying that every white person is this way, it is the teacher and Oakley and a couple of other people."

In contrast, Matt, a college student, is more open to discussing issues of racism than is Andy. He recognizes his own sense of privilege: "I'm actually rather lucky and privileged. It stands better generally to be white because we don't have as high of a mortality rate. And we don't have institutional racism against us as much, so I feel very lucky." At the same time, his sense of white privilege leads him to object to having to read texts in which authors portray their victimization according to their race. In responding to Native American poet Diane Glancy, Matt notes:

> I am sick of victimization writers. It seems we moved from center-ing on the individual to centering on the group, and now we focus on the victim in the arts and Diane Glancy is just another of the var-ious tag-alongs. And where does she get off being this Champion of the Native American plight when only one of her many grandpar-ents was a Native American, Cherokee? Because of this she writes that she has always felt this presence inside of her. Give me a break. One of my grandparents was one-hundred percent German, yet I have never once felt any hatred toward the Jewish. What I mean is this, often when someone is so wrapped up in something they are unable to see very clearly. They can only look for the inside out and not vice versa. . . . She is too close to her subject.

Matt is irritated with Glancy's portrayal of herself as "victim." He seems uneasy with her openness in discussing her "presence inside of her"—her feelings about her victimization. He also resents having to read the Japanese American writer David Mura, "because it makes me feel as though no matter how hard I try I will always be racist, my society will always be unfair. I get apathetic and start seeing all the instances of domi-nation throughout history." While Matt identifies instances of racism, he is reluctant to empathize with others' experience of racism, empathy that might lead to an analysis of institutional causes of racism.

Denial of Racial Difference

Another stance of resistance reflects students' denial of racial difference. In adopting this stance, students minimize the role of race, assuming that racial differences can be bridged simply by changing how people per-ceive or feel about each other. In response to the story about interracial dating, Kari notes that: "I think that if two people love each other, it shouldn't matter what color they are. To me, love doesn't see color. It just sees what's inside . . . for the most part we're all the same." Similarly, Amy posits that "People are people, why should it matter . . . maybe someday, we will also grow to a point where everyone believes in equality." And Nicole argues that "in the book that we're reading now, you don't see black and white; it's like it can be anybody. You can get into their role . . . I don't see any racial differences so I get into it. Like in *Sula*, I didn't feel like she is a black character. I felt like she could be anybody, Indian, white." She interprets a scene in "The Kind of Light That Shines on Texas" in which Clinton is "looking out the window and seeing prisms of all different colors" as representing the need for people not to "see because of somebody's color of skin that they are different. Everybody would be the same; he wanted everyone to be the same."

Denial of racial difference reflects a moral relativism—the assumption that everyone has the right to espouse their own feelings about race as individual opinions even if these opinions reflect a racist perspective. For example, because Mike assumes that individuals have a right to their own opinions, expressions of prejudice do not disturb him. As he notes:

> I don't care too much about what people say. I'll laugh or I don't really take it offensively. A lot of jokes don't really bother me because I don't really act stupid. My dad's a successful businessman and Polish. I think it's all in people's head what they think and it's their problem. I mean I don't get into people's problems; people believe what they want to believe.

Assuming that everyone is entitled to their own opinions serves to circumvent consideration of ideological issues associated with racism.

The extent to which students deny or accept racial differences is related to the degree to which they define their own identity in ethnic or racial terms (Helms, 1990; Phinney, 1992; Tatum, 1992). As they develop a sense of their racial or ethnic identity, they become increasingly aware of how their ethnic orientation shapes their responses and perceptions. These developmental phases have been explicated by Janet Helms (1990) in her model of white racial identity development. In the initial "contact" phase of Helms's model, white students lack awareness of or deny their own privileged status and often perceive people of color in stereotyped ways. They are also less likely than students of color to perceive themselves as part of a racial group, acknowledging their own racial attitudes only when challenged by alternative perspectives (Ferdman, 1990). At the subsequent stage, "disintegration," white students experience a sense of guilt or shame related to their own advantages as whites, but they still deny their own privileged stance. At the "reintegration" stage, students blame people of color for their discomfort and anxiety. At later stages, white students abandon their sense of white superiority, seeking out information about racism and openly confronting racism in their daily life. In a related study, 65% of first-year college students' thinking about racism was characterized as that of an "individual prejudice" perspective (Bidwell, Bouchie, McIntyre, Ward, & Lee, 1994). This suggests that many secondary and even college students conceive of racism in terms of dualist categories of victim/victimizer having to do with an individual's bias or discrimination. As they then acquire more information about racism through their own experience or in reading literature portraying racist actions, they begin to conceive of racism as a more complex phenomenon involving a range of factors within a larger social context.

Voyeuristic Reaction to False Portrayal of "the Other"

Students may also respond to portrayals of racial difference with a voyeuristic fascination, particularly in responding to texts such as gangsta rap music that seemingly portray a cultural world different from their own middle-class, suburban worlds. However, simply being fascinated by a sense of difference or "the other" does not necessarily lead to an examination of the issues of racism. It may even serve as a false substitute for grappling with authentic portrayals of racial difference.

The popularized versions of gangsta rap music that appeal to these students differ considerably from music geared to a black audience that directly confronts issues of institutional racism. This popularized version is marketed primarily to appeal to suburban students' adolescent fascination with images of deviant macho gangsters. Ewan Allison (1994) describes this appeal as based on

> a long-established romanticization of the Black urban male as a temple of authentic cool, at home with risk, with sex, with struggle. Mimicry is rife: baseball caps turned backwards; street mannerisms learnt from watching Yo MTV raps!: "wack", "dope", "chil", "yo", uttered with blackward prowess. These safe voyeurisms of rap allow whites a flirtation with the coolness of ghetto composure, the hipness of an oppositional underclass, without having to deal with the actual ghetto. (p. 445)

This romanticized portrayal of racism provides middle-class adolescents with a stereotyped conception of blacks in urban settings as "the other" without having to examine the underlying economic and political causes for the decline in urban life. As David Samuels (1991) argues,

[T]he more rappers are packaged as violent black criminals, the bigger their white audience became . . . rap's appeal to whites rested in its evocation of an age old image of blackness: a foreign sexually charged and criminal underworld against which the norms of white society are defined, and by extension, through which they may be defined (p. 25).

The emotional appeal of this gangsta rap not only serves to perpetuate stereotypes of black males as being predominantly criminals; more importantly, it diverts attention away from the institutional critiques found in other rap music. Further, students may pretend to "understand" racial issues simply because they listen to rap, without any reflection on their own privileged middle-class status. They may also avoid music that deals explicitly with racism, particularly when they sense that this music is not rhetorically geared to a middle-class audience. As Allison (1994) notes, "[T]he muteness of so much in hip-hop to white ears comes down in part to the ghetto's economic, political, and geographic and even legal dislocation from the rest of America" (p. 453). Middle-class adolescents' alienation from this more authentic form of rap music reflects their resistance to all forms of multicultural texts.

Reluctance to Adopt Alternative Cultural Perspectives

In responding to literature, students enter into a different cultural world, requiring them to suspend their disbelief and accept alternative cultural perspectives. For example, in responding to "The Kind of Light That Shines on Texas," set in the 1960s, students needed to adopt the perspective of a different historical era, one in which racial discrimination was blatantly and openly expressed. However, many students in the study had difficulty entering into what was an alternative fictional world of the past. In explaining this difficulty, they cite their lack of background knowledge of cultural differences given the lack of attention to diversity in their school curriculums. When, for example, a speaker at one of the suburban high schools analyzed Christopher Columbus from a more imperialist perspective, the students in the audience were astounded by the fact that in all of their history courses, they had never been exposed to such an interpretation. To their credit, these students were beginning to sense the need to broaden their perspectives, recognizing that they need to begin somewhere in their understanding of diversity.

Other students refer to their lack of direct experience with diversity. For example, Melissa notes, "I don't think I have a deep knowledge of any other culture or experience feeling of being in the minority; it is hard for me to relate to multicultural literature without very much background

information." However, her conception of what constitutes cultural difference reflects a parochial conception of diversity. She describes herself as

> mostly Swedish and Polish and I don't feel like it has a big effect on
> me, but I think it's because I'm in the majority. There is one time
> that I had an allergic reaction—my lip swelled up and it is so differ-
> ent for me to feel like people are staring at me and like there is
> something wrong with me. That's one of the few experiences that
> I've has where I felt not mainstream.

Her conception of diversity is limited to observing surface behaviors. This
was evident in her comment that "I went on a field trip to [the urban
school in this study] the other day to see the different cultures and the
ethnic diversity." Given her somewhat superficial conception of diversity, she may have difficulty adopting an alternative cultural perspective.
Adopting an alternative perspective requires momentarily assuming a
cultural worldview based on differences in beliefs and attitudes, as opposed to phenomena such as observed physical appearance.

Reluctance to Challenge the Status Quo

Another stance of resistance is related to a sense of paralysis that stems
from students' sense of guilt or shame about their newfound sense of
racism. Students certainly recognize instances of racism in their schools.
As Matt notes:

> One thing that's gotten into is the idea of white bashing because our
> class is almost entirely white persons. A lot of people get really de-
> fensive when we see people depicting white people in a derogatory
> way. I'll admit to it and agree that's not very good, but even as
> white people we have to admit that our culture has done a lot of re-
> ally negative things in the past and they have oppressed a lot of cul-
> tures . . . it hits us right at home.

However, students then have difficulty knowing how to act on or
channel their guilt or shame in responding to racial conflict. In some
cases, they espouse simplistic solutions to racial conflict, such as the use
of physical violence. In responding to Mrs. Wickham, the teacher in "The
Kind of Light That Shines on Texas," who tells racist jokes at the expense
of the three black students, David comments that "I felt like if I was one
of the black students I would have knocked Mrs. Wickham out. I couldn't
believe that the teacher is this mean and racist." Other students were

more perplexed about their own feelings. Roman (1993) argues that white students need to focus on their own sense of shame, analyzing reasons for their shame in terms of a social structure that privileges them:

> If white students and educators are to become empowered critical analysts of their/our own claims to know the privileged world in which their racial interests function, then such privileges and the injustices they reap for others would necessarily become the *objects* of analyses of structural racism. This allows white students and educators, for example, to move from *white defensiveness* and *appropriate speech* to stances in which we/they take effective responsibility and action for "disinvesting" in white privilege. (p. 84)

Students in the study explain their reluctance to act openly on their beliefs as based on fear of social repercussions. In response to the story about interracial dating, Heather notes:

> I look at black students or people of different color and wish to date one of them, but know deep in my heart that if I did my parents would scream at me, my friends would look at me funny, and people would stare, even though I think it might be fine to date a person of another color.

Similarly, Dan observes that "I don't worry about racism because you can't really do anything by worrying about it. . . . I just go with the flow because I just don't like a lot of controversy." In response to the portrayal of interracial dating in "Judgment," he recalls his own experience of social embarrassment:

> A girlfriend dumped me to go with a black male, for which I took some harassment at school. We broke up and two weeks later I met her at a summer baseball game or something. She has a black boyfriend and she introduced me and he seemed like a nice guy; I really never got to know him that well. But you say to yourself all those things under your breath and you kind of walk away. It's just that your own people stared at him, and you're just, like, "Well that's the way the ball bounces."

His reference to his peers as "your own people" reflects his concern with his own status with his white peers. The fact that Heather and Dan are reluctant to openly challenge their peers' racist views reflects their social concern with their peers' perceptions.

These, then, are some of the stances of resistance students adopt in responding to multicultural literature, stances that serve as barriers to exploring cultural perspectives that transcend an "individual prejudice" perspective. These stances of resistance mirror the larger society's reluctance to critically examine those institutional forces that serve to perpetuate racism in American society.

MOVING BEYOND RESISTANCE: EXPLORING ALTERNATIVE STANCES

In Chapter 2 of this volume, McGinley and colleagues argue that responding to literature entails more than simply reacting to a text. Responding also entails a range of life-transforming functions by which students construct alternative versions of reality and self. Central to this transformation is an awareness of how one's own ideological stance shapes the meaning of one's experience with literature.

Some students in the study moved beyond stances of resistance to assume a more transformational perspective. By openly exploring their beliefs and attitudes regarding racism as an institutional phenomenon, they reflect on the implications of portrayals of racism for changing their own attitudes and behaviors.

Empathizing with Experiences of Discrimination

In order for students to break down resistance to engagement with multicultural literature, they need to empathize with characters grappling with racism and then connect that experience to their own real-world perceptions. These vicarious experiences are certainly no substitute for the actual experience of discrimination. For example, a suburban student, Josh, describes his experience with working with low-income people: "I worked with the elderly, battered women and children, lower-income housing kids, and the Native Americans who go to Red Cloud School; and then I've worked in a reservation in South Dakota." He then connects his experience working on the reservation with his responses to characters who suffer from similar racial and economic discrimination. He also reflects on the limitation of his own perspective. As he notes, "I'm advantaged given my background . . . while I have a house, car, and shoes, and breakfast every morning, we had to give these kids in the housing projects their breakfast." Josh recognizes his own stance as that of an "advantaged" student. Similarly, by comparing her experiences in a private and a public school, Elizabeth perceives the relationship between institutional attitudes and racism: "In private school, they are racist and a little bit cocky . . . it opened up my eyes because I have always been around diversity. It is just interesting to see how the other half of the world lives . . . it just didn't feel like the school knew anything about the real world." Jason, an African American student, contrasts his experience of living in the city and the suburb: "I really learned what a stereotyped black is when I moved into the city. Because there you've got the gang bangers and all of that in the neighborhood and that's why my mom pulled me out of the neighborhood, because I started to turn into one." He notes that in the suburb he was "trying to play the 'Tom' role, something I remember doing when I was young. I didn't really know that is what I was doing until I moved into the city and started to learn different ways of acting other than what my parents are teaching me." Jim, an "American-Mexican" who was born in Mexico and lived his first five years in Mexico City—which he visits every summer—notes that his experiences in Mexico shaped his perceptions of racial and social discrimination: "You realize that a lot of these countries need a lot of help in order to make themselves better." He attributes his attitudes to experiences such as hearing jokes about Mexicans: "People remember that I come from Mexico and look at me and say, 'no offense intended,' or 'not of course you.' But I know that if I wasn't in the room they wouldn't say we mean this about all Mexicans except for Jim over there." Given these experiences, he is aware of how racism is shaped by institutional forces. In reacting to the portrayal of the teacher's discrimination against black students in "The Kind of Light That Shines on Texas," he notes that "the teacher seemed to care more about the twenty-seven white students than the three black students. And the rest of the community or society just seemed to let this happen."

Some of the female students in the study link their experience with gender discrimination to racial discrimination, seeing both as being shaped by institutional forces. For example, Lori notes:

> It's bad enough to be a white woman in the work force but to be a black woman in the work force is even worse. Race and gender kind of mix in together because both minorities and females feel the same kind of racial and sexist tension in the work place or in school, sports especially.

While the two forms of discrimination certainly differ in many ways, by linking the two, these students begin to define larger institutional forces shaping both gender and racial discrimination. As Pam notes,

> Thirty years since the beginning of the civil rights movement, women still don't have equal right to men. Even white women who are part of the majority race aren't treated equally. I couldn't imag-

ine being a minority race and being a woman. As a young female, I see that I'll have many odds stacked against me.

These students are not reluctant to challenge the status quo, even though they are discouraged from doing so. For example, Lori recalls her experience with confirmation class:

I'm Catholic and I'm very pro-choice on abortion. Last year I went through a confirmation class and the issue for one night was abortion. I did voice my opinion but I was shunned because right away I'm perceived to believe in killing and all of this so I could not voice what I wanted to say because it was against my religion. So you have to keep your mouth shut.

In describing these experiences, students begin to recognize that discrimination derives from dominant institutional forces, whether they be racial, patriarchal, or religious.

Recognizing the Limitations of One's Cultural Stance

In addition to connecting one's experiences to portrayals of racism, some students are able to stand back and reflect on the limitations of their own stance as cultural outsiders. As Jamie notes in reading *Sula*, "it might be hard to read from a nonwhite point of view. None of us know what it feels like to be black. We just assume that they think and feel the same things that we feel. Maybe they do, maybe they don't." In describing her response to *The Joys of Motherhood* (Emechete, 1979), a novel about Nigeria, Elizabeth perceives herself as "an intruder: I'm trying to learn about Nigeria and it just doesn't seem right sometimes. I feel bad because we make so many assumptions about blacks like in *The Joys of Motherhood* what it is they are feeling." In defining her role as an "intruder," she notes that she is adopting "an objective, sterile, controlled viewpoint of a white middle-class female." She perceives herself as "a scientist, observing, picking apart, and categorizing multicultural literature as if I'm not a part of it, only looking down and observing and only being objective." She therefore realizes that understanding a different cultural perspective requires some understanding of how those norms shape people's lives.

Students also recognize their ambiguous attitudes toward experiences with racism. For example, regarding her upbringing in a small North Dakota town that was "generally pretty racist," Andrea, a college student, believes that "because of my socialization I make a conscious effort to not make assumptions about other people." When asked in an interview to recount an incident in which she had difficulty openly challenging racist actions, she recounted her experience of going to a nightclub with a Philippine male. While at the nightclub, she noticed that another male with the same appearance as her partner was harassing some females. She was approached by a female employee of the nightclub, who asked her if her partner was bothering her and, if so, whether she wanted him removed from the premises. She then realized that the woman had confused her date with the other male in the nightclub primarily because he was also a Philippine male. She then reflects on whether she should have confronted the woman who had falsely accused her partner because of his race:

> I thought if she wants to think that he's like this and I'm a certain way for being with him, then that's her problem. I just didn't want to deal with it. And I just told her fine, don't worry about it, I'll keep an eye on him. She left and I felt really bad afterwards because I really wished I would have said something because it would have been one more person on his side. . . . It really annoyed me but what was I really going to do about it? In a way I really didn't feel like I had a right to say anything because as a woman I was glad she was there. If I was having problems with somebody, she would get rid of them. So it took me a minute to think now wait a minute, where did that come from. So who was I to stick my face in there and say anything?

Andrea is reflecting on her own shame in not confronting the woman about her racist assumptions. She is conflicted about the differences between her own sense of being insulted by the woman and her need for protection. She is also aware of her concern with potential social embarrassment from openly challenging the woman's implicit racism. Examining these tensions leads her to reflect critically on her own stance.

Reflecting on One's Stance as a Privileged White

In responding to portrayals of white privilege in texts such as Conrad's *Heart of Darkness* (Conrad 1902/1990), students begin to reflect on their own stance of white privilege. In her response to that novel, Elizabeth examines the nature of a white European colonialist perspective:

> *Heart of Darkness* can be seen as making a very strong case against colonialism, not only through the symbolism of Kurtz/Europe in a savage land, but also through the constant images of waste and

death. The black African's victimization is obvious; the picture that sticks with Marlow is that of the pristine accountant who writes numbers all day long while outside there are moaning, dying people. . . . When Europeans go to places where their own society is unknown, they lose themselves.

Elizabeth then considers whether Conrad himself is racist, but has difficulty coming up with a definitive answer. She notes:

There are two basic elements of prejudice: ignorance and fear. We might call Conrad ignorant or Eurocentric, but he and his hero Marlow do not hate or fear the Africans; indeed, they admire their strength and grace. I suppose that it's as racist to stereotype positively as it is to stereotype negatively. So is Marlow/Conrad racist? Not hatefully so. Almost forgivably so. But, yes.

By analyzing Conrad's racism, Elizabeth is defining a historical perspective that helps her perceive racism as constituted by institutional forces.

Other students examine the ways in which school-endowed privileges represent a form of institutional racism. In describing the racial diversity in the urban high school, Alison also notes that the ability-grouping system in the school creates classes that are not racially balanced, something that bothers her:

I really think that part of your education is not the classes you take but that you're learning to deal with all kinds of different people. The classes here are not racially diverse at all and I'm not sure why. I think that maybe we don't like to talk about class in our society, but most of the kids in this class are probably from upper-middle-class backgrounds . . . maybe we aren't as multicultural as we could be here.

From her analysis of institutional structures such as the ability-grouping or tracking system, Alison perceives how race and class intersect in the school to create structures that privilege certain groups.

Students are also aware of how punitive administrative policy can create conflict between racial groups in schools. As Jim notes:

We get privileges taken away, and sometimes people base that on a group or something. They say "Oh, well, it was these people," and then everybody turns you against them. I think that's kind of a pass-

word that this group did this and this group did that and then it
starts to become discrimination.

Jim is recognizing that discrimination stems from "competition among
and inequality across groups . . . that results from group conflict much
more than natural endowment or individualistic factors" (Sleeter, 1993,
p. 14).

Thus some students are able to move beyond stances of resistance to
explore how experiences in their own lives, and with texts, are shaped
by ideological forces. These students then examine how their own behaviors as well as those of characters are shaped by institutional racism.

HELPING STUDENTS MOVE BEYOND RESISTANCE TO ENGAGEMENT

The students in this study who resist engagement with multicultural literature either see little reason for caring about the plight of characters or
react defensively to challenges to their own sense of white privilege. As
a result, they rarely grapple with issues of institutional racism. In contrast, those students who are engaged with multicultural literature are
more likely to reflect on their own perspective as privileged whites. By
empathizing with characters who are victims of discrimination, they begin to vicariously experience the impact of institutional racism. This may
then lead to some self-reflection on their own perspective of white privilege.

These findings suggest the need to help students empathize with
characters' perceptions and analyze how those perceptions are shaped by
institutional forces. For example, students could read August Wilson's
play *Fences* (Wilson, 1986), about an African American working-class family living in Pittsburgh in the 1950s. The play revolves around conflicts
between a domineering father and a rebellious son who returns home
after serving in the military. Both the father and the son are angry about
their treatment in a racist society. As in all of Wilson's plays, characters
frustrated with their inability to vent their anger on the outside society
turn this anger inward in self-destructive ways.

In responding to the play, students could write a narrative from the
perspective of the son who is returning home from the military and confronting his father. For example, a student could depict the son's anger
with his controlling father as well as his father's reluctance to attack racism. Students could then write a narrative about their own autobiographical experience evoked by their description of a character's experience.

Students could also engage in role-play activities in which they adopt a character's role. For example, students could assume roles in which they confront one of their own parents regarding that parent's racist statements. At the completion of the role-play, students could stand back and reflect on the positions they assumed in the role-play and discuss how those positions are linked to allegiances to certain social groups. For example, a student could adopt the role of a parent who seeks to prevent low-income housing from being built in a suburban community because of the need to limit potential crime. That student could link such a stance to racist assumptions equating low-income people and crime. By reflecting on these links, students could begin to examine how their own perceptions are related to institutional perspectives.

Students could then reflect on their narratives or role-play in terms of the competing voices or ideological stances adopted in their narrative. In doing so, they could consider the following questions:

Who is speaking and in what voices?
What attitudes and beliefs are being espoused?
What are the motives for assuming a certain voice?
How do these voices reflect attitudes toward gender, class, or race?
How are these voices constituted by discourses of religion, the law, education, management, merchandising, and so forth? (Gee, 1990; Lemke, 1995)

By reflecting on these voices and the implied attitudes, they may begin to recognize ways in which their voices represent certain institutional forces or allegiances. Or, as did Andrea, they may recognize ways in which they are silenced by a concern with offending or criticizing certain institutional forces.

Discussing Issues of Race

While many students in my study are often reluctant to openly share their opinions about race with others, they do perceive a need to discuss an issue that shapes their everyday lives. Given this need, students, teachers, or administrators may want to create a forum in a school that serves to promote such discussions. When, for example, the students in the urban high school in my study experienced an incident involving written racial slurs in the lavatories, they organized a series of forums to discuss ways of combating such incidents (Tevlin, 1994). At the university level, Joe, a college student, in commenting about his willingness to openly discuss issues of racism, recalled his participation as an intern in a Diversity Institute in his university. In the Institute, they "discussed issues and listened to speakers who would tell you about racism being institutional and that you can't be racist unless you have the power to affect other people."

These forums can also provide ways to help students discuss strategies for actively coping with racism. For a number of students in my study, their sense of guilt simply immobilizes them from taking action to cope with their concerns. This suggests the need for what Beverly Tatum (1994) describes as "white allies" who would provide the necessary support for sharing concerns about racism. These allies consist of role models in biographies or autobiographies or in real-world contexts who reflect white practices that are nonoppressive. For example, Tatum asked a antiracist political activist to speak to her class at Mt. Holyoke College about her own awareness of racism and coping with the social repercussions of taking antiracist stands. One of her students commented that this person's presentation highlighted the need for a

> support group/system; people to remind me of what I have done, why I should keep going, of why I'm making a difference, why I shouldn't feel helpless. I think our class started to help me with those issues, as soon as I started to let it, and now I've found similar support in friends and family. They're out there, it's just finding and establishing them—it really is a necessity. Without support, it would be too easy to give up, burn-out, become helpless again . . . when the forces against you are so prevalent and deep-rooted as racism is in this society (Tatum, 1994, p. 23).

These "white ally" role models provide students with what, for Tatum, is a sense of hope for combating racism.

Students can also examine portrayals of discrimination in literature not simply as expressions of individual prejudice, but as manifestations of institutional power. Fiske (1993) defines these top-down expressions of institutional power as "imperializing ways of knowing [that] tend to produce cultures of representation, ones that reproduce both a sense of the world and the power to control that world" (p. 15). These "imperializing ways of knowing" are often insensitive to "localizing ways of knowing" that are based on the particulars of unique cultural and economic circumstances. For example, in discussing issues of welfare, conservative politicians represent single mothers in a manner that fails to appreciate the particular circumstances of these women's lives as part of their daily need for survival.

One aspect of representation has to do with the selection of multicultural literature in the literature curriculum. A number of the students in the study, particularly middle-class African American students, noted that most of the characters they were reading about were victims of oppression. The very selection of these texts may itself reflect a process of representing racial groups in a manner that serves those in positions of power. For example, African American characters in literature anthologies or frequently used novels in secondary and college literature classes are typically shown as poor and/or working-class. Also, background information about authors of color often tends to emphasize their own struggles with poverty. Having documented the existence of numerous African American middle-class writers who are usually not taught in schools, McHenry and Heath (1994) argue that multicultural literature is often represented for students as written by writers who are not middle-class and who lack "the same degree of variation in class, region, and ideology as other writers" (p. 437). They note that the choices of multicultural texts in the literature curriculum reflect a much narrower socioeconomic range, such that middle-class African American writers are ignored:

> The major choices as exemplars of African American literature tend to depict characters whose impoverishment and exploitation challenge them to survive as individuals that rise out of and above the circumstances of other victims of discrimination. The writings of Harriet Jacobs as an ex-slave are far more often read and referred to than those of Ida B. Wells as newspaper publisher and lecturer. Stories of Zora Neale Hurston's background in poor rural areas of north Florida receive much more attention than accounts of the elite backgrounds of her Harlem Renaissance contemporaries, such as Dorothy West or Jessie Fauset. (p. 437)

In examining this exclusion of middle-class African American writers as an issue of representation, students might question whether these curriculum decisions are themselves a reflection of institutional racism. The exclusion of these writers itself serves the larger goals of perpetuating the value of white, middle-class attitudes as the norm. Students might also reflect on how their attitudes toward class differences shape their responses to multicultural literature.

By participating in activities such as these, students may learn to be engaged with multicultural literature in ways that lead them to deconstruct their own white perspective of privilege that underlies much of their resistance to reading multicultural literature.

REFERENCES

Allison, E. (1994). It's a black thing: Hearing how whites can't. *Cultural Studies, 8,* 438–456.

Beach, R. (1993). *A teacher's introduction to reader response theories.* Urbana, IL: National Council of Teachers of English.

Beach, R. (1994). *Students' responses to multicultural literature.* Paper presented at the National Reading Conference, San Diego.

Beach, R. (1995, December). Applying cultural models in responding to literature. *English Journal, 84,* 87–94.

Beach, R., & Freedman, K. (1992). Responding as a cultural act: Adolescents' responses to magazine ads and short stories. In J. Many & C. Cox (Eds.), *Reader stance and literary understanding* (pp. 162–190). Norwood, NJ: Ablex.

Bennett, T., & Woollacott, J. (1987). *Bond and beyond: The political career of a popular hero.* New York: Methuen.

Bidwell, T., Bouchie, N., McIntyre, L., Ward, L., & Lee, E. (1994, April). The development of white college students' conceptualization of racism within the context of cultural diversity coursework. Paper presented at the annual meeting of the American Educational Research Association, New Orleans.

Buckingham, D. (1993). Boys' talk: Television and the policing of masculinity. In D. Buckingham (Ed.), *Reading audiences: Young people and the media* (pp. 89–115). New York: Manchester University Press.

Cherland, M. (1994). *Private practices: Girls reading fiction and constructing identity.* London: Taylor & Francis.

Conrad, J. (1990). *Heart of darkness.* In C. Watts (Ed.), *Heart of darkness and other tales.* Oxford, England: Oxford University Press. (Original work published 1902)

Eckert, P. (1989). *Jocks and burnouts.* New York: Teachers College Press.

Emechete, B. (1979). *The joys of motherhood.* New York: Braziller.

Ferdman, B. (1990). Literacy and cultural identity. *Harvard Educational Review, 60,* 181–194.

Fiske, J. (1993). *Power plays, power works.* London: Verso.

Gee, J. P. (1990). *Social linguistics and literacies: Ideology in discourses.* New York: Falmer.

Giroux, H. (1983). *Theory and resistance in education: A pedagogy for the opposition.* South Hadley, MA: Bergin & Garvey.

Goebel, B. (1995). "Who are all these people?": Some pedagogical implications of diversity in the multicultural classroom. In B. Goebel & J. Hall (Eds.), *Teaching a "new canon"?* (pp. 22–31). Urbana, IL: National Council of Teachers of English.

Helms, J. (1990). Toward a model of white racial identity development. In J. Helms (Ed.), *Black and white racial identity* (pp. 78–94). New York: Greenwood.

Jordan, S., & Purves, A. (1993). *Issues in the responses of students to culturally diverse texts: A preliminary study.* Albany, NY: National Research Center on Literature Teaching and Learning.

Keating, A. (1995). Interrogating "whiteness," (de)constructing "race." *College English, 57,* 901–918.

King, J. (1995). Race and education: In what ways does race affect the educational process? In J. Kincheloe & S. Steinberg (Eds.), *Thirteen questions: Reframing education's conversations* (pp. 159–180). New York: Peter Lang.

Lee, V. (1986). Responses of white students to ethnic literature. *Reader, 15*, 24–33.

Lemke, J. (1995). *Textual politics: Discourse and social dynamics.* Bristol, PA: Taylor & Francis.

Many, J., & Cox, C. (Eds.). (1992). *Reader stance and literary understanding.* Norwood, NJ: Ablex.

McCarthy, C. (1993). After the canon: Knowledge and ideological representation in the multicultural discourse on curriculum reform. In C. McCarthy & W. Crichlow (Eds.), *Race, identity, and representation* (pp. 289–305). New York: Routledge.

McHenry, E., & Heath, S. B. (1994). The literate and the literacy: African-Americans as writers and readers—1830–1940. *Written Communication, 11,* 419–444.

McIntosh, P. (1989). *White privilege: Unpacking the invisible knapsack.* Philadelphia: Women's International League for Peace and Freedom.

McKnight, R. (1992). The kind of light that shines on Texas. In R. McKnight, *The kind of light that shines on Texas: Stories* (pp. 59–64). Boston: Little, Brown.

Morrison, T. (1974). *Sula.* New York: Knopf.

Oakes, J. (1985). *Keeping track: How schools structure inequality.* New Haven, CT: Yale University Press.

Peck, J. (1994). Talk about racism: Framing a popular discourse of race on Oprah Winfrey. *Cultural Critique, 27,* 89–126.

Peck, R. (1989). I go along. In D. Gallo (Ed.), *Connections: Short stories by outstanding writers for young adults* (pp. 184–191). New York: Dell.

Phinney, J. (1992). The Multigroup Ethnic Identity Measure: A new scale for use with diverse groups. *Journal of Adolescent Research, 7,* 156–176.

Radway, J. (1988). The Book-of-the-Month Club and the general reader: On the uses of "serious" fiction. *Critical Inquiry, 14,* 516–538.

Roman, L. (1993). White is a color! White defensiveness, postmodernism, and anti-racist pedagogy. In C. McCarthy & W. Crichlow (Eds.), *Race, identity, and representation* (pp. 71–88). New York: Routledge.

Samuels, D. (1991). The real face of rap. *The New Republic, 34,* 21–26.

Scheurich, J. (1993). Toward a white discourse on white racism. *Educational Researcher, 22,* 5–10.

Sharpe, R., Mascia-Lees, F., & Cohen, C. (1990). White women and black men: Differential responses to reading black women's texts. *College English, 52,* 142–158.

Sleeter, C. (1993). Advancing a white discourse: A response to Scheurich. *Educational Researcher, 22,* 13–15.

Tatum, B. (1992). Talking about race: Learning about racism: The application of racial identity developmental theory in the classroom. *Harvard Educational Review, 62,* 1–24.

Tatum, B. (1994, April). *Teaching white students about racism: The search for white allies and the restoration of hope.* Paper presented at the annual meeting of the American Educational Research Association, New Orleans.

Teens and race. (1995, August 18–20). *USA Weekend,* pp. 5–10.

Tevlin, J. (1994). Fast times, good times at Henry High. *Minnesota Monthly, 28,* 80–85, 149–150.

Thompson, C. (1990). Judgment. In T. McMillan (Ed.), *Breaking ice* (pp. 615–629). New York: Penguin.

Times Mirror Center for the People & the Press. (1994). *Americans' political attitudes regarding current issues.* Washington, D.C.: Author.

Wilson, A. (1986). *Fences: A play.* New York: New American Library.

CHAPTER 4

No Imagined Peaceful Place

A Story of Community, Texts, and Cultural Conversations in One Urban High School English Classroom

THERESA ROGERS

THIS CHAPTER TELLS a story (not *the* story) of a teacher and her eleventh-grade English class in a midwestern urban high school. The teacher, Chris, developed her practices not out of any theoretical epiphany as a result of university courses, but out of a shared need among her students and herself to reform the kind of reading and writing instruction that typically takes place in classrooms such as hers.

It is important to set this story in the context of the 1990s debates, or, as they have been labeled, "culture wars," surrounding the teaching of English at all levels. While these debates have varied manifestations when it comes to policy, there is basically an argument on one side for the canon, basic instruction, and the pursuit of truth through literature. On the other side is a plea for the recognition of cultural difference, the awareness of subjectivity in relation to truth, and an expanded canon. As Peter King (1993) argues in the introduction to a book on critical teaching in England, teachers may be forgiven for becoming cynical about both extremes, but "nevertheless they must be urged not to . . . turn away to seek some imagined peaceful place of straightforward teaching" (p. xiii).

It is unlikely that teachers such as Chris would or could turn away. They are there in the classroom looking out at the faces of young adults who demand something different. They will ultimately have much more influence on these students and, as a result, on the larger society, than those of us in academia. Many of Chris's students had what would be their last school literature lesson in her classroom, since there is a high dropout rate: Many don't even reach eleventh-grade English. Some came to class only occasionally and then not at all. So what does it mean to be an urban English teacher at the end of the twentieth century in the United States, standing in front of students whose mere presence demands something different?

THE TELLING OF THE STORY

This is primarily my story, since I am telling it, but it is integrated with Chris's story and the students' stories by the intermingling of their voices. A colleague and I visited Chris's classroom regularly over the course of a year and documented what we saw, heard, and felt in journals, transcripts, videotapes, and field notes. Chris also kept a journal and occasionally provided time for us to interview her on audiotape. Some students were also interviewed. This chapter explores the nature of the literacy or interpretive community that was built during the year we visited, with a particular focus on *what, how,* and by *whom* texts were read, written, shared, and critiqued.

The class consisted of 34 students of "average" ability at the beginning of the year, about equally divided between white and African American, with one Asian student. About half of the students were girls. The majority of African American students were bused in from an inner-city housing project. The white students generally came from the neighborhood—so students came from a mix of poor, lower-middle-class, and middle-class families. Chris is a white teacher who, although now firmly a middle-class professional, grew up quite poor in the south side of the city. She has often been recognized by colleagues as a particularly dedicated and compassionate teacher. In fact, in her journal and interviews, she often spoke of teaching as a spiritual calling (cf. McLean, 1991). In every other way, this classroom was a fairly typical urban English classroom.

The story begins with a discussion of the notion of an interpretive community as it is proposed by reader-response critics—the usefulness of the concept in general as well as the ways in which it falls short of actually shedding light on what it means to be part of a contemporary urban high school English classroom.

REAL CLASSROOMS AND THE IDEA OF AN INTERPRETIVE COMMUNITY

At the center of reader-response theory is the notion that it is the reader who creates literary meaning (e.g., Bleich, 1987; Fish, 1980), given that literary texts themselves are indeterminate (Iser, 1978). However, in recent critiques of reader-response criticism as it is manifested in classrooms, a focus on personal responses as the basis for community responses is seen as somewhat limited. For example, Willinsky (1991) eloquently argues that students and teachers "should look up from their private and shared responses, to study how a poem is part of a larger literate enterprise . . . to trace texts out into the world" (p. 190). He also argues that works of literature should no longer be seen apart from other kinds of texts as though they are written or read in a social or cultural vacuum, as we sometimes pretend to be the case in English classrooms. In such class-rooms, there is a focus on authoritative interpretations rather than on inquiry into texts as personal, social, and cultural constructions.

Students learn ways of reading from the particular contexts of the classroom communities in which they reside (e.g., Rogers, 1991); however, they also draw on previously learned conventions of reading and writing as well as on cultural situatedness, such as race, class, and gender (cf. Rabinowitz, 1987). Classrooms may include students and teachers who take on various identity or subject positions in relation to a particular literary work, and these positions may complement or even contradict one another (cf. Beach, Chapter 3; Enciso, Chapter 1; Hines, Chapter 5; all in this volume). Reader-response critics fail to acknowledge this "struggle of interpretations" of texts within communities or institutions that may result when "certain meanings are elevated by social ideologies to a privileged position" (Eagleton, 1983, p. 132).

In fact, literature study is increasingly viewed as the study of culture (cf. Smithson, 1994; Trimmer & Warnock, 1992), because literary texts are, in fact, cultural texts and because readers read from various cultural positions. Therefore literary works and readings can be seen as symbolic con-structions of particular cultural meanings (cf. Campbell, 1994). In the communities constructed in English classrooms, students and teachers are necessarily negotiating social and cultural meanings and discourses as they engage in literary study.

What kinds of interpretive communities, then, are urban high school classrooms? How are they socially constructed? What are the boundaries? Are these communities sites of consensus or sites of struggle? How does the teacher affect this community and how do the students? What counts as text? What role do the texts of students play in these communities?

How are texts talked about, and how do they get "traced out into the world"? In what configuration do issues of culture or of race, class, and gender enter into the conversations? We felt that many of these questions could best be explored in the specific, or the case—that is, the particular instantiation of one classroom in one year. As Brodkey (1994) has argued we have too long reified theory while separating it from, and devaluing, local acts and local practice.

This chapter explores these questions through three lenses: through the study of the kind of literacy or interpretive community that was built among the teacher and students in this classroom from a sociolinguistic perspective; through a close look at the relationship of texts, or intertextuality, in the classroom; and through an examination of the cultural content of classroom discussions. The chapter is structured such that these issues are described as they unfolded across the academic year.

One Classroom, One Interpretive Community: Beginning Steps

We spent time in Chris's classroom in order to see how she and the students constructed a literacy community through their spoken interactions. Drawing on a sociolinguistic perspective (e.g., Bloome & Green, 1984; Saville-Troike, 1982; Weade & Green, 1989), we analyzed how classroom norms were created through these interactions across the year. This perspective illustrates how the rules for interacting in classrooms (such as who can talk to whom, about what, when, and for what purposes) are socially constructed through talk. "From this perspective, members of a classroom form a social group in which a common culture is constructed" (Green & Meyer, 1991, p. 141). In earlier analyses, I have illustrated how norms of literary interpretation are typically constructed in English classrooms through social interactions such as questioning cycles (Rogers, 1991; Rogers, Green, & Nussbaum, 1990).

To begin to understand this classroom culture, we recorded everything that was said during the first few weeks and systematically recorded for the rest of the academic year. We listened in particular to what Chris said about how classroom life would be managed, and *what, how, and by whom* texts would be composed, shared, and critiqued (Rogers & McLean, 1993). That is, we were interested not only in the building of literary interpretations but also in the interrogation of the ways of reading and interpreting in a particular community (Rabinowitz, 1987).

One of the first things we noticed in Chris's classroom was her constant and consistent attempts to build a particular kind of classroom literacy community. This was explicitly articulated through many specific comments on what kind of classroom she was hoping to create in general and what kinds of literacy events she was attempting to bring to life. Her comments signaled to the students that she hoped to construct a community in which members listened to each other and honored what they heard. In literacy events, she signaled a true personal interest in what the students had to say as well as a concern that they become skilled readers and writers with "voice" as well as mastery of conventions. For instance, an example of how literary texts were to be read in this community is illustrated in an early example across two days in September in which she models for them her way of reading a poem:

> When I read anything I try not to think too much about it when I read it for the first time . . . so take a couple of minutes to look over—begin first with the title. I think titles particularly have a lot to say . . . If you could read the poem once silently through . . . Is there anyone in here who would feel like they would need to read this a second time to get a better understanding or do you all feel like when you read a poem that immediately the meaning comes to you? Can I just get your initial reaction?. . . . Anything else . . . any other sort of feeling about this?

Here Chris seems to be both directing their attention to specific aspects of the text (thus to particular meanings) *and* encouraging immediate personal responses. She goes on to say:

> Now I always hated teachers when I was in school that used to rip poetry apart and then it was like you talked about it so much you never wanted to read another poem in your life. I really believe that poetry like other literature speaks to you as an individual. That your interpretation might be a little different from my own, but I don't think mine is necessarily better than yours. There are specific things that I should be able to ask you and you should be able to get from this and . . . there are some terms . . .

Again, Chris is displaying to the students the seemingly conflicting aspects of a literature curriculum in which students are encouraged to give individual, subjective responses but must also display knowledge of literary conventions and the ability to extract "an interpretation." Yet her overriding concern is that students be given a chance to construct their own meanings while moving herself away from the role of the interpreter, and so she provides them with models or ways of reading that would facilitate that process.

> Let me say I don't have the right answer and that this group may
> have a different view from that group, but I think that is sort of in-
> teresting. . . . See, the value of talking with other people is that ideas
> come out that you may never have thought of . . . and I really want
> you to know that you far surpassed my reading of it.

In her journal from that time, Chris expresses her concern about the
silence of some students even in the face of her continual prodding: "I
am concerned that a few students respond and *many* are silent" (journal,
9/6). And still a few weeks later, the concern appears in her journal that
the students are still looking toward her as the interpretive authority: "I
realize that if I speak, the group takes on my views and abandons their
own" (journal, 9/18).

By November, however, students who are interviewed recognize
Chris's efforts to build a particular kind of community. Jimmy (from the
inner city and the first male in his family who didn't drop out and who
had hopes of going to college—in part, so that he could set an example
for his younger cousins) comments:

> Well, OK, she'll have like a class discussion and like she wants to
> learn from what you say and we learn from each other. And she's al-
> ways asking questions. Makes you want to listen. Wants to add lit-
> tle comments and then we learn off each other. I like that.

Even so, it is not until later in the year that she begins to hear the
kinds of responses or "voices" that she hopes to hear. This usually happens in the context of discussions in which students reveal their personal
responses, freely relate their own texts and other kinds of cultural texts
to literary texts, and respond in ways that reflect their social and cultural
stances in the world. In other words, it is not until the texts of the classroom "were traced out into the world" that Chris feels she is hearing
what the students have to say.

Texts and Intertextuality in One Classroom Community

The texts in Chris's classroom include a traditional American literature
anthology, student writings, a multicultural reading list, and movies,
magazines, and other noncanonical bits of literacy that serve the purpose
of creating responses and dialogue among students. The first thing Chris
notices about the new anthology is who is represented and who is not:

I think what's interesting is when I go through the textbook it started out with the pilgrims and haven't we left someone out? The American Indians. Are there American Indians here? (class, 9/5)

In her journal (9/4) she writes:

> The materials [in the anthology] are in chronological order, but the text has omitted Native American Literature. . . . I want them to be able to compare the Puritans' view of America and the Indians', versus the Indians' values and beliefs. I want the students to compare these to their own values.

Simple decisions and recognitions such as this in a classroom become political acts for teachers such as Chris. Indeed, as bell hooks (1994) has argued, no education is politically neutral. Chris's notion of what counts as texts worthy of sharing and interpreting, both within and beyond the canon, is also open and fluid. Student texts, in particular, are seen as the stuff of the curriculum, and much time is spent carefully modeling ways in which students can respond to each other's work. In one example, which we call "Larry's story," a student's story is held up for sharing and critique in a writing lesson, and then it is briefly reintroduced in the context of a discussion of a canonical poem.

Larry's Story. The following excerpt, from one of Chris's early transcripts, is part of a lesson in which she asks student volunteers to share their written "memory pieces." She gives the autobiographical assignment to get "some insight into who they are and what they think/feel" (journal, 9/3). This is the first piece of writing to be included in their portfolios, and it is also a way for Chris to come to know the students and for the students to come to know each other. The students share stories about a range of experiences, including being seriously injured in a sports-related accident, giving birth, and, in Larry's case, being shot.

CHRIS: I'm real anxious to hear some of your memories. Larry, you decided to go first. All right.
LARRY: I did mine on the worst memory I ever had. It was May 4th, 199—. I got shot three times. . . . It was my oldest brother's birthday that day. I stayed home most of the day waiting for a phone call. . . . Around 10:30 I left and went over (inaudible) and she was already drinking some beer and I had some and I drove home. . . . Deana and I got punked up a little bit. I got real high. I thought I was bad and my little brother came over and we was all sitting

down talking and he pulled out a gun from nowhere and I was like I don't believe it was real so I asked to see it and it was real and it had six bullets in it. From there he asked me if I wanted to go to a party and so I went to a party again. After I left the party I went to another party and then I saw a guy that spit on me and I was going to beat his—you know so when I seen him you know that's what I did. I kicked him bad. Then he was holding on to me for some reason and then the next thing I know he just pulled out a gun and shot me in my arm and my chest. The next thing my little brother heard the gunshot. He turned around and pulled his gun and shot me in my leg while shooting the other guy. Then from there—I've got more but that's all I wrote because I didn't have enough time to write the rest.

CHRIS: So Larry, how did you feel? This is terrible to have to ask one of my students this, but how does it feel to have a bullet in you?

LARRY: Still in. They took one of them. I got shot in my arm right here and then they had to cut me open because of the bullet. He shot me with a hollow-tip bullet and the first one is inside my stomach. He cut me from here (*gestures*) all the way down. My little brother shot me with a .38 in my leg and the gun that he shot me with was a .22. I got shot three times. It was a mistake but if he wasn't there I would probably be dead.

During his sharing of his story, there are signs that in this early draft Larry is already creating a text that has a personally transforming function (McGinley & Kamberelis, 1992; McGinley et al., Chapter 2, this volume) for him. That is, the classroom dialogue helps him to reflect on the incident, on the irony of thinking his brother was killing him but was actually perhaps saving his life. He brought up the incident again in his interview and reflected on how the incident made him realize he wanted to do something with his life—"I don't want to be a bum. I don't want to live off other people." He also talked about how it changed his attitude toward conflict: "Now I don't care if somebody spit on me. They can spit on me. I just wipe it off and keep going. Not important to me anymore. Not if my life is involved."

CHRIS: Larry, I'm curious. This is such a terrible thing. I mean I'm glad you survived that and it would make a great story if you ever decided to write a short story. I think this would be a great story where you actually could tell what people said and what happened and carry that thought over. . . . Thanks for being willing to share that with everybody. That's a scary thing. . . . Proba-

bly a lot of you have personal experiences. . . . Are there any questions you thought to ask Larry when he was reading his story?

STUDENT: Did it hurt?

LARRY: I thought my little brother was trying to kill me and the other
guy tried to kill me but when the doctor put the tubes in my
body that was the worst part of all.

CHRIS: What was the worst part?

STUDENT: Just the IVs hurt?

LARRY: The whole thing. (*Many people talking.*)

CHRIS: I can visualize that, can't you? I want to thank those people
who volunteered to read. I know that it is not always easy to do
in front of your peers . . . but sometimes it's easier to take criticism from your peers than from a teacher. The one thing I try to
point out by asking you if there were any questions that you had
as you were listening is that, like in any good story, a good teller
never leaves out the details. And they were obviously important
enough for people to ask. . . . Larry, what you were feeling physically was something that I wanted to know and maybe that was
something you would include in your story, but like any writer
you always have the option to accept someone's advice or to dis-
regard it. . . . We are going to be doing a lot of writing. We are
going to be doing a lot of sharing of our writing with other students and you have to learn that criticism isn't something to hurt
you. Hopefully, it will be used to improve your writing. We'll be
talking more about that later.

Chris displays her many reasons for sharing and critiquing student
texts: to build community, to make them feel like writers, to help them
with the skills of writing, and to connect their lives to the more traditional
curriculum. Aware of the need to make these connections between what
the students experience and what they read, Chris provides opportunities
to make these links explicit. In the following discussion, which took place
almost three months later, Chris asks the students to write a journal entry
on their thoughts about or experiences with death prior to reading
"Thanatopsis" by William Cullen Bryant. During their sharing of journal
entries in November, a student spontaneously reintroduces Larry's story
into the discussion.

STUDENT 1: I'm not scared of [death]. I don't want to die right now
but I'm not going to be scared when it comes.

STUDENT 2: You can't be scared of something that has to happen to
you at a certain time in your life.

STUDENT 3: Until you've got children or a whole family. . . . Somebody comes to you and says . . .

STUDENT 1: I know what you're saying.

STUDENT 3: . . . if you don't give me your money then I'll shoot you, you ain't going to be ready to leave.

STUDENT 2: I just don't see why I would be—I'm not scared. I don't see why people would be scared of something that has to happen.

STUDENT 4: (inaudible) in a painful way. It's not that they're scared of dying. It's just dying in a painful way.

CHRIS: Well, see, you know what my fear is? It's like Joe says—you die and we really don't know what happens because no one has really come back to tell us so I think for myself—I can only speak for myself—the fear is not knowing.

STUDENT 4: That's normal.

CHRIS: That's what you're scared of?

STUDENT 1: But I go on faith because I don't know the specifics but I know there is a better place and I have faith in at least that. Whether it's going to be some cloudy place where I float around with planes . . .

CHRIS: Uh huh (*Laughs.*)

STUDENT 1: . . . or just living out the fantasies of my life or whatever. Maybe as a spirit living it out the way I want to live . . .

STUDENT 5: I have a question for Larry. When you were shot did they put you under anesthesia in the hospital?

LARRY: Yeah.

STUDENT 5: You could have died. . . . So when you were put asleep did you have a feeling like you would come back?

LARRY: I was praying. I was afraid I wouldn't come back.

CHRIS: You know what's interesting is when I talk with young people, in my mind I still think that you haven't had a lot of experiences with death and after talking with young people that's so untrue. Because many of you have had such close experiences with death. Some of you have had surgery. Some of you have had near-death experiences with being shot or in auto accidents. Some of us have had a lot of experience. . . . Well, I really want to read these [journal entries] and if you want to finish that thought or idea and then turn them in tomorrow to me that's fine. If you're finished if you wouldn't mind I would like to see them. Um, the poem we are going to read today—it's really interesting and the reason I like it is because supposedly the author was about your age . . . and he was contemplating this very thing. He was contemplating death and he was thinking, gosh, I wonder what is going to happen ... and he was considered a deist and I'm not expecting you to call that up in your memory but what do you surmise he might think about death based on that. Just knowing he is a deist?

STUDENT 6: That once he's dead, it's over with ... (inaudible). Is that a deist?

CHRIS: Uh ... that God sort of created things and then he let them follow their natural order and what is that—natural order?

STUDENT 6: That's what I just said.

CHRIS: Right. You said it. There is a belief in God but not in predestination. Just sort of a cycle. The natural cycle of things (*compares to cycle of seasons*). If our author sort of believes in the natural cycle of things—if he believes this then we're going to guess now what is his perception of death, or how does he view death. Can we—can we speculate? Your speculation is as good as anyone else's. Someone said when you're dead, you're dead. Someone else said reincarnation and there might be some others. Actually, what he does is he goes out and he is sort of wandering and he starts looking at these things in nature and evidently he wrote this poem after that experience and in this poem nature speaks. Could we have a nature speaker?

After reading and discussing the poem, including the author's view of death, Chris says:

Someone said to me yesterday, "Miss Gibson, are we going to read poetry and enjoy it or are we going to rip it apart?" I don't want to rip it apart. I just wanted to show you that this man at 16, 17 was having some thoughts about death and this was his belief or explanation. This is how he dealt with it and I'd like to talk, after I have a chance to look at your responses, about how this compares to your view.

In these excerpts Chris again signals the worth of the students' own responses, which are "as good as anyone else's" and indicates that part of the process of reading in this classroom is to set their own beliefs against those articulated in texts. In this way she keeps an unswerving and sympathetic eye on what the students are expressing personally about themselves and their lives and their beliefs, while at the same time she is able to see these expressions as texts worthy of analysis, comparison, and critique. In this classroom, then, we begin to see an intermingling of texts: of students' written and spoken texts, canonical texts, and the texts surrounding those primary texts, so that authors and readers become members of the same community (Rabinowitz, 1987). In their interviews many students feel that Chris is mixing up history with English in her attention to authors' social and cultural backgrounds, and at the same time they feel, as one student said, "she is more of a real person interested in us." What Chris is beginning to accomplish is to create a community in which authors are readers, readers are authors, and both readers and authors are seen as situated in particular social and cultural places from which they can construct particular meanings about their lives and the lives of others.

Social and Cultural Conversations in One Community

In February, Chris reads student responses to F. Scott Fitzgerald's *The Great Gatsby* and feels once again that there is a lack of "voice" in their writing and that they miss the race and class implications in the novel. So on the advice of a friend she shows them a documentary film called *The War Between the Classes* and then distributes a survey to get their responses. When there still isn't much discussion, Chris thinks, "Now I know they have had similar experiences but maybe I'm treading too close . . . I know they want to say something but they are hesitant."

Eventually, as Chris encourages them to share their survey responses, the discussion becomes a lively debate. At one point, a student says he agrees with the student in the film who says people don't want to be responsible for historical racism and prejudice. Chris responds by acknowledging his comment and bringing up a comment by another student in the film who had talked about the subtleties of contemporary racism.

> CHRIS: You know, I think there's a point here. We're saying OK, we're not putting Asians in camps anymore, enslaving blacks and we're not. . . . I hear there clearly is a difference but I think the subtleties that Ann is talking about, unless you walk in someone's shoes it can be a little difficult to understand and I think that's why the teacher [in the film] went to the extreme he did to make the point about what it is like to be a victim of racism.
>
> SUSAN: It's like they're trying to say they're not enslaving people, putting them in a place and saying you do this, but they give them these jobs and it's hard for them because like they put them in poor conditions. Like Jesse's mom [in the film] wasn't a slave but she got paid minimum wage and they wanted her to do extra

work and she had to do it or lose her job. That's enslaving her right there.

SAM: I don't think you should live that way. I don't think you should worry about what happened 20 or 30 years ago. Worry about what will happen now and how you're going to change that.

CHRIS: And Adam [in the film] says that. He says I don't know why you're bringing up all this old stuff, all these old feelings. Bob, you made a comment to that point.

BOB: I don't think you should forget it either. The human race isn't perfect and I believe that if you forget about something you will probably fall back into that pattern again. You have to rehash the mistakes of the past.

After a brief discussion on the acting in the film, another student, Susan, suddenly shifts the topic to a current concern of the students: a new proficiency test that would be tied to high school diplomas throughout the state.

SUSAN: What I gotta say is not pertaining to this movie, right? They say racism and prejudice is not going on. But this proficiency test . . . in a couple of years from now, people that live in the lower class, they gotta go out and make money you know, but if they can't pass that test that's keepin' them down in the lower class . . .

CHRIS: Right, you see, my purpose in showing you this film was not to talk about the film, per se, but to get you to think and write about your own experience and Susan, I'll tell ya, that's my fear as an educator, and there are a lot of educators out there expressing the same fear of this proficiency test and what it does to keep people where they are and keep people under control. . . . Is this test designed to keep you at a certain level? That's something that affects you people directly, and Susan, you may want to write about that.

BOB: And they published those scores and like ——— [a suburb] had like 99% and in city schools, there's like 16% that passed and it went down from the ones that had money to the ones that had nothing. The ones that have money have the grades and the ones that have nothing have nothing.

CHRIS: And do you think the people in ——— are more intelligent than you?

STUDENTS: No.

CHRIS: Then why do they do better on the test?

JAY: They have the support they need.

JOE: I think the parents push them more. There's more influence to do well.

ANN: I used to go to school there and it was, like, what are you going to do tonight and they would say, "I'm gonna do my homework" and it's like they know their parents got to where they are and they want to get there, too.

CHRIS: It's that self-fulfilling prophecy. It's understood you will do well. It has a lot to do with environment.

JOE: Yeah, like my mom has to work and she doesn't have time to help me. I'm not putting her down or anything, but she can't help me and stuff. So like in ———, they've got all the money and maybe those parents have time to sit down with them and show them how to do it. My parents, they don't have enough time. Not that they don't care or don't want to but they're tired when they come home.

CARL: I'll go with Joe. People in ———, I mean everyone is success-ful around there and they've got good school buildings, every-thing. But if they had to live in my neighborhood and see what I see every day they would probably lock themselves in their house and cry. There wouldn't be anything to do because they couldn't deal with it.

CHRIS: I don't know—if some of the things that some of you live with I don't know if I could get up in the morning. I've even said that out loud to people. Sometimes when I think about your experi-ences I try to put myself in that experience and I say, "Could I get up in the morning and go on?" I'm not sure. I'm not so sure about that.

At this point the discussion turns to opportunities for work and college, focusing on the relative difficulties of blacks and whites to "make it," with various personal anecdotes to illustrate points made. One anecdote from the film centers on a humorous story that also contains a racist inci-dent, to which Chris responded:

CHRIS: We laugh about that but if you remember what Amy said in the film, she said I smiled but I cried inside. . . . I wanted to give you a thought before the bell rings. Really, truly, my purpose in the film was to give you some things to think about. . . . And if you would talk or write about an experience that you have had or that someone you know had I would like you to begin drafting and I would like you to bring that draft tomorrow. I think when you open your feelings . . . you took a lot of risks here today and

I'm asking you to risk something in writing. I don't think these are issues to be resolved easily and I think the teacher in the film was saying this is only a beginning. I think what we have done here in a small way is to make people aware, maybe a little more sensitive. There are going to be people in this room that will just walk away. I would like you to draft something. If you have had any experience that you would like to talk about and maybe it's dialogue you want to write or maybe a conversation. Maybe something that happened at work or in your neighborhood. Would you bring that back tomorrow?

Afterward, in an interview, Chris says, "I was excited about their understanding of social issues and what these mean in their own lives." Initially, the students, for whatever reason, make no connection between race and class issues in the novel and similar issues in their own lives. What Chris is able to do is to find another kind of cultural text (the film) that would stimulate these connections, which spontaneously extends the inquiry into the ways in which social issues are related to literacy practices—that is, the assessment of literacy by the state actually serves to reinforce both inequities due to race and class (Rogers & McLean, 1991) and, for some children, the related discontinuities between home and school (Heath, 1983). In supporting this kind of discussion, Chris gives the students an opportunity to critique texts and discourses, such as the "violent" (Stuckey, 1991) discourses of assessment, as well as to respond to them, making literacy "discourses themselves the object of study" (Luke & Baker, 1991).

The intertextual nature of the discourse in this classroom provides a place where the students can begin to see the relationships between the texts of their own lives and the lives of others who are like them as well as different from them—which eventually enables them to connect to texts across historical, cultural, and social borders:

> When we isolate literature from the world, allowing only for a brief background of the author and the times to introduce the work, students have little chance of understanding how books work and how readers make something of real importance out of them. . . . What is public, historical, and cultural about [the literary transaction] is most often left unspoken, although these are arguably aspects of literary accomplishment. (Willinsky, 1991, p. 195)

The writings the students bring in the next day range from brief historical analyses of racism related to the present, to personal experiences with racism or prejudice, to inequities between working men and women.

Chris feels that their writings reveal understandings that they gained from the discussion that followed the film, and she encourages the students to revise and include them in their writing portfolios (Gibson, 1991).

By the end of the year, students are able to share the personal, social, and cultural nature of their responses or their identity positions openly, but not without some struggle of interpretation. During a sharing of poetry projects in May, for instance, an African American girl presents her research on Countee Cullin to the class. She reads two poems, "Tableau"—about the response to a white boy and a black boy walking arm in arm—and "The Incident."

> DAWN: I'm not a reader of poetry but this really involves—he writes about something that had to do with like blacks and whites. It really makes the poem interesting. The first poem is "Tableau." As I read it, think about it. I'm serious, really do think about it (*She then reads the poem.*) Do y'all have thoughts about this? You have to think about what it means. . . . What I got out of it was there was a black boy and a white boy . . .
>
> STUDENT: Were they holding hands or something . . .
>
> DAWN: Just walking along like past houses or villages or something and that people out of their houses were looking out of their blinds not understanding why a black and a white was walking with each other. I'm serious. I'm serious. It's more common maybe if a white and a white walk together or a black and a black but they couldn't see—they just couldn't understand. Okay, the next one is called "The Incident." I really liked this one.
>
> "The Incident"
>
> Once, riding in old Baltimore,
>   Heart-filled, head-filled with glee,
> I saw a Baltimorean
>   Keep looking straight at me.
>
> Now I was eight and very small,
>   and he was no whit bigger,
> And so I smiled, but he poked out
>   His tongue, and called me "Nigger."
>
> I saw the whole of Baltimore
>   From May until December;
> Of all the things that happened there
>   That's all that I remember.

What do you all think about that one? Now that was deep. I'm serious. It is deep.

AIMEE [another African American girl]: Everybody's had an experience like that. If you ever went somewhere, you know, you just happen to be there and somebody—they ain't going to stick their tongue out and call you nigger. They're just like (*turns her head and stares*) "what're you doing here?"

DAWN: There are just certain things, like places you'll go when you're younger you remember every detail. Like if you go somewhere fascinating, a lot of fascinating . . .

SARAH [a white girl]: I was going to say if you go someplace—well, he's so excited to see this place and it's new and everything, but out of his time there's this one thing that brought him down and it ruined his whole time down there.

DAWN: Well, sort of. See, everyone has their own opinion about stuff but what I was saying is like when you're young you block out stuff. There is just a certain thing in your life you'll always remember. You know she'll always remember this guy calling her a nigger. Out of all the things that happened in her life, she'll never forget someone calling her a nigger.

TIM [a white boy]: Isn't she just asking why? Wondering why this happened?

DAWN: I know a lot of y'all have been places but it's just one thing, one instance that may have happened that you'll always remember. I liked both these poems because it had to do with blacks and whites. Not because they were short but they were interesting. The last poem really gets to you. You've got to take time out to read them.

This exchange is particularly interesting because of the kind of struggle for meaning it represents. Dawn is trying to situate the poem in the context of the profound effects racism can have on a child; and, in fact, in the middle of her speech she begins to reference the speaker of the poem as "she." In this way it becomes her own experience, "populating it with [her] own intention" so that the poem "lies on the borderline" between herself and the narrator (Bakhtin, 1981). Aimee attempts to expand the conversation by suggesting that racism is still a common experience even if it may take more subtle forms; yet the white students seem to want to understand the poem in a more restricted context. They want to understand the incident as isolated and as affecting the narrator's experience in a more circumscribed way—that it ruined his or her trip, or that it was somehow momentarily puzzling. While Dawn attempts to share her understanding of the poem again, from her identity position, as a powerful statement on the personal effects of racism, the issue is essentially left unresolved apart from a plea for them to read it (again). This plea echoes Chris's earlier comment that some will just walk away from this kind of conversation but that she hopes they will be more aware.

This discussion illustrates a kind of resistance by some students to hearing or understanding Dawn's response to the poem. Resistance to certain understandings takes many forms and can be understood only by examining the context of classrooms in which it is manifested. In her work in another high school classroom, Fairbanks (1995) describes what she calls the "relational waters of culture, context, and gender" that shape classroom interpretations of literary works (p. 50). By studying one African American girl's response to *The Bluest Eye* by Toni Morrison, Fairbanks takes a closer look at these relational waters in order to understand the girl's uncharacteristically resistant stance to the story as a situated act. As she argues, students need curricular spaces in which they can explore complex and conflicting images in their social and cultural worlds, and in which they can communicate with others about matters that concern them.

RE-PLACING TEXTS

Across the year in Chris's classroom curricular spaces were gradually opened up so that literature became a subject of critical and social as well as literary inquiry, rather than an exercise in close reading of texts that remain irrelevant to students' experiences—an exercise that directs attention to "words on the page rather than to the contexts which produced and surround them" (Eagleton, 1983, p. 44). As Poovey (1992) points out, when culture is put at the center of classroom inquiry, we can begin to understand historical transformations and the place of texts considered to be "the best that has been thought or said" (p. 5). When the traditional canon is decentered, a focus on student voices is a natural consequence. Indeed, embracing multiculturalism compels educators to ask who speaks, who listens, and why (hooks, 1994).

Over time, Chris carefully crafted a community in which responses that reflected some risk-taking on the part of the students could be voiced and were encouraged to be voiced. She did this by gradually shifting textual interpretive authority away from herself and back to the community, and by gently encouraging the most personal responses so they could be understood in the larger social and cultural realm. At the same time, the literary canon was shifted away from center in favor of an intermingling of texts and voices both within and beyond the classroom and discourses of critique and resistance as well as consensus. Without developing this kind of community with an emphasis on intertextual readings, it is unlikely that expanded cultural conversations such as these could take place (Greene, 1994).

This kind of teaching is not sanctioned by the larger culture of high schools and by the norms for teaching reading or English in the United States. Many high school English teachers still view their job as one of transmitting culture rather than critiquing or transforming it and of teaching the skills of reading and writing as though they were not themselves cultural artifacts—products of particular ways of doing literacy in schools. That is, few teachers see issues of culture (e.g., race, class, and gender) or literacy practices themselves as open to critical inquiry in the classroom (cf. Bigler & Collins, 1995; Fine, 1987).

Teachers like Chris are not starry-eyed about what the task in front of them consists of. As Chris (Gibson, 1991) wrote of the students,

> They are there in school, for whatever reason: for the free lunch, for the heat, for the escape from responsibility, for the attention. . . . While they are in my class they are going to learn. I can't control their environment, take them home with me, give them money, but I can try to teach them to read and write. (p. 4)

Nor do teachers like Chris turn away from cultural difference, from the role of power and ideology in social institutions and interactions, or from the facts of racism, violence, poverty, and discrimination in hopes of finding some timeless truth in texts and some imagined peaceful place of straightforward teaching.

NOTES

A very special thank you to Chris Gibson for allowing us to spend time in her classroom and for responding to an earlier draft of this chapter.

Chris's real name has been used in this and in other reports with her permission. The names of the students have been changed to protect their anonymity.

Other reports from this project have provided a glimpse into the teaching characteristics of Chris and her colleagues (Rogers & McLean, 1994), the ways in which they themselves are at risk for dropping out of the system (McLean, 1991), a more complete analysis of the classroom transcripts (Rogers & McLean, 1993), and the teachers' own descriptions of their practice in an edited journal (Rogers & McLean, 1991).

REFERENCES

Bakhtin, M. M. (1981). Discourse in the novel. In M. Holquist (Ed.), *The dialogic imagination: Four essays by M. M. Bakhtin* (pp. 259–422). Austin: University of Texas Press.

Bigler, E., & Collins, J. (1995). Dangerous discourses: The politics of multicultural literature in community and classroom. Report series 7.4, National Research Center on Literature Teaching and Learning, State University of New York at Albany.

Bleich, D. (1987). *Subjective criticism.* Baltimore: Johns Hopkins University Press.

Bloome, D., & Green, J. (1984). Directions in the sociolinguistic study of reading. In P. D. Pearson, R. Barr, M. Kamil, & P. Mosenthal, (Eds.), *The handbook of reading research* (pp. 395–422). New York: Longman.

Brodkey, L. (1994). Lecture at Ohio State University.

Campbell, R. (1994). Cultural studies. In *The encyclopedia of English studies and language arts.* New York: Scholastic.

Eagleton, T. (1983). *Literary theory: An introduction.* Minneapolis: University of Minnesota Press.

Fairbanks, C. M. (1995). Reading students: Texts in context. *English Education, 27* (1), 40–52.

Fine, M. (1987). Silencing in public schools. *Language Arts, 64* (2), 157–174.

Fish, S. (1980). *Is there a text in this class: The authority of interpretive communities.* Cambridge, MA: Harvard University Press.

Gibson, C. (1991). Listening to what they say: Using portfolio evaluation with "at-risk" high school students. *Literacy Matters, 3*(2), 4–8.

Green, J. L., & Meyer, L. A. (1991). The embeddedness of reading in classroom life: Reading as a situated process. In C. Baker & A. Luke (Eds.), *Towards a critical sociology of reading pedagogy* (pp. 141–160). Philadelphia: John Benjamin.

Greene, M. (1994). Multiculturalism, community and the arts. In A. Dyson & C. Genishi (Eds.), *The need for story: Cultural diversity in classroom and community* (pp. 11–27). Urbana, IL: National Council of Teachers of English.

Heath, S. B. (1983). *Ways with words: Language, life and work in communities and classrooms.* Cambridge, England: Cambridge University Press.

hooks, b. (1994). *Teaching to transgress: Education as the practice of freedom.* New York: Routledge.

Iser, W. (1978). *The act of reading: A theory of aesthetic response.* Baltimore: Johns Hopkins University Press.

King, P. (1993). Introduction to N. Peim, *Critical theory and the English teacher: Transforming the subject* (pp. xiii–xvi). New York: Routledge.

Luke, A., & Baker, C. (1991). Toward a critical sociology of reading pedagogy: An introduction. In C. Baker & A. Luke (Eds.), *Towards a critical sociology of reading pedagogy* (pp. xi–xxi). Philadelphia: Johns Benjamin.

McGinley, W., & Kamberelis, G. (1992). Personal, social, and political functions of reading and writing. In C. Kinzer & D. J. Leu (Eds.), *Literacy research, theory, and practice: Views from many perspectives* (Forty-first yearbook of the National

Reading Conference) (pp. 403–413). Chicago, IL: National Reading Conference.

McLean, M. M. (1991) *The plight of the at-risk teacher.* Unpublished doctoral dissertation, Ohio State University, Columbus.

Poovey, M. (1992). Cultural criticism: Past and present. In J. Trimmer & T. Warnock (Eds.), *Understanding others: Cultural and cross-cultural studies and the teaching of literature* (pp. 3–15). Urbana, IL: National Council of Teachers of English.

Rabinowitz, P. (1987). *Before reading: Narrative conventions and the politics of interpretation.* Ithaca, NY: Cornell University Press.

Rogers, T. (1991). Students as literary critics: A case study of the interpretive experiences, beliefs and processes of ninth grade students. *Journal of Reading Behavior, 23,* 391–423.

Rogers, T., Green, J. L., & Nussbaum, N. (1990). Asking questions about questions. In S. Hynds and D. Rubin (Eds.), *Perspectives on talk and learning* (pp. 73–90). Urbana, IL: National Council of Teachers of English.

Rogers, T., & McLean, M. (Eds.) (1991). Theirs are voices we need to hear: Teaching literacy in urban high schools [Special issue]. *Literacy Matters, 3*(2).

Rogers, T., & McLean, M. (1993, December). *Reading, writing and talking our way in: The social construction of literacy communities in three urban classrooms.* Paper presented at the annual meeting of the National Reading Conference, Charleston, SC.

Rogers, T., & McLean, M. (1994). Critical literacy/Urban literacy: A case study of three urban high school English teachers. *Urban Review, 26*(3), 173–185.

Saville-Troike, M. (1982). *The ethnography of communication: An introduction.* Oxford: Blackwell.

Smithson, I. (1994). Introduction: Institutionalizing culture studies. In I. Smithson & M. Ruff (Eds.), *English studies/ Culture studies: Institutionalizing Dissent* (pp. 1–22). Urbana: University of Illinois Press.

Stuckey, J. E. (1991). *The violence of literacy.* Portsmouth, NH: Heinemann.

Trimmer, J., & Warnock, T. (1992). *Understanding others: Cultural and cross-cultural studies and the teaching of literature.* Urbana, IL: National Council of Teachers of English.

Weade, R., & Green, J. L. (1989). Reading in the instructional context: An interactional/sociolinguistic perspective. In C. Emihovich (Ed.), *Locating learning across ethnographic perspectives on classroom research* (pp. 17–56). Norwood, NJ: Ablex.

Willinsky, J. (1991). *The triumph of literature/ The fate of literacy: English in the secondary school curriculum.* New York: Teachers College Press.

CHAPTER 5

Multiplicity and Difference in Literary Inquiry

Toward a Conceptual Framework for Reader-Centered Cultural Criticism

MARY BETH HINES

I think they don't want me to make it. I mean they just want me to stay low. . . . They all have me down. They all . . . think I'm gonna be a junkie or something. I just think what I can. If I keep on keeping on, I can leave. . . . School's for stupid people.
—Kevin, a 14-year-old African American student

They don't be treating us right in schools and stuff. They say the only way a black person can be real good or make the grades is like they gotta act white or something. All the black people who got good grades, they ain't been suspended, they ain't been in trouble, and they don't act like their self. They try to fake it and be somebody else. . . . I know they do it to get along; I see it every day. . . . They gotta suck up, and I mean they act like other white students and stuff; they act like the teachers and stuff. Well, they gotta suck up to the teachers, and they don't be their self—they act all stupid.
—David, a 15-year-old African American student

FOR DAVID AND KEVIN, middle school students living in a housing project nestled against a row of brick colonial homes with manicured lawns, "school's for stupid people." Consequently, they choose the margins and refuse to "act like other white students . . . and teachers" because such behaviors seem antithetical to the social and cultural traditions they value, those that texture their daily experiences and provide a grid of intelligibility for their lives as African American adolescent males living in a housing project. To "fake it," by being successful in school, as David explains, is to not "be their self."

Given these views, it should not surprise us that, although bright, both boys have failed a series of classes, garnered a string of truancies, and tendered a number of disciplinary infractions—all before the eighth grade. School is a "battle ground," as Kevin says, where race, class, gender, authority, and ideological issues intersect, circulate, and escalate in school halls and classrooms. The boys, in turn, respond with a variety of forms of resistance to those who want them to "stay low." Although the boys seem headed for failure, they are fighting furiously to stay in school, determined to graduate from middle school and eventually attend a post-secondary institution. During that schooling process, however, they have no intention of surrendering their racialized identities, and they speak disparagingly of teachers and students who thwart their efforts to learn about African American culture.

But if David and Kevin's efforts to retain, rather than to obscure, their identities remind us of the value of community and the importance of selfhood to adolescents, they also remind us that we have failed in some ways to make schools in general, and English classrooms in particular, spaces of community for nonmainstream and oppositional students. As is obvious, David and Kevin's alienation will constitute the "prior knowledge and experience" that they bring to their respective English classes. As a result, their behaviors, attitudes, and practices may complicate or deflect efforts by the district's English teachers to "build community," "foster success," and "honor differences," as our slogans go, even when their English teachers stand firmly committed to multicultural education.

As David's and Kevin's teachers move beyond the narrow confines of the canon, they might also enrich inquiry by cultivating new understandings of what it means to know texts, selves, and culture. In this chapter, I draw from case studies of four literature classrooms to illuminate the principles of a reader-centered cultural criticism, informed by recent work in literary and cultural studies and focused on the concepts of multiplicity and difference. In conceptualizing interpretive communities that foster appreciation for multiplicity as they sensitize students to diversity, teachers can make spaces for David and Kevin in the name of effective literary inquiry.

EXPLORING TEXTUAL AND ACTUAL WORLDS

Because our ways of reading are always inherently linked to our ways of seeing society, current approaches to texts can be examined for the ways in which they explicitly and/or tacitly promote particular conceptions of the world. Belsey (1980) explains:

> No theoretical position can exist in isolation: any conceptual framework for literary criticism has implications which stretch beyond criticism itself to ideology and the place of ideology in the social formation as a whole. Assumptions about literature involve assumptions about language and about meaning, and these in turn involve assumptions about human society. (p. 29)

This chapter uncovers the "assumptions about human society," as Belsey says, that are tacitly and explicitly promoted in literature discussions, shaped by the teacher's understanding of multiplicity and diversity. I trace the conceptions of multiplicity and diversity issuing from literature classrooms taught by Barb, a middle school teacher; Paul, a high school teacher; and Richard and Michael, college instructors. Despite variations in their approaches, all take the view that knowledge, language, and truth are socially constructed; thus students can assert, contest, and complicate truth claims in the classroom. All believe that effective literary inquiry invites discussion of personal, social, cultural, and textual matters in communities where the teacher makes interpretive priorities and practices explicit through his or her discourse. In naming the salient principles of a reader-centered cultural criticism, I hope that we can begin to imagine new possibilities and responsibilities for English/language arts classrooms, just as we can begin to create homespaces in English classrooms for David, Kevin, and their friends in the housing project. In the next sections I turn to the four classrooms to consider the "assumptions about human society" at play in those particular interpretive communities.

A NEW CRITICAL PERSPECTIVE

Paul, an Anglo teacher of an American literature class for high school juniors in a predominantly Anglo, middle-class suburban district, advocates the text-centered practices of New Criticism as a way of knowing literature. Thus he engages in practices that reflect and constitute the current-traditional text-centered and teacher-led orientations to literature instruction that prevail in the research on literature classrooms (Applebee, 1993; Marshall, Smagorinsky, & Smith, 1995). From Paul's perspective, a multiplicity of responses can be generated by students who use social, economic, and historical knowledge to better comprehend the text. He explains:

> I know that with *The Great Gatsby* I'm trying to decide how much I teach from the book, what—do I point out every little detail—and you know, I feel compelled to do so. You know, there's a great little line here, and a great one there; Fitzgerald writes these magnificent little lines. . . . What I want to do is to ask a question that forces students to look at the novel as a whole piece of work rather than asking yes-or-no questions. . . . I wonder if it's a bias on my own part. I'm very much interested in the techniques that an author uses in a novel, and particularly Fitzgerald with his use of symbolism and characterization and all that. How else can you discuss it without looking directly at it?

For Paul, the formal properties of a text provide entrance into the social and culture worlds created by an author. "Knowing" in this case focuses on "symbolism and characterization" issues that, in turn, prod students into looking at the "techniques that an author uses" or "the novel as a whole." We can see the logic of this approach in the following excerpt, where Paul and his students explore *The Great Gatsby* (Fitzgerald, 1925/ 1953) and learn about its sociohistorical context:

> PAUL: Let's finish up on our characterization of Tom. . . . What's the one word you'd use to characterize Tom after he talks about this book [Goddard's *Rise of the Colored Empires*]?
>
> MEGAN: He's a bigot.
>
> BILL: He's racist.
>
> PAUL: (*Sarcastically.*) Yeah, you know, blacks are going to take over. We gotta watch out. It's in the book; it's scientific. I've read it. Whatever is in the book must be right. OK, now you have to wonder how he could get an attitude like that. He's a relatively educated man. I mean, he graduated from Yale, and it helps to know a little bit about the 1920s, the attitudes about the times. To help me with that will be Bob and Carrie, who have done some research about the KKK and racism in the 1920s. Go ahead and tell us what you know.
>
> CARRIE AND BOB READING ALTERNATE SECTIONS: The KKK was the Ku Klux Klan in the 1920s. The reason of this was that people were worried that the United States was going to this industrial business and what not, and there was more immigration coming in

with the blacks of South Africa and what not, and they were worried about the takeover of the blacks, so they formed the KKK and in a way to make them [blacks] feel uncomfortable and not to try going out and taking over the United States. The KKK was basically a group of prejudiced white people, and they'd start with their children basically. Even the older people from the KKK would bring their children to the meetings and burn crosses, carry torches. They'd go around sometimes and torch 'em, sometimes with a Negro on them. They'd drag them behind cars and do all sorts of bad things basically to try to drive them from the community.

PAUL: Did you see that movie on cable the other night, *Mississippi Burning?* . . . That, of course, took place in the 1960s; it wasn't that long ago. . . . The KKK is still prevalent today; the numbers are greater, I think, than they ever were. You'd think what happened 70 years ago we could forget about; it still continues. The KKK was prejudiced not only against blacks but against who else, Mike?

MIKE: Minority groups.

PAUL: Yeah, OK, anyone who wasn't . . .

MIKE: Anglo-Saxon.

PAUL: Yeah, have you heard this term before, WASP? W–A–S–P. Do you know what that stands for? What's the term for that acronym?

SUE: White, Anglo-Saxon.

TERRY: Protestant.

PAUL: Protestant, right. So not only that any immigrant came in, but anyone who is Catholic, Jewish, black. Minorities could take over the country, all right, so we gotta watch out. It's been proved in this book by Goddard. I don't know who he is, but it's proof. All right, Tom literally, physically pushes people around. Mentally, he is not very open-minded; he is unwilling to accept other people that are different from him, and that's shown in his belief in this book, *Rise of the Colored Empires.* Thank you for that presentation, very well done. OK, that's all for Tom, so let's move on to Jordan.

This excerpt suggests several of Paul's priorities. First of all, he encourages multiplicity by providing an array of inroads into the nature of Tom's character. He invites connection to the quality of "bigot" by evoking a movie, by appealing to the antiracist sentiments of students, by noting the prevalence of racism in contemporary culture, and by asking for clarification of terms.

In this section Paul also tacitly and explicitly conveys his attitudes about diversity. He playfully picks up on the racism suggested by the texts and times evoked in *The Great Gatsby* ("Minorities could take over the country, all right, so we gotta watch out."). Implicit in his ironic tone is an antiracist sentiment that becomes manifest in his follow-up questions about the KKK's targets. His mention of the popular movie *Mississippi Burning* suggests not only the resurgence of KKK affiliations but also his antiracist convictions ("You'd think what happened 70 years ago we could forget about; it still continues.").

In this exchange Paul and his students also dramatize Belsey's (1980) claim that a specific way of reading a text also promotes a particular way of seeing the world. For instance, students are invited to contribute to the discussion of racism, but they simply recall and recite facts and definitions, that is, "W–A–S–P," missing opportunities to hypothesize and problematize social, historical, and cultural forces in their own worlds as well as that of *Gatsby*. Paul's first and last turns in this episode suggest that the knowledge generated in relation to racism is rendered to understand Tom. That is, Paul does acknowledge racism, but he and his students construct it as a character trait, an attribute of Tom's persona. Hence inquiry about racism folds into a lesson on characterization.

As this exchange illustrates, inequities are elicited and acknowledged, but they are glossed over, appropriated as cues to analyzing the textual world, its characters, and events. If Paul's students explore social and historical issues, they do so within the context of learning about a textual universe, given the framework that guides and shapes Paul's understanding of literary inquiry. In light of the limits of teacher-led, text-centered approaches, many experts now turn to reader-response theories because they promote multiplicity and figure readers into "the meaning" of texts, as the next section illustrates.

A READER-RESPONSE ORIENTATION

As Paul invites his secondary students into a community where textual knowledge is privileged, Michael encourages his college literature students to join a classroom community where reader knowledge and experience are valued dimensions of the reading experience. Michael, an exemplary, award-winning teacher, attempts to enact lively discussions by invoking Rosenblatt (1938, 1978) in a transactional version of reader response. Michael encourages students to bring their prior knowledge and experience to bear on the text, recognizing "both the openness of the text, on the one hand, and on the other, its constraining function as a guide or check" (Rosenblatt, 1978, p. 88).

However, Michael is not only interested in promoting multiplicity in response to texts; he is also particularly aware of diversity issues. An Anglo male who recently married a woman of a different race and culture, he is working in both personal and professional ways on multiculturalism. In Michael's view there is a direct connection between promoting multiplicity and encouraging sensitivity to linguistic and cultural diversity. As students generate multiple ways of seeing society, texts, and citizens, they gain a greater understanding of diverse selves, societies, and texts, thereby gaining a greater understanding of difference.

In spite of his personal and professional priorities, Michael nonetheless objects to those who would measure a teacher's commitment to multiculturalism by the number of noncanonical texts students read in a course. He argues that classroom social dynamics, rather than the array of texts used in a curriculum, offer a more accurate index to an instructor's commitments to social justice:

> Just because he's teaching *Sula* and I'm not doesn't mean I'm less politically conscious. Does that make his class more politically correct? Somehow there's a slippage of logic, but that's what goes on. . . . You bring your questions, your interests, and we'll see what we'll do with them. If somebody says gender issues are important here, it's theirs; and then I can say, "What can we do with it?" . . . It's more important for me to echo what other people say about a text or about an idea. So I'm not saying, "I'm a feminist; therefore, I'm interested in issues of gender." I'm saying, "We're going to read closely. We're going to learn to read, and we're going to talk about the things you're interested in [with] this text."

His taking the role of facilitator allows students to bring various perspectives to the class, just as it enables Michael to enact his commitments to democracy—intent as he is on returning power and authority to students by vesting in them responsibility for discussion. Consequently, issues of social justice enter the classroom as students, not the teacher, raise and discuss them. "If you try to look at the story through somebody else's eyes, you will see some other picture," he explains. That new image, he believes, will lead to greater understanding of social, cultural, and individual differences.

Michael believes that patterns of language and patterns of society are necessarily linked. Consequently, as he says, when students "look closely at language," they can "question the construction of ideas, the ways we inherit certain ways of seeing things." If students do this, then it might be through the promotion of multiple perspectives that students can come to understand other ways of seeing things. However, Michael wants students to freely choose "without thinking about the political implications" of a differential system of values or knowledges because, as he explains, he isn't after "disruption and destabilization."

We can see the effects of his priorities in this excerpt from a discussion of Ellison's "Battle Royal" (1947/1990) with his predominately Anglo, middle-class students:

LINDA: What does he mean by "keep this nigger boy running"?

JASON: I kind of thought it was motivation. It was kind of like the message said it will always be like that. It was a general thing to say keep running. If you persist, you'll make it through. If you don't make huge strides, if you at least persist, then you've won.

MICHAEL: Sort of like the war is never over.

JASON: The war is never over. If you give up, you've lost; but if you don't give up, that's good.

MICHAEL: Add on to that?

JAY: You see "keep the nigger boys running." You see that in society anywhere throughout the history of the blacks. You fight it through your meekness. If you fight it through your meekness, you'll never get anything accomplished. So that's where he has to contemplate being meek or actually doing anything about it. It's a struggle.

MICHAEL: It is. Lee is still struggling with it, right? How many of you have seen *Do the Right Thing?* Martin Luther King and Malcolm X both on one wall of a building. The one preaching passive resistance and the other preaching take arms. Is there a point at which passive resistance no longer works? That seems to be what you're getting at. You're wondering if in here somewhere the story isn't suggesting "be hoping up to a point and when you're ready, take arms." I'm not sure if that's there or not. It's tricky.

JAY: I was just going to say that black people have, like you said, two selves, their outer self and their inner self. I think that represents white people, too. They try to be nice to black people on the outside, but behind closed doors they say the opposite. Sort of the same way on both sides.

This dialogue illustrates the ways in which students understand multiplicity. As Linda initiates the exchange with the question that sparks a discussion of racism, Jason elaborates by focusing on the theme of persistence as a key to overcoming oppression. Michael then "reads back" Jason's comment, prompting Jay to analyze the value of another trait, meekness, in relation to black history. Students explore racial difference by tracing it through what they know and believe about history, media, and psychology, generating similes and expressing their prior experiences and understandings. Meekness, persistence, history, and culture are all glossed, thereby evoking multiplicity in the spirit of Rosenblatt.

But if we also use this excerpt to understand how racial difference is constructed in this discussion, then we see both the power of reader response and its limits. For instance, when Jay and Jason speak, they conceive of racial difference in terms of individual personality character-istics—meekness, passivity, resistance, honesty. In articulating a liberal-humanist view—that individuals are "free" to lift themselves up by their bootstraps—students miss opportunities to explore the complex ways in which social, historical, ideological, economic, institutional, and material forces affect and constitute the self and society (cf. Beach, Chapter 3, this volume). The view that life is "sort of the same on both sides," issuing from students, actually fails to take difference into account because it obscures and appropriates the specific struggles and experiences that mark the lives of persons of color. Racial difference is repressed as human sameness is promoted; oppression is named but not analyzed.

In celebrating multiplicity with Rosenblatt—or any of the first gener-ation of reader-response theorists (Tompkins, 1980)—we need to consider that there are no theoretical linkages that systematically move from *ac-knowledgment* to *analysis* of social justice issues. That is, reader theories do not take up the political dimensions of reading texts, selves, and worlds; they do not explore how access to opportunity is structured dif-ferently for those who are not male, not Anglo, and not middle-class het-erosexuals (Mailloux, 1990; Pratt, 1982; Tompkins, 1980). Therefore such issues are, at best, glossed by politically oriented students or, at worst, occluded from view.

Given changing demographics and the importance of multicultural education, we need to create reader-centered approaches with conceptual frameworks for "reading" the histories, lives, and literacies of linguisti-cally and culturally diverse students, characters, and citizens. By explor-ing the interplay of complex and contradictory forces in various arenas—ideological, material, social, historical, and institutional—students can not only learn to respond to textual worlds; they can also be challenged to assume responsibility for their world.

From this perspective, reader response might best be viewed as a necessary but not sufficient set of principles to explore social justice is-sues; however, multiplicity can be recuperated by articulating it with a theory of difference, as it is elaborated by materialist-feminists and others in cultural studies (e.g., Barrett, 1988; Brodkey, 1989; Newton & Rosenfelt,

1985). Teachers can undertake analyses of the social, historical, material, and discursive forces at play as certain individuals and groups gain power and privilege at the expense of others, typically those who are not of the dominant race, class, and gender. While "liberal" versions of multicultural education encourage students to "see and even honor cultural differences," they do not require them to "examine, change, or be responsible to the economic and political power structures difference [that] is entangled within" (Hennessy, 1993, p. 11). However, to understand difference is to invite students not only to acknowledge diversity but also to trace the effects and sources of difference through cultural, economic, and political spheres. From this vantage point, the focus is on "acquiring the critical frameworks to understand how and why social differences are reproduced" (Hennessy, 1993, p. 11) in order to challenge instances in which diversity equals inequity. In the next section, we turn to teachers who dramatize forms of reader-centered cultural criticism capable of acknowledging, honoring, and interrogating difference.

A SOCIAL JUSTICE FRAMEWORK

Barb is an eighth-grade teacher in David's and Kevin's school. Committed to social justice, she spends summers developing curricula on thematic units related to diversity issues. For instance, her students recently completed a unit on gay and lesbian issues, and they have read texts about apartheid in Africa and Bosnia. She has taught units on the physically and mentally challenged as well. Like Michael, she values multiplicity in classroom discussion, and she believes that the experience of reading literature can be transformative because it offers possibilities for students to imagine lives and experiences that may be unlike their own:

> When you read, when you're exposed to literature, you can be anything and anywhere. You can have any experience in the world. And you take on points of view that you normally don't, because when you read a book, in effect, you become the character for a little bit of time. . . . For example, in *Monsoon* when you experience what the young girl does when she goes to India—the rampant hunger—it makes a stronger impression on you than seeing coverage in the news or reading it in a newspaper because it's *you* who becomes affected.

For Barb, a literary text provides a personalized transaction not simply with a text, but with a world, a personalized cultural odyssey. Therefore, in her view, literary inquiry can foster respect for and understanding of those marked as "other," those different from the culturally diverse urban students she teaches:

> What kinds of citizens will they become? How will they react to social issues? I totally believe in putting your money where your mouth is. I see certain problems with my world, and I want to help fix them. Teaching English is the best way I know how to do that. . . . Our world is about choices. But too many people don't have choices.

Consistent with her commitments to social justice, her students discuss the differences in experiences between male and female Delaware and Navajo Indians in relation to *Sing Down the Moon* (O'Dell, 1970) and *A Light in the Forest* (Richter, 1953). After small-group discussions, students present their opinions to the class and then attempt to defend their stances on how gender roles in the two tribes resulted in gendered divisions of labor. Barb then shifts the focus from textual to social issues, inviting students to make personal connections with the text by turning to an exploration of contemporary gender roles:

> BARB: Do you think they covered everything? Do you believe everything that James just said? What do we have to add from the book? Do you think that men and women today are completely equal?
>
> STUDENTS: (*Multiple students shouting indignantly.*) No! No way! No!
>
> BARB: Young women in the class, do you think that you are completely equal to the young men?
>
> STUDENTS: (*Multiple students.*) No! No! No!
>
> MARK: I was going to say like with football and basketball games on TV, there's no way that women can join these teams!
>
> SUE: We can't play!
>
> JOHN: Y'all can play!!
>
> BARB: Please be quiet, everyone, and let Glenda speak.
>
> GLENDA: My dad told me that they tried to let women in the NBA, only they didn't have enough money or spectators as the men's stuff.
>
> BARB: Why do you think that is?
>
> GLENDA: Because I mean—not me—but not a lot of people think this way, but some do: Some of it has to do with that they don't, they think we are as good as men and that the men are *more interesting* to watch.

JOSH: I just think that girls can play any sport, like girls playing hockey— a girl plays hockey, and we don't think it's nothing.

MAX: I think . . . now that women are equal and have every right to be equal and everything, they are like—grrrrr!—now *WE'RE* better than you! . . .

RONA: It's not that, "Oh yeah, we are better than you or anything," but it's just that we are sick of people—guys—saying that we are afraid that we are going to break a nail or something. (*Students clap enthusiastically.*)

JOSH: (*Standing, gesturing to gain the floor.*) That's a ster–e–o–type!!!!

BARB: Great, you are referring to a lesson we had before. Explain how.

JOSH: You are saying "guys." Like every male, all guys—

TRAVIS: Just like saying *all* of us are brutal!

This episode of discussion occurs between episodes in which students closely analyze the details of the two texts to illustrate social and cultural traditions in the tribes. Barb's initial question sparks a heated discussion in which speakers contribute with enthusiasm. Like Michael's discussion, this one, too, places an emphasis on multiplicity. Students not only volley back and forth with "yes" and "no," but they supplement those opinions with knowledge of sports, with knowledge of how "ster–e–o–types" circulate through popular culture as "one man" becomes "all men" in gross overgeneralizations. While in prior and subsequent episodes students focus closely on the text, in this exchange they consider social and cultural patterns.

Barb's turns in this episode suggest that she ostensibly works as a facilitator in many of the ways that Michael does, nudging students to elaborate and defend positions. But like Paul and unlike Michael, it is she who introduces the topics, that is, gender roles in the American Indian tribes and U.S. culture. While she promotes multiplicity, she also intervenes in discussions of diversity by raising social justice issues and by providing classroom time for students to "read" culture. Like Paul and Michael, Barb sees herself as a facilitator; but unlike them, she does not see herself as value-free. As a teacher who values and respects others enough to insist that her students do likewise, she consciously formulates questions that provide opportunities for students to crystallize their views on social justice issues. Obviously, the momentum of the episode suggests that students were excited and engaged, practicing "uptake" by elaborating on one another's comments and filling in words before speakers on the floor would ever have the chance (Nystrand & Gamoran, 1991).

The excerpt also suggests how students conceptualize and construct difference. Students highlight the variable and differential access to sports available to men and women in our society, and they suggest a variety of reasons for such inequities—revenues from media coverage, attitudes about women's abilities, and competing conceptions of women in the larger society. Glenda holds the view that "not a lot of people think this way, but some do," while Rona, Josh, and Travis collaboratively construct and explain the notion of stereotypes in relation to gender issues. Although these culturally diverse students do not complicate their analyses with overlays of class, race, ethnicity, and so forth in this instance, they explore competing ideologies and argue that gender differences result in and reinforce variable access to opportunity. In short, difference is not only acknowledged, it is also analyzed. In the next section, I turn to a classroom in which discussions of difference are mediated by a teacher who is able to advance a more sophisticated version of cultural critique because he teaches college students.

CULTURAL CRITICISM

Richard, a literature teacher who, like Barb, is committed to social justice, explains his priorities in an interview:

> If you go into your classroom and say that we're going to talk about how this piece of literature enriches us all as human beings, how it teaches us all as human beings to respond in the same way to love or to death—big universals—then that is very biased because it allows the political status quo in society—which exploits women, which exploits through the class system—to continue. It doesn't engage with them at all, and it doesn't even try. It says we're all the same, which of course we're not—you're a different class, a different color, and I would say, then, that your relationship to love and death is different.

While Paul wonders if his approach to literature is biased because it focuses on textual details, Richard suggests that approaches rooted in liberal-humanist tendencies—"We're all the same"—obscure diversity issues by refusing to take into account the ways in which individual, social, and cultural differences complicate and shape one's perceptions of "love and death," for instance. For Richard, challenging and critiquing received "ways of seeing" is at the heart of the literary enterprise. As he explains in an interview:

Teachers have been taught to believe that in literature classrooms we don't bring in too much of the outside world because that is not something that you teach. We're supposed to be teaching what's in the novel, the play, or the poem . . . digging out. . . . What I explain is that we're not interested in formal ways of writing, how great a text is put together, or anything like that. We're interested in the message that's being sold to us. . . . What I'm really doing is not teaching text, but context, so I'm decentering the text. I'm saying that it is a catalyst. . . . I want to stress that the text is a social construction, and if it's a social construction, then who constructed it, what's it doing, and what are the mechanisms that are at work here?

Richard's orientation to reading texts and worlds stands in almost direct opposition to Paul's. If Paul emphasizes the world in order to illuminate the text, then Richard uses the text to focus on the world, "the mechanisms that are at work." Like Barb, he is passionately committed to social justice, seeking to make visible the marginalized and obscured, infusing discussions with popular culture, media, social issues, and history.

In fact, his students learn to generate multiple responses to texts as they explore issues of difference. A good example of this process is the way they responded to the following passage from *Out of Focus* (Davies, Dickey, & Stratford, 1987), discussing the *Oxford English Dictionary* (*OED*):

Its definition of the verb "to beat" is truly unbelievable (or is it) in these supposedly enlightened days: "to beat—to strike repeatedly, as in to beat one's wife." Not only does this show the presumed sex of the reader (at least one-half of the population does not have a wife), but it also clearly demonstrates that beating "one's" woman is an acceptable way for men to behave. Would it not otherwise have been struck from the "thinking man's bible"? (p. 98)

The discussion that ensued opened up the perspective:

GREG: On page 98 talking about wife beating, "not only does this show the presumed sex of the reader . . . but it also clearly demonstrates that beating 'one's' woman is an acceptable way for men to behave." I can't draw that conclusion from what's found in the dictionary.

RICHARD: Why would they put that in the dictionary? It makes it very commonplace. As in beating one's wife. Like it happens all the time, right? And the dictionary is supposed to be the definitive meaning of the word.

JAN: The author sends subtle unconscious messages which shape our attitudes.

GREG: But a dictionary isn't the place where you make comments.

STAN: When you're little you don't hear them say to a little girl, "You're not supposed to hit little boys." But it comes to that; little boys aren't supposed to hit girls, but they play with GI Joes and stuff. So the whole thing is that they get those messages when they're little, from basketball players or cartoon characters, who are mostly male. A kid is too little to say, "Yeah, but that's not the way real life is." That's the point of the cartoon character. It is directed toward little kids, and that's the way life goes on.

JAN: When we look in the dictionary, what you see is what you believe. That's what you're taught. I think that what they're trying to say in this one quote is that something like that in there almost condones it. Like it's OK. Like a message if you're male it's something that is done or is OK to be done. It's tied in with a definition. It's just a message. But it's there. . . .

LINDA: By being in the dictionary it's something that people look at every day; they are stating that it's commonplace. You open a dictionary every day. If you read "beating one's wife," it may seem that that's what happens. . . .

TODD: It's kind of, I guess to add on to this, I was looking in my friend's room the other day and on his bulletin board, Charles Barkley, the NBA basketball player—I guess he was losing a game and was talking to a reporter and said, "Yeah, this is the kind of game that after you're done with it you go home and beat your wife." . . . The newspaper person was like, do you want me to just quote you on that or do you want it off the record. He said, no just quote me on that. That's kind of glamorizing. That it's OK. Some little boy might think, Charles Barkley is my hero, my idol, after a game you just go beat your wife. This kid will grow up and think that's OK. . . .

GREG: I sort of find it degrading to women, but some people do beat their wives, and it does explain the word *beat*. Striking repeatedly. But as I see it, they're putting the word *beat* in a certain context, and I don't think they should have used it. But at the same time I don't necessarily think it is a statement that it's OK to beat your wife.

JAMES: I think they have a valid point; I can see the point. But my question is, how are we supposed to respond to the knowledge that we have? How are we supposed to change ourselves and our attitudes? How do we go about doing that?

RICHARD: . . . I don't think there are any ready-made solutions. But
I think the biggest step is to be aware of this stuff. . . . The next
step is to tend to your own ways of seeing and to tell other people
to change their ways of seeing.

Salient here are distinguishing features of a reader-centered approach
that fosters cultural critique (see also Rogers, Chapter 4, this volume).
First of all, the discussion explores a multiplicity of meanings and purposes for the use of "wife-beating" as part of an OED definition. Students
in this class understand that texts—and dictionaries—not only carry
meanings, but also serve ideological functions in the larger society.
That is, as cultural artifacts, they do cultural work by promoting, in
subtle ways, a set of values. As Richard says in his interviews, he wants
students to understand texts as social constructions so that they can question those values. In this exchange, personal experience, opinion, and
popular culture infuse the "knowing" of texts, thereby complicating
and enriching the discussion of the representation of women in various texts. Gender issues then become a point of analysis, resulting in cultural criticism and the interrogation of misogynistic forces that circulate
in texts, media, toys, families, and history. As a result, gender is "read"
as a set of complex, frequently conflicting set of material and ideological
forces, visible in institutions, sports, and families as well as in dictionaries.

READER-CENTERED CULTURAL CRITICISM AND SOCIAL JUSTICE INQUIRY

We can, with Paul, Barb, Michael, and Richard, construct approaches that
not only acknowledge and honor diversity but also interrogate its effects
on selves, worlds, and texts. If David and Kevin remind us of what's missing from our current conceptions of the English classroom, then Paul,
Michael, Barb, and Richard invite us to consider how we might reenvision
instruction to make it relevant, engaging, and productive for these students. David and Kevin signal how important it is for English/language
arts teachers to "honor students in all their pluralities" (Greene, 1993),
just as the four case study teachers remind us to value texts in all their
multiplicities. In so doing, Kevin and David can, as Kevin says, "keep on
keeping on," cultivating new possibilities as they explore texts and
worlds in their English classrooms.

REFERENCES

Applebee, A. (1993). *Literature in the secondary school: Studies of curriculum and instruction in the United States.* Urbana, IL: National Council of Teachers of English.

Barrett, M. (1988). *Women's oppression today* (2nd ed.). London: Verso.

Belsey, C. (1980). *Critical practice.* London: Methuen.

Brodkey, L. (1989). Opinion: Transvaluing difference. *College English, 51,* 597–601.

Davies, K., Dickey, J., & Stratford, T. (Eds.). (1987). *Out of focus: Writings on women and the media.* London: Women's Press.

Ellison, R. (1990). Battle royal. In P. J. Annas & R. C. Rosen (Eds.), *Literature and society: An introduction to fiction, poetry, drama, nonfiction* (pp. 62–75). Englewood Cliffs, NJ: Prentice-Hall. (Original work published 1947)

Fitzgerald, F. S. (1953). *The great Gatsby.* New York: Scribners. (Original work published 1925)

Greene, M. (1993, April). *Reciprocity, an ethic of care and social justice.* Fourth Annual Joshua Weinstein Memorial Lecture, presented at the University of Houston.

Hennessy, R. (1993). *Materialist feminism and the politics of discourse.* New York: Routledge.

Mailloux, S. (1990). The turns of reader-response criticism. In C. Moran & E. Penfield (Eds.), *Conversations: Contemporary critical theory and the teaching of literature* (pp. 38–54). Urbana, IL: National Council of Teachers of English.

Marshall, J., Smagorinsky, P., & Smith, M. (in collaboration with Dale, H., Fehlman, R., Fly, P., Frawley, R., Gitomer, S., Hines, M. B., & Wilson, D.). (1995). *The language of interpretation: Patterns of discourse in discussions of literature.* Urbana, IL: National Council of Teachers of English.

Newton, J., & Rosenfelt, D. (Eds.). (1985). *Feminist criticism and social change: Sex, class and race in literature and culture.* New York: Methuen.

Nystrand, M., & Gamoran, A. (1991). Student engagement: When recitation becomes conversation. In H. Waxman & H. Walberg (Eds.), *Contemporary research on teaching* (pp. 257–276). Berkeley: McCutchan.

O'Dell, S. (1970). *Sing down the moon.* Boston: Houghton Mifflin.

Pratt, M. (1982). Interpretive strategies/strategic interpretations: On Anglo-American reader response criticism. *Boundary 2, 11* (1–2), 201–231.

Richter, C. (1953). *A light in the forest.* New York: Knopf.

Rosenblatt, L. M. (1938). *Literature as exploration* (4th ed.). New York: Modern Language Association.

Rosenblatt, L. M. (1978). *The reader, the text, the poem: The transactional theory of the literary work.* Carbondale: Southern Illinois University Press.

Rosenblatt, L. (1985). Viewpoints: Transaction versus interaction—A terminological rescue operation. *Research in the Teaching of English, 19,* 96–107.

Tompkins, J. (1980). *Reader response criticism: From formalism to poststructuralism.* Baltimore: Johns Hopkins University Press.

PART II

Authors, Teachers, and Texts

CHAPTER 6

Exploring Multicultural Literature as Cultural Production

ARLETTE INGRAM WILLIS

THOSE OF US IN teacher education are preparing a predominantly white teaching force of preservice educators to teach an increasingly culturally and linguistically diverse student body. My crusade for improving the current generic approaches to literacy training of preservice teachers is both professional and personal. Professionally, I believe as teachers in institutions of higher learning we should equip our "charges" to meet the challenges of tomorrow—the challenges of cultural and linguistically diverse students—armed with theories and practical experiences that are inclusive. Personally, I want the future teachers of my own children to understand that children bring with them rich and culturally mediated language, experience, and knowledge to the classroom. Furthermore, I want these future teachers to understand that language and culture are inseparable. That is, the manner in which culturally and linguistically diverse students give meaning to the world is culturally understood and may differ from a mainstream perception. In addition, I want my preservice teachers to respect, value, and affirm the culturally mediated knowledge that my children (and others like them) bring to the classroom and to know how to build upon that knowledge for literacy development.

I use multicultural literature as an avenue to traverse the chasm between formal definitions of literacy and school realities of literacy (Willis, 1995). Moreover, in the undergraduate preservice classes I teach, I use multicultural literature to open discussions of history, knowledge, power, culture, language, class, race, and gender.

One of my goals is to sharpen the ability of my students to think critically about the choices they make when teaching literacy. Giroux (1987b) puts it this way: "The task . . . is to broaden our conception of

how teachers actively produce, sustain, and legitimate meaning and experience in classrooms" (p. 14). The task, I believe, can be performed with
the sagacious use of multicultural literature. I encourage and challenge
my students to become informed decision makers about the instruction
and use of multicultural literature for positive social change.

A CRITICAL PEDAGOGY

In addition to Freire, I ground my work in the thinking of the critical
pedagogues Macedo, Giroux, Shor, and McLaren, among others. My interpretation of Freirean theory, as applied to the instruction and use of
multicultural literature, begins with the adoption of the definition of literacy offered by Freire and Macedo (1987). They write of literacy as "a set
of practices that function either to empower or disempower people. In
the larger sense literacy is analyzed according to whether it serves a set
of cultural practices that promotes democratic and emancipatory change"
(p. 14). Further, they clarify their position on literacy by noting that "for
the notion of literacy to become meaningful it has to be situated within
a theory of cultural production and viewed as an integral part of the way
in which people produce, transform, and reproduce meaning" (p. 142). I
see multicultural literature as an artifact of cultural production. As such,
multicultural literature is an expression of how groups outside of the
dominant culture view themselves and their life experiences, of how they
read the world. All multicultural literature, in my opinion, must be evalu-
ated in light of what Freire (1994) calls the "complex set of circumstances"
(p. xi) that gave rise to it. In my courses the importance of attending to
the relationships among ideology, history, power, and knowledge in the
reading of multicultural writings is emphasized. I believe that it is important for students to be knowledgeable of the historical significance of
how those holding certain ideologies and positions of power have determined who can be literate, what is important to learn in literacy, how
literacy is to be learned, and when one is said to have become literate.
Exclusive use of Western Eurocentric ideology, situated in a celebratory
description of its historical and social contexts within the United States,
has given rise to an exclusionary literary canon. The required teaching of
this canon serves to cultivate the continual production of a literary culture
based on Western Eurocentric views. For groups that have lacked power,
their histories, language, and literature have been marginalized to the
status of "supplemental" to the literary canon. Henry Giroux's (1987a)

interpretation of this phenomenon in school literacy programs is worth quoting at length:

> [S]chools are not merely instructional sites designed to transmit knowledge; they are also cultural sites. As cultural sites, they generate and embody support for particular forms of culture as evident in the school's support for specific ways of speaking, the legitimating of distinct forms of knowledge, the privileging of certain histories and patterns of authority, and the confirmation of particular ways of experiencing and seeing the world. Schools often give the appearance of transmitting a common culture, but they, in fact, more often than not, legitimate what can be called a dominant culture. (p. 176)

Adopting a critical pedagogy for the training of educators in the United States has its risks. As Freire and Macedo (1995) point out, there is a growing mechanistic approach to the implementation of critical pedagogy. Like Freire and Macedo, I am disturbed by the interpretations of the critical position that give lip-service to a democratic pedagogy but fail to address the history of race, class, and gender oppression as experienced in the United States. Further, there is a tradition in U.S. educational circles of downplaying the importance of race, class, and gender; of minimizing the importance of acknowledging a history of forced servitude; of ignoring the history of legal denial of access to literacy; and of ignoring the history and role of privilege. Beneath the surface of the rhetoric and methodological rigidity lies the refusal to deal with the ideological positions that have supported and maintained race, class, and gender oppression. Whether educators are unwilling or unable to make explicit the role of oppression is unclear. I believe the reluctance to acknowledge a history of oppression in the United States may be due to the realization that such an acknowledgment would impose an obligation to adopt alternative ideologies and instructional practices.

Critical pedagogues are not without their critics. Especially vocal are those who believe that Freire's theory acts as an umbrella for all forms of oppression, while not adequately addressing specific forms of oppression, namely, gender and race. In their most recent installment of a decade-long dialogue of critical pedagogy, Freire and Macedo (1995) directly address some of their harshest critics. The critics have raised questions in an effort to understand how Freire's theory can account for the varying forms of oppression. In *Pedagogy of the Oppressed*, Freire (1970) focuses on social-class differences and political barriers to literacy attainment. Freire's (1994) response situates his early work within the historic and social contexts in which it was written. He states that "readers have some responsibility to place my work within its historical and cultural context. . . . I believe that what one needs to do is to appreciate the contribution of the work within its historical context" (p. 109).

By situating Freire's work within the historical and social contexts in which it was written, his critics can see how his original work cannot account for contemporary concerns of racial and gender oppression. Moreover, current application and translation of critical pedagogy should identify the unique ideological, historical, and social contexts in which it is used. Macedo (1994) also responds to critics by adding that "what we need to do is to understand the fact that the different historical locations of oppression necessitate a specific analysis with a different and unique focus that calls for a different pedagogy" (p. 110). While I strongly support Freire and Macedo's (1995) call for a review of specific histories, situated in the contexts that gave rise to them, I believe that it is also important to understand the forms of ideology that were present and remain as part of ongoing oppression. When reading specific histories, as in multicultural literature—told from the historical perspective of the oppressed (not through a marginalized view written by the oppressor)—we read the product of a cultural artifact.

Expressly and plainly addressing the history of class, racial, and gender oppression in the United States—in their varying forms—appears to be a risk-taking position for those seeking to adopt a critical pedagogy. The failure to acknowledge a history of oppression may have impeded the progress of education in the United States for oppressed groups. For example, the ideological, historical, and social burden of racial oppression in American society is poorly admitted in education. In a recent work, Ladson-Billings (1994) argues that "while it is recognized that African-Americans make up a distinct racial group, the acknowledgment that this racial group has a distinct culture is still not recognized. It is presumed that African-American children are exactly like white children but just need a little extra help" (p. 9). Importantly, ideological positions that gave rise to oppression and the ideologies that have sustained them, when examined in light of their specific historical and social contexts, illustrate how intimately power and knowledge have worked together to limit access to literacy in the United States.

My use of a critical literacy approach to the teaching of multicultural literature emphasizes the various forms of ideologies as part of the contexts that underlie the relationship between power and knowledge in the United States. I believe that it is important that future teachers understand these relationships historically as well as currently. Teachers' understanding of the contexts that supported the writing of oppressed people will help them better inform their students and make wise decisions on instructional and evaluative materials. Reading the text, in the mechanical sense, is not a problem for the majority of secondary students. However, gaining an understanding and appreciation of the literature may be difficult for those new to multicultural literature. Freire, among others, suggests that literacy is more than the construction of meaning from print: Literacy must also include the ability to understand oneself and one's relationship to the world. I support his thinking and in my course require a fresh reading of historical and social contexts of oppressed people. That is, I use the voices of the oppressed, as told through their literature, to foreground a study of multicultural literature.

While Freire offers a compelling argument for adopting a critical literacy position as a matter of policy, he does not offer suggestions for its implementation. Adopting a critical literacy stance does not come with a manual. In fact, he is concerned about the translation of "purist" notions into some sort of method. Thus I have relied heavily on the work of Shor, among others, to create a multicultural literature course for preservice teacher educators. In a broad sense the use of multicultural literature as inquiry, even in the exploration of issues of diversity, is not an innovation on my part. Current research in the area of multicultural literature by Harris (1992), Barrera (1992), Spears-Bunton (1992), Bishop (1992), Au (1993), Diamond and Moore (1995), among others, emphasizes the importance of using multicultural literature for understanding cultural differences, building community, and preparing students for the twenty-first century. Multicultural literature, however, should not be limited to use with traditionally underrepresented groups. The use of multicultural literature can be empowering to all children since it offers a more expansive context for students than the traditional literary canon. Moreover, multicultural literature can include differences that arise within race, class, and gender writings.

My course is in a constant state of redesign. With each new class comes a review of the histories underrepresented in most U.S. curriculums and, thus, new challenges. I begin, as Giroux (1987a) suggests, by reinventing the literature curriculum for preservice secondary English majors. My reading of Freire and Macedo (1995) suggests that they would be in agreement with my creation of a critical pedagogy that encourages preservice teachers to adopt a multicultural perspective toward literature. A brief overview of some of the barriers to curriculum reform will prove insightful.

THE MULTICULTURAL LITERATURE CURRICULUM:
BARRIERS TO REFORM

James Banks (1994) suggests that in preparing teachers for increasingly culturally and linguistically diverse student populations teacher educators need "to acquire an understanding of the meaning of cultural and ethnic diversity in complex Western societies, to examine and clarify their racial and ethnic attitudes, and to develop the pedagogical knowledge and skills needed to work effectively with students from diverse cultural and ethnic groups" (p. vi). This is a rather tall order for teacher educators. In the field of English/language arts there are several issues that complicate a smooth transition of multicultural literature from teacher educator to student and from teacher to student: (1) the demographics of teacher educators, (2) the history of English methods courses, (3) the teaching of the canon, and (4) the issue of diversity in literacy education for preservice teachers.

Demographics of Teacher Educators

Most preservice teachers have very limited experiences with diverse populations. As Fuller's (1992) statistics reveal, the majority of the preservice teachers are European American (92%), female (75%), and middle-class (80%), and most grew up in suburbs, small cities, or rural areas (80%). Preparing students to meet diverse school populations will require more than a tourist approach (Sleeter, 1994) to multicultural education. Students will need knowledge, experiences, and skills to effectively conduct classroom dialogues that support democratic values and include the language and literature of increasingly diverse student populations. Multicultural education is needed by all students. It is imperative, in a pluralistic society, to help preservice teachers acquire experiences and skills that will allow them to understand multiple perspectives, multiple voices, and multiple ways of knowing.

A History of English Methods

The training of English educators has a long history of maintaining the status quo. Graff's (1992) findings of the undergraduate English curricula offered nationwide suggest that there has been little substantive change in the literature offered to English majors since 1965. Generally, the literature that dominates college and high school English curricula offers a very narrow view of the world, one that is not part of the cultural schema of every student. Giovanni (1994) declares:

> In the universities we have seen white men declare time and time again that they cannot teach women, they cannot teach Blacks, they cannot teach Native Americans, because they do not have any "experience" in this area. Yet we who are Black and women and not white males are expected to teach literature written by them because it is "universal"? I think not. It is called education because it is learned. You do not have to have had an experience in order to sympathize or empathize with the subject. (p. 109)

Research by Bonnie Sustein and Janet Smith (1994) on the use of methods textbooks over a 75-year period indicates that the discussion of the teaching of the literary canon as part of English methods instruction has had a cyclical history. Debates over the selections to include have been waged since the late 1800s. They cite the earliest "standard authors" list, issued by Harvard in 1874, as the beginning of the debate. The debate has considered student choice, minority literature, and gender issues but has not changed significantly. They discuss the difference between English methods courses that reflect the need for change and the lethargic response of publishers to adopt change. Finally, they expose the difficulty encountered by English majors as they try to make sense of opposing forces:

> [O]ur preservice teachers arrive in our methods courses not only with institutionalized values about what literature makes them successful in school, but with a treasury of other reading experiences which broadens their personal definition of "literature" and "great books." (p. 53)

This is not the case just in English methods courses. Research by Au (1993) notes that most preservice teacher education courses are dominated by traditional transmission models of literacy instruction that support a mainstream middle-class perspective of literacy and inadequately address the needs of culturally or linguistically diverse students. Preservice teachers need to be taught strategies to help make implicit cultural knowledge explicit for students reading outside of their culture. These strategies need to permeate all teacher training courses.

The Literary Canon

When considering teaching English at the secondary level, there is a tacit assumption that, with varying degrees of competence, all secondary students have mastered the mechanics of reading. What becomes more important at this stage is not teaching students how to read, but helping them understand what they read. Many researchers believe that this begins with helping students make a connection between what they read and their personal lives. No teacher can be assured that all students will always be able to make a connection between the assigned reading and their life experiences; however, continued use of the literary canon assures that the experiences of underrepresented groups will remain unvoiced and marginalized in school settings. Multicultural literature clearly offers a wide range of literature choice for teachers. The selection of literature has been at the heart of the debates in the culture wars. Gates (1992) has pointed out that this is where the debates in the culture wars get messy: Whose values are most important for the succeeding generations to emulate? Gates (1992) argues:

> [T]he teaching of literature *is* the teaching of values; not inherently, no, but contingently, yes; it is—it has become—the teaching of an aesthetic and political order in which no women or people of color were able to discover the reflection or representation of their images, or hear the resonances of their cultural voices. The return of "the" canon, the high canon of Western masterpieces, represents the return of an order in which my people were subjugated, the voiceless, the invisible, the unrepresented, and the unrepresentable. (p. 35)

The most comprehensive look at secondary literature curricula is offered by Arthur Applebee (1993) in his current text *Literature in the Secondary School: Studies of Curriculum and Instruction in the United States*. In this text he examines literature and literature instruction in public and private schools. Applebee notes that literature instruction includes a variety of facets, but none so important as the book-length works used to convey a sense of who and what literature is important to study.

Applebee's (1989, 1992) nationwide survey reports the consistent use of canonical literature in our nation's high schools. He cites the continual use of works by Shakespeare, Steinbeck, Dickens, and Twain, yet few works by women and minority authors. (Similar traditional approaches to high school literature had been observed by Tanner [in Applebee, 1989] and Anderson [in Applebee, 1989]). Further analysis by Applebee of his findings reveals only one European American female author and two African American authors (one female, one male) among the top 50 listed authors. Applebee (1992) draws several important conclusions from his study:

1. A comparison of the studies reveals little change in the nature of the selections in the 25-year period.
2. There have been only marginal increases in titles by women and diverse authors.

3. Few book-length works by women and diverse authors have entered the canon.

If Applebee's conclusions about the importance of book-length works is correct, students are receiving a very narrow view of what literature, values, and people are important. As Applebee (1991) puts it, "Whether intentional or not, schools have chosen to ignore diversity and assimilate everyone to the classical culture that found its way into schools before the turn of the century" (p. 235). He goes on to state that "we are failing in a fundamental way to open the gates of literacy to the majority of the students we teach" (p. 235). Applebee's conclusions suggest that the literature used in classrooms today does not offer the best possible link with the children who are required to read it daily. His conclusions are supported in the research of Barrera (1992) and Diamond and Moore (1995), among others. Applebee offers suggestions for change that include the challenge of expanding the canon to be more reflective of the history, life experiences, culture, and literature of all Americans. Applebee argues that the expansion of the canon begin with preservice programs that require students to read and discuss book-length works written by authors of underrepresented groups. Moreover, Applebee suggests that preservice English courses may help students develop a repertoire of effective teaching strategies to use when teaching the literature. Although I support Applebee's suggestions for an updated canon that is more inclusive and the improved training of preservice English teachers, I believe his argument can be strengthened by offering a framework in which preservice teachers can be educated.

Additionally, Applebee's suggestion for canon expansion does not acknowledge the need for increased understanding of the complex issues surrounding the ideological, historical, and social contexts of multicultural literature. Such expansion without sufficient understanding of the contexts will give preservice teachers inadequate knowledge with which to instruct students. Expansion of the literary canon should be accompanied by a rearticulated theory that includes an understanding of the ideological, historical, and social contexts. If we as a nation are committed to the democratic values we espouse and to the development of a more just society, teacher training can be a starting point for change.

Substantiating Applebee's findings, Karen Peterson (1994) reports on a recent College Board survey citing the following 20 books and plays as those most frequently recommended for high school seniors and college freshmen: *The Scarlet Letter, Huckleberry Finn, The Great Gatsby, Lord of the Flies, Great Expectations, Hamlet, To Kill a Mockingbird, The Grapes of Wrath, The Odyssey, Wuthering Heights, The Catcher in the Rye, The Crucible, Gulliv-*

er's *Travels, Julius Caesar, Of Mice and Men, The Old Man and the Sea, Pride and Prejudice, The Red Badge of Courage, Romeo and Juliet,* and *Death of a Salesman.* According to spokesman Fred Moreno, The College Board examined curriculum guides, private school reading lists, research surveys, federal reports, and other sources in conducting the survey. A review of the titles shows that the list favors the literature of European or European American males and includes only three titles by women authors. The list does not include any works by authors from historically underrepresented groups. The marginalization of the works by women and people of color even prompted the well-known traditionalist E. D. Hirsch to observe that "this is a very traditional list that doesn't reflect new thinking. . . . It is clearly defective in not including books such as *Black Boy* (Richard Wright), *Song of Solomon* (Toni Morrison) and *I Know Why the Caged Bird Sings* (Maya Angelou)" (quoted in Peterson, 1994, p. 17). He later predicted that it may take another decade before the list is more representative. It is not clear from the article what has prompted Hirsch to alter his position on the use of multicultural literature.

ADDRESSING ISSUES OF DIVERSITY IN THE TRAINING OF PRESERVICE TEACHERS

Research in the area of literacy by Delpit (1988), Barrera (1992), and Reyes (1992), among others, has suggested that teacher education courses may offer the best opportunity to make significant inroads into how literacy is redefined and taught. Barrera (1992) argues that there is a desperate need to fill in what she refers to as a "cultural knowledge gap" (p. 227). Barrera argues that teachers need to improve their understanding of culture in three specific domains: cultural knowledge, cross-cultural knowledge, and multicultural knowledge. This cultural knowledge is needed by teachers to meet the literacy needs of all students, but most especially those of culturally and linguistically diverse children. Barrera's argument finds support in recent research by Reyes (1992) that indicates the importance of not assuming that theories of literacy designed with a homogeneous cultural group somehow magically meet needs of diverse cultural groups. Diamond and Moore's (1995) longitudinal study of multicultural literacy issues, the most complete to date, suggests that "teachers need additional cultural and social knowledge as they work with increasing numbers of students from varied cultural and linguistic backgrounds" (p. ix). The call for increased cultural and social knowledge can be met during preservice teacher training.

As stated earlier, my response to meeting the needs of preparing teachers for future generations of learners has been the development of a multicultural literature course that sees literature as an artifact of cultural production. To better understand this viewpoint, let us begin with a definition of multicultural literature. Harris (1992) defines multicultural literature as literature that focuses on people of color (such as African Americans, Asian Americans, Hispanic Americans, and Native Americans), on religious minorities (such as the Amish or Jews), on regional cultures (such as Appalachian and Cajun), on the disabled, and on the aged. This definition fits well with my notions for developing a better understanding of the historical, ideological, and social contexts of oppressed groups. Moreover, the definition is broad enough to include variance in the broad categories of race and class. Gender issues are not defined separately but are subsumed under race and class. The definition also includes forms of difference (religious, regional, etc.) that are often unmentioned.

I am fortunate to work at a university that respects and honors attempts to work collaboratively among departments. I teach what is known, informally, as the "combined course." The course is so called because it combines high school literature and reading methods for grades 9–12. The English Department agreed to permit me to teach the course if I would agree not to delete all the dead white men (their words) from the reading list. I actually found this quite funny, but in all fairness, the concerns of select members of the English Department are quite valid. There has been constant, often heated, debate in the professional and public literature over the literary canon. I had no intention of excluding the works of these men; however, I did not intend to make their works the center of my attention or concern. I do not take an either/or position on the canon debate. It seems to me that there is enough literature for expanded notions of the canon to include both "Western classics" and multicultural literature.

CREATING A MULTICULTURAL LITERATURE COURSE FOR PROSPECTIVE ENGLISH TEACHERS

How I translate critical pedagogy and the recent research on the instruction and use of multicultural literature to preservice teachers is the subject of this section. How is a teacher to know which literature to select? How is it that certain works of literature are valued more than others? If literature reflects the language, life experiences, values, interests, and beliefs we hold dear, whose values are celebrated and learned? Whose values are not? In a pluralistic society, should we recognize, read, and learn about the multiple voices that represent literary contributions? Or is there one set of readings that form American literature? The question of what becomes part of the curriculum, then, becomes what Giroux (1987b) calls "a battleground over whose forms of knowledge, history, visions, language and culture, and authority will prevail as a legitimate object of learning and analysis" (pp. 19–20). In my course students are offered an alternative to the traditional course on literature for the high school in that they are required to read multicultural literature.

Questions may arise as to the willingness of high school and college students to read multicultural literature. Research by Beach (1994; Chapter 3, this volume), among others, suggests that white high school and college students often have negative reactions to multicultural literature. However, Spears-Bunton's (1992) study of the use of multicultural literature with African American and European American students proposes that literacy lessons can be used to alter students' negative responses to multicultural literature. Her research found that some European American students were forced to rethink some of their previously held stereotypical notions of African Americans as a result of reading and discussing literature written by African Americans. Importantly, Spears-Bunton's study reveals that the responses of African American students to literature written by African Americans improved their self-esteem, involvement, and performance. She states that African American students "personally identified with the language, theme, characterization and world view of the text" (p. 394). From her study, Spears-Bunton concludes that there are "multiple ways in which the students took ownership of the process and products of their reading and the ways in which they used their reading of the text in combination of their reading of the world to construct meaning" (p. 400). The willingness of all students to read and respond to multicultural literature may be a product of the classroom environment, the instructional strategies used, students' option to enroll in the course, the specific works included, and students' educational background (Beach, 1994).

The need for a multicultural pedagogy that is transforming is perhaps best captured by bell hooks (1993). She articulates the need in this manner:

> Despite the contemporary focus on multiculturalism in our society, particularly in education, there is not nearly enough practical discussion of ways classroom settings can be transformed so that the learning experience is inclusive. If the effort to respect and honor the social reality and experiences of groups in this society who are non-White is to be reflected in a pedagogical

process, then as teachers on all levels, from elementary to university settings, we must acknowledge that our styles of teaching may need to change. (p. 91)

An Alternative Approach to English Methods

New holistic approaches to literacy have influenced the ways in which literature and language arts courses are taught in preservice teacher education. Reading and writing workshops, journal writing, reading logs, literature circles, reader responses, and portfolios are becoming commonplace. Yet the actual literature required has changed little (Applebee, 1989; Graff, 1992). Despite an increase in the number of books written and published by authors from groups that have been historically underrepresented in the canon, multicultural literature still does not have a permanent place in high school or college curriculums. I submit that to continue to maintain the literary canon means to ignore the needs of culturally and linguistically diverse students and to ignore the literary contributions of their forefathers and foremothers. Soon this will mean ignoring the needs of the majority of the students in our classrooms. Maintenance of the literary canon also suggests that teacher-training institutions are ill preparing a future teaching force to adapt to the changes in student populations.

An excellent reference for developing instructional strategies, grounded in Freirean theory, is Ira Shor's (1987) *Freire for the Classroom.* I have adopted and adapted several instructional strategies described in the text for my course. A number of activities that students engage in on the first day of class sets the tone for participation and dialogue for the remainder of the semester. My goal throughout the course is to model practice that is worthy of emulation. For example, the first day of class begins with oral self-introductions and oral responses to six questions requiring a sharing of personal preferences (e.g., what is your favorite color, animal, etc.). Each student is expected to participate and does so naturally. I, too, participate as a member of the class. Use of this introductory technique creates an early impression and atmosphere for the participatory nature of the course. Responses offered by the students are recorded and used throughout the course for small-group assignments.

Next, students are asked to list every book they have ever read that was written by a person of color. Responses to this activity vary with each student's tastes in academic and pleasure reading. Their responses reveal that, as English majors, my students are familiar with canonical literature but less familiar with multicultural literature. The first day ends with students responding to the following question: "How does your cultural perspective affect the students you teach?" (Hansen-Krening, 1992, p. 125; permission to use this question was granted in a personal communication with Nancy Hansen-Krening). Written responses to this activity also vary in length and completeness. However, generally all students try to give a response they believe answers the questions. A few responses will help to illustrate my point:

STUDENT A

I have so often heard people say that they are not biased, or prejudiced, and are completely open-minded to everyone and their perspectives. I suppose we'd all like to believe that we are without fault and values that maybe aren't so liberating. The truth is that we all contain within ourselves a very unique set of values and perspectives that have developed largely from what we have experienced in our lives.

STUDENT B

My own cultural perspective, because it shapes who I am in the classroom, will affect my students. I am a mixed-blood Central American Indian, Mexican, and Western European. . . . I do have a cultural point of view; despite working at being open-minded, my beliefs and values may conflict with [my] students values.

STUDENT C

I believe that your cultural perspective has a significant impact on the students that you teach. As a teacher you will interact daily with students from various cultural backgrounds who have various ideas and beliefs. It is important for a teacher to not only respect each student and his or her background but also to have some understanding of the students' cultures and the personalities that accompany their cultural perspective.

I repeat this final activity on the last day of class. Content analysis of the students' precourse/postcourse responses reveals how their thinking and attitudes have changed over the course of the semester as they have explored multicultural issues and multicultural literature.

Students are also required to write two autobiographies. In the first autobiographic sketch they are to trace their families' cultural and linguistic heritage back four or five generations. This activity is always quite revealing to students, since most young people know little of their family history beyond their maternal and paternal grandparents. Each year I am amazed as students discover who they really are as a person from long-distance calls around the country to parents and relatives. An example helps to illustrate this point. In a concluding paragraph, a female student observed:

> It is often asked what we second-generation "Korean Americans" consider ourselves as Korean or American. It's a difficult question to answer because our "Korean-ness" and our "American-ness" are in conflict. We cannot consider ourselves as fully Korean because we were born and raised in America. At the same time, however, it is also difficult to say we are fully "American" for a number of reasons. First, the families, cultures, customs, traditions, and lifestyles are not typically "American." They are, in fact, very different from some of the traditional American customs people have held since the beginning of American history. Secondly, our outward appearance must confuse people into thinking that we are foreigners to the American way of life. Lastly, it is just plain difficult to define what "American" really is, especially now, in the X-generation and the politically correct wave of thought.

The discovery of our varied cultural backgrounds is shared in small groups. Volunteers may share with the whole class any portion of their autobiographic sketch. I also share my autobiographic sketch with the class. While I appear to be an African American female, most of my students are also surprised to learn that my lineage includes English and French slave owners who fathered my grandparents. Moreover, they are amazed to learn that I have an Irish great-grandfather who married his African slave and a great-grandmother who was a Cherokee Indian (full-blooded). After sharing our autobiographic information, students are more aware of the variety of histories, languages, cultural values, and culturally mediated traditions that each of us brings to the classroom.

Students are also asked to write autobiographies of their school literacy experiences. Britzman (1986) describes the experiences that preservice teachers bring with them as "their implicit institutional biographies—the cumulative experience of school lives—which, in turn, informs [sic] their knowledge of the student's world, school structure, and of curriculum" (p. 443). Students have shared memories that include learning to read and write, their favorite childhood books, and experiences in junior and senior high school language arts classes. The most hurtful memories tend to be those associated with being placed in a low reading group or being asked to read aloud in class. For most students, it is their college experiences that have provided the most diverse settings for literacy instruction.

An Alternative to the Canon

The literature selected for my course centers on the literature produced by groups who have historically been underrepresented in the canon and also includes literature produced by European American males and females. I have created a technique I call *freedom within structure* in selecting the titles to be reviewed and chosen for class readings. Each year I update a list of multicultural titles by following an adapted version of guidelines for the selection of multicultural titles offered by Rudine Sims Bishop (1992). I also read widely, ask for recommendations from colleagues and local high school English teachers, browse in bookstores, and scan lists of award-winning books for young adults. While it is impossible to have read every book written, it is necessary to make some decisions about what the students are asked to read. Furthermore, in an effort to support my notion of literature as an artifact of cultural production, I offer my students a list of titles that I believe can be used to uncover the ideological, historical, and social contexts of oppression. Hence students have the *freedom* to select which titles to read, yet I have supplied a *structure* that supports my pedagogical position. With these parameters in mind, below is a sample of the title list I distribute. This is by no means an exhaustive listing of all the available multicultural titles. Please note that on this abbreviated list I have included European and European American authors as well as works by women in each cultural group.

EUROPEAN AND EUROPEAN AMERICAN TEXTS

Growing Up, Russell Baker
The Great Gatsby, F. Scott Fitzgerald
The Outsiders, S. E. Hinton
Death of a Salesman, Arthur Miller
The Optimist's Daughter, Eudora Welty

AFRICAN AMERICAN TEXTS

I Know Why the Caged Bird Sings, Maya Angelou
Narrative of the Life of an American Slave, Frederick Douglass
The Autobiography of Malcolm X, Malcolm X with Alex Haley
Their Eyes Were Watching God, Zora Neale Hurston
The Darkside of Hopkinsville, Ted Poston with Kathleen Hauke

ASIAN AMERICAN TEXTS

Donald Duk, Frank Chin
The Year of Impossible Good-byes, Sook Nyul Choi
The Floating World, Cynthia Kadohata
The Joy Luck Club, Amy Tan
Farwell to Manzanar, Jeanne Wakatsuki Houston and James D. Houston

LATINO/A TEXTS

Bless Me, Ultima, Rudolfo Anaya
The Last of the Menu Girls, Denise Chavez
Chronicle of a Death Foretold, Gabriel Garcia-Marquez
Silent Dancing: A Partial Remembrance of a Puerto Rican Childhood,
    Judith Ortiz Cofer
Days of Obligation, Richard Rodriguez

NATIVE AMERICAN TEXTS

Ceremony, Leslie Silko
Two Old Women, Velma Wallis
House Made of Dawn, N. Scott Momaday
Winter in the Blood, James Welch
The Education of Little Tree, Forrest Carter

My students receive a longer and more contemporary list than can be included in this chapter. The list includes literature that has been written by insiders (members of a minority group) and outsiders (people from outside the minority group about which they write); literature that offers a balanced representation of specific cultures and literature that does not; and literature that is appropriate for grades 9–12 and literature that is not. The literature that is not appropriate for grades 9–12 (usually adult novels or novels that are stereotypical or written by those outside the culture) is generally unknown to the students. I have "planted" the literature in the list so that the students can discover areas of concern. My goal is to have them read carefully enough to be concerned about the inclusion of multicultural literature that may be seen as problematic when used in school settings. When questions arise in class, out of discovery and concern, we have some very lively discussions.

Course readings begin with European and European American novels. Situating the ideological, historical, and social contexts of the novels is easiest at this point. For the most part, the contexts are familiar to the students, since these works have been the meat of their literature and history courses to date. However, as we begin to venture into the other groups, students bring far less understanding and knowledge about the history and literature of underrepresented cultural groups as a whole. Moreover, they lack information and understanding of the groups as part of U.S. history. Having students supply the ideological, historical, and social contexts for discussions of the novels is important for their understanding of the literature.

Cultural Production of African American Literature

A history of the genesis of African American literature offers an excellent example of literature as an artifact of cultural production. It is imperative that members of each new generation know and understand these roots before approaching the task of teaching them to the next generation. Many of the early Africans brought to the New World were kidnapped from the shores of western Africa. It is difficult to pinpoint one dominant language of the people from this region, for many languages were spoken. Although diverse languages and cultures existed among various African clans, there were also commonalities. There were, however, few written languages. Because these were predominantly oral societies, the literature and history of each tribe of west Africa was also oral. Franklin and Moss (1994), two respected experts on the history of African Americans, declare that "the oral literature was composed of supernatural tales, moral tales, proverbs, epic poems, satires, love songs, funeral marches, and comic tales" (p. 23). The oral literature that grew from their everyday activities served many functions in the African way of life, such as to educate, govern, and entertain. Bell (1987) suggests that the varying forms of verbal art used helped to

> transmit knowledge, value, and attitudes from one generation to another, enforce conformity to social norms, validate social institutions and religious rituals, and provide psychological release from the restrictions of society. (p. 16)

As men, women, and children were kidnapped, sold, transmitted, and resold to colonists in the New World, old folkways, languages, rituals, and beliefs gave way to acculturation to a new language and way of life.

Initially African slaves were brought as indentured servants who could work to earn or purchase their freedom, as many of them did. They also bought property and initially lived as other groups did, even enjoying some political rights. However, as the economic demand for increased labor mounted and more African slaves were brought to the colonies, the more stringent laws became in forcing people of African descent into servitude. The rights, land, and property of the "free" African Americans were not protected by the laws of the colonies—nor was their freedom. Any slave owner could, in effect, rescind any promise of freedom, land, or property. An analysis of class, or of economic social constructions, cannot account for the continued racial oppression endured by the African Americans.

There is a long and unfaltering history of legal barriers to literacy acquisition—from the enactment of Virginia slave codes in 1636 to the 1990 court battles over Africentric schools in major U.S. cities with large African American school populations. Using one of the earliest slave codes as an example will help to illustrate this point. One of the laws in the slave codes called for maintaining control over the travel of slaves in order to limit the number runaways and to prevent revolts. Slaves were required to have written permission to travel away from the master's property. It was reasoned that since slaves could not read or write they could not produce written travel documents, and thus slave owners were assured of maintaining control. Further, it was reasoned that if slaves became literate they would no longer submit to the inhumane treatment of slavery. Barksdale and Kinnamon (1972) suggest that it is important to understand the circumstances of America's "peculiar institution" in situating African American literature. They note that "slavery had the negative effect of divesting Africans of a substantial portion of their own culture [and] denied Blacks the opportunity and the occasion to create written literature" (p. 2). There were, of course, exceptions to the enforced illiteracy of slaves. There were some "benevolent" slave owners who allowed their slaves to acquire literacy skills. Most common among this group of slaves were the children of the slave owner and a slave woman.

An analysis of the early writings of people of African descent after their capture and arrival in the New World notes how Africans adapted the language, style, and genres of European American writings with their own interpretations. The early writings also depict a longing for freedom and their homeland in the midst of their inescapable lives as slaves. One of the most important genres of African American literature began during the eighteenth century with the publication of fugitive slave narratives. These were most similar to autobiographies which were popular during this period. Stepto (1984) has called the slave narrative the beginning of "the creation of an Afro-American fiction based upon the conventions of slave narratives" (p. 178). Two popular themes in slave narratives were the need for self-actualization through literacy and the call for literacy to help stay the hand of the oppressor. Thus literacy was linked to the fight for individual and group liberation from the ideology of a slave-owning society. The fugitive slave Frederick Douglass best captures the sentiment of slave holders' perception of the threat of liberation through literacy acquisition. In his autobiography, Douglass (1845/1968) quotes the objection of one of his masters, Mr. Auld, to his being taught to read:

> A nigger should know nothing but to obey his master—to do what he is told to do. Learning would soil the best nigger in the world. "Now," said he, "if you teach that nigger (speaking of myself) how to read would be no keeping him. It would forever unfit him to be a slave. He would at once become unmanageable, and of no value to his master." (p. 49)

Douglass's literacy acquisition is pivotal to his understanding of freedom in two important ways. Literacy freed Douglass intellectually and allowed him to use the language of the oppressor to state his case (Smith, 1987). Smith observes another important issue unveiled in Douglass's narrative. She writes that "Frederick Douglass' narrative participates in one of the major ideological controversies of his day, the dispute over the question of Negro humanity and equality" (p. 21). The ideological controversy continues in the misunderstanding of the role of ideology in shaping the social and political constructs of race and how they are actualized in U.S. society. I have used this short historical perspective to make explicit the role of race in the cultural production of literacy.

It is my belief that there is no escaping the centrality of race and class as key factors in the politics of literacy acquisition and in the production of a unique literature as a cultural artifact in the United States. W. E. B. DuBois (1903/1989) prophetically declared:

> This history of the American Negro is the history of this strife,—this longing to attain self-conscious manhood, to merge his double self into a better and truer self. In this merging he wishes neither of the older selves to be lost. He would not Africanize America, for America has too much to teach the world and Africa. He would not bleach his Negro soul in a flood of white Americanism, for he knows that Negro blood has a message for the world. He simply wishes to make it possible for a man to be both a Negro and an American. (p. 3)

Although the above description is helpful in the understanding of the racial and class oppression of the African American male, it does not reveal the special case of oppression that can be made for African American women. In contextualizing their oppression it would be necessary to include the sexual exploitation to which many women were subjected. The only accounts available that tell of the ideological position of a society that would tolerate forced concubinage, of the privilege of white women and their children over the black family of the slave owner, and of the breakup of families—sold to other slaveowners—can be found in the writings of slave women. The few fugitive slave writings by African American women (*Our Nig*, by Harriet E. Wilson, and *Incidents in the Life of a Slave Girl*, by Harriet Jacobs) are not included on traditional lists. Yet they, too, tell a story of oppression—one that crosses race, class, and gender lines. Similar historical, social, ideological, and cultural contextualizing is done by the students for each novel they read.

As students share their written responses to the novels and their investigations into the ideological, historical, and social contexts of the novels, it often becomes clear that they are working from a narrow understanding of the history of oppression in the United States. Moreover, their written responses reveal that, for most of them, their college lives, both academically and socially, are the most diverse settings they have ever experienced. It is in discussions of the contexts of multicultural literature that unvoiced assumptions about culture, class, and power begin to be recognized and addressed. Many students seem unaware of the ideological, historical, and social privilege they have experienced in an educational system designed to support Eurocentric views of history, norms, and values. It is difficult for the students to examine the ideological, historical, social, and institutional structures that have aided their success. McIntosh (1989) argues that "absence of a racial discourse on whiteness reinforces the widely accepted myth that whiteness is morally neutral, normal, and average, and also ideal" (p. 2).

King (1991) suggests that some preservice teachers may unknowingly bring with them dysconscious racism. She defines dysconscious racism as

> a form of racism that tacitly accepts dominant White norms and privileges. It is not the *absence* of consciousness (that is, not unconsciousness) but an *impaired* consciousness or distorted way of thinking about race as compared to, for example, critical consciousness. (p. 135)

Many students have not considered their whiteness. One student writes:

> I have always considered myself to be very open-minded, not racist. Now I realize that I can, or do, carry around certain stereotypes even though I have good friends from many cultures. It is a hard thing to admit . . . white racism is hard for people to talk about because racism is usually hushed up. People do not like to claim responsibility for some of their ideas. I do not choose to carry around some of mine—they were handed down to me, not necessarily by parents but by [the] environment. By sharing these misconceptions

aloud and acknowledging them for what they are, it may be easier to dispel them.

I believe it is important for students to begin to assess their personal responses to their newfound knowledge of the larger ideological, historical, and social contexts that are part of a history of oppression in the United States. Moreover, it is important for students to reflect upon their responses to multicultural literature as they anticipate teaching others. As an artifact of the process of cultural production, multicultural literature can be the heart or source for rearticulating literacy.

The class has been challenged and required to consider the relationship among notions of ideology, culture, and history through their explorations of multicultural literature as an artifact of cultural production. Student voice, whether written or oral, continues throughout the semester, as on the first day, to be an important and welcome facet of the course. From the first day's sharing of personal preferences to later sharing of students' responses to text (both oral and written) during discussions, we have grown. The students have not come to the course as tabulae rasae, nor should they expect to leave without gaining some knowledge. Acknowledgment of the history, attitudes, and sometimes baggage we bring to class helps to move us toward change. This acknowledgment also allows us to deconstruct the past and build toward a shared understanding of the present as we plan for the future. Therefore it is necessary to include students' cumulative social experience—as they understand and analyze it—as part of the content of the classroom discussion (Britzman, 1986; Florio-Ruane, 1994; Giroux, 1987a). In small-group discussions and in small working groups based on responses given the first day of class, students begin to negotiate the meaning of multicultural literature, often extending their knowledge and understandings to personal and work situations. Small groups learn to work and cooperate as they select novels to read and write individual response during the semester. Small-group discussions follow the reading of each novel and the sharing of written responses. It is during the small-group discussions that students reveal their lack of historical, ideological, and cultural awareness. As a facilitator I often supply this information, but students who are more knowledgeable are encouraged to supply documentation of alternative views of history. For example, after a student wrote a response, she proudly shared it with her group. The response reflected her thinking (and later she explained her background). She was surprised to learn that in her small group, her response was in the minority. She sought to make others understand her point of view, citing historical references. They listen patiently and told her they understood but did not agree with her viewpoint. They shared their interpretations of the text and offered historical, political, and ideological data to support their claims. As a group they were required to summarize the text for the class. The student with the dissenting voice asked if she could reconsider her position. During the course of the class, she became an active listener to the opinions of others and more sensitive in her responses to text. Thus in small-group discussions students become aware of the multiple interpretations of text and the need to negotiate among themselves about the meaning of the text. After the small-group meetings we reconvene and share our readings, responses, and reflections with the class.

A CONTINUING PROCESS

The course I have described is based on a theory of critical literacy that views multicultural literature as an artifact of cultural production. The instruction and use of multicultural literature is designed to address the specific ideological, historical, and social contexts of the novels read. Using multicultural literature, I believe, offers preservice teachers some direct experiences in gaining knowledge about different ethnic and cultural perspectives. My hope is that the experiences will motivate preservice teachers to sensitively consider the decisions they make about the school literacy experiences they design and plan for their students.

I would like to continue this research by tracking former students through their student teaching experience and into the first year or two of teaching. It occurs to me that Giroux (1987b) is correct in assuming that schools are sites "where dominant and subordinate cultures collide and where teachers, students, and school administration often differ as to how schools' experiences and practices are to be defined" (p. 17). I would like to know of the support or resistance teachers face when they bring a critical literacy approach to the instruction and use of multicultural literature in the classroom. Several students have managed to stay in contact with me through their early careers. Recently a former student who uses many of the methods and materials from class wrote:

> I am teaching at West Somewhere High School. The school is 75% EuroAmerican and 25% Latino/a. Kids are the same in this small community as they are in a bigger one. I have an outside reading requirement of 3,000 pages over the course of the year, and students must select one book each quarter written by one of the authors that we used in your class. These kids are beginning to see outside of their own little world and get a look at situations that have not

been distorted by television. Many of the girls are "hooked" on the list of authors that I provided. One girl actually told me that I was the first teacher who had introduced any Hispanic authors to her and said I was the first teacher she has ever had who made her proud to be Hispanic, instead of ashamed of it.

Wouldn't it be grand if every child could be similarly influenced?

NOTE

My sincerest thanks to Ed Buendia, Eunice Greer, Robert Jimenez, Cameron McCarthy, and Shuiab Mechem, who read and critiqued earlier drafts of this chapter.

REFERENCES

Applebee, A. N. (1989). *A study of book-length works taught in high school English courses* (Report No. 1.2). Albany, NY: Center for the Learning and Teaching of Literature.

Applebee, A. N. (1991). Literature: Whose heritage? In E. Hiebert (Ed.), *Literacy for a diverse society: Perspectives, practices, and policies* (pp. 228–236). New York: Teachers College Press.

Applebee, A. N. (1992). Stability and change in the high school canon. *English Journal, 81*(5), 27–32.

Applebee, A. N. (1993). *Literature in the secondary school: Studies of curriculum and instruction in the United States.* Urbana, IL: National Council of Teachers of English.

Au, K. (1993). *Literacy instruction in multicultural settings.* Fort Worth, TX: Harcourt Brace.

Banks, J. (1994). *An introduction to multicultural education.* Boston: Allyn & Bacon.

Barksdale, R., & Kinnamon, K. (1972). *Black writers of America: A comprehensive anthology.* New York: Prentice-Hall.

Barrera, R. (1992). The cultural gap in literature-based literacy instruction. *Education and Urban Society, 24*(2), 227–243.

Beach, R. (1994, April). *Research on readers' response to multicultural literature.* Paper presented at the Annual Meeting of the American Educational Research Association, New Orleans.

Bell, B. (1987). *The Afro-American novel and its tradition.* Amherst: University of Massachusetts Press.

Bishop, R. (1992). Multicultural literature for children: Making informed choices. In V. Harris (Ed.), *Teaching multicultural literature in grades K–8* (pp. 37–54). Norwood, MA: Christopher-Gordon.

Britzman, D. (1986). Cultural myths in the making of a teacher: Biography and social structure in teacher education. *Harvard Educational Review, 56* (4), 442–456.

Delpit, L. (1988). The silenced dialogue: Power and pedagogy in educating other people's children. *Harvard Educational Review, 58,* 280–298.

Diamond, B., & Moore, M. (1995). *Multicultural literacy: Mirroring the reality of the classroom.* White Plains, NY: Longman.

Douglass, F. (1968). *Narrative of the life of Frederick Douglass: An American slave, written by himself.* New York, NY: Penguin Books. (Original work published 1845)

Du Bois, W. E. B. (1989). *The souls of black folks.* New York: Bantam. (Original work published 1903)

Florio-Ruane, S. (1994). The future teachers' autobiography club: Preparing educators to support literacy learning in culturally diverse classrooms. *English Education, 26,* 52–66.

Franklin, J., & Moss, A. (1994). *From slavery to freedom: A history of African Americans. Seventh Ed.* New York: McGraw-Hill.

Freire, P. (1970). *Pedagogy of the oppressed.* New York: Continuum.

Freire, P. (1994). Foreword to Macedo, D., *Literacies of power: What Americans are not allowed to know.* Boulder, CO: Westview.

Freire, P., & Macedo, D. (1995). A dialogue: Culture, language, and race. *Harvard Educational Review, 65*(3), 377–402.

Freire, P., & Macedo, D. (1987). *Literacy: Reading the word and the world.* Westport, CT: Bergin & Garvey.

Fuller, D. (1992). Monocultural teachers and multicultural students: A demographic clash. *Teaching Education, 4*(2), 87–93.

Gates, H. (1992). *Loose canons: Notes on the culture wars.* New York: Oxford University Press.

Giovanni, N. (1994). *Racism 101.* New York: Morrow.

Giroux, H. (1987a). Critical literacy and student experience: Donald Graves' approach to literacy. *Language Arts, 64,* 175–181.

Giroux, H. (1987b). Introduction. In P. Freire & D. Macedo (Eds.), *Literacy: Reading the word and the world* (pp. 1–27). Westport: CT: Bergin & Garvey.

Graff, G. (1992). *Beyond the culture wars: How teaching the conflicts can revitalize American education.* New York: W. W. Norton.

Hansen-Krening, N. (1992). Authors of color: A multicultural perspective. *Journal of Reading, 36*(2), 124–129.

Harris, V. (Ed.). (1992). *Teaching multicultural literature in grades K–8.* Norwood, MA: Christopher-Gordon.

hooks, b. (1993). Transformative pedagogy and multiculturalism. In T. Perry & J. Fraser (Eds.), *Freedom's plow: Teaching in the multicultural classrooms* (pp. 91–97). New York: Routledge.

King, J. (1991). Dysconscius racism: Ideology, identity, and the miseducation of teachers. *Journal of Negro Education, 60*(2), 133–146.

Ladson-Billings, G. (1994). *The dreamkeepers: Successful teachers of African American children.* San Francisco: Jossey-Bass.

Macedo, D. (1994). *Literacies of power: What Americans are not allowed to know.* Boulder, CO: Westview.

McIntosh, P. (1989, July/August). White privilege: Unpacking the invisible knapsack. *Peace and Freedom*, pp. 10–12.

Peterson, K. (1994, December 27). "Scarlet letter has 'A' position on reading lists." *USA Today*, p. 16.

Reyes, M. (1992). Challenging venerable assumptions: Literacy instruction for linguistically different students. *Harvard Educational Review, 62,* 427–446.

Shor, I. (1987). (Ed.). *Freire for the classroom: A sourcebook for liberatory teaching.* Portsmouth, NH: Boynton/Cook.

Sleeter, C. (1994). White racism. *Multicultural Education, 1,* 5–39.

Smith, N. B. (1987). *Self-discovery and authority in Afro-American narrative.* Cambridge, MA: Harvard University Press.

Spears-Bunton, L. (1992). Literature, literacy, and resistance to cultural domination. In C. Kinzer & D. Leu (Eds.), *Yearbook of the National Reading Conference: Vol. 41. Literacy research, theory, and practice: Views from many perspectives.* Alexandria, VA: National Reading Conference.

Stepto, R. (1984). Storytelling in early Afro-American fiction: Frederick Douglass's "The heroic slave." In Henry Louis Gates, Jr. (Ed.), *Black literature and literary theory* (pp. 177–180). New York: Methuen.

Sustein, B., & Smith, J. (1994). Attempting a graceful waltz on a teeter totter: The canon and English methods courses. *English Journal, 83*(8), 47–54.

Willis, A. (1995). Reading the world of school literacy: Contextualizing the experience of a young African-American male. *Harvard Educational Review, 65*(1), 30–49.

CHAPTER 7

Reflections on Cultural Diversity in Literature and in the Classroom

LAURA E. DESAI

Do you feel safe when you visit your husband's family in New Delhi, India? I mean, isn't it dirty, overcrowded and dangerous? Can you talk to the people? Do they accept you?

— Conversation with author

WHILE I HAVE TAKEN some poetic license with the above quote so the reader will understand the context that framed its occurrence, it does capture the essence of a recent conversation. The questions, not meant to be offensive, were asked with a genuine desire for knowledge and understanding. My companion, aware only that India is a third-world country and extremely poor, could not imagine how I could enjoy or appreciate visits to my Indian in-laws. However, hers is not an unusual concern. A fourth-grade teacher, with whom I was speaking about my 10- and 15-year-old Indian nieces, expressed the assumption that once they had the opportunity to visit the United States they would be reluctant to return to India. Again, a comment made without malice—but perhaps also without an understanding of people and places beyond the borders of her own life.

While these incidents might be a reflection of a lack of understanding about a people and a place to some extent removed from the United States, I offer another personal example that has been a recurring experience throughout my life. While I would define myself as a white American woman, I could also add the term *Jewish* to the preceding cultural and ethnic description. However, over the years I have found that this final term can prompt a great deal of consternation for some. Apparently,

I do not look the part nor fit the stereotype that many hold of Jewish Americans. In fact, there have been times when people have vehemently argued that I could not possibility be Jewish. Again, I would suggest that these comments were uniformly made without apparent prejudice—but also without an understanding of someone from a background different from their own.

I have offered these personal anecdotes based on a belief in the importance of narrative. As noted by Connelly and Clandinin (1990), "education and educational research is the construction and reconstruction of personal and social stories; learners, teachers, and researchers are storytellers and characters in their own and other's stories" (p. 2). It is my own story that has prompted my interest in the role that the stories of others might play in the development of our students' multi-ethnic understandings. While there has been a great deal of support (Harris, 1991; Norton, 1985, 1990; Sims, 1982; Sims Bishop, 1990) for the role that literature plays in classroom instruction, and while many have suggested that multicultural literature can provide students with valuable examples of the unique differences among people while also highlighting the universality of the human experience, there has been little consideration of exactly how a child interacts with multicultural texts. How do the stories in the texts impact the stories that comprise the lives of our students? What is the link between multi-ethnic understanding, the classroom, and children's literature?

My choice of topic does not come by accident. It is shaped by who I was, who I am, and those I wish to affect who are in the process of becoming, as a result of their experience with literature. While I believe that literature has the power to enable children to experience more fully what they already know, as well as to be touched by people, situations, and events that they might otherwise never encounter, I am, as yet, uncertain as to how this happens. It is, however, a journey toward understanding on which we must embark. We need to carefully consider the issues that frame the discussion. If, as Rabinowitz (1987) suggests, the writer and reader exist as members of a shared social interpretive community, we need to determine the impact a society with multiple communities has on our interpretations and understanding of text. We need to look at the definitions of terms, the claims made about multicultural literature, and the studies that have framed our understandings. As we look at the role of culture in a reader's response, we must consider the multiple communities that frame our social, cultural, and political context, and we can then begin to consider the role that a teacher and the classroom play in this process.

THE POWER OF THE STORY

Joshua is 9 years old now, but he has been going to visit his grandmother almost every Sabbath since he was 5. These Sabbath visits are a special time, because not only does Joshua have the chance to help his grandma Goldina light the Sabbath candles, he also has the opportunity to hear her remembrances about the past. Through the objects in her remembering box he learns about his grandmother, her life, and their religion, a way of life that frames both their worlds. He also learns about the willow stick that can find water, the ribbons his grandmother placed in her horse Mazel's mane, the money kept in her knippel, and the silver bell that called the people of her childhood village to their Sabbath prayers.

Eth Clifford's (1985) *The Remembering Box* is a story about family love across the generations, but it is also about tradition and about a young boy who comes to realize the value of the past as well as the present. As such, it is a book that has the power to speak to all of us regardless of ethnic background, but I would suggest for those readers who happen to be Jewish, it can bring a smile, a tear, and a feeling of warmth.

How does this happen? What impact does culture have on a reader's response to a text? There are layers of meaning that we need to understand as we consider a reader's "cultured" response to a text. The search for an answer necessitates an understanding of the reading process, the notion of culture, and the nature of response. None of these concepts is simple, nor is there universal agreement regarding definitions of the terms. Consequently, before the question can begin to be answered, the terms must be unpacked and defined.

WHAT ARE CULTURE AND ETHNICITY?

Culture, or ethnicity, as defined here is an adaptive system, or the way of life of a particular human society, which is composed of learned, shared group behavior. Erlich (1990), an anthropologist, notes that anthropologists see culture as a survival mechanism for a way of life created by human groups. The paradox, as suggested by Erlich, is that while on the surface cultures appear to be all different, they are, in reality, all the same. They all represent "adaptations to similar demands of living a group existence" (p. 3) and are all organized around the same set of basic institutions: kinship, legal and political, religious, and economic. Each of these institutions is part of a set of integrated interrelationships, and, as a result, change within one institution will have repercussions in all other parts of the culture. Cultures are, therefore, systems that operate as a whole and that are continually adapting to specific environmental settings.

Banks (1979) defined ethnicity almost exactly as Erlich defined culture. His definition stated that "an ethnic group is an involuntary group which shares a heritage, kinship ties, a sense of identification, political and economic interests, and cultural and linguistic characteristics" (p. 239). On the other hand, he defined culture as consisting of "the behavior patterns, symbols, institutions, values and other human-made components of society" (p. 238). Based on these definitions, Banks suggested that "multi-ethnic education is also a form of multicultural education since an ethnic group is one kind of cultural group" (p. 239).

In *Teaching Strategies for Ethnic Studies,* Banks (1991) has expanded on these definitions and explanations of ethnicity and culture. He suggests that while ethnicity is an important part of American culture, there remains a strong American culture and identity. Using the phrases *microcultural groups, ethnic groups, ethnic minority groups,* and *people of color,* Banks suggests that there are many smaller groups within the American culture. He notes that "these microcultural groups share many characteristics with the common national group but have some distinguishing characteristics that set them apart from other cultural groups" (p. 14). He differentiates between these various group terms by suggesting that while microcultural groups are voluntary groups, an ethnic group is, for the most part, involuntary, although identification with that group may be optional. Ethnic minority groups are also ethnic groups but are groups with "a numerical minority that have minimal economic and political power" (p. 14). He makes one further distinction, which provides an explanation of race by saying that within an ethnic minority group there are people of color who are nonwhite and share unique physical and cultural characteristics. Finally, we exist in a global society in which the American culture is but one of many global cultures.

Given the strength of the American cultural identity as suggested by Banks, how do we incorporate in our classrooms, as well as in society itself, the multiple ethnic minority groups that exist as part of the American culture? At what point do we exist in a shared interpretive community and at what point does our cultural or ethnic affiliation become the lens through which we view our lives and their stories?

A young fifth-grade child sits quietly at her desk on what, even for Texas, is a somewhat warm November day in 1964. Suddenly her teacher asks if anyone in the class is Jewish and would be willing to bring in a menorah to help represent the upcoming Jewish holiday of Hanukkah. Our young student does not immediately raise her hand but considers her options. If the teacher does not know that she is Jewish, why should she admit something that has remained hidden for the past year and a half? On the other hand, what happens if her deception is uncovered? Slowly and extremely reluctantly, she raises her hand. No one in this class of 10-year-olds cares or for that matter really even notices, but a lingering question remains. Of what was I afraid? Why did I think it would matter that my religion or ethnic group differed from that of every other child in the classroom? Could something or someone have made a difference in my reaction?

VALUE OF MULTICULTURAL LITERATURE

"Literature," writes Itty Chan (1984),

> is a literary record of our collective human experience. It introduces us to other human beings, and invites us to share their lives—their thoughts and convictions, feelings, sufferings, and joys. Our outlook on life is broadened, our understanding of it deepened, and our own life takes on added meaning and significance as it is interpreted in the context of other lives. . . .
>
> Minority children too, seeing their own lives and cultures represented in the literature they read, will no longer feel that minority means insignificant or inferior, and will come to cherish their own cultural heritage, and be proud of it. (pp. 19–20)

Esther Jenkins (1973) writes:

> A multi-ethnic literature program which introduces each child to his own heritage along with that of others and which is flexible enough to allow him to sample according to his own needs yet, at times, focuses his attention on the universalities of human experience should add another dimension to current efforts to improve the image of each minority group and could make learning more relevant to all. (p. 694–695)

Donna Norton (1985) suggests that the benefits of sharing multicultural literature are so powerful and persuasive that they are beyond dispute and that they not only shape attitudes but also stimulate children's language and cognitive development. Violet Harris (1991) sees similar benefits from children's interaction with African American literature, and she suggests that this exposure not only increases general knowledge but also supports reading processes, develops visual literacy, increases understanding of literature and how it works, explores critical issues, prompts imagination, inspires the creation of literary and artistic products, and, last but certainly not least, entertains.

However, while these experts suggest that children's literature allows our students to vicariously experience their own culture as well as that of others and to learn about the similarities and differences among the peoples who comprise our world, the research to support this view is just now slowly beginning to emerge. At this point it is not only that the claims outweigh the evidence, but also that the questions being asked do not necessarily reflect the complexity of the issues. Should literature in fact be a vehicle for cultural understanding? Given the multiple communities that frame our world, and frame the stories that we write and read, how are we to make sense of the role that literature plays in determining our cultural understandings? Although I exist as an individual when reading a text, I am a product of numerous interpretive communities. So, too, is the author of the text I read. As Rosenblatt indicates, we are each members of numerous cultures and subcultures. As individuals existing within a culture, we all impact each other. However, all of us are products of numerous ethnic and cultural backgrounds. So in reality we each talk with multiple voices. We need research that considers not only the role of literature but also the role of the multiple communities that comprise the interpretive communities of our classrooms. Such questions add a new level of complexity to what is already a complicated issue.

The research that does currently exist can be found in three areas of work that provide in-roads but often result in more questions than answers. The first two areas look at the impact of literature on children's cultural attitudes and understandings. One is a set of experimental studies looking at the impact of cross-cultural books on children. The first of these studies was done in 1944, but they appeared predominantly in the 1960s and 1970s. The other area includes a set of studies loosely grouped under the category of "reader response." While these began in the late 1970s and were largely experimental at that time, they continue today, using a variety of research methodologies. Their purpose is to study the nature of a reader's response to various pieces of culturally diverse literature. Finally, the third area looks at the nature of a reader's response from the perspective of literary theory. While there is little agreement among literary theorists regarding the nature of interpretation, they share the common goal of seeking to understand what happens when a reader reads a text, or how the interpretation, or accomplishment of meaning, occurs. Although, for the most part, their work has not specifically asked questions regarding the role that culture plays in interpretation, their theories leave much room for speculation regarding the impact that culture might have on the accomplishment of meaning.

RESEARCH ON CULTURALLY DIVERSE LITERATURE

Campbell and Wirtenberg (1980), in their review of the literature, note that the majority of the early experimental studies were comparison studies looking at the effects of what was then termed to be curriculum containing "multicultural" books and curricula said to have more traditional, less equitable materials. For the most part, these studies found that these "multicultural" materials had positive effects on children's attitudes and achievements.

Those studies grouped under the broad umbrella of reader response focus on six basic areas: cultural impact as tied to *schema;* cultural impact on *personal response;* cultural influence and *gender* differences; *race* as a cultural issue; the impact of cultural *views of literacy;* and *literature's* impact on cultural understanding.

By far the largest group of these studies looks at the role of cultural schemata in the comprehension and recall of stories (Kintsch & Greene, 1978; Malik, 1990; Reynolds, Taylor, Steffensen, Shirey, & Anderson, 1982; Rogers-Zegarra and Singer, 1985; Steffensen, Jaog-Dev, & Anderson, 1979). These studies suggest that cultural schemata not only influence how material is read and interpreted but also affect the amount of information retained after reading. The studies show that readers remembered far more, and elaborated and extended their retellings more appropriately, after reading culturally familiar texts than after reading those that were culturally unfamiliar. It seems apparent that current research suggests that culture or ethnic background impacts understanding and response. However, the nature of that impact is still being questioned. Culture is often broadly defined and fails to consider the true "multicultural" nature of any given culture. Therefore, when studies suggest that the cultural content of a story affects understanding (Kintsch & Greene, 1978; Malik, 1990; Pritchard, 1990; Steffensen et al., 1979) and that subjects remember more, provide correct elaborations, and offer fewer distortions when they retell texts taken from their own culture, there is little indication that the complexity of the issues involved in bridging multiple voices has been considered. There is also no indication that a reader's response is linked to "understanding" the text. Readers from different cultures within a culture have arrived at different responses and understandings from reading the same text (Reynolds et al., 1982). Given the current reading-response research, this is worth stating but is not surprising. Interpretation or "understanding" results not only from the text but also from the reader and from the interpretive community of the classroom. As a result, it is important that the multiple voices become part of the research.

The studies (Bunbury & Tabbert, 1989; Ho, 1990; Tobin, 1990) that looked at the relationship between culture and personal response focused on the response of students to characters and settings both familiar and unfamiliar to their own culture and found an ability to appreciate those texts at different levels. Rogers-Zegarra and Singer (1985) found that "since cultures are not homogeneous, even within a nation, groups of individuals can be identified whose perspectives on issues and events will vary considerably" (p. 615). Tobin (1990) also noted that an important component in cultural literary interpretation is access to the interpretive community of the classroom. She suggested that when readers are deprived of interaction with their interpretive community, their understanding of and response to text are missing an important component. Given the perceived importance of the role of an interpretive community in understanding and response, research needs to look more carefully at the nature of that interaction. How do we bridge the multiple voices that are part of the classroom's interpretive community, and what role does literature play in this process?

It is equally important, when involved in cross-cultural research, to look at issues of race as related to issues of culture. Sims Bishop (1983) has looked at the portrayal of African Americans in literature for children and has examined the texts in terms of author, intended audience, and perspective. Spears-Bunton (1990) has looked at the impact that literature might have on students' cultural understandings. In an ethnographic study of one teacher's attempts to include African American literature in the curriculum of her eleventh-grade honors English class, Spears-Bunton found that students were forced to deal, on an individual and on a group basis, with important cultural and ethnic issues. Through case studies, she documented the change and growth of two female students, an African American and a white American, and noted the positive impact the change in curriculum had on both of these students.

A related issue is the acknowledgment and understanding of varying views of literacy held by diverse cultures. The work of Heath (1983) and Fishman (1987) has pointed to the fact that cultural views of literacy learning have a strong influence on the nature of language learning and success in school.

A weakness in studies that have considered culture as a factor in response is that they have only examined the issue from one perspective, the effect that a reader's own culture has on his or her own understanding of text. Few studies have followed Spears-Bunton's (1990) lead and have investigated the role that literature can play in determining our cultural understandings. I would like to suggest that as such our response studies need to carefully consider the roles that the culture or ethnic background of the author, reader, and interpretive community play in the development of our responses. An equally important issue is the role that literature plays in the growth of our cultural and ethnic understandings, and the insight that our responses to that literature might provide. The work of literary theorists provides some interesting possibilities, but again we are left with as many questions as answers.

LITERARY THEORY

At the outset I would like to suggest that it is difficult to answer a question which considers the impact that culture might have on the processes of an individual reader's meaning-making. Response theorists strive to answer the question of where meaning resides: in the reader, the text, the interaction between the reader and the text, or the context. According to Mailloux (1989), all the theorists "share a common assumption: Validity in interpretation is guaranteed by the establishment of norms and principles for explicating texts and such rules are derived from an account of how interpretation works in general" (p. 5). However, there is no single reader-response theory. These "norms" and "rules" are more reflective of a "critic" culture than an "ethnic" one. Rosenblatt (1991) suggests that there is a "spectrum" of response theories, with theorists grouped under reader-oriented theories (Holland, Bleich), text-oriented theories (Culler, Scholes, Fish), reader-plus-text-oriented theories (Iser, Rosenblatt), and feminist, ethnic, and other critical theories (Mailloux). Rogers (Chapter 4, this volume) argues that these views are limited because they fail to consider the society or culture in which the reader or any literary text originates. I would suggest that while each of us is an individual, there is no such thing as an individual reader. We are each a product of our interpretive communities and of our ethnic and cultural backgrounds. By this I do not mean that we do not each have our own personality and beliefs, because we do, but these beliefs did not develop in isolation. Therefore, when we read, we bring our own individuality to what we read, but we also need to consider what it is that framed and continues to frame our personality. I would like to suggest that it is our cultures that frame us and that our interpretive communities are in many ways synonymous with our cultures.

Literary theory reminds us that we do not live in isolation, nor do we read and interpret in isolation. We understand what we read through some combination of ourselves as the readers and the text with which we interact, but this is never free of the multiple contexts that frame us. Contexts have determined our personal identity (Bleich, Holland), the way we transact (Rosenblatt), the gaps we find in the text (Iser), the conventions we use to interpret the text (Culler), and our public shared interpretive strategies (Fish).

Scholes (1989) has suggested that all life is a text and that we read our lives as we read books. He says that we are reading culture. Given the mobility and changes in our lives, perhaps it is more accurate to say that all life may constitute one or more texts, as life is rarely seamless or continuous. I would also argue that our culture reads us, or, as Fish (1980) says, we are writing ourselves as we read. The theorists argue for the importance of the reader in developing an understanding of a text. They all acknowledge the significance of the communities from which the reader emerges and the impact those communities have on the reader. Mailloux (1977) suggests that it is the power of the rhetoric which exists in our communities that frames our interpretations. He also suggests that the context which frames our interpretive conventions is impossible to define. If we cannot define the context, does this mean we cannot define our interpretive communities and cannot define our cultures? How can we judge culture's impact if we cannot define what it is that is influencing our reactions? While, as I indicated earlier, this is a difficult and complex question to answer, I believe that it is important to make the attempt. When we begin to ask questions about culture, we need to consider issues of difference, multiple voices, and multiple communities, and our research must acknowledge this complexity.

Although I exist as an individual when reading a text, I am a product of numerous interpretive communities. So, too, are those with whom I interact. Our strength comes from these voices. Our interpretive community is richer for the multiplicity of voices that exist within it. As individuals we need to listen to the voices, listen to the rhetoric, and arrive at our own ethics of understanding. However, we need to acknowledge the voices and to celebrate their diversity. Therefore, the questions with which we are left are: What voices impact an individual reader's response to a text? How might this response be ethically negotiated within the community of voices that surrounds it?

THE CLASSROOM

What happens in a diverse classroom when children are given the opportunity to respond to literature? How is the response ethically negotiated when multiple communities exist together? What is the shared social interpretive community? How is a teacher to bridge the multiple voices and to celebrate the diversity?

To begin to answer these questions I spent the 1994–95 school year in a fourth-grade classroom as the teacher, Martha Klingshirn, and I collaboratively developed a culturally diverse literature program for her classroom. The site for the study was an urban public school. Ninety-two percent of the school's students receive a free or reduced-price lunch. Through an English as a Second Language (ESL) program, the school serves students from 22 different countries. Many of the neighborhood students attending are from the Appalachian regions of Ohio, West Virginia, and Kentucky. A large proportion of the African American students attending the school are bused in from a nearby housing project. The result is a rich and diverse, albeit economically poor, group of students.

Given the collaborative nature of the study, my focus was to document changes in the grounded theoretical understandings of the need for culturally diverse literature held by the teacher and the researcher, and the resulting change, if any, in the teacher's classroom practice. Seven specific units were taught over the course of the year using culturally diverse literature, and more than 85 culturally diverse picturebooks were shared during read-alouds. Field notes, researcher and teacher journals, videotapes of selected lessons, structured interviews, interviews with focal students, copies of the students' work, and transcribed audiotapes of the teacher's and researcher's conversations regarding the units and the literature used have helped to frame the emerging insights.

The story that emerges from the data documents our concerns and questions as we struggled together to determine how best to bring multicultural literature to the children and how to negotiate ethical issues. As teachers, we believed that we held responsibility for the development of the classroom's shared interpretive community. It is not enough merely to use the literature. As teachers, we need to understand what our purposes are for introducing books to the children, and we must carefully consider the issues that arise through our book discussions. Throughout the study we found that we often had more questions than answers as we struggled with the issues.

In February, we had just finished a unit that focused on Mildred D. Taylor's *Roll of Thunder, Hear My Cry* (1976); *Song of the Trees* (1975); *Mississippi Bridge* (1990); *The Friendship and the Gold Cadillac* (1989); and *The Well* (1995). We were very concerned about how we were negotiating the issue of similarities and differences, particularly as it was tied to issues of racism and discrimination. This became apparent in one of our debriefing conversations.

LAURIE: What do you think the children learned from these books?
MARTHA: I think they learned that at that time in history African

Americans were treated differently and unfairly. Maybe they learned a little bit about prejudice, what it is and what it entails. Maybe, not thinking that it happens now, but what it is.

LAURIE: I don't think they believe it exists today. But I think they learned it was a terrible thing to believe. I think they learned that we're really all alike. I think they've got that concept—that people are alike regardless of their cultural background. I don't think they've got the concept that they're also different.

MARTHA: But I think it's because they don't want it to be. They want it to be that we're all alike. African Americans shouldn't be treated any differently because we're all alike. So they can't separate the *shouldn't be treated any differently* from being different.

LAURIE: OK. That makes sense.

MARTHA: And I think that's why they don't—because they kind of don't want to see that—they don't want to admit differences because they think if they're admitting differences that's treating people differently and they're not separating those two things.

Later in the conversation this dichotomy between similarities and differences arises again:

LAURIE: After finishing these books, what are your opinions about the value of multicultural literature for use in the classroom?

MARTHA: Teaching prejudice and racism. I think the main thing is to value differences. I think that is more important than teaching that people are alike.

LAURIE: To value differences, but all we're teaching is that they're alike.

MARTHA: I know, that's where we need to make the distinction that the kids aren't making and we're not either—that being treated differently and being different are two separate things.

LAURIE: I can do a little bit of talking about that with *The Carp in the Bathtub*. I can talk about how people treated me because I was Jewish. As much as I've talked about being Jewish and liking *Elijah's Angels*, I've never talked about any other stuff. I've never talked about anti-Semitism.

MARTHA: And I don't think they have any idea that that exists.

LAURIE: That goes right into your concern about whether we are introducing something that they don't even know about by talking about it.

MARTHA: Are you saying that's wrong?

LAURIE: That was your concern.

MARTHA: I don't know—stated that way it doesn't sound like . . .

LAURIE: What I heard you say was that it's OK for fourth graders right now to feel that we're all alike.

MARTHA: I'm struggling really hard with this whole thing.

LAURIE: I am, too.

MARTHA: Every time a different situation comes up, I change my mind.

LAURIE: But let's just think about it.

MARTHA: But then when you said what I said before it doesn't jibe. A lot of things that I think we should do and teach don't jibe with what I think is happening.

LAURIE: I think maybe we're not as clear on what to do with the multicultural literature because we haven't decided for ourselves what's appropriate to do yet. You can't talk about Mildred Taylor books without talking about differences between the African American and white people. You just can't, but we're not sure how far to push it. Although, I think your question about "niggers" really pushed . . .

Mildred Taylor often uses texts that contain the word *nigger*. In the rural South, during the Depression, that was often the term used by white people when they spoke about, or to, anyone who was African American. However, Martha noticed that when portions of the text that contained that term were read aloud, many students in the classroom looked uncomfortable. She felt that the feeling "needed to be aired" and that the students needed to "look at where the feeling was coming from." She also wanted the students to know that while the author might write words that are offensive, it is not her saying them but the characters whom she has created. As a result, Martha asked the students to respond, in their reading journal, to the question "What would be your reaction if someone called you a nigger?" After the children responded in their reading journals, they shared and discussed their responses.

While the question was not an easy one to answer, the children's responses give some indication of the thought they put into the question. The question itself and the students' developing insights became integrated into the interpretive community of the classroom. The students, the stories, and Martha and I all brought multiple voices to the ongoing discussions.

AFRICAN AMERICAN GIRL: I really don't like the word *nigger* because when the Simms be calling the Logan family niggers and stuff it makes me feel awful and it makes me feel like I'm a nigger when the white people be calling the black people niggers.

WHITE GIRL: It probably feels as they're calling them a bad word or a wimp. When black people get called a nigger they probably feel that they don't have no pride.

WHITE BOY: If someone called me a nigger I would not show them that they hurt my feelings because if they know that they hurt my feelings then they would keep calling me that. Instead I would just walk away so they would not get any satisfaction out of it.

AFRICAN AMERICAN BOY: I feel like I'm being talked about. I feel like they're putting down my color and it really hurts my feelings. And when someone calls me a black [*nigger* is written and erased] I would say and I'm proud to be a black. And I am very proud that I am a black man.

ASIAN AMERICAN GIRL: It hurts my feelings and it will hurt your feelings, too, if someone called you that. If I was a black African American and they called me names I would just call them back just like Hammer did.

While Martha and I had very real concerns about the issues we chose to present to the students, we often felt that we had a "moral imperative" to present issues that might make us or the students feel uncomfortable. When Martha asked the students to consider how they would feel about being called a "nigger," she did so because she believed the issues were present because of the language of the text yet were not being addressed; as a result, many students were feeling uncomfortable. By making this issue part of the conversations of this community, Martha could share her own discomfort with the term and allow the students the opportunity to deal with a difficult issue.

However, as our conversation indicated, we were not always clear about how to negotiate the issues surrounding our use of culturally diverse literature. We were concerned about what the students were ready to deal with and what they were able to understand. The decisions we were making existed within the social, cultural, and political context of the classroom, but they were framed by who we are and what we believe. My background as a white Jewish American clearly influences my choices, as does Martha's Catholic upbringing in a small, rural town in the Midwest. As suggested earlier, it is our culture that frames us and writes our lives, and our interpretive communities in many ways become, or are synonymous with, our cultures.

MULTIPLE VOICES AND INTERPRETIVE COMMUNITIES

As we consider the role of culture or of the interpretive communities in a reader's response to a text, many questions remain. The search for an understanding of the ethics of response in a society framed by multiple communities is challenging and complex. As literary theory suggests, we understand what we read through some combination or transaction among the reader, the text, and the context. However, given the diversity that exists within our culture, this transaction or creation of a shared interpretive community must be carefully negotiated. This is particularly true of the classroom.

While it seems apparent that literature has the power to open eyes and change lives, it is also apparent that this does not happen merely by reading a piece of culturally diverse literature in a classroom. The multiple voices brought to our interpretive communities makes the use of literature as a vehicle for cultural understanding quite complex. As the work done in Martha Klingshirn's fourth-grade classroom indicates, there are important questions that must be considered. While in some cases these questions are experientially or aesthetically related, there are important ethical issues that must be considered.

If we are to use culturally diverse literature in the classroom, we must be sensitive to the multiple communities that exist as we create a shared social interpretive community of unique and special diverse readers. Our lives, our stories, our cultures are framed by our social and political context. All of us are individuals with our own personalities and beliefs. However, as stated earlier, these beliefs are shaped by the multiple communities that frame us. In bringing our individuality to the stories of our lives that we read and write, we have the potential to create a shared social interpretive community. In so doing, it is hoped that readers will see themselves and others in what they read and will grow to appreciate their own uniqueness as well as the diversity that exists in the stories of their lives.

REFERENCES

Banks, J. A. (1979). Shaping the future of multicultural education. *Journal of Negro Education, 48*(3), 237–252.

Banks, J. A. (1991). *Teaching strategies for ethnic studies* (5th ed.). Needham Heights, MA: Simon & Schuster.

Bunbury, R., & Tabbert, R. (1989). A bicultural study of identification: Readers' responses to the ironic treatment of a national hero. *Children's Literature in Education, 20*(1), 25–35.

Campbell, P. B., & Wirtenberg, J. (1980). How books influence children: What the research shows. *Bulletin, 11*(6), 3–6.

Chan, I. (1984). Folktales in the development of multicultural literature for children. TESL TALK, *15*(1&2), 19–28.

Clifford, E. (1985). *The remembering box*. Boston: Houghton Mifflin.

Connelly, F. M., & Clandinin, D. J. (1990). Stories of experience and narrative inquiry. *Educational Researcher, 19*(4), 2–14.

Erlich, A. S. (1990, November). *Reading the world cross-culturally: An anthropologic view*. Paper presented at Understanding Cultures Through Literature Conference, Moorehead State University, Moorehead, MN.

Fish, S. E. (1980). *Is there a text in this class? The authority of interpretive communities*. Cambridge, MA: Harvard University Press.

Fishman, A. (1987). Literacy and cultural context: A lesson from the Amish. *Language Arts, 64*(8), 842–854.

Harris, V. J. (1991). Multicultural curriculum: African-American children's literature. *Young Children, 46*(2), 37–44.

Heath, S. B. (1983). *Ways with words*. Cambridge, England: Cambridge University Press.

Ho, L. (1990). Singapore readers' responses to U.S. young adult fiction: Cross-cultural differences. *Journal of Reading, 33*(4), 252–258.

Jenkins, E. C. (1973). Multi-ethnic literature: Promise and problems. *Elementary English, 50*(5), 693–699.

Kintsch, W., & Greene, E. (1978). The role of culture-specific schemata in the comprehension and recall of stories. *Discourse Processes, 1*, 1–13.

Mailloux, S. (1977). Reader response criticism? *Genre, 10*, 413–431.

Mailloux, S. (1989). *Rhetorical power*. Ithaca, NY: Cornell University Press.

Malik, A. A. (1990). A psycholinguistic analysis of the reading behavior of EFL-proficient readers using culturally familiar and culturally nonfamiliar expository texts. *American Education Research Journal, 21*(1), 205–223.

Norton, D. E. (1985). Language and cognitive development through multicultural literature. *Childhood Education, 62*(2), 103–108.

Norton, D. E. (1990). Teaching multicultural literature in the reading curriculum. *The Reading Teacher, 44*(1), 28–40.

Pritchard, R. (1990). The effects of cultural schemata on reading processing strategies. *Reading Research Quarterly, 25*(4), 273–295.

Rabinowitz, P. J. (1987). *Before reading: Narrative conventions and the politics of interpretation*. Ithaca, NY: Cornell University Press.

Reynolds, R. E., Taylor, M. A., Steffensen, M. S., Shirey, L. L., & Anderson, R. C. (1982). Cultural schemata and reading comprehension. *Reading Research Quarterly, 17*(3), 353–366.

Rogers-Zegarra, N., & Singer, H. (1985). Anglo and Chicano comprehension of ethnic stories. In H. Singer & R. Ruddell (Eds.), *Theoretical models and processes of reading* (3rd ed.) (pp. 611–617). Newark, DE: International Reading Association.

Rosenblatt, L. M. (1991). Literary theory. In J. Flood (Ed.), *Handbook of research on teaching English language arts* (pp. 57–62). New York: Macmillan.

Scholes, R. (1989). *Protocols of reading.* New Haven, CT: Yale University Press.

Sims, R. (1982). *Shadow and substance.* Urbana, IL: National Council of Teachers of English.

Sims, R. (1983, May). What has happened to the "all white" world of children's books? *Phi Delta Kappan,* pp. 650–653.

Sims Bishop, R. (1990). Walk tall in the world: African-American literature for today's children. *Journal of Negro Education, 59*(4), 566–576.

Spears-Bunton, L. A. (1990). Welcome to my house: African-American and European American students' responses to Virginia Hamilton's *House of Dies Drear. Journal of Negro Education, 59*(4), 566–576.

Steffensen, M. S., Jaog-Dev, C., & Anderson, R. C. (1979). A cross-cultural perspective on reading comprehension. *Reading Research Quarterly, 15*(1), 10–29.

Taylor, M. D. (1975). *Song of the trees.* New York: Dial.

Taylor, M. D. (1976). *Roll of thunder, hear my cry.* New York: Dial.

Taylor, M. D. (1990). *Mississippi bridge.* New York: Dial.

Taylor, M. D. (1989). *The friendship and the gold Cadillac.* New York: Bantam.

Taylor, M. D. (1995). *The well.* New York: Dial.

Tobin, B. (1990, April). *Australian readers' responses to the cross-cultural folklore-based fantasy novels of Patricia Wrightson.* Paper presented at the meeting of the American Educational Research Association, Boston.

CHAPTER 8

Out of the Closet and onto the Bookshelves

Images of Gays and Lesbians in Young Adult Literature

MARI M. McLEAN

IN A LITERATE and multicultural society such as exists in the United States, books are powerful vehicles for conveying images of diversity. Because multicultural education has helped bring about "a heightened sensitivity to the needs of all people in American society" (Norton, 1987, p. 502), and because we are "increasingly recognizing the role of children's literature in shaping attitudes" (Norton, 1985, p. 103), we are seeing an increasing emphasis placed on including multicultural literature for children and young adults in the curriculum. This is because multicultural literature is seen to be both a mirror to validate a group's experiences and knowledge, and a window through which those experiences and knowledge can be viewed—and perhaps understood—by "outsiders" (Cox & Galda, 1990). It provides an invaluable opportunity for teachers and students to glimpse into the lives of the "other," to know for a time what it feels like to be a member of a group that is not in the mainstream. Through literature,

> [The reader] will experience . . . other life styles; he may identify with others or find his own self-identity; he may observe from a different perspectives; . . . [and] feel he belongs to one segment of all humanity (Huck, Hepler, & Hickman, 1987, p. 4).

Yet when I look at multicultural education materials, I usually find that one particular "segment of all humanity"—the 10% of the population that is homosexual—is conspicuously absent.

THE INVISIBLE MINORITY

The hypocrisy of multicultural education in the United States is that while emphasizing the importance of increased awareness and understanding among people from diverse cultures, it is selective about which groups qualify for its benefits. Multicultural educators such as Banks (1979), Garcia (1982, 1984), and Austin and Jenkins (1983) caution us to avoid hurtful and hateful racial, ethnic, or gender slurs; call for equality of opportunity and fair treatment; and champion the right of all people to live in dignity. However, time and again these educators fail to specifically mention homophobia as a dangerously prejudiced attitude that contributes to institutionalized discrimination and even violence against lesbian and gay[1] Americans. For example, homophobia is not included in a list of biases that, Garcia (1984) cautions teachers, can lead to discrimination against individual students and, therefore, must be eradicated from classrooms.

Some might argue that the reason references to homosexuals do not appear in many multicultural materials is that there is no "homosexual culture," because homosexuality has no racial or ethnic basis for existence. In our vastly diverse world, however, color and national origin are rather narrow ways to define which groups of people have a right to have their way of life accepted and to be individually respected as valuable members of society. Culture often transcends the boundaries of race and ethnicity. It may be more broadly defined, wrote the anthropologist Franz Boas, "as the totality of the mental and physical reactions and activities that characterize the behavior of the individuals composing a social group" (cited in Garcia, 1982, p. 23).

Because their uniquely shared ways of thinking and doing make them a "specific 'kind' of people" (Tinney, 1983, p. 4), gays and lesbians can and do form a general cultural group, as well as cultural subgroups, which are independent of and frequently cross groupings based on race or ethnic origin. Like members of racial or ethnic groups, people who are homosexual can point to a history, to cultural artifacts, to famous people, and to a celebration of life that is uniquely their own. Like those who belong to racial or ethnic groups, homosexual women and men are often the victims of stereotyping, prejudice, discrimination, and sometimes violence. Like nonwhites and non-WASPs, gay and lesbian Americans have had to struggle, and continue to struggle, to gain both legal rights and human dignity in a society that lauds individualism while demanding conformity.

The need to conform enough to fit in and be accepted is a very real need for many people, especially adolescents. Aileen Nilsen and Kenneth Donelson (1985) point out that finding one's identity is considered by some psychologists to be "the major challenge of adolescence" (p. 5). Having taught middle school and high school students, I can verify that the search for self is nearly all-encompassing for most young people. The adolescent/young adult years can be a troubling time of questioning, self-doubt, real and imagined humiliations, isolation, and even fear for any young person.

Adolescence is an even more traumatic time for the young person whose "different affectional nature" (Tinney, 1983, p. 4) sets him or her apart as possibly the most despised "other" in American society: a queer, a lezzie, a fag, a dyke. Just how traumatic this time can be is evidenced by the fact that gay and lesbian adolescents commit suicide at a higher rate than do adolescents in general (Walling, 1993). The results of a U.S. Department of Health study of youth suicide completed in 1986 (and suppressed for three years by the Bush administration) showed that suicide was the leading cause of death among gay and lesbian youth, who accounted for approximately 30% of all youth suicides annually (Chandler, 1995).

BECOMING VISIBLE TO OURSELVES AND OTHERS

Advocates of multicultural literature such as Rudine Sims Bishop (1987) and Donna Norton (1987) believe that, in addition to helping us appreciate our common humanity, this kind of literature sensitizes us to the way in which people's lives may be affected by things beyond their control and provides validation of one's self and culture. From a psychological point of view, the right literature can be a means of helping any young reader understand others', as well as to accept his or her own, differences. In fact, according to Michael Angelotti (cited in Gallo, 1984), a therapeutic function is one of the four main functions of young adult literature. For the adolescent who must, because of the social stigma attached to homosexuality, wage a very private struggle to understand and accept his or her sexual orientation, good literature can be invaluable in providing the information, validation, and positive role models so necessary to the development of a healthy self-esteem (Wilson, 1984). "Vicariously experiencing the life of a character in fiction," Rosenblatt (1983) wrote, ". . . may enable the [adolescent] reader to bring into consciousness similar elements in his own nature and emotional life. This may provide the basis for a release from unconscious fears and guilt" (p. 201).

How well young adult literature with gay and lesbian characters and/or themes meets the multicultural goal of validating personal experiences and perspectives is best determined by a literary analysis based on certain reader-response theories. While other poststructuralist theories such as feminist and Marxist theories can also inform such issues, reader-response theories are the most appropriate bases for analysis because, across the spectrum of these theories, the reader's personal experience, knowledge, and perspective in the interpretation of a text is honored to varying degrees (cf. Bleich, 1980; Holland, 1980; Iser, 1980; Rosenblatt, 1978). Especially meaningful for analyzing the multicultural value of a text is the work of psychoanalytic response theorists, such as David Bleich (1980) and Norman Holland (1980), who maintain that the interpretation of a piece of literature is very much tied to the individual's personality. Bleich asserts that "the personal need of the critic-reader for self-understanding is definitely a guiding factor in the search for knowledge" (p. 137), so that an adolescent might be expected to read in order to gain self-enlightenment. According to Holland, "interpretation is a function of identity" (p. 123), and "all of us, as we read, use the literary work to symbolize and finally to replicate ourselves" (p. 124). Clearly, to him, a piece of literature can provide the means of validating the self, of raising one's self-esteem.

Of those literary critics who take a psychologically oriented response perspective, it is the feminist response theorists, rooted in psychosociology (Kennard, 1986), whose work most directly addresses the issues related to the portrayal of gays and lesbians in literature. Just as feminist critics see gender as an all-important consideration of *how* they read (Schweickart, 1986), so might lesbians and gays see their own sexuality as an all-important consideration in their interaction with a text. Responding to Fetterley's (cited in Schweickart, 1986) reference to "the powerlessness which derives from not seeing one's experiences articulated, clarified, and legitimized in art," Schweickart argues that reading texts by and about men "draws her into a process that she uses against herself" (p. 42), causing the woman reader to emphasize the male identity at the expense of her own female identity. The response of the gay and lesbian reader to the predominance of texts by and about heterosexuals is no different.

Whether texts structure the reader's experience or whether the reader's experience structures the text, the fact is that the ignoring or denial of a group's existence in literature invalidates the experience and self-identity of members of that group by rendering them invisible, not only to themselves, but to all other groups in a society. A primary value assigned to multicultural literature is that it mirrors the minority youth's culture and experience in positive ways. Yet, like women, lesbian and gay youth are surrounded by books that are neither by nor about themselves. The precious few mirrors that do exist in young adult literature contain many distortions that fail to project a good, clear image.

The inaccurate portrayals, the misinformed assumptions, the failure to even admit to the existence of gay and lesbian culture in literature is played out in the reality of our schools, says gay activist Eric Rofes (1989), and "[t]he result has been the creation of a population [of gay and lesbian adolescents] within our schools who exhibit significant indications of lack of self-esteem, emotional problems, and substance abuse" (p. 445). If this were any other minority population, educators would not allow the situation to continue unaddressed.

MIRRORS AND WINDOWS:
MEETING THE GOALS OF MULTICULTURAL LITERATURE

There are relatively few young adult novels dealing with lesbian and gay issues. At the time of this writing, I have read 34 such novels (see the selected bibliography at the end of the chapter); however, Jenkins (1993) lists 60 titles published between 1969 and 1992. Of the 30 novels used in this analysis, 10 have been written since 1990. The remainder, with the exception of 2, were written prior to 1984, with 2 of the novels written between 1984 and 1990. The decline in the number of titles published about the gay and lesbian experience since 1983 is attributed, in part, to the ascendancy of neoconservatism, the stridency of the so-called Moral Majority, and the subsequent censorship and book-banning campaigns launched during the Reagan–Bush era. In fact, the same decline can be seen in the number of titles published about *all* minority groups during the 1980s (Sims, 1985), a rather bleak commentary on how very "discriminating" an era that prided itself on restoring American values could be.

From a psychosociological reader-response perspective, I have analyzed most of these novels in order to determine whether or not they meet the stated goals of multicultural literature: providing validation of one's self and culture, and contributing to our understanding of "other." Perhaps more significantly, I have also analyzed this literature from an insider's perspective, which makes me very aware of the presence of stereotypes and misinformation that perpetuate damaging myths about nearly 10% of our population. Such myths not only impair the development of a healthy self-identity among gay and lesbian youth, but they prevent members of the lesbian and gay culture from gaining full acceptance in society. One need only look at the recent furor over the issue of gays and lesbians in the military to understand how lack of information (or an abundance of misinformation) distorts judgment and results in protests against the equity demands of the members of a minority.

Jan Goodman (1983) lists several damaging stereotypes and inaccuracies about lesbians and gays that can distort the judgment of heterosexuals and to which we need to be alert in young adult literature. Among these stereotypes and inaccuracies are that lesbian and gay adolescents (1) have been traumatized into homosexuality, (2) are just going through a phase toward heterosexuality, (3) want to change their sex, (4) can expect a lonely, isolated adulthood characterized by a series of unhappy love relationships, (5) are interested in seducing heterosexuals, particularly younger ones, and (6) will be punished for their sexuality. From my analysis of young adult novels with gay and lesbian characters and themes, I would add that—especially in the older novels—gay and lesbian adolescents are frequently depicted as guilty, ashamed, bitter, desperately unhappy individuals who would give anything to be "normal." Also, among all of the books, the stereotype of the "artistically inclined" homosexual is all too common.

Like other minority-group adolescents, lesbian and gay youth need literature that provides "validation for their feelings and hope for a bright future that involves self-affirmation" (Goodman, 1983, p. 15). Books that promote the above stereotypes and misinformation cannot provide such validation and will only complicate the struggle toward self-identity. Rather, these adolescents need to read about stable, committed, and loving gay and lesbian relationships, and about contented, productive, and quite "normal" lesbian and gay characters.

Several questions were in my mind as I read these young adult novels with lesbian and gay characters and/or themes: (1) Do these novels meet the goals of multicultural literature? (2) What images of gay and lesbian characters and culture are depicted in these novels? (3) What is the overall characterization of gays and lesbians, how are same-sex relationships depicted, and what are the societal and personal consequences of following one's affectional nature? (4) What might be the effects of these images on a homosexual adolescent's self-esteem, or on a heterosexual student's perceptions about alternative lifestyles? To attempt to answer these questions, I will discuss examples from a number of these novels.

YOU CAN ALWAYS SPOT ONE: GAY AND LESBIAN STEREOTYPES

To the credit of the authors of these young adult novels, the physical descriptions of the gays and lesbians are uniformly complimentary—and "normal." This is a relief, considering that we live in a society obsessed with noting physical differences and in which many people erroneously believe that all lesbians are tough and brutish and all gays are mincing and limp-wristed. In *A Boy's Own Story,* the narrator does describe himself as "effeminate" and a "sissy," but this is a semi-autobiographical novel, and, as an insider, Edmund White is allowed some license. The closest any other author comes to perpetuating the idea of a stereotypic appearance is Rosa Guy (*Ruby*), whose character Daphne is 6 feet tall and embraces her lover with "powerful arms." Daphne is redeemed, however, by being very beautiful. In Marilyn Levy's *Rumors and Whispers,* Sarah describes her gay brother as "the beautiful one," but there is no other indication that this could be construed as meaning he is effeminate. In general, however, all of the authors except Holland (*The Man Without a Face*), whose character Justin is unattractive because of a disfiguring scar over half of his face, describe their gay and lesbian characters as either attractive or unremarkable in appearance.

A recurring stereotype that, as an insider, I found annoying was that of the artistically sensitive homosexual. Among the lesbian and gay characters depicted in these novels are four actors, four writers, two singers, one pianist, five artists, and three lovers of poetry or music. While I have no quarrel with artistic sensitivity itself, this quality is sometimes used by heterosexuals to "excuse" or "explain" why a friend or family member is gay or lesbian: "You know, those sensitive people are just *that* way." These books pander to the idea that being gay or lesbian is more likely, more tolerable, perhaps more "understandable" and acceptable if the person has an "artistic temperament."

The books written prior to 1984 generally perpetuate the stereotype that gays and lesbians are ashamed, guilt-ridden, and bitter. Nearly all of the characters in these novels struggle to understand their homoemotional and/or homoerotic feelings, not only bearing their own shame and guilt but also having to deal with that of family and friends. Because the early novels are more interested in the struggle than with the end result of that struggle, they deprive the reader, both homosexual and heterosexual, of an important insight: After the adolescent's struggle for self-acceptance, a happy and well-adjusted lesbian or gay adult usually emerges. Although it might be argued that the intent of the authors is to show how societal pressure is responsible for placing unfair burdens of guilt on individuals, the subtlety of that intent might lead the burdened adolescent to find confirmation that one *should* feel guilt, shame, and bitterness about being gay or lesbian.

For many people, a homosexual encounter or even a relationship can be more easily "accepted" if it is believed to be a temporary aberration. It is therefore no surprise that, stereotypically, the development of a same-sex relationship in young adult literature is frequently linked to some traumatic event(s) in the life of a young person (Goodman, 1983). Since some heterosexuals regard being homosexual as a condition deserving of pity, it is convenient to believe that, like any noncongenital disfigurement, homosexuality is something that results from being in the wrong place at the wrong time. Also, it is known that people who have been traumatized can, with the proper treatment, be returned to a "normal" life. Thus the message from the novels that imply a connection between trauma and the development of a same-sex relationship is that homosexuality, contrary to recent scientific discovery of a "gay gene" (Henry, 1993), does not have to be a permanent condition.

Guy's *Ruby,* Scoppettone's *Happy Endings Are All Alike,* Donovan's *I'll Get There. It Better Be Worth the Trip,* Futch's *Crush,* Holland's *The Man Without a Face,* White's *A Boy's Own Story,* and Winterson's *Oranges Are Not the Only Fruit* all have characters who have to deal with the trauma of loneliness, alienation, and a ruptured or dysfunctional family. Ruby contends with the recent death of her mother, a domineering father, an unsatisfactory relationship with her sister, and a school life that only contributes to her feelings of loneliness and alienation. Peggy, in *Happy Endings,* has also lost her mother and must put up with an inattentive father and a psychologically unbalanced older sister. Lexie, in *Crush,* is left in the care of a guardian by her wealthy, indifferent parents. Davy's parents, in *I'll Get There,* are divorced, and he lives alone with his alcoholic mother. In *The Man Without a Face,* Charles lives with two half-sisters, one of whom continually bullies and torments him, and an indifferent mother. The mothers and fathers in the semi-autobiographical novels are extremely eccentric characters who do not provide anything approaching a "normal" family life for their children. Readers of Hall's *Sticks and Stones* might get the idea that since Ward's first "homosexual involvement" was "with another guy in my [Army] barracks" (p. 183), it resulted from the trauma of separation from family and friends. Whatever "caused" Ward to give in ("I do have these—tendencies," p. 183) is really peripheral to this story, however, since the book is not really as much about homosexuality as it is about the stigma of being accused of it.

As befits the idea that conditions related to life trauma are reversible, Ruby, Charles, and Davy eventually head off into the heterosexual sunset. We suspect that Peggy might opt out of same-sex relationships because she *is* confused about her sexuality: She admits to Janet that "the trouble is I still do care what people think but I have to try not to" and "I can't make you any promises" (p. 201). Only in *A Boy's Own Story*, in *Oranges*, in both of Garden's novels, and in *Rumors and Whispers* do the characters remain true to their sexual identity, belying the myth that homosexuality is a temporary condition, a phase that will eventually pass along with adolescence.

If the implied message from these novels is that same-sex relationships are "one-shot deals" that develop "accidentally" out of the confusion and pain of adversity, then an accompanying implication is that such relationships must be short-lived. This implication is clear in these novels. Among these novels, only one prior to 1980 depicts a loving, long-term same-sex relationship. Norma Klein's 1978 novel, *Breaking Up*, stands out among the early books as offering a positive, upbeat view of a mother's lesbian relationship and its effect on her teenage children and their father. After 1980, however, the depiction begins to change. In Garden's *Annie on My Mind*, two lesbian teachers at Liza's school have lived together for many years. Perhaps more important for young lesbian readers is the fact that the book ends with the strong suggestion that Annie and Liza will, despite the obstacles, reestablish their loving relationship and develop their own long-term commitment. In Garden's later novel, *Lark in the Morning*, Gillian and Suzanne have already made a long-term commitment when the story begins, and nothing occurs to shake that commitment in the course of the novel. In *Rumors and Whispers*, Sarah's brother and his lover live together and are committed to a monogamous relationship.

INCURRING GOD'S WRATH: THE BIBLICAL INFLUENCE ON IMAGES

Perhaps because the Judeo-Christian ethic prevails in American society, there exists the fairly common belief that those who engage in homoerotic relationships will be punished in some way for their "sin." (This notion is so widely accepted that recently an antigay protester in Harlan County, Georgia, could be shown on television daring to display a sign reading "Thank God for AIDS.") True to the belief that homosexuality does or should result in punishment, all of the earlier novels involve some kind of loss (most notably, death) or violence that is either overtly or implicitly linked to a homoerotic act. The loss in Reading's *Bouquets for Brimbal* is relatively minor: A close friendship nearly ends because Macy cannot accept Annie's lesbian relationship with an older woman. In *Happy Endings* and in *Oranges*, parents are faced with loss of prestige in their communities when their daughters' lesbianism becomes public knowledge. In both stories, parents and children become estranged from one another, which is also a theme in one later novel, *Rumors and Whispers*.

Punishment through loss of livelihood occurs in *Annie on My Mind*, in which the lesbian teachers are fired for unwittingly providing a place for 17-year-olds Liza and Annie to make love. Peggy's father, in *Happy Endings*, has his livelihood threatened when a number of his patients desert his medical practice because of his daughter's lesbianism. In *Crush*, both Lexie and Jinx are expelled from their prestigious private school, and Jinx is faced with the possibility that she will not be able to pursue her career choice because her expulsion might affect her college admission. In *Ruby*, the main character is beset by several losses: Ruby's shaky relationship with her father is further damaged by her lesbian relationship with Daphne, Ruby eventually loses Daphne, and then she almost loses her life in a suicide attempt.

In light of the presumed effect of Judeo-Christian ethics on the messages in young adult literature, it is important to note that the only Old Testament injunctions against homosexuality are directed toward males (Leviticus 18:23 and 20:13). It is not surprising, then, that in five novels about gays, a death occurs that the reader might easily link to homosexuality. In Scoppettone's *Trying Hard to Hear You*, Phil is killed while trying to "prove" to himself and others that he is really "straight." Tom, the protagonist in *Sticks and Stones*, is so angered and confused by the gossip that he is a homosexual that he causes an accident in which another boy is killed. A reader influenced by fundamentalist beliefs could see 47-year-old Justin's sudden death by heart attack in *Man Without a Face* as divine punishment for his homoerotic attachment to 14-year-old Charles. Certainly that same fundamentalist reader would see divine retribution in the impending death of the art teacher who is dying of AIDS in *Rumors and Whispers*. We presume that the teacher has contracted the disease as the result of homosexual activity: "He's queer," Jimmy said. "Either that or he's shooting up heroin, and I ain't seen any track marks on his arm" (p. 101).

In both Donovan's and Holland's novels the violent death of a beloved pet is directly linked to a homoerotic act. In *I'll Get There*, Davy's dog is killed when his mother takes him for a walk so that Davy's father can speak to him privately about Davy's relationship with Altshuler. "She took him out because of me," says Davy, "She wanted to leave me alone with my father to talk. Is that why it happened? Yes, God, yes. It's my fault. Because of everything I did" (p. 172). Charles's cat in *The Man Without a Face* is killed because Charles, who has spent the day with Justin, was not home to protect him from his sister's boyfriend, Percy. "Moxie died about an hour later. Percy was telling the truth. It was his boot. But it was as much my fault as his" (p. 138).

If the message to young adult readers is not "If you're gay or lesbian (but especially if you're gay), you'll die," then it is "If you're gay or lesbian, you can get badly hurt." Both of Sandra Scoppettone's novels strongly suggest that being gay or lesbian can drive heterosexuals to commit bodily assault. Even though Scoppettone—an insider—portrays the heterosexual assailant in both books as psychopathic, and even though her sympathies are clearly with the gay and lesbian characters, a naive reader may still see these acts of violence as, at best, a warning or, at worst, justified. In either case, the message is that gays and lesbians can expect to be victims of prey. They can also be the victims of excessive religious piety, as with Winterson's character, who undergoes an exorcism that falls just short of torture.

DIFFERENT IMAGES OF SAME-SEX LOVE

It is interesting to note the different ways in which the authors of these young adult novels treat lesbian and gay sexuality, a difference that reflects the importance society places on males and the unimportance with which females are regarded. Male homosexuality is obviously more offensive than female homosexuality since gays and their pets die because of same-sex relationships, but lesbians do not. Centuries after the Leviticus passages (see above) labeled the male homosexual act "an abomination," authors of young adult literature are still carrying out the sentence on their gay characters: "They shall be put to death; their blood shall be on their own heads." That lesbian characters escape such a fate is undoubtedly linked to the fact that nowhere in the Old Testament is lesbianism even mentioned. Apparently, God did not want Abraham, Isaac, and Jacob to engage in homosexual activity but was not overly concerned about what Sarah, Rebecca, and Rachael might do with each other.

The different treatment of male and female homosexuality is also shown in what the authors tell of the homoerotic act itself. In the lesbian novels, authors have the young women touch or kiss intimately and sometimes even admit to sexual arousal: "Peggy put her hand inside Jaret's blouse" (*Happy Endings*, p. 85); "Her mouth was being kissed, and she responded eagerly to those full, blessedly full, lips" (*Ruby*, p. 55); "I kissed Annie, somehow moved away from her and reached for my clothes" (*Annie on My Mind*, p. 163). In *Crush*, there are several scenes in which Futch describes Jinx's physical and emotional response to the intimacy of being in bed with Lexie. While no intimate lesbian scenes are described in *Bouquets for Brimbal* or *Lark in the Morning*, the characters do refer to themselves as "lovers" or to the act of "making love."

By contrast, with the exception of *A Boy's Own Story* (which, it must be remembered, is semi-autobiographical), sexual intimacy is only hinted at in the gay novels, and arousal is never mentioned. In *The Man Without a Face* the characters are in bed together, but when Justin puts his arms around Charles, it is a comforting, rather than sexual, embrace. The homoerotic act is only alluded to by Charles's statement ("Even so, I didn't know what was happening to me until it had happened" [p. 141]) and by the fact of his changed attitude toward Justin the next morning. Although Jeff and Phil are mercilessly tormented for their relationship in *Trying Hard to Hear You*, the only glimpse the reader gets of homoeroticism in this book is when a third party reports, "We found these two creeps kissing, for godsake" (p. 182). In *Rumors and Whispers*, a hint of sexual activity is given by the mention of a single queen-sized bed in the apartment of Sarah's brother and his lover.

There is no homoerotic act in *I'll Get There*, but there is the damaging accusation of it. In Donovan's novel, Davy playfully gives his friend Altschuler "a dumb kiss" (p. 158), and after drinking whiskey, they fall asleep together on the floor, but only in Davy's mother's mind does anything erotic happen. In *Sticks and Stones* there is no sexual activity between Tom and Ward, although they obviously have a close and loving friendship. As in *I'll Get There*, all the homoeroticism in *Sticks and Stones*, just as in Tolan's lesbian novel, *The Last of Eden*, happens in the minds of other people.

However, as an interesting aside, it should be noted that in neither the gay nor the lesbian novels is any consummation of the sex act described, although some of the novels rather graphically describe heterosexual sex. Perhaps the authors are responding to the sensitivity of many heterosexuals that they not be told what homosexuals actually do in bed! More likely, the authors do not want to be accused of tempting teenagers who are not so inclined into homosexual experiment. Also interesting to note is that heterosexual "immorality" is portrayed by some of the characters themselves as far less serious than corresponding homosexual behavior. Thus, in *The Last of Eden*, students react violently to the idea that a woman teacher might be having an affair with a female student but are indifferent to or condone the fact that the teacher's husband is having an affair with a female student.

Returning to the different treatment of the gay and lesbian homoerotic act in these novels, we may find that the explanation for it is that all women, and what they do, are relatively unimportant in male-dominated societies. Male homosexuality has apparently been far more worrisome and disturbing to these societies than female homosexuality. For example, of the six biblical references to homosexuality, only one (Romans 1:26–27) deals with lesbianism, and that reference is so vague that we cannot even be certain that lesbianism is the "abomination" being mentioned. In the United States, lesbianism per se is not illegal, although it is sometimes prosecuted under widely interpreted sodomy statutes (Scanzoni & Mollenkott, 1978). If lesbian love-making is more openly depicted in young adult literature than is gay love-making, the reason may be that society agrees with Peggy's father in *Happy Endings:*

> "Are you horrified?" she asked tentatively.
> Was he? Of course not. That was much too strong. Actually, Tom realized, sex between two girls, two women, just didn't seem important to him.
> "No, I'm not horrified, Peggy. As a matter of fact, I think it's hard for me to take lesbianism very seriously." (p. 187)

Related to the "seriousness" with which American society seems to take male homosexuality but not lesbianism is the message the reader might get from the earlier books that gays are, or should be, more tormented by guilt than are lesbians. None of the gay novels written before 1982 include a character comfortable with his sexuality, although two books written by insiders, Scoppettone's *Trying Hard to Hear You* and White's *A Boy's Own Story,* have characters who seem to have, with great difficulty, come to terms with their sexuality. In contrast, over the past 20 years, a number of lesbian characters seem to have been spared the agonizing struggle to accept their sexuality that besets their male counterparts. Liza, and to some extent Annie, in *Annie On My Mind,* Jaret in *Happy Endings,* Annie and Lola in *Bouquets for Brimbal,* and Gillian and Suzanne in *Lark* all are fairly content and well-adjusted. The narrator in Jeannette Winterson's semi-autobiographical novel even manages to accept her sexuality despite the hellfire and brimstone atmosphere of her fundamentalist home.

Overall, the earlier novels support the stereotype of instability in homosexual relationships: How would the tormented and guilt-ridden characters in Guy's, Donovan's, Holland's, and Hall's books turn out? What future togetherness could Janet have with Peggy, who is committed only for "now"? What happiness could embittered Daphne ever have for herself, or give to anyone else? How could Jinx ever make a commitment to a relationship when her first lesbian relationship was filled with such betrayal and terrible consequences? The outlook for happiness is bleak; the gloomy message might not be so easily shaken off by a gay or lesbian adolescent and is only likely to confirm for outsiders that life in the lesbian and gay culture is either pitiable or contemptible—but certainly *not* acceptable.

BRIGHTER WINDOWS AND MIRRORS: THE MOST RECENT IMAGES

There is cause to hope, however, that authors might be leaving some of those negative messages about gays and lesbians behind: The more recent books, those written since 1990, all have strong homosexual characters who accept themselves and seem quite capable of establishing stable, long-term relationships; dispel some of the myths about homosexuals used as discriminatory excuses; and present a new and very positive picture of families headed by gay or lesbian couples. I think the most striking thing about the most recent novels, from the perspective of an insider, is a change in "tone." Although a reader could point to parts of the novels written since 1990 as contributing to the stereotypes Jan Goodman warns about (e.g., Slim's gay father, Mack, in Nelson's *Earthshine,* dies of AIDS), the overall characterizations are so positive and so "normal" that any possible stereotypic images are stripped of their power. Since most gays and lesbians must remain invisible in order to protect themselves from discrimination and abuse, it is almost impossible to say whether or not this change is because more insiders are writing about the gay or lesbian experience.

As "coming-out" stories, Brett's *S.P. Likes A.D.,* Walker's *Peter,* and Sinclair's *Coffee Will Make You Black* depict the struggle that young people beginning to question their sexuality must go through in a dominantly heterosexual society. Yet these stories all conclude with the young persons working through the imposed guilt and fear to the point where they are accepting of their possible homosexuality and hopeful of their future happiness in a same-sex relationship. It is also significant that in each of these stories, the young person is counseled by a homosexual adult in ways that belie the myth of the predatory gay and lesbian seeking to "recruit." In Walker's novel, Vince fends off the advances of the younger man because he is too young, but his gentle and sensitive counseling, similar to Nurse Horn's in Sinclair's book and to Kate and Mary's in Brett's novel, gives comfort to the younger person that sets him on the path to self-acceptance. In each of these novels, we are left not knowing for certain whether or not the young person will become involved in a homosexual relationship. What is refreshing, though, is that each book ends with the possibility, even the likelihood, that it will happen and that when it does, it will be a positive life experience.

A major change in the tone of the books since 1990 is that despite the centrality of the issue of homosexuality in these books, the treatment of it has a matter-of-factness to it. My hope is that this indicates a subtle shift away from seeing homosexuality as an abnormality to be shunned toward seeing it as one more aspect of human diversity to be understood and accepted. Recent novels are showing, in positive ways, that homosexuality is an unchangeable fact of some people's lives. Garden's *Lark in the Morning* is a wonderful example of the way in which a novel can have a homosexual protagonist without making homosexuality its focus.

Toward this tone of acceptance, we are seeing in these novels a new consciousness-raising phenomenon: the positive portrayal of gay and lesbian family life, complete with children and dogs and cats and casserole dinners and taxes to pay and lawns to be mowed. Even though the father is dying in *Earthshine*, the "normalcy" of the family life cannot be overlooked. The same is true for Salat's *Living in Secret*, even though the lesbian family must adopt new identities and be very secretive about themselves in order to keep the court from removing Amelia from her mother and her lover's home. It is also important for the "recruitment" myth that in both families, neither child sees herself as homosexual, even though she lives in the midst of the lifestyle.

AIDS, which might be considered a topic that lends itself to stereotypic images, is receiving the kind of treatment in these more recent books that can help to change readers' perspectives. In an older novel (*Night Kites*, published in 1986), M. E. Kerr gave the first really sympathetic and sensitive portrayal of a young man dying of a dread disease and of his family's struggle to come to terms with it. Although it might be argued that Kerr has bought into the idea of God's punishment of male homosexuals, it must be noted that the author's central message is that by its ostracism of those who are different, society pushes people into a self-hate that often leads to self-destructive behavior. By his own admission, Eric's brother, Pete, says that contracting AIDS was the result of his sexual promiscuity. But why did he think he had been promiscuous? He tells Eric:

> I think relationships scared the hell out of me. I guess it was because if one lasted, I'd have to face a lot of shit I didn't want to. I'd be seen with one guy all the time. How could I explain that to the family . . . ? I've always had a problem with being openly gay. . . . That's probably why I couldn't get used to being with just one person. . . . (pp. 178–179)

In Durant's *When Heroes Die* and in *Earthshine*, AIDS is viewed in an entirely different way. How the disease might have been contracted is simply not an issue. The focus of both of these more recent novels is on the way in which a loving family comforts and supports both the dying loved one and each other. Neither book looks to blame or excuse whatever behaviors might have led to the illness, but rather strongly suggests that in a plague time, loving care and seeking a cure are the things that really matter.

Gay and lesbian activism in demanding the search for treatments and cure of AIDS is well-documented. *Earthshine*'s protagonist, Slim, learns the importance of activism, of doing something positive in the face of disaster, in the course of the novel. In fact, the authors of recent novels are portraying gay and lesbian activism in sympathetic ways, and they are also sending the message to readers that activism for social justice issues takes great courage and commitment from individuals. One of the many redeeming messages of Bette Greene's otherwise depressing and horrifying novel of homophobia, *The Drowning of Stephan Jones,* is the positive portrayal of those organizations fighting for the civil rights of gays and lesbians. Their Ghandian response to the cruelty and violence of the Christian Right makes them heroic and belies the myth of the wimpish, cowardly homosexual. The appearance of such organizations in young adult literature also provides assurance to the reader that there are certainly a great many more homosexuals around than the invisibility of the culture allows people to realize.

Finally, along the lines of "invisibility," I want to return to the stereotype of appearances. These recent novels are showing evidence, by the ways in which characters are physically portrayed, that we have progressed to a point where we can accept the full spectrum of differences among homosexuals. It is a fact that most gays and lesbians are invisible because they do not fit the physical stereotypes that still dominate many people's thinking. However, stereotypes frequently embody some truth, and another fact is that some gays and lesbians do fit those stereotypic images: There are effeminate gays and mannish lesbians. The genre has progressed to the point where an author can now honestly and sympathetically tell the story of a character who some years ago would only have represented a bad example. M. E. Kerr has refreshingly and sympathetically portrayed butch lesbians in *Deliver Us from Evie.* In this novel, very butch Evie is the seduced rather than the seducer, and her seducer is a very feminine stereotype herself. The novel not only admits to the reality of some stereotypes but dispels the myth of the butch predator as well as the myth that such stereotypic people will never find happiness. Evie and Patsy are mutually loving and clearly destined for a long-term relationship. As Evie explains to her mother:

Some of us *look* it, Mom! I know you so-called normal people would like it
better if we looked as much like all of you as possible, but some of us don't,
can't, and never will! And some others of us go for the ones who don't, can't,
and never will. (p. 86)

In a sense, we have come almost full circle, but that circle appears to be
ending on a more positive note than the one on which it began.

BREAKING THE SILENCE

Multicultural literature for young adults is a promising vehicle for developing awareness, understanding, and acceptance among cultural groups.
It is also a potentially valuable took for validating one's own knowledge
and experience. In doing so, it may help the reader discover him- or herself and build self-esteem. But for this to happen, the reader must be able
to find familiar, friendly images in the literature. As the feminist critics
point out, reading the androcentric canon is destructive to women's self-
images because they are always reading against themselves. Likewise,
because literature, whether of the canon or not, is predominantly heterosexual, gays and lesbians are always reading against themselves, since
they never see themselves reflected. How unfortunate, especially for gay
youth, that when a book that seems to mirror readers finally turns up, it
presents such an unattractive distortion that readers find that they are
reading against themselves once more.

Those students who are gay or lesbian are looking for respectable
role models and for validation of their feelings and experiences as surely
as African American, Hispanic, Asian American, Native American, or heterosexual female students are. Because there is still considerable misunderstanding, fear, and hostility actively directed toward homosexuals,
lesbian and gay youth can rarely speak or ask openly about their concerns. There are virtually no role models (allowed into the curriculum)
for them to look to, and their gay and lesbian teachers must suffer with
and for them silently out of fear of losing their jobs. Along with the psychosociological damage, the increasing physical threat of AIDS makes the
continuation of such enforced silence immoral. Under these repressive
circumstances, there is an even greater need for these students to have
literature that offers positive images of people like themselves, gives an
honest portrayal of the gay and lesbian culture, and helps them develop
into emotionally healthy and happy adults.

Unfortunately, there is not enough young adult literature about the gay and lesbian culture, and a number of the older books convey some troubling messages. But even if there were an abundance of "good" litera- ture, it would not be enough in and of itself. Heterosexual teachers need to deal with their own homophobia before they can help heterosexual students deal with theirs, and certainly before they can help build the self-esteem of their gay and lesbian students. Ideally, these young people would benefit if lesbian and gay adults, especially teachers, were free enough to become advocates for them. Sadly, as Rofes (1989) points out, that is unlikely to happen as long as homosexual teachers continue to be victims of "witch hunts" and as long as local laws continue to be passed that "forbid *positive* discussion of homosexuality in public school class- rooms" (p. 451; emphasis added).

The best hope for combating homophobia in our schools and our society is *not*, however, through multicultural education or with multicul- tural literature, but through the recognition by various racial/ethnic and cultural groups of their common oppression. Only when such groups realize that they "belong to each other [and] suffer at the hands of the same oppressor . . . [can they] attain liberation by jointly beating down the door to those whose fortunes are due to [their] misfortunes" (Tinney, 1983, p. 5). Any minority group that demands liberation for its members in the name of equity and justice is morally bound to demand liberation for all. If they do not, then they need to change their particular demand to what it really is, favoritism and the right to become oppressors themselves.

If multicultural education is sincere in its goals of countering discrim- ination, fostering cross-cultural respect and understanding, and assuring equal opportunity for all Americans, then it must be morally committed to eradicating *any* oppression that is based on diversity, including oppres- sion directed at gay and lesbian Americans. If the goals of multicultural education are partly achieved through literature that "permits children whose lives are mirrored to know that their ways of living, believing and valuing are important, legitimate, and to be valued . . . , [and] also permits them to reflect on the human condition" (Sims, 1984, p. 155), then we need to take a close look at the accuracy of the portrayal of *all* minority and oppressed cultures: We cannot behave as if the eradication of one oppression is more "worthy" than another. As Audre Lorde (1983) wrote, "Among those of us who share the goals of liberation and a workable future for our children, *there can be no hierarchies of oppression* [emphasis added]" (p. 9). The oppression of lesbians and gays "is usually the last oppression to be mentioned, the last to be taken seriously, and the last to go. But it is extremely serious, sometimes to the point of being fatal" (Smith, 1983, p. 7).

NOTE

1. The term *gay* is sometimes used to refer to all homosexual people, male and female. It is increasingly being used, as in this chapter, to refer only to homosexual males.

REFERENCES

Austin, M. C., & Jenkins, E. (1983). *Promoting world understanding through literature.* Littleton, CO: Libraries Unlimited.

Banks, J. A. (1979). Shaping the future of multicultural education. *Journal of Negro Education, 68,* 237–252.

Bleich, D. (1980). Epistemological assumptions in the study of response. In J. P. Tompkins (Ed.), *Reader-response criticism: From formalism to post-structuralism* (pp. 134–163). Baltimore: Johns Hopkins University Press.

Chandler, K. (1995). *Passages of pride: Lesbian and gay youth come of age.* New York: Random House.

Cox, S., & Galda, L. (1990, April). Multicultural literature: Mirrors and windows on a global community. *The Reading Teacher,* pp. 582–588.

Gallo, D. (1984, November). What should teachers know about YA lit for 2004? *English Journal,* pp. 31–34.

Garcia, R. (1982). *Teaching in a pluralistic society.* New York: Harper & Row.

Garcia, R. (1984). Countering classroom discrimination. *Theory Into Practice, 23,* 104–109.

Goodman, J. (1983). Out of the closet, but paying the price: Lesbian and gay characters in children's literature. *Interracial Books for Children Bulletin, 14,* 13–15.

Henry, W. A. (1993, July 26). Born gay?: Studies of family trees and DNA make the case that male homosexuality is in the genes. *Time,* pp. 36–39.

Holland, N. N. (1980). Unity identity text self. In J. P. Tompkins (Ed.), *Reader-response criticism: From formalism to post-structuralism* (pp. 118–133). Baltimore: Johns Hopkins University Press.

Huck, C. S., Hepler, S., & Hickman, J. (1987). *Children's literature in the elementary school* (4th ed.). New York: Holt, Rinehart & Winston.

Iser, W. (1980). The reading process: A phenomenological approach. In J. P. Tompkins (Ed.), *Reader-response criticism: From formalism to post-structuralism* (pp. 50–69). Baltimore: Johns Hopkins University Press.

Jenkins, C. A. (1993). Young adult novels with gay/lesbian characters and themes 1969–92: A historical reading of content, gender, and narrative distance. *Journal of Youth Services in Libraries, 7*(1), 43–55.

Kennard, J. E. (1986). Ourself behind ourself: A theory for lesbian readers. In E. A. Flynn & P. P. Schweickart (Eds.), *Gender and reading: Essays on readers, texts, and contexts* (pp. 63–80). Baltimore: Johns Hopkins University Press.

Lorde, A. (1983). There is no hierarchy of oppressions. *Interracial Books for Children Bulletin, 14,* 9.

Nilsen, A. P., & Donelson, K. L. (1985). *Literature for today's young adults* (2nd ed.). Glenville, IL: Scott, Foresman.

Norton, D. E. (1985). Language and cognitive development through multicultural literature. *Childhood Education, 62,* 103–107.

Norton, D. E. (1987). *Through children's eyes.* Columbus, OH: Merrill.

Rofes, E. (1989). Opening up the classroom closet: Responding to the educational needs of gay and lesbian youth. *Harvard Educational Review, 59,* 444–453.

Rosenblatt, L. (1978). *The reader, the text, the poem: The transactional theory of the literary work.* Carbondale: Southern Illinois University Press.

Rosenblatt, L. (1983). *Literature as exploration* (4th ed.). New York: Modern Language Association.

Scanzoni, L., & Mollenkott, V. R. (1978). *Is the homosexual my neighbor?: Another Christian view.* San Francisco: Harper & Row.

Schweickart, P. P. (1986). Reading ourselves: Toward a feminist theory of reading. In E. A. Flynn & P. P. Schweickart (Eds.), *Gender and reading: Essays on readers, texts, and contexts* (pp. 31–62). Baltimore: Johns Hopkins University Press.

Sims, R. (1984). A question of perspective. *The Advocate, 3,* 145–156.

Sims, R. (1985). Children's books about blacks: A mid-eighties report. *Children's Literature Review, 8,* 9–14.

Sims Bishop, R. (1987). Extending multicultural understanding through children's books. In B. E. Cullinan (Ed.), *Children's literature in the reading program* (pp. 60–67). Newark, DE: International Reading Association.

Smith, B. (1983). Homophobia: Why bring it up? *Interracial Books for Children Bulletin, 14,* 7–8.

Tinney, J. A. (1983). Interconnections. *Interracial Books for Children Bulletin, 14,* 4–6 and 27.

Walling, D. R. (1993). *Gay teens at risk.* Bloomington, IN: Phi Delta Kappa Educational Foundation.

Wilson, D. E. (1984, November). The open library: YA books for gay teens. *English Journal,* pp. 60–63.

SELECTED BIBLIOGRAPHY:
YOUNG ADULT NOVELS DEALING WITH LESBIAN AND GAY ISSUES

Barger, Gary W. *What Happened to Mr. Forster?* New York: Clarion, 1981.

Brett, Catherine. *S. P. Likes A. D.* East Haven, CT: Inland Press, 1990.

Chambers, Aidan. *Dance on My Grave.* New York: Harper & Row, 1982.

Donovan, John. *I'll Get There. It Better Be Worth the Trip.* New York: Harper & Row, 1969.

Durant, Panny Raife. *When Heroes Die.* New York: Antheum, 1992.

Ecker, B. A. *Independence Day.* New York: Avon, 1983.

Forster, E. M. *Maurice.* New York: Norton, Inc., 1971.

Futcher, Jane. *Crush.* New York: Little, Brown, 1981.

Garden, Nancy. *Annie on My Mind.* New York: Farrar, Straus & Giroux, 1982.

Garden, Nancy. *Lark in the Morning*. New York: Farrar, Straus & Giroux, 1991.

Greene, Bette. *The Drowning of Stephan Jones*. New York: Bantam, 1991.

Guy, Rosa. *Ruby*. New York: Viking, 1976.

Hall, Lynn. *Sticks and Stones*. Chicago: Follett, 1972.

Hautzig, Deborah. *Hey, Dollface*. New York: Bantam, 1978.

Holland, Isabelle. *The Man Without a Face*. New York: Bantam, 1972.

Homes, A. M. *Jack*. New York: Macmillan, 1989.

Kerr, M. E. *Deliver Us from Evie*. New York: HarperCollins, 1994.

Kerr, M. E. *I'll Love You When You're More Like Me*. New York: Harper & Row, 1977.

Kerr, M. E. *Night Kites*. New York: HarperCollins, 1986.

Klein, Norma. *Breaking Up*. New York: Pantheon, 1978.

Levy, Elizabeth. *Come Out Smiling*. New York: Delacorte, 1981.

Levy, Marilyn. *Rumors and Whispers*. New York: Fawcett Juniper, 1990.

Mosca, Frank. *All-American Boys*. Boston: Alyson, 1983.

Nelson, Theresa. *Earthshine*. New York: Orchard, 1994.

Reading, J. P. *Bouquets for Brimbal*. New York: Harper & Row, 1980.

Salat, Cristina. *Living in Secret*. New York: Bantam, 1993.

Scoppettone, Sandra. *Happy Endings Are All Alike*. New York: Harper & Row, 1978.

Scoppettone, Sandra. *Trying Hard to Hear You*. New York: Harper & Row, 1974.

Sinclair, April. *Coffee Will Make You Black*. New York: Avon, 1994.

Snyder, Anne and Pelletier, Louis. *The Truth About Alex*. New York: Bantam, 1981.

Tolan, Stephanie S. *The Last of Eden*. New York: Bantam, 1980.

Walker, Kate. *Peter*. Boston: Houghton Mifflin, 1993.

White, Edmund. *A Boy's Own Story*. New York: Dutton, 1982.

Winterson, Jeanette. *Oranges Are Not the Only Fruit*. New York: Atlantic Monthly Press, 1985.

CHAPTER 9

Reader-Response Theory and the Politics of Multicultural Literature

MINGSHUI CAI

IN RECENT DISCUSSIONS of multicultural children's literature, critics and educators often debate an author's responsibility for creating culturally authentic works. Contrary to belief in the "death of the author" or the banishment of the author from the interpretation of the text, many hold that the author's perspective has tremendous impact on the outcome of the literary creation and that the author's cultural identity, in turn, has great bearing on his or her perspective (e.g., Harris, 1992; Huck, Helper, & Hickman, 1993; Silvey, 1993; Sims, 1982; [Sims] Bishop, 1992; Yokota, 1993). At present, the "battle about books" is still very much a "battle about author . . . as a social constituency" (Gullory, cited in Gates, 1991, p. 26).

Who should write multicultural books for children? Should an "outsider" write about the experiences of another culture? Can an "outsider" succeed in creating authentic representations of an alien culture? These are some of the major questions raised about the authorship of multicultural literature. As Anita Silvey (1993) of *The Horn Book* magazine observes:

> On the one hand there are those who fight for artistic freedom and license. No one should prescribe what a writer or illustrator attempts, and creative genius allows individuals to stretch far beyond a single life and to write about lives never lived or experienced. On the other side are those who argue with equal conviction that only those from a particular culture can write about that culture or can write valid books about it. (p. 132)

The focus of the debate over multicultural literature is whether the author's or illustrator's cultural identity and perspective have any significant impact on the outcome of their artistic creation. This debate entails many complicated issues, such as the relationship between imagination and experience (Cai, 1995), authors' social responsibilities (Noll, 1995), and censorship. It is beyond the scope of this chapter to deal with all these issues adequately. Here I attempt to justify the concern with the author's cultural identity and perspective in terms of reader-response theory.

The current concern with the author's influence on the text of multicultural literature seems to run counter to the assumptions of reader-response theory, which has shifted the focus of literary criticism from the author and the text to the reader. The author's intention is no longer the locus of meaning. To some critics, emphasis on the author's identity and perspective appears to be outmoded, perhaps even a kind of atavism. In "'Authenticity,' or the Lesson of Little Tree," the noted African American critic Henry Louis Gates, Jr. (1991), argued against preoccupation with authenticity and the author's identity, lamenting that the "assumptions" that "ethnic or national identity finds unique expression in literary forms hold sway even after we think we have discarded them" (p. 26). He went on to say, "After the much-ballyhooed 'death of the author' pronounced by two decades of literary theory, the author is very much alive" (p. 26).

Is the concern with the author's or illustrator's identity and perspective, then, a legitimate one? Does it violate the principles of the presently prevailing reader-response theory? I try to answer these questions by first examining the basic principles of reader-response theory regarding the role of the text and author and then, in the light of these principles, justifying the concern with the author's cultural identity and background.

THE ROLE OF THE AUTHOR IN READER-RESPONSE THEORY

The role of the author in literature is played out through the text he or she creates. From the reader-response perspective, "the communication with the author becomes in fact a relationship through the text" (Rosenblatt, 1978, p. 76). An overview of the position on the status of text taken by various reader-response theorists will shed light on the extent to which they accept the author's role in the process of reading.

It should be noted that reader-response criticism "is not a conceptually unified critical position, but a term that has come to be associated with the work of critics who use the words 'reader,' 'reading process,' and 'response' to mark out an area for investigation" (Tompkins, 1980, p. ix). Varied as they are, all brands of reader-response theories recognize the reader's contribution to the making of meaning. The controversy centers around the status of text and the role of its creator—the author—

in the process of meaning-making. While emphasizing the reader's role, most reader-response theories, to varying degrees, also acknowledge the role of the text and author.

UNIACTION, INTERACTION, AND TRANSACTION

Positions on the relation between the reader and text, in my view, can be classified into three categories: uniactional, interactional, and transactional. The root *action* in the three terms can be operationally defined as the contribution of the agent (reader or text) to the making of meaning. The extreme uniactional view admits only the action of one of the two co-ordinates or elements in literature, namely, either the text or the reader alone has a role to play in the making of meaning.

E. D. Hirsch's (1967) theory of validity is a variant of reader-response theory in the sense that it accepts the fact of the text's openness, that the text can have different significations. Yet his theory is uniactional because it rejects the notion that there can be more than one valid interpretation for a text. For him, the only acceptable meaning of a text is the meaning the author encoded in it. What an individual reader reads into the text is not meaning, but "significance." Therefore, a text can have a constant "meaning" intended by the author but shifting "significances" decoded by the reader.

Stanley Fish's (1980) theory, which claims that all the meaning is supplied by the reader, is uniactional at the other extreme; it is actually a theory of "reader action" instead of reader response. Fish claims that "the interpreters do not decode poems; they make them." The epistemological assumption beneath this assertion is: "It is not that the presence of poetic qualities compels a certain kind of attention but that the paying of a certain kind of attention results in the emergence of poetic qualities" (p. 326). As the author's text has become a nonentity, literature exists only in the reader, whose interpretive strategies can mold the text, like plasticine, into any desired shape. From this theoretical perspective the author is driven totally out of the scene.

David Bleich's (1978) "subjective criticism" is also a uniactional model of reading. He considers the text as a series of symbols, the meaning of which depends entirely upon the reader's mental activity in constructing it. The reader becomes the independent self and the sole agent in the reading process. He rejects the active nature of the text—the guidance and constraints built into the text that the author can give to the reader.

Holland's (1968) psychoanalytical approach borders on uniactional theory. He sees the relationship between reader and text as the self and the "other." He admits that the text as the "other" exists prior to the reader's experience of it and puts constraints on the reader's interpretation. However, his main concern and interest centers on the function of the reader's identity. He later defined interpretation as "a function of identity" (1980, p. 123). Reading becomes a process of re-creating the text in terms of the reader's personal identity.

In contrast to the uniactional theories are the interactional and transactional theories, which incorporate both the reader and text as significant contributors to the reading experience but do not assign a central intended meaning to the text as the universal criterion for validity of interpretation. Both interactional and transactional theorists view the reading process as a reciprocal one, rather than a uniactional one in which a passive reader is acted on by the text or a passive text is acted on by the reader. However, the transactional theory (Rosenblatt, 1937, 1978) collapses the traditional subject/object dichotomy. The transaction between the reader and text is not a process of the subject (reader) responding to the stimuli of the object. It is a "highly complex ongoing process of selection and organization" (1978, p. 49) that results in the evocation of the literary work as distinguished from the text, the sequence of verbal symbols. Rosenblatt does not exalt the reader's creativity. As she notes, "the view that the reader in re-creating the work reenacts the author's creative role superficially seems more reasonable" (1978, p. 49). Nor does she deny the text's constraints on the reader's re-creation.

Robert Scholes's (1985) dialectic view of the relation between reader and text is compatible with Rosenblatt's. He believes that the reader is engaged in three kinds of activity: "reading, interpretation, and criticism. In reading, we produce text within text; in interpretation we produce text upon text; and in criticizing we produce text against text" (p. 24).

Iser's (1974, 1978) phenomenological theory carries some similar assumptions. Like Rosenblatt, who sees meaning-making as experiential, Iser holds that "meaning is no longer an object to be defined, but is an effect to be experienced" by the reader (1978, p. 10). A literary text does not formulate the meanings itself but "initiates performances of meaning" (1978, p. 27). It is this nature of indeterminacy that brings about the text–reader interaction. While the text contains "gaps" (i.e., what is only implied) that stimulate the reader to "concretize" (1978, p. 21) them with their projections so as to synthesize an aesthetic object, it also provides instructions and conditions for the production of that object.

Jonathan Culler's (1975) structuralist reading theory is primarily concerned with literary conventions, the knowledge of which enables a reader to understand literature. The literary conventions are a system of rules governing the operation of literary discourse, like the grammar of a language. Both author and reader have internalized this "grammar of literature" (p. 114) that makes literature intelligible. Reading, metaphorically, is a rule-governed game played by both the author and reader in the court of the text.

Rosenblatt's transactional theory and the interactional theories of Iser, Scholes, Culler, and others acknowledge the constraint and guidance of the text to the reader. These theories justify the investigation of the "textual power" (Scholes, 1985) of literature and the role of the author who infuses the text with that power. Rosenblatt admits the author into the scene of literary experience in this way: "He [the reader] will be conscious always that the words of the author are guiding him; he will have a sense of achieved communication, sometimes, indeed, with the author" (1978, p. 50). In some works, the author intrudes into the text with open comments; in others the author withdraws behind the characters. The author–reader relationship has evolved down through literary history. Yet, whether in the traditional "closed" texts or more modern "open" texts (in Barthes's [1974] terms, "readerly" or "writerly" texts), the author is always there. In children's literature, especially, the author's voice always speaks out loud, conveying attitudes, values, and assumptions that serve to shape the younger reader's mind and heart, even though it is no longer as openly didactic as in the past.

Fish's and Bleich's uniactional and Holland's near-uniactional theories not only put the reader at center stage in literary criticism but have also eliminated the role of the author and text. Their theories constitute the most subjectivist trend in the reader-response movement. In terms of influence, however, their theories by no means represent the mainstream of the movement; the critic most often quoted in educational research is Rosenblatt, not Fish or Bleich. These widely accepted reader-response theories have not banished the author from the criticism of literature.

In reading, as Terry Eagleton (1983) suggests, readers do not merely engage textual objects but also involve themselves in "forms of activity inseparable from the wider social relations between writers and readers" (p. 206). While it is an outdated notion to view the author's intention as the objective of reading, the dynamic of reading certainly lies in the interaction between the author and the reader. This occurs through the latter's reaction to the text, especially when there are discrepancies between the author's and reader's beliefs, assumptions, and values (as frequently happens in reading multicultural literature). According to one feminist view of reader response (Schweickart, 1986), "literature—the activities of reading and writing—[is] an important arena of political struggle" (p. 39). In the case of a female reader reading a male text, she asserts herself against the control of the text, "reading the text as it was not meant to be read, in fact, reading against itself" (p. 50). The reader then becomes a "resisting reader" (Fetterley, cited in Schweickart, 1986, p. 42). If the author were dead and his voice silent, there would be nothing to resist.

Just as female readers resist male-chauvinistic texts, readers from nonwhite cultures have been resisting literature showing racial bias and prejudice. The well-known author Milton Meltzer's (1987) response to the stereotyping of Jews in many literary masterpieces by major writers in history, such as Scott's *Ivanhoe*, Dickens's *Oliver Twist*, and Shakespeare's *The Merchant of Venice*, offers a typical example of reader's resistance to authorial sensibilities. Although he liked these works in his early years, he "tried to ignore everything in the novel that nourished anti-Semitism" (p. 493) and was "anxious to get on to passages less painful to me as a Jewish child" (p. 494). Meltzer speaks for all those who feel strongly about racial bias and prejudice encountered in literature.

These authors of classic literature—many of them were great humanitarians—might not have been aware of the anti-Semitic prejudices in their works. As their perspectives were shaped and conditioned by their times, they might have unconsciously reflected in their works the prevalent prejudices of their times. The prejudices might have been implied rather than intended. This is still the case with some authors of multicultural literature of our times. In whatever age, authors do not live in a social vacuum; their consciousness is determined by their social existence. In short, authors are social beings. If we accept the notion that "the author is dead," we would do nothing less than excuse the authors from their social and ethical responsibilities. A more realistic view is that authors live on, although their authority is reduced, their intention no longer wholly determining the meaning of their texts. We cannot deny the social nature of writing and reading; fiction and other forms of literature are "a contract designed by an intending author who invites his or her audience to adopt certain paradigms for understanding reality" (Foley cited in Rabinowitz, 1987, p. 23). It is up to the readers to decide whether they will accept the author's contract. Meltzer found the author's invitation to view Jews disparagingly in the classics unacceptable and rejected the contract.

THE REAL AUTHOR AND THE IMPLIED AUTHOR

Some reader-response theories not only acknowledge the author's role in reading but also provide new terms to deal with it, such as "implied reader" (Iser, 1974), "authorial audience" (Rabinowitz, 1987), and "implied author" (Booth, 1961). All these terms point to the author's presence in the text and acknowledge his or her role in the event of reading.

While reader-response theories reject the author's intended meaning as the objective of interpretation, as Rabinowitz (1987) observes, reading the author's intended meaning, or "authorial reading," provides a basis for critical reading from "some perspective other than the one called for by the author" (p. 32). Rabinowitz's theory dovetails with Scholes's theory of "producing text against text."

The author's intention may not be realized by the text he or she creates. There may exist a discrepancy between the actual author and his or her implied image in the text. Booth's concept of implied author addresses this discrepancy. Booth is not generally regarded as a representative reader-response theorist, but his concept of implied author is endorsed by Wolfgang Iser, one of the leading reader-response theorists. Iser (1974) states that "we should distinguish, as Wayne Booth does in his *Rhetoric of Fiction*, between the man who writes the book (author) and the man whose attitudes shape the book (implied author)" (p. 103).

According to Booth (1961), the author's presence is implied in his or her artistic creation. Different from the real author who writes the book, the implied author is the real author's "second self." A real author has "various official versions of himself" in different works he or she creates:

> Just as one's personal letters imply different versions of oneself, depending on the differing relationships with each correspondent and the purpose of each letter, so the writer sets himself out with different air depending on the needs of particular works. (p. 71)

The implied author is not to be identified with the speaker in the work, often referred to as "persona," "mask," or "narrator" (p. 73), who is only one of the elements created by the implied author. The narrator could be a dramatized character in the work, but the implied author can not. "The 'implied author' chooses, consciously or unconsciously, what we read . . . he is the sum of his own choices" (pp. 74–75). In fiction, some aspects of the implied author may be inferred from the style and tone of the work, "but his major qualities will depend also on the hard facts of action and character in the tale that is told" (p. 74).

The implied author's attitudes that shape the book are equivalent to what Iser (1978) termed "schematized views" in a literary work. The "schematized views" are not plainly stated but are hinted at by various perspectives offered by the text. In the novel, for example, "there are four main perspectives: those of the narrator, the characters, the plot, and the fictitious reader [the intended reader]" (p. 35). As the reader tries to use these perspectives to relate the "schematized views" to one another, he or she brings the text to life, and their meeting place, which the reader finds at the end, is his or her experienced meaning of the text. Different readers may find different meeting places. However, the network of perspectives predisposes the reader to read in certain ways.

Iser's (1978) term for the series of perspectives, the "network of response-inviting structures," is "implied reader" (p. 34). The term seems to be opposite to Booth's implied author, but in fact they refer to essentially the same thing from different perspectives. Both are theoretical constructs formulated to designate the conditioning force that the real author builds into the text when he or she creates the literary work. Both denote the "perspective view of the world put together by (though not necessarily typical of) the author" (Iser, 1978, p. 35). The relationship of the two concepts is footnoted by these remarks of Booth's: "The author creates, in short, an image of himself and another image of his reader; he makes his reader, as he makes his second self" (1961, p. 138).

An example may help to make these terms less abstract. In 1984, there was a debate between Rudine Sims (1984) and Belinda Hurmence (1982), author of *A Girl Called Boy,* in *The Advocate.* According to Sims, Hurmence's book presents a white perspective that perpetuates stereotypes of African Americans although it is a well-intended attempt to depict their experiences. She bases her argument on the sum of choices the author made consciously or unconsciously in the novel—choices of details to include, of words in the descriptions of things and people, of what to emphasize or deemphasize. For example, while mentioning the cruelties of the slave system throughout the book, according to Sims, the author also emphasizes the benevolence of some slave owners and the slaves' ambivalent attitude toward them. Implied in her literary choices is the author's perspective, or, in Iser's terms, "schematized views" on the reality presented in the book. The reader, such as Sims, would create from the author's choices the implied author—the image the real author created of herself when she created the book. According to Sims's reading, the implied author is a person who is sympathetic to black Americans but is not yet able to look at the world through their perspective. One may argue that Sims's inference about the implied author in the text is inaccurate and that one may then create from the text another very different implied author. Different inferences of the implied author are possible and natural, which explains why there is controversy over a multicultural literary work. In a sense the implied author may also be termed the *inferred author.* The implied author, as its name indicates, is not portrayed by the author in definite terms; it has to be inferred by the reader from the literary choices the author makes. The reader's inference, however, is a "struc-

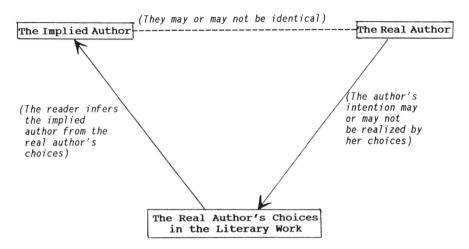

Figure 9.1. The Real Author, the Implied Author, and the Reader

tured act" (Iser, 1978, p. 35), not a random guess. The literary choices the author makes sketch a contour of his or her image in the text. The reader fills in the blanks with shade and color to form a clear picture of the implied author. Figure 9.1 illustrates the relationship among the actual author, the implied author, and the reader.

Despite her good intention to contribute to the representation of black experience in children's literature, the author of *A Girl Called Boy* implies in her choices an author whose perspective is not acceptable to some black readers.

This tension between the reader's and the implied author's perspectives is always present in any process of reading, but it is particularly conspicuous in reader response to "cross-cultural literature," because, conditioned by cultural differences, the gap between the reader's and the implied author's perspectives is often wide. When the implied author and the real author are different, the perspective of the world presented in the text, as Iser notes, is not necessarily typical of the real author. An author who writes about a culture other than his or her own may take on the alien beliefs and values of that culture. The author may give an authentic presentation of the culture in his or her works. The implied author, or the second self the real author creates, may be accepted by readers from that culture.

A typical example of the gap between real author and implied author is the novel by Forrest Carter (1976), *The Education of Little Tree*. This book is about the life of a Native American orphan who learned the ways of his culture from his Cherokee grandparents in Tennessee. When recently reprinted, it was an instant success and was well accepted by some Native American reviewers. Then suddenly it became a cause of controversy, an embarrassment to those who praised it, when the author's true identity was revealed. Forrest Carter turned out to be a pseudonym for a late racist. If a racist can write an authentic book about a minority, then one may ask, do we need to concern ourselves with the real author's perspectives and ethnic identity?

We may counter the question with another question: How many racists have written books like *The Education of Little Tree?* It is only rarely that a racist is willing and able to write an authentic book about the experiences of an ethnic minority group. While some authors may be able to build into their works an implied author that is completely different from themselves, others may not. This is especially true in multicultural literature. In many cases, the implied author and the real author are not two utterly different persons. In creating a literary world, the real author cannot put the complete reality into it but has to choose what to include. The choices the author makes often consciously or unconsciously reflect his or her experiences and perspectives of the real world. It is not easy, as Staples puts it, "to be under somebody else skin" (cited in Swayer & Swayer, 1993, p. 166) or, as Yep states (1987), to become an "invisible man" erasing all the features on your own face, "a blank mirror reflecting other people's hopes and fears" (p. 485). For authors of multicultural literature, this is a remarkable achievement, because they are not only aware of cultural differences but also are able to fill in the cultural gaps in their literary creation.

The distinction between the real author and the implied author makes it possible to explain the existence of such books as *The Education of Little Tree*. The relation between the real author's identity and his or her literary creation is not one of determinism (Gates, 1991). It is possible for authors of the mainstream culture to write authentic books about minority experiences. Minority authors can also write successful works about the mainstream culture. Among the numerous works of cross-cultural literature, there are well-written ones. Outsiders are not doomed to failure when they write about cultures other than their own. The lesson—if there is one—we may draw from *The Education of Little Tree* is not that the author's cultural identity is no longer significant, but rather that, while emphasizing the influence of an author's cultural background on his or her works about another culture, we should not claim an absolute causal relationship between the two. How can we if Forrest Carter, "a Ku Klux Klan terrorist," succeeds in creating a "second self" "who captures the unique vision of Native American culture" (Gates, 1991, p. 26)?

The author's experiences (direct and indirect) and imagination may help him or her surmount cultural barriers and create an implied author acceptable to the reader from a specific culture, but the gaps are not as easy to cross as one might imagine. What Rabinowitz (1987) calls "brute facts" impose great constraints and limitations on the author's imagination. Writing about another culture is comparable to writing about a historical period. Many "brute facts" are independent of the author's imaginations. Careful research is needed before the author can grasp the reality beyond his or her own world. Relying on imagination alone may result in making a laughing stock rather than a respectable self-image of the author (Cai, 1995). There is no lack of examples in the past or present. In a popular picture book *Tikki Tikki Tembo* (Mosel, 1968), the architectural style of the houses, the dresses and hairdos of the characters, and other details are Japanese, but the story is presented as a Chinese story. In a more recent picture book, *The Dwarf Giant* (Lobel, 1991), which is set in Japan, food is served in a manner only appropriate for offering it on the family altar and characters wear kimonos in a manner in which only deceased people would be dressed (Yokota, 1993). To a knowledgeable reader, these ludicrous misrepresentations show the authors and/or illustrators as culturally ignorant.

From the standpoint of ethical criticism, Booth (1988) holds that the actual writer should create for his or her work an implied author that represents a wise ethos. This often means "giving up a beloved fault or taking on an alien virtue" (p. 128). We can apply Booth's notion of an implied author representing wise ethos to multicultural literature. In doing so, we suggest that the actual writer should create in his or her work an implied author that represents the attitudes, beliefs, and values—in short, the perspective—of the culture he or she tries to portray and is thus identified with the readers from that culture. An outstanding example of such an author is Paul Goble, a non–American Indian who has created many pictures that authentically reflect American Indian culture. His works are highly acclaimed for their authenticity and distinct style. His success has been attributed to his long-term relationship with American Indian cultures (Noll, 1995).

THE AUTHOR'S CULTURAL IDENTITY IN MULTICULTURAL LITERATURE

Reader-response theory shifts the focus of critical attention from the text as the sole locus of meaning to the reader as an important constituent of meaning. This shift does not entail the death of the author. While uniactional theories deny the role of the text in literary interpretation, interactional and transactional theories recognize the text as a constraining and guiding force and admit the author's participation in the reading event. These theories justify the concern with an author's cultural identity and perspective as reflected in the text of multicultural literature. The concept of implied author in particular defines the author's presence in the text: The literary choices the actual author makes combine to form an image of the author or his or her second self. This concept also explains possible discrepancies between the author and his or her "second self," between the author's intention and the actual effects of his or her literary creation. This has two significant implications, among others, for the creation of multicultural literature.

First, an author can write about a different culture and create a "second self" that shares the perspectives of the people from that culture, even though he or she has not become one of its members. While we emphasize the influence of an author's cultural background on his or her works about another culture, we should not hold a deterministic view that claims an absolute causal relationship between the two.

Second, a well-intended author may create a literary work about an ethnic culture unacceptable to the people of that culture. The author's cultural identity and background may adversely influence his or her literary choices without the author's knowing it. From the perspective of social progress, multicultural literature is intended to inform people about other cultures, to liberate them from the bondage of stereotypes (Howard, 1991), to foster respect for one's own cultural heritage as well as others, and to promote cross-cultural understanding. Many authors who write multicultural literature for children may be motivated by these lofty purposes, but good intention does not guarantee that the implied author in their books will achieve the desired effects. Instead of insisting on good intentions, authors would be better off turning an eager ear to readers' responses to their works and taking responsibility for the social effects their works may have produced. As promoters and gatekeepers, publishers share some of this responsibility with authors.

The battle over the role of the author will continue in the political arena of multicultural literature. The mainstream reader-response theories are on the side of those who uphold the relevance of the author's cultural identity and perspective regarding the creation of multicultural literature.

REFERENCES

Barthes, R. (1974). *S/Z*. (R. Miller, Trans.). New York: Hill and Wang.
Bishop, R. S. (1992). Multicultural literature for children: Making informed choice.

In V. J. Harris (Ed.), *Teaching multicultural literature in grades k–8* (pp. 37–54). Norwood, MA: Christopher-Gordon.

Bleich, D. (1978). *Subjective criticism*. Baltimore: Johns Hopkins University Press.

Booth, W. C. (1961). *The rhetoric of fiction*. Chicago: University of Chicago Press.

Booth, W. C. (1988). *The company we keep: An ethics of fiction*. Berkeley: University of California Press.

Cai, M. (1995). Can we fly across cultural gaps on the wings of imagination? Ethnicity, experience, and cultural identity. *The New Advocate, 8*(1), 1–17.

Carter, F. (1976). *The education of Little Tree*. New York: Delacorte.

Culler, J. (1975). *Structuralist poetics: Structuralism, linguistics and the study of literature*. Ithaca, NY: Cornell University Press.

Eagleton, T. (1983). *Literary theory: An introduction*. Minneapolis: University of Minnesota Press.

Fish, S. (1980). *Is there a text in this class?* Cambridge, MA: Harvard University Press.

Gates, H. L., Jr. (1991, November 24). "Authenticity," or the lesson of Little Tree. *The York Times Book Review*, November 24, pp. 1, 26–30.

Goble, P. (1988). *Her seven brothers*. New York: Bradbury.

Harris, V. J. (Ed.). (1992). *Teaching multicultural literature in grades k–8*. Norwood, MA: Christopher-Gordon.

Hirsch, E. D., Jr. (1967). *Validity in interpretation*. New Haven, CT: Yale University Press.

Holland, N. N. (1968). *The dynamics of literary response*. New York: Oxford University Press.

Holland, N. N. (1980). Unity identity text self. In J. Tompkins (Ed.), *Reader-response criticism: From formalism to post-structuralism* (pp. 118–134). Baltimore: Johns Hopkins University Press.

Howard, E. F. (1991). Authentic multicultural literature for children: An author's perspective. In M. Lindgren (Ed.), *The multicolored mirror: Cultural substance in literature for children and young adults* (pp. 90–94). Fort Atkinson, WI: Highsmith.

Huck, C. S., Helper, S., & Hickman, J. (1993). *Children's literature in the elementary school*. New York: Holt, Rinehart & Winston.

Hurmence, B. (1982). *A girl called boy*. New York: Clarion.

Iser, W. (1974). *The implied reader: Patterns in communication in prose fiction from Bunyan to Beckett*. Baltimore: Johns Hopkins University Press.

Iser, W. (1978). *The act of reading: A theory of aesthetic response*. Baltimore: Johns Hopkins University Press.

Lobel, A. (1991). *The dwarf giant*. New York: Holiday House.

Meltzer, M. (1987). A common humanity. In B. Harrison & G. Maguire (Eds.), *Innocence and experience* (pp. 490–497). New York: Lothrop.

Mosel, A. (1968). *Tikki Tikki Tembo*. Illustrated by B. Lent. New York: Holt.

Noll, E. (1995). Accuracy and authenticity in American Indian children's literature: The social responsibility of authors and illustrators. *The New Advocate, 8*(1), 29–43.

Rabinowitz, P. J. (1987). *Before reading: Narrative convention and the politics of interpretation*. Ithaca, NY: Cornell University Press.

Rosenblatt, L. M. (1937). *Literature as exploration*. New York: Appleton-Century-Crofts.

Rosenblatt, L. M. (1978). *The reader, the text, the poem: Transactional theory of the literary work*. Carbondale: Southern Illinois University Press.

Scholes, R. (1985). *Textual power: Literary theory and the teaching of English*. New Haven, CT: Yale University Press.

Schweickart, P. P. (1986). Reading ourselves: Toward a feminist theory of reading. In E. B. Flynn & P. P. Schweickart (Eds.), *Gender and reading* (pp. 31–62). Baltimore: Johns Hopkins University Press.

Silvey, A. (1993). Varied carols. *The Horn Book Magazine, 69*(2), 132–133.

Sims, R. (1982). *Shadow and substance*. Urbana, IL: National Council of Teachers of English.

Sims, R. (1984). A question of perspective. *The Advocate, 3,* 145–156.

Swayer, W., & Swayer, J. (1993). A discussion with Suzanne Fisher Staples: The author as writer and cultural observer. *The New Advocate, 6*(3), 159–171.

Tompkins, J. (Ed.). (1980). *Reader-response criticism: From formalism to post-structuralism*. Baltimore: Johns Hopkins University Press.

Yep, L. (1987). A Chinese sense of reality. In B. Harrison & G. Maguire (Eds.), *Verbal icon* (pp. 485–489). New York: Lothrop.

Yokota, J. (1993). Issues in selecting multicultural literature. *Language Arts, 70*(3), 156–167.

Reading Literature of Other Cultures

Some Issues in Critical Interpretation

ANNA O. SOTER

Hence, people enjoy looking at images, because as they contemplate they understand and infer each element (e.g., that this is such-and-such a person). Since, if one lacks familiarity with the subject, the artifact will not give pleasure qua mimetic representation but because of its craftsmanship, color, or for some other such reason.
—Aristotle, Poetics

The perspective of cross-cultural literatures has given explicit confirmation to the perception that genres cannot be described by essential characteristics, but by an interweaving of features, a "family resemblance" which denies the possibility either of essentialism or limitation.
—Bill Ashcroft, Gareth Griffiths, and Helen Tiffin,
The Empire Writes Back

IN ALDOUS HUXLEY's *Brave New World*, the Savage, an outcast in that utopian society, stumbles across Shakespeare's *The Tempest* and is transformed through its offering of another world that to him is wondrous in all its possibilities until he discovers that it is not what it seems to be (Huxley, 1933; Shakespeare, 1611/1964). In Australia, a young child in the outback enters the world of the English romantic poets, dreaming of "verdant lands" in the midst of a rocky, red-dirt landscape.

Questions of what constitutes "literature" and, related to this, questions of truth, values, knowledge, and culture have always been with us even in our study of the classics as incorporated in high school and college curricula in the past century. We could argue that a student living and studying Jane Austen's *Emma* (Austen, 1816/1969) or Shakespeare's *The Tempest* in the Australian outback is nearly as far removed from the contexts that created both of those works as are current students in American urban and suburban school settings. Yet the power of literature to transport readers into other worlds has never been doubted by those who, despite their own sometimes narrow worlds, have been captured by writers no matter how different the culture they inhabit. Certainly, we could also argue that an understanding of the political context in Czechoslovakia would enable us to better understand and appreciate ironies in Milan Kundera's *The Book of Laughter and Forgetting* (Kundera, 1986). Or, if we were familiar with the sociocultural and political character of contemporary Israel, we might make much more of A. B. Yehoshua's *A Late Divorce* (Yehoshua, 1984) than we are able to as outsiders. However, it would be utterly inaccurate to suggest that lacking such knowledge always precludes both enjoyment and even critical appreciation of such literature. In addition, much of our reading would be severely curtailed.

Yet not all readers in our schools will so readily connect with Bloom's (1994) claim of the "autonomy of imaginative literature," although they may well agree with the "sovereignty of the solitary soul," even if not in the way Bloom intended (p. 10). To understand and appreciate the significance of the arguments put forth by many scholars for the necessity of including literature of other cultures, and not necessarily canonical texts within those cultures, we must, I believe, return to the beginnings of the literary history of our diverse, individual students. If we do not, we assume a literary sophistication and experience that more resembles our own, with frequently disappointing consequences.

LITERATURE OF OTHER CULTURES IN THE CLASSROOM

To date, the focus of much discussion on the use of literature representative of other cultures—whether within or outside of the United States—has been on *the content* of that literature. Our concern with using that literature in classrooms has centered, and rightly so, on the following: the relevance to readers in school (Chisunka, 1991); the appropriateness to students at different ages and levels (Applebee, 1990; Diamond & Moore, 1995); issues related to negative stereotyping (Ramirez, 1992; Viehmann, 1994); questions of accessibility (Perkins, 1992); and questions related to the range of selections (Applebee, 1991; Harwood, 1993). We are now at a point at which the notion of using literature representative of other cultures (within and outside the United States) is well established in the professional literature and is increasingly accepted in schools, which suggests that at least some progress has been made in addressing the concerns described above. My concern in this chapter, as in much of this book, is to address the question of what we *do* with these books once they are in the classroom. I am particularly interested in exploring the notion of aesthetic restriction in terms of how it influences us as readers of often quite unfamiliar content found in the literature of other cultures, and what we as teachers can do about this.

AESTHETIC RESTRICTION IN THE FACE OF THE UNFAMILIAR

While educators may readily admit that reading books by writers of other cultures provides us with a rich and immensely enjoyable literary experience, as well as some understanding of those cultures, our starting point for engagement *and* interpretation will be different from that of "insiders." Therefore we are faced with new critical challenges if we intend to use literature representative of different cultures in our classrooms. Dasenbrook (1992), however, suggests that this need not be an insurmountable obstacle, for "the informed position," he asserts, "is not always the position for the richest or most powerful experience of a work of art. And this becomes even more true when crossing cultural barriers" (p. 39).

I was recently reminded of these and other insights when discussing with a class the concluding chapter of Katherine Susannah Prichard's novel *Coonardoo*, first published in Australia in 1925 and since reprinted in a variety of editions (Prichard, 1925/1994). The novel is about, among other things, the unacknowledged love between a white man and an Aboriginal woman. Unacknowledged love (and more frequently, sex) between white men and Aboriginal women was not entirely uncommon in the outback of Australia. However, it did not do to speak about the subject. Nor is it, even now, a subject many want to address.

Drusilla Modjeska, in her introduction to the recent edition, observed that, in an rather unusual step, Prichard had originally explained this particular work of fiction in the following way:

> Life in the north-west of Western Australia . . . is almost as little known in Australia as in England or America. It seems necessary to say, therefore, that the story was written in the country through which it moves. Facts, characters, incidents, have been collected, related, interwoven. That is all. (1994 edition, p. v)

Given both the critical acclaim and the public outrage following the novel's original publication, Prichard seems to have been gifted with special insight in presenting her justification of the work for its "imaginative, historical and social accuracy" (1994 edition, p. v).

I was interested in seeing how a group of American graduate students in a large midwestern university would respond to the novel. Reluctance to declare "outrage" was evident in my class, although it is also likely that none was felt. Only one person in the class wished to talk about it in depth. However, others felt the power of the novel, which in its concluding stages approaches the scope of grand tragedy. Nevertheless, there was strong reluctance to talk about it, for, seemingly, the following reasons: Students felt they did not know enough about the context to comment on the events and characters; the setting and events seemed so far-fetched in the midwestern American context that a starting point for discussion was difficult to find, despite the empathy that everyone felt for the Aboriginal woman, the main character; and the mixture of fact and fiction also made students feel that they lacked "background knowledge" that they admittedly did not have. Unlike me, my students had not grown up in Australia, let alone the outback. None had any previous contact with Australian Aboriginals. Unlike me, they could only connect with the relationship between Hugh (the white man) and Coonardoo (the Aboriginal woman) through urban and suburban eyes, in a markedly different context. I had known of such relationships in a firsthand experience—one of my close childhood friends was the son of a white man and an Aboriginal woman. I had also known of white men and Aboriginal women whose relationship went beyond sex to the similarly unacknowledged emotional bond the novel describes between Hugh and Coonardoo.

The begged question became: What is the starting point for this and other similarly "foreign" works? Where does a teacher begin to help students make the connections at the personal level and at the aesthetic level that establish the ground to engage in interpretive criticism, to evaluate the novel as a work of art, and to commence what Geertz (1979) described as "entering into a kind of conversation" with these "depicted lives of other peoples" (p. 226). In *Coonardoo*, as in other works, readers might also have to overcome aesthetic restriction (my term) brought about by ethical and, possibly, religious repugnance (Gunn, 1987). At the same time, it is worth noting that an uncritical acceptance may also occur simply because the context and its representation in the literary object are unfamiliar. I find myself in this quandary when reading a collection such as Fauzia Rafiq's *Aurat Durbar* or Masha Gessen's anthology, *Half a Revolution: Contemporary Fiction by Russian Women* (Rafiq, 1995; Gessen, 1995).

Similarly, what adjustments must I—a well-seasoned reader—make when confronted with the following excerpt, powerful as it is in its effect, from Marina Palei's "The Bloody Women's Ward"?

> Razmetalsky delivers his lectures only when he has temporarily set aside his razor blade, sat himself down in the abortion theater with a martyred air and is bearing his cross in the form of a pair of uplifted female legs. Then, with Darya Petrovna lovingly maneuvering the surgical basin into which the bloody tatters are to slop, Razmetalsky delivers his lecture in his dull monotonous voice, and seems to the woman the lord of all creation. (Palei, 1992, p. 75)

The widely experienced reader will more readily accord this and other "different" literature sufficient distance from the reading "self" in order to grant it literary merit. In general, as I read, I am already contextualizing the literary text. If it is by a writer from another culture, I am prepared for "difference"; if it is a novel, I more readily suspend my judgments, disbeliefs, resistances because I must read further than a few pages to give the book a chance to "work" on me; if it is a contemporary work, I must be prepared for a greater degree of directness, bluntness, perhaps even shock-effect; and so on. Most, if not all, readers who are naturally drawn to a rich and varied literary diet will not have great difficulty in accepting the initial strangeness sometimes experienced when reading literature representative of different cultures. However, the inexperienced or young reader is, as a rule, not so readily accommodating. The reader inexperienced in reading literature outside of his or her cultural context may have considerable difficulty in finding "fits," in making space so that the unfamiliar, the potentially shocking, will not create aesthetic shut-down. This aesthetic shut-down is the core of my earlier use of the phrase "aesthetic restriction."

Aesthetic restriction is not, I think, the same as the notion of "aesthetic distance" described by Jauss (1982), although the concepts are related. Jauss's use of the concept of aesthetic distance implies the possibility of the acceptance of a literary work because the readership is *receptive* to it. He argues that the "sum total of reactions, prejudgments, and verbal and other behavior that greet a work upon its appearance" is capable of being altered (cited in Godzich, 1994, p. 40) such that there can be acceptance. Jauss acknowledges that resistance, implied in distance, may also result in the rejection of the work until such time that a "horizon of expectation" for that work is "forged" (Godzich, 1994, p. 41). My notion of aesthetic restriction, on the other hand, dismisses the work out of hand *because* of elements in the text that the reader finds unacceptable, and it is often as much because of *content* as of form that the rejection occurs. Thus the literary text cannot "work on the reader"—it is at the level of personal response related to values, tastes, life experiences, predilections, openness to possibilities of other lives and values that the work is untenable for the reader. The distance necessary for the values to be held in suspension, allowing for a dispassionate evaluation of its other possible merits, cannot occur with this kind of reading.

I also do not see the notion of aesthetic restriction operating in the same way as Fetterley's (1978) notion of "the resisting reader," for in my use of the term, "restriction" is primarily an unconscious act, and in Fetterley's case it is proposed as a conscious act:

> Clearly then, the first act of the feminist critic must be to become a resisting rather than assenting reader and, by this refusal to assent, to begin the process of exorcising the male mind that has been implanted in us. (p. xxii)

Let me explore how the notion of aesthetic restriction might work when applied to a story written by a writer from a different literary tradition. The author, Alifa Rifaat (1989), draws much of her material from her experience of living in the Egyptian countryside, according to the editor of the collection in which her story is found. We are moved into the story, "Another Evening at the Club," somewhat innocuously as a woman waits for her husband:

> In a state of tension, she awaited the return of her husband. At a loss to predict what would happen between them, she moved herself back and forth in the rocking chair on the wide wooden veranda that ran along the bank and occupied part of the river itself, its supports being fixed in the river bed, while around it grew grasses and trees. (p. 148)

The long, multi-embedded sentence winds its way into our minds but also suspends the action and, in doing so, suspends us, too—we seem to be caught in the seemingly breathless moment before action. Rifaat maintains the suspense as she describes, in great detail, the setting for the main event, the loss of an emerald ring given to the woman by her husband as part of her betrothal package. The story is told in retrospect as the woman recalls her husband coming to her parents' house to meet her for the first time. The emerald ring is subsequently bought by her husband-to-be as a birthday present. We move through her memories to her marriage, when on her wedding night, her husband instructs her that she must pretend that she comes from a well-known Barakat family and that her father is a judge. He then gently pats her cheeks "in a fatherly, reassuring gesture that he was often to repeat during their times together" (p. 150).

From that point we move quickly to the critical event—the loss of the emerald ring—a result of a somewhat tipsy evening prior to the telling of the story when the woman accidentally drops the ring and falls asleep to awaken next morning and discover the ring gone. She alerts her husband, who interrogates the maid, who, in turn, is interrogated by the police, who have "their ways and means" to make people talk (p. 152). The following day the woman finds the ring, which had slipped between the legs of the table and the wall. She informs her husband, who does nothing, because to inform the police would mean a loss of face in having to admit that his wife had been tipsy the night before. He then asks her to give him the ring. He will sell it when he next goes to Cairo to get something else in its place. In the face of her surprisingly uncharacteristic protest,

> he gently patted her on the cheeks . . . the gesture telling her more eloquently than any words that he was the man, she the woman, he the one who carried the responsibilities, made the decisions, she the one whose role it was to be beautiful, happy, carefree. Now, for the first time in their life together the gesture came like a slap in the face. (p. 154)

The situation described in the story is not totally unfamiliar even for a Western female reader. However, this is a story set in modern Egypt, by a modern Egyptian writer. That is, it is not a story set in a contemporary U.S. context. In reading this tale, we know almost nothing about the author, almost nothing about the tradition of Egyptian modern writing; therefore we must start, in effect, with what is in the story. As modern readers in a culture where the rights of women are a "given" and where women expect to be equal to men in all respects (at least, rhetorically), what aesthetic resistance to the story itself will result from the passage quoted above?

Furthermore, both the husband's and wife's nonchalance concerning the potential fate of the maid is very disturbing. At no point is any concern expressed for her treatment by the police. Can we assume an implied author who *is* concerned for the maid? Can we read the husband's and wife's indifference as a critique of that indifference? Although we *can* read the foregoing extracts as a critique of a culture that imposes a dependent status on women, issues of class or economic status remain unsolved.

Will this reading result in Jauss's (1982) "aesthetic distance," which, in turn, may result in the rejection of the work? Or will it do what Jauss suggests as the alternative effect, that is, make the public (reader) alter its horizons so that the work is accepted? (Godzich, 1994). How is the teacher to deal with the personal resistance to the content that may, in turn, result in what I have termed "aesthetic restriction"? In effect, the reader is unable to enter the domain of the story from the perspective of the woman. We could, after all, argue that the writer is critical of the context in which a woman has to "put on the right face" in order to "get on" with the rest of her family and with her community. Is the subtext really about acquiescence, or is it a clever way of raising the issue, of critiquing the accepted status of women who must deny their knowledge of truth? At one level, the story is quite a powerful statement about the status of women in the culture inhabited by the writer. But it is very differently expressed than writing that is more familiar to us, as I think this excerpt from Doris Lessing's short story, "Two Old Women and a Young One," will illustrate:

> The Modigliani girl answered her, and her voice was just as much in a local pattern as the American's. . . . For often and everywhere is to be found this voice. . . . a little breathy high voice that comes from a circumscribed part of the women who use it, not more than two square inches of the upper chest, certainly not a chest cavity or resonating around a head. . . . Oh dear, poor little me, they lisp their appeals to the unkind world; these tough, often ruthless young women who use every bit of advantage they can. (Lessing, 1992, p. 177)

The portrait is not a charming one but it *is* recognizable; and we, as Western women, know exactly what is meant and acknowledge the quest for power implicit in the depiction of the use of womanly wiles, even while not necessarily liking it—it is, after all, an unflattering portrait. But as readers situated in a shared cultural context, we do not have to work hard to *overcome initial alienation*. Indeed, we want to know more: How does this story evolve; what happens to the use of the female wiles; is the author addressing us tongue-in-cheek? In contrast, we may resist wanting to know more about the Rifaat story—it has greater potential to cut us out because of its content, making it more difficult for us to pursue at other levels.

Although I have argued that the Rifaat story may bring about aesthetic restriction because of its content, I would hastily add that distinctions between form and content cannot, as a rule, be so neatly made. Even as we read the Rifaat story, we could be influenced (in terms of the content) by the subtle juxtaposition of a serene, luxurious setting described in the opening lines with the jarring indifference of the couple toward the maid and the undercurrent of the wife's warring emotions, which are *not* expressed in her surface features and behavior. That is, *how* something is said will influence *what* is perceived by the reader. As Scott Walker (1989) notes in his introduction to the collection containing Rifaat's story:

> As in other forms of friendship, in order to understand and appreciate, one must meet the other a bit more than halfway. . . . [We] open ourselves to a different aesthetic model. If we perceive and are put off by stiffness in the plot, a static character, or clumsy language, we may entirely miss the music of these tales. . . . It can be a struggle for a reader unaccustomed to reading the myths and stories of another culture to overcome *resistance and predisposition* [emphasis added]. (p. xii)

One way out of the thicket of critical difficulty implied in the previous pages is to define our goals as teachers of literature representative of diverse cultures in terms of creating a literary dialectic, a conversation that prepares the ground for the movement from "uncritical" response (which may include aesthetic restriction) to "critical" appreciation, that is, to evaluative interpretation. Bogden (1992) describes the full literary response as a "dialectic that legitimizes and capitalizes on the responses of partial form by building on whatever emotional and intellectual raw material presents itself at the precritical level in such a way that response can be deepened, refined, and enriched through aesthetic distance" (p. 119). The way in which this kind of distance is accomplished is through perceiving the literary object as a "separate reality," or, as Frye says, as an "alien structure of the imagination" (cited in Bogden, p. 120). The teacher's role, then, becomes one of creating spaces to allow for the transmutation from the real to the imaginative, from similarities with to differences from the real versus the imagined, and to ground the responses more firmly in the world of the text, *having begun them* in the world(s) of the reader.

AESTHETIC RESTRICTION AND AESTHETIC EVALUATION

In my experience, the teacher of literature of other cultures, no matter how liberal, must be prepared to encounter and deal with readers' puzzlement and negative reactions to content so that "initial responses can be deepened, refined, and enriched through aesthetic distance" (Bogden, 1992, p. 119). An exploration of how aesthetic restriction can influence subsequent engagement and evaluation of literary works follows, with a description of responses to Ding Xiaoqi's (1994) collection of short stories, *Maidenhome,* used in a recent summer institute on the teaching of global literature. No easy solution appeared in terms of how to prepare readers for the unfamiliar literature they encountered. All of the participants had volunteered to take the institute, all were eager to experience literature representing diverse cultures and wished to use the information in their own classrooms. In many respects, the institute was an ideal starting point for our exploration of unfamiliar territory, given that its participants had a high level of motivation, were all skilled and experienced readers who loved literature, and were open and tolerant of new experiences.

A reading journal was utilized to help the participants connect with the texts and to aid the process of articulating responses. It also provided participants with the opportunity to reflect on how they responded to the selections. Some background information was provided for each of the cultures represented in the course by cultural informants who responded to questions from the participants. Brief historical and cultural background information was also provided to contextualize the literature used in the selections.

The following excerpts from responses to Ding Xiaoqi's stories illustrate how difficult even these experienced and eager readers found it to accept literature that, while gripping and fascinating, was "foreign" to them. At the same time, they also reveal much that teachers can work with, using the initial responses as a foundation for further exploration. One explicit reaction to the contents of the story is the following:

> The thought of parents selling children/young adults [14-/17-years-old] was shocking. She didn't even know she was being sold—just like in the short story, "Maidenhome," in which the girl did not know she was joining the military the day her father signed her up. . . . The lack of information and discussion of the child's future in what seems a family-centered culture is surprising. . . . I was shocked to read "Killing Mom" and I started thinking about other pieces of literature that deal with insanity—"The Yellow Wallpaper" and "The Tell Tale Heart."

This member of the institute attempted to connect (and, therefore, make sense of) some of the *Maidenhome* stories with stories about insanity. Another reader sought to find an "explanation" for what was difficult for him to articulate in the possibility that the author was a cultural anomaly:

> The book of short stories, *Maidenhome,* was fascinating but I wonder whether the stories are very typical. Perhaps the very fact that this author found translators into English and a publisher makes her unusual.

Some members of the institute attempted to give the book its "due" rather than dismiss what they found difficult to accept:

> I am still trying to come to terms with the sterile concept of love of Party above all else. I think I would surely have gone mad under such a regime. Perhaps that is the impetus which drives artists and revolutionaries to acts of courage and risk. Death as the better alternative.

Some were more explicit in their response to individual stories but explained the effect in terms of contextual (in this case, cultural) differences:

> *Maidenhome* was excellent. It was disturbing to think about women in those roles. Actually, it was quite depressing. Love and marriage are not perfect in the United States but at least we have the freedom to make our own choices. I cannot imagine being in a situation like the daughter-in-law in "Indica, Indica." It made me think about how sex is discussed in the United States. Many people feel that it is in the media too much, but I think more people know about it as a result.

Most striking in all the responses was a tension between shock and repulsion at the events described and fascination *because* those events were described—among them, subtle rape (not known until it was over), teenage brides, killing a mother, government control, and breakups in relationships. As some members of the institute noted, some events were universal but many were not. One member observed that the collection of stories "really helped destroy my stereotypical conceptions of what it means to be Chinese, especially a Chinese woman. I thought this book would contain stories about demure, obedient, well-behaved women who suffered at the hands of men. I couldn't believe the women in these stories." Paradoxically, however, the collection does show stories of women who "suffer at the hands of men" and who, on the surface, are "demure, obedient women." The rage, the revenge, the passion is *internal* rather than *external*.

Participants in the institute were required to read the selections prior to its commencement. Many observed that it was not until the presentation by the Chinese cultural informant, who talked of the power and influence of the Cultural Revolution, that they began to understand *Maidenhome*, written as it was after the Cultural Revolution by an author who left China as a refugee in the early 1990s.

These examples are representative of responses made by all of the institute's participants. They are meaningful in terms of my earlier discussion because they illustrate in several ways some of the challenges we face when using literature of other cultures. First, the session on Chinese literature provided participants with cultural and literary information and participants appeared to find this valuable, although they did not use the information directly in "interpreting" the literature. Second, each reader was at a very different "place" relative to background information needed to move beyond very superficial readings of the texts. We found that we had difficulties in assuming shared understandings of meaning and intention in the literature being read. Third, while participants engaged with and interpreted the literature selections from the perspective of their own cultural frames, they nevertheless also approached them as individuals, with quite varying responses (the responses were always written *prior to* discussions). Fourth, content in the literature must be taken into account, especially when considering why readers connect the way they do (as illustrated in some of the responses to the *Maidenhome* stories).

Indeed, the institute substantiated Jauss's claim that "we never come to cognitive situations empty but carry with us a whole world of familiar beliefs and expectations. The hermeneutic phenomenon encompasses both the alien world we suddenly encounter and the familiar one we carry" (cited in Godzich, 1994, p. 41). Like Godzich (1994) we were forced to recognize that readers "are awash in the tradition that has given rise to the object of his or her reading" (p. 41) *only if* the literature being read is representative of the culture that the reader also inhabits. Otherwise, our conceptions of reading and what readers bring to the experience of reading are often in conflict. Such contradiction must also include questions of what we see as aesthetically satisfying to us and, at times, even as aesthetically recognizable.

A Vignette

The time frame and purpose of the institute did not allow for in-depth explorations of how we can assist students in overcoming aesthetic restriction to the works read. However, the following example (discussed in greater detail in Soter, 1996) may help to illustrate how we can guide readers to Jauss's "altered horizons ... leading to an acceptance of the work which was previously rejected" (cited in Godzich, 1994, p. 44). Students in a college young adult literature course found the novel *Where the Lilies Bloom* (Cleaver & Cleaver, 1960) implausible for several reasons but primarily because they had little familiarity with the lifestyle and values of the Appalachian community that is depicted in the novel. They were unable to accept that the heroine, 14-year-old Mary Call, could be as competent and mature as she appears to be. For example, students found her wildcrafting expertise difficult to accept; they found her clever ruses in covering up her father's death absurd; they could not accept her inability to see her older sister (Devola) as anything but "cloud-headed"; and they were reluctant to believe that Mary Call could outwit her apparent adversary, 30-year-old Kiser Pease. Despite evidence later in the novel, Mary Call was perceived as "too good to be true."

Given that authenticity was an issue in the reading of the novel, one would have thought that discussions centering on the book as an authentic rendering of the lifestyle of an Appalachian community might soften the students' resistance. This was not the case. Having encountered similar responses in past uses of the novel, I chose to have students examine it structurally—from the perspective of point of view. I wanted them to see that Mary Call was indeed "flawed" and, at the same time, authentically represented. The focus on first-person point of view developed into a discussion of reliable and unreliable narrators and, subsequently, to a consideration of how Cleaver and Cleaver maintained their control over their narrative. The students came to see that as Mary Call developed insight into the *actual* capabilities of other characters, so did they. As the narrative developed, they came to perceive her as an unreliable narrator prior to her maturing understanding and thus, paradoxically, found her more plausible than had been the case in their first readings of the novel. To help the students understand how significantly a particular point of view influences the reader's perspective of the characters and events in a novel, they were also asked to rewrite the opening chapter from another perspective—some chose an omniscient third-person narrator close to the action; others chose to introduce the narrative from a first-person perspective using one of the other characters. As a result of these approaches, the earlier resistance ("aesthetic restriction" apparently influenced by the students' limited understanding of the role of narrative perspective on our perceptions) gave way to an acceptance that the main character *could* indeed have been authentically cast. More significantly, I think, these approaches resulted in richer readings of a novel that, while deceptively simple, is remarkably complex in its narrative structure.

JOURNEYING THROUGH THE IMAGINATION

To deny that behind this book lies an agenda would be a denial of the obvious: There is a pedagogical agenda, apparent in several ways. First, such obvious phenomena as the title of the book, titles of individual chapters, and, perhaps, the reputations and previous works of many of the authors all indicate that we favor multiple perspectives in the teaching of literature, that we favor sensitivity on the part of teachers toward ethnic and gender diversity, and that we favor the return of authors—not just texts and readers—to discussions of the reading act. Second, we all believe, although to differing degrees, that readers, writers, and texts are culturally situated and bound. Third, as educators, we all believe in the value of teaching literature from such a cultural perspective. Yet, if we argue that teachers already have enough on their hands teaching nineteenth- and twentieth-century American and British literature to classrooms filled with students who find many of these literary experiences irrelevant and difficult because of lack of background knowledge and experience, how can we argue for the inclusion of literature that seems even more removed from them and for which there is relatively little accessible critical material available?

In response to these and other challenging questions raised in this chapter, we could consider the literary journey as comparable to the physical one we take when venturing to another country and culture. No matter how much we may prepare ourselves, arm ourselves with information about the unfamiliar culture, we can be sure of encountering the unpredictable; we can be sure of our own surprise expressed perhaps in terms of "But it wasn't in the guidebook!" We can also be overprepared. Armed with too much preliminary information, we may seek to find what will confirm our "prior knowledge" (albeit limited). Such information may function as a frame or a lens through which the actual is then perceived. We may, therefore, be so preoccupied with confirming what "the guidebook" said that we miss the opportunity for the experience to speak directly to us and not see that:

> This is where the artist begins to work: with the consequences of acts, not with the acts themselves. Or the events. The event is important only as it affects your life and the lives of those around you. The reverberations you might say, the overtones: that is where the artist works. (Hellman, 1989, p. 128)

Similarly, Scholes (1989) brings us back to the *artistry,* to the *imaginative dimension* that is a characteristic of all good literature by which we find ourselves affected. This suggests that we might also give more play to the capacity of humans to *imagine outside their present or immediate realms and experiences* than we frequently do in our discussions of literature and its teaching. Granted, "artistry" and "imaginative dimensions" are culturally loaded terms, accompanied as they are with concepts such as taste, experience, and value. Nevertheless, if we were always to be limited by these, we could not find ourselves moved, despite them, to "enter . . . passing through the looking glass and seeing ourselves in the other" (Scholes, 1989, p. 27). Thus, while I cannot pretend to have shared the space, time, and experience of Ding Xhiao as represented in *Maidenhome*, I can "pass through the looking glass" as much because of her capacity to invite me there as mine to put aside disbelief and resistance. Perhaps we have fallen too far into the trap of thinking first of the text, then of the reader; we may find it provocative in our discussions to consider again the artistry, the power to move, of the writer.

In suggesting that readers are capable of receiving the "reverberations" of artistic works, I am also suggesting that, given the appropriate contexts and approaches for the cross-cultural literary experience, the inclusion of literature of other cultures can provide us with opportunities for widening "our own narrow cultural horizons" (Dasenbrook, 1992, p. 45). The greatest challenge, perhaps, is that in teaching literature representative of other cultures, the teacher, as often as his or her students, must also be prepared to not know, to learn how to experience the unknown afresh, and thus to accept that "the meaning" of the text in hand will no longer function as his or her safe haven when students wander off on uncharted trails.

NOTE

I am very grateful to the following colleagues and friends for their very valuable contributions in helping this chapter become a reality: Mary Ellen Tyus, Denise Wollett, Heather Lewis, Barbara Epstein, Stephanie Connell, Alan Purves and James Phelan.

REFERENCES

Applebee, A. N. (1990). *A study of book-length works taught in high school English courses*. Albany, NY: Center for the Learning and Teaching of Literature.

Applebee, A. N. (1991). *A study of high school literature anthologies* (Report Series 1.5). Albany, NY: Center for the Learning and Teaching of Literature.

Austen, Jane. (1969). *Emma*. New York: Harper & Row. (Original work published 1816)

Bloom, H. (1994). *The Western canon: The books and school of the ages*. NY: Harcourt Brace.

Bogden, D. (1992). *Re-educating the imagination: Toward a poetic, politics, and pedagogy of literary engagement*. Portsmouth, NH: Boynton Cook/Heinemann.

Chisunka, C. (1991). The impact of cultural background and worldview on the literary responses of American and African college students. *Dissertation Abstracts International, 53,* 744A. (University Microfilms No. 92–22, 247)

Cleaver, V., & Cleaver, B. (1960). *Where the lilies bloom.* New York: HarperKeypoint.

Dasenbrook, R. W. (1992). Teaching multicultural literature. In J. Trimmer & T. Warnock (Eds.), *Understanding others: Cultural and cross-cultural studies and the teaching of literature* (pp. 35–46). Urbana, IL: National Council of Teachers of English.

Diamond, B. J., & Moore, M. A. (1995). *Multicultural literacy: Mirroring the reality of the classroom.* NY: Longman.

Ding Xiaoqi. (1994). *Maidenhome* (C. Berry & C. Silber, Trans.). San Francisco: Aunt Lute Books.

Fetterley, J. (1978). *The resisting reader: A feminist approach to American fiction.* Bloomington: Indiana University Press.

Geertz, C. (1979). From the native's point of view: On the nature of anthropological understanding. In P. Rabinow & W. Sullivan (Eds.), *Interpretive science: A reader* (pp. 225–242). Berkeley, CA: University of California Press.

Gessen, M. (1995). *Half a revolution: Contemporary fiction by Russian women.* Pittsburgh: Cleis.

Godzich, W. (1994). *The culture of literacy.* Cambridge, MA: Harvard University Press.

Gunn, G. (1987). *The culture of criticism and the criticism of culture.* Oxford: Oxford University Press.

Harwood, J. D. T. (1993). A content analysis of high school American literature anthology textbooks. *Dissertation Abstracts International, 54,* 932A. (University Microfilms No. 93–20, 207)

Hellman, L. (1989). Interview. In G. Plimpton (Ed.), *Women Writers at Work* (pp. 122–146). London: Penguin.

Huxley, A. (1933). *Brave new world.* New York: Harper & Brothers.

Jauss, R. (1982). *Towards an aesthetics of reception* (T. Bahti, Trans.). Minneapolis: University of Minnesota Press.

Kundera, M. (1986). *The book of laughter and forgetting* (M. H. Heim, Trans.). New York: Penguin.

Lessing, D. (1992). Two old women and a young one. In D. Lessing, *The real thing: Stories and sketches* (pp. 169–179). New York: HarperCollins.

Palei, M. (1992). The bloody women's ward. In N. Perova & A. Bromfield (Eds.), *New Russian writing: Women's view* (pp. 74–93). Moscow: Glas Publishers.

Perkins, E. D. (1992). Response patterns of third-grade African-Americans to culturally conscious literature. *Dissertation Abstracts International, 53,* 2667–2668A. (University Microfilms No. 92–38, 791)

Prichard, K. S. (1994). *Coonardoo.* Sydney, Australia: Angus & Robertson Publications. (Original work published 1925)

Rafiq, F. (Ed.). (1995). *Aurat Durbar.* Toronto: Second Story Press.

Ramirez, G. (1992). The effects of Hispanic children's literature on the self-esteem of lower socio-economic Mexican-American kindergarten children. *Dissertation Abstracts International, 52,* 07A. (University Microfilms No. 91–29, 388)

Rifaat, A. (1989). Another evening at the club. In S. Walker (Ed.), *Stories from the rest of the world* (pp. 148–155). St. Paul, MN: Graywolf.

Scholes, R. (1989). *Protocols of reading.* New Haven, CT: Yale University Press.

Shakespeare, W. (1964). *The tempest.* New York: Signet Classics. (Original work published 1611)

Soter, A. O. (1996). Applying critical perspectives to *My Brother Sam Is Dead* and *Where the Lilies Bloom. Focus: Teaching English Language Arts, 22*(1), 59–68.

Viehmann, M. L. (1994). Writing across the cultural divide: Images of Indians in the lives and works of Native and European Americans. *Dissertation Abstracts International, 55*, 1265. (University Microfilms No. 94–26, 211)

Walker, S. (1989). Introduction to S. Walker (Ed.), *Stories from the rest of the world.* St. Paul, MN: Graywolf Press.

Yehoshua, A. B. (1984). *A late divorce.* New York: Doubleday.

About the Editors and the Contributors

Theresa Rogers is an associate professor of language, literacy, and culture at Ohio State University. Her specializations include response to literature, literacy instruction in urban settings, and drama and literary response. She previously taught English and reading in middle and high schools in Boston, Massachusetts. She is the co-author (with A. C. Purves and A. Soter) of *How Porcupines Make Love II* and *How Porcupines Make Love III* (1990, 1995). Other publications include articles in the *English Journal, Journal of Literacy Research,* and *Urban Review.* She is also co-editor of the *Ohio Journal of English Language Arts.*

Anna O. Soter is an associate professor of English education at Ohio State University. Her specializations include comparative rhetoric, writing instruction and assessment, ESL and writing instruction, applications of critical theories to young adult literature, and teacher learning. She has taught English in Australian secondary schools, taught courses in children's and young adult literature, and, with James Phelan, co-taught two NEH seminars on rhetorical approaches to literature teaching. Since 1994, she has co-edited the *Ohio Journal of the English Language Arts.* She is the co-author (with A. C. Purves and T. Rogers) of *How Porcupines Make Love II* and *How Porcupines Make Love III* (1990, 1995), the co-editor (with G. Hawisher) of *On Literacy and Its Teaching* (1990), and the author of several chapters in edited volumes and articles in various journals.

Richard Beach is a professor of English education at the University of Minnesota. He is the author of *A Teacher's Introduction to Reader Response Theories* (1993), co-author (with J. Marshall) of *Teaching Literature in the Secondary School* (1991), co-author (with C. Anson) of *Journals in the Classroom: Writing to Learn* (1995), co-editor (with S. Hynds) of *Developing Discourse Practices in Adolescence and Adulthood* (1990), and co-editor (with J. Green, M. Kamil, and T. Shanahan) of *Multidisciplinary Perspectives on Literacy Research* (1992). He has published numerous book chapters and journal articles on teaching literature and composition and has served as President of the National Conference on Research in English and Chair of the Board of Trustees of the NCTE Research Foundation.

Mingshui Cai is an assistant professor in the Department of Curriculum and Instruction at the University of Northern Iowa. He received his Ph.D. from Ohio State University. His areas of research interest are reader response, multicultural literature, and children's literature. He has published several articles in *The New Advocate, Children's Literature in Education,* and other journals.

Laura E. Desai is a doctoral candidate at Ohio State University. Her research interests include alternative assessment, urban teaching, and the use of multicultural literature for children. She is the co-author (with R. Tierney and M. Carter) of *Portfolio Assessment in the Reading-Writing Classroom* (1991).

Patricia E. Encisco is an assistant professor at the University of Wisconsin–Madison, where she teaches courses in reading and children's literature and graduate courses in culture, reading, and response to literature. She is currently studying preservice teachers' interpretations of those books that are recipients of the Americas Award, a new award recognizing Latino/a children's literature. Recent publications include an article in *Language Arts* and a forthcoming book chapter.

Mary Beth Hines directs the English education program of the School of Education, Indiana University. She received her Ph.D. from the University of Iowa. Her current research focuses on social justice inquiry in literature classrooms. Her recent publications include an article in *English Education* and several chapters in edited volumes.

George Kamberelis is an assistant professor in the departments of Speech Communication and Curriculum & Instruction at the University of Illinois at Urbana-Champaign. He teaches courses and conducts research on sociocultural dimensions of children's reading and writing development, discourse and identity, and multicultural literacy pedagogy. His recent publications include articles in the *Journal of Contemporary Legal Issues, Linguistics and Education,* and *Research in the Teaching of English.*

Daniel Madigan is an associate professor of English at Bowling Green State University, where he is the director of the Center for Teaching, Learning, and Technology. He has published articles in *Language Arts,* the *Journal of Children's Literature,* and the *National Reading Conference Yearbook,* and is the co-author (with V. Rybicki) of a forthcoming book focusing on the overlapping narratives that impact on and contribute to the stories that children tell and eventually write about.

Timothy Mahoney is a doctoral student at the University of Colorado in the School of Education. His research interests include the cultural and historical foundations of literacy, critical theory, and qualitative research methods. In his dissertation, he is exploring the school- and home-based literacy practices of Mexican immigrants in a small rural community.

William McGinley is an assistant professor of English and literacy in the School of Education at the University of Colorado. His research focuses on the role of humanities and the visual arts in public education, literature education, critical literacy, and narrative theory. His recent publications include articles in *Research in the Teaching of English* and in *Statement*.

Mari M. McLean is a high school reading and English teacher in the Columbus, Ohio, public schools. She is also an adjunct assistant professor in the College of Education of Ohio State University, where she coordinates a program that prepares teachers for urban settings.

Jeff Oliver teaches 10- and 11-year-old children at University Elementary School in Boulder, Colorado. He also teaches undergraduate courses in literacy education at the University of Colorado. He is interested in how children's imaginative engagement with stories and literature provides them opportunities for understanding themselves and their worlds.

Victoria Rybicki has been an elementary school teacher in Detroit, Michigan, for 31 years. She is interested in creating a curriculum for her 9- and 10-year-old students that provides them with opportunities to experience some of the imaginative and humanizing possibilities that are associated with learning to read and write. She is presently a doctoral student in literacy education at the University of Michigan. Her dissertation is an autobiographical exploration of her own literacy teaching practices and experiences, and a forthcoming book (co-authored with Daniel Madigan) examines overlapping narratives in stories children tell.

Arlette Ingram Willis is an assistant professor at the University of Illinois, where she teaches courses in secondary reading methods, multicultural literature for grades 6–12, and trends and issues in reading research. Her research interests focus on the history of reading research in the United States from a critical perspective and on teaching and using multicultural literature for preservice teacher educators. Her publications include articles in the *Harvard Educational Review* and *Discourse*.

General Index

Index of Literary Works for Children and Young Adults

ECO-COMPUTER